JUDE DEVERAUX

JUDE DEVERAUX

The Princess

The Temptress

The Enchanted Land

INDEX

This edition published in 1993 by Index
by arrangement with Random House UK Ltd
20 Vauxhall Bridge Road
London SW1V 2SA

The Princess © Deveraux Inc 1987
The Temptress © Deveraux Inc 1986
The Enchanted Land © Jude Gilliam White 1978

ISBN 0 09 182493 1

Printed and bound by Mackays of Chatham

Contents

The Princess

Chapter One

Key West, Florida
1942

J. T. Montgomery stretched his long legs out in the motorboat, resting his injured calf against one of the crates in the bottom of the boat. He was the remarkably handsome product of generations of remarkably handsome people. His dark hair had been cut too short by the navy but that did not detract from his good looks: brilliant blue eyes, lips that could be as cold as marble or as soft and sweet as the balmy air surrounding him, a slight cleft in his chin, and a nose that on a smaller man would have been too large. His mother called it the Montgomery nose and said it was God's attempt to protect their faces from all the fists aimed by people who didn't like the Montgomery hardheadedness.

"It still doesn't make sense to me," Bill Frazier was saying as he maneuvered the stick on the motor. Bill was a striking contrast to J.T. Bill was six inches shorter, hair already thinning at age twenty-three, and built like a stack of concrete blocks. Bill was grateful

1

to have J.T. as a friend because, wherever J.T. went, the chicks followed. Six months ago, Bill had married the pick of the bunch.

J.T. didn't bother answering his friend, but just closed his eyes for a moment and smelled the clean salt air around him. It was heaven to get away from the smell of oil, from the noise of machinery, and away from the responsibility of taking care of others, of answering questions, of—

"If I were a bachelor like you," Bill was saying, "I'd be down on Duval Street having the time of my life. I can't understand anybody wanting to spend time alone on one of these godforsaken islands."

J.T. opened one eye at Bill then turned and looked out over the ocean at several mangrove islands surrounding them. He couldn't explain what he felt to Bill, who had grown up in a city. J.T. had grown up in Maine, away from the noise and confusion of people and their machines. And there had always been the sea. When other boys had bought their first cars at sixteen, J.T. had received a sailboat. By eighteen he had been sailing three-day trips alone. He had even dreamed of sailing around the world alone. But then the Japanese bombed Pearl Harbor and the war began and—

"Hey!" Bill was calling. "Don't leave this world yet. Are you sure that's enough provisions? Don't look like much to eat to me. Dolly says you're too skinny as it is."

J.T. smiled at the mention of Bill's pretty little wife. "It's enough," he said, and closed his eyes again. City people were never able to look at the sea as one long banquet table. He had brought a net, a fishing pole and hooks, a couple of pots, a small box of vegetables, and his mess kit. He planned to live like a king for the next few days. The thought of the silence, the solitude, and the lack of responsibility made him shift on the hard seat.

Bill laughed, his very ordinary face crinkling. He was a man who would have made an excellent spy since he could have faded into any crowd. "All right, point taken. But I still think you're crazy. Anyway, it's your life. The commander wants you back next Monday and I'll be here to pick you up. And Dolly said to tell you that if you don't swear you'll use that burn salve she'll be out here tomorrow to apply it herself."

Bill snorted when J.T.'s eyes flew open with a look of horror on his face. "Now that would be *my* idea of a visit to a island," Bill said. "I'd lay in a hammock and have two beautiful—no, three—gorgeous dames feeding me mangoes."

"No women," J.T. said, his blue eyes darkening. "No women, please."

Bill laughed again. "What happened with that little WAVE was your own fault. Anybody could see marriage was in her eyes. And why *didn't* you marry her? I can highly recommend the state."

"That's my island over there," J.T. said, ignoring Bill's comments about marriage.

"Beats me how you can tell one island from another, but it's your funeral. One good thing is you'll be so lonely out here you'll be glad to get back to work."

J.T. grimaced at that. Peace, he thought, that's all he wanted. Nothing but the sound of the wind and the rain beating down on his tarp. And the food! No more navy chow, just fish, lobster, shrimp, conch, and—

"Cut your motor," he half shouted at Bill. "You're going to hit the beach."

Bill obeyed and eased the motorboat onto the narrow white sand beach.

Holding his left leg stiff in order to minimize the

pulling of the burned skin, J.T. untangled his six-foot-long body and stepped out of the boat and into the shallow water. The heavy navy boots felt awkward on the slippery bottom and he suddenly couldn't wait for Bill to be gone so he could get out of the stiff uniform.

"Last chance," Bill said, handing J.T. the first crate. "You can still change your mind. If I had time off, I'd get drunk and stay that way until I had to sober up."

J.T. grinned, showing even white teeth and making the cleft in his chin almost disappear. "Thanks for the offer and tell Dolly I swear I'll use the salve and try my best to fatten up," he said as he took the second crate ashore.

"She'll probably still worry about you and when you get back she'll no doubt have twenty pretty girls lined up to meet you."

"I'll be ready for them by then. You'd better go, it looks like it might rain." J.T. couldn't keep the eagerness out of his voice.

"I can take a hint, you want me gone. I'll pick you up on Sunday."

"Sunday night," J.T. said.

"All right, Sunday night. But you don't have to live with Dolly. She's going to worry me to death about you."

"All right," J.T. said, stepping toward the boat. "Now you've made me a decent offer. I'll live with Dolly and you stay here."

"Some joker," Bill said, the smile leaving his face. His buxom little wife was the love of his life; each day he still marveled that she had married someone like him. For all that J.T. was his friend and had even introduced them, J.T.'s looks aroused Bill's jealousy.

J.T. laughed at his friend's expression. "Go on, get out of here and don't get lost on the way back."

Bill revved the engine and backed off the narrow beach with J.T.'s help.

J.T. stood at the edge of the water and watched his friend until Bill rounded another island and was lost to sight, then J.T. opened his arms and breathed deeply. The smell of decaying sea matter, the salt air, the wind on the mangrove trees behind him made him feel almost at home.

In another minute he had grabbed most of his things and was heading north along the beach. Nearly a year ago when the navy had first sent him to Key West to supervise their ship repair operation, he had seen this island through binoculars from the deck of a ship. He had known then it was a place where he would like to spend time.

Over the past year he had read a few books about the land around Key West and he had gotten an idea of what was involved in camping on a hostile mangrove island.

Saying that the interior of a mangrove island was impenetrable was an understatement. The branches of the trees that had formed the island hung down to the ground, creating a prison of woody stems.

J.T. removed his shirt, took up his machete, and began slashing a narrow path through the growth. He meant to reach the freshwater cut in the center of the island.

It took him four hours of hard work to reach the cut and by that time he was down to his skivvies. Dolly was right in saying that he was too thin. He had lost weight in his three weeks in the hospital and the burns on the left side of his body were still pink and now beginning to itch from sweat. He stood panting for a moment and looked about him. He was completely enclosed on three sides by the short, glossy-leaved mangrove trees, but in front of him was the cut of water and a small area of land and sea debris. The water flowed out before him, its source hidden under the trees. There was room here for his tarp tent, a campfire, and his few provisions, it was all he needed.

He wiped the sweat from his face and turned back down the path he had just made. The track had many twists and turns, and twice he had let it lapse, crawling under the looping, low branches for a while before starting to hack away again. He didn't want a freshly made path leading to his sleeping area. Several times German submarines had come into the Keys and J.T. had no desire to awaken one night to a bayonet at his throat.

It was sundown by the time he dragged all his things down the serpentine path, then, wearing only his shorts, boots, and a knife about his waist, he grabbed a johnny mop from his kit and went back to the beach. He removed his boots and walked into the warm water.

"There are definitely things to recommend this place," he said aloud, remembering the cold Maine water of his hometown.

When he was in water to his chest, he dove and easily swam underwater to the nearest bit of wreckage protruding from the water. Unfortunately, the war had left the shallow water near Key West littered with debris. The water was dark but J.T. could see the deeper shadows. He stuck the mop into a hole in what had once been part of a ship and twisted. When he pulled the mop out, the antennae of four lobsters were entangled in the threads of the mop.

One lobster got free before he got it to shore but he quickly pegged the claws of the other three and carried them back down the path.

Moments later he had a fire going and a pot of water boiling. Deftly, with a practiced gesture, he pierced the spine of each lobster before dumping it into the water. These lobsters were different from the ones he had grown up with, smaller, with spotted shells, but they turned red when cooked just the same.

An hour later he tossed the empty shells into the water and smiled as he climbed into his hammock strung between two trees. The air was balmy, the wind just barely moving. The water was lapping at the shore and his belly was full. For the first time since he had left home, he was at peace.

He slept soundly, more soundly than he had in a year, and dreamed of mounds of shrimp for breakfast. For the first time in weeks he didn't dream of the night he had been burned, didn't dream of being surrounded by fire.

The sun rose and J.T. kept sleeping. Somewhere his mind was rejoicing that there were no starched nurses shoving stainless steel trays under his nose at five A.M. and saying, "And how are we this morning?" He smiled in his sleep and dreamed of yellowtail snapper roasted over an open fire.

When the shots came, he was too deeply asleep to even hear them, much less recognize them. He had slept knowing that he was safe and now he somehow knew the shots were not aimed at him.

When he did awake, it was with a jolt, sitting upright. Something was wrong, he knew it, but he didn't know what it was. He leaped from the hammock, ignoring the pain on the left side of his body, pulled on his boots, laced them as fast as possible, grabbed his rifle, and left the clearing, wearing his shorts and knife.

When he reached the beach and he still had heard

or seen nothing, he began to laugh at himself for being skittish. "It was a dream," he muttered, then started back toward the path.

He heard another round of shots before he could take another step.

Crouching low, staying at the far edge of the beach, he began to run toward the sound. He had not gone far when he saw them. Two men were in a motorboat, one sitting by the motor, the other standing, aiming a rifle at something in the water.

J.T. blinked a few times then saw the dark, round shape in the water dive. It was a human head.

J.T. didn't consider what he was doing. After all, it was wartime and perhaps the head in the water was a German spy who deserved to die. All he thought was that two against one was unfair. He put his rifle behind a tree, flung off his boots, and eased into the water.

J.T. swam as quietly as he could, trying to watch the men and the head. When the head went down and didn't surface, he dove, swimming under the tip of the boat and heading downward.

"There!" he heard above him just as he dove. Moments later bullets came zinging through the water, one of them cutting into his shoulder.

He kept diving down, down, his eyes wide as he searched.

Just when he knew he was going to have to resurface for air, he saw the body, limp, bent over, and floating downward. He kicked harder as he dove deeper.

He caught the body about the waist and started clawing his way upward. He could see mangrove roots to his right and tried to reach them. His lungs were burning, his heart pounding in his ears.

When his head broke the surface, his only concern

was air, not the men. Fumbling, he grabbed the hair of the person he held and pulled the head out of the water. As he tried to determine his position, he knew he heard no gasping of air from the body he held. The men had shut off their motor and were now only a few feet from J.T. but their backs were to him.

Silently, J.T. swam into the tree roots. Involuntarily, he gasped as a razor clam clinging to the roots cut into his burned side. But he made no more sound as he backed further into the roots, the clams cutting into his skin. The men used oars to maneuver the boat.

"You got her," one man said. "Let's get out of here."

"I just want to make sure," the man with the rifle said.

Her? J.T. thought, then turned to look at the face of the head lolling on his shoulder. She was a delicate-featured young woman, quite pretty actually—and she didn't seem to be alive.

For the first time J.T. felt anger. He wanted to attack the two men in the boat who would shoot at a woman, but he had no weapon except a small knife, his body was covered with half-healed burns, and he had no idea how deep the bullet wound in his shoulder was.

Impulsively, he pulled the woman closer to him, shielding her slim body from the razor clams, and encountered the curve of a female breast. He suddenly felt even more protective of her, holding her to him in a loving way.

He glared at the backs of the men who searched the water.

"I hear something. It sounds like a motor," the seated one said. "She's dead. Let's get out of here."

The other one shouldered his rifle, sat down, and nodded as the first man started the motor and they sped away.

J.T. waited until the boat was out of sight then protected the woman's body as best he could with his own as he made his way out of the jungle of roots and into the open water. He held her with his injured arm while swimming with the other until he reached the beach.

"Don't be dead, honey," he kept saying as he carried her to the shore. "Don't be dead."

As gently as he could, he put her on her stomach on the beach and began to try to pump the water from her lungs. She was wearing a long-sleeved, high-necked, full-skirted dress, her dark hair coiled and pinned about her head. The dress clung to her in a way that allowed him to see that she had a beautiful body: tall, slim-hipped, a waist he could span with his hands, and big breasts that swelled against the fabric. Her face was turned to one side, her eyes closed, thick, dark lashes lying against a cheek as pure and pale as porcelain. She looked like some rare, precious flower that had never been exposed to sunlight. How could anyone have tried to kill this delicate beauty, he thought with anger. All his protective instincts rose within him.

"Sweet lady," he said, squeezing on her ribs in a way that was half caress then lifting her arms. "Breathe, baby, breathe for Daddy Montgomery. Come on, sweetheart."

Blood ran down his shoulder from the bullet wound and more blood flowed from half a dozen cuts from the razor clams, but he didn't notice. His only concern was the life of this beautiful young woman.

He prayed, asking God to spare her.

"Come on, sweetheart, please try," he begged. "You

can't give up now. You're safe now. I'll protect you. Please, baby. For me."

After what seemed to be hours, he felt a shudder run through her body. She was alive!

He kissed her fragile-looking cheek, felt the cold skin, then resumed pumping with increased vigor. "That's it, honey, just a little more. Take a big deep breath for Daddy. Breathe, goddamn you!"

Another shudder passed through her body and she gave a great gagging heave. J.T. felt so much empathy for her that his own sides tightened. A huge amount of water came from her mouth and she began to cough as she struggled to pull herself upright.

J.T. smiled, feeling a great joy flood through his veins, and thanked God as he pulled her into his lap. "That's it, baby, get it all out." He stroked her damp hair, caressed her small, frail back, and felt as God must have when He created man. J.T. didn't know when anything had made him feel as good as saving this girl. He caressed her pretty cheek with the back of his fingers, cradled her like a child, and soothed her more. "You're safe now, sweetheart. Perfectly safe." He held her face against his neck.

"You—" She coughed.

"Don't talk, honey, just rest. Get all the water out and I'll take you home." He began to rock her.

"You"—cough, cough—"may"—cough, cough.

"Yes, love? You can thank me later. Let's get you into dry clothes for right now. How about some hot fish soup?" His voice was deep and loving.

The girl seemed to want desperately to say something so J.T. allowed her to move back a few inches so she could look at him.

He pulled her back into his arms, cradling her as if she were the most precious object on earth. "It's all right, baby. No one will try to hurt you again."

She struggled against him and he let her pull away again as he smiled at her indulgently.

Again he was struck with the sheer prettiness of her. Not beautiful in a modern sense but in an old-fashioned way. Her small features and perfectly shaped head made her look as if she had stepped out of an old photograph. She reminded him of the ladies in the fairy-tale books his mother read to him as a child. She was a damsel in distress and he was her rescuer. Warmth flooded him.

He kept his hands lightly at her back in a protective way. "All right, honey, what is it you want to say?" he said caressingly.

Trying to talk made her cough again but he waited patiently, his eyes filled with tenderness while she made the effort to gain control.

"You may not"—cough, cough—"touch me"—cough, cough—"I am"—cough, cough—"royalty."

By the time she finished, her back was ramrod stiff.

It took J.T. a moment to comprehend what she had said. He stared at her stupidly.

"I am a royal princess and you"—she looked down her nose at his bare chest—"may not touch me."

"I'll be damned," J.T. breathed, and dropped his hands from her back. Never in his life had he felt such betrayal. He was on his feet in seconds, leaving her sitting. "You ungrateful little—" he began, then stopped. His jaw hardened and his eyes glittered like blue fire as he looked at her before turning away and leaving her where she was. "Find your own breakfast, Princess," he muttered, and stalked away from her.

Chapter Two

ARIA sat where she was on the beach. Her head hurt, her lungs hurt, her legs ached, and what she most wanted to do was lie down on the beach and cry. But a royal princess must never cry. A princess must never show anyone what she is feeling. To the outside world she must always smile even when she is in pain. She had been taught these things until they were second nature to her.

Once when she was a little girl, she had fallen from her pony and broken her arm. Even though she was only eight years old, she didn't cry, but stood, holding her arm close to her body, and went inside to her mother. Neither her groom nor her governess knew that she was in pain. Later, after her arm had been set—through which ordeal Aria shed not one tear—her mother had congratulated her.

Now here she sat in a strange country after having had to fight for her life all night and the man who had rescued her was behaving very oddly. She glanced toward the tangle of trees and wondered when he was going to return with that fish stew he had promised. Of course she would have to insist that he clothe himself. Mama had told her never to allow a man to appear before her unclothed, whether he was a servant, a husband, or a native of some strange island.

There was a single palm tree a few feet down the beach and she slowly rose and started walking toward it. Her head swam with the effort and her legs were weak from exertion, but she pulled herself up as stiff as possible and began to walk—no slouching or staggering for someone of the blood royal. A princess is always a princess, Mama had said, no matter where she is or how people around her are behaving. She must remain a princess and let others know of their status or else they'll take advantage.

Take advantage, Aria thought, such as that man did this morning. The names he had called her! She willed her cheeks not to blush in memory. And the way he had touched her! No one, ever, in all her life had touched her like that. Didn't he understand that he wasn't supposed to touch a royal princess?

She sat down under the tree in the shade. She wanted to lean against the trunk and rest but she didn't dare. She would probably fall asleep and it wouldn't do for that man to see her sleeping when he returned with her meal.

Instead, she sat up straight and looked out at the ocean and, without willing them to, the events of the last twenty-four hours came back to her.

This past night had been the worst of her life, perhaps the worst night of anyone's life. Three days ago she had left her country of Lanconia for the first time in her life. She was to be the guest of the American government, and while the officials were talking to her ministers, the Americans planned to take Aria on a round of official engagements. Her grandfather the king had explained that their hospitality was merely an effort to persuade him to sell Lanconia's vanadium but he thought Aria might benefit from the experience.

There had been a long, tiring journey on trains then an army plane that had hastily been outfitted with antique chairs and brocade that was taped to the walls. Some of the tape came unstuck but Aria did not let the Americans know that she saw. Later she planned to laugh about it with her sister.

The Americans had treated her well if a bit strangely. One minute someone would bow to her and the next minute some man would take her elbow and say, "Watch your step, honey."

They landed in a place called Miami and immediately she was led to a small plane that was to take them to the southernmost tip of America, Key West. Here Aria was to be escorted about the big naval base and see where ships that had been injured in the war were repaired. Unfortunately, her two-week itinerary was full of visits to naval bases and army hospitals and luncheons with dowager societies. She wished that one afternoon could have included a gallop on a good horse but there didn't seem to be any time. Grandpapa had said the Americans wanted to impress upon her the need their country had for the vanadium and they didn't think that parties with handsome young men were likely to do that.

Straight off the plane Aria was greeted with a red carpet, and several overweight ladies wearing dresses of pastel chiffon—dresses that were indecently short—and carrying heavy bouquets of flowers. Aria accepted the flowers, smiling even though her feet were killing her and the heat of Key West made her feel light-headed. Three times she had to stifle a yawn as she handed the flowers to her lady-in-waiting who handed them to an American officer who handed them to an enlisted man who handed them to the chauffeur who put them in the trunk of a long black limousine.

Aria was escorted to a room in a building on the naval base that made her gasp. It looked as if the Americans had scoured the island for every piece of gilt furniture they could find and had put it all in the room. The hastily built, plain building with its purely functional rooms looked incongruous with the carnivallike carved, gilt furniture.

Aria gave her lady-in-waiting a quelling look lest the woman offend the Americans, but she was afraid the room would give her nightmares. There was an hour for her two dressers to ready her for a banquet.

At the banquet, she sat at a long table set on a dais surrounded by generals and town officials wearing suits smelling of mothballs. Every one of them had to give a speech and Aria tried not to show her sleepiness. She was also hungry but could not eat because the Americans had allowed photographers into the room for the entire meal. Royalty could not be photographed while ingesting food. So she sat, her plate taken away barely touched.

By the time she got back to her room, her long black heavy dress was weighing her down and she knew that even though it was midnight she had to be up at six A.M. for breakfast with a politician, then at seven she was to see something called a gyro compass laboratory.

Standing in the middle of the room, waiting for her dresser to come and remove her dress, waiting for her maid to draw her bath, in those few minutes when she was alone, someone threw something heavy over her head and carried her out of the room, and, as far as she could tell, out of the building.

She was nearly suffocated before the two men removed the covering.

"You will be paid if I am returned unharmed," she had begun, but a gag was put over her mouth then her hands and ankles tied. She was shoved into the backseat of a car and driven away.

Her mother and grandfather had often lectured her on the hazards of being royal, and once before, when she was twelve, there had been an attempt on her life. Aria lay quietly in the back of the car but she never lost her wits. She began to work the cords on her wrists, wriggling them looser and looser.

The men in the front seat didn't speak, just drove. They stopped, got out, and Aria could smell the ocean. She had freed her hands then untied her feet, but she had wrapped the cords lightly back around them. By now she thought the alarm would have been given and people would be looking for her, but she had to wait until there was a good opportunity to escape.

The men returned, but before she could see where she was, they covered her with a cloth again. This time she was put into what felt like a boat.

"Let her breathe," one of the men said as he started the motor, and the cloth was removed from her face.

Aria had a good look at the men. With a jolt, she realized that if they allowed her to see them, then they did not mean for her to live. She could smell the ocean and see the sky but nothing else.

After an hour or more one of the men said, "We're out far enough. Let's get it over with." He slowed the motor and over her feet, Aria thought she could see tree leaves.

She saw the other man lift a rifle and check to see if it was loaded.

Aria made her move as quickly as possible. Under the cover she had removed the loose bindings and now she jumped up and over the side of the little motorboat. The action rocked the boat and startled the two men, giving her a few precious seconds. She dove, but when she came up for air the man was shooting at her. She dove again. After she dove the fourth time, she remembered nothing until that man was holding her and saying outrageous things to her.

So here she was now, sitting under a palm tree in a country that was entirely too hot, having had no sleep and no food, and the only other person who seemed to be on this island was a half-naked commoner.

She stood, tried to straighten her dress, smoothed her hair back, and decided to look for him. Americans certainly didn't seem to know how to act. Why hadn't he apologized for touching her? And why wasn't he bringing her food? She would have to find him then allow him to return her to the American government. They would be frantic by now.

He wasn't easy to find. It took her an hour to walk around the narrow, smelly little beach but there was no sign of him. What a very odd way to treat royalty. Of course she had read that America had never had a king but surely even that couldn't excuse this man's behavior. In her own country the commoners were anxious to please her. Every time she left the palace they lined the streets to wave at her and present her with gifts. Perhaps this man was a prince and that was why he acted as if he had rights of familiarity. She dismissed that idea. He was an American and all Americans were equal—they were all commoners—no royalty, no aristocrats, just a nation full of commoners.

She sat down on the beach. So why wasn't he bringing her food? Even an American should know enough to bring a princess *food*.

At noon she moved back to the palm tree. The heat, her hunger, and the lack of sleep were too much for her. She stretched out on the sand and went to sleep.

When she woke it was dark. There were the calls of strange birds and she could hear movement in the bushes behind her. She moved nearer the palm tree and drew her knees up, wrapping her arms around them. She dozed a bit but mostly she stayed awake and wondered what was happening on the naval base. If they told her grandfather the king she was missing, he would be very worried. She had to get back as soon as possible and let the world know she was safe.

The sun rose and she sat up straight. Perhaps the naked man had left the island and she was alone here. Perhaps she would die after all.

A shadow blocked the sun and she looked up to see the man standing over her. He wore an unbuttoned shirt that exposed a great deal of his chest which was covered with dark hair. She could not possibly look directly at him.

"Hungry?" he asked.

"Yes," she answered.

He held a string of fish in front of her but she looked away. He tossed the fish onto a patch of grass then began gathering wood.

"Look, I guess we got off to a bad start," he said. "Maybe I *was* a little too friendly and maybe getting shot before breakfast doesn't put me in the best of

temper, so what do you say we start again? My name's
J. T. Montgomery."

She turned to look at him as he squatted over a fire,
the fish on sticks as he turned them. With his shirt
open and hair on his chest and black whiskers on his
face, he looked very primitive, more like something
out of a history book about Attila the Hun than what a
proper man should look like. Her mother had warned
her about men like him, or at least her mother had
warned her about improperly attired men. She
doubted if her mother had ever imagined that men
such as this one existed. Such men were never to be
allowed to take liberties.

"What's your name?" he asked, smiling at her.

She didn't like that overly familiar smile. It was
imperative to stop it at once. "Your Royal Highness
will do," she answered, her jaw set.

The man looked away, his smile gone. "Okay,
Princess, have it your way. Here." He thrust a fish on
a stick at her.

She looked at it in bewilderment. A princess was to
eat whatever was offered to her, but exactly *how* did
one eat this?

"Here," J.T. said, and dumped the fish on a leaf of
the palm tree. "Have at it."

Aria looked at the fish with horror, then, to add to
her horror, she saw the man was about to sit down on
the other side of the fire and eat his fish.

"You cannot," she gasped.

"Can't what?" he asked, squinting at her, a piece of
fish halfway to his mouth.

"You cannot sit with me. You are a commoner and I
am—"

"That's *it!*" he shouted, coming to his feet and
towering over her. "I've had it with you. First I risk
my life to save you and all the thanks I get is a 'you

20

can't touch me, I'm royalty!'" he mocked. "Then I
bring you food that you won't eat and I'm told to call
you Your Serene Highness and now—"

"Royal," she said.

"What?" he sputtered.

"I am a Royal Highness, not Serene. I am a crown
princess. Someday I will be queen. You must address
me as Your Royal Highness and you must take me to
the naval base immediately. Also, I need a knife and
fork."

The man said a few English words her tutor had not
taught her.

Was it possible, Aria thought, that the man was
angry? She couldn't imagine why. He would have
the honor of escorting her back to the base—it
would be something he could tell his grandchildren
about.

It was better to ignore commoners' outbursts. It was
their lack of breeding and training that made them so
emotional. "I should like to leave as soon as I've
eaten. If you wash that knife you're carrying, I will eat
with it."

The man removed his knife from his belt, opened
it, and tossed it blade down so that it stuck into the
ground an inch from her hand. She didn't flinch.
Commoners were so unpredictable—and their tem-
pers made them dangerous. One must take the upper
hand.

She took the knife from the ground and waved it at
him in dismissal. "You may go now and prepare the
boat. I will be ready."

Above her, she heard the man give a little laugh.
Good, she thought, at least he was in better humor.
Even he had to see how childish his temper was.

"Yeah, Princess, you just sit there and wait." With
that he turned away.

Aria waited until he was out of sight before looking back at the fish. "Princess," she murmured, "makes me sound like a collie."

It took her a while to figure out how to eat the fish. Food was not something to be touched with one's hands. She found a stick, cleaned it in the dying fire, and at last tackled the cold fish with the stick and the knife. To her amazement, she ate all three fish the man had left behind.

Noon came and the man did not reappear with the boat. He certainly took long enough to do things, she thought. It had taken him an entire day to catch three fish so it would probably take two days to bring a boat around. The day wore on and still he did not return. Were all Americans like this? Her grandfather would not tolerate such behavior in a palace servant. America was very young compared to Lanconia and she wondered about the survival of the country if all Americans were as slow and uneducated as this one. How could they possibly win their war with men as undisciplined as this one? The Americans needed more than vanadium—they needed a new population.

In the afternoon it began to rain. It was a light, warm drizzle at first but the wind rose and it grew colder. Aria huddled under the tree and wrapped her skirt about her legs.

"I'm not going to recommend him for a medal," she said, rain pouring down her face, her teeth beginning to chatter. "He is failing in his duties to me."

Lightning flashed and the rain began to come down in lashing sheets.

"Don't you know enough to get out of the rain?"

She looked up to see the man standing over her. He was still wearing very little clothing and his cheeks had even more black whiskers on them. "Where is the boat?" she called up at him, over the rain.

"There *is* no boat. We're stuck here together for three more days."

"But I can't stay here. People will be looking for me."

"Could we discuss this another time? Much as I dislike the idea, you have to come back to my camp. Get up and follow me."

She stood, using the tree for support. "You must walk behind me."

"Lady, I don't know how you've lived so long without somebody murdering you. Go ahead, then, lead."

Immediately, she realized she had no idea which way to go. "You may go first," she said graciously.

"How kind you are," he replied, the first decent thing he had said to her.

He turned away and she waited until he was several feet ahead then followed. It would not do to get too close to him. He didn't seem to be a trustworthy man. She followed him a few yards behind then the rain obscured him and she lost sight of him. She stood absolutely still and waited, willing even her eyes not to blink against the driving rain.

He returned after several long minutes. "Stay close to me," he shouted over the rain. Shouted unnecessarily loudly, she thought. He turned away then looked back and grabbed her hand.

Aria was horrified. He had *touched* her after she had told him he could not. She tried to pull away from him but he held fast.

"*You* may not have any sense but I do," he yelled, and began to pull on her arm.

Really, she thought, the man was too insolent for

23

words. He plunged ahead, hanging on to Aria's hand as a dog holds on to a bone. Once in a while he shouted orders at her, telling her to duck, and one time he grabbed her shoulders and pushed her to the ground. He expected her to *crawl* through the underbrush! She tried to tell him he had to cut the growth away but the man didn't listen to her. She was faced with being dragged, on her stomach, through the swampy land or crawling. Disgusting sort of non-choice.

When they at last reached the clearing, it took a moment to get her bearings. She was completely disoriented after her treatment by this man. She stood in the rain and rubbed her wrist where he had held her. Was this where this man *lived?* There was no house, nothing but a few crates and a piece of black fabric forming a little tent. No one in Lanconia lived this poorly.

"In there," he shouted, pointing to the piece of fabric draped over tree branches.

It was the most humble type of shelter, but it was dry. She knelt and crawled inside. As she was wiping water from her face, to her utter disbelief, the man crawled in beside her. This was too ridiculous even for an American.

"Out," she said, and there was an edge to her voice. "You will not be allowed—"

He put his face nose to nose with hers. "Listen to me, lady," he said as quietly as he could over the rain. "I've had more than enough from you. I'm cold, I'm wet, I'm hungry, I got a bullet wound in my arm, I got cuts on top of burns, and you've ruined the first vacation I've had in this war. You got a choice: you can stay in here *with me* or you can sit out there in the rain on your royal ass. That's it. And so help me, if you say one more word about what I'm allowed or not allowed to do, I will take great pleasure in throwing you out."

Aria blinked at him. So far, America was not what she had imagined. Perhaps she had better try a different tack because this man seemed to have an extraordinarily violent nature. Perhaps he would begin shooting at her as the other men had done. "May I have some dry clothes?" she asked, and gave him the smile she gave to one of her subjects who had just pleased her.

The man groaned, twisted toward a corner of the tarp, and opened a metal chest. "I got navy whites and that's it." He tossed them into her lap, then turned away, lay down on the rubber floor, stretched out, pulled a blanket over himself, and closed his eyes.

Aria had difficulty hiding her shock. Was *all* of America like this? Full of men who abducted one, then shot at one, other men who called one honey and tossed knives at one's hand? She would not cry, under no circumstance would she cry.

She knew it was no use trying to unbutton her dress. She had never undressed herself and had no idea how to do it. She clutched the dry clothes to her and lay down, as far away from the man as possible, but she could not control the shivering.

"Now what?" he muttered, and sat up. "If you're afraid I'll attack you, don't be. I've never found a woman less interesting than you."

Aria kept shivering.

"If I go outside in the rain, will you get out of that piece of sail you're wearing and into dry clothes?"

"I don't know how," she said, clenching her teeth to still the chattering.

"Don't know how to what?"

"Would you mind not shouting at me?" she said, sitting up. "I have never undressed myself. The

25

buttons . . . I don't know how . . ." The man's mouth fell open. Really, what did he expect? What did he think royal princesses did anyway? Did he think they polished silver and darned stockings? She sat up straighter. "I have never needed to dress myself. I'm sure I could learn. Perhaps if you told me the rudiments I—"

"Turn around," he said, then shoved her shoulder until her back was turned to him. He began unbuttoning her dress.

"I think that your touching of me is more than I can allow—what was your name again?"

"J. T. Montgomery."

"Yes, Montgomery, I believe—"

He turned her around to face him. *"Lieutenant* Montgomery of the United States Navy, not just Montgomery like your damned butler, but lieutenant. Got that, Princess?"

Did this man shout every word he spoke? "Yes, of course. I understand that you wish to use your title. Is it hereditary?"

"Better than that, it's *earned.* I got it for . . . for buttoning my own shirt. Now, get out of that dress—or do you want me to undress you?"

"I can manage."

"Good." With that, he turned away from her and lay back down.

Aria kept watching him as she removed her dress. She didn't dare remove her several layers of wet underwear, so she was still uncomfortable as she pulled his white uniform on over her head—and that took some concentrated effort to figure out. All in all, it took quite some time before she was able to lie down.

The rubber ground cover was damp, her underwear

was soggy against her skin, and her hair was wet. In minutes she was shivering again.

"Damn," Lieutenant Montgomery said, then rolled over, flung the blanket over her, and pulled her to him, her back against his front.

"I cannot possibly—" she began.

"Shut up," he said. "Shut up and go to sleep."

His big body felt so warm that she didn't offer any more protests. Her last thoughts before she fell asleep were a prayer of hope that her mother in heaven would not see her like this.

Chapter Three

WHEN Aria woke in the morning, she was alone. For a few moments she lay still and went over the events of the previous hideous day. She had to get back to the naval base and let the world, and especially her grandfather, know that she was safe. She crawled out of the little shelter and stood. There was a small fire made, but no sign of the man. His uniform, which she wore, hung past her hands, the top reaching to her knees and the cuffs under her feet. Tripping on the thing, she turned back to pull her damp dress from the ground.

It had stopped raining and it was a clear morning that was already beginning to grow hot. The clearing was really very small and hemmed in by the shiny-leaved trees. There was no sign of the man.

Cautiously, after listening for him, she removed the naval uniform.

"It's too hot for all that underwear," said the man from behind her.

Aria gasped and clutched her dress to her.

29

J.T. picked up his white uniform from the ground at her feet, frowning at the stains. "You sure don't respect other people's property, lady."

"Not 'lady.' I am a—"

"Yeah, I know. You're my royal burden, that's what. Why couldn't you have waited until Sunday morning to get yourself shot at? Are you going to put that rig on or stand there and hold it?"

"You must leave here. I cannot dress in front of a man."

"Princess, you overestimate your charms by a long way. You could parade stark naked in front of me and I wouldn't be interested. Hurry up and get dressed. You can peel the shrimp."

It took Aria a moment to recover. "You cannot be allowed to talk to me like that."

He stopped in front of her then grabbed the heavy black dress she was clutching. As she watched, horrified, he took his knife and slashed away the long sleeves then tore off about a foot of the skirt. He handed it back to her. "That should help. And you ought to throw away about half of that underwear. You pass out from the heat, don't expect me to rescue you. I learned my lesson the first time."

He took a fishing net from the ground, walked away, and stood at the end of the little stream.

Aria could not believe what had just happened. Her aunt had told her that Americans were barbarians, that they had no manners, and that the men were not to be trusted, but surely this man was worse than the rest. Surely the whole country was not populated by men like him—men who had no respect for authority.

Ten minutes later Aria was still standing there when he turned back with a net full of wriggling shrimp.

"You waiting for your maid? Here, let me help." He tossed the shrimp down then grabbed the dress from her and roughly pulled it down over her head, scraping her nose on the buckram in the waist. He jerked it into place, shoved her arms through the now-short sleeves, then buttoned the back with as much gentleness as a shark attacking its prey.

Throughout this, Aria kept her back rigid. This man was insane. This man's mind was not functioning properly. She moved away from him and sat down on a wooden crate. Her dress was quite short now, to the middle of her calves, and her arms were bare. "You may serve me breakfast now," she said as politely as possible.

He didn't look at her but threw the net of squirming shrimp into her lap.

Aria did not scream, did not jump up, did not show the revulsion she felt. "May I borrow your knife?" she whispered.

He turned toward her, a look of interest on his face, and handed her the knife.

A princess ate whatever was put before her, she chanted. One must never offend one's subjects by refusing to eat their food. She carefully opened the net, her stomach backing up at the sight of the bug-eyed creatures with their many legs. Taking a deep breath to still her churning stomach, she speared a shrimp with the knife point then brought it slowly, ever so slowly to her mouth. A leg touched her lip and she closed her eyes, her stomach rebelling.

The man's hand clamped down on hers just as she was about to put the shrimp into her mouth. She opened her eyes to look at him.

"Are you that hungry?" he asked softly.

"I'm sure your food is delicious. It's just that I've never eaten it before. I'm sure that I'll enjoy it just as much as you do."

He looked at her oddly then took the skewered

31

shrimp and the netful from her. "First they have to be cleaned then cooked."

She watched as he dumped the load of shrimp into a pot of boiling water.

"Have you never seen a shrimp before?"

"Of course, but they have been served to me on a plate and they bore no resemblance to those pink wiggling things. I did not recognize them."

"Yet you were going to eat it raw. Where do you come from?"

"Lanconia."

"Ah yes, I've heard of it. Mountains and goats and grapes, right? What are you doing in America?"

"Your government invited me. I'm sure they are frantic since I have disappeared. You must—"

"Don't start that again. If there was any way to get you off this island, I would. Believe me, sister."

"I am not your sister, I am—"

"A royal pain in the neck. Here, cut the heads off these and shell them while I make a sauce."

"I beg your pardon. I am not a scullery maid, nor am I your personal maid."

He was standing over her, blocking the sunlight. Once again he had on shorts and an unbuttoned shirt. His legs were in front of her face and they were too large, too brown, too hairy.

"You're in America now, Princess, and we're all equal here. You eat; you work. I'm not serving you meals on a gold plate." He tossed the knife and a flat piece of driftwood at her feet. "Cut and shell."

"I don't think your government will like the way you're treating me, Lieutenant Montgomery. They very much want the vanadium my country has and I'm not sure I'll sell it to America if I'm not treated well."

"Treated well!" he sputtered. "I saved your skinny

ass and look what it cost me." He pulled his shirt from his left shoulder and she saw a deep, puffy, ugly furrow across his skin and around that were half-healed scars that ran down his upper arm, his ribs, and into his shorts. His leg was also scarred and the wounds there looked deeper and not as well healed.

She turned away from the sight. "You should not show me such things. Please keep yourself dressed in my presence."

"You *expect* people to risk their lives for you, don't you?"

"My subjects—"

"Subjects, hell! Here, get busy on these shrimp. If I have to do them, you don't eat them."

"I cannot believe you'd refuse me food."

"Baby, you just try me."

"Lieutenant Montgomery, you cannot call me—"

"Cut!" he yelled at her.

She picked up a boiled shrimp with the knife, put it on the piece of wood, then tried to slice downward with the knife. The shrimp moved but did not cut.

"Don't you know how to do *anything?*" He took the knife, grabbed a shrimp in his left hand, and deftly cut off the head then broke the tail off and slipped the shrimp from its shell. "See? Easy."

Aria was looking at him with all the horror she felt. "You touched it."

"The shrimp? Of course I touched it."

"I cannot do that. One does not touch food with one's hands."

He looked at her in disbelief. "How do you eat corn on the cob? Hot dogs? Hamburgers?"

"I have never eaten any of those things, and if one must touch them I do not plan to eat them."

"Apples?"

"With a knife and fork, of course."

He didn't say anything for a moment but looked at her as if she were an alien from outer space. He took her hand in his, turned it palm up, and dumped a fat shrimp in it. He kept holding even when she tried to jerk away from him. He forced her to hold the shrimp in one hand, the knife in the other, and guided her through the motions of cleaning the shrimp.

Aria willed herself not to gag. She tried to close her eyes but the horrid man waited until she opened them before proceeding.

"Got it, Princess? When I get back, I expect the lot of them to be done."

She breathed a sigh of relief when he was gone but the mound of shrimp looked enormous. She felt like the princess who had to spin straw into gold or be beheaded in the morning. Tentatively, she picked up another shrimp. It took her a full five minutes to get the thing cleaned and then there wasn't much of it left.

"The American government will not like this," she said under her breath. "When they hear of this, they will no doubt use their trial system to condemn this man to a long prison term. He will wear chains about his ankles and live in a rat-infested dungeon. Or better yet, they'll send him to Lanconia. Grandpapa will know how to deal with him."

The man's snort from directly overhead made her jump.

"You must announce yourself. You cannot enter my chamber without my permission."

"This is *my* chamber. You haven't done ten shrimp. At this rate we'll starve."

She expected him to take the knife and finish them but he didn't. Instead, he had another string of fish. He used a big knife to remove the heads then tied a string to the heads and secured them so they dangled in the water.

"We'll have blue crab for lunch—that is, if we ever have breakfast."

He made her so nervous that she cut her thumb. In shock, she sat there staring at the blood welling from the cut.

He grabbed her hand and looked at it. "What do you know? It's red like the rest of us peons. Go stick your hand in the water."

When she didn't move, he pulled her upright and dragged her toward the stream and pushed her down until her hand was in the water. "Lady, you are the most useless human I ever met. You're not good for much but living in an ivory tower. What do you people do, just marry each other and produce more useless brats?"

Aria's hand was beginning to throb. "I am engaged to marry Count Julian of Borgan-Hessia."

"Oh?" J.T. lifted her hand and inspected the cut. "Ever met him?"

"Of course. I've met him three times and danced with him four times."

"Four times! It's a wonder you didn't get pregnant. Don't look so shocked, get over there and finish the shrimp."

Crude, vulgar man. The dungeon would be too good for him. She'd have to come up with a better punishment, something humiliating and disgusting. "My hand is injured. I cannot . . . Where are your . . . your . . . private facilities."

"See all these trees? They are one big toilet."

Trying to keep her composure, she walked away toward the narrow path. Once she started, she didn't stop. The man was hideous. No one had ever spoken to her as he had. She had never realized anyone ever spoke to anyone else as this man did. But she would not stoop to his level of crudity. She was hungry, thirsty, tired, and hot but at least she was away from him.

It wasn't easy for her to find her way to the beach but she finally made it. Perhaps there would be a boat to come by the island and she could hail it. She walked along the beach, stepping into ankle-deep mounds of rotting seaweed and straining her eyes to see across the ocean's horizon.

There were few shells on the beach but she did see what looked to be long, narrow blue balloons. She stopped to pick one up.

"Don't touch that!"

Her hand came away and she turned to glare up at him. He was on the rise of land above the beach. "Are you following me?"

He had his military rifle with him and he dropped it, butt down on the ground. "You say your country has vanadium?"

"A great deal of it." She bent again to touch the balloon.

"That's a man of war," he said quickly, "and on the bottom are tentacles that can sting. The pain often kills people."

"Oh," she said, straightening and starting back down the beach. "You may leave me now."

He followed her. "Leave you to get yourself killed? You have a propensity for getting into trouble. I don't want you on the beach. Those two jokers who tried to kill you before might come back."

"Perhaps your navy will send ships looking for me."

They were at the palm tree now and he sat down,

leaning his rifle against the tree. "I've just thought about it and I figure it's my duty to protect you—or at least to protect the vanadium you own. You'll have to come back to the clearing."

The edge of the beach disappeared into water. "No thank you, Lieutenant Montgomery. I would rather sit here and watch for ships." She sat down on the edge of the beach, her back straight, her hands in her lap.

J.T. leaned against the palm tree. "Suits me, just don't get out of my sight. We have three more long days here and I plan to deliver you to the U.S. government safe and sound. When you get tired of eating your pride, let me know. I got blue crabs at the camp."

Aria ignored him as he lay down and appeared to be dozing. The sun was hot and her stomach was growling with hunger. She imagined spring lamb and green beans with thyme. The sun flashed off the water but there was no sign of any sailing vessel.

Before her, swimming lazily in the water, was a large fish. She remembered how the man had speared a fish and cooked it over an open fire. It was the last meal she had had, so very many hours ago. She thought maybe she could make a fire, but how did one catch a fish?

She looked back at the man and saw he was sleeping. A foot from him rested his rifle. Rifles were something she understood since she had hunted game since she was a child.

Quietly, so as not to wake him, she climbed up the bank and had her hand on the rifle before he grabbed her wrist.

"What are you planning to do with that? Get rid of me?"

"I was going to catch a fish."

He blinked a couple of times before he grinned. "What? Use a rifle as a fishing pole? Bullets for bait?"

"I have never met a man more absurd than you. I am planning to shoot a fish."

He grinned broader. "Shoot a fish. With an M-1 rifle? Lady, you couldn't even fire the thing, much less hit anything with it. The recoil would knock you flat."

"Oh?" she said, and raised the rifle, drew back the bolt to check if it were loaded, and before he could speak, she had tossed it to her shoulder, aimed, and fired. "Another bullet," she said, stretching out her hand to him.

Speechless, J.T. put one of the long M-1 cartridges in her hand.

She loaded again, but this time she swung the rifle overhead, aiming at a flock of ducks. She fired and a duck fell a few feet out into the ocean. She put the rifle down and turned to look at him.

J.T. walked past her, down the bank, and stepped into the water. He picked up a large red snapper, the tip of its head blown cleanly off. Turning, he walked a few more feet out and retrieved a duck, its head missing.

"Princesses *can* do some things," Aria said, turning on her heel and starting down the path toward camp. "You may serve them to me for luncheon."

He caught up with her, the rifle slung at his back. He pulled her arms up and dumped the duck and fish into them. "You eat what you kill and you clean it. You're going to learn that I'm not your servant if I have to beat it into you."

She smiled at him. "Men are always angry when I outshoot them. Tell me, Lieutenant Montgomery, can you ride a horse?"

"I can dress myself and I'm not starving. Now go to

38

the camp and start plucking feathers. And this time you finish the job."

"I hate him now," Aria said as she pulled out a duck feather. "I hate him tomorrow." She plucked another feather. "I hate him yesterday."

"You haven't finished that yet?"

Aria jumped. "You *must* announce your presence."

"I did." He looked at her bare arms. "Do you realize that you're sitting in the sun again?"

"I will sit where I please."

J.T. shrugged, bent over the crabs, and began to clean them.

"I hate him for always," Aria said under her breath. "I think this is complete," she said, standing; then, to her consternation, the land began to twirl about her.

When she woke, she was lying in the hammock, Lieutenant Montgomery looming over her with a frown on his face.

"Damned dame," he muttered, then louder, he said as he glowered at her, "you're too hot in that damned dress, you're sunburned, and you're hungry." He turned away, muttering to himself, "I ought to get a Silver Star after this."

Aria did feel awful, and as she looked at her arms, she saw the pinkening flesh. In minutes he returned with a metal plate full of fish and crab. She had some difficulty trying to sit up in the hammock, so after a few more mumbled curses, Lieutenant Montgomery set the plate of food down, bent, and picked her up in his arms.

"You cannot be allowed to do this," she gasped, sitting rigid in his arms.

He set her down on the wooden crate and shoved the food into her lap. "I could have brought three kids with me and they would have been less trouble than you." When she didn't start eating, he groaned and handed her his knife. "Aren't the words 'thank you' in your vocabulary?"

Aria ignored him but began to eat. It was difficult to remember her manners and not eat with the gusto she felt. She sat absolutely rigid, daintily picking up the knife, eating one bite, and putting the knife down. The man huddled over the fire, doing things to the spitted duck.

Before she had finished the crab, he dumped a quarter of the roasted duck on her plate. It took her a few moments to figure out how to do it, but by using the knife and the tip of one finger to hold the meat, she managed to eat all of it.

The man seemed surprised when he saw her empty plate but she gave him a look that dared him to say anything.

"Now we get you out of those clothes."

"I beg your pardon."

"You fainted, remember? Florida is too hot to wear that many clothes. I'll unbutton you then you go into the trees and remove your underwear. Don't look at me like that; if I wanted a woman it would be one with a little meat on her and one with a sweeter temper." He turned her around and unfastened the back of her dress then pointed her toward the trees.

As Aria went into the trees she kept her head high. She knew he was right, she couldn't continue fainting, but right had nothing to do with his ordering her about.

She removed her dress then stood and looked down at her layers of underwear. She removed her petticoat first, which she had had to roll up at the waist to keep from showing below her abruptly shortened skirt. The silk camisole came off next and that left her with a pink satin corset laced in tightly over a girdle, under-pants, and hose.

She could not reach the laces of the corset, twist and turn as she might. She put her dress back on, picked up her slip and camisole, and left the trees.

He took one quick look at her and said, "Not enough off."

"I will not—"

He turned her around, opened her dress at the back and cut away the fasteners on her corset. He pointed toward the trees.

Aria removed the rest of her undergarments and felt heavenly. The tight, restricting girdle, which left marks on her skin, came off, and the removal of her hosiery allowed her skin to breathe. When she put her dress and low-heeled slippers back on, she felt abso-lutely decadent. The silk of the dress against her bare skin felt marvelous.

Of course now the dress was a little snug in places. Without the heavy elastic confining her, she seemed to be larger in places—both top and bottom. She had never appeared in public without her foundation garments before. At fourteen, at the first sign of growing breasts, her mother had ordered foundation garments made for her. "A princess does not move about under her clothes" was what she had told her daughters. Except at night, in bed, Aria had worn them ever since.

She hesitated before leaving the cover of the trees, but then she put her head up, her back straight—and her eyes widened. More of her protruded than before. Well, if she ignored this fact, she was sure that dreadful man would also.

She was mistaken. He glanced at her as she entered the clearing, turned away, then looked back for a long, hard look. Aria ignored him. She turned toward the path to the beach.

"Where do you think you're going?"

"To the beach to watch for boats."

"No you're not. You're staying here."

"Lieutenant Montgomery, I do not take orders from anyone lower than a king."

"Well, baby, I'm king here. I figure that if you have something the American government wants, then it's my duty as a sailor to protect it. You stay here where I can see you and you don't get out of my sight."

Aria just looked at him then turned toward the path again.

He grabbed her arm. "Maybe your hearing doesn't work too well. There aren't just Americans out there. German submarines have been spotted in this area."

She jerked away from him. "My cousins are Germans. Perhaps they will take me home to my grandfather. I don't think I care for America anymore."

The man stepped back from her and looked as if she were a monster. "We are at *war* with Germany," he whispered.

"*Your* country is at war with Germany, mine is not." She took a few steps down the path before he caught her.

"Look, you little traitor, you're staying here with me whether you like it or not. And tomorrow when my friend comes, I'm delivering you to the government—to the United States government." He took her arm and pulled her back into the clearing, then proceeded to ignore her as if there was nothing more to be discussed after his order was given.

She sat on the ground against a tree and waited. She wasn't going to try to explain to this man who saw only his side of a problem, but every minute she delayed was taking months off her grandfather's life. He would know by now of her disappearance and he would be very worried. He had trained his only son, Aria's father, to take his place as king but he had had to survive the tragedy of the young man's death when Aria was five. From then on, his hopes had centered on his young granddaughter. Aria had been trained to be queen. She had been immersed in history and politics and economics.

This man who now lay in his hammock reading thought he understood patriotism, but here he was enjoying himself while his country fought a war. No king or queen ever rested while his or her country was at war. The people looked to their royal family to set examples.

Her grandfather had been able to keep his country out of this awful war that waged through most of the world and he dreaded what the Germans were going to do if he sold the vanadium to the Americans, but Lanconia so needed the money. When Lanconia declared itself neutral in this war, it had cut itself off from the imports of the outside world.

This Montgomery had said Lanconia was mountains, goats, and grapes—and now the grapes were dying. Knowing how valuable she was, how likely a kidnap attempt was, her grandfather had still sent her to America—selling the vanadium was that important.

Yet here she sat, a virtual prisoner of this stupid man who was much too provincial to understand, and she could not get off the island.

She hoped the Americans would delay telling her grandfather that she was missing—but the American papers seemed to love telling *everything*.

She glanced up at the man and saw that he was

sleeping. As quietly as she could, she left the clearing and went down the path.

She made it to the beach but the sun was going down and she couldn't see very far.

Suddenly, she heard what was distinctly the sound of a motor. She took off running as fast as her feet would move. Around the curve of the island was a motorboat just docking, three men hauling it onto the sand. She raised her hand and opened her mouth to hail them but the next minute she was flat in the sand, a weight on her that could only be the lieutenant's body.

"Don't say a word," he said in her ear. "Not one word. I don't know who they are but they aren't picnickers."

Aria was chiefly concerned with catching her breath. She lifted one hand and waved it.

He rolled off of her but pulled her close to him so that she was still half under him.

"You cannot be allowed—"

He clamped his hand over her mouth. "Quiet! They're looking this way."

She pried his fingers away then looked at the men. One stood by the boat and lit a cigarette while the other two, carrying a heavy crate, disappeared into the trees. When they returned, they were empty-handed.

J.T. held Aria tightly while the men climbed into the boat and motored away.

"You may release me now," she said when the men were gone.

J.T. kept holding her, his one hand creeping down toward her hip. "What kind of underwear did you have on? It sure made a difference."

Her mother's training had not included this situation. She reacted out of a primitive female instinct:

she elbowed him in the ribs then rolled away and stood.

The man lay there rubbing his ribs. "I've been here too long if *you're* starting to look good. Go back to the camp."

"What did the men leave in the box?"

He rolled up on his feet. "Well, well, the princess is curious. I should have let you tell them you'll not allow them to litter your island."

"This is an *American* island," she said, confused.

"Come on," he said, groaning. "Does anyone in your country have a sense of humor?" He started down the beach and she followed.

"Only when they are not being held prisoner. Keep your hands off of me."

"Someone should have put his hands on you long ago. How old are you?"

"I don't think—" she began, then sighed. "Twenty-four."

"That's an old maid in wartime America. What's this prince you're going to marry like?"

"He's a count and he's related to the English and Norwegian thrones."

"Ah, I see, you'll breed pure-blood brats. Is he related to you?"

She hated his tone. "Just barely. We are fourth cousins."

"No blithering idiots out of that. Who picked him out?"

"Lieutenant Montgomery, I very much resent these personal questions."

"Maybe I'm just trying to find out about your country, your customs and such. Aren't you curious about Americans?"

"I have studied your customs. Your Pilgrims arrived in the seventeenth century, all the Texans were killed at the Alamo, your government is based on a constitution, your—"

"No, I mean about us."

She was quiet a moment. "I find Americans to be a very strange sort of people. So far, this has not been the most pleasant of trips."

He gave a laugh at that and stopped where the boat had landed. "Stay here—and I mean that. *Stay here.*" He disappeared into the trees, returning a moment later.

"Stolen navy property. There's a big stash of it. I'm sure they're black-marketing it."

"Black market?"

He grabbed her arm. "Let's get out of here. They could make a couple of more trips tonight. When I get back, the navy will hear of this."

Aria pulled out of his grasp and walked ahead of him down the beach.

"Only kings walk *with* you, is that right? Tell me, does Count Julius walk beside you?"

She stopped, turned, and glared at him in the moonlight. "He is Count Julian, and in public, no, he does not walk beside me."

She turned and started walking away.

"What about when he's your husband and king?"

"He'll not be king unless I decree it, which I will not do. I will be queen and he will be made a prince consort."

"If he's not going to be king, then why's he marrying you?"

Aria clenched her fists inside her skirts. This man had a way of making her forget that she was not to show emotion. "Lanconia," she answered simply. "And he loves me."

"After four meetings?"

46

"Three," she corrected. "That will be all the questions I will answer. I'm sure there must be some books on Lanconia in your libraries. What are you serving for dinner?"

"*We* are preparing seviche. Ever cut up onions, Princess? You're going to love the job."

Chapter Four

ARIA sniffed her hands and they did indeed smell as bad as she remembered. No amount of washing would rid them of the awful smell of those onions. She turned back to the campsite and saw Lieutenant Montgomery settled in his hammock for the night. There was no bed for her.

"Where am I going to sleep?"

He didn't bother opening his eyes. "Wherever you want, Princess. Ours is a free country."

It was beginning to turn cool and she rubbed her arms. "I would like to sleep in the hammock."

Eyes still closed, he stretched out his arm. "Be my guest, baby. I'm willing."

Aria gave a sigh. "I suppose it's too much to hope that you'd leave that and let me have it."

"Much too much. I came prepared for one camper —one bed, one blanket. You can share what I have, though, and be assured that I won't do anything except sleep."

Aria sat on the ground against a tree, feeling the

night grow cooler. A breeze came up and chills broke out on her arms. She looked at him, warm and sleepy in the hammock. She leaned back and closed her eyes but her chattering teeth kept her from relaxing. She stood and walked about the camp.

When she looked back at him again, he seemed to be sleeping but he extended his arm out to her. Without thinking what she was doing, she climbed into the hammock beside him. She tried to turn her back to him but the hammock pulled them together and the stiff, cramped position made her back ache.

"Pardon me," she said, as if she were passing him on the street, and turned so that her head was on his shoulder. She made an attempt to pull his shirt closed but it was caught under him so she had to put her head against his chest. To her surprise, the sensation wasn't unpleasant at all.

He curled both arms around her and she heard him chuckle softly. It was better not to think seriously about what she was doing. A desperate situation called for desperate measures. Besides, his big warm body felt so very good. She moved her leg by his, then crooked one knee and put it over his leg. She sighed happily and went to sleep.

"Wake up, it's morning," said a cross voice in her ear.

She had no desire to wake up, so she just snuggled closer to the man.

He grabbed her shoulders and pushed her away to stare at her. "I told you to get up. And fix your hair! It's come down."

She wasn't fully awake. Her eyes were half open, her hair falling over her shoulders. She gave him a soft smile. "Good morning."

The next minute he pushed her out of the hammock

and onto the ground. Wide-awake now, she rubbed her bruised posterior.

"You're the dumbest broad I ever met," he muttered angrily. "Didn't you ever go to school and learn the facts of life?"

"If you are referring to a public school, I have never attended. I had tutors and governesses." She stretched. "I slept very well, did you?"

"No!" he snapped. "I slept rotten. In fact, I didn't sleep much at all. Thank God this is our last day together. After this 'vacation' I am going back to the war to rest. I told you to go fix your hair. Pull it back the way you had it, just as tight as you can get it. And put your underwear back on." With that he stomped away down the path.

Aria stared after him for a moment then began to smile. She wasn't sure what was wrong with him but it was making her feel absolutely heavenly. She walked to the water and looked at her reflection in a clear little pool.

Many men had asked for her hand in marriage but quite often they had done so without having met her. They wanted to marry a queen, regardless of what she looked like. Count Julian, sixteen years her senior, had asked her grandfather's permission to marry her when Aria was eight.

Aria felt her hair. It was dirty right now but when it was clean . . . She glanced down the path, didn't see the man, so she looked inside his crate of provisions. There was no shampoo but she did find a fat bar of soap and a skimpy towel.

Hurriedly, she undressed and stepped into the stream. She was lathering her hair when he returned. He stopped and stared, eyes wide, mouth dropped open.

She grabbed the tiny towel and tried to hide her

nude body behind a tree branch. "Go away. Get out of here."

With a look of dumb obedience, he turned and left the camp.

Aria smiled and then she grinned. She began humming. That odious man and the awful things he had said to her: "skinny ass," "you could walk stark naked in front of me and you wouldn't interest me." How utterly lovely his stares had made her feel. Of course he wasn't really anyone, but sometimes that type of man . . . She wasn't supposed to know about it but a cousin of hers had borne a child without being married and it was said that the father was the footman who wound her bedroom clock each night. Aria had heard her mother say that of course the footman had hypnotized the poor girl. Smiling even more broadly, Aria wondered.

She took her time dressing—and didn't put her underwear back on—and began to comb her hair. She was still combing when he returned.

"I got lobster for breakfast and there's crackers in the crate."

He stopped talking and she was aware that he was watching her. She smiled slightly as she played with her long, dark hair in the early morning breeze.

Suddenly, he grabbed her shoulders and hauled her up to face him. "Lady, you are playing with fire. You may think I'm some servant of yours you can tease and still be safe with but you're wrong."

With his fingers digging into her shoulders, he pulled her to him and kissed her in a fierce, hungry way. When he had finished, he pushed her away.

"You're a twenty-four-year-old child, an innocent little girl, and I'm willing to leave you that way for your Duke Julian, but baby, don't push me. I'm not your servant and I'm not safe. Now get over there and haul up that net and give me those shrimp."

It took Aria a moment to react. She put her hand to her mouth. Julian had kissed her once but only gently and only after asking her permission. It was not a raw, hot thing like this man's kiss.

"I hate you," she whispered.

"Good! I don't feel any love for you either. Now scat!"

Breakfast was a quiet, sullen thing with neither of them talking.

After they had eaten, he lit a cigarette. Aria opened her mouth to tell him he didn't have her permission to smoke but closed it again.

She didn't feel inclined to speak to him and now she was somewhat afraid of him. How very much she wished she could get off this island and away from him.

After his cigarette, he stood, gruffly told her to stay in the camp, then disappeared down the pathway.

Aria sat for a long while, hugging her knees to her and thinking of her grandfather. How she wished she could go home where people and places were familiar.

After a few hours, when the man didn't return, she made her way down the path to the beach. He was lying under the single palm tree, his eyes closed, his shirt open, his rifle leaning against the tree.

"Planning to go fishing again?" he asked, not opening his eyes.

She did not reply as just then they heard a motorboat.

J.T. was on his feet in seconds. "Get down," he commanded. "And stay there. Don't come out until I say it's okay." He grabbed his rifle and started running along the beach.

Aria crouched behind the tree and watched, but then she saw the man stand up straight and wave his arm in greeting. Feeling a bit foolish, she stood, smoothed her skirt, and tidied her hair. With a dress with no sleeves, a too short skirt, and hair that had not seen a hairdresser for a week, she did the best she could.

With all the grace of her years of training, she walked down the beach toward Lieutenant Montgomery and the man who was not getting out of the motorboat.

"I've never been so glad to see anybody in my life," J.T. was saying to the man, who was a great deal smaller than Lieutenant Montgomery.

"Dolly made me come early. She imagined all sorts of things happening to you. And besides, I thought I might stay here and do a little fishing before we go back."

"No thanks. I want to go back where it's nice and safe."

"You *did* get lonely then. I told you—" He broke off when he saw Aria. "Well, you devil," he said, chuckling and looking at Aria admiringly. She was obviously a classy dame, he thought. The way she walked, the way she stood, reeked with class. Bill knew J.T.'s family had some money and this was just the type of dish he had imagined J.T. would go for. He would like to see J.T. married—maybe he wouldn't be so jealous then of J.T.'s friendship with Dolly if J.T. had his own wife. "You certainly put one over on me."

"It's not what you think," J.T. snapped at Bill, then turned to Aria. "I told you to stay out of sight."

Bill smiled knowingly. A lovers' spat. Then he looked at Aria more intently. "Haven't I seen you somewhere?" Bill asked. "And, J.T., aren't you going to introduce us?"

J.T. sighed. "Bill Frazier, this is Her Royal Highness—" He whirled on Aria. "I don't know your name."

"Princess!" Bill gasped. *That's* who you look like, that princess who visited the plant day before yesterday."

"But I was here," Aria said, eyes wide. "I have been here for many days." Years actually, she thought.

J.T. was frowning as he grabbed Aria's arm and pulled her toward the palm tree.

"Hey," Bill said nervously, "you think you ought to treat a princess like that? I mean, isn't her country valuable or something?"

"Yeah, something." J.T. stopped under the tree. "Now tell me why those men were shooting at you."

"Shooting?" Bill asked, running up behind them. "When I saw her, she was surrounded by about fifty servicemen. I never heard anything about any shooting."

"Bill," J.T. said. "When your princess was visiting the plant, *this* princess was here with me."

Bill looked confused. "You have a sister?"

"She does not look like me," Aria said, equally confused.

"Start talking," J.T. said.

As quickly as possible, Aria told of being kidnapped and of escaping.

"You can untie your hands but you can't unbutton your clothes?" J.T. said, one eyebrow arched.

"One does what one must." She glared at him.

"Ahem," Bill said, drawing their attention. "You think the guys that kidnapped you slipped in a double?"

"A double?" Aria asked.

"Someone is impersonating you," J.T. explained, and shocked Aria into silence.

Bill gave J.T. a hard look. "How do we know which one's fake?"

J.T. looked Aria up and down. *"This* one is the real princess. I'd stake my life and the lives of my family on that. *No* one could put on an act like hers."

Bill looked at Aria as if he had never seen her before. "My wife sure wanted to meet you. When I got home the other day, she asked me a hundred questions about you—her. She wanted to know what you were wearin', what you looked like, if you wore a crown." He stopped. "But I guess that wasn't you."

Aria gave him a hint of a smile. "Perhaps I will grant your wife an audience someday."

Bill looked back at J.T., his eyes wide. "Is she real?"

"More or less. We have to figure out what to do about this."

Aria thought the problem had an obvious solution. "You must take me back to your government officials. I will explain what has happened and they will remove this imposter."

"And how are they going to know which one is the real princess?" J.T. asked with the voice of a father talking to an annoying child.

"You will tell them. You are an American."

"I'm a commoner, remember?" J.T. said with anger.

"I thought all Americans were equal," she shot back at him. "According to my studies, each American is as important as another. You are each one a king."

"You—" J.T. began.

"Wait a minute," Bill interrupted. "Could we do this without you two fighting?"

J.T. looked at Aria. "Do you know any higher-ups in Washington? Generals? Senators?"

"Yes, General Brooks stayed a week in Lanconia

56

trying to persuade my grandfather to allow me to go on this trip. My grandfather will not like—"

"Her grandfather is the king," J.T. said to Bill. "Then what we have to do is get you to D.C. and General Brooks."

Aria straightened her back. "I am ready to go. As soon as I get my clothes, I will be ready to travel with you. Oh," she said, and for the first time she realized the enormity of what was happening. She couldn't go back to her clothes or her dressers or her ladies-in-waiting. She had no way to even get back to Lanconia. "Did the woman actually look like me?" Aria whispered.

"Come to think of it, she wasn't nearly as pretty as you," Bill said, grinning.

J.T. gave Bill a look of disgust. "Look, the important thing is to get the vanadium for America. I imagine that the reason you were replaced is so the imposter can turn the vanadium over to an enemy."

"Vanadium?" Bill asked.

"It's an alloy that you put in steel to make it harder," J.T. said impatiently. He gave Aria a critical look. "No general will see you looking like that. Bill, you think we can make it to Miami in that boat?"

"Miami! That'll take hours."

"That's all the time we have. We'll buy her some clothes, put her on a train to D.C., and that's the end of it. We've done our part."

"But she's a stranger in a strange country. Shouldn't someone go with her?" Bill asked.

"It's war, remember? We both have to report to work at nine tomorrow morning. In war, they don't dock you for being late, they shoot you. She'll be all right as soon as she gets to General Brooks." He hesitated. "Besides, I *can't* go with her." J.T. turned toward the path. "Come on, let's go shopping."

Bill gave Aria a nervous smile then ran after his friend. "J.T., you're crazy. It'll be midnight by the time we get to Miami and besides that it's Sunday. No stores will be open and how are you going to pay for clothes for her? She doesn't have any money and you can't very well buy her new clothes at Woolworth's, you know. And then there's clothing coupons. I think you're going to have to turn her over to the government and let them handle her."

"No," was all J.T. said.

"I don't guess you could give me a reason, could you? I mean, after all I'm in this too."

J.T. stopped and turned. "Somebody in Key West tried to kill her. If she walks up to this imposter princess and declares herself, I figure she'll be dead in two days. I've heard of General Brooks, he has some brains. He'll know what to do with her."

"You have more faith in the brass than I do." Bill followed J.T. as they crawled on all fours through the brush.

Thirty minutes later they had J.T.'s gear in the boat and were ready to go. Bill held out his hand to help Aria.

"She'll fall flat on her face before she touches you," J.T. said with disgust.

Aria concentrated on stepping into the swaying boat without falling.

"Oh hell," J.T. said, "we haven't got all night." He picked Aria up, and half tossed her over the side. "Now sit there and behave yourself."

Aria kept her back rigid and refused to look at him but she couldn't keep the blood from reddening her cheeks. A dungeon was going to be too good for this man.

They took off with more speed than she liked but she held on to the single seat in the boat as tightly as she could. It would no doubt give that odious man a good deal of satisfaction to see her tumble over the side of the boat.

After a few moments J.T. took the controls of the boat away from Bill and somehow got even more speed out of it. The salt air hit Aria's face, and after her initial shock, it began to feel good. Now and then Bill would ask her if she was all right, but Lieutenant Montgomery just kept his eyes on the water.

In the late afternoon they stopped in Key Largo for gas. Although her muscles were stiff from holding on for so long, Aria sat in her place on the boat. She had been trained to sit still for hours at a time.

"Where can I get some sandwiches?" J.T. asked the dock owner.

"Gertie's at the end of the pier."

Bill stayed with the boat and Aria while J.T. got the food.

"What's this?" Bill asked when J.T. returned. He was looking inside the bag of food. "A knife and fork for sandwiches? And a china plate?"

J.T. took the bags from Bill's hand. "You ready to go?" he snapped.

"Just waiting for you," Bill answered with a matching snap.

Bill boarded while J.T. shoved off then jumped in. As soon as they were headed north again, J.T. slammed an egg salad sandwich on the cheap plate he had had to pay dearly for and handed it to Aria with the knife and fork.

Aria, for the first time in days, felt comfortable eating. She didn't notice the way Bill kept gaping at her.

"A *real* princess," he said. "Wait'll Dolly hears about this."

"Dolly isn't going to hear about this," J.T. said

emphatically. *"Nobody* is going to hear about this. We keep it to ourselves."

Bill started to say something, but after looking at J.T., he closed his mouth.

They arrived in Miami at midnight.

"We'll have to wait until morning when the stores open," Bill said, then groaned. "The navy frowns on being late. Think we'll get the brig?"

J.T. leaped off the boat before it was fully docked. "Secure the boat and get her off. I have to make a phone call."

Aria unsteadily stepped onto the dock and made her way up the ladder. She was determined not to show her weariness.

"It's settled," J.T. said. "There'll be a cab here in a few minutes and my friend will meet us at a clothing store. There's a train out of here at four A.M. Come on, Princess, you're not too tired to buy clothes, are you?"

Aria straightened her shoulders. "I am not tired at all."

The taxi arrived with a squeal of brakes and J.T. lost no time in pushing Aria into the back seat.

"She seems awfully nice to me," she heard Bill saying. "Maybe you shouldn't treat her like that."

J.T. didn't answer as he climbed into the front seat and gave the driver the address. They rode through the deserted, dark streets.

"Are you sure this place is open, bub?" the taxi driver asked J.T.

"It will be by the time we get there."

They stopped in front of a small shop in a residential area of big, expensive mansions that were hidden behind vine-covered walls.

"Don't look like much to me," Bill said. "Maybe we oughtta try downtown."

J.T. got out of the car. "There he is," he said,

walking toward a long black Cadillac that was pulling to the curb.

Bill jumped out.

"Sorry for the inconvenience, Ed," J.T. was saying, hand outstretched. "If it weren't for helping with the war, I'd never have asked you."

"Think nothing of it," an older, gray-haired man said. He had the plump, well-cared-for look of a wealthy man. "The clerk isn't here yet?" he asked, frowning.

"No," J.T. answered. "How's your family?"

"Fine, one boy at Yale, the other in the air force. How's your mother?"

"Worried about her sons, of course."

The older man smiled and took out his wallet from his inside coat pocket. "I hope this is enough."

Bill's eyes widened as the man handed J.T. a four-inch-thick wad of money.

"It should be," J.T. said, grinning, "but you know ladies."

"May I meet her?"

J.T. went to the taxi door and opened it. Aria gracefully left the car.

"Your Royal Highness, I am honored," the older man said.

Aria would never get used to American manners. The man was not to speak until spoken to and he was to be presented to her. But considering the way she had been treated by the odious Lieutenant Montgomery on the island, this man's behavior was the height of protocol. She inclined her head in his direction.

J.T. seemed about to reprimand her about something when a dark Chevrolet pulled up beside them and a thin, hawk-nosed woman got out. She was obviously angry about something.

As every woman knows, there is no snob like a

61

saleswoman in an exclusive dress shop. And this particular clerk had been ordered from her bed in the middle of the night.

She looked at the men. "I don't appreciate this," she snapped. "I don't care if there *is* a war going on. I won't stand for this." She turned to Aria and looked down her long nose. *"This* is what I'm to work with?"

All three men opened their mouths to speak but Aria stepped in front of them. "You will open your little shop and show me your wares. If they are good enough, I will purchase an item or two." She said it in such an autocratic way, as if she were granting the woman a favor, that the men were stunned. "Now!" Aria said in a clipped voice.

"Yes, miss," the woman said meekly as she fumbled at her keys.

Aria entered the store as soon as the lights were turned on. It was the first store she had ever entered and it intrigued her. Rather than being presented with drawings of dresses and swatches of fabric, here were dresses already made. How very odd to think of wearing a dress that had not been designed for her alone.

Behind her the saleswoman was talking to the lieutenant and Aria touched a blouse hanging from a long rack. The ivory silk crepe was rather nice. Next to it was a yellow blouse with small black dots on it. She had always wanted to see how she looked in yellow. Perhaps she could see if the blouse fit.

She began to see possibilities in this idea of previously made clothes. She might be more inclined to be adventurous if she could see what something looked like before it was sewn.

"Here!" the saleswoman hissed at J.T., handing him a piece of paper with a telephone number on it. "Call this and tell Mavis to get over here instantly."

J.T., like all men, was out of place in the female atmosphere and docilely did as he was bid.

"Who is he?" Bill whispered as J.T. was dialing, nodding toward the older man who had managed to open the store in the middle of the night.

"A friend of my mother's. He owns a bank or two," J.T. said as he dialed. "Hello, Mavis?" he said into the telephone.

"I am waiting," Aria said impatiently from the dressing room.

The banker left, Mavis arrived, and Bill and J.T. sat down on little gold chairs to wait. Bill dozed while J.T. shifted on his chair impatiently.

"This will not do at all," Aria said, examining herself in the mirror.

"But it's a Mainbocher," the woman protested. "Perhaps a tuck taken in here and one here, and with the right gloves . . ."

"Perhaps. Now, about this one."

"The Schiaparelli?"

"I will take it. You must pack it carefully."

"Yes," the woman said hesitantly. "Does madam have her luggage here?"

"I have no luggage. You will have to provide it."

"But . . . but, madam, we do not sell luggage in this shop."

Aria found the woman quite tiresome. "Then you must obtain some. And I want the clothes packed carefully, with tissue paper." As far as Aria could tell, Americans were so odd, it was no telling what they would do with one's clothes.

The woman was backing from the dressing room. She whispered something to Mavis, who ran out of the shop. She turned to J.T. "This will take a while. There are alterations."

J.T. stood. "We don't have time. I have to report for

duty in Key West in a few hours. What size does she wear?"

"Six. She is a perfect six but sometimes the dresses are not perfect," the woman said diplomatically.

"Then give her one of every size six you have in the shop."

Her eyes widened. "But that will cost a great deal. And the clothing coupons—"

J.T. took the roll of money from his pocket. They were hundred-dollar bills. He began counting off bills. "Perhaps you can say that all your size sixes were damaged and they had to be discarded. Believe me, Uncle Sam won't mind giving up a few pieces of clothing for what this lady will bring him in return."

The woman's eyes were on the money. "There are shoes."

J.T. kept unrolling layers of bills.

"And gloves. And hosiery. And, of course, underwear. We also carry a line of costume jewelry."

J.T. stopped counting. "Princess," he yelled, startling Bill awake so that he nearly fell off the chair, "you want jewelry?"

"I'll need emeralds, and a few rubies, but only if they're deep red. And of course diamonds and pearls."

J.T. winked at the saleswoman. "I don't think she'll wear glass and gold paint, do you?"

"We do have a pair of diamond earrings."

J.T. unrolled a few more hundreds. "She'll take them. Give her whatever you have in her size."

At that moment Mavis appeared at the door. Behind her was a sleepy-looking man with a hand truck piled high with matching blue canvas luggage trimmed in white leather. "Where you want it?" he asked sullenly.

J.T. stepped back as the saleswoman took over.

"Beautiful, madam," the saleswoman said moments later to Aria in the dressing room. "You are utterly lovely."

Aria studied herself in the mirror. All her life she had been on display and how to look good was something she had learned at an early age. Yes, the clothes were beautiful, very little fabric used because of the war, of course, but they were cut well and they draped and clung to her body in a very pleasant way. But from her neck up she thought she looked very different from these Americans. Her long hair was scraped back and untidily wrapped into a knot and her face was pale and colorless.

"Your handsome young man is growing impatient," the saleswoman said, some apology in her voice.

"He is neither mine nor do I find him particularly handsome," Aria said, twisting to look at the seams in her stockings. "Are you sure American women wear dresses this short?" The clerk didn't answer so Aria looked at her and saw her staring.

"Not handsome?" the woman said at last.

It occurred to Aria that she had never actually looked at Lieutenant Montgomery. She opened the curtain to the dressing room and peered out.

He was sprawled across a small antique reproduction chair—and not a very good one at that—his legs stretched out across the floor so that Mavis had to walk around him, his hands deep in his pockets. He was broad-shouldered, flat-bellied, with long and surprisingly heavy legs. He had dark hair that waved back from his face, blue eyes under thick lashes, a straight thin nose, and perfectly cut lips above a slightly cleft chin.

Aria returned to the dressing room. "I believe this hat will do."

"Yes, madam. He *is* handsome, isn't he?"

"And I'll take all the hosiery. You may pack the dark green silk suit also."

"Yes, madam." The woman went away without an answer to her question.

When she was alone, Aria smiled at herself in the mirror. She had spent days alone on an island with an exquisitely handsome man—and she hadn't even noticed. Of course something had to be said for his despicable manner, which overrode any physical beauty. Before she had left Lanconia, her sister had teased her about spending time with the handsome American soldiers and here she had spent what would seem to be a romantic time alone on an island with a *very* handsome man and she had never once looked at him.

"Princess, we got to go. That train leaves in one hour and we have to drive there yet," J.T. said angrily from the other side of the screen.

Aria closed her eyes for a moment, braced herself, then left the dressing room. So much for handsome, she thought. She had heard the devil was handsome and now she knew it was true.

The man Bill gave a sort of whistle when she walked into the room that Aria found offensive, but before she could speak, it was echoed by the man who had delivered the luggage. As far as she could tell, the whistle seemed to be a type of compliment.

Of course Lieutenant Montgomery said nothing but grabbed her arm and started pulling her toward the door.

She jerked away from him—how good she had become at that motion since she had met him—and sat down. "I am not traveling with my hair like this."

"You'll do what you're told and be grateful that—"

The saleswoman cut him off by stepping between

Aria and him and removing a comb from her dress pocket. "If I may be so bold."

"We don't have time for anything fancy," J.T. said.

The woman combed Aria's tangled hair then quickly braided it and wrapped it atop Aria's head. "It looks like a crown," she said, pleased.

Aria looked in a hand mirror and saw the arrangement was neat but then she saw Mavis snickering at her. Mavis's hair was shoulder length, pulled back at her temples in a becoming way, and looked cool and very modern. Aria's hair, perfectly all right at home in Lanconia, looked old-fashioned here in America.

J.T. took the mirror from her. "You can admire yourself on the train. Come on. We got two taxis waiting, one for us and one for all your damned luggage." He pulled Aria from the store.

As he was shoving her into the taxi, the saleswoman came running out carrying a bottle of perfume. "For you," she said. "Good luck."

Aria held out her hand to the woman, palm downward.

Through some basic instinct that years of American freedom had not erased, the woman took Aria's fingertips then half curtsied. She caught herself in midbend and straightened, her face red. "I hope you enjoy your new clothes." She backed away.

J.T. started pushing Aria again but Bill stepped forward and placed himself between them. "Your carriage awaits, Your Royal Highness."

Aria gave him a dazzling smile then gracefully entered the taxi. Bill entered from the other side, J.T. next to him.

"I sure wish my wife could hear about this," Bill said as they sped away. "She'll never believe I met a real princess."

"Perhaps you could visit Lanconia one day. My house will be open to you."

"House? You don't live in a palace?" He sounded like a disappointed little boy.

"It is made of stone, is three hundred years old, and has two hundred and six rooms."

"That's a palace," Bill said, smiling in satisfaction.

Aria hid her own smile because she was glad she had not disappointed him. She vowed to greet his wife and him wearing the Aratone crown, the one with the ruby the size of a hen's egg in the center.

"If you two are finished playing old home week, we have some business to conduct," J.T. said, "Here, Princess." He held out a stack of green papers.

"What is that?" she asked, looking at them in the dim light.

"Money," he snapped.

Aria turned away. "I do not touch money."

"She *is* a princess," Bill gasped, obviously impressed.

J.T. leaned across his friend and grabbed the elegant little leather handbag from Aria's lap. It contained a lace-edged handkerchief and nothing else. "Look, I'm putting the money in here. When you get to D.C., get a porter to carry your bags and give him this bill, the one with the 'one' on it. No zeroes, understand? Get him to get you a taxi that'll take you to the Waverly Hotel. Give the driver a five. At the hotel ask for Leon Catton. If he's not there, have them call him. Tell him you are a friend of Amanda Montgomery."

"I do not know such a person."

"You know me and she's my mother. If you don't mention her name, you'll never get a room. Leon keeps a suite for emergencies, but you'll have to mention her name to get it. It won't hurt to show a little green either."

"Green?"

"Show them a hundred-dollar bill, that'll get their attention, and I imagine your attitude and all that luggage will make them take notice too. Oh, here." He pulled a box from his pocket and handed it to her.

She opened it to find a pair of earrings consisting of five small diamonds on each one. She held them up to the light of a passing car. Not very good quality at all, but she put them on.

"Don't you ever say 'thank you' for anything?"

"I will give America the vanadium," she said, looking straight ahead.

"You can't beat that, J.T.," Bill said.

"*If* she gets back to her country. *If* she can persuade our government that there has indeed been a switch. *If* she can—"

Bill patted Aria's hand, making her start. "Don't you worry, honey, anybody can see you're the real princess."

"Don't touch her and don't call her honey. She is royalty," J.T. said sarcastically.

"Lay off, will you?" Bill snapped.

The rest of the journey was made in silence.

Chapter Five

ARIA sat very still in the suite at the Waverly Hotel. Her ears were still ringing with the laughter of the hotel personnel. Never before had she been laughed at and it was not something she wanted to experience again.

The train had been dirty, cramped, and filled with hundreds of soldiers who kept trying to touch her. They had laughed uproariously when she had told them they were not allowed to touch her.

Upon arrival in Washington, she had been so flustered that she had become confused about the money. The porter nearly kissed her feet at the bill she had handed him, but the taxi driver had been abusive and yelled at her because of all the luggage she had.

There was a line at the hotel desk, and when she told the people to move out of her way, they became quite unpleasant. There were also many comments about her huge pile of luggage.

Aria had no idea how to wait in line but she soon learned. By the time she got to the desk, she was very tired and very impatient. Unfortunately, the hotel clerk was feeling the same way. He laughed in her face when she said she wanted a suite of rooms, then to further her embarrassment, he told the people in line behind her what she wanted. They had all laughed at her.

Remembering Lieutenant Montgomery's advice to show her "green," she thrust her purse at the awful little man. For some reason, this made him laugh harder.

By that time, after a night without sleep, Aria was feeling awful. She hated America and Americans and she couldn't remember half of what Lieutenant Montgomery had told her. Also, her command of the English language was failing. Her words became accented as she grew more tired and more confused.

"Amanda Montgomery," she managed to say.

"I can't understand you," the clerk said. "Are you German?"

The crowd had grown utterly silent at that and began to stare at her hostilely.

Aria repeated the name just as another man walked from the back.

The second man was the manager of the hotel and it seemed that the name Amanda Montgomery was magical. He berated the clerk, snapped his fingers at the bellboys, and within minutes was ushering Aria into an elevator. He apologized profusely for the clerk's rudeness, saying that the war made it impossible to get good help.

Now, alone in the room, Aria was still lost. How did one draw a bath? The manager, Mr. Catton, had said to ring if she needed anything but she could find no bellpull anywhere.

There was a knock at the door and when she did not

answer it a man walked in wheeling her baggage. Once the baggage was put in the closet, the man stood there looking at her. "You may go," she said. He gave her a little sneer and started toward the door.

"Wait!" she called, grabbing her purse. As far as she could tell, Americans would do anything for the green bills—and it made them so happy when the bills had zeroes on them. She pulled out a bill. "I need a maid. Do you know someone who can help me dress, draw my bath, unpack for me?"

The man's eyes bulged as he looked at the hundred-dollar bill. "For how long? My sister might do the work but she ain't nobody's maid forever."

It was Aria's turn to be stunned. In her country it was no disgrace to be someone's maid. Her ladies-in-waiting were aristocrats. "For a few days," she managed to say.

"I'll call her," the man said, and went to a black telephone on a table by the window.

Aria had used a telephone but someone else had always dialed it for her. She watched with interest as the man turned the dial. He turned away from her as he began to talk to his sister. Aria went to the bedroom.

The woman arrived two hours later. She was sullen, angry, and made it clear to Aria that she wasn't really a maid, that only because it was wartime was she willing to wait on anyone. She did what Aria asked but only reluctantly.

At four P.M. Aria lay down. She had bathed and washed her hair, eaten a mediocre meal, and now planned to sleep for several hours.

She had barely closed her eyes when the loud ringing of the telephone woke her. Groggily, she answered it. "Yes? This is Her Royal Highness."

"You don't lay off it even when you're asleep, do you?" said a familiar voice.

"What do you want, Lieutenant Montgomery?" She sat up straighter in bed.

"Bill wanted me to call to make sure you were all right."

"Of course I'm all right."

"No problems getting into the hotel?"

"None whatever. Everyone has been very kind," she lied.

"Did you see General Brooks yet?"

"I will see him tomorrow."

"Tomorrow? What did you do today?"

She wanted to scream at him that she had waited in line, been laughed at, had to deal with a maid who hated her, and been accused of being the enemy. "I washed my hair and spent hours in a tub of hot water."

"Of course. I should have known. A princess would put luxury before everything else. I'll call tomorrow night and see what he said."

"Please do not bother. I'm sure your government will rid itself of the imposter."

He paused a moment. "I guess you haven't seen the papers. That princess is a dead ringer for you and she's a hit wherever she goes. Maybe Americans will like her so much they won't want the real princess."

She glared at the telephone then slammed it down. "Hideous man!" she said as she left the bed and went into the living room of the suite. They had brought a newspaper with her dinner but she had left it where it lay.

On the second page was a photograph of a woman who looked very much like her, smiling at two men in uniform and cutting a wide ribbon. The caption told how Her Royal Highness, Princess Aria of Lanconia, was spreading peace across America. Instantly, she recognized her cousin Maude. "Were you always jealous of me, Cissy?" she asked in wonder, calling her cousin by the royal family's pet name. As she looked closer at the photo, she saw that in the background, smiling and hovering, was Lady Emere, Cissy's aunt. It was obvious that Lady Emere was protecting Cissy, probably keeping Aria's other attendants at a distance, but surely, Aria thought, one of them must be suspicious.

"Doesn't anyone know that's not *me?*" she said, blinking back tears.

She went back to bed but she didn't sleep very well.

Morning brought more problems. The woman she had hired to be her maid walked out when Aria held out her leg for her hose to be put on, so it took Aria three hours to get dressed. She was very glad for the black, veiled hat that covered her attempts at hairdressing.

When she left the hotel, she was feeling less than confident, but she kept her head high and her shoulders back. Once again she heard those low whistles from the men as she walked through the lobby, but she ignored them.

The doorman was someone she understood. She told him she wanted to see General Brooks, he blew a whistle, and a taxi came forward. Aria pointed at a long black Cadillac with a chauffeur leaning against the hood. "I want that car." The doorman walked across the traffic and talked to the chauffeur, who nodded.

"He'll take you to the Pentagon."

Aria had already realized that every American expected to be paid for everything he did. She handed the doorman one of the bills with the two zeroes on it, and he nodded gravely to her, then opened the door to the limousine.

Aria leaned back against the seat and closed her eyes. In the back of this luxurious car she felt at home for the first time since she had been kidnapped.

The chauffeur opened the car door for her and later, held the door that led into the Pentagon.

"I have been paid," he said solemnly when she offered him one of the few bills left in her purse.

She smiled at him, glad for any kindness from an American.

The time in the car was only a pause before the storm. Nothing she had experienced so far prepared her for the Pentagon during war. Everywhere people rushed back and forth, machines printed, people shouted orders, radios played news.

She stopped at a desk and asked for General Brooks.

"Over there," the woman said, her mouth full of pencils. "Ask over there."

Aria walked down the corridor and asked again.

"I'm not his secretary," a man snapped. "Don't you know there's a war going on?"

Aria asked a total of five people and they all shuffled her to someone else. Twice she started down hallways and men drew rifles on her. Someone told her to come back next week. Someone else told her to come back when the war was over. Someone else grabbed her arm and half shoved her out the door into a parking lot.

She straightened her suit jacket, squared her hat, and went back inside. If Americans didn't want to listen to the truth, then she would give them a good story. She walked into the middle of the busiest room and said in a normal voice: "I am a German spy and I will give my secrets only to General Brooks."

One by one the people stopped what they were doing and stared at her. After one brief second of absolute silence, all hell broke loose. Soldiers with guns came from every corridor and seized her.

"Do not touch me," she called, the men lifting her by her arms so her feet did not touch the ground.

"I knew she was German the minute I saw her," Aria heard a woman say.

She was pulled down a long corridor, people leaving their offices to have a look at her. Aria was glad her hat had slipped down to obscure half of her face. I am never leaving Lanconia again, she vowed to herself.

After what seemed to be ages, the soldiers dropped her into a chair.

"Let's have a look at her," said a voice with a great deal of anger in it.

Aria lifted her head, and pushed back her hat to look up at General Brooks. "So good to see you again," she said as if they were at a gala reception, and extended her hand to him.

General Brooks's eyes widened. "Out!" he commanded the many soldiers jammed in the room.

"But she may be dangerous," said a man holding an ugly black pistol aimed at Aria.

"I will somehow manage to fight her off," the general said sarcastically. When they were alone, he turned to Aria. "Your Royal Highness?" He took her hand, touching her fingers lightly. "The last I heard, you were in Virginia."

"Not me but someone who looks like me."

The general looked at her for a long while. "I'll send for tea and we can talk."

Aria ate everything that was on the tea tray, then

lunch was ordered, and still the general asked her questions. He made her repeat nearly every minute of their time together in Lanconia. He wanted to know anything that would make him *sure* she was the real princess.

At two he had her taken to a small sitting room where she could rest. At three-thirty she was led into a room where four generals and two plainclothesmen sat and had to tell everything over again.

Throughout this time she showed no impatience, no anger, no fatigue. The seriousness of the matter was coming through to her. If these men did not believe her and therefore did not help her get back to her country, she would lose everything. She would lose her identity, she would lose the people she loved, and she would lose her nationality. And Lanconia would have an imposter for queen—a woman eaten with jealousy who must want something besides the good of Lanconia.

She sat upright and answered their questions—over and over and over again.

At ten o'clock they sent her back to the hotel under armed guard. A WAC drew her bath and, Aria knew, searched her new clothes. Aria stayed in the tub until her skin wrinkled to give the woman plenty of time. At midnight, she was at last able to go to bed.

The big Pentagon room was filled with a blue haze of cigarette and cigar smoke. The mahogany table was littered with empty glasses, overflowing ashtrays, and crumbs from a meal of dried-out sandwiches. The preeminent smell was a mixture of sweat and anger.

"I don't like it!" General Lyons shouted as he shifted the wet cigar butt from one side of his mouth to the other.

"I think we have more than enough evidence that she's telling the truth," Congressman Smith said. He was the only one of the six men to still look somewhat fresh; nevertheless, there were dark circles of sleeplessness under his eyes. "Did you see the scar on her left hand? Our records say she fell while on a hunting trip when she was twelve years old.".

"But who knows which princess is better for America?" General O'Connor said. "Lanconia doesn't really mean much to us except that now we need the vanadium. If the imposter princess will give us the vanadium, I don't think we should involve ourselves."

"Lanconia lies near Germany and Russia. Russia is our friend now but it is a communist country. After the war—"

"Who knows what will happen to Lanconia after the war? Say we restore this princess to the throne. Didn't that report say she was related to some German royals? What if she marries one?"

The six men began to talk at once.

General Brooks slammed his fist on the table. "I say we *need* her on the throne. You heard her promise to give America the vanadium if we help her. And she would be sure to give it to us if she were married to an American."

"An American?" Congressman Smith gasped. "Those bluebloods marry only bluebloods. We abolished monarchy in this country, remember? So where do we find an American prince?"

"That little girl will do *anything* for her country," General Brooks said. "You mark my words. If we told her we'd help her only if she married an American and later made him king, believe me, she'd do it."

"But didn't we hear she was already engaged?"

"I met him," General Brooks said. "A pompous little runt, old enough to be her father. He only wants our princess for her money."

"*Our* princess?" General Lyons snorted.

"She will be ours if we help her and put an American there beside her. Think of having military posts so near Russia and Germany."

The men considered this.

"So who do we choose to make king?" Congressman Smith asked.

"Someone we can trust. Someone who believes in America. None of these bleeding hearts."

"He has to have a good family history," General Brooks said. "We can't ask a princess to marry a gangster or an imbecile. We put only America's finest on the throne."

General Attenburgh yawned. "I vote we adjourn and present some names tomorrow."

The men readily agreed.

The next morning six sleepy-eyed men met. Four of them, without giving away the actual facts of the problem, had asked their wives what American would make a good king. Clark Gable won hands down, with Cary Grant a close second. Robert Taylor also received a few votes.

After four hours of arguing, six names were selected. Two of them were young congressmen, one a wealthy businessman not so young, and three were sons of America's oldest families, one of whose ancestors came over on the *Mayflower*.

Each name was given to a committee and rated as top priority. The men were to be researched as thoroughly as possible and it was made clear that the staff was to look for dirt. If this man was going to be crowned king, whatever skeletons were in his closet had better come out now.

"And check out that man Montgomery," Congressman Smith said as an afterthought. "Let's see if we can trust him to keep his mouth shut."

For three days Aria was kept as a prisoner in her hotel room. Two men with rifles were outside her door twenty-four hours a day and more soldiers were stationed on the street below her windows. On the morning of the second day a large package of magazines was delivered courtesy of General Brooks.

Aria sat down and got her first real look at Americans. They seemed to be a frivolous lot, interested mainly in movie stars and nightclub singers. A *Life* magazine had several pages neatly cut from it and the contents showed that it had been an article on Lanconia's regal princess.

At six A.M. on the fourth day, three WACs came to her room to help her dress. They were very professional and very cool, did what Aria asked, and made no complaint.

At eight she was again at the Pentagon, seated at the end of a long table with the same six men as before. They explained that she was to marry an American and crown him king.

Aria did not let her horror show. It seemed that these Americans believed they could ask *anything* of her. Patiently, she tried to explain why an American husband was an impossibility. "My husband will be prince consort and no American has a kingdom to unite with mine."

"You have the 'kingdom' of America," one man said sarcastically.

"It cannot be done," she answered with less patience. "I am engaged to be married. My people would not like my breaking my engagement, nor will my grandfather, the king." She was sure that would end the matter but it did not. A Congressman Smith began to explain to her an utterly preposterous plan.

"If we switch you with the imposter without first knowing who set this whole thing up, your life could be in danger. You make one error and you're a dead duck."

"Duck?"

"Dead princess, then. We have to find out who tried to kill you and who doesn't want America to have the vanadium. It had to be someone close to you."

Aria didn't respond to that but she knew the man was right. She tried to control the blood she could feel leaving her face. It was no use telling them her cousin was the imposter because she knew quite well that Cissy was not the instigator. Cissy was a nervous, easily frightened weakling, and if she was acting in Aria's place, it was because someone else was telling her what to do and how to do it.

"We have a few things going for us," said a large, gray-haired man with a chestful of medals. "First of all, they have no idea you're alive, so they won't be looking for you."

"So here's the plan we've come up with," said another man. "We let the imposter princess finish her tour, return to Lanconia, then we take her. At the same time you will appear in Lanconia and we figure someone will approach you to take the place of the missing princess."

"That way we can find out who engineered the switch," Congressman Smith said.

General Brooks cleared his throat. "The only catch is that you will have to be an American with an American husband."

Aria wasn't sure she was understanding. They were going too fast for her. "But I am not an American. How will they think I am American?"

"We'll teach you."

"But *why?*" she gasped. Suddenly, she just wanted to go home. She was tired of strange food, of strange customs, of using a language she had to think about before every word. She was tired of people acting as if she were a spy and maids who cursed her because she wanted her hose put on. She was tired of dealing with things and people that she did not understand. Desperately, she wanted to go *home*.

General Brooks took her hand and squeezed it and she didn't pull away. "If we take the imposter princess and then you show up talking as you do, walking as you do, eating cookies with a knife and fork, the men who first tried to kill you are going to do it again—but this time they may succeed. We want to create a need for another woman who looks like you, then we hand them an American who they'll probably want to train to be a princess."

"Train *me* to be a princess?" The absurdity of that statement brought her out of her homesickness.

General Brooks smiled at her but the others watched with faces of great seriousness.

Aria decided she had better try to comprehend their plan. "I am to learn to be an American and then learn to be a princess?"

"Think you can do it?" Congressman Smith snapped.

She looked down her nose at him. "I shall do quite well at the princess impersonation."

All the men except Congressman Smith laughed.

"But I do not need an American husband for this," Aria said. Perhaps if she went along with part of their plan, they would forget the more ridiculous aspects.

General Lyons leaned forward. "The fact is, the only way we're willing to risk our necks for you is if you put an American on the throne beside you. If you don't agree, you can walk out that door and we've never heard of you."

She took a moment to respond. They could *not* be serious. "But I have agreed to give you the vanadium."

Congressman Smith looked at her and his eyes were cold. "The truth is, we want more. The vanadium is for now, during the war. We want military bases in Lanconia after the war. We want a place where we can keep an eye on Germany and Russia."

"*If* you win this war," Aria said, some of her growing anger showing. "If Germany wins, then Lanconia will have an American prince consort—an enemy." She had to protect her own country.

"We won't lose and he's to be made king," Congressman Smith said in a cold, cutting voice.

"I cannot—" Aria began, but closed her mouth. They asked so *much*. They asked for diplomatic sacrifices and military sacrifices as well as personal sacrifices. She looked at her hands. But if she didn't agree, what did she have? America was the strangest place she had ever encountered and to have to live here forever . . .

She looked up and saw the men staring at her. The door opened and a woman in uniform came in and whispered something to General Brooks. He nodded at the others.

"Princess," he said, rising, "we have to leave you for a while. I will have someone escort you to a rest area."

The men walked out, leaving Aria sitting. She would never get over being horrified at American manners but at least they had given her time to think. She followed an armed guard to a waiting room.

* * *

The six men walked into a room that held fourteen tired, red-eyed enlisted personnel. None of them had had any sleep in the last three days as they had gathered information on the candidates for Princess Aria's husband. They had been given carte blanche for military transport to return to hometowns to talk to anyone who remembered a candidate. One woman had had three permanent waves in three days in three towns because she knew that the best place for gossip was the beauty parlor. Now, the fourteen researchers were too tired to do anything but sit and stare.

As the six men entered, the group wearily stood and saluted, and one lieutenant stepped forward, papers in hand.

"What did you find out?" Congressman Smith asked impatiently.

"I'm afraid it's not very good. Charles Thomas Walden," the lieutenant read. He told of the magnificent family tree of this young man.

"Sounds pretty good to me," General Brooks said. "What's wrong with him?"

"He's a homosexual, sir."

"Next one," the general barked.

The next man, the businessman, had married a woman from the wrong side of the tracks when he was sixteen and now paid her enormous sums to keep out of his life. There had been no divorce.

Another man was a compulsive gambler, another one's family was making a fortune off the war with black-market goods. One of the young congressmen was selling his votes.

"And the last man?" General Brooks asked wearily.

"German grandparents. We could never be sure of his loyalty."

"Now what do we do?" General Lyons asked.

"We're running out of time. The imposter returns to Lanconia in two weeks and she'll award the vanadium contract then. If she gives it to Germany, we'll have to take the war onto Lanconian soil and then no mining will be done."

"I have a brother," one of the WACs said, but no one laughed.

After a moment of silence, a young second lieutenant stood. "Sirs, I have a report that might be of interest to you. It's on the Lieutenant Montgomery who saved the princess's life."

"We don't have time—" Congressman Smith began.

"Read it," General Brooks barked.

"Jarl Tynan Montgomery grew up in a small town on the coast of Maine, a town which his family virtually owns. They are Warbrooke Shipping." The lieutenant paused a moment because he had the room's attention now. Warbrooke Shipping was vast, and when the war broke out the company was the first to convert its plants to making warships. The navy owed much to Warbrooke Shipping.

"His family first came to America during Elizabeth the First's reign—some of them were here to greet the Pilgrims. The family motto is 'Never sell the land,' and they've kept the vow. They still own land in England that once belonged to an ancestor, Ranulf de Warbrooke, who lived in the thirteenth century. In eighteenth-century America they were rich by any standards, but one of the men married a woman named Taggert and the two of them ended up owning half the state of Maine. In the early nineteenth century, some of the Taggerts left the East Coast to seek their fortunes and lost everything until in the 1880s one Kane Taggert made the money back in spades. An aunt of Lieutenant Montgomery's went to

Colorado around the turn of the century and ended up marrying the son of this Kane Taggert. They now live in a marble mansion and own Fenton-Taggert Steel." This was another supplier for the war.

The lieutenant took a breath. "Lieutenant Montgomery is also related to Tynan Mills in Washington State. Besides the money, which the Montgomery family is rolling in, he's got an ancestor who was a grand duchess in Russia, another one who was a French duchess, and several English earls as well as a few gunslingers. His ancestors have fought in—and been decorated in—every American war. Hell, even the *women* in his family have been decorated.

"As for Lieutenant Montgomery himself, I couldn't find a hint of scandal. He's worked in his father's shipyard with his three brothers since he was a kid. He's a loner, spent more time on his boats than on anything else. Good grades in school, three years captain of the local rowing team. Enlisted the morning after Pearl Harbor—as did his brothers—and after boot camp was sent to Italy. A year and a half ago he was brought back to the States, given a commission, and put in charge of converting civilian vessels to military use in Key West. Two months ago a PBM came in too low and hit an ammo igloo and caught fire. Eleven people were killed but Lieutenant Montgomery got the fire out before the ammo blew. He was badly burned, spent a few weeks in the hospital, and was recuperating on the island when he saved the princess."

The lieutenant put down his papers. "In conclusion, sirs, I'd say that this man Montgomery is about as blue blood as America has to offer."

"Absolutely not!" Aria gasped. "Under no circumstances will I marry that rude, boorish man. I will beg on the streets before I marry him." For once in her life she didn't bother trying to cover her emotions. She allowed her disgust, her horror, her repulsion to show to everyone. These Americans were *insane!*

Congressman Smith looked at her with contempt. "If it were only you involved, there would be no problem. I hate to think what this imposter princess and her advisers will do to your country. I hope they don't kill your grandfather." He closed his briefcase. "It was nice meeting you, Princess. I wish you well, whatever happens to you."

Images flew through Aria's mind: Cissy on the throne with someone—a murderer—controlling her. Lanconia had once been a warlike country. Would the murderer enter Lanconia in this war that raged around the world? Some Lanconians, usually older men without children to lose, said the lagging Lanconian economy would be helped greatly if the country joined the war.

Aria imagined living in some American hotel and reading about the war-bombed Lanconian country-side. All those deaths would be *her* fault. To prevent hundreds, maybe thousands of deaths, all she had to do was marry a man she disliked greatly.

"Wait!" she called to Congressman Smith.

He stopped at the door but didn't turn.

"I . . . I will do what you want," she whispered. She kept her back straight, her muscles tight. She felt that if she loosened one little bit, she would dissolve into a heap of tears.

"Lieutenant Montgomery has already been sent for," Congressman Smith said with a smirk before he left the room.

"Bastard," the WAC behind Aria muttered. She took Aria's arm. "Honey, what you need is a good cry. Come with me. I'll take you to General Gilchrist's

88

office. He's away right now and you can be private in there. Is this Montgomery a real jerk?"

Aria allowed herself to be pulled along and the lump in her throat prevented her from talking. She managed to nod.

"Brother!" the WAC replied. "Am I glad I'm an American. Nobody tells an American what to do. I can marry whoever I want." She unlocked a door. "Now, you stay in here. Leave the lights off and nobody'll know you're here. I'll come pick you up at five. Until then I won't have any idea where you went." She winked at Aria and shut the door.

Aria sat down on a little leather-covered sofa and clasped her hands together tightly. If she started to cry, she was afraid she would never stop. She forced herself to visualize her country under attack, then she thought how she was saving it from destruction by this selfless, noble act of hers. Unfortunately, she also kept remembering Lieutenant Montgomery sneering at her, his rudeness, the way he pulled her about, tossed her into boats.

How could such a man be trained to be a prince consort?

The more she thought, the worse she felt. She prayed that her grandfather would understand that she had had to do this.

Chapter Six

TWENTY-FOUR hours later the six men who were working on what had become known as the Lanconia Project had dwindled to four. Two men pleaded that they had more pressing matters to attend to and left the conference room. The truth was that if they had found the princess difficult, they weren't prepared for the muleheaded stubbornness of Lieutenant Montgomery.

General Brooks's eyes were red and his throat raw from talking. "The son of a gun still laughing?"

Congressman Smith was too angry to do more than nod.

"What's the latest?" General Brooks asked the pretty young WAC. They had tried using men to talk some sense into Montgomery and that hadn't worked, so they had started using women. So far that had met with no success either.

"J.T. . . . . er, ah, Lieutenant Montgomery says he'll stand a court-martial before he marries the princess. When I told him he was wanted because of his family history, he did, however, suggest that we offer Her Royal Highness to one of his brothers. He said that they might be tempted since they hadn't met the—" She looked up. "Expletive deleted."

"His brothers?" General Brooks's face showed a little hope.

"I checked, sir," said a young captain. "The eldest brother is in intelligence, so far underground that only the president and two others know where he is. The second brother is now in a hospital. Last week his leg was nearly blown off by machine-gun fire. The third brother married an English girl last month. The family doesn't know of it yet."

General Brooks's face fell. "Any cousins?"

"We don't have *time!*" Congressman Smith said, slamming his fist on the table. "This Montgomery is perfect. He's about as American as a human can get, and he has the looks of a prince." He raised an eyebrow at the fervent agreement from the WAC. "His IQ tested out at one hundred forty-three and he's rich. According to our reports, Lanconia is barely surviving. The Montgomery family's money could put it on its feet."

"And spread American goodwill throughout the country," General Brooks added.

Congressman Smith stacked the papers in front of him. "We can't threaten him and risk losing the support of Warbrooke Shipping—"

"Or Tynan Mills or Fenton-Taggert Steel," the captain added.

"So we'll lie to him."

That succeeded in quieting the room.

Congressman Smith continued. "He can't stand the princess, right? He laughs at the idea of being king so we tell him the marriage is a sham, that he's to think of this as a temporary intelligence operation. He's to live with her, teach her to be an American, take her to Lanconia, then, when she's on the throne again, he can walk away."

"But in Lanconia he finds out the marriage is permanent and he's to be king?" General Brooks added.

"Something of the sort. We do what we can now to get them married and America's foot in the door. We worry about the consequences later."

"Won't the princess give it away?" the captain asked.

Congressman Smith snorted. "She'd sell her soul for her country. She'll lie to him or do anything else to keep her country. I have a feeling that she has no plans to make Montgomery king. We shall see what he says about that. Well, shall we go? I don't want to give him time to think about this. How long has he been without sleep now?"

The captain looked at his watch. "Thirty-eight hours."

"And food?"

"He's had a sandwich and a Coke in twenty-two hours."

The congressman nodded. "Let's go."

Aria had difficulty concealing her astonishment. "Lieutenant Montgomery did not want to marry a royal princess? He does not want to be married to a queen?"

The WAC was not going to tell Aria the dreadful things J.T. had said about her, that she was inhuman, a piece of marble, that she wasn't anything like a woman, that he would much rather give his love to the statue of Venus de Milo. Instead, the WAC explained what they had had to do to get J.T. to agree to the marriage.

93

"He believes there will be a—what is that word?"

"Divorce, or annulment."

"But royalty is not permitted to separate—no matter what. A royal princess marries once and that is all." Aria looked at a picture of President Roosevelt on the wall. Too clearly she remembered the time on the island with this insolent, despicable man named Montgomery. For the sake of her country she had agreed to marry him, agreed to spend the rest of her life with him, but now he was saying he didn't want to marry *her*.

"I will not tell him we are to be married for always," she whispered.

"I'm afraid there's more." The WAC cursed Congressman Smith for detailing this job to her. She rather liked the princess, liked anyone who was willing to fight for her country.

"The army had rented a house for the two of you in Virginia, complete with horses and a butler, but the lieutenant refuses to have anything to do with it. He says he wants to return to his job in Key West and you two are to live in a single-family house—no servants, no special privileges. You're to live on his military pay also."

The WAC was well aware that no one had told the princess of J.T.'s wealth, and now, looking at her, the WAC thought she had no idea what J.T. was demanding of her. She couldn't imagine this elegant woman donning an apron and washing a sinkful of dishes. "He says that if you're to learn to be an American, he wants it done properly."

"The lieutenant certainly has many opinions, doesn't he?"

You don't know the half of it, the WAC thought. "Then you agree to his terms?"

"Do I have a choice?"

94

"No, I guess not. If you're ready, the chaplain's waiting."

Aria didn't say a word but stood, her head held high. What she was doing was so much more important than the romantic nonsense of a white wedding gown and people wishing her joy and happiness. It didn't matter that the dress she was wearing was one she had had on for two days, that it was wrinkled and sagging in places.

She stood before the door until the WAC opened it.

Outside were waiting six other WACs, all of them smiling happily.

"They don't know who you are," the first WAC whispered. "They think the army's reunited you with your lover and you're to be married today."

"Something old," said one woman holding out a little gold locket. "It's also something borrowed. It was my grandmother's."

"Something new," said another, offering her a pretty little handkerchief.

"And something blue." A third woman gave Aria a corsage of blue-dyed carnations. She pinned it on Aria's shoulders as another woman took Aria's shoe and slipped a penny inside for good luck.

Aria was bewildered by this treatment. So far, the women in America had been very good to her, but the men . . .! She wondered how the women coped with the rude, ill-mannered men.

The conference room was to be used for the ceremony. No one had so much as bothered to push the table out of the way so there was no aisle for her to walk down, no older man to give her away. She walked along the wall beside the WAC toward the group of men at the far end. There were a few men in suits but about a dozen men wore uniforms, their chests resplendent with medals. It seemed that at least there was enough significance to this wedding that some of the higher officials attended.

Lieutenant Montgomery was sitting in a chair, half asleep, his head propped on his arm. His cheeks and chin were dark with unshaved whiskers. His uniform was dirty and rumpled.

Aria's anger rose immediately. Perhaps these men were afraid to tell him how disrespectful he was, but she wasn't afraid. She stood in front of him. "How dare you appear before me looking like that," she said, glaring down at him.

He didn't even open his eyes. "The dulcet tones of Her Royal Highness."

General Brooks took Aria's arm and pulled her to stand in front of the chaplain. "He's had a long few days. Perhaps we shouldn't annoy him until after the ceremony. He might change his mind again."

Aria clenched her hands at her sides. Was she worth so little that she had to beg a man to marry her?

Lazily, J.T. stood. "Want to change your mind, Princess? I'm willing."

She didn't look at him but instead concentrated on an image of Lanconia.

The chaplain hesitated over Aria's name.

"Who?" J.T. said, scratching at his whiskers.

"Victoria Jura Aria Cilean Xenita."

"Yeah, I take her," he said.

Aria glared at him. She promised to love and honor Jarl Tynan Montgomery but she left out the word "obey."

"Your Royal Highness," the chaplain said. "It's love, honor, and obey."

Aria looked at J.T. and didn't say a word.

"We have enough lies today," J.T. said. "Get on with it."

The chaplain sighed. "I now pronounce you man and wife. You may kiss the bride."

J.T. grabbed Aria's wrist. "Hell, I'm going to bed."

Aria barely had time to return the little gold locket to the WAC before J.T. pulled her out of the room.

General Brooks was chuckling. "It looks like they're off to a fine start."

Congressman Smith grunted.

Aria leaned back against the seat of the plain black car the army had provided and concentrated on controlling the smile that was threatening to escape. At the other end of the seat, as far from her as he could get, sat the man who was now her husband. His head was resting against the window and she couldn't see his face, but he had certainly made his feelings clear.

Again Aria had to control her smile. While they were marooned on the island together, he had pretended she wasn't a woman to him. He had also ignored the fact of her royal birth, but somehow that hadn't hurt as much as when he had told her he didn't think she was pretty or appealing. No matter how royal a woman was, she still wanted to be desirable.

Aria closed her eyes a moment. It had been a long two weeks since she had been kidnapped and many awful things had happened to her, but now it was over. She was married—she stole a look at Lieutenant Montgomery as he sprawled in the back seat—and she could have done worse. He might look all right in evening dress and he certainly looked strong enough to carry the heavy state robes. Of course she still had to learn how to be an American, but how difficult could that be? There seemed to be many people doing it with ease.

97

But first there was her wedding night. Her mother had talked to her about this night, had explained what men did to one and how they were driven to it by a passion not felt by women. Her mother said Aria was always to look her best for her husband and she was to encourage this desire in him—it perpetuated the line.

So tonight was to be her wedding night. Of course her husband was virtually a stranger but then Aria had always expected to marry a man she barely knew. Perhaps after tonight Lieutenant Montgomery wouldn't be so rude to her. Perhaps tomorrow morning he would kneel by her bed and kiss her hand and beg her forgiveness for the terrible things he had said to her. Perhaps after tonight . . .

She hadn't realized that the car had stopped until the driver opened her door. They were back at her hotel. She got out then waited while the driver opened the door for her husband. He had to catch J.T. before he fell.

"We're here, sir," the driver said as J.T. untangled his long body from the car.

J.T. looked at the hotel as if he had never seen one before. "Good," he mumbled, and went inside, leaving Aria standing. He returned a few seconds later, grabbed her arm, and pulled her along behind him.

"Which room is yours?"

"It is a pink one."

J.T. stopped and turned to look at her. His eyes were red and his beard was darkening by the minute. "When you get back here after being gone, how do you find your room?"

"I have to go there." She pointed to the desk. "Sometimes I have to wait, then someone escorts me."

"They didn't give you a key?"

98

"A key to the city? Why no, no one has mentioned it."

He closed his eyes a moment. "Stand right here. Don't move, understand?"

She nodded, then looked away to hide her smile. He was certainly anxious to keep her near him.

After some discussion at the desk and after shaking hands with Mr. Catton, J.T. returned and led her to the elevator. "I'll never be more glad to get into bed in my life," he said when the doors closed.

Aria did smile at that.

He unlocked the door to the room, went inside, leaving her standing in the hallway. A moment later his arm shot out, caught her hand, and pulled her inside. He stood very close to her as he locked the door and Aria modestly looked at her clasped hands. Now they were alone.

J.T. yawned and stretched. "Bed. I can see it," he said, and began to stagger through the living room into the bedroom. He got one shoe off then fell across the bed and was asleep.

Aria was still standing by the door. She waited a few minutes but heard no sound from the bedroom, so she timidly crossed the room. He was already in bed. He seemed to be asleep but she knew he was waiting for her.

"I'll . . . I'll get ready," she whispered, and went to the bureau to get a nightgown.

She saw immediately that there was nothing appropriate for her wedding night. This was a night that happened only once in a woman's life and she wanted to look her best.

She glanced at J.T. and thought he looked suspiciously as if he were asleep. A moment later he twitched and made a noise like a snore.

Glancing at the little clock by the bed, she saw that it was only four P.M. Perhaps she could go to one of those American stores she had seen on the way here and get a proper nightgown—one that would keep a new husband from sleeping.

Softly, she crept from the room after checking that her handbag had a clean handkerchief. All the green money papers Lieutenant Montgomery had given her were gone.

She did what she always did when she wanted to go out: she asked for Mr. Catton and he got a car for her and paid the driver. She had some difficulty explaining where she wanted to go without losing her dignity. He finally asked a pretty young girl who worked in the hotel and soon Aria was on her way.

The taxi driver let her off in front of a very large building; Aria had never seen a department store before. Perhaps it was the way she carried herself or perhaps it was the sight of a Paris original dress, but three women nearly ran to wait on her. She chose the oldest woman.

"I wish to be shown ladies' sleeping attire."

"Right this way, ma'am," said the saleswoman, feeling superior for having been chosen.

Two hours later, the woman was not so pleased. Aria had tried on every nightgown in the store and discarded most of them on the floor. The saleswoman had difficulty keeping up the supply and refolding them, as well as having to help Aria take them off and on.

At last Aria seemed to settle on a low-cut, off-the-shoulder, heavenly concoction of pink silk voile and satin.

The saleswoman sighed in relief. "If you'll come with me, I'll box it for you." When she found she had to help Aria dress, she also found she was losing her temper.

Moments later the saleswoman was slamming the nightgown into a box. "Expected me to wait on her like I was her damned servant or something."

"Shh," said her fellow employee. "The floor walker will hear you."

"I'll let *him* deal with her."

Aria came out of the dressing room just in time to see the clerk close the lid on the pink nightgown. As the woman turned away to make out the sales slip, Aria picked up the box and started walking toward the door.

"Oh my God!" the clerk gasped. "She's *stealing* it."

The telephone rang eleven times before J.T. awoke fully enough to answer it. "Yes?" he said groggily.

"You Lieutenant Montgomery?"

"Last I heard I was."

"Well, this is Sergeant Day at the Washington Police Department and we got a lady down here under arrest for shoplifting. Says she's your wife."

J.T. opened his eyes more fully. "Have you booked her?"

"Not yet. She says she's valuable to the war effort, but then she's sayin' a lot of things. She's too much of a screwball for us to make out. She says she has no last name and that she's a queen and we're to call her Your Majesty."

J.T. ran his hand over his face. "Princess, and it's Your Royal Highness."

"How's that?"

"Sergeant, it may seem hard to believe but she *is* valuable—at least to somebody. If you lock her up, it could cause a lot of problems with the government.

Could you just put her in a room and give her a cup of tea? And give her a saucer with her cup."

There was a pause from the sergeant. "You really *marry* this fruitcake?"

"Lord help me but I did. I'll be there as soon as I can."

"We'd sure appreciate your takin' her off our hands."

J.T. hung up the phone. "Who's going to take her off *my* hands?" he mumbled.

Chapter Seven

ARIA sat in the chair in the glass-walled office in the police station and tried her best to ignore the gaping people on the other side of the glass. They had put a heavy white mug of what they had told her was tea beside her, but for some odd reason, they had put the cup in an ashtray. She hadn't considered touching it.

The last few hours had been miserable, what with people touching her, shouting at her, and asking the same questions over and over—and they hadn't believed her answers.

She was almost glad when she saw Lieutenant Montgomery's unshaven face appear in the room outside. He gave her one quick, angry glance then was surrounded by all the people who had moments before been shouting at Aria. She wanted to see how an American handled these other Americans. He distributed several of the green money papers, signed some white papers, and all the while talked to the people, but she couldn't hear what he was saying.

She was sure she could have done the same thing if she had just understood what they wanted. Perhaps it was going to be *very* easy to learn to be an American.

The crowd moved away from Lieutenant Montgomery and he strode toward her.

"Let's go," he growled after throwing open the door. "And not one word from you or I'll let them have you."

Aria held on to the box containing her nightgown and left the room, her head held high.

He didn't speak to her on the way back to the hotel and constantly he walked in front of her. Once inside the room, he went to the telephone.

"Room service?" he said. "I want dinner sent up to the Presidential Suite. No, I don't have a menu. Send me dinner for four, whatever you have, and a bottle of wine, the best you have in the cellar. Just hurry it up."

Aria stood there blinking at him when he had hung up.

"Could you keep out of trouble for a while? All I want is a decent meal, some sack time, a shower, and I'll be all right. Just give me that and maybe then I can tackle you and the U.S. government."

Aria didn't understand half of what he was saying, but she did understand that he planned to eat dinner now. She blushed. After dinner he would make her his wife.

"The woman who was my maid did not return. If you would draw my bath, I will ready myself," she said softly.

"Haven't even learned to fill your own bathtub yet?" he said with wonder in his voice. "Come on then and I'll show you."

She gave him a hesitant smile. "Don't the maids of American wives draw their baths? Perhaps we should call Mr. Catton and ask for someone?"

"Honey, American wives don't have maids, and from now on, neither do you. From now on you dress yourself, bathe yourself, and, what's more, I'm going to teach you how to take care of a husband."

Aria looked away to hide her red cheeks. He was a little rough, and more than a little rude as he showed her how to adjust the water, but she learned. He left her alone when room service knocked.

She took a long time in the tub, soaping herself and contemplating the coming event. Lieutenant Montgomery called to her twice that her food was getting cold but she still didn't rush.

It wasn't easy dressing alone, but the beautiful nightgown did just slip over her head so she managed. For several minutes she had not heard anything from the other side of the door and she supposed he was readying himself also.

Cautiously, she opened the door.

In the living room stood a large table with the remains of a banquet. The cad had eaten their wedding supper without her! Nose wrinkled, she looked at the dirty dishes, which seemed to be all that was left of the feast. This man might teach her how to fill a bathtub but she planned to teach him some manners.

She turned toward the bedroom. He was sprawled on his back on one side of the bed, a newspaper over his face. He didn't move when she tried to pull back the spread and get into the bed. Even when she gave an unladylike yank, he didn't move.

Taking a deep breath, she lay down on top of the spread beside him, her hands clenched at her side. "I am ready," she whispered.

He didn't move, so she repeated herself. He still didn't move.

Even for a husband, this man's conduct was beyond the limits of decent good taste. She pushed the newspaper off his face. He was sleeping with his mouth half open, and with his whiskers he looked like the town idiot.

"I am ready!" she bellowed into his face in a very unprincesslike fashion, then lay down again.

"Ready?" he mumbled, coming awake slowly, then sitting up with a jolt. "Fire!" he said, then seemed to realize where he was. He turned and looked at Aria, his eyes going up and down her lavishly clad body.

Aria kept her hands at her sides, her legs stiff, and her eyes on the ceiling. This was it. This was when men turned into basic animals—all men did this, her mother had said, whether king or chimney sweep. And now was her turn to be ravaged.

"Ready for what?" Lieutenant Montgomery asked groggily.

"The wedding night," she said, and closed her eyes against the coming pain. Would he hurt her terribly?

She opened her eyes when she heard him laugh.

"The wedding night?" he said, laughing. "You think that I . . . ? That you and me . . . ? That's a good one. Is that why you spent half the night in the bathroom?"

He was *laughing* at her.

"Listen, lady, I married you only to help with the war. No other reason. I don't have any designs on your body, no matter what silly thing you wear, but most of all, I don't want anything to stand in the way of our ending this marriage once you get back on your throne. I somehow think your Count Julie will frown on your carrying my brat. Now, will you go in the other room and let me get some sleep? But don't leave the hotel! Next time you'll probably do something that'll cause another country to declare war on us."

Aria was thankful for her years of schooling that had shown her how to control her emotions. To be rejected as a princess was one thing but to be rejected as a woman was hurting her deeply.

"Out!" he said. "Get out of my bed. Go sleep in the other room. Here, I'll call housekeeping and have the couch made up for you."

With all the dignity she could muster, Aria rose from his bed. "No, Lieutenant Montgomery, I will manage on my own." She did not want another woman to know she had been rejected on her wedding night. She walked into the living room. Behind her, he closed the door loudly with a muttered, "Damn!"

Aria sat on the couch for the rest of the night. She did not close her eyes once. She kept thinking of all the things she should have done, should have said, but what she remembered most clearly was how much trouble she had gone to to please him and he had rejected her.

She hated him.

She wasn't well acquainted with the emotion but she certainly recognized it. Several of her ancestors had made marriages, for political reasons, with husbands or wives they hated. In the eighteenth century one couple had not spoken for over twenty years. Of course the woman had three children during that time, all of them looking like her husband the king, Aria thought.

She sat rigidly on the couch waiting for daylight. She would learn what he had to teach her so that she could get her country back, but all hope of anything else between them was gone. Perhaps her sister could produce an heir to the throne.

Aria did not cry—and holding the tears back now was much more difficult than when she had broken her arm.

* * *

J.T. woke slowly, his mouth tasting foul, his eyes heavy, and a pain in his back. He lifted himself and removed his twisted belt from where it was gouging in his kidney. He still wore his uniform and his shirt was twisted tightly about his body.

He knew without looking that the princess wasn't in bed beside him and he also somehow knew that she was in the living room of the suite. Probably sulking, he thought with a grimace. Probably hating him even more because he wasn't doing what she thought he should.

He closed his eyes a moment and thought of the past events. She had been impossible since the day he had rescued her. She had been demanding, overbearing, autocratic, always wanting more from him. No matter how much he gave, she expected more. He handed her an enormous amount of money—his money, which he had been saving for a new boat—and she never so much as said thank you.

He had never been so glad to get rid of anyone in his life as when he put her on that train and sent her to Washington. He sincerely hoped he would never have to see her again.

But he had not been so privileged. A few days later, by order of the president, J.T. was "requested" to go to D.C. They did everything but put a gun to his head in order to enforce their "request."

No one would tell him what was wanted of him but he knew it had something to do with Her Royal Pain in the Neckship. Repeatedly, he cursed having met the woman.

Almost as soon as the army plane landed, they started on him. They wanted him to *marry* that bitch. At first he had merely laughed at them but he couldn't laugh for long. They denied him food, drink, and sleep. They pounded at him hour after hour, preying on everything he held sacred. They talked about how he was betraying his country, how he was betraying his family's name. They said they would give him a dishonorable discharge and send him home to live with the disgrace. They sent a woman in to talk to him. She purred at him, said the marriage would only be temporary and America needed him so badly.

He had agreed at long last because he realized they were telling him the truth. America did need someone to help the princess, and her country's mineral deposits and strategic location were important to the war effort.

He was exhausted by the time he entered the conference room where some of the biggest brass of both army and navy were waiting for him. Someone had pity on him and gave him a chair and he immediately put his head down and was nearly asleep when he was woken by the princess giving him orders as if he were her lackey.

He would have liked to wring her little neck. He had agreed to help her get her country back—this was something *she* wanted—yet she had the audacity to belittle him.

All through the short service she stood like a martyr readying herself for sacrifice. J.T. saw the other people giving him hostile looks, as if he were doing something vile to this lovely woman. *Lovely, ha!* he wanted to yell. He had already saved her life, spent two years' savings on her, put up with one nasty remark after another from her, yet *he* was being cast as the villain.

Even the WACs were giving him hostile looks, and that was something else that was further angering J.T. He had never had trouble with girls before. At home his family was the richest in town, he and his brothers weren't bad to look at, and he had always liked girls. It had, until now, seemed to be a devastating combination. But since he had met the princess, every woman seemed to look at him as if he were the devil incarnate. Yet as far as he could tell, he had done nothing wrong. He had saved her from drowning and he had even agreed to marry her—but everyone seemed to think he had done something horribly wrong.

After the ceremony, all he had wanted to do was sleep. It had been an ordeal getting the princess back to the hotel. She didn't lead and she refused to follow. Every two minutes he had to turn around to see if she was still with him—which she usually wasn't—then he had to go back and get her. He barely made it to the bed before he was asleep.

When the telephone rang and the man said she had been arrested for shoplifting, it seemed a perfect end to a hideous week. He dragged himself to the police station and there she sat with that haughty look on her face, as if she expected someone to save her.

Of course she didn't say one word of thanks to him for once again saving her ass. She just sat there as if expecting a red carpet to be rolled out for her to walk on.

At the hotel *he* had almost apologized to *her*. He had tried to explain how tired he was, how hungry, but it didn't affect her. She could have been carved out of marble. Her perfect little face was set into a cold, perfect little mask.

He ordered food, then had to show her how to work the bathtub. He planned to nip this trend in the bud right away or she would have him playing her maid.

He was glad to get rid of her when room service knocked. She stayed in the tub the entire time he was eating. He was a little chagrined at himself for having eaten all four dinners and he meant to tell her to order herself something else, but the bed seemed to be calling him. He fell asleep before she left the bathroom.

The next thing he knew someone was yelling "Ready!" in his ear. He came awake suddenly, sitting upright and thinking there was another ammo fire. It took him a moment to get his bearings.

The princess was lying beside him, wearing some frilly pink thing, her fists clenched at her side, her legs stiff—in fact her whole body was so rigid she could have been made out of steel. It took him a minute to understand that she expected him to ravish her. He had never seen anything as undesirable in his life as this cold, unfeeling woman.

He didn't know whether to laugh or rage at her. It made him angry that she seemed to have successfully reduced him to her idea of a primitive male who wouldn't be able to control himself at the sight of a beautiful female in his bed wearing a low-cut, gossamer-thin nightgown that clung to and outlined every one of her not-inconsiderable curves.

The next thing he knew he was yelling at her.

Her expression didn't change—after all marble didn't move. She got up from the bed and left the room.

Immediately, he had felt guilty, as if *he* had done something wrong. He turned on his stomach and punched his pillow with his fist. If she would just smile at him, just show him that she *could* be human. *If* she could be human, that is. It took him awhile before he could go back to sleep.

Now, he looked at the clock and knew it was time to get up. Maybe he had dreamed the whole thing. Maybe he wasn't married to the haughty princess after all. Maybe he was just plain Lieutenant Montgomery and not Public Enemy Number One.

At nine the next morning Aria looked up as Lieutenant Montgomery emerged from the bedroom, still wearing his rumpled uniform, his jaw now black with whiskers. He looked like a pirate.

"It's true then," he mumbled, looking at her with eyelids still heavy with sleep. "I thought maybe I dreamed all of it."

She rose from the couch, not letting him see her stiffness.

"About last night . . ." he began.

She started past him toward the bathroom.

He caught her arm and pulled her around to face him. "Maybe last night I was a little too harsh. The brass kept me awake for hours, then when I finally got to sleep I get a call saying you're in jail."

She looked at him with cold eyes.

"Is that what you stole?" he asked, his voice lowering, one hand moving to touch her shoulder. "It's nice."

"It is a—as I believe you called it—'silly' garment." She moved away from him but he grabbed the long, flowing skirt of her negligée.

"I'm trying to tell you that I'm sorry about last night. You could have been Rita Hayworth and I wouldn't have touched you. I didn't mean to hurt your feelings."

"You did not," she lied, chin up. "I merely misunderstood the situation. If you will release me and allow me to dress, we can get started on my learning to be an American."

"Sure," he said with anger. "The sooner we get this done, the sooner you can get your kingdom and I can go back to controlling my own life."

She did not slam the bathroom door; she was able to control herself that much. She looked at herself in the mirror. Was she so unattractive? Perhaps her nighttime braid was too tight, perhaps she didn't look so young and carefree as the pretty American girls she saw, but was she really so undesirable?

She dressed in a simple little Mainbocher suit: slim skirt, padded shoulders, a little veiled hat perched over her left eye. She had a devil of a time with the seams in the hose but she managed at last.

Lieutenant Montgomery was lounging in a chair when she emerged. "Finally," he muttered, barely looking at her before entering the bathroom.

He emerged shaved and showered, a towel around his waist. Aria left the room.

He started lecturing her the moment they left the suite. He showed her how to use the room key, and the elevator. He lectured her about menus and American waiters. They ate breakfast and he said nothing to her that wasn't a criticism: she was holding her fork in the wrong hand, she was to use her hands to eat her bread and not cut it with a knife and fork, she was not allowed to return her eggs, which she had ordered soft-boiled and received scrambled. And in between his corrections he handed her change and told her how to count it, laying little piles of coins on the tablecloth and making her total the amounts in her head between bites. He was ready to leave when she was only half finished.

"We haven't got all day," he said, pulling back her chair. "Every American should know about the nation's capital."

He made a telephone call then half pulled her along to a waiting military car.

All day they went sightseeing. He dragged her through one building after another, lectured her on the history of the place, then impatiently waited while she got back into the car and they were off again. When they were in the car, he told her about glorious American women who had died for their country, women who were afraid of nothing, women who lived for their men. He seemed especially taken with someone named Dolley Madison.

"What's that?" Aria asked just as he was shoving her back into the car after seeing a statue of someone named Lincoln.

"It's a drugstore. Come on, let's go. We still got the Smithsonian to go to and the Library of Congress."

"What are they drinking?"

"Cokes. We don't have time for lollygagging, let's go."

Aria watched the drugstore until it was out of sight. How she would like to do something pleasant.

At the Smithsonian, they met Heather. She was a plump little blonde who came hurrying around a corner and nearly ran into them.

"Excuse me," she said, then the next moment she squealed and said, "J.T.!" She dropped the leather portfolio she was carrying, threw her arms around J.T., and kissed him passionately.

Aria stood by and watched without much interest except to note that Americans acted this way on public streets.

"J.T., honey, I've missed you so much. How long are you in town? Let's do the town tonight. Then later we can go back to my place. My roommates can leave us alone for a few hours. What do you say?"

"Baby, there's nothing I'd like better. You don't know how good it is to see a woman smile at me. The last few days of my life have been sheer hell."

Aria walked away at that. She didn't halt when J.T. yelled, "Wait a minute!"

He caught up with her, holding Aria's arm with one hand and the blonde's with the other.

"J.T., who is this?" the blonde demanded.

"This is Prin . . . I mean—" He looked at Aria. "What *is* your name?"

"Victoria Jura Aria Cilean Xenita."

After a moment's pause, J.T. said, "Yeah, that's right. Vicky. And this is Heather Addison."

"Aria," she corrected. "My family calls me Aria."

Heather looked at J.T. suspiciously. "And what do *you* call her?"

Aria smiled sweetly. "Wife," she said.

Heather gave J.T.'s cheek a resounding slap then turned on her heel and walked away.

"Stay here," he ordered Aria, and took off after Heather.

Aria smiled to herself and felt good for the first time in days. It had been very nice to see that man slapped. Across the street was one of those drugstores. She waited for the light just as J.T. had instructed her then crossed the street and went into the store. Several people, young men in uniform and girls in thick socks and brown and white shoes, were sitting on red stools.

Aria sat on an empty one.

"What'll you have?" asked an older man in a white apron.

She searched her memory for the word. "A coat?"

"What?"

A handsome young man in a blue uniform moved down to the stool beside her. "I think she means a Coke."

"Yes," Aria said, smiling. "A Coke."

"Cherry?" the man asked.

"Yes," she answered promptly.

"You live around here?" the soldier asked.

"I live—I am staying at the Waverly Hotel."

"Plush. Listen, I got a few friends in town and tonight we're going out to do the town."

"Do the town," she murmured, just what Miss Addison had said. The man served her a Coke in a strange glass that was metal with a paper cone in it. There was a straw in it. She glanced at the teenage girls and mimicked them. Her first sip nearly choked her, but when her mouth and throat adjusted to the bubbles, she found the drink delicious.

"What do you say?" the soldier beside her asked.

Another soldier walked up behind her. "A babe like this to go out with scum like you? Listen, honey, I know a couple of nightspots where we can dance 'till dawn then—"

A third soldier moved behind her. "Don't listen to them. Neither one of them knows how to treat a *real* lady. Now, I know a place over on G Street that—"

He broke off as J.T. shoved his way between them. "Take your turn, buddy, we saw her first."

"You want to *eat* all those teeth of yours? I married the woman yesterday."

"Don't look to me like you're taking very good care of her."

Aria kept her head bent over her Coke but she was smiling. Oh how she was smiling. She glanced down the bar toward the teenage girls who were also smiling. One of them winked at her and Aria decided that this was a part of America she rather liked.

"Come on," J.T. said angrily, grabbing her arm. "Let's get out of here."

"Wait! I have to pay for my Coke." After her bout with the police, she knew she had to pay for everything.

"That's all right, I'll do it," the soldiers said in unison.

"No, no, I must learn your money." Deftly, she

116

moved out of J.T.'s grip and made her way through the hovering soldiers. She asked the man behind the bar how much the Coke was then took her time opening her handbag and her change purse. "A nickel is this one, isn't it?" she said, holding up a quarter.

The men fell all over themselves helping her find the correct coin.

"You're French, aren't you? I knew it the moment I saw you."

"*Oui,* I speak a little French."

J.T. pulled her out of the crowd and out of the store. He didn't say a word until they were in the car.

"You just can't obey, can you? I'm doing my best to teach you how to be American and what do you do but run off and display yourself like a common tramp."

"Not like Heather," she said under her breath, not meaning for him to hear.

But he did hear. "Leave my friends out of this. In fact, leave *me* out of this. I *am* an American. *You* are an American *wife.* You are not some French floozy who sits in drugstores and lets men ogle her. You conduct yourself in a proper manner. You'd think that being a princess you'd have some idea of decent conduct, but it's obvious you don't. The American wife is a lady. She is respectful to her husband, she obeys him—which you wouldn't even do in our phony marriage ceremony. And she—"

"You remember that but you do not remember my name?"

He ignored her. "The American wife helps her husband in every way that she can. She listens to him; she learns from him; she—"

He lectured her every minute during their sightseeing excursion until Aria began to feel that her brief adventure in the drugstore had branded her as a cross between Nell Gwyn and Moll Flanders. She tried her best to pay attention to the American pictures in the National Gallery but she saw other couples holding hands, the men sneaking kisses, the women giggling. "I don't guess they're married, are they?" she asked J.T. "Or else they wouldn't be acting like that. The women would be doing something dutiful."

He didn't answer but read aloud another paragraph from the guidebook.

Waiting in their hotel room was a three-foot stack of history books.

"I had them sent," J.T. said, "and they're all textbooks with questions at the end. You're to read a chapter then I'll quiz you on it. Get started while I take a shower."

"Get started while I take a shower," Aria mocked, and held up a book to throw at the closed bathroom door but then she saw a newspaper on the bureau and above one column the words LANCONIA'S PRINCESS TO VISIT NEW YORK MONDAY.

"Lanconia," she said to herself. "Lanconia. I must learn to be an American so their government will help me get my kingdom back." She opened the first textbook and began to read.

J.T. came out of the bathroom, wearing only his trousers, just as the telephone rang. He listened to the person on the other end. "No, baby, I'm not mad at you," he said in a tone she had never heard him use before.

Aria looked up from her history book. His bare back was to her and she found the sight not unpleasant. Muscles moved about as he talked. There were scars on one side of him, more healed than they were on the island, but she did not find them unattractive.

"Yeah, I might be able to get away. After the work I've done today, I need a break." Abruptly, he turned

118

to look at Aria, who looked back at her book. "No, no problem at all. I'll see you here in half an hour."

Aria didn't say a word when he hung up the telephone nor did she say anything when he emerged from the bedroom in a dark blue uniform, clean shaven, and she could smell the fresh scent of lotion across the room.

"Look, I'm going out for a while. You have enough to do that you don't need me. Call room service and order yourself dinner. I might be late." He didn't say another word but left the room.

Aria's mother had explained about men's infidelities and said that they were something a wife had to bear, but she had not described how they made a woman feel. Aria went to the window and looked down at the street. J.T. was leaving the hotel, his arm around the plump Heather, and as Aria watched, he kissed her.

Aria turned around, her fists clenched to her side. *"Kneq la ea execat!"* she muttered, then put her hand to her mouth at her use of such language.

She called room service and ordered caviar, pâté de foie gras, champagne, and oysters. She glanced at the stack of history books. "And send me a selection of your American magazines."

"You want movie mags, confessions, or what?" the bored woman on the other end asked.

"Yes, anything. And I'd like a Coke, no, two Cokes and . . . and a whiskey."

There was a pause on the other end of the phone. "How'd you like a couple of rum and Cokes?"

"Yes, that will do fine." She dropped the telephone.

The meal arrived with a stack of the oddest magazines Aria had ever seen, all about people she had never heard of with the most intimate stories told about them. She read while she ate, while she bathed, and after she climbed into bed wearing a sedate white nightgown. She thought that Lieutenant Montgomery could sleep on the couch. The thought of him made her bury her nose deeper in the magazines. MY HUSBAND BETRAYED ME WITH ANOTHER WOMAN. She read that story avidly.

Chapter Eight

THE next morning an awful sound woke Aria and she opened her eyes to see Lieutenant Montgomery lying beside her, on top of the covers, snoring loudly. She hadn't been aware of when he had returned to the room.

The telephone rang, and as it was on his side of the bed, she wasn't going to lean across him to answer it. He picked it up on the sixth ring.

"Yeah, this is Montgomery." He listened for a moment then turned and looked at Aria. "Yeah, she's right here with me. Yeah, in the same bed, not that it's any of your business." He moved the phone away from his mouth. "How soon can you be ready to fly to Key West?"

"As soon as someone packs my—"

"An hour," J.T. interrupted. "Pick us up in an hour."

He dropped the telephone then sat up. "An American wife packs her own bags and her husband's. Oh

121

damn, my head. You can get started while I take a shower."

Aria had no intention of obeying him. She called room service and ordered herself breakfast then picked up a magazine that carried photographs of Mr. Gary Cooper.

Minutes later, J.T. snatched the magazine from her hand. "What is this trash? Where did you get this and why aren't you dressed yet? You ought to have half the bags packed. Listen, Princess, if you want to be an American, you better make an effort to learn. How many of the history books did you read last night?"

"The same number that you did. If you think that I am going to pack your suitcases—"

She was interrupted by a loud knock and a call of "Room service."

When he saw that she had ordered only one breakfast, he was furious. He said she had no idea what it meant to be a wife and she pointed out that she couldn't order for him as she had no idea what he liked to eat. He said it was obvious to him that she wasn't really interested in being an American or in helping her country.

That made Aria stop arguing. Very calmly, she went to the telephone and ordered a second breakfast, the particulars of which he dictated to her with an air of smugness that she hated.

She kept trying to remember how she had come to be under this detestable man's rule and how important Lanconia was to her, but it was difficult. He sat at the table and ate while she tried to pack all their clothes, eating her eggs while packing. He ate; she worked. He read the newspaper; she worked.

"Why do American women *do* this?" she muttered. "Why don't they revolt?"

"Are you ready yet?" he asked impatiently. "Why does it always take women so long to dress?"

She looked at the back of him and imagined hitting him with a suitcase. Her mother's lessons in princess-like behavior had not prepared her for this.

The telephone rang and it was a soldier saying their transportation was downstairs.

"Does an American wife also *carry* the luggage?" she asked innocently.

"If her man wants her to, she does," he answered. He called the bellhop and they brought a cart for Aria's many bags.

They were given transport on an army carrier, but this time there was no attempt to make the interior luxurious. J.T. dozed in his seat, opening his eyes only now and then to make sure Aria was reading the history book he had brought with him. He quizzed her on Christopher Columbus and then on the Pilgrims. She answered all his questions correctly but he didn't give her one word of praise.

When she started on the third chapter, he fell asleep, so Aria removed one of her movie magazines from her purse and placed it in front of the history book. She might have succeeded if she hadn't leaned her head back and also fallen asleep. The book fell open on her lap.

"What is this?" J.T. demanded, startling her awake.

"It's swell, isn't it?" she asked, half awake.

To her surprise, she saw J.T. almost smile but he seemed to catch himself. "You're supposed to be reading about Colonial America," he said softly. The noise of the plane enclosed them and their heads were close together.

He was quite good-looking from this distance. "Isn't there more to America than history?"

123

"Of course. There's entertainment." He nodded to her movie magazine. "But you've seen that. And there's family. Maybe I can explain how the American family works."

"Yes, I would like to hear something besides history."

He thought for a moment. "Everything in the American family is absolutely equal, divided fifty/fifty. The man earns the money; the woman takes care of the house. No, wait, it's not really fifty/fifty, it's more sixty/forty or perhaps seventy/thirty since the man's duties carry a backbreaking responsibility with them. He's the one who always has to provide for his wife and children. Whatever they need, it is his duty to give it to them, to make sure they want for nothing. He works day after day at his job, always giving, always there with that check, asking little in return but giving much. He . . ." J.T. stopped and straightened in his seat. "Well, you get the picture. We men do very well at holding up our end, even while you ladies spend your afternoons drinking tea." He sighed. "And war is our duty too."

"I see," Aria said when he had finished, but she didn't see at all. "By 'take care of the house' do you mean that if the roof leaks she fixes it?"

"No, of course not. She calls a roofer. I mean she cleans the thing, washes the windows and such. Cooks. Of course she doesn't fix the roof."

"She washes windows? What about floors?"

"She cleans *all* of it. It's not such a big deal. After all, it's only housework. Anybody can do it, even a royal princess."

"You say she cooks. Does she also plan menus? Clean the dishes?"

"Of course. The American housewife is very versatile, and self-reliant."

124

"What if there are guests? Does she cook for them? She doesn't *serve,* does she?"

"I told you that she takes care of the house and whatever's in it. That includes guests."

"Does she take care of clothes?"

"Yes."

"Children?"

"Certainly."

"Who helps her with correspondence?"

"The man usually turns his paycheck over to his wife and she pays the bills, buys the groceries and whatever the kids need."

"I see. And she drives a car?"

"How else can she get to the grocery?"

"Amazing."

"What's amazing?"

"As far as I can tell, the American housewife is a secretary, bookkeeper, chambermaid, chauffeur, caterer, butler, maid, chef, treasurer, lady-in-waiting, and nursemaid. Tell me, does she garden also?"

"She takes care of the yard if that's what you mean, although, if he has time, the man may help on that."

"One woman is lord chamberlain, lord steward, and master of the horse all in one. And yet she has time to spend her afternoons drinking tea. Utterly amazing."

"Could we drop this?" His earlier softness was gone. "It's not like you make it sound."

"Of course men did start the war, didn't they? I don't remember any woman wanting to bomb another woman's children. But then she may have been too busy drinking tea or clipping the hedges or washing the dishes or—"

"I'm going to the can."

Aria picked up her history book but she didn't read

it. Perhaps being an American was going to be more difficult than she thought.

When the plane landed in Key West, there was transportation waiting for them and the driver took them through narrow streets overhung with bright flowers to a two-story house next to a large cemetery. The houses next to it were very close.

J.T. opened the wooden gate with its peeling paint as the car drove off. "I don't know how the navy got us a house. There's a year-long waiting list."

Aria had a hideous vision of standing in line for a full year.

The house was tiny to Aria. The lower floor consisted of one room that was living–dining room, then a half partition hid some of the kitchen. There was a bathroom containing a large white machine also on the first floor. Up steep, narrow stairs was a long room, a double bed at one end, a single bed concealed behind the bathroom wall. The house was filled with wicker furniture and painted in pale blues and pinks.

J.T. hauled all of Aria's luggage upstairs. "I'm going to the base. Unpack our clothes and hang them up. The army said they'd furnish the place so I hope that means food. When you get done, hit those books again." He paused a moment at the head of the stairs, seemed about to say something, then turned and left the house.

There was a balcony leading off the upstairs and Aria went outside to look at the narrow street below and across to the cemetery.

"Hey! Is anybody home?" she heard a man's voice from downstairs.

"J.T.?" she heard a woman call.

How odd, Aria thought. Did people always walk into one another's houses in America? She walked to

126

the head of the stairs. Below her, coming in the door, were three couples.

"Wow!" said one of the men looking up at her. "Are you J.T.'s heartbreaker?"

They all stopped to stare up at her. Aria might not know how to dress herself or how to count money but she was quite confident of herself as a hostess. "How do you do?" she said regally, descending the staircase as if she were floating.

"Princess!" came another voice as Bill Frazier entered the door, a pretty blonde behind him. "I mean . . ." He trailed off, embarrassed.

"I am——" Aria began.

"Princess will do," one man said, laughing. "It suits you. Princess, let me introduce this clan. We came to welcome the new bride." He introduced Carl and Patty, Floyd and Gail, Larry and Bonnie. Bill introduced his lovely wife Dolly to her. There was another guest, a bachelor named Mitch.

Mitch took her arm. "J.T.'s a fool to leave a beauty like you alone."

"*Where* did you get that dress?" Patty asked. They had each brought casseroles and grocery bags of food.

"Is that *silk?*" Bonnie asked. *"Real* silk?"

"I thought you two just flew in today. If I had on a dress like that, it'd be a mass of wrinkles!"

"I think I'd die for a dress like that."

Aria desperately wanted these American women to like her. They wore pretty, flowered cotton sundresses and cool-looking sandals. Each had short hair that looked so young and carefree, and they wore dark red lipstick. Standing before them in her silk suit, her long hair drawn severely back, she felt old-fashioned—and very foreign. They were looking at her expectantly and she searched her mind for something that would please them.

"Lieutenant Montgomery bought me several dresses that are still packed. Perhaps you'd like to see them."

One minute Aria was standing in the living room and the next she was being pushed up the stairs before a herd of stampeding women.

"What about dinner?" a husband called, but no woman answered him.

Ten minutes later the upstairs was a flurry with women pulling clothes from Aria's many suitcases. She began to smile and in another ten minutes she was having *fun!* For the first time in America, she was enjoying herself. She asked if Bonnie would like to try on a Schiaparelli and the next minute the four women were in their underwear.

"I have to show Larry this," Bonnie said, wearing a gorgeous red Worth evening gown.

"In those shoes?" Aria said softly. "With socks? Perhaps these would be better."

She held up a pair of silk stockings.

Bonnie looked as if she were going to cry and reached for them.

Aria held them back. "There's a price."

The woman hesitated. There was something a little daunting about Aria.

"Will you find me a hairdresser who can cut my hair like yours?" Aria asked. "And a place where I can buy cosmetics?"

The evening turned into a fashion show, with the women modeling Aria's gowns, suits, and dresses for their husbands. Dolly was a little too plump for the suits, but what she did for one strapless dress was a sight to behold. The women laughed at the men who started cheering when Dolly descended the stairs.

"Bill was horribly jealous," Dolly said triumphantly.

The smell of roasting meat drifted upward from the tiny backyard.

"J.T. better get back soon or he'll miss the hamburgers," Gail said. "Where is he anyway?"

The women paused, their hands on the clothes.

"He went to his job," Aria said. "Do you think I look all right in this lipstick?"

The women were obviously very curious about her marriage. J.T. went away to rest after his hospital stay, came back exhausted, snapping at everyone, and a few days later a black limo pulled up on the dock, J.T. got in, and then he was gone for days. When he did return, he had a wife.

"I think you look swell," Dolly said, smoothing over the awkward moment. "Let's get this cleaned up and get downstairs. There won't be anything left to eat by the time we get there."

Aria was in her element as hostess. She quietly made sure everyone had enough to eat and that no one's glass was ever empty. It was a little difficult coping without servants but she managed. She caught Dolly watching her a few times and smiled.

J.T. arrived for dessert.

"Here's the bridegroom," Gail called. "Move over, Mitch, and let J.T. sit by his bride."

"This is fine," J.T. said, moving toward Bill and Dolly. "Anything left to eat?"

"No more meat but there's coleslaw, potato salad, shrimp salad, whatever, over there. Help yourself."

J.T. gave Aria a hard look. "My wife will fix me a plate."

For a moment the group was silent, then Aria put her plate aside and stood. "Larry, would you like more apple pie?"

"No thanks, Princess, I've had more than enough."

"Princess?" J.T. asked.

"It's my nickname for her," Bill said pointedly.

Aria took a plate and began filling it with food.

J.T. moved to stand across the table from her. "American women wait on their men. They are also good hostesses. Did you make demands that everyone serve you? You didn't use a knife and fork on your hamburger, did you?"

"Lay off her," Bill hissed. "She's doin' just great. Real nice party, Princess."

"Does this please you, master?" Aria asked, handing J.T. a plate heaped with food.

"Don't get smart with me, I'm—Oh, hello, Dolly." He took his plate and left.

Dolly stood for a moment watching Aria, then took her arm. "Let's you and me get together Monday and have a nice long girl talk."

At that moment, someone put on a Glenn Miller record inside the house and Bill asked Dolly to dance. One by one the couples went inside and began to dance in the living room. Only Mitch, J.T., and Aria were left outside.

"Mrs. Montgomery, may I have this dance?" Mitch asked. J.T. never looked up from his plate of food as Mitch escorted Aria inside the house.

Her first encounter with American dancing was shocking to Aria. Even the man to whom she had been engaged had never held her this close.

"Come on, honey, loosen up," Mitch said, holding Aria's stiff body.

"Are American wives, as you say, loose?"

"Where are you from?"

"Paris," Aria answered quickly.

"Ah," he said, and tried to pull her closer but she wouldn't bend. "If you're French, you ought to know a little about love."

"Absolutely nothing," she said quite seriously.

Mitch laughed aloud at that and hugged Aria. "I've always wondered about ol' J.T."

Dolly pulled Bill to dance by Mitch and Aria. "You'd better behave yourself," Dolly said to Mitch, nodding her head toward the back door where J.T. was entering.

The other couples held their breaths as J.T. strode purposely toward Mitch and Aria. But he walked past them as if he didn't see them. "Bill, you got a minute? I want to talk to you about installing the radar."

"Now? This is Saturday night."

"Yeah, well, a war doesn't have weekends. You want to go to the base tomorrow and look at it again?"

"On Sunday?"

J.T. rubbed his jaw. "It's the first radar we've installed and I'm concerned about it, that's all. The damned thing is from Britain and I don't know if it's going to fit our American ships. Probably make the ship sail on the wrong side of the ocean."

Bill smiled but Dolly didn't. "I still think you should spend the day with your wife."

"I got more important things to do. Doll, did you bring any of your chocolate cake?"

"Yes. Can you cut it yourself or should I get your big strong wife to do it for you?" Dolly turned on her heel and left them.

"Is she mad about something? You do something to tee her off?"

"It's not *me*, buddy," Bill said. "How are you and the princess getting along?"

J.T. yawned. "As well as can be expected. She's pretty well useless. I had to teach her how to turn on the bathtub."

"Mitch doesn't seem to think she's useless."

131

"That's thanks to my teaching. A week ago she'd have been demanding he serve her oysters on a gold platter."

Bill shook his head. He knew the story of why J.T. had married Aria. "She must really want that country of hers. When I met her she wouldn't let anyone touch her and now she doesn't seem to mind Mitch's hands all over her." He looked up at J.T. but J.T. didn't react.

"Is everything about ready for the conversion of the distillation ship?"

"Yeah," Bill said, and there was disgust in his voice. "I think I'll get another beer."

J.T. walked toward Aria and again everyone held his breath as Mitch removed his hands from J.T.'s wife. "I've got some work to do upstairs," J.T. said. "You take care of everybody. And I mean that. Get them whatever they need." J.T. looked at the group of people who were standing quietly. "Stay as long as you want. Have a good time. Good night."

They watched as he mounted the stairs.

"Talk about a wet blanket," Gail muttered.

"What happened to the J.T. I used to know?" Larry asked.

All eyes turned toward Aria as if expecting an answer.

Dolly stepped forward. "How about if we all meet at the ice cream parlor on Flagler tomorrow at eleven?"

"I think J.T.'s going to work," Bill said.

"Well then we'll have to do without him, won't we? We'll pick you up at ten-forty-five . . . Princess," Dolly said, smiling.

It took them only minutes to clean up and get ready to leave. Mitch kissed Aria's hand. "Until tomorrow, Princess," he said.

Aria stood at the door and said good night. She heard Dolly say, "You're going to tell me what's going on, Bill Frazier, if you stay up all night doing it."

Upstairs, J.T. was ensconced in the big bed, a sheet covering the lower half of him, the upper half bare. Papers were all around him.

"I guess the little bed is mine," she said.

"Mmm," was all J.T. answered.

Aria wrinkled her nose at him, but he didn't look up. She opened a chest of drawers and looked at her pile of nightgowns. On impulse she removed the pink silk one she had bought for her wedding night—a wedding night that had never come.

In the bathroom she began humming one of the tunes she had heard that night and remembered being in Mitch's arms. Of course it had been very awkward, and by Lanconian standards, it was very improper, but all in all it had been rather pleasant.

After her bath she brushed her hair loose, letting it flow over her shoulders and down her back. She was still humming and smiling when she left the bathroom and took her clothes to hang them in the closet across from J.T.'s bed. She was getting quite used to taking care of her own wardrobe and was beginning to feel some pride at seeing her clothes neatly hung.

"Who is this Mitch?" she asked J.T. behind her.

"What? Oh, he runs the optical shop."

"Optical? He makes eyeglasses?"

J.T. put down his papers. "His department repairs chronometers and ship watches."

"Then he's an important person?"

"Everyone's needed in the war effort."

"Yes, but how does he rank? Is he your superior?" She sat down on the edge of his bed.

"Oh, I see, you want to know if he's a duke or a prince. Sorry, Princess, but he's not my superior. I have only one boss and he's the industrial manager. I'm Mitch's boss—and Bill's boss and Carl and Floyd and Larry's boss. What's that smell?"

"Perfume from the saleswoman in Miami. He seems very nice."

"You always wear perfume at night?"

"Yes, of course. The others were very nice too. America seems so free and there don't seem to be many rules governing conduct."

"Get off of my bed and go to your own. And don't wear that nightgown again and put your hair in a pigtail. Now get out of here and leave me alone. And take that history book with you. You'll have a test over chapters seven through twelve tomorrow."

"Not if I'm eating ice cream all day," Aria whispered defiantly as she left him. In bed she looked at pictures in the movie magazines and tried to decide how she wanted her hair cut.

"Well, I'll be damned," Dolly Frazier said, leaning against the headboard of the bed.

"Dolly, I don't like my wife using such language." Bill stayed snuggled under the covers, refusing to sit up.

"And I don't like my husband keeping such secrets from me."

Bill turned over to face her. "I thought the whole thing was J.T.'s business. Heaven help the married man who thinks he can keep a secret."

"A princess. A *real* princess right here in Key West and I met her. Do you realize that someday she'll be a *queen?* And if J.T. stays married to her, maybe he'll be king. I would know a king *and* a queen."

Bill turned back again. "J.T. doesn't *want* to be king. You know his background. He's got more money than ninety percent of the kings of this world. He married the princess to give her a cover and to teach her to be an American. As soon as everything is set up in Lanconia, he takes her back there and the marriage is annulled."

"Teaching her to be an American, ha! Did you see that stack of history books? And the way he made her wait on him! I think the two of them didn't get along too well on that island and J.T.'s still mad at her."

"He says she's a nuisance, that she's been waited on all her life and expects everything to be done for her. She'd never even dressed herself and he says she expects him to walk two paces behind her."

"I didn't see anything like that."

"She was arrested for shoplifting in D.C. Didn't know she had to pay for things, and he says she hands out hundred-dollar bills to porters."

"So what did he do, make her learn to count money?"

"Of course," Bill said, bewildered. "What else was he supposed to do?"

"Take her shopping. That's the only way to learn about money."

"He took her shopping in Miami. Spent a bundle. Dolly, baby, could we get some sleep now?"

"Sure. I was just thinking, though. What if J.T. fell in love with her? Then he wouldn't want to leave her and he'd stay and be king."

"I'm not sure an American can be king."

"Of course he can. If he's married to the queen, then he's king. I wonder if Ethel would open her beauty parlor on Sunday? I think I'll call right now and ask her."

"Dolly, it's two o'clock in the morning," Bill said, but Dolly was already out of bed.

' "She won't mind. We'll make the princess so beautiful J.T. won't be able to resist her. By the time they get to Lanconia he'll face a firing squad before giving her up."

Bill groaned and pulled the pillow over his head. "What have I done?"

Chapter Nine

"GET up," J.T. said. "This morning you're going to learn to cook my breakfast."

Reluctantly, Aria opened her eyes. J.T., fully dressed in his tan uniform, was standing on the far side of the room and yelling at her as if she were in the next state. She stretched. "What time is it?"

"Breakfast time. Now get up."

"Are you always so loud this early?" She lay back against the pillows. "At home my maid brought a pot of tea to me every morning in bed. It was always served in the Lily set of china. Such a peaceful way to start the day."

J.T. didn't say a word, so Aria turned to look at him. He was watching her with a strange expression on his face and she began to blush as her eyes met his.

"Get up," he repeated, then turned on his heel and went down the stairs.

Smiling to herself, Aria took her time dressing in a silk shantung suit, hoping it was all right for an ice cream parlor visit.

J.T. was sitting in the living room reading a newspaper. "You took long enough." He stood and went into the kitchen.

"This is a skillet. These are eggs. This is butter—or it's what we have instead of butter during a war. Put the butter in the skillet, drop in the eggs. Damn! I forgot the bacon. Get it out of the fridge."

"Fridge?"

He pushed past her and opened the refrigerator. "This is bacon. You'll have to learn to cook it, and before long you'll have to learn to go to the grocery and buy it. Get another skillet out of the bottom of the stove and put the bacon in it."

Aria opened a door and a drawer before finding a second pan like the egg pan but there was nowhere to set it. The top of the stove was covered with an egg carton, a loaf of bread, a pan from last night, eggshells, and odd-looking shiny metal utensils. She thought she could make room by moving the handle of the egg pan.

The hot handle seared her palm and she moved away quickly but she didn't say a word.

"Have you got that bacon in there yet?"

She tried using only her left hand to move the bacon but it was difficult. Pain was shooting through her body.

"Can't stand to touch it?" J.T. asked angrily. "Here, use both hands."

He grabbed her right hand and Aria gave a slight intake of breath that made J.T. stop and look at her white face. He turned her hand over to look at it. The skin was beginning to blister. He slapped margarine onto her palm.

"You burned yourself that bad and didn't say a word?"

She didn't answer but was grateful for the cooling relief of the grease.

"Hell," he said in exasperation. "Stand over there and watch." He finished cooking his breakfast while muttering things about Aria being useless. Then, as he put his food on the table, he again cursed because he realized Aria had no breakfast. While his grew cold, he cooked her bacon and eggs.

At last, they both sat down to eat in absolute silence.

How unpleasant this place is, Aria thought. How different from breakfast at home with her grandfather and sister. She smiled as she thought of how she would entertain them with stories from last night. Her grandfather would laugh loudly at the absurdity of the Americans.

"Care to share that with me?" J.T. asked.

"I beg your pardon."

"You were smiling and I wondered why. I need something to cheer me up."

"Actually, I was thinking of how I'd describe last night to my grandfather."

"And?"

She looked at her breakfast, a bit repulsed by the greasiness of it. "I don't think you'd like it. They are your friends."

J.T.'s eyes narrowed. "I want to know how you'd describe my friends to your royal family."

He said the words with such a sneer that Aria didn't care what he thought. Her grandfather often said that commoners had no sense of humor, that they took themselves very seriously and were always concerned about their dignity.

Aria's face immediately changed expression as she opened her mouth a bit, shifted her head to one side, and began to look somewhat dazed. "Bonnie, where's the ketchup?" she said in a deep voice that conveyed the idea of a little boy lost. "Bonnie, I need some tomato. Bonnie, where's the mayonnaise? Bonnie, didn't you bring an apple pie? You know how I like apple pie."

J.T.'s eyes widened. "That's Larry. Dolly said he'd starve to death if Bonnie weren't around."

Aria's face changed again; this time she made her eyelashes flutter rapidly. "I just loved that red dress. Here you are, honey. Of course red isn't usually my color. It's right there, honey. But I did wear red as a child. You don't think my hair's grown too dark for red? To your right, honey. But maybe I'm getting too fat for red. Here it is, honey. I have put on some weight since I got married. You want a slice of onion, honey?"

J.T. began to smile. "Larry's wife, Bonnie."

Aria smiled and resumed eating.

"What about Patty?" J.T. asked after a moment.

Aria's eyes sparkled as she put down her fork. She stood, turned her back to J.T., then perfectly imitated Patty's walk, an odd walk with her knees together, her feet flat, not bending, and her arms bent at the elbow, her hands stuck out like chicken wings. "Carl, I do believe I shall have a lamp like this," Aria said in a high, singsong voice. "It gives out the most wondrous color. So good for one's skin."

Aria stopped and looked back at J.T. He was beginning to laugh, and Aria thought how good it was to have an audience again. She had always been able to mimic people and her grandfather and sister had begged her for her performances after every official engagement. Of course she had only performed for her closest relatives.

She performed for J.T. with all the gusto she had

used at home. She went over each of their visitors of the night before and ended with a full parody of all of them talking at once. According to Aria's portrayal, the men were lazy, a little dumb, and as helpless as infants. The women handed them food and utensils, catered to them and pacified them as if they were large children, all the while talking a mile a minute about clothes, money, hairdos, money, cooking, money, and money. Yet her portrayals were never spiteful, and somehow made the people seem quite lovable.

J.T. was laughing hard when she finished.

Who would have thought, she wondered, that the American male had a sense of humor?

"We're that bad?" he asked, smiling at her.

"Mmm," was all Aria answered.

He was still smiling. "Come on and I'll show you how to wash dishes. You're going to love this little task."

For the first time ever he didn't snip at her as he showed her how to fill the sink with water and add the liquid soap. "Now you stick your hands inside and start washing."

Aria started to obey but he caught her wrists.

"I forgot about your burned hand." He held her wrists and looked at her for quite some time before releasing her. "I'll wash, you dry. Tell me something about your country," he said as he handed her the first clean dish.

Aria began to enjoy the task as she told him about her country, about the mountains and the cool night air.

"A lot different from Key West, isn't it?"

"From what I've seen, yes," she said. "But the flowers here are very pretty."

"Maybe we can go sightseeing."

The word made Aria shudder. Sightseeing was what

141

they had done in Washington, D.C.—that day he had pulled her in and out of a car, the day he had screamed at her for drinking a Coke.

J.T. saw her shudder and looked back at the sink full of dishes. "Maybe it could be a bit more pleasant this time. Look, I need to go to the base. You have anything to read today?"

"I have the history books."

"Yeah, well . . ." he stammered.

"Dolly said she was taking me to an ice cream parlor at eleven."

"Good, then you won't be here alone." He let the water out and dried his hands. "I better go." He went upstairs and returned a moment later with a handful of papers. "Have you seen my briefcase?"

"Here it is, honey," she said, mocking Bonnie's answers to Larry.

J.T. laughed as he walked forward to take it from her. "See you tonight, baby," he said, then caught himself. He smiled. "I mean, Your Royal Highness." He left the house.

Aria leaned against the door and smiled. "I think I like 'baby' better," she said.

Dolly arrived exactly at eleven. "Is that what you wear to an ice cream parlor? You look like Merle Oberon."

"I have nothing else. It isn't suitable?"

"If you were meeting a grand duke, it would be great." Dolly was watching Aria's eyes. "Come on, we'll go to Gail's first and see what we can scare up for you to wear. J.T. already go to the base?"

"Yes."

"Well, maybe we can fix that. I have a surprise for you today. The others aren't meeting us until three."

Aria had no idea what Dolly had planned but she followed her out the door.

J.T. looked at the stack of papers on his desk. There were new plans for changing a ship into a water distillation plant, other plans for installing English radar in an American ship, and other plans for something else under those. He rubbed his eyes. He hadn't slept well last night, not after Her Royal Highness had sat down on the edge of his bed wearing some exotic scent and two thin layers of silk. And this morning he had watched her awhile before waking her.

He had a job to do, he told himself. He was to teach her to be an American and then get rid of her. That meant no involvement with her personally—and definitely not physically. But there were times when all he could remember was the time on the island when he had stepped around the path and seen her standing nude in the pool. She wasn't built bad for a princess. Hell! Who was he kidding, she wasn't built bad for Miss America.

But staying away from her had been easy so far. She was so damned haughty, so cold and inhuman. But this morning she had thawed a little. He smiled at the memory of her imitation of Patty's walk.

What a strange person she was, he thought. So helpless but at the same time so fearless. Why hadn't she said a word when she had burned her hand? And the eggs he had cooked! He seemed to remember now that eggs didn't take as long as bacon to cook but he had put the eggs on, then the bacon, and taken them out at the same time. They were awful but she had eaten them just the same.

"J.T., you still here?"

J.T. was on his feet instantly and saluting smartly to Commander Davis. "Yes sir, I'm still here."

"I heard you just got married."

"Yes sir, three days ago."

"Then why are you here now? Why aren't you home with your new bride?"

"I wanted to go over the radar plans and the—"

The commander waved his hand. "I'm glad you're so conscientious but there are other aspects of life besides work—even in wartime. Now this is an order, Lieutenant: go home and spend the rest of the day with your new wife."

J.T. began to smile. "Yes sir, I'll obey that order immediately."

Aria looked at her reflection in the mirror as if she were hypnotized. She didn't know the young woman who looked back at her. She put her hand to her hair, now a shoulder-length bob that felt so light and cool. Instead of a somber silk suit she wore a yellow-and-white-print cotton sundress that exposed her arms and shoulders and neck.

"Well?" Dolly asked. "You like it?"

"Very much," Aria said breathlessly, then held out her skirt and turned about. "It feels so free, so . . . so . . ."

"American?" Dolly prompted.

"Exactly. Do I look American? As American as Dolley Madison?"

"Dolley Madison?" Gail laughed. "You look as American as Coca-Cola. You're one hundred percent red, white, and blue."

"Do you think Mitch will think so?" Aria asked, still looking at herself in the mirror.

"Mitch?" Bonnie gasped. "But J.T.—"

Aria caught herself. "Of course I meant my husband. It's just that Mitch laughs. I mean, I'm sure that Lieutenant Montgomery does too. I've even seen him laugh. But as a general rule . . ." She trailed off as the four women watched her with interest.

Dolly broke the silence. "J.T.'s a barrel of laughs. A regular riot. He's just had a lot to think about lately what with this new radar and all. He'll cheer up as soon as he's sure everything's gonna work. You'll see. Hey! It's quarter after three. We better get going. The guys'll be waiting."

Bonnie, Gail, and Patty left through the front door of Gail's house while Dolly caught Aria's arm. "J.T.'s a really great guy. He's had every single woman and half the married women on the island after him since he arrived."

Aria was incredulous. "Really? Perhaps there is a shortage of single men."

"In a navy town during a war?" Dolly gave Aria a long look. "J.T. hasn't been very good to you, has he?"

"He is my husband." Aria realized that these American women had a way of making her forget herself. "He has been very kind to me."

"Bill starts being 'kind' to me and I'll think there's another woman. Come on, let's go get some ice cream."

The husbands, except for J.T., were there, and Mitch was waiting for them. The way Mitch looked at Aria made her lower her head and blush. Involuntarily, she wished the army had chosen someone like this man for her husband.

"You are gorgeous," he said, taking her arm and leading her to a chair.

It never occurred to Aria to tell this man he wasn't allowed to touch her. The other couples, all newly married, were wrapped around each other, acting as if they hadn't seen one another for months. Aria, with her new haircut and her borrowed sundress, felt almost as if she were one of them instead of a foreign princess. It seemed natural when Mitch moved his chair very close to hers and put his arm around the back of her chair.

"I can't get over how different you look," he said softly. "You were beautiful before but now you could stop traffic. Maybe later we could get together for a moonlight drive."

Aria looked at her hands. This man was making her feel heavenly, as if she were enormously desirable, so very different from the way she had been feeling since she had arrived in America. "My husband," she murmured.

Mitch moved a little closer to her. "It's obvious that J.T. doesn't appreciate a dish like you. Princess, I'm serious about you. I like the way you look, the way you move. I've never met a girl like you. You and J.T. don't seem to be exactly in love. There must be some other reason why you married him. A baby on the way?"

"Certainly not," Aria said, but gently.

Mitch's hand moved to her shoulder, his fingers caressing her skin, and his touch felt delicious. No man had ever touched her skin like this before.

She looked up into his eyes, their noses almost touching.

"Let's get out of here," Mitch whispered.

She was on the verge of agreeing when all hell broke loose—the hell being in the form of Lieutenant J. T. Montgomery.

"Jesus H. Christ!" he bellowed. "What have you done to your goddamned hair?"

In an instant, Aria went from being an American wife to being a royal princess. She was on her feet.

"How dare you use such language in my presence!" she yelled back at him. "You are dismissed! Go! Leave my chamber."

The crowd in the ice cream parlor had come to a halt at J.T.'s first shout. Some of them had smiled at his words. But Aria's command left them stunned.

Dolly recovered first and, at the moment, she feared J.T. less than she did the autocratic Aria. "J.T., honey, sit down and stop glaring so. Waitress, bring this man a root beer float." She turned to Aria, her voice automatically lowering. "Your Royal—I mean, Princess, please have a seat."

Aria was recovering and she realized how she had called attention to herself and how she had reestablished herself as a foreigner. She felt Mitch take her hand and give a gentle tug. She sat, J.T. still standing, still hovering, still frowning.

"Sit down, J.T.," Dolly commanded, her voice filled with disgust. "Newlyweds," she said loudly to the watching crowd, and gradually they turned back around, although one ensign muttered, "Who's married to who?" as he nodded from J.T. to Aria to Mitch.

J.T. sat down at last and fastened his glare on his root beer float.

Gail patted Aria's hand. "I think you were right, Princess. Never let a man use the Lord's name in vain. Once he starts, he'll never stop."

Aria looked at the strawberry sundae someone had ordered for her and wished the floor would open up and swallow her. Mitch still had his arm around the back of her chair but it was different now. He was no longer leaning toward her but, instead, leaning a little back.

Once again she was a freak. Just as she had been the day they had arrested her. They had put her in a

147

glass-walled cage and stared at her and laughed at her. Everything she did seemed to amuse them. And the only person she had known in America—Lieutenant Montgomery—had treated her the worst of all. Yet she had tried so very hard to please these new people. She had tried so hard to fit in.

"Let's go to the beach," Dolly said cheerfully. "We'll get our suits and go swimming at sunset, and J.T., you can catch us some lobsters and we'll grill them."

"I have work to do," J.T. muttered, moving his straw up and down in his untouched drink.

Dolly leaned forward. "Then maybe you'd be so kind as to drive your *wife*"—she emphasized the word—"to my house so I can loan her a bathing suit."

"Sure," J.T. said, fumbling for his keys. "You want to go now?"

Dolly stood. "On second thought, why don't you and I go and we'll all meet at Larry and Bonnie's apartment in an hour? Take care of our princess," she told Bill, then had J.T.'s arm and was leading him out the door.

"You bastard," Dolly said as soon as they were in the military car that was at J.T.'s constant disposal. "Bill told me everything and I think you're being a bastard."

"I've had all the abuse from women today that I can take. Don't you start on me."

"*Someone* should. The way you're treating that lovely girl is disgraceful."

"Lovely? Lovely girls don't allow men who aren't their husbands to drape themselves all over them."

"Hallelujah! You noticed," Dolly said sarcastically. "Mitch likes her, as we all do except you." Suddenly, she softened. "J.T., I've seen you charm lady sergeants, tough old broads who terrified every other man, but you had them eating from your hands. So why aren't you using some of your charm on your wife?"

J.T. turned a sharp right. "Maybe it's because she hates me, or maybe it's because she looks down her nose at me. She thinks I'm a commoner. Or maybe because she can't do anything useful. My job is to teach her to be an American and I'm doing that."

There was something in his tone that made Dolly change hers. "She's pretty, isn't she?"

"She's all right if you like the overbred type."

"I see," Dolly said.

"You see what?" he snapped.

"You're afraid of her."

"What?" he yelled, and slammed on the brakes at a stop sign.

"You're afraid that if you unbend a bit, you'll find she's quite courageous and rather likable. I'd never be able to do as well as she has. Bill said she couldn't even dress herself when she came to America but now she's cooking your breakfast."

"Sort of. She burned herself."

"Yes, but she's trying. Did you ever think how lonely she must be? She's in a strange country married to a man who despises her, but she's made the best of it. In spite of you, she's surviving."

"In *spite* of me? *Because* of me she's surviving."

They were silent for a while then J.T. spoke quietly. "I don't want to get involved with her. As soon as the army takes the imposter princess, she goes back to her throne. Then, no doubt, she'll hold out her hand for me to kiss and say 'so long, sucker.' Or maybe she'll give me a medal on a ribbon and she'll hang it around my neck."

"You didn't mind getting 'involved' with Heather Addison, or Debbie Longley or Karen Filleson or— what was the redhead's name?"

J.T. smiled. "Point taken. Aria's different, as you well know. You can't very well have a one-night stand with a royal princess. She doesn't dream of cottages with white picket fences, she dreams of castles and land management and lifelong servitude. Kings have no privacy or freedom."

"So you'll be mean to her instead."

"I'm not mean exactly, I just keep my distance. As that Mitch goddamn well better do. Oh, sorry."

Dolly turned away to hide a smile. Her Royal Highness had made her point about cursing. "I think she may be falling in love with Mitch."

"What!" J.T. slammed on the brakes again as the car skidded into the parking lot of the Marina Hotel.

"I don't blame either one of them. She needs a little kindness and every woman needs a man to tell her she's beautiful. She looked great today, didn't you think so?"

J.T. seemed to be deep in thought as he got out of the car and started toward the hotel, leaving Dolly sitting. She smiled as she got out of the car and went after him. At least she had made him think.

The hotel had once been a resort for the rich but the war had changed that and it was now used as temporary quarters for married officers. But the magnificent old lobby was the same and there was still a gift shop off to the side.

"Wait!" J.T. said as they walked past the window.

"Think she'd like that?" He pointed to a Catalina swimsuit, straight cut legs, a deep, square neckline.

"Sure," Dolly said, following J.T. into the store. She helped him choose a beach cover, a straw hat, "to protect her white skin," he explained, and a big matching straw beach bag.

"What else does she need?"

Love, Dolly almost said, but didn't because she didn't want to push too hard too fast. "Something to take her mind off Mitch."

J.T.'s smile left at that. "You have any jewelry?" he asked the saleswoman. "Any diamonds? Emeralds maybe."

She swallowed. "No sir, but we do have a rather fine selection of French perfumes."

"Good. I'll take a quart of whatever you've got. No, make that a half gallon."

"It's sold by the ounce," the woman said meekly.

"Then add up the ounces," he said impatiently. "You ready to go?" he asked Dolly.

"As soon as I go upstairs and get my suit."

J.T. smiled at her. "Need a new one?"

Never pass up a gift from a handsome gentleman, Dolly's mother used to say, and worry about the price later. "I would love a new suit."

Chapter Ten

ARIA was quiet during the drive to Larry and Bonnie's apartment. The others tried hard to lighten the atmosphere but she kept thinking that they were watching her and that they somehow knew she was different from them.

And it was Lieutenant Montgomery's fault. That awful, dreadful man had been the cause of everything bad that had happened to her in America—except the kidnapping, of course. He had saved her life then. At this moment she wished he had let her drown.

She was standing in Bonnie's tiny living room when the door opened and in walked J.T. and Dolly. Immediately, Aria went to the kitchen and J.T. followed.

"I brought you something," J.T. said softly from behind her.

She turned. "A biography of George Washington including ten essay questions at the end?"

He gave a little laugh then held out a paper sack.

Tentatively she took it and withdrew the dark blue swimsuit. She gave him a skeptical look.

"I picked it out myself. And there's a hat and purse and a little robe in here. And I got a sack of perfume in the car." His eyes sparkled. "And not one history book."

Aria didn't smile.

"What did you get?" Gail squealed from the doorway.

Aria held out the bag and Gail took it and rummaged inside.

"Not a bad apology, J.T.," Gail said. "You might make a good husband yet. Well?" she said, looking at Aria.

Aria realized Gail was expecting something from her but she didn't know what.

"When a husband apologizes, you kiss him and make up. Now get to it. I'll give you two minutes, then it's upstairs to change and we go to the beach. I'm hungry." She left them alone in the room.

"I . . . ah, I guess it is a peace offering," J.T. began. "I guess I shouldn't have said what I did. It was just such a shock seeing you look so different."

"I guess so," Aria said. "I wanted to look American and the long hair was so old-fashioned."

"I liked it."

"Did you?" she asked, surprised. "I never knew. I mean, you never said one way or the other."

He took a step closer to her. "Well, I did like it. It suited you."

"This feels so nice," she said, touching her hair.

"Does it?" He put his hand up and wrapped a fat curl around his fingers. "It does at that."

"I meant—"

"Time's up," Gail called. "Let's go."

Confusion showing in her eyes, Aria stepped past

him and left the kitchen. Upstairs she forgot about the curious incident when she found that the bedroom was to be a communal dressing room. It was one thing to be nude before your ladies-in-waiting, but before *strangers!* Besides, it took her forever to get in and out of clothes and this swimsuit had a zipper down the back.

But Dolly didn't give Aria time to think. She unbuttoned the back of Aria's sundress and began to help her out of it. "Now me," she said when Aria was wearing only a borrowed rayon teddy.

Thanks to Dolly, the disrobing was easier than Aria expected, and when she pulled on the boned, stiff swimsuit, she felt as if she had accomplished something grand.

She was smiling when she went downstairs. And there stood two men, the handsome, smiling Mitch and her husband. But this husband was someone she had never seen before. He was lazily leaning against the staircase and laughing at something Bonnie was saying. Now what does he plan? Aria thought. Is this some special American torture he had planned for her?

"Princess?" Mitch said, holding out his arm for her. Smiling, she took it.

J.T. pushed his way between them. "I think I'll escort my wife myself."

"It's about time," Mitch muttered, and after one sad look at Aria, he excused himself from the night's revelries.

They all piled into J.T.'s car, the women sitting on the men's laps except that J.T. drove and Aria sat beside him. He kept smiling at her, and the more he smiled, the more suspicious she grew. What terrible thing was he planning now?

At the beach the men stepped into the darkness to

don swim trunks while the women gathered driftwood for a fire.

Dolly whistled when J.T. came into the light wearing nothing but the black trunks.

He winked at her then turned toward the ocean waves. "Want to swim, Princess?" he called back.

"Not at night in that water," she answered.

J.T. did what he was supposed to and returned with a dozen lobsters, which the group dispatched in a hurry. After dinner, with the fire nearly out, the couples entangled themselves about each other and began kissing.

Aria looked away in embarrassment.

"J.T.," Dolly called when she came up for air, "why don't you introduce your princess to the good old American custom of necking?"

"I think I will," he answered, then picked up Aria's hand.

Before he could get it to his lips, she pulled away. "You cannot possibly consider doing to me—in public—what they are doing," she hissed at him.

"Is everyone in your country frigid?"

"I live in a warm country," she said, confused. "We have winters but they are mild."

"You want to be an American or not?" he snapped.

"I am trying to learn."

He calmed himself. "Yes, and you're doing a fine job of it. Look at them." He gestured to the other couples. "They wouldn't be aware of a German invasion right now so they won't notice us. What they're doing is called, among other things, necking, and it's what newlywed couples are supposed to do."

"All right," she said, leaning away from him and holding out her hand. "You may kiss my hand if you do not twist my arm or pull it or do any of the other painful things you are inclined toward."

"Listen, lady—"

"It's Your—"

He slipped his hand behind her head and kissed her before she could say another word.

Only twice before had she been kissed on the lips, once when Count Julian asked her to marry him and once by Lieutenant Montgomery on the island. Neither time had prepared her for this.

First one of his hands and then the other enveloped her head in a gentle, protective gesture and his lips played on hers softly. Aria kept her eyes open and her hands moved as if to push him away, but then she began to feel quite different. Her hands moved to his shoulders and she liked the feel of his bare skin under her palms. Gently, he moved her head to one side and his kiss deepened.

Aria closed her eyes and leaned forward ever so slightly.

When he moved away from her she stayed where she was, eyes still closed. *"Lantabeal,"* she murmured. Then slowly her eyes fluttered open. He still had his hands on the side of her face.

"That's one of our American customs. You don't have that in Lanconia?"

She knew he was teasing her, but she didn't care.

"And how does my kiss compare to Mitch's?" he asked.

She straightened at that, and before he knew what hit him, she gave him a resounding slap. "I learned *that* American custom from your friend in Washington." She stood. "Someone may take me home now."

"Listen," J.T. said, standing in front of her, "we aren't your servants. You *ask* for things here, you don't command them."

"Then I *ask* to leave this place."

"*I'll* take you. I'm your husband, remember? Although a fat lot of good it does me." He turned to Dolly. All the couples were gathering their gear. "I tried. I bloody well tried. Come on, Your Royal Highness, I'll take you home."

The trip around town to let the other couples off was made in silence. Aria's heart was still pounding. She knew she had made too big a fuss over something that wasn't such a terrible thing to say—in fact she rather liked her husband's display of jealousy—but what had prompted her attack was fear.

From the time she could walk, decorum and self-discipline had been drilled into her. At all times she was to control her emotions. She had attended the funerals of her beloved parents and never shed a tear in public. She had suffered a couple of physical injuries and never cried. She had been through two kidnappings and never lost her wits. She had *always* controlled herself.

Yet, tonight she had come closer to losing control than she ever had before. What that man's kiss had made her feel!

She wished she could talk to her grandfather about this. Was this right? Count Julian had never made her feel like this. But then she had never lived with him, slept in the same bed with him, had never even dined alone with him. Maybe this feeling would have come if she had married the count.

Right now she could feel Lieutenant Montgomery's side pressed against hers and he touched her knee every time he shifted gears. It made her heart beat harder.

When they were alone in the car, she wanted to apologize to him, but he said, "Over there. I want you to move to the far end of the seat. As far away from me as possible."

Aria did as he bid and they didn't speak again.

The next two days were miserable. She went shopping with Bonnie and Dolly, had her hair done, went swimming, but it wasn't the same. J.T. returned to his old, cool self, no more laughing and asking where his briefcase was, and he lost patience with trying to show her how to cook and do laundry.

"But I washed dishes yesterday," Aria said.

"Yes and they have to be done again today. They have to be done three times a day, seven days a week."

"You are making a joke, aren't you? If I wash dishes every day, dust the furniture every day, wash the clothes, cook the food, buy the groceries, when do I get to read a book? When do I get to shop with Dolly and Bonnie? When do I get to be Aria and not Mrs. Montgomery? When do I get to think about something besides which dishwashing detergent to buy?"

"I have to go to work."

Later that morning a Mrs. Humphreys, hired by J.T., showed up to clean the house and bake a casserole for dinner.

That night Aria set the table with candles and made the room as attractive as she could with the little the navy had used to furnish the house.

J.T. turned on every light and blew out the candles. She knew he was very angry with her and she wanted to make him smile at her again. He thought their marriage was temporary but she knew better. She no longer hated him but he was still a stranger to her.

She served Mrs. Humphreys's cold lobster salad, then on impulse, she arched her back, thrust her chest forward, and said in a southern drawl, "Would you rather have that little ol' lobster or little ol' me?"

Her excellent imitation of Dolly made him smile.

She sat down across from him. "What do American couples do when they're alone?"

"Outside of bed I have no idea."

She blinked a few times at that. "Don't American women find this life somewhat boring? Do they *really* enjoy cleaning even if it is for their families?"

J.T. smiled again. "Maybe 'enjoy' isn't the right word. What did you do as a princess?"

"I always got a great deal of exercise. My sister and I rode horses, fenced, had dancing classes."

"That's why you look—" He broke off.

"I look what?"

He grinned. "Look so good in a bathing suit."

"Thank you," she said.

"The first time I've heard those words."

"The first time you've deserved them," she shot back.

"Oh? Saving your life didn't rate a thank-you?"

"For all I knew you were worse than the kidnappers. 'Breathe for Daddy Montgomery,'" she mocked.

He started to say something then stopped. "Maybe you'd like to see the blueprints for the new distillation ship. Maybe that'll help relieve the boredom."

"Yes, please," she said.

It was very pleasant sitting on the couch together leaning over the blueprints. The war needed ships that could distill fresh water from seawater and deliver it to troops. J.T. was in charge of converting the first of these ships.

Her mind was hungry for something of interest, something of the present instead of the past.

160

"Could a plant like this be made on land?" she asked.

"It would be easier on land than on a ship. Why?"

"At home in Lanconia our major crop is grapes for wine, but in the last five years we've had a drought. We are losing our grapes. But seeing this I wonder if such a plant could be made and we could irrigate the grapes. The young people are leaving my country because we are losing a major source of income."

"You'd have to have some engineers look at it but I imagine something could be done."

"You'd look at it? I mean, when we go home, you'd help my country?"

"I don't know what I can do but I'll try."

She smiled at him. "It would mean a great deal to my people if you did. Dolly says you know as much about shipbuilding as anyone alive today."

J.T. laughed. "Not by a long shot, but my family knows a lot." He looked at his watch. "You ready to go to bed, baby?" He caught himself. "I mean—"

She smiled at him. "I'm beginning to like the 'honeys' and 'babies,' although I'm not sure about 'Princess.'"

"It fits you," he said, yawning. "Cool, stiff, unbending, not quite human. The name means someone untouchable and that's what you are."

"Oh," she said softly, and turned away. "Someone not quite human." She went upstairs, and as she was creaming her face and putting a net over her hair she thought about his words. Was she like he described? Two nights ago he had kissed her and she had felt such passion that she had been afraid. Hadn't he felt anything? Maybe when he kissed Heather she was warmer. Maybe Heather knew a great deal about kissing.

161

Aria went to her narrow bed on the other side of the partition from J.T. and lay awake. It was hot, as always, and she wore a thin peach-colored nylon nightgown, more a slip than a gown. "Rita Hayworth style," Dolly had said when they bought it.

It began to storm around midnight and the wind lashed at the thin-walled little house. The thunder cracked and the lightning lit the room. Aria threw off the covers, the nightgown feeling heavy and confining. It grew hotter and closer in the room and she began to perspire.

Another crack of thunder made the windows pop. Aria tried to get comfortable but she couldn't. Images floated through her mind: J.T. on the island standing over her, his big body nearly nude; J.T. in his swim trunks. She remembered the look in his eyes as he had entered the clearing and seen her bathing in the pool. She remembered his two kisses.

She started and pulled the sheet over her body as she heard the floor creak behind her. In the dim light she saw J.T. walk past her bed and close a window.

He turned back, glanced at her, then stopped. "Are you awake?" he whispered.

She nodded.

He came closer to the bed. "The storm wake you?"

She shook her head.

Frowning, he sat down on the edge of the bed. "Are you all right?" He put his hand on her forehead.

Aria caught his hand and held it in both of hers.

"What's wrong, baby, have a bad dream?" He pulled her into his arms as if she were a child who needed comforting.

But what Aria needed wasn't comfort. She held on to him, pressed her body against his, feeling her breasts against his bare chest.

162

J.T. understood instantly. "I am lost," he murmured in the tone of a man going down for the third time, then he pulled her face to his and began to kiss her hungrily. "Oh, baby," he said, "my sweet beautiful princess. You're mine, you know that?" He was kissing her neck as a man who was dying of hunger. "I saved your life and you're mine. You wouldn't be alive now if it weren't for me."

"Yes," she gasped. "Yes. Make me alive. Make me glad to be alive." She said more but it was in Lanconian and J.T. didn't understand her, but words weren't needed.

He hadn't realized how much he had been wanting her. Ever since he had seen her nude on the island, her big-breasted, slim-hipped body had haunted him. And seeing her every day, her back straight, her chest thrust forward, made him sweat.

He tore the nightgown off of her, hungry to get at those breasts he had dreamed of so many times. He buried his face in them, made them cover his ears while his hands held them.

Aria groaned, her head back.

J.T. tried to tell himself to go slowly, that she was a virgin and probably frightened, but he couldn't control himself any more than he could have stopped a freight train.

He began kissing her body, her arms, her breasts, her shoulders, back up again to her neck, briefly touching her lips, then down again. It was as if in the past few weeks he had memorized her skin. There was a mole on her collarbone and he kissed it.

His head moved downward, kissing whatever he came in contact with: her hips, her belly, her thighs. She made not a sound but her skin grew hotter and hotter as if her temperature were rising by degrees.

163

"Jarl," she whispered.

"Right here, baby," he answered, and climbed on top of her.

He had to guide her since she had no idea what to do, but she was a quick learner. Oh, heavens yes, she was quick. And after his first slow entry, he was beginning to believe she was possessed of a very natural talent.

He kissed her lips and he kissed her breasts as he made long, slow strokes. She was right: she had exercised a great deal in her life and her body was strong and agile and she followed his lead easily. Once he even had to hold her back, but then he could no longer hold himself back.

He finished in a satisfying explosion that shuddered through his body and he collapsed on her, pulling her into a tight little roll in the tangle of his arms and legs.

It took him quite a while to recover. "Are you okay?"

He felt her nod under his chest and he smiled. "Can you breathe?"

She shook her head and he chuckled, then moved just a bit so she could get some air. He held their sweaty bodies close together as outside the rain began to fall.

"Did I hurt you?" he asked softly.

"A little sore," she said, "but not terribly. I . . . I liked that."

He had been a little afraid to look at her, afraid of what would be in her eyes, but now he pulled back to see her face. She was more beautiful than he remembered. Her hair was soft about her head, with sweaty tendrils clinging to her cheeks. Softly, he kissed her mouth.

"How about a bath?" he asked. "Together. The two of us in a tub."

She opened her eyes wide. "Is that . . . done? Do men and women do that?"

"This man and woman are about to." He stood and she turned away modestly from his nudity. She searched for her nightgown while holding a sheet over her breasts.

J.T. pulled her out of bed. "No coverings. I want to *look* at you."

"Oh," she said, blushing, eyes downcast.

He stepped back, still holding her hand, and gave a low whistle. "You, lady, are a sight to behold. No, not lady, I mean, Your Royal—"

She stepped forward so the tips of her breasts were touching his chest and put her finger to his lips. "You may call me baby or honey or lady or whatever you want tonight."

"Keep talking to me like that and we'll never get bathed. Come on, sweetheart, let me wash you."

Chapter Eleven

"Well, you've done it now," Bill Frazier said. He and J.T. were sitting in one of the many sleazy beer joints on Duval Street, working their way through their fourth beer. "How are you going to hand her over to her prince?"

"He's not a prince, merely a count, and he doesn't have any money, and he also happens to be shorter than she is."

"I can tell you weren't interested enough to do any research on the man."

J.T. downed the beer and held up his hand to the waitress for a fifth one.

"The SPs will have your hide if you're drunk."

"I'm not drunk," J.T. snapped. "Although I'd like to *get* drunk. How could I possibly involve myself with an overbearing woman who keeps ordering me from her presence?"

"You get those circles under your eyes from her being overbearing last night?"

J.T. smiled. "She isn't useless after all." He stopped

smiling. "That isn't the problem. Look, she's been raised to marry somebody she's never met, so she'll do fine with her Count Julie. Besides, I hear that all those royals take lovers."

"So stay around and be her lover."

J.T. slammed the beer mug down so hard half of it sloshed onto the table. "Like hell I will. *She* may regard this marriage as a lark but it's not that way to an American."

"That's not what you said when you called from Washington. You said you were marrying her to help America and you'd be glad to get rid of her when the time came. You said no man could love such an idiot of a dame. You said—"

"What are you? A wire recorder? I know what I said. Now the problem is, this marriage is getting a little too intimate. I'm sure this would have happened with *any* woman. You can't put two young healthy people together like the army's done to us and not expect something to happen. I just need some perspective, that's all. I've been around her so much I'm beginning to *like* her."

"Not difficult to do."

"Yes it is," J.T. said. "You don't know her like I do. She argues about *everything*. Acts like housework is a death sentence. And she spends money like there's no tomorrow. Do you have any idea what last week's bill from Ethel's Beauty Parlor was?"

"I bet it wasn't any more than Dolly's and your wife sounds just like mine."

"That's just it—she's not my wife. I guess it's like the difference between borrowing a car and owning one. It's not the same. You can use the borrowed car but someday you have to give it back."

"You sure borrowed one hell of a car in that little lady."

J.T. finished his beer. "Yeah, I borrowed a Rolls, but, unfortunately, I'll have to spend my life with some Buick."

Bill laughed. "So what do you do now? You got another week before she goes back, right?"

"One more week and then I take her to her country, slip her back into her castle, and turn her over to her scrawny little count. They deserve each other."

Bill looked at his watch. "We better go. Dolly said to meet her at the pool at seven and it's quarter after now."

They walked from Duval Street to the swimming pool opened by the navy for the officers.

"You two smell like a brewery," Dolly said. "J.T., what did you do to Aria? She looks positively radiant."

Before J.T. could answer he saw Aria, wearing only her swimsuit, walking away from the concession stand beside Mitch, who was in uniform, both of them laughing. J.T. didn't think; he just acted. He strode the few steps around the edge of the pool, grabbed the smaller Mitch by the back of his collar and the seat of his pants, and threw him into the water.

"Stay away from my wife, you understand me?" he yelled down when Mitch came up for air.

"Of all the primitive displays I have seen, this is the worst," Aria said, then bent to offer her hand to Mitch.

J.T. grabbed her shoulders and pulled her around so that Mitch fell back into the water. "We're going home."

Their little house wasn't too far away, and when Aria was dressed, he started walking home, Aria barely able to keep up with him. She didn't say a word to him on the way because she didn't want a public

169

scene but she meant to speak to him once they were home.

How could he be so disagreeable after last night? She could still feel his soapy hands on her body, still feel his lips on her skin. They had bathed each other last night, except that she had been too shy to fully explore his body. He had laughed and said, "There's time for that." After their bath he had dried her then carried her to his bed and made love to her again. She had felt no pain the second time and they had fallen asleep in each other's arms.

When she woke, it was morning and he was gone. There was no note, no message left for her. All day she had hoped the phone would ring but it hadn't. At two she made an emergency trip to Ethel's to have her hair done so it would look nice when he got home. She again set the table with candles.

At 5:30 Dolly had come by and told her they were to meet the boys at the officers' swimming pool. She was surprised J.T. hadn't told Aria.

The next thing she knew J.T. was throwing Mitch in the pool.

When they arrived at the house, he unlocked the door for her but he didn't enter. "I got to go somewhere," he muttered, and turned toward the gate.

She ran after him and put her hand on his arm. "Jarl, is something wrong? Did something bad happen today?"

He moved his arm from her touch. "No one calls me Jarl except my mother and she's not borrowed. It's J.T. Got that?"

She stepped back. "Certainly, Lieutenant Montgomery. I will not make that error again. Should I keep supper warm for you? I believe that is an American wifely custom."

"I'll get something somewhere else. And sleep in your own bed tonight."

She schooled her face not to betray her feelings. "Yes, Your Sublime Highness. Will there be anything else you desire of this poor concubine?"

He glared at her then slammed out the gate.

"I will not cry," Aria whispered. "He will not make me cry."

J.T. buried himself in his work. He felt as if he were fighting for his life, that he was the one drowning—but there was no one to save him. She was getting under his skin like no one ever had before. Every day she changed dramatically. She laughed; she danced; she made jokes. He had shown her plans for the ships and she had understood everything he told her. She was smart and sexy and funny. And she was *not his*. He tried to remember that but then he would make a fool of himself when another man so much as looked at her.

He just wanted to stay away from her and try to get her out of his mind, so he stayed at work and slept on the ratty couch outside the officers' mess. But it didn't help much. He dreamed about her.

As if he didn't have enough trouble in life, he received a telegram saying his mother was coming to visit. J.T. knew Amanda Montgomery had hundreds of friends, and no doubt she had heard of her son's marriage from one of them. It was not going to be pleasant because he knew she was going to tell her son what she thought of his marrying and not telling his family.

"Women!" J.T. muttered. He wished he could row out to an island and spend some time alone. He groaned at that thought when he remembered his last time "alone" on an island.

He braced himself before he went to see Aria to tell her about his mother. Aria was wearing a sundress with little bows on her shoulders, her neck and arms bare, and she was as delicious looking as a peach. He tried to explain to her that he would like her to not request his mother to kiss her royal hand, but Aria stuck her nose in the air in that way that only she could do, and it made him so mad he ended up slamming from the house.

Aria hadn't counted on two whole days of J.T.'s absence. He didn't come home at all that first night and the next night he stayed less than an hour—only long enough to lecture her.

"My mother sent me a telegram and she'll be here Saturday. She'll come to the house first, then the three of us will attend the Commander's Ball. Do you have anything proper to wear? Do you know how to ballroom-dance? Do you know the proper forms of address to navy officers?"

Aria was too astonished to answer. She was a royal princess and he was treating her as if she had just come in from the fields. "I believe I can manage to not disgrace myself," she murmured. But her sarcasm didn't reach him.

He went on to tell her about his mother, this woman who was a cross between Attila the Hun and Florence Nightingale. She was a Daughter of the American Revolution and a Daughter of the May-flower.

"And she married a Montgomery," J.T. said as if that explained everything else.

"Perhaps we should send her my family tree for approval. I am descended from every royal house in Europe thanks to the English Queen Victoria. Or do

172

foreign kings not matter when pitted against your American heroines?"

J.T. glared at her then left the house.

He came back the next morning to change clothes, barely said anything to her except to remind her that his mother was arriving and he wanted the house spotlessly clean, then left for work.

Dolly came over at one o'clock, just after Mrs. Humphreys left. "What's going on?" she asked by way of greeting.

Aria had always lived surrounded by servants and she knew that the only people in whom one could confide were blood relatives. "I was about to have luncheon. Will you join me?"

"I'm not interested in food. Floyd told Gail who told Bill that J.T. was out all night last night. You two have a fight?"

"There is a lovely shrimp salad and cold tomatoes."

"Honey," Dolly said, putting her hands on Aria's shoulders. "I know everything. I know you're a princess and I know you want to get back to your country and I know how this marriage came about. But I also know something bad has happened, and I want you to talk to me."

Perhaps Aria was more American than she thought. In the last few days she had sat by quietly while the other women talked and revealed the most intimate secrets about themselves.

To Aria's disbelief, she burst into tears. Dolly's arms about her felt good and Dolly led her to the couch.

After Aria had regained some control, Dolly urged her to talk.

"He . . . he made love to me." Aria sniffed, part of her mind not believing what she was revealing. Royalty could never trust anyone not royal, as outsiders tended to write books—one couldn't even trust the aristocracy. "But then he hated me. I don't understand. What did I do wrong?"

"Absolutely nothing. Bill and I fought about it but he finally told me some of what J.T. said. Who is Count Julie?"

"That is Lieutenant Montgomery's name for the man I was engaged to marry." She blew her nose.

"Did you know J.T. thinks you're still going to marry this count?"

Aria didn't answer.

Dolly leaned forward. "*Why* does J.T. think that?"

"He wouldn't marry me unless he believed our marriage was temporary. Of course I cannot get a divorce, it isn't thinkable."

Dolly leaned back. "Then J.T. *will* be king."

"Prince consort." Aria waved her hand. "But I don't understand why he's so angry with me now."

"Easy. Of course he never admitted it to Bill, but he's afraid he's falling in love with you. He thinks he has to turn you over to someone else and he doesn't want it to hurt so much."

"Perhaps I should tell him the marriage is permanent."

Dolly's mouth dropped open. "Tell a red-blooded American male that he's been snookered? Bamboozled? Taken for a ride?"

"Not the done thing?"

Dolly laughed. "I think you ought to make him finish falling in love with you."

"Wear low-cut dresses, feed him strawberries and wine?" Aria said, having no idea how to make a man fall in love with her.

"First you have to get his attention. You can wear a sexy dress to the Commander's Ball."

"For his mother," Aria muttered.

Dolly laughed. "I heard she might be here. She's some bigwig, isn't she?"

"Enough that the manners of a royal princess are considered to need work to meet her."

Dolly put her hand on Aria's arm. "*Every* man is that way about his mother. Bill told me so many glowing stories about his mother that I was ready to worship at her feet. He constantly bragged about her cooking and he insisted that I beg and plead if necessary to get her fabulous recipes. So when we went to visit the first time I took along a pad and pencil to take notes. Some cook she was! You know how she made spaghetti sauce? Two cans of tomato soup and one can of tomato paste. It was ghastly. Her 'famous' turkey dressing consisted of nine slices of bread cut into cubes, a half cup of water, and an eighth of a teaspoon of sage. No onion, celery, or anything else. She stuffed it into the turkey and cooked the bird until it was so dry you could have used slices of the breast for powder puffs. Then the old biddy had the gall to ask me if I thought I was a good enough cook for her little boy."

Aria's eyes twinkled. "Count Julian's mother curtsies to me and addresses me as Your Royal Highness."

Dolly laughed. "A dream come true. I'd like to see Bill's fat ol' mother curtsy to me. Does she kiss your ring?"

"She touches her forehead to the back of my extended hand," Aria said airily.

"*That* I'd like to see."

"If I ever get home, you have an invitation."

"Deal. Hey! How'd you like to go to a movie? There's a matinee on today."

"I would love it."

The women had heaping plates full of shrimp salad

for lunch and they drank most of a bottle of wine. They were laughing as they set off to walk to the movie theater.

Aria was smiling and laughing when she heard Dolly gasp. When she turned to look, Dolly placed herself in front of Aria. "Let's go this way," Dolly said. "The cannonball tree is in bloom. I hear it's the only one on the island. It's really very beautiful and—"

Aria stepped around Dolly to look across the street. J.T. sat at a tiny table at a cafe, a pretty redhead across from him. While she watched, he lifted the woman's hand and kissed it.

"Yes, let's see the cannonball tree," Aria said, starting to walk briskly.

Dolly ran after her. "So what are you going to do?"

"A wife ignores her husband's infidelities."

"What!" Dolly grabbed Aria's arm and halted her. "That may be the way in *your* country but that's not American. You should have gone over there and snatched that floozy bald."

"The woman? But what has she done? She merely accepted his invitation. Perhaps she doesn't know that he's married. It is Lieutenant Montgomery who has committed the wrong."

"I never saw it like that, but I guess you're right. So, anyway, what are you going to do to get him back?"

"A royal princess is above revenge," she said, her nose in the air.

"There's the difference between you and me. I'd *do* something."

They were silent the rest of the way to the theater. The movie was *Springtime in the Rockies* and one of the players was an outrageously dressed woman named Carmen Miranda. To Aria, she was a caricature of what Americans seemed to think all foreigners

176

were like. Dolly kept laughing at the woman's eye rolling and mispronunciations but Aria did not find the performance amusing.

That's what Jarl thinks the people of my country are like, she thought. He's not sure but what I won't show up at his American ball with a dozen bananas on top of my head. He worries that I'll embarrass his pedigreed mother when the truth is my ladies-in-waiting have more exalted family trees than she does. *He* worries about *my* conduct while he publicly consorts with a redheaded harlot—a *fake* redhead, at that.

Dolly's words—*What are you going to do to get him back?*—echoed in her head.

Maybe she was becoming an American, maybe the short hair and the flowered cotton dresses were making her an American, because she didn't feel like ignoring Jarl's (*Only my mother calls me Jarl,* she thought with disgust; one's initials were what was embroidered on one's linens) infidelity.

She looked up at the movie. Carmen Miranda was wearing a purple and white frothy concoction now.

Aria began to fantasize about meeting her illustrious mother-in-law with her belly bare, a slit up her skirt, and an eighteen-inch headdress weaving about on her head.

"Something that sparkles," she whispered.

"What's that?" Dolly asked.

"Has this woman recorded any of her songs?"

"Carmen Miranda? Sure. She has lots of records out."

Aria smiled and began studying the woman's movements. She was so exaggerated that she would be easy to imitate.

After the movie Dolly saw by Aria's eyes that she was happier than she had been. "Cheer you up?"

"I am going to be just what my husband thinks I

am. I am going to the Commander's Ball dressed as Carmen Miranda. I am going to meet Lieutenant Montgomery's mother and pinch her on the cheek and say, 'Chica, Chica.' "

"I . . . I don't think you should do that. I mean, the Commander's Ball is the biggest event of the year and it's very formal—only the top brass. Bill and I aren't invited. J.T. is because his mother's coming. And, Aria, you *have* to be nice to your mother-in-law. I think it's a law somewhere. She can treat you like dirt but you're always supposed to be nice to her. Believe me, an angry mother-in-law can make your life hell."

"More hell than it is now? I don't have a country; my husband spends his time with another woman and treats me as if I am nothing. He said I was cold and inhuman. I shall show him that I am not."

"J.T. said that? You definitely should get him back but there has to be a better way. I'd rather face a firing squad than anger my mother-in-law."

"Who can we get to make the dress? I think I'll have it made in red and white and we shall use the very cheapest fabrics. What is the sparkling powder?"

"Glitter. Aria, really, I don't think the Commander's Ball is the place—"

Aria stopped walking. "If you help me with this, when I get back to my country, you can come for a month-long visit and I will let you try on every crown I own. There's twenty-some of them."

Dolly swallowed, her eyes wide. "We could put red Christmas balls in your hair and Bonnie's landlady has the biggest, ugliest pair of seashell earrings from Cuba that you've ever seen. They're red and white polka dot."

"Perfect," Aria said, smiling. "Now let's go buy some records. I plan to sing while I dance. I shall get Jarl Tynan Montgomery's attention all right."

"I hope you can handle it. His mother is going to hate you." Dolly brightened. "But men do like women with spunk. They don't like cowards. You know, this might work."

"He'll look at me and not that redhead."

"I can guarantee that. It's just how he's going to look at you that worries me."

Chapter Twelve

"WE made it," Dolly said, leaning against the rest-room door. "Did J.T. believe your reason about why you couldn't attend the ball?"

"I gave him something to think about. I said I was suffering from morning sickness."

"You didn't," Dolly said, giggling. "I almost feel sorry for him. Here, let's get you dressed. I gave the maid five dollars to keep people out for fifteen minutes, so let's get to work."

Aria removed her long raincoat, then untied her skirt so it fell to the floor. It was made of cheap white satin, tight across her hips and slit from her hip to the floor. The slit and the hem were covered with three layers of one-foot-wide gathered nylon that was sprinkled with dots of red and white glitter. The white satin halter top left her stomach bare. Red satin ribbon trimmed the waist and halter. The sleeves were three layers of nylon dotted with more glitter.

On her arms were gaudy red bracelets that reached from wrist to halfway up her forearm. Around her neck she wore fourteen strings of cut-glass beads that hung almost to her waist.

But the *pièce de résistance* was the headdress of five seven-inch-wide nylon flowers and a half-moon piece of cardboard covered in glitter set on top of a white satin turban. The earrings were sewn to the turban.

"Now, if we can get this thing on," Dolly said, holding the headdress aloft. She halted when, behind them, a toilet flushed. "I didn't check," Dolly whispered miserably.

Out of the stall came a pretty woman, tall, slim, with dark chestnut hair and wearing a stunning draped, black Molyneux. She had beautiful skin that refused to tell her age.

Both Dolly and Aria stood frozen, Dolly with the turban held above Aria's head.

"Is there to be a show tonight?" the woman asked.

"An impromptu one," Aria answered.

"Oh. May I help with that?" she asked Dolly, referring to the turban.

"Sure."

The woman adjusted Aria's hair in the back and pulled the turban in place. "Is it heavy?"

"Not bad," Aria said. "I guess I'm ready."

"Oh no, my dear," the woman said. "Your makeup isn't nearly enough; your face is lost against the glitter. I have a few cosmetics with me. May I assist?"

Obediently Aria sat down in front of the mirror and the woman went to work.

"I didn't mean to eavesdrop but I take it this has to do with a man."

Aria didn't say a word but Dolly let go. "It's her husband. He's been . . . well, the SOB has been seeing another woman and Aria and I decided to pay him and his mother back."

"His mother?" the woman asked.

182

"She's some Yankee snob, came down here to give her daughter-in-law the once-over, and J.T. acts like Aria hasn't got sense enough to pour—"

"Dolly," Aria cautioned.

"I see," the woman said, standing back to look at Aria's face. "I think that's much better. Now, why don't I give the maid another five, then I'll persuade the band to play a little calypso and you can make an entrance?"

"This is awfully kind of you," Aria said.

"I've had a mother-in-law and I have a husband. Don't *ever* consider allowing a man to get away with infidelity. I hope he's *very* embarrassed and you teach him a good lesson. I have a feeling he'll not be so neglectful in the future. Oh, what shall I have the band play?"

"I know the words to 'Chica Chica Boom Chic,' 'Tico-Tico,' and 'I, Yi, Yi, Yi, Yi, I Like You Very Much.'"

"All of my favorites," the woman said, and they all laughed. "Wait until you hear the music."

Aria let the calypso music play for a couple of minutes before she burst from the rest room. She had been practicing for days and had seen Carmen's movie four times, so by the time she entered the ballroom with its sedate lighting, its conservatively dressed matrons, its hushed music and conversation, its polite and genteel laughter, she *was* Carmen Miranda.

She had a thick Spanish accent and an exaggerated wiggle as she made her way through the astonished crowd.

"You are so cute," she said to one admiral as she pinched his cheek. "It is so many stars on his shoulder, no?" she said to the admiral's wife.

One by one the crowd stopped and watched her.

She plopped down on a lieutenant commander's lap and moved her bottom back and forth. "You want we should chica-chica-boom-boom?"

"Young lady!" the man said, astonished. "Were you invited to this?"

"Oooh yes," she squealed. "I am zee wife of a very powerful man."

"Who?" the man bellowed. He was trying to get her off his lap.

"Zere he is."

J.T. had been watching this with amusement, having no idea who the woman was.

"Oh my God," he said when he realized it was Aria. He bounded across the room and pulled her off the lieutenant commander's lap.

"I'm *very* sorry for this, sir," J.T. said. "I had no idea she . . . I mean, sir . . ."

"You seem to like women in red," Aria said so only he could hear, "so I wore red. Maybe this red is dyed with the same dye she uses on her hair." She turned to the crowd. "He ees so forceful, no? So . . ." She rolled her eyes then stuck her rear end out, baring one leg to her hip, and moved her bottom down J.T.'s leg. "Ooooh," she squealed.

"Lieutenant Montgomery!" an admiral shouted.

"Yes sir," J.T. said weakly.

"Oh, but I want so bad to meet hees mother," Aria said petulantly. She broke away from J.T. and undulated over to a captain. "Men can be so cruel, do you not think?"

"I am Jarl's mother," said someone behind her.

Aria turned and her face fell. It was the woman from the rest room. "Oh my God," she said, for the first time in her life using the Lord's name in vain. "I . . . I . . ." she sputtered. I want to die, she thought. Please, God, strike me dead now.

Mrs. Montgomery leaned forward to kiss Aria's cheek. "Don't give up now," she whispered. She turned to the others. "My daughter-in-law and I are going to sing you a song. Jarl, loan me your pocket knife."

"Mother, I'm going to take the two of you home."

"Yes, Lieutenant, I think that would be wise, and tomorrow morning I want you in my office," said an admiral.

"Yes sir." J.T. saluted smartly and took Aria's arm firmly.

"Coward!" said Mrs. Montgomery to Aria as she was pulled past.

Aria jerked away from J.T. "He is a tyrant, no?" she said loudly. "He makes me to clean the dishes, to scrub the floors, to wash his back, but he never lets me to sing."

Several people laughed.

"Let her sing," called someone from the back.

"Yes, do let her sing," said the admiral's wife.

"Your knife, Jarl," said Mrs. Montgomery. She took his knife and slit the skirt of that divinely beautiful and very expensive dress to above her knee, exposing a shapely leg. She took three huge red hibiscus from a table decoration and tucked them in her hair.

"Tell the band to play 'Tico-Tico,'" she told J.T.

Aria and her mother-in-law put on an extraordinarily good performance in spite of the fact that they had never rehearsed. They played well off one another because neither was afraid of an audience. Aria had a repertoire of sexy moves she had seen Carmen Miranda do, but Mrs. Montgomery had the lifelong experience of being a sexy woman. They began to play a game of who-can-top-this? If Aria moved one way, Mrs. Montgomery moved another. They passed the song back and forth, moving their shapely bodies to the music. The band began to participate with drum rolls and long instrumental sections. All Aria's years of dancing lessons paid off.

When at last the song ended with the two women with their arms around each other, the applause was thunderous and many flashbulbs went off. After many bows they made their way to the rest room.

"Can you ever forgive me?" Aria said to Mrs. Montgomery as soon as the door closed. Dolly was waiting for them. "I had no idea you were . . . Lieutenant Montgomery said you were . . . Oh, I am so sorry."

"I haven't had so much fun in years."

"You'll come home with us now?"

Mrs. Montgomery laughed. "You, my dear new daughter, are going to have to face your husband alone. Just remember that the Montgomery bark is worse than the bite. Stand up to him. Give him a good long hard fight, then another good long time in bed, and you'll be fine."

Aria blushed.

"I have to go now. I have my own husband waiting for me in Maine. I hope the two of you come to visit very soon. Oh, by the way, were you actually suffering from morning sickness?"

"No," Aria said, smiling. "But give me time."

"The first one will probably be here before the year is out if I know my son. He's always liked girls." She kissed Aria's cheek. "Now I really must go. Come see me soon." She left the rest room.

"She's not like *my* mother-in-law at all," Dolly whispered. "*That* woman would never pour tomato soup over spaghetti."

Aria looked toward the door. "Your American men do not deserve the women."

"Uh-oh," Dolly said, and ran to lean against the door as the first people reached it and began trying to enter.

"Grab your raincoat and climb out the window. I'll hold them off. And you're right about the women," she called as Aria's foot disappeared out the window.

J.T. was waiting for her.

"Of course," he said before she was halfway out the window, "where else would I find my royal wife but climbing out the bathroom window?" He took her about the waist and helped her down. "You go shopping and you get arrested for shoplifting. Of course you've more than conquered that problem. All the shop owners in town now genuflect at the sight of you. You go to a ball and you humiliate me. You have my own *mother* prancing about half dressed."

He led her to his car, opened the door for her, and she climbed in. As she waited for him to walk around the car, she stuck her hands in the pocket of her raincoat and found his pocket knife. Mrs. Montgomery must have put it there.

"This is not the way an American wife acts," J.T. said as he opened the car door and got inside. "Nor is this the way a royal princess acts. *Nobody* acts as you did tonight."

"You are right," she said contritely. "This is a terrible dress for anyone to wear." Very solemnly, she took the knife and cut the inch of ribbon that connected the two cups of the halter top, and exposed her breasts to the dark interior of the car. "And the skirt must go too," she said, holding the knife at the slit and moving so her leg was exposed from hip on down.

J.T. started to speak, then he glanced out the back window. He was on her instantly, covering her body with his.

"I want to see you in the morning, Lieutenant Montgomery" came a man's voice from outside.

"Yes sir!" J.T. replied, still covering Aria.

The admiral looked embarrassed at the intimate scene and walked away.

J.T. and Aria looked at each other then burst out laughing.

He kissed her passionately, his hand fumbling under her coat and searching for her breast. "You were great, baby, absolutely great."

She kissed him back, moving her hands to the buttons on his dress uniform. "Was I? Better than your redhead?"

"She's my secretary, that's all."

She pushed at him. "You kiss your secretary's hand?" She was getting out of breath. He was tearing at her skirt.

"When she stays up all night typing a report for me, I do. What did you sew this with? Fishing tackle?"

His elbow hit the horn, making them both come to their senses. He looked at her, his eyes hot and hooded, then he rolled off of her and started the car.

Using the same techniques she had used to free herself from her kidnappers' ropes, Aria wriggled out of the remnants of the Carmen Miranda dress so that she was nude under the raincoat.

J.T. drove too fast to reach their house and he must have cooled off some too because he started lecturing her again as soon as they were inside. "You don't want to draw attention to yourself, yet you display yourself like tonight. This was *not* American behavior. This was not the behavior of *my* wife."

She dropped the raincoat and stood nude before him. "Is *this* American? Is *this* the behavior of your wife?" she asked innocently.

He blinked a couple of times. "Not exactly, but it'll

THE PRINCESS

do for the moment." A split second later he was on top of her, knocking her to the floor. "I'm tired of fighting," he whispered. "I'm going to enjoy what time we have together."

They made love on the living-room floor, then J.T. carried her to the stairs and, in a contortionist's nightmare, made love to her with her back against a stair tread. She began backing up the stairs and he followed. They finished on the floor at the head of the stairs, both of them out of breath, sweating, and limp with exhaustion.

"What do I get if I dress as Jean Harlow?" Aria whispered, her body feeling like rubber.

"Not more of the same because I'm done for."

"Oh?" she said, wiggling under him, but it was a halfhearted motion.

"You are definitely a quick learner. Now go take a bath."

"You'll wash my back?"

"Maybe, but not your front. Your front gets me in trouble."

She laughed at that.

He sat in the bathroom while she bathed and she asked him questions about his mother. He was still in a state of shock over his mother's performance, saying that the woman he knew was quite a bit different from the high-stepper of that night. He remembered milk and cookies.

"And your father remembers begetting you," Aria said, smiling, and she smiled broader when she thought she saw him blush.

"You want your back washed or not?"

"*Sí*, meester, I do," she said in her Carmen Miranda accent.

J.T. groaned but when he washed her back he kissed her neck.

189

He bathed next and she washed his back. Aria put on a lilac spaghetti-strap nightgown and stood quietly outside the bathroom.

"What are you waiting for?" J.T. asked.

"I wondered which bed was to be mine tonight," she said shyly.

He pulled her into his bed. "With me, of course." He cuddled her to him and went to sleep right away.

"I got his attention," she murmured.

"What, honeybunch?" J.T. muttered.

"A new name," Aria said happily, and snuggled closer to him and went to sleep.

The next morning she woke slowly, smiling at the sunlight coming into the room. It was already growing hot but she didn't mind. Her body felt heavenly. She moved a bit to see J.T. lying beside her. Last night had been a dream come true. No pain, no discomfort at all, just pure sensual happiness.

She eased onto her elbow to look at him. My, but he was good-looking. Wasn't it odd how the more time they spent making love, the more handsome he became? He was much better-looking than Count Julian. In fact, right now she thought he was better-looking than any other man on earth.

How would it be, she wondered, if he opened his eyes and whispered, "I love you"? How would it feel to have a man say those words to you? Of course Count Julian had said them to her but they both knew he had only wanted her kingdom. This man didn't want her kingdom. In fact, all he wanted from her was her body.

She smiled at that. On the island she had been a princess and he hadn't obeyed her, hadn't done anything she had wanted, but when she acted as a woman acts . . . *then* he did anything she desired.

She realized that she wanted to please him. She had been taught to believe that the only persons she had to please were those of higher rank than she. But here in America she had wanted to please the wives of the other officers, she had wanted to please her mother-in-law (she swallowed at that memory), and now she wondered what it would be like to please her husband.

She knew he wanted her to learn to be an American and she vowed to try even harder to be as American as she could be. Maybe she would barbecue hamburgers for him; American men seemed to love big pieces of meat.

He stirred in his sleep, opened his eyes, and looked at her. "Good morning," he murmured as he pulled her to him and cuddled her against his big, hairy body.

"What is that American bear the children hold?" she asked.

"A teddy bear?"

"Yes. That's the one. You make me feel like your teddy bear."

"You don't feel like any kind of bear to me," he said softly, running his leg up hers. "You're too thin and not enough hair."

"Too thin?" she said in alarm, turning toward him.

"Too thin to be a teddy bear."

"Oh." She slipped her leg between his. "But not too thin otherwise? Not, oh, what did you say? 'A skinny ass'?"

"I think it would be better if we both forgot what was said on the island," he said before he kissed her.

"It is . . . all right to make love during the daylight?"

"I don't know. Let's try it and see. If the earth opens up and the devil takes us, at least we'll go happy."

Aria made a sound remarkably like a giggle just before J.T. began to kiss her neck.

He took his time caressing her body and she, for the first time, began to touch him too. How different his body felt from hers, no softness, just angles and planes and hard muscle. His skin was different too, coarser feeling, and his hairiness was a delight.

"Happy?" he asked, looking at her, smiling.

"Yes," she whispered.

"Perhaps I can make you happier."

He did.

Later, they lay together, sweaty but holding each other close, both of them content.

"I have to get up," Aria said. "I have to wash my hair and Ethel showed me how to set it in pin curls. It has to dry before this evening."

"Pin curls? Not those awful bobby pins that poke a man's eye out?"

She twisted away from him. "What do you know about women's pin curls?"

"Less than you know about Count Julian's mustache."

"How did you know he has a mustache?"

"A guess," J.T. said, but Aria smiled, knowing he was lying. She hummed in the bathroom while she washed her hair.

She managed with washing and rinsing her hair but the curling was beyond her.

J.T. had stayed in bed, half dozing, half smiling at the sound of her in the bathroom.

"Lieutenant Montgomery," she called. "I need your help."

Stubborn wench, he thought. He had told her not to call him Jarl and for some reason she refused to call him J.T., so she insisted on Lieutenant Montgomery.

Fifteen minutes later, to his utter disbelief, he was

wrapping her hair about his fingers and fastening it with bobby pins. "I cannot believe I am helping you deceive me," he muttered, making Aria laugh.

But later, as he was getting dressed, Aria ran past, gave him a quick kiss, and said she was going to cook him lunch. He leaned back and smiled. There were redeeming features to this marriage: lovemaking for breakfast and home cooking for lunch.

Later J.T. was just coming down the stairs when there was a loud knock at the door. Before he could answer it, the door burst open and General Brooks barged in. J.T. stopped on the third step, came to attention, and saluted.

"What is this?" General Brooks roared as he shoved the door shut in the face of his adjutant. He was holding aloft a copy of the *Key West Citizen* and pointing at the front-page photo of Aria dressed as Carmen Miranda arm in arm with Amanda, both women doing a high kick. "Is this Her Royal Highness?" he bellowed. "Is this Princess Aria?"

"Yes sir!" J.T. said smartly, eyes straight ahead.

General Brooks began to pace, punching the newspaper as he walked. "Do you know what you've done? You've exposed our plan to the world, that's what. Or you will have if anyone from Lanconia sees this."

"I don't think anyone will recognize her, sir."

"Don't get smart with me, young man. This is *your* fault. The army gave you a solemn responsibility and you have failed. What coercion did you use to get that poor young woman to do this? You were to teach her to be an *American,* not some South American hootch dancer."

"Sir! The idea was hers alone. It was a surprise to me." J.T. was still standing on the stairs, still at attention.

"Who's playing that confounded radio?"

"It's—" J.T. began.

"*Her* idea? You expect me to believe that? For God's sake, man, the woman is a royal princess. She's been raised in style and elegance, yet here she is wearing"—he held the paper up—"wearing platform shoes."

"Again, sir, it was not my idea."

General Brooks sat down on a wicker chair, the stiff straw creaking under his weight. "Well then, maybe you should have allowed her a little freedom. Sometimes women are like wild ponies: you can't keep them locked up all the time, sometimes you have to let them run a little free or else they break the traces altogether." He ran his hand over his face. "I've been married thirty-two years and I'm no closer to understanding my wife today than I ever was. What a day this has been! I've been on that plane for hours. You have any bourbon?"

"Yes sir," J.T. answered, but didn't move.

"Then get it!" General Brooks snapped.

J.T. went to the kitchen while the general continued talking.

"To pull this off, the princess has to act like an American. American women don't dress up in bare-legged skirts and dance at a Commander's Ball. It seems like a simple thing to ask that you could explain that to her. Did she think it was one of her blueblood masquerades? And who is that harlot with her?"

"My mother, sir," J.T. said, handing the general his drink.

"Lord," General Brooks gasped, and downed the drink. "I thought they checked you out. Look, Lieutenant, this is an order, you take control of the princess or I'll give you a desk job under the stupidest officer in the navy. You understand me? What the princess did was obviously a reaction against too tight a rein. My wife once reacted like that when we were first married." He waved his hand. "That's neither here nor there. Let the princess have a little fun now and then and maybe she'll learn to be an American. Time is running out. She'll never fool the Lanconian kidnappers this way. Damnation, but that radio is loud! Tell whoever is playing it to turn it off."

"Sir," J.T. said, "perhaps I could show you something."

The general looked tired and greatly put out but he heaved himself up from the chair and followed J.T. to the kitchen window.

In the backyard was a smoking barbecue grill and a cord stretched through an open window leading to a radio blaring "Don't Sit Under the Apple Tree with Anyone Else But Me." Aria was wearing baggy jeans rolled up to her knees, triple-rolled bobby socks, brown and white saddle oxfords, a plaid shirt of J.T.'s, and her hair was in pin curls with a polka-dot scarf tied over her head. She was chewing gum to the tune of the music while slapping hamburger patties between her hands.

"*That* is Her Royal Highness?" General Brooks gasped.

"She does look like an American housewife, sir."

"She looks *too much* like an American housewife." He turned to glare at J.T. "There is such a thing as going too far in the opposite direction." His expression changed and he put his hand on J.T.'s shoulder. "You want to talk about it, son? I mean, this isn't exactly the usual wartime assignment. Has it been very difficult?"

J.T., seeming to forget the general's rank, poured out two glasses of bourbon and took a healthy drink of his. "I can't make her out at all. One minute she's stretching out her hand to me like I'm one of her damned subjects and the next she's embarrassing me in front of hundreds of people and the next she's—" He broke off. "Let's just say that she's not shy when we're alone." His eyes narrowed. "And she refuses to do what I tell her to do. I explained to her about ironing and she laughed at me."

"My wife refuses to iron too," General Brooks said sadly. "Always has."

"I guess I don't know much about wives, sir, only women, and this woman doesn't fit into either category."

"You like her, do you?"

J.T. grinned. "I'm beginning to, but I sure as hell don't want to. I plan to fight it. I'm going to turn her over to her fiancé count with a clear conscience."

A look of guilt crossed General Brooks's face but he didn't say anything. "It looks to me like she's got your lunch ready and I better go. Don't tell her I was here. Tomorrow someone will come and tell you the details of returning to Lanconia. Do me a favor and don't let her pack her Carmen Miranda dress when she goes. Who knows what she'll do."

"No, sir, I won't," J.T. said, smiling as he walked the general to the door. He stood for a moment, thinking that the Carmen Miranda dress was in shreds, still lying on the floor of his car.

Aria called that the hamburgers were almost ready and, still smiling, he went outside.

The radio was blaring "Shorty George" and Aria took his hand. "Let's dance."

"Wait until something slower is on. I'm not good at this dancing."

"Okay," she said, turning back toward the hamburgers. "I'll ask Mitch the next time I see him. He's a great jitterbugger."

J.T. grabbed her hand, spun her around, and began a wild jitterbug with her. He had been rowing since he was a boy and his arms were very strong. He tossed her over his head, slid her beneath his legs, then whirled her out at arm's length.

She was breathless when the song finished.

"I told you I wasn't any good," he said smugly, making Aria laugh.

Companionably, they sat down to eat their lunch and J.T. watched Aria. Her hair in pin curls, her chewing gum stuck on the side of the plate, her fingers tapping to the music, eating a hamburger with her hands and drinking beer from a bottle, she was a different person from the princess on the island.

He began to realize that the general's visit had upset him because it made him aware that soon he would have to return his borrowed princess.

Since the war, it seemed that every man he knew was getting married, but J.T. had thought he was too wise to get trapped by a woman. More than once, he had seen a man marry some beautiful dish then two weeks later she would look like Aria looked now. J.T. had been disgusted. He liked his women combed and powdered and perfumed. But right now, looking at Aria, he wouldn't trade her for a beauty queen.

"Where did you get that shirt?" he asked over the radio, referring to the oversize, beat-up plaid she wore.

She gave him a level look over her beer. "From a box in your closet."

"The box way in the back? The one that is—was—taped and tied and has 'private' written in three-inch-tall letters on all six sides?"

"That sounds like the one," she said, watching him.

J.T. grunted and she smiled at him. He had always

197

heard men complaining about the lack of privacy in marriage and he had always thought that if he had a wife she would never invade *his* privacy. But now he found it didn't matter at all. In fact, he rather liked that she had been curious enough to search his belongings. It made it seem as if they really were married.

He looked back at her. He was going to have to turn her over to another man.

Right then he made a vow that he would be like a man falling off a horse—he would get right back on. As soon as he gave her to her short, old, effeminate count, he would get himself another wife. He liked having someone to come home to. He liked sitting in the backyard on a Saturday afternoon and eating hamburgers. He even liked the intimacy of rolling a woman's hair.

Of course he wondered if he would be able to find another wife as interesting as Aria. He smiled at the memory of last night. Most young officers' wives were terrified of any man with a star on his shoulder, but Aria hadn't cared one way or the other. And maybe he *had* been a little overbearing about his mother's visit—of course who knew that one's mother would act as his had?

He leaned his chair back and turned down the radio. "Yesterday you said you were suffering from morning sickness. Was that true or did you just want to get rid of me?"

"It wasn't true," she answered.

"What would happen if you were going to have my kid? Would your blueblood count still accept you?"

"I would still be queen, and as he wants to marry a queen, I don't believe it would interfere in any way."

"And what about the kid?"

198

"If he were a boy, as the oldest, he'd someday be king. If the child were a girl and I had no male issue, she would become queen."

J.T. took a deep drink of his beer. "I see. No objection from your short husband?"

Aria coughed to cover a laugh. "I will be queen and the decision about the child would be mine."

"Ol' Julian would be a father to someone else's kid?"

"He wouldn't be involved much in the upbringing even if the child were his. Royal children are reared by governesses and tutors. My father died when I was quite young and until I reached womanhood at fourteen, I only saw my mother from six to six-thirty each evening."

"And that's how your children would be raised?"

"I know of no other way."

"In America we do things differently. If we had a kid right now, he'd be here with us. You'd be feeding him and I'd be tossing him a ball."

"Another example of American equality," she said. "The woman does the work and the man gets to play."

J.T. looked like he might get angry but then he laughed. "It beats giving the kid to strangers. If you fell and cut yourself, who hugged you?"

Aria looked puzzled. "A doctor would be called. But a royal princess is too well guarded to get hurt very often, although I have injured myself falling from a horse."

"Guarded? When I was ten I rowed myself out to an island and camped for two nights alone."

"Royal children are never alone. Even at night someone sleeps in their room. At fourteen I was given my own room but a maid slept in an adjoining chamber."

"I see," J.T. said, taking a big bite of his hamburger. "And our kid—I mean, if we made one—would be raised like that?"

"It is tradition." She was quiet a moment. "But you could visit him whenever you wished."

"No," J.T. said slowly. "I'm not sure I could do that." He leaned back, turned the radio back up, and fell silent.

Chapter Thirteen

O_N Monday morning J.T. received a telegram from General Brooks saying that all was arranged and the two of them would be shipped out to Lanconia on Tuesday.

"The beginning of the end," he murmured as Bill entered his office.

"Something bothering you?" Bill asked.

"The princess and I leave for Lanconia tomorrow."

"I'm going to miss her, and Dolly's not going to be fit to live with. Those two have become as thick as thieves. And the merchants around town are going to cry too."

J.T. crumbled the telegram in his hand. "I better call her so she can pack," he said solemnly.

"And I'll call Dolly so she can help."

Later that day Dolly called J.T. and said she was inviting everyone to a cookout on the beach. "A farewell party for her," Dolly said, and there was a catch in her voice.

You aren't going to miss her more than I will, J.T. thought.

It was a subdued Aria who met him at the beach. He took her hand in his. "Cheer up, baby, you're going home."

"I shall miss America," she said softly. "I shall miss its freedom and its music and its feeling of progression."

Not to mention missing me, he thought with some anger. "I guess I'm to catch the lobsters."

"Yes," she said disinterestedly. "Probably."

Aria couldn't cheer up, no matter how hard she tried. And Dolly was as bad as she was. A princess never shows her emotions in public, Aria chanted.

J.T. brought back lobsters and the men put them on the grill.

"Oh no," Dolly said. "Look what the cat dragged in."

Aria looked up to see a plump Heather Addison on the arm of Mitch. "Good evening, everybody," Mitch called, then looked at Aria. "You look lovely, as usual. J.T. taking better care of you?"

"I take *great* care of her," J.T. said, holding a barbecue fork as if it were a weapon.

Heather gave a contemptuous look at Aria then wiggled over to J.T. She took his arm and snuggled her breasts into his side. "J.T., honey, I haven't seen you since Washington. Remember the night we did the town? The day after you got married?" she added loudly.

"Just what we need—fireworks," Gail groaned. "J.T., let's make this evening pleasant, okay?"

Mitch went to sit by Aria. "I hear you're shipping out tomorrow. We're going to miss you. J.T. going too?"

J.T. turned around. "She's going with *me*, not the

other way around. This country of Lanconia needs some shipbuilding advice, and I'm giving it. My *wife* goes with me."

Mitch moved closer to Aria. "I hear Lanconia is very pretty with long, cool nights, nothing but cowbells ringing."

"True," Aria said sadly. "No McGuire Sisters, no garbage trucks at three A.M., no honkytonks, no beach parties."

"You've been there?"

"No," J.T. and Aria said in unison. "We've just been reading about it," J.T. added.

"J.T., honey, I left my wrap in the car. Would you get it for me?" Heather asked.

"Somebody watch the grill," J.T. called, and stepped away from the light of the fire and into the darkness.

Heather lost no time in following him. "J.T.," she called, "wait for me."

He halted. "You shouldn't have come."

"Don't give me that," she said. "I know what's going on. I had to pay three lipsticks and four pair of nylons to get the information about you and that . . . that princess. If she's royalty, I'll eat my bathing suit."

"You better start chewing." J.T. turned away.

Heather hurried after him. "I also know the marriage is temporary and that she's going to dump you as soon as you two get to her country. I hear she's going to throw you over for a skinny little duke with blue blood."

"Heather, you have a big mouth." He stopped at Mitch's car, opened the door, grabbed her beach cover-up, and shoved it at her.

"You used to like my mouth," she said, leaning into his chest. "Honey, I'm only concerned about you. What are you gonna do when she ditches you? You aren't fool enough to end up with a broken heart, are you?"

The words hit too close to home. "Let's go back," he said, but there was no conviction in his voice.

"I'll be here, sweetie. When you come back here all alone, I'll be waiting."

He looked at her a moment. "I might take you up on that offer," he said.

They walked back to the firelight together.

"Are you going to stand for that?" Dolly asked, looking up at Heather and J.T. bending over the grill.

"That's a nice suit," Aria said absently. "Do you think she bought it here?"

Dolly rolled her eyes then got up and pushed herself between J.T. and Heather. "Your *date* is over there," she said pointedly to Heather.

"My date for tonight," Heather said smugly.

The evening grew worse. Aria and Dolly were depressed and Heather was angry at J.T. for having married someone other than herself, Mitch kept making hints to Aria about having a night of farewell, and the rest of the group wished they hadn't come.

Aria watched J.T. and Heather and saw that J.T. was making no effort to keep Heather's hands off his body. In fact, he kept looking at Aria as if he expected something from her. But the more Heather oozed over J.T., the straighter Aria's back became. She felt closer to being a royal princess tonight than she had in weeks.

By the time the group said good night, Aria's manners were very formal. "So good of you to have invited me," she said, and held out her hand to shake—not a hearty American shake but the fingers-only type royalty used to save their hands from hundreds of handshakes in a few hours.

"I'll see you off tomorrow," Dolly said softly, a little intimidated by Aria's manner.

"Thank you very much," she said to J.T. when he opened the car door for her. "A most pleasant party," she said as he drove away.

"What, no mimicking of Heather?"

"She is a lovely young woman," Aria said. "Such lovely hair."

"It's not a natural color."

"Oh? One would never have guessed." They were both quiet the rest of the way home.

"You must pardon me," Aria said when they were home. "I am most tired and think I'll go to bed. I wish you a pleasant good night."

"Damn!" J.T. said when she was upstairs. Did the woman have no feelings? How many times had he made a fool of himself out of jealousy over her? But tonight he had allowed Heather to make the most outrageous remarks and Aria had said nothing. He went into the backyard to smoke a cigarette and drink a strong gin and tonic. Perhaps she was looking forward to getting rid of him. Perhaps she was too cold-blooded to feel such an emotion as jealousy.

As usual in Key West, it was starting to rain. He crushed his cigarette out and downed his drink as he glanced up and saw the light go out in the window above. It looked like she was sleeping in her single bed tonight. Good, he thought, it was better to start breaking apart now.

The upstairs was dark and he made no effort to be quiet as he stumbled about and undressed.

He went to Aria's end of the room to close the windows. A bolt of lightning showed her to be lying with her face buried in the pillow.

"Damn," he said under his breath, and went to

stand over her bed. "Look, it's almost over. You'll be home soon. You'll be back in your castle and you'll never have to wash a dish again and you'll never have to look at my ugly mug again."

"Or see Dolly," she said into the pillow.

"Are you okay?" He sat down on the bed. "You and Dolly get into it?"

She whirled around like a tornado and came up with fists clenched, pummeling at his bare chest and arms. "You humiliated me," she yelled. "You embarrassed me before people who have become my friends."

He grabbed her fists. "Look who's talking! You with your 'Chica Chica' in front of my commanding officers."

"But you deserved that! You insinuated that I wasn't good enough for your mother."

"I never did such a thing in my life." He was aghast.

"Then what was that 'Do you know how to act at a formal ball?' 'My mother hates chewing gum so don't blow bubbles in her face.' 'You are to be courteous and respectful to my mother. Treat her as if she were a queen so don't go telling her she does or does not have permission to speak.' 'And she can sit wherever she wants'? What was all that?"

J.T. grinned in the darkness. "Maybe I did go a little overboard."

"You deserved 'Chica Chica.' I did *not* deserve Heather. I've been very good the last few days."

J.T. moved his hands to her back. "You sure have, honey," he said, leaning forward to kiss her.

She drew back. "How can you have the audacity to touch me? Get away from me."

J.T. stopped abruptly. "Sure. Fine. I'll leave you alone. You can lie there and dream about the time when you never have to see me again."

He went to his own bed but he was too angry to sleep. He kept thinking of the injustice of it all, how he had saved her life and married her and taught her to be an American, and she screamed at him and told him to leave her alone. He flopped about in the bed and the sheets began to stick to him. He punched the pillow but sleep wasn't anywhere near.

Maybe he shouldn't have let Heather act like that. She always was a bit of a pest. She had wanted to get married and he acted as if he had no idea what she had in mind, but all along he had suspected that Heather wanted Warbrooke Shipping more than she wanted him.

Cursing women, cursing the army for marrying them, cursing his love of seafood that had made him want to go to that island where he had first met her, J.T. got out of bed and went to her end of the room. She still had her face buried in the pillow. He sat down on the edge of the bed.

"Look, maybe I shouldn't have behaved like I did. I know Heather can be a little cat and I'm sorry I embarrassed you."

She didn't say a word.

"You hear me?" He held out his hand to touch her temple. "You're crying," he said as if he didn't believe it. He pulled her into his arms. "Oh, sweetheart, I'm sorry. I didn't mean to make you cry. I didn't even know you *could* cry."

"Of course I can cry," she said angrily, sniffing. "A princess just doesn't cry in public, that's all."

"I'm not public," he said, sounding hurt. "I'm your husband."

"You didn't act like it tonight. You acted as if Heather were your wife."

"Well, maybe she will be."

"What?" Aria gasped.

"Well, honey, I have to think of the future. You're going to stay in Lanconia with your scrawny count and I find I'm growing rather fond of marriage."

"Oh? How so?" she asked, snuggling against him.

"I don't know. It's sure not the peace and quiet it's added to my life."

"I wonder, Lieutenant Montgomery, maybe you could stay in Lanconia and remain as my husband. My country could benefit from some of your knowledge."

"And be king? I'd just as soon be put in a zoo. No thank you. *No* woman is worth that. Hey, where you going?" he asked.

"As you say, to the can."

"Now what did I do wrong?" he muttered.

Dolly and Bill came to the plane to say good-bye and it felt natural to Aria when Dolly hugged her in public.

Dolly held out a package. "It's just a little something to help you remember America." There were tears in her eyes.

J.T. shook hands with Bill. "I'll be back as soon as . . . as soon as this is done." He was hovering over Aria as if he thought she might fly away.

"Good-bye," they called as Aria and J.T. boarded the airplane.

It was to be a long flight because they had to go north over Russia instead of risking being shot down over Germany.

Aria leaned back in the hard leather seat and looked out the window at Dolly and Bill on the ground.

"Cheer up," J.T. said. "You're going home. What did Dolly give you?"

Aria blinked away tears and opened the package. The box was filled with chewing gum. She laughed.

"I'll get her back," J.T. groaned. "A princess who likes bubble gum."

When they were in the air, the copilot brought J.T. a fat package. "It's our orders," J.T. said. "By the time we get to Lanconia you're to have memorized a new background and assumed a new identity. Look at this!" he said, scanning the cover letter. "General Brooks recommended that you come from Warbrooke, Maine, and that you and I have known each other all our lives. That way I can tell you about my hometown. And your name is Kathleen Farnsworth Montgomery. Okay, Kathy, let's get to work."

Aria couldn't help contrasting this trip to their earlier flight from Washington to Key West. J.T. didn't doze while she studied; instead, he told her about his hometown and the people who lived there. He told her about his father, who was now single-handedly running what J.T. described as the family's modest shipping business. He told her about his three older brothers, about the rowing races they used to have.

"I always won," he said smugly. "I was the smallest and strong for my size."

She looked at the length and breadth of him sprawled in the airplane seat. "You're not *still* the smallest, are you?" she asked, and her voice conveyed her fear of a family of giants.

"Of course not," he said, eyes twinkling, and leaned over to kiss her, then he shoved the papers off his lap and gave all his attention to kissing her.

"Not now!" she hissed at him, and he withdrew, grinning at her flushed face.

"Where were we?" he asked. "Oh yes, Warbrooke." He continued to tell about his town and his family until she began to feel she knew the place.

The plane landed in London for refueling and for

hurried dashes to the rest room for the two passengers. When they reboarded, they started again with the study. This time J.T. asked her questions about her upbringing in America and about her own vital statistics.

They fell asleep against each other somewhere over Russia and didn't wake until they landed in Escalon, the capital city of Lanconia.

J.T. looked out the window and saw blue-green, snow-topped mountains in the distance.

"Most of Lanconia is very high. We're about seven thousand feet elevation now, so the air is thin."

He kissed her. "You know *nothing* about this place, remember? Neither of us has been here before."

"Okay, babe," she said, snapping her gum.

"That's better—sort of. Do you have to chew that stuff?"

"It's very American, and besides, I'll have to give it up soon enough. Crowns and bubble gum don't go together. Hurry up and get off, I want to make sure no one hurts the box of records I brought my sister."

"*Kathy* has no sister, remember?"

He was looking at her very sternly, so she crossed her eyes and blew a bubble at him.

"Go!" he said, laughing.

The air was cool and fresh and sharp as only mountain air can be; even the fumes of the planes couldn't override the cleanness of it.

It was a small airport, and with the war there was very little traffic through it. A car was waiting for J.T. and Aria.

"Lieutenant," said a man who was wearing a dark suit and carrying a briefcase, "everything is ready for you. Good morning, Your Roy—"

"Good to meet ya!" Aria said, grabbing the man's hand and pumping it. "It always this cold in this place? It looks pretty dead around here. What's to do?"

The man's eyes sparkled. "Good morning, Mrs. Montgomery."

"Just call me Kathy, ever'body does. 'Cept him. Sometimes he calls me other things." Chomping away on her gum, she hugged J.T.'s arm and gave him an adoring look.

"Well, yes," the man said uncomfortably. "Shall we go to your hotel?"

"Who're you playing?" J.T. asked when he opened the car door for her.

"Every Lanconian's image of an American."

The man who drove them was James Sanderson and he was assistant to the American ambassador to Lanconia and only he and the ambassador knew the truth behind the imposter princess.

"Otherwise, your story is well covered," Mr. Sanderson said. "Tomorrow, Lieutenant, you will be escorted to the local water plant. You are supposedly an expert on distillation plants."

"Then someone is starting to work on the grapes?" Aria asked.

"We are working with the king every day," Mr. Sanderson answered.

"How is he?"

"Aging," Mr. Sanderson answered, but said no more.

Aria looked out the window. Lanconia looked the same as it had for centuries and she could feel the place creeping into her bones. The streets had been made for goatherders and for walking, so they were much too narrow for the long, wide American car. The cobblestones were hard on the tires and made for a rough ride.

The houses were plastered and whitewashed and

everywhere were the distinctive blue-gray roof tiles that Lanconia manufactured. In the twenties Lanconia had briefly become a fashionable resort and the people who were in the know took crates of the tiles home and had little Lanconian playhouses built. But the fashion hadn't lasted long and the factory was left with thousands of surplus tiles.

The people in the streets were on foot or on bicycles and there were a few horse-drawn carts, but no automobiles. Their clothes were simple, in a style that hadn't changed in centuries: long, dark skirts, white blouses, and pretty, embroidered belts. For a while, those belts had been fashionable too. The men wore heavy shoes, thick wool socks to their knees, and wool knickers. Their white shirts were covered by a sleeveless embroidered vest. The women were proud of their skill with a needle and showed off on their own belts and their husbands' vests. The children wore smaller versions of their parents' clothes, without the belts and vests, but with finely smocked shirts.

J.T. and Mr. Sanderson had stopped talking. "It's like going back in time," J.T. said softly.

"More than you know," Aria replied.

"Here we are," Mr. Sanderson said, pulling the car into the circular drive of the three-story white hotel. He leaned forward to look at Aria. "I don't think anyone will recognize you, but you should be prepared if they do. You want to be seen as much as possible, so when the imposter is taken—it's planned for tomorrow, by the way—they will have an idea of where to look for a replacement."

"No idea yet who 'they' are?" J.T. asked. "No idea who tried to murder the princess?"

"We have suspicions but nothing concrete yet. Okay, here's the bellboy, let's go."

"Wait," Aria said, her hand on J.T.'s arm. "I know

him." The bell "boy" was actually a man nearing seventy. "He was our third gardener. His wife used to bake me cookies. This isn't going to be easy."

"We've come too far to blow it now. You've never been here before and never seen this man before."

"Okay," she said, taking a deep breath.

She stood on the bricked entryway while Mr. Sanderson went inside and J.T. helped load the luggage on a cart.

The old man nearly dropped two bags when he saw Aria.

She smacked gum out of the side of her mouth. "Seen a ghost, honey?" she asked the old man. He just stood and gaped so Aria leaned over and pulled her skirt halfway up her thigh and adjusted her nylons. The man was still staring. "Seen all you want?" she said rather nastily.

J.T. grabbed her arm and pulled her inside the hotel. "You're going to lower America's reputation into the gutter. Use a little subtlety."

"Sure, ducky," she answered. "Anything you say, sugar."

J.T. gave her a warning look.

The inside of the hotel looked like a Russian czar's hunting lodge: log ceiling, plaster walls, big pine furniture scattered about. Above the desk was a flag of Lanconia: a red ground with a stag, a goat, and a bunch of grapes on it.

"Quaint," J.T. said under his breath. "Do they have bathrooms in this joint?"

"Remember America's reputation," she reminded him.

While J.T. signed the register, the hotel clerk looked up and did a double-take on Aria. He stared at her until she winked at him. He looked down at the book.

"Excuse me, Lieutenant Montgomery, I must get

something," the clerk said, and disappeared through a door behind the desk.

J.T. looked questioningly to Mr. Sanderson, who shrugged.

The clerk reappeared with what looked to be his entire family: a fat wife and two plump teenage girls. They all stood and stared at Aria.

Aria walked to the desk. "You got any postcards in this burg? Nobody back home will believe this place is for real."

No one moved; they just stared at Aria.

She leaned across the desk and into the manager's face. "What's the matter with you people?" she asked belligerently. "How come ever'body's starin' at me? You people don't like Americans? We're not good enough for you? You think—"

J.T. caught her arm and pulled her back. "Kathy, be quiet."

The manager began to recover himself. "Pardon our rudeness. We did not mean to stare. It's just that you look like our crown princess."

Aria's jaw dropped down. "You hear that, honey?" she said, punching J.T. in the ribs. "They think *I* look like a princess."

The manager's fat wife reached under the desk and withdrew a postcard and held it at arm's length to Aria.

She took it and studied the official photograph of Her Royal Highness, Princess Aria. Aria's face showed her disappointment. "Nice rocks but I've seen better-lookin' women. In fact Ellie down at the diner is better-lookin', ain't she, honey? Hey! Wait a minute! You sayin' I look like this stuck-up blueblood? I'll have you know I was Miss Submarine Romance of 1941. I was voted, by two hundred and sixteen sailors, mind you, the girl they most wanted to submerge with." She looked up at J.T. "I don't look like her, do I, honey? She looks like somethin' out of a silent movie."

He put his arm around her, took the postcard, and angrily slapped it on the desk as he glared at the clerk and his family. "My wife is much prettier than that woman. Come on, honey, we'll go upstairs and you can rest and try to forget about this insult." He led her away with her head buried in his chest.

When they reached the room, the three didn't speak until the bellboy had left.

Mr. Sanderson looked at Aria in amazement.

"Congratulations, Mrs. Montgomery, you are the *most* obnoxious American I have ever had the misfortune to meet."

She snapped her gum, grinned, and winked at him at the same time. "Thanks, toots."

Chapter Fourteen

Mʀ. Sanderson stayed in their room for three hours as he talked about the seriousness of the coming venture and how important Aria's return to the throne was. He talked about America's need for the vanadium and how much America needed to have military bases in Lanconia.

"Our plan is this," Mr. Sanderson said. "We will take the imposter princess and her aunt, Lady Emere, tomorrow just as they return from America, before anyone of her family in Lanconia sees Princess Maude, and I imagine the brigands who put her in Princess Aria's place will contact Her Royal Highness immediately. For them to be aware of your presence, you two will have to be seen as often as possible within the next twenty-four hours. Once Her Highness is taken, Lieutenant, your services will no longer be needed. She cannot reenter the palace with an American husband at her side. The ambassador and I have arranged for you to be returned to America as soon as contact is made."

"But—" Aria began, wanting to tell the man that Lieutenant Montgomery was to remain as her husband.

J.T. put his hand on her arm. "So we have a couple of days," he said softly.

"Yes," Mr. Sanderson said, looking from one to the other, taking note of their closeness.

"I am concerned for her safety," J.T. said. "I don't want her alone among her enemies. Someone tried to kill her before."

"Yes, but now whoever tried to kill her will think she is an American. I'm sure the murderers believe the actual princess to have been drowned in Florida. We plan to negotiate for the imposter princess's return with whoever contacts Her Royal Highness. Princess Aria—they think—will be discharged once the imposter is returned. Someone believes the real princess is dead, but it may not be the same person who contacts Kathy Montgomery."

J.T. stood, pacing and frowning. "I don't believe whoever planned this is as stupid as you seem to think. She's bound to give herself away. I think I—"

"Lieutenant," Mr. Sanderson said sharply, "your services will no longer be needed. We can protect Her Royal Highness."

Aria was trying to control her emotions but she was very pleased that the lieutenant wanted to protect her, that he was so concerned about her safety. Perhaps it was a camouflage of the truth. Maybe he wanted to remain with her forever.

J.T. turned his back to the two of them and looked out the window.

"We, the ambassador and I," Mr. Sanderson said, "thought perhaps that the two of you might give some evidence of not being a happily married couple; then, when Her Royal Highness is contacted, it will seem natural that she is willing to participate in this farce without her husband."

J.T. didn't turn around but continued staring out of the window. "Yes, that makes sense," he murmured. He turned back. "Shall we go to dinner? It's been a long flight for both of us and we'd like to get to bed early."

Mr. Sanderson cleared his throat. "Tonight, if possible, we thought perhaps you two could stage an argument at dinner, a loud, public argument, and Her Royal Highness could run to the embassy in anger and spend the night there. We need the time to brief her and we need to establish her contact with our embassy. There are many details to work out yet."

"So, I'm no longer needed," J.T. said, his eyes dark. He didn't look at Aria. "I'm going to take a shower— if I can find a bathroom in this place—then we can go to dinner and start our fight. That should be easy." He grabbed clean underwear from a suitcase, a towel from a rack, and left the room.

"No, no, no," Aria said to Mr. Sanderson the minute J.T. was out of the room. "You have everything wrong. We are not to be separated. The American government would not help me unless I agreed to put an American on the throne beside me. We are to remain married and it is better that he stay beside me." She felt a bit of panic. America was still in her veins and she didn't want to let it slip away. And she didn't want to lose this man who made her feel so lovely.

Mr. Sanderson gave her his best diplomatic look. "Of course we were informed of this aspect of your agreement, Your Royal Highness, but that was a military agreement, not a diplomatic or political one. You could not possibly consider putting an American on the Lanconian throne. He knows nothing of the duties of being prince consort, nor does he know about Lanconia. And from what I hear, he has no desire to become prince consort. He could not do a good job even if, by some freak chance, the Lanconian people would accept an American commoner as their queen's husband. You must think of Lanconia and not your, ah . . . personal feelings."

Aria could feel Lanconia seeping into her, rather like someone opening a window and letting a room gradually grow colder.

"But royalty does not divorce," she said softly.

"Your marriage will be annulled," Mr. Sanderson said. "It was made under duress and the Lanconian High Council will agree to it, as will the American government. We are trusting that you can persuade the king to award the vanadium to America and that, as a result of the help we have given you, in the future we may station American troops in your country."

"Yes," she said. "America has helped me and I will show my gratitude."

Mr. Sanderson's face changed. "I am sorry to cause you any unpleasantness. I had no idea the two of you had become fond of one another in so short a time. I was given to understand that you'd welcome an annulment."

"At one time," she murmured. Her head came up. "Let us have this time together, to say good-bye. We can part in anger when I am contacted. He can say that no wife of his will do such a thing and I can go against his orders. Later I can say that I like being a princess better than being a wife. The marriage can be dissolved when I am restored to my rightful place."

"Yes, but—"

"You may leave me now." As soon as Aria said it she realized how long it had been since she had given a regal order.

"Yes, Your Highness," Mr. Sanderson said, then stood and gave a little bow as he left the room.

Aria walked to the window and looked down at the narrow street, at the people walking there. They seemed so old. There was no spring to their step. There were no children in sight. Every year more young people took their children and left the country. There was no industry for them, no jobs, no modern entertainment.

As she watched, she became even more aware of how these people were her responsibility. The High Council passed laws, worked on the trial system, but it was up to the royal family to create interest in the country. In the last century she and her family had become a tourist attraction.

She glanced down at her dress, the easiness of it, such a simple dark brown thing with no diamonds, no royal insignia, and she began to remember how she had to dress as a princess. It took three women two hours each morning to dress her and to arrange her long hair. All day long she changed clothes. There were morning clothes, afternoon clothes, reception clothes, tea clothes, and long, formal dinner gowns.

She thought of her social calendar: every minute of every day was filled with engagements. From ten A.M. until six P.M. she was on public display. She inspected factories, listened to people's complaints, shook thousands of hands, sidestepped personal questions. Then there were the trips around Lanconia, for several days in a row when she did nothing but visit one hospital after another, comfort one dying child and his parents after another. Then at night she was escorted to some long, tiring ball where people talked to her with quaking voices.

Before she had gone to America, she hadn't minded her duties so much. They had been what she had done since she left the schoolroom and she had been trained for them. But now . . . now she had been able to shop in stores, she had gossiped with other women, she had jitterbugged in public. She had been able to be a normal ordinary person who wasn't watched and judged every minute.

She remembered once, when she was eighteen, that she had worn a dress with a low neckline to an afternoon garden party. At the party, a man had suddenly fainted at her feet. When she bent to help him, he whipped out his camera, snapped her picture, then scampered away. The next day every paper in the free world carried a photograph of the semiexposed bosom of Princess Aria of Lanconia.

That was her life. She lived in a glass box, her every movement scrutinized and examined then exposed to the world.

Yet she had considered asking this American husband of hers to share that life. How would he be as king? Would he toss reporters into swimming pools? Would he call people like Julian "Count Julie" to their faces? Would he dine with common-looking women in public places? Would he show up at dinner wearing his undershirt?

And how would the people of Lanconia react to him? Would he be contemptuous of the goatherders? Of the grape pickers?

All Americans seemed to think their country was the only one on earth. Could Lieutenant Montgomery give up his American citizenship to become a Lanconian? Would he bother to learn the language?

He was so quick-tempered, so impatient, so intolerant. She remembered their time on the island. She understood now some of his intolerance, some of his anger, but if he remained in Lanconia, he would be consorting daily with people whose lineage could be traced to generations of kings. Their snobbery made Aria's seem like that of a peasant. How would they treat this American commoner? How would he react to their treatment of him? She had a vision of Lieutenant Montgomery wrapping Cousin Freddie's pearls about his thin neck the first time Freddie looked down his nose at the American.

And then there was the fact that the lieutenant didn't *want* to be prince consort. She didn't think he could do a good job at best, but if he was reluctant, he would be like a large, spoiled two-year-old.

She took a deep breath and turned away from the window. Mr. Sanderson was right: it was over.

Her easy, happy American interlude was over. It was time now to return to her destiny. She had been born to be queen and now she must continue preparing for that duty—no, the honor of being queen, she corrected herself.

She was able to smile when J.T. reentered the room. He frowned. "I guess you're glad to be home."

"Yes and no. America will always be a fond memory to me. Dolly said she will visit me, so I don't plan to lose all contact with your country. Perhaps you will visit—"

"No," he said sharply. "Can we get this over? I mean our public argument?"

"It has been postponed." She was studying his face. Until today she had thought they were always to be married but now she knew these were their last few hours together. "We dine together and . . . and spend the night, then tomorrow or the next day I'll be contacted, I'm sure. Tomorrow we must be seen as often as possible by as many people as possible."

He wore only a towel about his middle and was

223

rubbing his wet hair with another towel. He looked so good her fingers ached to touch him.

"I wish you hadn't," he said. "I need to get back to the base as soon as possible and the sooner . . ." He trailed off.

She stiffened. "The sooner you get rid of me the better."

He looked at her for a long moment. "It'll be better for me to get this over with."

Dinner was one of the most difficult meals she had ever experienced. She felt like a fool because the idea of not seeing him again was making her very sad but he couldn't wait to get rid of her. He was cool and remote to her.

Aria had to hide her feelings and play the despicable American when any Lanconian was near.

"You think we want a table out in the middle?" she demanded. "J.T., honey, they want to stare at me. They want to point at me and say I look like their plain-faced princess. Do we have to stay in this town? I don't know if I'm gonna be able to stand it."

"This way, madame," said the haughty waiter, and led them to a secluded table in the corner.

"What will you do when you get back?" Aria asked when they were alone.

"Look at Buicks," he said, then glowered at her. "Work. Do what I can to help in the war."

"Will they let you keep our little house?"

"I don't want it."

Aria smiled at that. Perhaps he too was upset at their parting. "I shall miss America and I shall miss you," she whispered.

He looked down at his empty plate. "It'll be nice to have my time be my own again. I've been neglecting my work."

She didn't say anything in reply to him. Their food came and still she said nothing.

"Will you see Heather again?" she asked at last.

"I'm going to go out with every woman in the southeastern U.S. And you? You going to marry your little count?"

"Really!" she said, her eyes glaring into his. "Sometimes you can be most infantile. Count Julian is a perfectly suitable man and he will make an excellent prince consort. Better than you could do."

"Better than *I* could do? Let me tell you, baby, what this backward place of yours needs is a shot of new blood. You'd be lucky if I stayed with you, but I wouldn't have this place on a platinum platter. There's a war going on out there, but these people are so wrapped up in their own petty problems that they don't even see anyone else's."

"We are not involved in a *war* and that is what is *wrong* with us?" she seethed. "You aggressive, angry Americans could learn a lot from our peaceful country. We don't destroy ourselves and other countries with our war machines."

"Because you don't fight *for* anything. You just let the outside world take care of you. You're willing to profit from the war by selling the vanadium but you aren't willing to sacrifice your men for soldiers."

"Are you calling us cowards? Our country was founded by the greatest warriors in the world. In 874 A.D. we—"

"What the hell do I care about your history? *Now* you're a bundle of lily-livered extortionists with a petticoat ruler."

At that she rose and slapped him hard before storming out of the dining room. She ran out of the hotel and into the street, into the cool night air, past people who looked as if they were seeing a ghost, down one street after another. She had no idea where she was going. Her experience of the streets of Escalon was limited to rides in ceremonial carriages. When she was a little girl, she thought the driver merely followed the trail of rose petals to get where he was going.

How could she have considered that man as prince consort? How could she have allowed bed pleasure to influence her rational thinking? He was the pig-headed, intolerant bigot she had first thought he was. She was quite willing to learn American ways and to see thoughts and ideas through American eyes, but he could see no other way than his own. His country was very young, with an adolescent's energies. America wanted power and was willing to kill for it. Her country was old and had learned the power of peace. At one point her ancestors had ruled a big portion of Europe and Russia. In fact, the reason her family was in power was because they had bred the largest, strongest warriors.

Yet this American had called them cowards! Extortionists!

She walked for a long time, not seeing where she was going, just walking and cursing herself for being such a fool.

She halted when she ran into someone. "Excuse me," she said, still using the American expression. She looked into the eyes of her Lord High Chamberlain. He was an arrogant man who expected the streets to clear when he walked them. Intelligence burned in his black eyes.

Aria wanted him to see her and to remember her. "Path not wide enough for you, bub?" she said. "You knock ladies into the street here?"

He drew back from her as if she were a bit of fungus.

Aria leaned forward and put her hands on his badge of office. "Hey! Are you royalty or somethin'? What's that say on there? Is that Latin? We have Latin in America. Do you know the princess? People here say I look like her, but I don't think I do, but I was thinkin' maybe I could borrow a crown of hers and have my picture taken. It'll be real funny back home. How much do you think she'd charge to rent one of her crowns? Or maybe she'd just loan it bein' as we look alike an' all. What d'ya think, buster?"

The Lord High Chamberlain flared his nostrils at her and moved away.

"That's no way to treat an American citizen," she yelled after him, disturbing the tranquil street. "We own your country, you know. You ought to be nice to us."

People looked out of their doors and windows at her.

"I'm gonna report you to the American ambassador," she said loudly, then turned to an openmouthed bystander and demanded directions to the embassy.

It was after midnight when she arrived and she was surprised to see every light in the building on. Someone must have been watching the entrance because the door opened before she reached it.

A large, matronly woman who was desperately trying to hold on to her figure via the use of rigid corsets swooped into the room like a decorated snow shovel and ushered Aria up the stairs.

"Oh my dear," the woman said. "I mean, Your Royal Highness, it has been dreadful here. How could the American government do such a thing to you? You poor, poor darling."

"What has happened?" Aria asked, standing in the big bedroom, surrounded by sumptuous blue silk wall coverings and darker blue silk bed hangings. The Americans didn't skimp on their embassies.

"My goodness," the woman gushed. *"Everything* has happened. We didn't have much notice that you were coming, and with the war and all it was difficult to get what we needed. But I did manage a nightgown for you. It's made by French nuns and the sewing is exquisite. I do hope you like it, although I am sure it's not the quality you're used to."

"What has happened?" Aria insisted.

"That man was here, that awful man my own government married you to."

"Lieutenant Montgomery? Is he here now?"

"Oh no, although it wasn't easy to get rid of him. My husband the ambassador got rid of him but only after what could only be described as a brawl in the foyer. He had a fistfight with four armed guards."

Aria sat down on the edge of the bed. "Why was he here?"

"He said he wanted to see you and didn't believe anyone when we told him you weren't here. We have been so dreadfully worried about you. My husband insisted he leave but he refused, thus the brawl."

"Was he injured?"

"No, a bruise or two, no more. My husband finally had to tell him that he was not going to be king no matter what. That news made him calm down and they went to my husband's study. I just hope the guards didn't understand what my husband meant. It has been so difficult keeping all this a secret. I am to treat you as a niece, not as Your Royal Highness. I do hope you can forgive me. We have tried so hard to make everything comfortable for you but we were given such short notice that—"

"What did your husband say to Lieutenant Montgomery?" Aria asked.

"He explained that the bargain you'd made with the army could not possibly be kept and that no matter how hard he fought he'd never be allowed to be king."

Aria looked away from the woman. "So he's been told," she murmured.

"My husband told him in no uncertain terms. The very idea of an American as king. I mean, it is my own country, but an American—especially one such as him—as king! The idea! Such a crude young man. Fisticuffs in the foyer!"

"You may leave me now," Aria said.

Startled, the woman stopped speaking abruptly. "Yes, Your Royal Highness. Will you need help dressing?"

"No, just leave me." She waved her hand at the woman.

Once she was alone, Aria took her time undressing and putting on the long, high-necked nightgown. It was indeed like she had worn all her life—no more Rita Hayworth style, she thought with regret. It seemed that minute by minute she was losing America and returning to Lanconia. Already she was dismissing people from her presence.

She climbed into the empty bed and thought about her husband. He must be very angry about what he had heard tonight.

She drifted off to sleep wondering why he had come to the embassy in the first place.

J.T. looked out the car window in silence. He had been told that he was to lunch with his wife, then he was to be taken on a token tour of Escalon then put on a plane and shipped out. After his initial rage, he was glad that that had been changed and it was at last over, that he could return to America and get back to work on something of importance.

Last night he had felt guilty about their argument—not that every word he had spoken hadn't been true—but because, after all, it was her country and no one wanted to hear the bad things about his country. So he had gone to the embassy to talk to her. He had been attacked as soon as the door opened.

He had barely got himself out of that mess when he was informed he couldn't be king no matter how much he tried to blackmail himself into the position. He listened to the pompous little ambassador for twenty minutes, somehow managing to keep his blood from boiling over.

While the man postured and lectured and talked to J.T. as if he were semiretarded, J.T. was able to piece the story together. Aria had told the army she would put her American husband on the throne if America would help her. Now she was reneging on her word.

J.T.'s anger was quiet, running through his body like poison. He had been used, duped into something that he stupidly had believed on a surface level. He had been told he was to marry her to teach her to be an American, but now he realized that a gaggle of women could have done that.

As he watched the ambassador pose and strut as he lectured, J.T. thought of the *real* reason he had been married to Her Royal Highness. No doubt Warbrooke Shipping had something to do with it. Then there were the lumber mills and steel mills owned by the Montgomery family. How useful all that would be to this poor, desolate country.

Wonder what she demanded, he thought. The richest American available? What a fool he had been. He had thought he was chosen because he saved her scrawny neck. He was angry at her, sure, but part of him had been flattered that he was chosen. Yet she had just wanted his money. No wonder she agreed to put him on the throne beside her. Montgomery money was needed in this poor country.

He had stood. "I'll be going now and I won't bother you again," he told the ambassador. "I'll find my own transportation back to America. Tell the princess so long for me and I'll arrange the divorce or annulment —whatever is needed." He turned to go.

The ambassador began sputtering and said that J.T. *had* to help them. He had to continue in his role as husband until the imposter princess was taken and Aria was once again princess.

J.T. said he had had enough games and lies to last him a lifetime and he just wanted to get out of the country.

The ambassador changed his tune after that. He began to ask rather nicely that J.T. remain as long as Lanconia and America needed him.

"You are to be seen together today, at luncheon, then you will have another spat and separate. Her Royal Highness will take a walk by herself into the hills. We think she will be contacted there. At dinner a waiter will drop soup on you, and the two of you will be so angered, you will pack and leave Lanconia. Her Royal Highness will be taken off the plane a hundred miles south of here. You will return to America."

"You seem awfully sure they will contact her," J.T. said.

"The American government has said that if the papers giving the vanadium to us are not signed within eight days, America will consider Lanconia an enemy. The papers will not be delivered until after the princess is taken and I'm sure the king's advisers will do anything to prevent the king from finding out that his granddaughter has been kidnapped, or he might be too upset to sign the papers. Or worse, it might give him another heart attack."

"Then the Lanconian government would have to sign the papers."

"The vanadium is on land personally owned by the king's family."

J.T. was torn. He wanted to help his country and make sure it got the vanadium but he wanted to get away from the intrigue. Most of all, he wanted to get away from Aria, the woman who had made such a fool of him. Everything she had done in America, the lovemaking on the stairs, the grilled hamburgers, the being nice to his friends, it had all been to get his money for her country. All of it had been false.

"I will stay in this country for twenty-four hours more and that's all."

The ambassador gave a weak smile and held out his hand to J.T. but J.T. ignored it.

Chapter Fifteen

AT eight A.M. tea had been brought to Aria's room on a tray, served in a Lily set of Limoges china. All morning, as close as possible, her life in the palace had been duplicated. She could feel herself slipping back into the former pattern of her life. She allowed the ambassador's wife to help her dress; she sent the strawberries back to the kitchen; she complained because her shoes had not been polished during the night; she berated the maid for not putting toothpaste on her brush. Part of her didn't like what she was doing but another part of her seemed to have no control.

At twelve forty-five she hurried down the stairs, eager to greet Lieutenant Montgomery. When she saw him, she could feel her petulance falling away, and she began to think of beach cookouts and Tommy Dorsey's band.

But J.T.'s expression was one of controlled rage. He pulled her into a reception room. "So," he said, his eyes black with fury, "you double-crossed me. You never meant for there to be an end to our marriage."

There was no need to ask what he was talking about. "It's the only way your government would help me. I had to agree to make my American husband prince consort."

"King," he snapped.

She looked at him.

"So, you lied to me and lied to them as well. I've always viewed this marriage as temporary."

She didn't answer him.

"When did you plan to tell me about this? Some night when we were in bed, you'd say, 'By the way, you have to live in this godforsaken country the rest of your life'? 'You have to give up your family, the sea, ships, and everything in America so you can ride around in a broken-down horse and buggy and wave at a bunch of people who'll hate you because you're an American'? Is that what you expected of me?"

"I never considered you at all. I thought only of my country."

"You thought only of what *you* wanted. Let me tell you that I'm an American and I plan to stay one. I don't want to live here and I sure as hell don't want to be a wind-up toy king. I'm not trading my freedom to live in a cage. I'm leaving for home today. The army's deal was with you, not me. I'll have our marriage annulled as soon as I return. It'll be like it never existed and you'll be free to once again dupe some other sucker into being a half-king." He grabbed her arm. "Now let's get this over with."

Aria's body was so rigid, it's a wonder she didn't snap in half. She relied completely on her royal training to get her through that long, silent walk back to the hotel and into the dining room. "I believe we

234

are to argue," he said coolly as soon as they were seated.

"I do not feel like arguing," she answered haughtily.

"So, the princess has returned. I guess you got tired of pretending to be an American. You've returned to being the spoiled brat I met on the island. Am I supposed to bow to you? Kiss your hand? Lady, you should be given an Academy Award for your performance in Key West. You'll have some great laughs when this is all over. Will you tell your royal relatives what fools we were, how we believed your act? Will you do your imitations of Dolly and Bill and the rest of us for your bluebloods? Will you tell your new husband of the sexual acts you had to perform with me in order to get your country back?"

Aria went from stunned to hurt to a feeling of wanting to protect herself all in a few seconds. "I love my country as much as you do yours and one does what one must."

He glared at her. "Well, you lost out on this one. I'm returning to America tonight and I'll have the marriage annulled immediately. You'll never touch Warbrooke Shipping."

She had no idea what he was talking about but she wasn't going to let him know that. "I can do without it."

"You'll have to, baby."

"It is Your Royal Highness," she said, looking down her nose at him.

He started to say something else but the waiter arrived and J.T. didn't speak.

Aria began to chew as if she had gum in her mouth. "So! You'd rather have fat little Heather Addison than me," she said loudly for the waiter's benefit.

"I'd rather have *anybody* than you," he said, his

eyes deadly serious. "You are a liar, a money-grubbing little bitch, and besides that you're the worst in bed I've ever had."

There was no need for Aria to fake the tears in her eyes. "Really?" she whispered.

"Really."

Slowly, she rose from the table and left the dining room. Her mother had been right: one cannot trust people not of one's class. Right now she greatly regretted how much she had relaxed in his presence. She had let him see her as no one else ever had. She had even let him see her cry.

The ambassador had shown her on a map where she was to walk, the place where she would be most visible to the townspeople. As a side street curved around, there was a dirt goat path winding up around the mountain.

Her shoes weren't made for climbing but the exercise felt good and she began to walk faster.

She was startled when a man jumped from behind a bush at her. In her bewilderment, she almost greeted him by name. He was the king's third secretary, a mild, quiet man one rarely noticed and certainly never thought of as a villain.

"Mrs. Montgomery, would you come with me?"

"Not on your life, buster," she said, and turned to go back down the hill.

Another man blocked her path. He was the Master of Plate's assistant. "This is more than a request." He took her arm and led her away as she yelled in protest, but they were too far away from town for anyone to hear her.

She was taken to a goatherder's hut and sitting inside was the Lord High Chamberlain. Aria had to conceal her anger. This was a man her grandfather had always trusted.

He didn't conceal his contempt for her. "Mrs. Montgomery, I have a proposition for you."

Twenty minutes later, Aria leaned back in her chair. "Let me get this straight. You want *me* to be your princess?"

"For a short time only. We fear that the news of his granddaughter's kidnapping will kill the king. He is old and his heart is bad and this news could be too much for him. You won't have to do anything but stay in Her Highness's apartments and be seen from a distance now and then. We shall say that you have an illness and cannot leave your room. Now and then someone will look in on you and you will have to play the invalid in bed, but for the most part you will be free to read or listen to records or whatever you Americans do." There was a sneer in his voice.

"So I'm to be a prisoner in a couple of rooms. I see what you get out of this but what's in it for me?"

The Lord High Chamberlain stiffened. "You will be helping an old man who is near death, and our country needs you."

"That's just what I said: what's in it for me?"

The man's eyes blazed. "We are not a rich country."

"Well, maybe you can pay me some other way. How about a title? I'd like to be a duchess maybe."

The man's face showed his revulsion. "Duchess is a hereditary title. Perhaps a directorship. You would be addressed as Mistress."

"Mistress!" she gasped. "That's what my husband's got. I'll not be called a mistress."

"It does not mean the same thing in our country. It is a title of great honor."

She stood. "Look, I gotta go. It's been real nice meetin' you, but no go. I don't wanna sit in some rooms for a couple of weeks and pretend I'm sick."

"All right then, what can I offer you?"

237

Aria thought a minute then sat back down. "Me and my husband ain't been gettin' along so well. I'd like to *be* this princess for a while, know what I mean? You teach me how to talk like her and act like her and maybe I can get somethin' on with one of your dukes or somethin'. Then when your real princess gets back maybe I can stay and be married to a duke. Or maybe a prince. A prince would be nice."

The Lord High Chamberlain could not conceal his horror.

"Take it or leave it, buddy," Aria said, rising. "And who knows about what you're tryin' to do? This sick ol' king know about this? The American ambassador? Are you sure this is on the up and up?"

The Lord High Chamberlain left the room and a second later returned with Princess Aria's lady-in-waiting, Lady Werta.

"Can it be done? Can she be trained not only to meet Princess Aria's family but also to carry out her rigorous schedule?" he asked.

Lady Werta gave Aria a condescending look. "Stand," she ordered. "And walk."

It was on the tip of Aria's tongue to tell the woman to mind her manners, but she did as she was told. She slouched across the room, putting lots of wiggle in her hips.

"Impossible," Lady Werta said. "Totally impossible."

"Oh yeah?" Aria said. "Watch this, honey." She strode across the little room until she was inches from Lady Werta's face. "You will address me as Her Royal Highness and nothing else. And I will not tolerate such insolence of manner again. And you"—she whirled to face the Lord High Chamberlain—"how dare you sit in my presence? Now bring me my tea."

"Yes, Your Highness," they said in unison, then looked in shock at Aria as she grinned and blew a bubble.

"I used to be an actress. I can play a part real good."

"Humph!" Lady Werta sniffed. "Perhaps she is trainable after all." She left the hut.

"Old biddy," Aria said under her breath. "Well, I got the part or not?"

"We will give you two days of instruction and we shall see at the end of that time."

"You'll be amazed at how fast a learner I am."

"Mrs. Montgomery, I am beginning to believe you cannot further amaze me. Now, shall we discuss details?"

Aria sat in her hotel room, sitting utterly still, and waited for J.T. It had been a hideous afternoon. Her instruction in being Princess Aria had begun immediately and it had been as if she were training for prison. Her few short weeks in America had made her forget the loneliness and isolation, the rigidity of being a princess. Rules, rules, and more rules. Lady Werta had spit out one rule after another, all the things a princess was not to do. With each word the haughty old woman spoke, Aria could feel herself getting closer to being the crown princess than to being Mrs. Montgomery.

Tomorrow Lady Werta said she would bring corsets and see if they could fit Aria's expanded body—too much good American food—into them.

Right now, more than anything, Aria wished she could return to America and go with Dolly to Ethel's Beauty Parlor and cook J.T. some spaghetti for supper.

The thought of J.T. made her stiffen. She didn't like

to think how much his words hurt her. She had grown fond of him while all she had been to him was a pain—no, a *royal* pain—in the neck from beginning to end.

When the door opened and he entered the room, she was sitting as she had been taught to sit for hours at a time: back utterly rigid, seated away from the back of the chair. "Good evening," she said formally.

"It's Her Royal Highness," he said sarcastically, then pulled his suitcase from out of the closet and opened it. "You pack this?"

"Yes," she said softly. "Wives pack for their husbands. You taught me that."

He didn't turn around and his shoulders were hunched as if in protest of something. "Let's go down and get this over with. I'd like to go home."

She rose stiffly and formally.

"Did they contact you today?" J.T. asked on the way down the stairs.

"Yes."

He took her arm and halted her. "Look, I feel some responsibility toward you. I'm worried they'll find out you're the real princess. Somebody tried to kill you before, they may try to again."

"There will be people there to save me. People who will not be so burdened with my presence as you have been."

He looked at her for a long while and Aria held her breath because he looked as if he might kiss her. "Sure. You'll be fine. You'll have your country and you'll get to sit on your gold throne—I assume you have a gold throne."

"It's only gold leaf."

"Such hardship. Come on, baby, let's go have our last meal together."

Aria had a great deal of difficulty trying to maintain her guise of obnoxious American. They were to wait for the waiter to spill soup on one of them before leaving in anger.

"The embassy was to take you on a tour of Escalon today," Aria said. "Did you see anything of interest?"

"I saw a country living in the nineteenth century. No, maybe it was closer to the eighteenth. As far as I can tell, the newest car in town, not owned by an American, is a twenty-nine Studebaker. People don't even have wells, they carry water from the rivers. I can understand this in some poor, uneducated country, but you have schools and you have access to modern communication."

"But we have no money. We are a poor country with no resources except the vanadium, and when the world isn't at war, there is the tourist trade."

"You have the grapes. The only thing wrong with them is lack of water because of the drought."

"Yes, we pray for rain but—"

"In the meantime, have you people ever heard of irrigation, of dams, of wells?"

"I told you that we cannot afford such—"

"Afford, hell! Two-thirds of your men sit on their duffs in cafes and drink bad wine and eat goat cheese all day. If they got up and did some work, maybe they could help this country."

"You have called us cowards and now we are also *lazy?*" she hissed at him.

"If the shoe fits, baby."

"And I guess your country is so much better. Your people have the energy to create bombs."

"Your country is so peaceful that they kidnap their own princess then try to shoot her."

"You shot your Abraham Lincoln."

"That was generations ago. Look, let's not talk about this. I'd like to eat one meal in this town and not get indigestion."

They began to eat in silence but they had taken no more than a few bites when the waiter spilled soup on J.T.

J.T.'s exclamation was one of genuine anger. "I've had it," he yelled. "I've had it with you and this country. There's a troop ship coming through here to refuel tonight and we're going to be on it." He grabbed Aria's arm and pulled her up the stairs.

"That was foolish," she said once they reached their room. "Lanconia cannot refuel military planes from any army. We cannot take sides in this war."

He didn't say anything but grabbed their two suitcases and started out of the room. At the desk he plunked down a hundred-dollar bill and left. A taxi was waiting nearby and jumped at J.T.'s whistle. J.T. slammed the luggage into the trunk. "To the airport," he said, nearly pushing Aria into the back seat.

"You should have changed your uniform," she said softly. "You have soup all over you." He didn't answer as he looked out the window and Aria wondered what he was thinking.

For her, she knew he was her last connection to the freedom she had enjoyed in America. She tried to control herself and remember that all this was for her country. In another couple of weeks she would barely be able to remember this man, and if she did remember him it would be as someone who was rude and boorish. She would remember that dreadful week on the island when he had thrown fish in her lap. She would *not* remember the way he held her at night or the afternoon when they had grilled hamburgers in the backyard or dancing with his mother.

242

"We're here. You getting out?"

Aria boarded the plane silently. On board was Mr. Sanderson with a lapful of papers. The plane took off and he started talking. The plane was to develop engine trouble a hundred miles south of Escalon and at that time J.T. and Aria were to separate, with her remaining in Lanconia and traveling back to the capital city in a goatherder's cart. She could keep her early morning meeting with the Lord High Chamberlain.

"We have no idea if he is the man who ordered Princess Aria's execution," Mr. Sanderson said. "The Lord High Chamberlain may just be reacting to the kidnapping of the woman he believes to be the actual princess. Lady Werta must know something. She's too close to the princess not to know."

The plane had barely taken off before it was landing again.

Mr. Sanderson looked out the window. "The goatherder is waiting for you. He's one of our men and he'll make the journey as pleasant as possible. There has been a bed made in the back of the wagon. I hope you can sleep."

Mr. Sanderson was waiting for her at the door, but J.T. sat in his seat looking out the window.

She held out her hand to J.T. "Thank you so much for your help, Lieutenant Montgomery. Thank you for saving my life and I apologize for the inconvenience I have caused you. Please tell Dolly I will write her as soon as possible."

J.T. seemed to move in one lightning-swift motion. He pulled her into his arms and onto his lap and kissed her with passion.

She clung to him and part of her wanted to beg him not to leave her.

"Good-bye, Princess," he whispered. "Good luck."

"Yes," she said, realizing that he didn't feel the way she did.

"Your Royal Highness," Mr. Sanderson said impatiently. "We must go."

She rose from J.T.'s lap. "I wish you the best of luck also," she said formally, and left the plane.

Minutes later she was hidden in the back of a smelly goat cart, its jarring making it impossible to sleep. It was over, she told herself, and from now on she must only look ahead. She would try her best to forget America and her American husband. From now on she must think only of her country.

Perhaps she should marry Julian right away. He had been trained to be a king. Even though the monarchy had been abolished in his country in 1921, Julian's father had reared his son to rule, and it was one reason her grandfather had chosen Julian for her husband.

She snuggled deeper in the straw. Yes, Julian was the man she should look to. He was handsome, knew what the word "duty" meant, and had been trained for the monarchy. *He* understood protocol. *He* knew to walk two paces behind his queen-wife.

For a moment Aria had a vision of J.T. as prince consort. The two of them would be mounting the stairs into the High Council building wearing the twelve-foot trains of state when J.T. would suddenly become impatient because their sons were playing in Little League—which he coached—that afternoon and he would grab Aria's arm and pull her into the building.

It wouldn't do at all, she thought, but she smiled at the thought of their sons.

Absolutely not! She was to be a queen, not an American housewife, and she couldn't have a husband who knew nothing of duty and responsibility. She *had* to concentrate on Count Julian. She remembered their single kiss and wondered if Julian were capable of more. Before she went to America, she had no idea she was capable of passion, so how could she judge Julian? She would have to find out about him, not just as a prince consort but as a husband.

Toward dawn she began to grow sleepy. How did one build a dam? she wondered. How could one irrigate crops growing on the sides of mountains? Perhaps Julian would know. Or perhaps she could hire an American engineer to help her.

She slept.

"Lieutenant," the pilot said. "It looks like we *do* have engine problems. It's going to be a while before we take off, so if you want to get out and stretch your legs, we'll have a few minutes."

"Sure," J.T. mumbled, and left the airplane.

It was dark out but the moon was bright and he walked to the far side of the runway, looking out at the short, sparse mountain vegetation. He lit a cigarette and drew deeply on it, wanting something to calm him.

He had never wanted anything as badly as he wanted to get out of this country. He wanted to put as many miles as possible between himself and his princess.

"Not *my* princess," he muttered as he threw the cigarette down and crushed it.

"You will come with me," said a voice behind him.

J.T. turned and saw an armed man. He hadn't heard him approach. Behind them, the airplane started its engine.

"You will come with me, Lieutenant Montgomery," the man repeated.

"I've got to get on that plane." J.T. started to push past the guard but three more men slipped out of the darkness, guns in their hands.

"You are to accompany us."

J.T. knew when it was senseless to fight. Two men were in front of him, two in back; he followed them to a black car hidden in the darkness. From the car window, he watched the plane take off. "Damn her!" he muttered because he knew that what was going to happen now directly resulted from his having met Princess Aria.

They drove for forty-five minutes until they came to a large stone house surrounded by towering trees.

"This way," one of the guards said.

Inside, the house was lit by hundreds of candles in old silver candelabra. There were flags hanging from the ceilings and old, dusty tapestries on the walls.

One of the guards opened a door and motioned J.T. inside, then shut the door. It took a moment for his eyes to adjust. The stone-walled room was dark except for its far end.

A big, gray-haired man sat at the middle of a table covered with silver platters of food. Behind his high-backed, tapestry-covered chair stood a tall, gaunt man.

"Come in and sit down," called the gray-haired man. "Have you eaten?"

"I don't like being ordered about at gunpoint," J.T. said, not moving from where he stood.

"Very few people do, but one has to tolerate such indignities during a war. I have venison, hare, game pie, and some of your American beef. There's also quail that I shot myself. I don't believe you've had dinner."

J.T. moved closer to the table. The man looked to be in his fifties but with the strength and constitution of a younger man. He was strongly built and J.T. was tempted to ask if he had wrestled the steer to death.

"Ned," the man said, "pour our American some wine."

J.T. gave a shrug and took the seat across from the man and began to fill his plate. "What's so important that you made me miss my plane?"

"Your president and I have a favor to ask of you."

J.T. paused with a piece of venison on his fork. "Roosevelt?" He gave the man a hard look. "Who are you?"

"I'm the king of this country, such as it is."

J.T. looked at the man awhile longer than began to eat. "I heard you were on your deathbed. You don't look very sick to me."

"You will address His Majesty properly," snapped the gaunt man behind the king.

"Ned is very protective of me," the king said, smiling. "But I don't think we're going to teach an American to be subservient. I assume my granddaughter is safely on her way to Escalon to take her rightful place."

J.T. didn't answer. He had heard the king didn't know what was going on with his granddaughter, but he obviously knew something. J.T. wasn't going to play his hand and tell the king more than he already knew. "Why don't you tell me," he said at last.

"All right," the king said. "I believe it started right after my granddaughter began her tour of America. She was kidnapped, probably by someone from Lanconia, then she was to be shot. I believe you, at the risk of your own life, saved her. I will be eternally grateful."

"You're welcome."

"With your help, she went to the American government to ask for help in reinstating her to her throne.

247

Your army insisted she marry an American and put him on the throne beside her. I believe their objective is military bases in my country."

"Among other things."

"Ah yes," the king said. "The vanadium. But then Aria had already agreed to give that to America. Am I correct so far?"

"I'm not bored yet."

The king smiled. "You were chosen to be the husband and I must say, after looking at your family tree, for an American, your ancestry is quite good."

J.T. didn't reply to that but kept eating.

"The two of you lived in Key West, where you were stationed and where my granddaughter learned to be an American. You must tell me about the photograph that appeared in the *Key West Citizen* of Aria and your mother. Mrs. Montgomery looks to be a delightful woman."

"She's married. Could you get on with this? I'd like to find another plane leaving this country and get home. I have war work to do there and I can't afford to be gone any longer."

"Ah, your war job. More wine, Lieutenant?" the king asked, and motioned to Ned to refill the glass. "Now my granddaughter has returned and she has, with the help of that bumbling American ambassador, gotten herself reinstated as Princess Aria. And she has once again put her life in danger."

J.T. stopped eating. "I was told she'd be protected."

"Who can I trust? Ned here is the only person I know to be clear of this plot and he stays with me. I cannot trust Aria's advisers, her relatives, even her ladies-in-waiting."

"Can you find out who put the imposter princess on the throne? That woman has been kidnapped; maybe you can find out something from her."

"I sent her to America," the king answered. "When your president radioed me that my granddaughter had been taken while on American soil, I saw right away the hazards. It could have forced Lanconia into the war. I sent Ned south to get Aria's cousin, who, except for fifty pounds or so, looks like Aria. She was sent to America immediately to pose as Aria."

"Aria said that if you found out she was taken, it would kill you."

The king looked at his wineglass. "I am harder to kill than that. Duty and country come first, before personal involvement."

"She is just like you."

The king smiled. "Your spats are well known, both in America and Lanconia. She is a very good mime, isn't she?"

"What do you want from me?" J.T. asked.

"I want you to remain in Lanconia."

"Not on your life," J.T. said, rising. "I want out of this place. My country is at war and I am needed."

"You have already been replaced."

"There aren't many people who know as much about ships as I do," J.T. said. "I'm not easy to replace."

"How about Jason Montgomery? He took over two days ago. Think he'll be able to do the job?"

J.T. sat back down. His Uncle Jason was his father's youngest brother and J.T. hoped that someday he would know as much about ships as his uncle did. "He'll do quite well. Who is helping my father run Warbrooke Shipping?"

"Your mother and one of your brothers who was wounded. He prefers to convalesce behind a desk in the shipping office instead of in an army hospital."

"You seem to know a damned lot," J.T. said angrily.

The king put up his hand to halt Ned. "I have become very interested in you and your family in the last few weeks. I wanted to make sure I could trust you."

"I wouldn't trust anybody if I were you. I never saw a place so riddled with intrigue."

"I agree, which is why I want someone who I know is not involved to be near my granddaughter to protect her."

J.T. took a deep drink of wine. "Would you mind telling me why anyone would want this backward country? Is vanadium that valuable?"

"No, but uranium is," the king said mildly. "Just after the war broke out, Lanconia was found to have several deposits of uranium. I realized right away that if this were made public knowledge we would be part of the war because countries would want control of the uranium. I did my best to keep it secret, but obviously someone knows and someone wants control of the country. Whoever it is must know that Aria is not someone easily controlled so he or she tried to get rid of her."

"Then who is left? I don't imagine you'd go down without a fight."

"I was probably next on the list. My granddaughter Eugenia, Aria's younger sister, would be queen, and she could be controlled rather easily, I'm sorry to say."

"You have no idea who wants Aria dead?"

"It could be anyone or a group of people. I want you to stay and find out, or if not that, stay and protect her."

"She's too hardheaded for anyone to protect. Look, this isn't my fight. My own country is at war, and if I'm not needed in Key West, I can tote a rifle as well as any man."

"But this is something not any man can do. I have told your president that if he releases you to me, I will sell the uranium to America." The king handed J.T. a sealed envelope stamped TOP SECRET.

J.T. opened it reluctantly because he knew what it contained. It was a letter from President Franklin Roosevelt asking him to remain in Lanconia and help with this difficult matter. He said J.T. could help his country more in Lanconia than he could in America.

"Why couldn't he ask me to go to the front line?" J.T. mumbled, folding the letter away.

The king began eating grapes. "May I ask why such an assignment is so repugnant to you? You will be living in a palace surrounded by great beauty; the most strenuous task you will have is to accompany my granddaughter on her morning ride. You will have the finest food. Why would you rather be shot at?"

"Because I don't want to see your granddaughter again, that's why. She is a spoiled brat who uses people and I've had enough of her."

"I see. So it is personal. So Americans put personal relationships before duty to their country."

"No we don't. It's just that—" J.T. stopped talking. "My country means more to me. I want to help however I can."

"Then please stay and protect my granddaughter," the king said. "I'm not used to begging but now I am. She may be a problem to you but she is the comfort of my life. She is kind and warm and loving and she is the future hope of our country. I am sorry you do not see her as I do."

"She can be all right," J.T. said reluctantly, toying with his fork. He did not want to return to seeing Aria every day. "How would I do this?" he asked. "I mean, if I agreed, how would I be introduced into her circle?"

"As yourself. I would say I had met you when your plane stopped near here for repairs, liked you, and hired you as a technical adviser. Or we could say that your president ordered you here to take charge of the vanadium. Your wife, of course, returned to the United States. You would not have any duties either way except to protect my granddaughter. You would be given every courtesy and every comfort."

"What about the people who think Aria is Kathy Montgomery?"

"They will curse the luck of having a meddling old king."

J.T. sat silently for a moment, playing with one of the five forks to the left of his plate. "I can't do nothing but follow your granddaughter around. I want to make some changes in this country."

The king's face changed from that of a sweet old man to one of a man descended from centuries of warriors. "What changes did you have in mind?"

"Irrigation. Dams. I'd like to bring some of the twentieth century to this place."

The king's face showed amazement. "You know of such things? How utterly splendid. Of course you may help the peasants in any way you want."

"Peasants? No one has freed them?" J.T. asked sarcastically.

"Of course they are free. It is just an expression." The king paused. "Lieutenant Montgomery, there is something I want to ask you. There was a General Brooks who reported directly to your president. His description of my granddaughter, of what he saw at your little house in Key West, was it correct?"

J.T. smiled and let himself remember that afternoon. He seemed able to hear the blaring radio. "Pin-curled hair, blue jeans, my shirt, radio blasting away, slapping hamburgers, and dancing?" he asked.

"Yes." The king sounded incredulous. "I have never seen her like that. Her mother, my son's wife, was very aware that Aria would someday be queen and she raised Aria to have no emotions, or at least never to display them. Tell me, have you ever seen her cry?"

"Only once."

The king contemplated J.T. for a moment. "She allowed you to see that? I had no idea you were so close."

"There's two Arias. There's Aria, my wife, who can be . . ." J.T. smiled. "Who can be all right. Then there's Princess Aria, the little prig. *That* Aria I can't stand, and with every minute in this country she becomes more like the bitch I met on the island."

The king studied his wineglass. "Perhaps you could teach her to be less of a—what is that word? Prig."

"Not me," J.T. said, pushing back his chair. "I'm staying here to protect her and to help with this country. For my sake she can remain a prig. I'm safer that way. I'm not likely to get involved with her when she's like that."

"You worry about becoming involved with her?" the king asked quietly.

"Yeah, I do. It was hard enough saying good-bye to her once, and when I have to do it again, it'll be worse."

"Yes, I see," the king said. "Of course you'll have to say good-bye again. Your government should have researched our laws. No American commoner can be married legally to the queen. She would have to abdicate. Unless, of course, the people of Lanconia asked for you, which I doubt would happen."

"She won't abdicate, and even if she wanted to, I wouldn't let her. And it's good to hear I can't be king but I wouldn't accept the position if offered. Now, can somebody point me to a bedroom, or am I to spend the night in the dungeon with the other prisoners?"

The king nodded to Ned, who pulled a cord on the wall. Immediately, the door opened and the four guards entered.

"Take Lieutenant Montgomery to the red bedroom," the king said.

When J.T. was gone, Ned spoke. "An insolent man. He isn't worthy of touching Her Royal Highness's gown."

The king leaned back in his chair and smiled. "He is more than I hoped for. You'd better be nice to him, Ned, because if I have my way, that man is going to be the next king of Lanconia." He laughed at Ned's sputters.

Chapter Sixteen

N o, no, no, no!" Lady Werta screeched. "He is your *seventh* cousin and twenty-eighth in line for succession."

Aria placed the side of her tongue between her back teeth, hoping the pain would remind her to be quiet. She had been awake all night in the goatherder's cart and they had started her training lesson at six A.M. It was now four P.M. and she was past exhaustion. This morning she had been made to walk for hours. At first Aria had pretended to be a clumsy American trying to walk like a princess, but she was tired and she wanted to be allowed to sit down, so she started walking as she had walked when she was a crown princess.

It wasn't good enough for Lady Werta. She said it wasn't nearly right, that Princess Aria's walk was much more royal and that this American was never going to be able to carry off the impersonation.

It was Aria's first encounter with prejudice. From then on she didn't try to be anyone but herself—yet, in Lady Werta's eyes, she was a failure. The lady-in-waiting showed her photographs of people she had not seen since she was a child, quickly told her who they were, shuffled the cards, and expected Aria to have memorized them. And Lady Werta lectured her endlessly on the most trivial matters, such as how to get around the fact that she supposedly did not understand or speak Lanconian.

The Lord High Chamberlain came into the room at noon. "How does it go?" he asked in Lanconian.

"She is all right but she doesn't have Princess Aria's personality. I hand her a cup of tea and she says 'thank you'! I think if I served her in a tin mug, she would say 'thank you.' No one will believe this person is Princess Aria. She is so *nice.*"

Aria was jolted by this information. Had she always been a pain in the neck to everyone?

She didn't change her act for several hours but at tea break she was very tired and she let everyone know it.

"What are these dishes?" she asked. "What are these flowers on them?"

"I believe they are sweetpeas," Lady Werta said haughtily. "Hurry and finish so we can continue our lessons."

They were in the Lord High Chamberlain's country house, a place of such spaciousness and grandiosity that Aria vowed to look into the minister's finances. "I want roses on my tea dishes. Didn't you say Princess Aria always has roses on her dishes at tea? Then if I am to be her I want *roses.* And I want fresh cakes. Some of these look like they were left over from the servants' meal. Do you understand me? I want roses and fresh cakes and then I want a nap. I am tired and I must rest."

"Yes, Your Royal Highness," Lady Werta said, backing out of the room.

Aria smiled to herself. It had been a while since ill temper had got her what she wanted.

She made up for lost time. For the next twenty-four hours she ran Lady Werta's legs off. There was *nothing* she didn't complain of. If it was food, it was too hot or too cold or she didn't like it. Clothes had to be remade. The Lord High Chamberlain lit a cigarette in her presence and she sent him away with his ears ringing.

"She's doing better, isn't she?" the Lord High Chamberlain said in Lanconian.

"In a manner of speaking," Lady Werta said, pushing a stray tendril of hair out of her eyes. "She is almost as arrogant as the real princess."

"Shall we introduce her into the family?"

"Tonight. People are beginning to ask me where she is. Have you heard anything about the ransom?"

"They want millions," the Lord High Chamberlain said. "I do not know how we can raise it."

"Is His Majesty well? No one has told him yet of the kidnapping?"

"He's at his hunting lodge. As innocent as a child, although it's been difficult to keep the secret from him. He's demanding to see his granddaughter. Princess Eugenia is with him now."

Lady Werta sighed. "We'll have to ready her. The king is getting old. I hope he won't see through the farce. We should be grateful Princess Aria is such a cold woman. No one will miss her lack of warmth."

Aria listened to this stiffly. She hadn't been cold in America. "You are very rude to speak a language in front of me that I do not understand," she said angrily. "Now come and show me these photographs again. Who is at the palace now?"

* * *

The oldest part of the Lanconian palace had been built in the thirteenth century by Rowan the Bold. It was a magnificent structure of massive stone blocks, a fortress as strong as the ruler who built it, situated on land that fell away on three sides, the fourth side a gentle slope that in the fourteenth century was used for Hager the Hated's many public executions. A small river flowed at the bottom of the southeast slope and ran down to the town that the palace overlooked —and dominated.

In 1664 Anwen, the great lover of art, covered the old stone walls, enlarged the palace, and made it look like a very long, very large six-story Italian villa. The old castle was the east wing, with a new, larger central block and a new, matching west wing. At an expense that depleted the Lanconian treasuries, he imported a rare yellow sandstone from Italy for the facade.

In 1760, Princess Bansada, the wife of the king's fourth son, decided to do something with the grounds after overhearing a derogatory remark by an English duchess. She managed to put the kingdom in debt once again, but she made a splendid garden. There were a dozen hothouses that kept the palace supplied with fresh flowers at all seasons. There were formal gardens at the ends of the east and west wings, a twenty-acre wild garden, a rose garden, a man-made lake with a bridge across it that led to a ladies' outdoor sitting room. There were three gazebos: one Chinese, one Gothic, and one made to look like a medieval ruin. There were statues everywhere, mostly of handsome young men. Someone unkindly said they were Princess Bansada's lovers and that when her voracious appetite wore them out, she had them dipped in plaster. When Aria was an adult, she realized the statues were marble and therefore the story could not be true.

When the Lord High Chamberlain rode with Aria to the palace, it was done in great secrecy. She was veiled and swathed in heavy black cloth so that no one would recognize her. She sat in the back of the black limousine and didn't say a word. With every turn of the wheels, she came closer to the palace and she could feel the pull of the place. It was as if her ancestors were calling her home.

The palace, so remote to some, was home to her and her eyes teared at the beauty of it, the way the sunlight lit the yellow facade, the way the mountains rose behind it. She was glad the veil hid her face and she was glad for the training she had received that kept her from showing her feelings.

The Lord High Chamberlain, who had not deigned to speak to her for the entire trip, now spoke and his tone carried contempt in it, as if he refused to believe she had any intelligence. "You must remember *at all times* that you are a crown princess. You are to exercise the most rigid control. You must not relax for a second, not even when you think you are alone. For a princess is *never* alone. A princess is protected and watched and cared for."

He had not turned to look at her. "You are not to indulge in that despicable American custom of finding amusement in everything."

Aria opened her mouth to speak but closed it again. Her life could benefit from a little humor. She smiled at the thought of having a jitterbug contest in the Grand Salon. Perhaps she could introduce some of the more lighthearted and frivolous American customs to her relatives who lived in the palace.

She and Julian, that is, she amended. She wondered if Julian would like to grill hamburgers by the river. She would have barbecue grills made, and instead of dressing in a long gown for dinner, they would wear blue jeans. She smiled as she thought of trying to persuade Great-Aunt Sophie to wear jeans.

"You are not listening to me!" the Lord High Chamberlain snapped.

Again, Aria bit back what she wanted to say. While she was princess, he had been the epitome of fatherly gentleness to her and all her royal family. She had, of course, heard rumors that he was not well liked by the people, but she had dismissed the complaints. He was such a sweet old gentleman that Aria couldn't believe anyone disliked him. He had even generously refused to live in the house provided for his office. Aria had been touched, but now she had seen his country house and she understood he had other reasons for his magnanimous gesture. She vowed to look into her people's complaints more thoroughly.

He was droning on about her deportment, her duties, her responsibilities, telling how she was to be a machine, an automaton who did nothing but sign papers and dedicate factories.

"Don't this princess have no fun?" she asked loudly, enjoying his wince at her bad grammar. "I mean, she has a boyfriend, don't she? When do they get together and have a giggle? You know?"

"Count Julian does not"—he almost gagged—"giggle. He is the perfect choice of a husband for Her Royal Highness. When you are with him, you will not be alone—you are *never* to be alone together—so your conduct must be beyond reproach."

Aria kept looking out the window. Part of her was beginning to feel sorry for Princess Aria, who never got to play. But now she was a new Princess Aria. Her experiences in America had changed her—and she meant to change the life in her palace.

Lady Werta had shown Aria a floor plan of the palace but she had been told that the Lord High

Chamberlain would show her as many rooms as possible before taking her to her own chambers. Even with her heavy veil he predicted that many of the retainers would recognize her. The story they had spread was that, after her American tour, she had been felled with a particularly nasty strain of flu and had been taken to a private clinic in Austria until she recovered. No one knew when Aria was to return, and there were rumors that she had died.

The Lord High Chamberlain started to lead her into the palace, but Aria stood where she was, refusing to let him precede her. He gave her a look of hatred then stepped behind her.

The grand entrance hall was designed to impress people. Scrolled plaster work made panels on the walls and ceiling. The panels on the ceiling were filled with paintings depicting Rowan the Magnificent's exploits. The wall held carved oak medallions of the coats of arms of every monarch and his queen. Aria's arms were on the east wall, with a space below for the arms of her husband. For a moment she wondered what Lieutenant Montgomery would have put in that place. An UNCLE SAM WANTS YOU poster?

The Lord High Chamberlain cleared his throat behind her and she walked through the big doorway into the war trophy room—another room made to impress. One wall held a twenty-foot-square portrait of Rowan on a rearing horse. Since Rowan had left behind no likenesses of himself, it was an artist's conception of a magnificent warrior. Aria's grandfather said Rowan probably looked a good deal more tired and dirty and wore quite a bit less gold braid than the artist depicted.

Aria smiled at the memory and then remembered how Lieutenant Montgomery had said the people of Lanconia were now cowards.

She sniffed and walked ahead toward the grand staircase, a staircase that a six-horse carriage could be driven up—Hager the Hated had proved that. Of course the driver of the carriage's life depended on his winning his king's wager. He had succeeded but the deepest nicks in the marble stairs had never been smoothed out.

Behind her, the Lord High Chamberlain was whispering directions but she ignored him. At specific intervals along the stairs and outside the rooms stood the Royal Guard. They stood, with only one break, for eight hours at a time. Aria had never given them a thought before but now she knew a little more about waiting. Later, when this problem of her identity was solved, she might do something about these Royal Guards.

The Lord High Chamberlain's whispering became frantic with insistence as Aria approached her apartment, but she continued to ignore him. In the hall portraits of her ancestors looked down at her, their eyes solemn, as if they knew she was harboring unroyal thoughts. She could almost feel her mother's horror: shall we supply the guards with chairs? Perhaps Rowan would have won his battles sooner if he had fought with his men in lounge chairs.

Aria braced her shoulders and entered her bedchamber as the two guards opened the doors. Behind her the Lord High Chamberlain's voice died away as the doors shut.

On their knees in a deep curtsy before her were her four ladies-in-waiting and two dressers. They were all older women, all chosen by her mother, and Aria's first impulse was to tell them to get off their knees.

"Welcome, Your Royal Highness," they chorused.

She nodded to them but made no answer to their

welcome. She really knew very little about these women as her mother had trained her not to be intimate with her attendants.

"Leave me," Aria said. "I want to be alone."

The women looked at one another in question.

Lady Werta stepped forward. "Perhaps Her Royal Highness would like a bath drawn."

Aria gave the woman a look that sent her retreating. "Must I repeat myself?"

The women left and Aria breathed a sigh of relief. She lifted her heavy veil and looked about the room. This was *her* room, a room where she had spent many hours, a room she had had done, against her mother's wishes, in yellow. The walls were silk moiré with the same draperies surrounding her many tall windows that looked out onto the wild wood.

There were eleven tables in the big room, all of them with delicate legs, all of them in some way unique and precious. One was a gift from a sultan, inlaid with tiny bits of precious stones. Another had an enamel portrait of Aria, her parents, and sister, each holding a musical instrument. Several of the tables were covered with family photographs in silver frames.

There was a seating arrangement of a tiny couch and three chairs, each covered with yellow and white silk. On the floor was an enormous blue, white, and gold Aubusson carpet. A year after her mother's death, Aria had walked about the palace and chosen all the portraits and miniatures of the most beautiful women and had them moved to the walls of her rooms.

Her desk was here, a small, exquisite ormolu and mahogany creation. Each instrument—letter opener, fountain pen, stationery holder—was a work of art, none of it chosen by her but given to her as her right. "Rather like Julian," she whispered, but corrected herself immediately.

Through the sitting room was her bedroom, done in the palest of sea green, the walls painted over a hundred years ago for another queen with fantasy scenes set in an imaginary forest peopled with unicorns and wood sprites. Her bed had been made for Queen Marie-August in the seventeenth century and had taken six men two years to carve the delicate tendrils and leaves and vines winding their way up the four posts. It was said that Queen Marie-August's husband never saw the bed—nor did any man for that matter.

One wall of the bedroom was a series of semihidden doors that led into her four closets. Each closet was actually the size of the bedroom she had had in Key West.

The first closet contained her daily clothes, hundreds of silk blouses, many hand embroidered by the women of Lanconia. There were rows of tailored skirts and a wall-length rod hung with her silk dresses.

She took one off the rod and looked with dismay at the buckram in the waist. "No more loose-fitting little rayon numbers." She sighed, but then the feel of the silk made her smile.

The second closet contained her ballgowns and ceremonial garments, each in a specially made cotton sack with a transparent voile shoulder so one could see the dress. Even under the voile, the gold work, the sequins, the tiny diamonds, even the pearls, glowed and made the pale pink of the walls look like a sunset.

The third closet contained her accessories: hats, gloves, rows of handmade, hand-fitted shoes, purses, boots, scarves. One wall was lined with drawers filled with handmade underwear: slips, underpants, night-gowns. And the heavy, elastic Merry Widow foundations. She grimaced at those and shut the drawer.

The fourth closet contained her furs, her winter suits, and, behind a mirror, the safe for her jewels. She tripped the three latches to the mirror, swung it back, then turned the combination to her safe. Two six-foot-tall rows of velvet-covered drawers greeted her. Red velvet meant sets: necklace, bracelet, earrings. Black velvet was for rings, yellow for earrings, blue for watches, green for brooches, and white was for her tiaras: pearl tiaras, diamond tiaras, rubies, emeralds. Each piece was in its own fitted compartment.

Aria smiled as she opened drawer after drawer. Each jewel had a history; each had belonged to someone else. Aria had never purchased a jewel nor had she been given one that had not belonged to generations of royalty before her.

Frowning, she shut the drawers and mirror abruptly since she heard someone in the outer chamber. On walking out of the closet, she saw Lady Werta standing there.

"Very good. You are examining the princess's belongings."

Aria was not going to allow this woman to think she could rule her. "How dare you enter my room without permission," she said, all her anger showing.

Lady Werta looked surprised for a moment then recovered. "You can stop the act with me. I *know* you, remember? We have to talk about tonight. Count Julian is here."

"I'll discuss nothing with you." Aria started toward the door leading to the hall.

"Wait a minute," Lady Werta said, grabbing Aria's arm.

Aria was actually horrified at the woman's touch. She wasn't the new American Aria pretending to be the princess. She *was* the princess.

Lady Werta stepped back. "We have to talk," she said, but there was no strength in her voice.

"Call my ladies," Aria said, turning away. "I must dress for dinner."

Aria wore a long white gown that was embroidered with thousands of seed pearls to dinner. It was high-necked, long-sleeved, very prim, very proper—sexless. The diamonds she wore in her ears Lady Werta had fetched for her, not showing her where the major jewel chest was hidden, probably for fear the American would steal the contents. Instead, she had selected three pair of insignificant earrings and presented them to Aria. "This is all?" Aria had complained so only Lady Werta heard.

"We are a poor country," Lady Werta sniffed, her eyes showing she was angry.

"We are glad to see that you have fully recovered from your American illness, Your Highness," her three other ladies-in-waiting said as they moved about the room, waiting to obey Aria's merest whim.

One of her dressers looked her over critically. "You are thinner than you were in America."

Aria gave the woman a withering look. "You will keep your personal remarks to yourself. Now dress me."

It was difficult not to be impatient with the women because she knew she could have dressed herself in half the time. The long foundation garment felt familiar and strange at the same time, and she felt as if the last vestiges of the American Aria disappeared when her dresser pulled her much shorter hair back into a tight chignon. Her secretary sat in a chair behind a screen, the princess's social calendar in her hand.

"Tomorrow at nine A.M. is riding; at ten-thirty, you will visit the new children's hospital. At one you lunch with three members of the council to discuss the American vanadium contract. At two you will hand out gold watches to four railroad employees. At four you have tea with council wives. At five-thirty the Scientific Academy is giving a speech on the insect life of the northeastern Balean Mountains. At seven you return to ready for dinner at eight-thirty. And at ten—"

"There is a jitterbug contest in the ballroom," Aria said, making everyone in the room stop.

Lady Werta gave her a quelling look. "It is from Her Royal Highness's visit to America. She makes a joke."

Politely, the women laughed, but they looked at her oddly, as if her making a joke was a very, very strange thing to do.

"Don't do that again," Lady Werta warned under her breath.

Later, when Aria walked into the dining room, everyone came to a halt. They stared at her, waiting for some signal from her as to how to act. When the king was away, the crown princess set the tone.

Aria took a deep breath. "Well, Freddie," Aria said to her second cousin, Prince Ferdinand, "I can see you still have no manners. Do I deserve no greeting?"

He came to her and bowed over her extended hand. "We have been worried about you," he said in Lanconian.

For a moment, Aria hesitated. This man was her cousin, they had spent a great deal of time together, yet he greeted her after a long absence as if she were a slight acquaintance. "In English please. If we are to deal with these Americans, we must be able to understand them. They do not learn other people's languages." She looked at him as if she had never seen

267

him before. Freddie was a small man, a few inches shorter than Aria and quite thin. He slouched when he walked. Aria had always ignored Freddie—as everyone did—but now she thought she saw anger burning in his dark eyes. He was third in line for the throne after Aria and her sister. Could he want the throne enough to kill for it?

"You look good, Aria," her Great-Aunt Sophie shouted. The old woman was nearly deaf and compensated by shouting at everyone. She was dressed as only Aunt Sophie dressed, in layer upon layer of baby-blue chiffon, big blue silk roses around the indecently low neckline that exposed her wrinkly bosom. What was that American saying? Mutton dressed as lamb. Her grandfather said Sophie had always had hopes of snagging a husband but so far no man had been so stupid as to ask.

"Well enough, I guess, after having nearly died," Aria shouted back, making everyone in the room look at her in surprise. Princess Aria did not shout.

"Good!" Great-Aunt Sophie shouted back, and turned away to yell at a waiter that she wanted more brandy.

"I am glad too that you are well" came a suave voice, and she was face-to-face with Count Julian.

Lieutenant Montgomery had always referred to the man as Count Julie and had always insinuated that he was effeminate. But Aria saw virility in the man's eyes. He wasn't big and strong like Lieutenant Montgomery, but a woman could do worse. He was quite handsome, about the same height as she was, with the erect, straight carriage of a military man. Her grandfather said Julian had been forced to wear a steel back brace from the time he was four until he was sixteen.

"Welcome home," Count Julian said, taking her

hand and lightly kissing the back of it. "Would you like something before dinner? A sherry perhaps."

"Yes, please," she answered. She watched him walk away. What would he be like as a husband? Once the bedroom doors were closed, did he become a tiger? She smiled at him when he returned from the sideboard with her sherry. He stood silently by her and Aria realized how very little they had ever actually talked.

She looked at the other dinner guests. There were her cousins Nickie and Toby, her Aunt Bradley, and her young, beautiful cousin Barbara, who was seventh in line for the throne.

"Where are Cissy and Gena?" Aria asked Julian, referring to Freddie's sister and her own sister, knowing that Cissy was in the custody of the American government.

"Both are with His Majesty at his hunting lodge," he answered.

The meal was deadly boring. The men could talk of nothing but the number of animals they had killed in the last week—since blood sports were their only occupation, there was nothing else they knew about. Great-Aunt Sophie bellowed at the people around her, trying to carry on a conversation but not able to keep up with anyone's replies. Freddie, Nickie, and Toby's affectations made Aria want to shout at them. Barbara flirted with each man, batting her eyelashes and leaning forward to show her décolletage.

"I think a husband should be found for Cousin Barbara," Aria said under her breath.

Julian looked at her in surprise but made no comment.

Wouldn't they be surprised, Aria thought, if she began to flirt? She looked at Julian, so properly eating his sturgeon in dill sauce, and she wondered if he would be very shocked if she batted her lashes at him.

With her heart pounding, and quickly, before she lost her nerve, she reached out and touched Julian's hand. "Will you meet me in the King's Garden after dinner?"

He nodded once, but she could see the slight frown between his brows as he moved his hand away. She had just done something a crown princess did not do.

She turned away to answer a question Great-Aunt Sophie was bellowing her way.

After dinner she had to work to escape Lady Werta, whose face showed she believed the end of the world to be at hand. Aria slipped through the Green Waiting Room, through the Mars Room, ran past the Gallery of Kings, then out into the White Horse Courtyard, past the Greek Orangery, and finally reached the King's Garden. The garden was so named because it was believed to have a masculine air with its tall pine trees and secret, twisting paths. It was said that Rowan once had a camp in this place.

Julian was waiting for her, a slight frown on his face.

He was sixteen years older than she was and she had always been a little in awe of him. After all, now she realized that theirs wasn't to be an ordinary marriage. Their marriage was arranged for political and diplomatic reasons; theirs was a marriage of state.

"You wanted to speak to me, Your Royal Highness," Julian said politely, but there was disapproval in his voice.

She wished there was something snappy she could say, or something wise. "You are angry with me," she said in a little-girl voice, and cursed herself for doing so.

She thought she saw a hint of a smile on his lips. He

was actually very handsome—in spite of what Lieutenant Montgomery said—and the moonlight made him more so.

"I think only of your reputation. It would not do for us to be seen alone together."

Aria turned away. On their wedding night he was going to find out that she was not a virgin. She looked back at him and took a deep breath. "For an engaged couple, we have spent very little time together, alone or with others. Since we are planning to spend our lives together, I thought we should talk and get to know each other better."

He looked at her for a while before responding. "And what did you want to discuss? The coming elections? I am sure our current Lord High Chamberlain will remain in office. In fact I think he may pass on the office to his descendants."

"No," she said. "I mean, yes, I do want to discuss the council and its officers but I thought perhaps . . ." Her voice trailed off.

"Your trip to America?"

He was standing absolutely rigid, shoulders back, every hair, every medal in place, no flaw anywhere. Aria remembered Jarl coming home from work, his uniform dark with sweat, pulling it off as soon as he entered the door and saying, "Get me a beer, honey."

"Do you drink beer?" Aria blurted.

Julian looked startled for a second then seemed to be trying to control a smile. "Yes, I drink beer."

"I didn't know that. I know so very little about you and sometimes I wonder if we'll be . . . compatible. I mean, we are to live together, and marriage is, I mean, I have heard, that marriage is so very intimate and . . ." She trailed off again, feeling a bit silly and childish because Julian was still standing so stiff and rigid.

"I see," he said.

Aria didn't like his smug tone or maybe she didn't like the way she was feeling. "I am sorry to have imposed upon you with this trivial matter," she said royally, and turned away.

"Aria," he said in a voice that made her halt. He stepped in front of her. "Your questions are quite valid. Before I submitted my proposal of marriage to the king, I gave a great deal of thought to the matter. Marriage is indeed a serious undertaking, but I have every reason to believe we will be most compatible. We have been reared in the same way, I to be a king and you to be a queen. We know the same people; we know the protocol of the monarchy. I think we shall make an admirable marriage."

Aria's shoulders drooped. "I see. Yes, I think we will make an admirable royal couple." She looked down at her hands.

"Is there something else?"

He was standing very close to her but he made no effort to touch her.

There was no way to say it but to blurt it out. "But what about *us?* What about me as a woman? Do you feel anything for me besides as a *queen?*"

Julian's expression didn't change, but he reached out and put his hand to the back of her head and drew her to him, then kissed her with what could only be expressed as long-repressed desire. When he pulled away, Aria still had her eyes closed and her mouth open.

"I look forward to the wedding night with *great* anticipation," he whispered, and she could feel his breath on her face.

Aria opened her eyes and straightened her body. "I did wonder," she managed to say at last.

At that Julian smiled at her, and he smiled with

great warmth. "You are a beautiful, desirable young woman. How could you have doubted that I am longing to make love to you?"

"I . . . I guess I never thought about it." Once again he was standing away from her, looking at her.

"Has something happened?" he asked softly. "Tonight at dinner you seemed different, as if you were worried about something."

The thought that he had noticed made her smile. She had agreed to their marriage without giving the marriage much thought. She had been much more interested in his ancestors and his training than she was in Julian as a man. But now it was different. Now she understood more of what went on between a husband and wife.

"In America," she said, beginning slowly, "in America I saw young lovers holding hands, walking together, and kissing on park benches."

"I had envisioned America to be like that," Julian said with disapproval.

"America is a *wonderful* place," Aria snapped. "There is a feeling there of moving forward. Nothing remains the same. They are not burdened with hundreds of years of tradition; they accept what is new. In fact, they *seek* the new."

"Lovers in a park is not new," Julian said, amused and smiling. "I forget how young you are. You have never seemed to want courting. You accepted my marriage proposal without seeming to want more than a handshake and a ring. Was I wrong?"

"No, but things happened in America . . ."

"The sight of the lovers made you wonder what it would be like if you had your own lover?"

"Something of that sort," she murmured, then looked straight at him. "Julian, I want our marriage to work. I *need* for it to work. It has to be more than a

273

marriage for Lanconia. I am a woman and I want to be loved for myself and not just for my crown."

Julian looked even more amused. "No one has ever asked something easier of me. Shall I court you?" He took her hand in his and kissed her palm. "Shall I show up at your door carrying a bouquet of wildflowers? Shall I sing love songs under your window? Shall I whisper love words into your pretty ear?"

"That will do for a start," she said, watching him kiss her hand.

"I will meet you at dawn and we will ride."

"At dawn? But I am scheduled to ride at nine."

"Break it," he said commandingly. "I will come for you at dawn, but now I must escort you back to the White Horse Courtyard. We will be seen by fewer people if we enter there."

He turned around and motioned for her to lead, as was her right, but then he smiled and pulled her arm through his.

At the edge of the courtyard she turned to him. "Will you kiss me again?" He glanced at the windows of the palace and seemed to hesitate. "Please, Julian. I need to know that our marriage will be good. I need to forget—"

He put two fingers over her lips. "We all have things we wish to forget. I will kiss you until you can bear no more, my darling." Slowly, he drew her into his arms and kissed her as if she were Rita Hayworth and Betty Grable rolled into one.

He released her. "Now go!" he ordered, smiling. "I will see you in the morning."

She started to move away but he caught her hand.

"If it takes kissing to make you forget, you will have amnesia by noon tomorrow." He released her and she ran inside the palace.

Lady Werta was waiting for her. "What did he say?

Did he guess? He was close to Princess Aria so he might know that you weren't she. They may have shared lovers' jokes."

The woman was beginning to bore Aria. "Go to your bed. I have no more need of you tonight."

"But I—"

"Go!" Aria snapped.

"Yes, Your Royal Highness," Lady Werta said, and retreated backward.

Upstairs Aria stood still as her dressers removed her gown and put on her nightgown. She didn't speak to them as they worked, and when they turned out the light and bid her good night, she still didn't speak.

She settled down to sleep and she felt good for the first time in days. Perhaps her life was not going to come apart because she no longer lived with Lieutenant Jarl Montgomery. Perhaps she could forget him and make a life of her own.

Tomorrow she planned to give all of her attention to Count Julian. He was the man Lanconia needed and he was the perfect husband for her. All she had to do was make herself fall in love with him—and judging by his kisses, that wouldn't be overly difficult.

As she went to sleep, though, her self-control faded and she began to remember Jarl sitting in the bathtub, Jarl tasting her fried chicken and telling her she should have been a chef, Jarl touching her breasts.

Chapter Seventeen

SHE had just fallen asleep when the door burst open
and the light was turned on. In a flurry of silk
petticoats, blond hair, and layers of diamonds, Princess Eugenia jumped into Aria's bed.

"I've missed you," Gena said, throwing her arms
about her sister's neck. "Please don't tell me to
behave myself and please don't tell me to leave. I've
just ridden all night with the most divine man to get
here as soon as I heard you were well enough to
receive visitors." She hugged Aria tighter. "Aria, they
said you nearly died. I couldn't have borne to have to
be queen."

Aria, smiling, held her sixteen-year-old sister at
arm's length. "I wouldn't like for you to be queen
either."

"Are you going to send me away? Tell me so I won't
get comfortable."

"No," Aria said, "I'm not going to send you away.
Tell me what has happened while I've been away."

THE PRINCESS

Gena stretched out on the bed. She was very pretty, and pretty in a modern sort of way, Aria thought jealously. Put her in a bathing suit and she would win any beauty contest in America. Too bad she had cotton for a brain.

"The same as usual." Gena sighed. "Nothing ever happens here. But *you* went to America. Was it *filled* with soldiers? Were they all as divinely handsome as *my* American soldier?"

"What is this about?" Aria asked sharply. "Have you fallen in love again?"

"Don't scold me, Aria, please don't. Grans has hired him for something or other—something to do with the peasants—but my soldier allowed me to ride around the countryside with him. He even let me sit in the front seat beside him. He acted as if he were reluctant to have me, but I won him over. He is a most handsome man and he's smart—Grans says so. Oh, Aria, you're going to adore him, at least I hope you do, because Grans sent him here to work with you."

"With me? Doing what?"

"I don't know, but I think he may be coming here to put all of us in order. I've never seen Grans like anybody so much. They sat up late and drank and told each other vulgar stories. Ned nearly died, but Grans looked the best he has in years."

Aria set up straighter in bed. "I wish you'd stick to the story. *What* is this American to do here? Has he come about the vanadium?"

Gena's eyes were beginning to close. "Aria, may I sleep here with you? It's so far to my chamber. Call someone to undress me and fetch my nightgown."

"Here," Aria said impatiently. "I'll help you undress and you can wear one of my nightgowns."

Gena's eyes flew open. "Wear someone else's nightgown?"

278

"Don't be a prude. *I* have slept on sheets slept on by other people."

"No," Gena gasped, stunned into speechlessness.

Aria pulled her sister out of bed then began to remove Gena's clothes.

"Are you sure you know how to do this?" Gena asked.

"It would help if you weren't an inert weight. Lift your arms. Now tell me what Grans has hired this American for."

"Something about dams, I believe. He is *so* handsome. Ouch! I think I should call my dresser."

"Gena," Aria said softly. "What is this man's name?"

"Lieutenant Jarl Montgomery. He is *so* nice and— Aria! Where are you going? You can't leave me here in my underwear."

"Gena, look in the closet and find a nightgown and put it on yourself. It's very easy. Where is Lieutenant Montgomery staying?"

"The State Bedroom—Rowan's room—so you know Grans thinks he's important. But I'm sure he's in bed by now. Aria! Don't leave me," Gena called, but Aria was already out of the room.

Aria knew the palace well and she was able to make her way down twisting corridors, through state rooms where no guards stood, down a very narrow spiral staircase, where she hid in the shadows as two laughing guards walked past.

She threw open the door to the State Bedroom. It was the room reserved for Lanconia's most honored guests. Its big, old, carved four-poster was draped in specially woven red Italian brocade, the walls covered in a matching red silk. No one was sure but it was rumored that Rowan had used this room when this part of the palace was a stone castle.

J.T. was wearing only a towel about his middle, his hair wet. "What are you doing here?" she asked, leaning against the closed door.

"Her Royal Highness herself. Now this is a welcome. I was just wondering if I pulled one of these cords on the wall, would one of those pretty maids wearing a short skirt and black stockings come and warm my bed. Instead, I get the princess. Come on, honey, get your clothes off and let's get to it. I'm ready."

"Lieutenant Montgomery," she said through her teeth. "What are you doing in Lanconia?"

J.T. continued drying his hair. "I'm not here because I want to be. My president and your king have requested my services. Contrary to what I've been told, they think your life is still in danger. I'm to protect you and do what I can with your . . . ah, peasants."

"But my grandfather knows nothing."

"He's heard enough to know there could be some trouble," J.T. answered quickly.

"You cannot stay. It is not possible. I will arrange for your transportation back to America tomorrow. Good night, Lieutenant."

J.T. caught her as she was leaving and pulled her back into the room. His towel slipped and he grabbed it with one hand while leaning his other hand on the wall behind her head. "I told you: this is not up to me, but my war assignment is to guard your life. Roosevelt seems to think I'm of more value here trailing after you and picking up your hankies than I would be in a fighting zone. So I'm staying."

She ducked from under his arm and walked to the other side of the room. "How long must you remain?"

"Until I know you're safe or until your grandfather says I can go."

"There will have to be rules. You cannot treat me with the insolence that is your normal manner. You will have to use the proper forms of address." She turned back toward him and saw how he narrowed his eyes at her. "The time in America was not something that can be repeated. Here I am not your wife."

J.T. didn't speak for a moment. "I married you to help my country and I'm staying here for my country. No other reason. As far as I'm concerned, our marriage is over."

"Does that include your jealousy?" she asked, one eyebrow arched. "Count Julian and I will be planning our wedding. His family is a very old one and the marriage is advantageous to my family. I cannot have you throwing him in a swimming pool."

"You don't have to worry about me," he said, anger in his eyes. "I might be jealous of my wife, but Her Royal Highness stirs no such feelings." He looked her up and down, standing there in her prim, high-necked nightgown and heavy brocaded robe that looked as impenetrable as armor.

She turned away again because the sight of him in just his towel was beginning to make her remember their nights together. "How are you to be introduced?" she asked.

"Supposedly I have been sent here by my government to buy the vanadium, but I am also to discuss military bases here. The king wants you to show me Escalon and the outlying country because, the story is, America is considering buying your country."

"Doing what?" She whirled on him. "America is to *buy* my country?"

"That's the story I hear. Actually, from what I've seen, we wouldn't have the place. We're just getting over one depression and this place might send us into another one. But the story gives us a reason to spend

281

time together. You're to show me the household accounts. You're to teach me about your country and, in general, be very nice to me. You're to—dare I use the word—seduce me into liking your country."

"I . . . I don't think this is possible. Of course my grandfather knows nothing of what has actually occurred between us, but he cannot ask this of me."

"He knows enough to know that your life may be in danger. Look, are you sure it's good for you to be in here with me? People must have seen you enter."

Aria blinked a couple of times. She knew no one had seen her enter but the sight of Jarl and his bed was making her forget her newfound promise of happiness with Julian. "I must go." She started toward the door.

"Not that way," he said, clutching her arm. He went to his duffel bag lying on the floor and withdrew a sheaf of papers. "Your grandfather gave me some maps of underground passages in this place."

"He did what?"

"He said that each monarch inherited these maps at the reading of the will but he thought this was a time for extreme measures. Here we are," he said, looking at one of the maps. "This room is called the State Bedroom, right? I knew he had a reason for putting me in this room. He seemed to think it was special." He began running his hands along the oak paneling. "Here it is." He pushed a button but nothing moved. "I imagine the door needs oiling." There was a letter opener on the desk and he pried open the door until he could get his fingers into the opening then pulled the door open. A musty smell filled the room and they could hear the movement of wings.

"If you think I'm going down that, you are wrong," Aria said.

J.T. got a flashlight from his duffel bag. "If you leave this room dressed like that, you will have the whole place gossiping. Your Count Julian won't marry you because your reputation will be ruined and they'll probably hang me, a commoner, for daring to look upon the royal nightgown. Come on. How bad can it be?"

It was awful. It looked like no one had been inside the passage for centuries and cobwebs and bat droppings covered the damp stone steps that led downward. It was very dark and her slippered feet kept sliding.

"Why do I not know of this place?" she whispered.

"It seems that one of your past kings had everyone who knew about the tunnels put to death. He wanted only the king himself to know of them."

Aria put up her hand to protect herself from a hanging web. Her slippers were so filthy they would have to be discarded. "That would have been Hager the Hated in the fourteenth century. He used any excuse to put people to death."

"Fine relative to claim. Who built this place?"

"Rowan," Aria said, and something in the way she said it made him look at her.

"I take it he was a good guy."

"The best. Where does this lead?"

"Here," J.T. said, stopping at a rusty, iron-clad door. "Let's just hope we can get it open." He handed her the flashlight.

"Where does that lead?" she asked, pointing the light toward a corridor heading toward the left.

"Down to your dungeons then underground to somewhere in the town. Your grandfather said the way out was probably blocked now since a house was built over the old exit. I got it open! Turn off the light."

Aria looked at the cylinder. "How?"

He took the flashlight from her and turned it off.

"According to the map we're at the north end of the King's Garden. Do you know where that is and how to get back to your room?"

"Of course." She walked out into the cool night air.

"Wait a minute, Princess, you haven't told me where you'll be in the morning. I don't plan to let you out of my sight."

Aria wasn't about to tell him she was riding with Count Julian in the morning. "My calendar has my first engagement for nine A.M.," she said truthfully. "I will go riding."

"Stay in your room, I'll meet you."

"But I'm not supposed to know you. We'll have to arrange a formal introduction first."

"You can say your grandfather telephoned you—if this falling-down pile of stones *has* telephones."

"We are more modern than you believe," she said, her chin up. "Good night, Lieutenant Montgomery." She turned away.

"Wait," he said, putting his hand on her arm. He looked at her in the moonlight for a long moment. "Go on, get out of here."

She nearly ran from him, hurrying down the paths she knew so well, then through a servant's door, up the stairs, and into the newer wing where her rooms were.

"I am going to love Julian," she whispered to herself. She was going to compel herself to love Julian and she was going to forget about the crude, insolent American who was temporarily her husband. He had told her that he thought she was cool and remote, not quite human. She was going to show him how haughty a royal princess could be. No matter how much time they spent together, she was going to treat him as the lowliest commoner.

There was no one in the hallway except for the

THE PRINCESS

guard who stood outside her door. She had to get past the man and into her room and be there when her dressers arrived in the morning. If there was gossip that she had left her room wearing her bedclothes late at night, her dressers would say it was impossible since she was there in the morning and no one had seen her reenter.

American movies had taught her a great deal. She picked up a valuable egg-shaped piece of malachite from its stand on a table and sent it rolling down the hall at the feet of the guard. He watched it for a moment, then, as she had hoped, he went after it. Aria slipped into her room as fast as possible. Her heart was pounding as she leaned against the closed door.

Of course, she had to change her clothes and she was glad she knew how to dress herself. She was also glad she knew how to take a sponge and get most of the cobwebs from her dressing gown. The slippers were beyond hope, so, to keep her dressers from finding them, she stuffed each into a sleeve of a ceremonial gown.

It was late when she was able to slide into bed beside a warm, sleeping Gena. For a moment, Aria thought she was with J.T. and snuggled against her. Then she caught herself. She was *not* going to let that man back into her life. There were more important things to life than what one did in bed.

Tomorrow she would have time alone with Julian and she would allow him to help her forget.

"Your Highness!"

Aria woke slowly to her dresser's voice.

"Count Julian is waiting for you." The woman smiled smugly. "He seems most impatient to see you."

Sleepily, Aria pulled herself out of bed and made

her way to the bathroom. Slowly, she began to waken and remember the events of last night. This morning she meant to begin forgetting her American husband. She would have hours alone with Julian—alone in the dim early morning light in the mountain forest.

She was impatient with her dressers but she couldn't dress herself and make them wonder where she had learned how.

Once in her riding habit, she hurried out of the room. She stole a glance at the guard outside her room but he had his eyes straight ahead. She must remember his face because if there were rumors that she had not been in her room last night, he would have spread them.

"Good morning, Your Highness." Julian greeted her at the door to the stables, then, as the groom walked inside, he leaned forward and planted a kiss just below her ear. "Or should I say 'my darling'? You look ravishing."

Aria blushed prettily. "You may call me what you wish in private," she said demurely.

"Then I would like most to call you wife," he said seductively. "Shall we go? In an hour we can be deep within the forest. Just the two of us alone. We don't have to be back for hours."

Aria continued blushing.

"Well, Count, that being alone part isn't exactly right." J.T. lazily moved out of the shadows of the stable door.

"You!" Aria gasped.

"Do you know this man?" Julian asked, looking from one to the other.

She squinted her eyes at J.T. "I had the misfortune of meeting him in America. We had business dealings there."

286

J.T. smiled. "I'm in charge of buying the vanadium from Lanconia."

Julian stepped forward and took Aria's arm. "Her Royal Highness will see you when she returns from her ride."

"No," J.T. said, placing himself between them and the horses, "that's not the way it is. You see, there was a little trouble in America and we—"

"Trouble?" Julian asked seriously. "What does he mean?"

"Nothing big," J.T. said before Aria could speak. "Just some people who seemed to want to cause the princess a little discomfort. So, to protect its own interests, America sent a couple of us soldiers over here to make sure there was no more funny business. One guy stays with the king and I'm to stay with the princess here."

Julian kept a tight grip on Aria's arm. "I'm sure that is very thoughtful of your government, but I can assure you that when Her Royal Highness is with me, there will be no need for your protection."

He moved toward the horses but J.T. intercepted.

They were contrasting men: J.T. dark, tall, his skin weathered from a life spent outdoors, while Julian was the product of centuries of careful breeding: his skin cared for, his hands manicured, his short, trim body held rigidly.

"Sorry, Count," J.T. said. "I go with her or she stays here."

Impatiently, Julian snapped his riding crop against his tall, polished boots. "I will not tolerate—"

"What's a matter, Count?" J.T. said jovially. "'Fraid I'll interfere in your time with the lady? I'll stay way back and you two can moon all you want." He winked at Count Julian, whose face was beginning

287

to turn purple with rage. J.T. smiled. "Of course, you have to understand that if I don't go with the princess, then the deal with America is off. We won't buy the vanadium from a country that's hostile to us, and if we don't buy it, we'll sure as hell not let anybody else buy it, which means we may have to do something warlike to keep you from selling it. Then you'd be king of a country that's maybe been bombed and has no money since you can't sell the vanadium. That's up to you." J.T. turned and started to walk away.

Aria rolled her eyes skyward. "He doesn't mean a word of it," she said to Julian.

"You are risking war and poverty," Julian snapped at her. "I am surprised at you. Does your country mean so little to you?" He went after J.T.

Aria gritted her teeth and wondered which one Julian was most concerned with, war or poverty? He wouldn't like to marry the queen of a war-bombed country.

She chastised herself for her thoughts and allowed Julian to help her onto her horse.

"He will stay well back and we will be almost as if we were alone," Julian said as if in apology, and kissed her gloved hand.

She jerked away from him, then made herself smile at Julian. Lieutenant Montgomery was *not* going to ruin her outing. Perhaps she would give the American something to see. She wondered if he could ride a horse.

"We'll take the north path, to Rowan's Peak."

"Aria!" Julian gasped. "Are you sure? You haven't been on a horse for a while."

She leaned toward Julian. "Perhaps we can lose our escort and be alone," she said, looking at him through her eyelashes.

"I will follow you to the ends of the earth, my darling," he said under his breath.

J.T.'s horse plunged between them, breaking them apart and making Aria's mare dance on the cobblestoned yard. "Sorry," he said. "I sure wish they'd put a steering wheel on this thing. If you two don't mind, could we go on an easy path? I'm not used to horses." His horse was prancing about and turning sideways, making the distance between Aria and Julian even wider. "Where's the brakes on this thing?"

"Pull back on the reins," Julian called. "Damned Americans," he muttered. "Why did the English fight for the place? Aria, what is his name?"

"Lieutenant Montgomery," she called over her shoulder as she cantered out of the stableyard and headed for the mountain trail.

Julian followed her, J.T. still in the courtyard, his horse wildly turning around in a circle.

Aria knew that her only chance of escaping Lieutenant Montgomery was to outrun him or to lose him on the twisting path that branched off in many directions. Her horse was rested and needed the exercise, and she gave it, urging the animal higher and higher into the mountains.

The air was cool and dry, and as she went up the rocky dirt path, the air got thinner. Around her were tall pine trees, closing off the rays of the morning sun. Huge gray boulders sometimes made the path very narrow and a couple of times her horse's hooves slipped, but she kept going.

She was perspiring from the effort, and at a bend in the trail she paused to see Julian not far behind her. She smiled when there was no sign of Lieutenant Montgomery. She motioned to the right to show Julian which path she was taking. There was a mountain spring a few miles down the trail and she thought they would stop there and rest—or whatever.

She brushed branches from her face, buried her face in her horse's mane to keep from getting struck, and kept riding. By the time she reached the spring, she was exhilarated with the exercise. She dismounted and breathed deeply of the clean mountain air. How she had missed her country.

Julian arrived, his face damp and wearing an angry expression. "Aria, I must protest. A lady should never ride such a strenuous path. It is much too much for someone of your delicate nature."

"Are you going to sit up there and scold me or are you going to get down and kiss me?"

His face registered momentary shock, then he dismounted rapidly and took her in his arms. "You *have* changed," he murmured before kissing her. "Let's set a date, my darling," he whispered, clutching her to him. "I don't know how much longer I can wait for you. I think your subjects would frown on our first child being born an inadequate length of time after our marriage."

Aria moved her head back so he could kiss her throat. He felt so very good.

"Whoa there, ol' Dan Tucker. Whoa!" J.T. burst into the little clearing like a rocket, and making about as much noise. Aria had tied her horse but Julian had not and at J.T.'s noise the horse jumped and went trotting further down the narrow path.

"You will fetch my horse," Julian ordered J.T., his face red with suppressed rage.

J.T. looked the soul of contrition. "I'm real sorry, Count, but I can't leave the princess. I guess you'll have to run after him yourself. Or you can take my horse. Brother! What a climb that was. About twenty times I thought I was gonna fall off and now I'm plumb tuckered out." He dismounted.

Aria glared at him. He was obviously lying because he didn't look in the least tired. In fact, he looked ready for some "real" exercise.

"You okay, Princess?" he asked.

"I am Your Royal Highness, to you," she said, then turned to Julian. "I will walk with you to find your horse. *You,"* she said to J.T., "will stay here."

J.T. lowered his eyes. "I wish I could do that, Your Royal Mightiness, but—"

"Your Royal *High*ness," Julian snapped. "Aria, I refuse to spend another moment with this provincial idiot. I shall cable the American government as soon as I return to the palace and protest. Come, Aria. *You* remain here."

Julian took Aria's arm and they started walking.

"Darling, I am sorry," Aria said. "As soon as the vanadium is sold and we once again have some capital in the treasuries, I shall send him packing."

"I do not think I can bear him until then. He is an uneducated, boorish lout. He is stupider than most of the peasants."

"Not all of them are stupid," she said. "In America I met some who were quite intelligent."

"How did you get away from your protectors to meet American peasants? Is that how you got into 'trouble,' as this idiot American so eloquently puts it?" He was looking at her speculatively.

"Well, no, I . . . I mean I . . ."

"Lookee here," J.T. shouted. "Hey, Count, I found your horse for you." Like a knight's lackey, he ran up the path holding the reins to the stallion. "Black brute," J.T. said fearfully. "I'm glad I don't have to ride him. Here you go, Count." He handed the smaller man the reins. "Hey! I brought some whiskey with me. You two wanna share it?"

"*Share* whiskey?" Julian asked, sneering. "Aria, we must return so that I may send a telegram. No, I will radio that American—what is his name? Roosevelt. I will radio him and protest this intolerable position he has put us in."

"You can radio President Roosevelt?" J.T. asked, eyes wide in wonder. "You must be a real powerful man. That oughtta help make up for your size."

Aria stepped between the men just as Julian raised his riding crop. "Julian, please. It would be like striking the American government. Let me speak to him. Please?" She asked the last very sweetly.

Julian turned on his heel and went back to the spring.

"You are making a fool of yourself," she spat at J.T. when they were alone. "And where did you learn to ride so well?"

He smiled at her. "In Colorado on the back of the meanest broncos my Taggert cousins could find."

"Your country bumpkin act is bad enough but your jealousy is intolerable."

He lost his smile instantly. "Jealousy, hell! How do you know it isn't your little count who wants you dead? Maybe he arranged the kidnapping in Key West. Maybe he wants you out of the way so he can marry that featherbrained little sister of yours."

"You leave my sister out of this!" She stopped. "And by the way, just what did the two of you do when you were at my grandfather's? All she could talk about was you when she returned last night."

"Yeah?" J.T. grinned. "Luscious little piece, that."

"How dare you," she said, doubling up her fists.

"Better not get too familiar, Princess, here comes your little stud. You better warn him that if he hits me with his little whip, I may wrap it around his throat. Probably go around about four times," he added, smiling.

"Leave us alone," she hissed as Julian approached. "Just leave us alone."

"Not until I know he can be trusted. Howdy, Count," he said loudly. "The princess here has given me a talkin' to set my ears ringin'. I'm sorry if I don't know how to treat royalty. We Americans ain't used to kings and dukes and counts and such. You two go on ahead. I'll be as quiet as a mouse and stay way back here."

Count Julian had been surrounded by servants all his life—servants who were respectful and knew their place in life. He imagined that this American had at last recognized his place. He turned back to Aria. "Shall we walk, darling? Perhaps we should discuss our wedding preparations. I think we should be married within three months at the most. It will be autumn then and we shall honeymoon in that mountain retreat of the king's."

"I don't know, there is a world war going on."

"And there are many marriages being performed. People need a little happiness now."

"I agree, Princess," J.T. said from behind them as he moved forward. "You two make a fine-lookin' couple and you ought to share your future with the world. The princess could wear a long white dress, symbol of her purity, and one of those diamond crowns—but not too tall 'cause of his royal countship here. I can see it now."

Count Julian raised his riding crop.

"Of course," J.T. continued, "America will pay for the wedding—sort of an appreciation gift for selling us the vanadium."

The crop lowered.

"We will return to the palace," Julian said, taking Aria's arm and leading her away.

She was angry herself, and as they returned to the horses, she vowed she was going to elude Lieutenant Montgomery and spend some time alone with Julian.

Julian's face was a mask as he helped Aria mount then mounted himself. The three of them started down the mountainside.

"Was it something I said?" J.T. asked, eyes bright as he reined his horse next to Aria's.

She kicked her horse forward and reached for Julian's hand. "Tonight I will meet you alone, at nine-thirty in the Queen's Garden under the gingko tree," she whispered.

He gave a curt nod but kept looking straight ahead.

They rode halfway down the mountain without speaking, J.T. staying just inches away from the back of Aria's horse. She glanced back a few times but he was always looking at the scenery with an intent expression. When they were back at the palace, she meant to talk to him about what she would and would not tolerate. And interfering with her growing relationship with Count Julian was one thing she would not abide. Another was his seeming interest in Gena. Gena was very young and frivolous and Aria could not allow her to spend time with an older, experienced man like Lieutenant Montgomery.

J.T. made no sound before he leaped. One second he was on his horse and the next he was sailing through the air, leaping toward Aria. She heard a sound behind her and saw this enormous man flying toward her. Only half of her scream escaped.

The shot missed her by inches. She was tumbling down the side of the horse, J.T. clutching her when the bullet whizzed over their heads.

Julian's horse reared, he lost the reins, and the

horse tore down the mountainside, Julian barely hanging on. The other two horses, now riderless, followed Julian's.

J.T. twisted his body so that he landed first on the rocky ground, Aria on top, then he moved so that they rolled off the path and into a little gully hidden by bushes and tall undergrowth. He covered her body with his, completely protecting her as he lifted his head slightly to look at the steep mountainside facing them.

"Was it a shot?" Aria whispered, looking up at his face.

"Something big, is my guess, maybe a sporting rifle because it had a shiny barrel. I saw it glint in the sun."

"Perhaps it was a hunter."

He looked down at her. "And they thought our horses were bighorn sheep?" He looked back at the mountainside. "They were shooting at you, Princess."

"Oh," she said, and her arms came up to wrap around him. "You saved my life."

"Again." He looked back at her. "I think I like this time better."

He looked as if he were going to kiss her but he pulled away. "We have to get you home. We can't take the path, we'd be too exposed. We're going through the forest and we're going to stop and listen often. No talking. Where's the nearest point of civilization? I guess it would be too much to hope for a car, but maybe there's a telephone. We need to call your army and get some protection on the trip down."

"There is a hunting lodge up the mountain," she said. "There are caretakers there who can take a message down but there are no telephone lines on the mountain. The nearest telephone is at the bottom. But Julian will bring help."

"Don't count on it, baby. He didn't look like he'd

stop running for miles, and if he gets back to the palace, he'll probably hide under the covers."

"I resent your saying that. Julian is not a coward."

"There was a rifle shot and all I've seen is the back of him. He should have returned with the horses by now. How far is this lodge?"

"It's not far if we don't use the road, but it's straight up."

J.T. groaned.

"It is a difficult climb, I admit, but—"

"We'll be exposed on the side of the mountain. Stay down and keep in the scrub oak as much as possible. Try to keep something between you and the sight of the rifleman."

"Perhaps he has gone."

"And miss an opportunity to pick you off? Come on, get up and let's go."

Aria had never made the climb before and she only knew about it because the son of one of her ladies-in-waiting had been lost from the lodge. During the three-day search she had heard much about the surrounding terrain.

The climb was strenuous and made worse because J.T. insisted they take the most difficult way. But he helped her over rocks, through groves of five-foot-tall oak trees struggling to survive, and under brush too thick to navigate except at a crawl.

It was noon when they reached the hunting lodge. J.T. pushed Aria into some shrubbery then began pounding on the door. A frightened-looking older woman opened it.

"Sir, you cannot—"

J.T. pushed past her and pulled Aria inside.

"Your Royal Highness," the older woman said, bobbing a curtsy.

"It's all right, Brownie," Aria said. "This is Lieutenant Montgomery, an American," she said, as if that explained his manners. "Could we have some lunch?"

"No one told us of your coming. We aren't prepared." The woman looked as if she were about to cry as she stood there fiddling with her apron.

J.T. moved away from the window he was looking out. "What are you having for lunch?"

Brownie gave him a quick look up and down as if to determine what his status was. "A humble shepherd pie with a potato crust. It's not fit for a princess."

"Sounds great to me," J.T. said. "How about you, honey?"

Brownie's face showed her shock.

"He is an American," Aria reemphasized. "The pie sounds excellent. May we have one?"

"Yes, my lady." Brownie disappeared into another room.

"Stop calling me honey!" Aria said the minute they were alone.

"Is 'darling' the name royalty use?" He was looking out the window again.

"Do you see Julian yet?"

"No sign of the front or back of him." He turned toward her. "You seem to be taking this well. But then you always recover from assassination attempts rather quickly. They only seem to make you hungry."

"It is part of my training. Since the beginning of time, people have wanted to kill royalty, either for the attention it brought them, for personal grievances, or for political ideals."

"Who taught you to spout out that answer?"

"My mother," Aria said before she thought.

He looked at her awhile. "You know something? I think I'm beginning to get to know you. How about a double whiskey?"

"Please," she said gratefully, and he smiled.

She was doing her best to remain the princess, to keep her head high, but inside she was shaking. Someone here in Lanconia was trying to *kill* her. One of her own people wanted her dead. She was almost grateful when J.T. pulled her from the foyer into the parlor hung with medieval tapestries and filled with chairs covered in dark, threadbare needlepoint.

"Sit down," he ordered as he went to a sideboard and poured a Waterford glass three-quarters full of whiskey.

She gulped a third of it. Her eyes watered but she needed the whiskey's warmth.

"I know about the time on the island and now this. Have there been any other attempts on your life? Maybe some 'accidents'?"

"I tripped over something on the stairs a week before I left for America. Lady Werta was behind me and caught my dress or I would have fallen."

"What else?"

Aria looked away. "Someone killed one of my dogs," she said softly. "I felt it was perhaps a warning to me."

"Who did you tell about these things?"

"No one. There was no one I could tell. My grandfather is too ill—"

"He's as much ill from pampering as anything else," J.T. said as he poured himself a whiskey. "I'm going to stay by you every moment. You're not getting out of my sight. You're to go nowhere without me."

"But I cannot possibly do that. I have many responsibilities. My grandfather has never believed in a monarch who dies one day and leaves the country to an untrained person. I am always in the public eye. It is the price I pay for the privilege of being a princess."

"So far I can't see that it's much of a privilege."

"And I have a duty to my fiancé," she said, draining her glass. "Julian is right: a royal wedding would help our country."

"Luncheon is served, Your Royal Highness," Brownie said at the doorway.

J.T. drank the rest of his whiskey. "Great. Send me an invitation. I'll do everything I can to help just as soon as I'm convinced he's not involved in this. Let's eat."

Chapter Eighteen

T<small>WENTY</small> minutes later Count Julian arrived with what indeed looked to be an army. They were planning to use the hunting lodge for their headquarters while searching for the princess and her attacker, but Julian strode into the dining room to see Her Royal Highness sitting at a table with a commoner and sharing a disgustingly coarse meal.

"Good to see you, Count," the American called. "Thought we'd seen the last of your back."

"Seize him!" Count Julian ordered one of the four guardsmen behind him.

Aria stood. "No," she said to the guard. "He saved my life and he is not to be harmed. Leave us."

With a court bow, the guard and his men left the room.

"Julian," Aria said firmly. "The guard and you will escort me home. I have engagements this afternoon."

J.T. stood and walked back toward them. "You can't go into the public."

"What am I to do? Lock myself in a tower? Should I find a food taster to check for poison? Am I to incarcerate myself?" She turned to Julian. "To explain the appointments I missed this morning, we will say that I fell from my horse and had to walk down the mountain. It will be better to be laughed at than to frighten people." She walked ahead of him out the door.

J.T. stopped Julian. "We can't let her do this. It's too dangerous for her."

Julian somehow managed to look down his nose at the taller J.T. "You cannot possibly understand. She is a crown princess; she will be queen."

"I understand that you're supposed to love her," J.T. said.

"What has that to do with it?"

"Her life is in danger, you little—" J.T. stopped. "Or would you like to see her out of the way?"

"If this were another era and you were a gentleman, I'd call you out for that." He stepped around J.T. and left the room.

"I'm ready when you are," J.T. called after him.

For J.T. the rest of the day was a nightmare. He stayed as near as possible to Aria but too many people pushed them apart. They were eager people with their hands outstretched, people with tears in their eyes who wanted to see their princess. She had been away for so long and they desperately wanted to see that she was well and not as ill as had been rumored.

As an American, it was difficult for J.T. to understand what she meant to these people. An ancient man in a wheelchair burst into tears when Aria held his hands in hers. "I have not lived in vain," he croaked out. "My life has some meaning now."

J.T. tried to envision the Americans' reaction to

seeing the president. Probably half of them would use the opportunity to tell him what he was doing wrong. Also, there was always the feeling of impermanence. Four years and he was out.

But Aria was a princess for life—however long that would be, J.T. thought with a jolt.

These people lined the street as she walked wherever she could. At the Scientific Academy he stood against the wall and listened to an incredibly boring speech about bugs. He let out a loud yawn that made that lipless Lady Werta turn and glare at him.

At 6:45 Aria was ushered into an ancient, highly polished Rolls to be driven back to the palace. J.T. pushed his way through the crowd, opened the opposite door, and climbed in with Lady Werta and Aria.

"Get out!" Lady Werta shouted. "Stop the car," she screeched to the driver.

"It's all right," Aria said.

"No, it is not all right," Lady Werta sniffed. "You cannot be seen with him. You are going to make people suspicious and then we will never get the real princess back. We will never see her again."

Aria started to pat Lady Werta's hand but J.T. shook his head. "What do you want?" she asked angrily, playing Kathy Montgomery, but it wasn't easy for her. "I told you I never wanted to see you again."

"Yeah, well, the old king hired me to protect the princess and I can't do that if you're out in the middle of all these people."

"She *must* do her duties," Lady Werta said haughtily.

J.T. started to say more but he stopped. Didn't any of these people have a bit of sense? They adored their princess, but if they didn't *protect* her she wasn't going to exist anymore.

It was only with reluctance that J.T. left Aria once they were back at the palace. His rooms were far away from hers and he knew he couldn't get to her quickly enough should she need help.

There was a small man wearing what seemed to be the household colors of gray and gold standing in his room.

"What are you doing here?" J.T. asked suspiciously.

"His Majesty has asked that I take care of you during your stay in Lanconia. My name is Walters and I will dress you, deliver messages, whatever you need. His Majesty has instructed me to be perfectly discreet. Your bath is waiting and your dress uniform is pressed."

"I don't need anyone," J.T. began, but then he thought that perhaps Walters might be useful.

"Here is a letter from His Majesty," Walters said.

The letter, on thick cream-colored paper and sealed with red wax impressed with a coat of arms, told J.T. that he might trust Walters with his life, that he had been told everything, and that he was excellent at hearing things.

J.T. began to undress, brushing Walters's hands away when the older man started to unbutton his uniform shirt.

"Did you hear what happened today?" he asked Walters.

"It was put about that Her Highness had an accident."

J.T. gave Walters a sharp look. "Was that all you heard?"

"Count Julian said she'd lost her way, but I managed to overhear him telling Lady Bradley that someone shot at her. The count seemed to think it was a hunting accident." Walters turned his head away as J.T. finished undressing and stepped into the bathtub.

"What do you think?" J.T. asked.

"I buried her little dog, sir. Someone killed it with a knife, but it had been cut open from neck to tail then put under her bed while she slept. She saw its tail sticking out between her slippers. She called me to take it away before anyone else saw it."

J.T. leaned back in the old-fashioned, short, deep, recessed tub. All the bathrooms in the palace had been added about the turn of the century and were sumptuously done in squares of marble, with heavy porcelain fixtures and taps in the shapes of swans or porpoises. There was hot water but it took an eternity to get it up from the bowels of the palace. J.T. remembered Aria saying she had told no one of her "accidents," yet this servant, Walters, had taken her murdered dog away. How many other "no ones" knew nothing of what was happening?

"Walters," J.T. said, "tell me who lives in this place."

Walters recited a list of people and their lineages and titles that sounded like something from a fairy tale. There were three young princes, all direct descendants from a male monarch. There was Aria's Aunt Bradley, the Duchess of Daren, a woman who was directly related to nearly every royal house in the world. "Except the Asians, of course," Walters added. Her Royal Highness Sophie was the king's sister, and Barbara—"a mere child," Walters said—who was Aria's deceased father's deceased brother's only child.

"How did Aria's parents die?" J.T. asked suspiciously.

"Her father caught a cold but would not postpone or cancel a scheduled three-day trip to the southern part of the country. It rained and he stood in the rain to take the bows and curtsies of his subjects. He died two weeks later of pneumonia."

"And her mother?"

"Cancer. It might have been operable but Her Royal Highness told no one until she could no longer stand."

J.T. digested the information. No wonder Aria was the way she was. It was bred in her.

After he was shaved and dressed, J.T. followed Walters down to the Green Dining Room. This was supposed to be the dining room for intimate dinners but it was larger than a basketball court.

Walters pulled his watch from his vest. "We are a little early, sir. Royalty is always punctual. One could set one's watch by royalty."

"I'll have to remember that," J.T. said, one eyebrow raised.

J.T. wanted a cigarette but, somehow, the portraits of stern ancestors that lined the hallways seemed to frown on anything so modern. In the twenty or so hours that he had been in the palace, he had begun to conjure up a picture of the life of royalty: all duty and no laughter. He tried to remember his best table manners as his mother had taught him. If nothing else, he didn't want to embarrass Aria or have Julian laugh at him. At the moment he desperately wished he could remember the name of that ancestor of his who had been an English earl. Maybe he could just drop the name when Lady or Lord So-and-so was speaking of their relationship to Rowan the Twelfth or whoever.

"It's time," Walters said, and led J.T. to the door of a drawing room where everyone met before dinner. "Good luck, sir," he said as J.T. entered the room.

Aria handed her drink to a liveried servant, who

seemed to be waiting for the honor, and made her way to J.T. "Come, I will introduce you. Wait," she said, stopping and lowering her voice. "I cannot introduce you as . . . as . . ."

It took him a moment to understand. "As J.T.? What is it you have against my name?" he asked angrily.

"Initials are put on one's underclothes," she snapped. "It is an absurd American custom of abbreviating a name. I can only introduce you as Lieutenant Jarl Montgomery—that is, if you can part with your mother's hold on that name."

J.T. laughed, causing the others to turn and stare. "Honey, you can call me what you want." He reached out to touch her bare upper arm but she froze him with a look. "Okay, Princess, start the introductions."

The first person in line was a beautiful woman, about forty, but with skin like cream and a cleavage that made J.T. blink a couple of times. She held his hand just a second too long, and when she left, J.T.'s eyes followed her.

"Are you planning a liaison with my aunt?" Aria asked under her breath. "She is *much* older than you are, you know."

"So are all the best wines."

Next came a voluptuous little nymphet named Barbara. "But Aria, he is utterly divine. It is so kind of His Majesty to send us something like him." She clutched J.T.'s arm and started to lead him away.

But the door opened and in ran Gena, looking exquisite, her face flushed from a run down the stairs. "Sorry, Aria," she said quickly, then grabbed J.T.'s other arm. "He's mine, Barbara, and if you touch him, you'll draw back a bloody nub."

J.T. smiled from one young lady to the other. "I'm willing to share," he said pleasantly.

Aria started to separate the trio but Julian caught her arm. "Dinner is served and I think we ought to go inside."

The two young ladies led J.T. into the dining room, where he found place cards showing he was to sit between Lady Bradley and Princess Gena. Lady Barbara was across from him.

The meal was not what he expected. If he had ever thought about it—which he hadn't—he would have thought the best table manners in the world belonged to royalty, but that was not the case. They were a motley group, reminding J.T. of a group of spoiled children who had always been given their own way. Each person at the table, ten in all, had his own servant, and J.T. thought perhaps there should be two per person as each servant was kept busy with demands: one person liked cold wine, another warm wine; one person would not eat carrots, another ate an entirely different meal than what was served. One of the cousins, Nickie, ate with his mouth open while punching the air with his fingers to tell about his latest animal kill. And not one of them touched food with his hands. It was as if a curse had been placed on the food, that whoever touched it would die. The entire group came to an abrupt halt when J.T. reached for a roll on his bread plate. Defiantly, he picked it up in his hands, and after a moment they returned to eating and J.T. returned to his observations.

He looked at Great-Aunt Sophie, a loud, rude woman who did her best to dominate the table—while everyone else did his best to ignore her. Barbara and Gena seemed interested only in sex, and tonight he was their object of desire. Lady Bradley hardly spoke but gave him long looks over her wineglass.

As J.T. watched the people, he realized that the only one to interest him was Aria. She sat at the head of the table, ate with impeccable manners, and didn't shout or make demands.

"How you are observing us," Lady Bradley said softly. "Like animals in a cage."

He smiled at her. "As an American I'm not used to formal dinners. I'm used to hot dogs cooked on the beach."

She smiled in a knowing way. "There is breeding somewhere in you. I can sense it. Are you one of those very wealthy Americans?"

"I was hired to do a job, that's all." His eyes were on Aria.

"Mmm," Lady Bradley said. "You do not answer." She glanced at Aria. "Are you in love with her?"

J.T. told himself he would have to be more careful of what he revealed about himself. "She is different, that's all."

Lady Bradley's laugh rang out. "Aria has to behave herself. She has all the responsibility while the rest of us have the luxury. She does the work while we share in the rewards." She laughed at his expression. "The others will give you a long list of what they do to earn their keep, but the truth is, Aria supports us. She will make an excellent queen."

Barbara began demanding his attention and J.T. had to turn away from Lady Bradley, but the thought of Aria as queen brought him back to the present problem. Someone was trying to kill her and it was quite likely that that someone was sitting at this table. Maybe what Lady Bradley had said meant something. Aria supported them all. Perhaps someone wanted more than just room and board. Tomorrow he thought he would look into the household accounts and find out who needed money.

He looked at Gena, laughing at something the effeminate Freddie was saying, and J.T. knew that if

Gena were queen and personally owned the fortune that uranium would bring her, she would give it to whoever asked for it. She would probably go through the money and the resource in five years. And whoever had Gena would share the money. All that was needed was to get rid of Aria and the king and Gena would inherit.

The meal was long and tedious with course after course served on a different pattern of china. The royal family did not eat much, but seemed to drink a great deal.

"Why doesn't the king live in the palace?" J.T. asked Lady Bradley.

"He says the air near his hunting lodge is better for his health, but the truth is, he doesn't like us. Oh, he likes Aria and Gena all right, but no one else. In the fall we move to a much smaller palace south of here, then His Majesty moves into this palace. When we return, he leaves. It is most convenient for everyone, even Aria, because she is, in essence, queen while her grandfather is away."

J.T. thought he didn't blame the king one bit.

All through the long meal, which seemed to consist mainly of overcooked food laden with thick, rich sauces that after a while began to taste the same, J.T. watched Aria. She and Julian had their heads close together several times and once something Julian said made her blush.

J.T. began to remember their time in Key West. He remembered her laughter, how she had discussed the distilling plant with him, how she had danced at the ball with his mother. He remembered holding her, waking up with her, making love with her.

The wineglass stem snapped between his fingers.

Only Lady Bradley noticed as a servant covered the

stained tablecloth with a white brocade napkin and replaced his glass within seconds.

Aria lifted her eyes, met his, seemed to not like what she saw, then frowned and looked back at Julian.

You can't have her, J.T. told himself. She belongs here and you belong in America. You have to keep yourself remote from her. Guard her, protect her, but for your own sanity, don't fall in love with her. And, also for your own mental health, let Julian have her. He wants to be king and he may make a good one.

After dinner the men and women separated, the men going to a room to smoke cigars and drink brandy. Freddie, Nickie, and Toby were still talking about the number of animals they had managed to slaughter in their lifetimes and Julian refused to speak to J.T., so J.T. was not included in the group.

He gave a yawn, downed his brandy, and announced he was going to bed.

This effectively stopped everyone and he knew he had committed some great *faux pas.*

"You may not leave until Her Royal Highness has bid us good evening," Julian said, and his tone implied that any slug would know this.

"Tell her I hope she sleeps well," J.T. said with a wink. "See you around." He nodded toward the three princes.

"I'll be damned," he heard one prince gasp in disbelief before he got out of the room.

J.T.'s plan was to get Walters to show him where Aria's room was and somehow figure out how to guard her at night.

Walters was waiting for him with pajamas and robe—silk pajamas and a cashmere robe.

"I have to find a way to guard the princess at night," J.T. said, eschewing the nightwear.

"She is meeting the count in the Queen's Garden immediately after dinner," Walters said.

J.T. told himself he didn't care, told himself it would be better to allow them to meet alone. "Where is the Queen's Garden?" he asked after a moment.

"Over the bridge, go right, and follow the path. It's just past the tall hedges, a very secret place, sir. It was named so because it is a traditional assignation place for queens and their lovers."

J.T. left before he changed his mind.

The gardens around the palace consisted of acres of carefully tended grounds, some of which he had seen from his window. One part of it, about half an acre, was laid out with the Lanconian flag in five-inch-tall shrubbery, the insides filled with different-colored flowers: the grapes were green, the goat white, and there were bands of gray and gold.

Beyond the coat of arms he could see trees and brilliant patches of flowers and occasionally pieces of white that looked to be marble.

The path to the bridge was well tended and bordered on each side with drooping willow trees. He turned right past the bridge and the plantings became denser. The trees blocked the moonlight until it was so dark he could barely see the path.

"Julian?" he heard Aria whisper.

He stopped where he was, listened, then made a leap in her direction, catching her about the waist.

She opened her mouth to scream, so he did what came natural to him: he kissed her.

He missed her more than he thought possible. He held her so tightly he thought he might break her body in half—half for him and half for Lanconia. He drank of her lips and it felt very good when her arms went around his neck and she tried to pull him closer.

"Oh, baby," he whispered, kissing her neck and

burying his fingers in her hair. Her hair fell about her shoulders, soft and loose the way it was supposed to be, the way *his* Aria wore her hair.

It was a while before he realized she was struggling to get away from him. He was feeling a little dazed but he released her.

"Why are you doing this to me?" she gasped as if she were out of breath. "Why did you follow me? Can't you understand that I don't *want* to see you again? I didn't want you on the mountain and I don't want you now."

J.T.'s brain was beginning to clear of the fog that had invaded it when he was touching her. "I came to protect you," he said, but his voice had an unusual thickness to it, as if his tongue were swollen. He cleared his throat. "I just wanted to demonstrate how unsafe it is for you to be here alone. I could have been your attacker."

"You *did* attack me," she said. "Now will you please leave me alone? I am here to meet my husband-to-be."

"He's supposed to protect you? That little—"

"Stop it!" she said, and there were tears in her voice. "He's not big like you. He's not, as Gena says, divinely handsome, but he is suitable. Can't I make you understand that I have more to think about in a marriage than bed pleasure? You can*not* be my husband so please stop . . . stop touching me. I am going to love Count Julian. Do you understand that? I do not *want* you to protect me or even be near me. Now, would you please return so I can meet my lover in private?"

J.T. was glad the darkness hid his face and she didn't see him wince at her use of the word "lover." "You are right," he said at last. "But I do have a job to do." His voice was formal to the point of coolness.

"My president has asked me to guard you and I plan to do so. I am not sure that your little count isn't part of the conspiracy to harm you, so I plan to stay near you while he's here."

"What does Julian have to gain by my death?" she asked, exasperation in her voice. "He gains by my being alive."

"Does he?" J.T. asked softly. "He will marry a hardheaded, stubborn wench of a queen who will make him walk two paces behind her, and he will never be more than a prince. Knowing you, you would never allow him any control of the country. This morning he gave an order to a soldier and you countermanded the order—and the soldier obeyed *you*. I don't think a banty rooster like your count is going to like a lifetime of that."

Aria was silent for a moment. "And if I am dead?" she whispered.

"Your little sister will inherit. Whoever marries her will rule the country. He'd have to since Gena is incapable of governing anything."

"But Lanconia is so poor. Why would anyone *want* control of it?" she asked.

"It's not as poor as you think. Listen! Someone is coming." He leaned closer to her. "I'm not leaving you alone. I'm going to hide but I'll be near. And fasten your hair back up," he snapped before disappearing into the shadows.

Aria tried to pull her hair back but she had no pins to hold it. Her hands were shaking too badly to do much anyway. Until Jarl's words, she had made excuses for the attempts on her life because she hadn't been able to see any advantage to her death, but she knew what he said was right. What did he mean that Lanconia wasn't as poor as she thought?

"Aria, my darling," Julian said, pulling her into his

arms. "Alone with you. I never thought it would happen." He began kissing her face. "Your hair is down. How very *intime.*"

Aria was intensely aware that Jarl was near them and listening. She pushed Julian away but still held his hands. "It is good to see you alone at last. Come and sit down and talk."

"Talk in the moonlight? Oh, my darling, no. Let us make love."

"Julian, please," she said firmly, and drew him to a curved marble bench. "I think we need to talk. We have never talked about our future together."

He kissed her hands, first the backs then the palms. "I thought I was marrying a country but I find I am marrying a woman."

"After we are married, what do you plan to do? I mean in Lanconia. Do you plan to adopt charities? What form of sports do you play? I really know very little about you."

"How delightful that you are interested," he said, leaning forward to kiss her lips, but she drew back. He sighed. "I have never been interested in sports. Other than riding a bit, that is. I was trained to run estates. I believe my father hoped he could make back some of the wealth my grandfather frittered away. But he could not. Everything was lost." There was bitterness in his voice. "All I have left is my lineage and my knowledge. I came to Lanconia because I heard there was a crown princess to be had but I . . ." His voice softened. "I had not heard she was so beautiful. Aria, our marriage will be very happy."

"Yes, perhaps," she said, "but what do you plan to *do* after our marriage?"

"Be a king, of course," he said as if she were an idiot.

"I see."

He began kissing her hands. "Yes, my darling, you will be a beautiful hostess. I shall buy you Paris gowns once this foul war is ended and we will entertain nobility from all over the world. We will produce lovely children and I shall teach our son how to be a king."

"How will Lanconia pay for these gowns and entertainments? Shall we tax the peasants?" There was an edge to her voice. "Shall we take a third of their crops and leave them with hungry children?"

He dropped her hands and sat up straight. "You shall leave payment to me. I will manage everything. You have merely to plan the menus."

Aria was shaking, both with anger and fear. Here was a reason this man could want her dead. And if a man who was supposed to love her could want her death, what about the unknown people?

She put her hands over her face. "Oh, Julian, you don't know how heavenly that sounds. To not have to wake up every morning worried about making decisions! I should love to fly to Paris twice a year for the new collections. And I'd love to have children. I would spend a great deal of time with them if I didn't have to worry about . . . about serious, government problems."

In the darkness, J.T. nearly burst out laughing. It was a perfect imitation of Dolly, minus the southern accent. How many times had he seen Dolly pretend to be helpless then end up managing everyone? J.T. almost felt like warning Julian.

Julian took Aria's hands from her face. "My darling, I've never been sure how you felt. You are making me the most happy of men. Tomorrow I will begin work. I must look at Lanconia's revenues and we can begin planning our wedding."

"But the king—" Aria began.

316

"Bah! He is an old man. He knows nothing of what is going on. I must prepare for when I am king. Come, let us return to the palace."

"Do I get no more kisses?"

"Of course, darling." Quickly, he kissed her lips. "This cool air is not good for you. We must return."

"No," she said. "I will stay here awhile longer. A girl needs time alone to contemplate her marriage," she said flirtatiously.

"I don't like it, but all right." He kissed her hands again and turned swiftly down the path.

Aria stayed sitting on the bench for a moment until she heard J.T. move behind her. She fought back tears. Was it not possible for someone to love her for herself and not for her kingdom?

She stood quickly, hands clenched at her sides. "Are you happy now?" she spat at J.T. as he emerged from the darkness. "Did you enjoy finding out that you were right? Julian wants Lanconia, not me. He plans to become king and relegate me to the nursery. An American housewife has more power than I am to have. Why aren't you laughing?"

He pulled her into his arms, holding her hands down as she flailed against his chest. "I'm sorry, baby," he said, stroking her hair.

Much to her shame, Aria began to cry. "I used to know he only wanted to marry me for my country, but I seem to have forgotten. I thought maybe he did love me. I'm a fool! Is it not possible for someone to want *me*? Just me—without Lanconia."

J.T. turned her chin up to face him. "Baby, if you didn't have this damned country tied around your neck like it was the *Titanic* on its way down, I'd take you and run."

"Would you? You'd want me as a woman?"

"I'd want you home with me throwing your red

blouses in with my white T-shirts, telling me that you will not iron, and making me crazy by dancing in a skirt cut up to your hip." He moved his hands to her face. "Honey, I'd want you there to wash my back. I'd want you in my arms when I woke up in the morning."

He brought his mouth to hers and began to kiss her with all the lonesome hunger he felt for her. "Stay with me tonight. Don't let me wake up alone again."

"Yes," she whispered. She forgot where she was. She was once again Mrs. Montgomery and she was free to laugh, free to dress in an absurd costume and not worry that she was letting people down. She was free to eat with her hands, free to choose friends, not restricted to people who might not write stories about the intimate details of her life.

She clung to him, remembering and savoring those few glorious, heavenly weeks.

Then a bird called, giving its long sweet song to the night air. It was a rare bird, found only in the mountains of Lanconia and therefore treasured, protected, and honored as its national bird.

It made Aria remember where she was.

Violently, she pushed away from J.T. "No, no, no," she screeched. "You are the devil tempting me. I am *not* an American housewife. I am a princess—a *crown* princess—and my life belongs to my country. I *do* have Lanconia tied to me—no, we are part of each other. We are not separate. Do not touch me again, do not try to make me leave my country. If I did not love Lanconia so much, I would never have met you. Oh, how I wish I had never met you. I was content before. I didn't even know there was a life other than mine. You have made me very unhappy. I wish I had never seen you! I hate you!"

Still crying, she began to run down the path toward the palace.

J.T. followed at a discreet distance, making sure she was safe. He was torn between feeling miserable and elated. She *had* missed him. Underneath the princess was the woman.

But what she had said was true. Was he selfish to want to make her say that she wanted him and not some little blueblood? He was here to do a job and that job did not include making Her Royal Highness cry.

Love didn't matter; desire didn't matter. They could never be together except temporarily and she knew that even if he seemed to forget. From now on he swore he was going to keep his hands off of her. In fact, he was going to help her find someone to marry. Someone who would stay out of the way. Someone not overly ambitious. Someone who liked her as much as he did.

Someone impotent, so he wouldn't touch what belonged to J. T. Montgomery.

J.T. corrected himself, followed Aria until she went past her guard and into her room, then, sighing, he made the long trek to his own empty bedroom.

Chapter Nineteen

J. T. was waiting for Aria the next morning outside her bedroom door and started walking with her down to breakfast.

"You cannot do this," she hissed at him.

He paid as much attention to her protests as he usually did. "I want to have a look at the books of this place."

She smiled. "Our library is excellent. We have a few manuscripts from Rowan's time, even a map belonging to him."

"I want the books telling how much it costs to run this place. The ledgers. Accounts. Understand?"

"Like the household budget you put me on?"

"The one you overran every week," he said.

J.T. stepped back and allowed her to enter the dining room first and she was glad he did not embarrass her in front of her relatives, who were already eating. She took a plate from the end of a long sideboard and began to fill it from the many silver servers that were warmed by a candle underneath.

"This is a lot of food for so few people, isn't it?" J.T. grumbled as he filled his own plate.

He didn't say much during breakfast and Aria saw him watching the people at the table. She knew what he was thinking. Just what did these people *do* all day? Aria realized she had no idea. She saw Freddie snub J.T., looking at the American's plain uniform with no medals, no stars on his shoulders. Of course Freddie's uniforms were laden with gold braid and many medals but he had never done anything to earn them.

"Ready?" J.T. asked, standing behind Aria's chair, waiting to pull it out for her. "We have work to do."

He seemed oblivious to the open mouths around them, but Aria knew she had to obey him or he might cause a scene. Once they were out of the dining room, she let him have it. "You can*not* treat me this way. I am a royal princess. You are supposed to be a guest in my house. People are going to say—"

"I hope people will say, 'You'd better stay away from the princess, or that American will flatten you.' I want people to realize that if they get near you, they have to deal with me. Now, let's go look at the ledgers."

"I will take you to my treasurer and you two can look at the accounts. I have engagements today."

They were at the door to her bedroom. "Let's see your schedule."

"I do *not* have to get your approval."

"You bring it out here or I go in there. How do you think your old, little count will like my being in your bedroom?"

She returned with her secretary holding the big maroon leather-bound book that was her schedule. "The Royal Society of Entomology wants—" the secretary began before J.T. took the book from her.

He scanned the page. "There's nothing here but

more bug lectures and some ladies' societies doings. No sick kids or old people." He shoved the book back at the skinny little secretary. "Tell everybody Her Royal Highness is still weak from her illness and cannot attend. And from now on don't accept every invitation sent to her. She needs a little time to"—he looked at Aria—"to jitterbug. Come on, baby, let's go find your treasurer." He took her arm and started pulling her.

Aria knew she would die of embarrassment if she looked back at her secretary. "You cannot touch me," she said in exasperation.

J.T. dropped her arm. "Okay, so I forgot. So shoot me."

"And the names are intolerable. And you cannot cancel my schedule without my permission. You can't seem to remember that *I* am in control in Lanconia." He was walking so fast she had trouble keeping up with him.

"Uh-huh. You're so much in control that someone wants you dead."

"Here!" she said, stopping at a pair of carved walnut doors. There were two Royal Guardsmen standing on either side of the doors, their backs rigid, their eyes straight ahead. With a precise movement, they opened the doors and Aria sailed through without missing a step. J.T. looked at the two guards for a moment. "Thanks," he said, and went into the office.

Four men were on their feet instantly and it was easy to see that they were unaccustomed to visits from Her Royal Highness. They mumbled greetings and tried to hide dirty coffee cups.

J.T. stepped forward. He was going to drown in all the "Your Highnesses" going around the room. "I have been hired by the king to look at the economy of Lanconia and I'm starting with the palace accounts."

The four men of the treasury dropped their jaws. The oldest man's eyes bugged.

Aria stepped forward and said in a cajoling voice, "He is an American and he has been sent here by the king. Perhaps you could show us the household accounts and leave us."

The men didn't say a word as they put the books on one of the four desks in the room then left.

"You aren't helping America's image," Aria spat at J.T.

"I want to have the reputation of being an SOB. Maybe it'll put a little fear in somebody."

"All right, you have your books so I'll go now. Julian and I—"

"You are staying with me. You're not leaving my sight."

"But Julian and I—"

"You'd be *dead* now if you'd gone out alone with him yesterday. Now sit there and be quiet."

Aria sat down on the edge of a hard chair, her body as rigid as flesh and muscle could be. Lieutenant Montgomery was ruining her present life and her future life. She wouldn't blame Julian if he left her, but then she remembered his words of last night and she wondered if she cared if he left. Of course, she wasn't going to delude herself that she could get anyone better for a husband. A princess's choices were severely limited.

"What is this?" J.T. asked loudly, making her jump. "Is this an entry for *snow*?"

"It's probably for Freddie's snow cream." Perhaps she could put an ad in a paper seeking some royally connected man who didn't want to be a king.

"Snow cream?" J.T. asked, interrupting her thoughts.

On the other hand, maybe she could rule alone, a

virgin queen like England's Queen Elizabeth, but then it was a little late for the virgin part and she would rather like to have children.

"Aria!" J.T. snapped. "Answer me. What is this bill for snow?"

She sighed. Sometimes he could be so common. "Freddie loves snow cream so snow is brought down from the mountains for him."

"He eats this stuff every day?"

"Of course not. He only has it four or five times a year, but of course the snow must be ready for him should he decide he wants some."

"How stupid of me not to realize that," J.T. said quietly. "And are these other expenses for other necessities of life? Here are imported blueberries."

"For Great-Aunt Sophie." She was beginning to understand what he was saying. "These people are of the royal family, they are entitled to a few luxuries."

"Fresh salmon from Scotland?" J.T. questioned.

"For Aunt Bradley."

"How do you get these things during a war?"

Aria kept her face motionless. "My Aunt Bradley seems to have an 'arrangement' with a few pilots. I have never been inclined to look into the exact details of how she procures the supplies."

"I can imagine," J.T. said. "'Procure' might be the correct word. The Lanconian government pays for this and your Aunt Bradley—"

"Stop," Aria warned.

J.T. looked over the ledger at her. Minute by minute she was becoming more princesslike, more like the prig he had first met. "You've got your underwear back on, haven't you?" He was pleased to see her blush but she didn't relax her rigid posture. "Here," he said, holding out a stick of Juicy Fruit gum.

"Ooooh," she said with great pleasure in her voice. "*I* never got that reaction for anything I ever did."

She started chewing, the gum snapping. "You did, only you were making too much noise to hear me."

He looked at her with lowered lashes. "You'd better behave or I'll give you what you're asking for. Why don't you find something to do and stop sitting on the edge of your chair? You're giving me the heebie-jeebies."

"Sure thing, baby," she said, and got up.

He could hear her muttering "heebie-jeebies" under her breath, practicing the new word. It was difficult for him to concentrate on the books. The gum seemed to have transformed her back into *his* princess, the one who wore sundresses and pin-curled hair.

He forced himself to look back at the ledgers. As far as he could tell, the Lanconian royal family consisted of a bunch of parasites who had no idea they lived in a poor country that was surrounded by other countries at war. They were a large group of spoiled children who had never been made to grow up. If he had any control over the group, he would parcel out Aria's duties among them. That young Barbara would probably love getting out into the public and Gena could review troops. He didn't know what use Freddie, Nickie, and Toby could be but they could damn well sit through bug lectures. Great-Aunt Sophie could go to whatever ceremonies they had where cannons were shot off. At least she would be able to hear what was going on.

"What's that little smile for?" Aria asked.

J.T. leaned back in the chair. "I was thinking about your family."

"A bit of a mess, aren't they?" she said with some apology in her voice.

326

"Is that Princess Aria talking or Mrs. Montgomery?"

"American Aria," she said, slumping into a chair. "Freddie's snow cream seemed perfectly reasonable before, but it costs money, doesn't it? A lot of money."

"Too much."

"So what do we do?"

J.T. turned his head away from her for a moment. What do *we* do? He should have punched the king in the nose and hitchhiked out of the country before seeing her again. He was tempted to say, "Let's ask Count Julie," but he didn't.

Instead, he turned back to her and told her how he thought her work load could be shared by her relatives.

Aria was thoughtful. "They won't like it. Gena would enjoy looking at the young men of the Royal Guard—they're the only troops we have—and Aunt Sophie will *love* the cannons, but the others will protest."

"Then I'll have to persuade them. I mean, your husband will have to persuade them."

"My . . ." Aria said. "Oh yes, whoever I eventually marry."

There was a quick knock on the door and the doors were opened. "Your Royal Highness, Count Julian," said the guardsman.

Julian strode in, obviously already angry. "Aria, what are you doing in here alone with this man?"

Aria jumped out of her slouch and came to attention so quickly she swallowed her gum. "We are looking at accounts." Her eyes were wide.

"It won't hurt you," J.T. said under his breath. "Every kid in America would be dead if it did." He turned to Julian. "We were looking into Lanconia's debts and the princess is here so I can see that she's safe."

Julian looked at Aria as a father looks at a wayward child. "Aria, it is time for our ride."

Before Aria could reply, J.T. stepped in front of her. "The princess is busy. You got that, buster? *Busy.* Now skedaddle."

Julian gave J.T. a look of fury then turned on his heel and left. A guardsman closed the door behind him and J.T. thought he saw a glint of approval in the guard's eyes.

"Oh no," groaned Aria, sinking back into the chair. "Now you've done it. He'll never marry me now."

"Good!" J.T. said. "You deserve better than him."

"Where am I going to *find* better than him?"

"On any street corner in America."

"You really don't understand, do you? I have to marry someone with royal blood, someone who understands the monarchy, someone who—"

"Tell me about this Royal Guard of yours," he said, cutting her off. "Is it my imagination or do they all look alike?"

"They are matched."

"You mean like dishes?"

"Something like that. Their size is based on what is traditionally thought to be Rowan's size. They are from six foot one to two, have forty-eight-inch chests and thirty-two-inch waists. They cannot be larger or smaller. It is the greatest honor a Lanconian male can achieve to be a Royal Guard—but he must fit the uniform."

J.T. was thoughtful. "Forty-eight-inch chests don't grow, they have to be built. Do these guys have a training place?"

"Rowan's Field."

"Rowan again," J.T. groaned. "I think I've seen enough of these books for a while. We're going out to see the countryside. I want to see the grapes and I want you to tell me about this guard. Can they do more than open and close doors? And don't give me that princess look. Here, have some more gum," he said, leading her out the door.

Aria's dressers were horrified when she insisted on wearing a simple wool challis skirt and blouse and heavy-soled, short-heeled walking shoes when she planned to leave the palace grounds.

"But, Your Highness, please think of your responsibility to the people. They will expect to see a princess."

"And they'll see a human," Aria snapped. Lady Werta looked as if she were about to faint. "No, I don't want gloves and I'm going to let my hair hang." Aria swept from the room before they made her feel too guilty and so change her mind.

J.T. was outside her bedroom talking to one of the guardsmen, but he turned toward her when her door was opened. "You look great," he said, grinning, and Aria felt as if she had lost twenty pounds; her feet didn't quite touch the ground.

He led her down the stairs, quite improperly holding her arm, but she didn't reprimand him, not even after Aunt Bradley saw them and lifted her eyebrows. She led him to the garages at the back of the west wing and stood back and looked at the mountains while J.T. argued with a chauffeur about who was going to drive one of the cars. Just as she knew he would, J.T. won.

He backed out of the garage driving a cream-colored front-wheel-drive Cord, a low, sexy, gorgeous vehicle. "This is Aunt Bradley's car," Aria breathed, feeling very risqué as J.T. leaned across the seat and pushed the passenger door open to her. She could feel her chauffeur's horror at the gesture.

Aria rolled down the window and let her hair get mussed. She felt extraordinarily free and happy. She had a day of no duties, she was alone in a car with a handsome, sexy man, and she had left her heavy corset at home.

J.T. kept glancing at her until he could stand it no more. In a practiced American gesture, he put out his right hand, caught her by the back of the head, and pulled her over to kiss him while keeping his eyes on the road. "Good to see you again, baby," he said, releasing her.

She settled back in her seat, smiling. "Where are you taking me?"

"First we're going to your Royal Guard's training grounds. Ever been there?"

Aria laughed. "When I was fifteen I sneaked away one afternoon and hid in the bushes and watched the men train. They are all quite beautiful."

J.T. laughed. "They'll take away your princess badge if they find out."

She laughed again, feeling very unprincesslike.

The guards' training ground was nearly a mile from the palace on a broad plain that had always been free of trees and was traditionally used as the site of tournaments and trials by combat. Around the edge of the two-acre plain was a long, low open-front stone building.

When they were within sight of the men, J.T. stopped the car and looked. There were about a hundred and fifty men, all rather eerily the same size, all of them wearing nothing but a white garment that could only be described as a loincloth. Their nearly nude bodies rippled with muscles under sun-bronzed skin covered with sweat. They were involved in a great variety of sports: wrestling, archery, fighting with long thick sticks, sword fights with broadswords, hand-to-hand combat. Here and there was a gray-haired man wearing a red armband who now and then shouted at the combatants. Their gray hair did not lessen the magnificence of their bodies.

J.T. felt as if he had stepped into a time warp. This scene, these men with their old-fashioned weapons, their primitive garments, the stone shed in back, was something from long ago. "Straight out of your thirteenth-century Rowan, isn't it?" J.T. said softly, his voice filled with awe. Suddenly he realized he would like to train with these men. If there had to be fighting between men, it should be like this, not the dropping of bombs on anonymous thousands.

"Uh-oh, they've seen us," Aria said.

A moment later, one of the gray-haired men blew a whistle and the guardsmen disappeared from the field, returning in seconds wearing long gray robes and standing at attention in a perfect line. They were an impressive sight.

J.T. eased the car forward.

"They won't like that I'm here," Aria said.

"You're their princess, don't forget that."

"But they are very private people. Grans says—"

"Stick by me, honey, I'll protect you."

"Ha! They are *my* guard, *my* men, *my* . . ." She trailed off and smiled as the gray-haired man, now wearing a long, black robe, came forward to open her door.

"Your Highness," he said formally, "welcome."

J.T. and the captain of the guard looked one another over and judged each other quickly. "I need your help," J.T. said.

331

"You have it," the captain answered without question.

Medieval-looking wooden chairs were brought and J.T. and the captain were seated under one end of the stone building while Aria was given a chair several feet away. Contrary to Aria's belief that she would not be welcomed by the men, they made her a little *too* welcome for J.T.'s taste. One man brought out a fat-bellied guitar that J.T. supposed was a lute and began to strum it, another man offered her cakes from a plate, two other men held out silver goblets of drink. And whatever they were saying was putting an enormous smile on Aria's face. She looked like a princess of old surrounded by her handsome courtiers whose heavy, muscular legs stuck out bare beneath their scanty clothes.

The captain looked from Aria to J.T.'s frowning face and smiled. "We do not get many visitors to our training ground and our princess has never been here." He chuckled. "Except once when we were not supposed to know she was here."

J.T. smiled. "How much do you know about what is going on?"

"Someone shot at Her Royal Highness," the captain said, his mouth set in a grim line.

"It has been more than that." J.T. knew that he could trust this man. Perhaps because they were descended from the same warrior stock, but J.T. knew he could trust this man with his life. He told him that someone had tried to kill Aria in America. He told of the other attempts on her life and J.T. could feel the captain's growing anger.

"We have been told nothing of this," the older man seethed. "In the past hundred years we have been relegated to doing nothing but opening and closing doors. Our king may have forgotten our true use, but *we* have not. We are ready to lay down our lives for our king and his two granddaughters."

"And the rest of them be hanged," J.T. said. "I agree with you. I want her watched every minute of every day. I wish there were women who could stay with her in her bedroom. I don't trust any of those women with her now."

"Perhaps there is someone. Come with me."

J.T. was reluctant to leave Aria alone with those half-naked men but he followed the captain.

"There was a time," the captain said as they walked, "when Lanconian warriors were the finest in the world. Over the centuries most of the people have turned to farming but a few of us have kept the tradition of training. We are not as much in favor now since Lanconia has been declared a neutral country."

They turned a curve in the path and rounded a grove of trees. Opening before them was a small clearing and here ten women wearing white, draped garments that reached only to the tops of their magnificent legs were participating in games like the men's.

"My God," J.T. said with sharp intake of breath.

The captain smiled. "Centuries ago, the women were trained beside the men. Beautiful, aren't they?"

J.T. couldn't close his mouth as he looked at the six-foot-tall, bronzed goddesses wrestling and fighting. A whistle blew and the women lined up, and a dark-haired woman wearing a longer red garment started walking toward them.

The captain turned his back to her for a moment. "Jarnel trains the women. She is also my wife."

J.T.'s eyes were on the woman. "No wonder you stay so fit."

J.T. and the captain talked to Jarnel and it was agreed that, somehow, one of the guardswomen would be substituted for one of Aria's ladies-in-waiting.

Later, as he and the captain were walking back to the men's training ground, J.T. said, "Tell me, do the guardswomen welcome men like your men welcome the princess?"

"No," the captain answered. "Lanconian women are pursued. They do nothing to win a man; he must go to them. Of course there have been exceptions. In Rowan's day sometimes the women fought each other for a man. In fact, that was the case with Rowan himself."

"You mean this Rowan I keep hearing about was the prize in a contest? Some muscular broad *won* him?" J.T. laughed.

"I imagine the warriors looked somewhat like our guardswomen," the captain said mildly.

J.T. remembered the ten tall, beautiful women in the field behind him, their skin gleaming with sweat, and he stopped laughing.

It was nearly noon by the time Aria and J.T. drove off in the Cord, three carloads of guardsmen behind them in old but perfectly kept black Fords. J.T. wanted to see a vineyard. He followed the directions the captain had given him and arrived just as the workers were sitting down to their midday meal.

Aria often saw the city dwellers but these country people had too much work to do to stand in line to gawk at a pretty princess. They were stunned into speechlessness at the sight of her looking a great deal like their own daughters and sweethearts.

"Your . . . Your Highness," one woman stuttered while the others stood quietly, their lunches forgotten at their feet.

"May we join you?" J.T. asked. "We brought our own food."

The people nodded hesitantly.

Aria followed J.T. to the trunk of the car. "We did bring food? Are you sure this is all right? They don't seem very friendly."

"They're scared to death of Her Royal Highness but I bet they'll like Mrs. Montgomery."

He was right. It took Aria awhile to forget that she was a princess and the people a little longer to lose their awe of her, but it did happen. They ate and talked, Aria telling them about the wonders of America and the people answering J.T.'s questions about the drought and the state of the grapes.

The Lanconians were a tall, good-looking people, both men and women slim and muscular from years of going up and down steep hills carrying big baskets of produce. They planted on top of the hills and lived below in tiny villages.

Everyone worked, from toddler to ancient. Young women strapped babies to their backs and went up the hills. Quite often the men took care of the younger children and it wasn't unusual to see a fifty-year-old man trailed by three four-year-olds.

J.T. realized that he was looking at what had once been a great society but now he knew it was dying. There were so very few children in Lanconia. Here, sitting at lunch with twenty-seven people, he guessed the average age to be fifty-two. There were only four children under sixteen when there should have been a dozen or more. He knew that too often the young people left home at an early age, prowled the streets and cafes of Escalon for a while, then left the country altogether.

At three o'clock he realized the people were impatient with politeness and wanted to get back to work. He asked if they could see the vineyard.

He had been given a tour before but then he had

looked at the place with disgust. Now he wondered if there was something he could do to help the economy of the country.

Aria seemed to be happy, walking up the mountain with three women, one of whom had a baby that Aria seemed fascinated with, four guardsmen surrounding her about twenty feet away and watching the area with hawklike gazes.

The women started picking grapes and Aria, without thinking, joined them. He smiled at the looks on the faces of the Lanconian women but they recovered quickly and picked alongside their princess. Aria passed out sticks of Juicy Fruit and moments later he heard laughter.

He left her with the women and guards as he went back down the mountains to the old winery that was dug into the side of the hill. This year's grape crop was the best in four years, but it still wasn't enough to make a profit. The wine had to age for three years, so even if this year had been magnificent, it would be three years before the wine could be sold. And in three years' time hundreds more Lanconians would be forced to leave the country.

J.T. stood outside in the sunshine and held a bunch of ripe green grapes and watched the people carrying basket loads of grapes down the mountainside. If only there was a quick cash crop for grapes.

Raisins, he thought. Men at war living on canned field rations might welcome the freshness of raisins. Maybe he could persuade the U.S. government to buy raisins along with the vanadium. Maybe his majesty the king would refuse to allow American bases in Lanconia if America didn't buy raisins.

As J.T. thought, he wondered how the Lanconians would take to the idea of raisins. They were a proud people and they might refuse to have anything to do with something as lowly as a raisin.

"Have you ever thought of doing something with the grapes besides making wine?" he began, talking to the four older Lanconian men near him.

J.T. needn't have worried. Lanconians were proud but not stupidly so. They were willing to try anything to help their impoverished country. Their only concern was that if they used the grapes now for raisins, three years from now they would have no wine.

"Next year we irrigate and we have a bumper crop." The words weren't out of his mouth before he realized he wouldn't be there next year.

It was six before he got Aria back into the car and they headed back to the palace. She was sunburned, windblown, and tired—and he had never wanted anything so much in his life as he wanted to make love to her.

"Have a good time?" he asked in a voice that was little more than a whisper.

"Oh yes, a lovely time. You seemed to enjoy it too."

"I did," he said, somewhat surprised.

At the palace they were whisked back into the present. Lady Werta was there, angry beyond words at Aria. Julian was livid and wanted to discuss her behavior. J.T. thought a couple of her retainers were going to choke when Aria thanked her guardsmen for watching over her.

J.T. put his hands in his pockets and went off whistling.

He felt more secure now that the guardsmen were watching her. The day had been a good one and he didn't even mind the way Walters fussed over him. J.T. let the little man tell him all the gossip Aria's unusual day had caused. There were stories of the

crown princess drinking alone with goatherders, of
Her Royal Highness working as a field hand. And
some people were beginning to hate Lieutenant Montgomery, who was trying to make a monarchist country into a socialist one.

J.T. sat in the tub and smiled.

He didn't think he could face dinner with Aria's
disapproving relatives and he was pleased with the
palace system when he realized he could order dinner
to be taken wherever he wanted. Walters told him how
to get to the library and J.T. went there to eat and be
alone and think.

Aria left the drawing room as soon as she could get
away. It had been a heavenly day of laughter and then
she had returned to the palace to find everyone
treating her as if she were a traitor to her country.
Julian was angry because she had been alone with
"that despicable American." The Lord High Chamberlain had berated her because he thought she was
actually Kathy Montgomery and had been out with
her husband and because her behavior was very
common.

But no matter what anyone said, Aria was deli-
ciously happy. Maybe she had been so demanding all
her life because, in her heart, she felt herself to be
useless. Today she got some idea of how important
her role was to her country.

And how important Jarl Montgomery was to her
life.

It seemed that the happiest times in her life had
been spent with him: cooking out on the beach,
making love on the stairs, even crying in his arms had
been a pleasure.

She had been very disappointed when he had not

come to dinner. She walked down the hall and saw one of the Royal Guardsmen standing as if he were a statue instead of a man. A few days ago she would never have considered speaking to a guard.

"Excuse me," she said politely, "do you know where Lieutenant Montgomery is?"

"In the library, Your Highness," he answered.

"Thank you."

"You are most welcome."

She saw the briefest hint of a smile on his handsome face. Please and thank you, she thought. Magic words.

She found her husband in the big library bent over one of the four long walnut tables, books scattered around him, the green shaded lamp on while he sketched on a pad of paper.

"Hello," she said when he didn't look up. "Did you have dinner? What are you doing?"

He rubbed his eyes and smiled at her. "Come here, honey, and look at this."

He showed her a drawing of gears and pulleys that meant nothing to her. She moved closer to him as he began to explain his ideas for bringing the grapes down from the hills via a motorized pulley system. He planned to use the motors of the derelict cars rusting in the fields of Lanconia to run the pulleys. "That'll free more people to dry the grapes," he explained.

"Dried grapes?" she asked.

As he explained about the raisins, she looked at him—and realized that she loved him. This was where she wanted to be more than anywhere else in the world: sitting here at night close to him and talking about future plans. She wished she were wearing a nightgown and they were in their little Key West home.

J.T. was asking her a question. "What?" she asked.

"Your little count mentioned a radio. Is there a two-way radio around here that I can use to call the States?"

"I guess so. Who are you going to call?"

J.T. pushed his chair back and stood, and when she stayed seated he took her hand and pulled her up. "Come on, let's go find the radio. I'm going to call my father and see if he can get Frank out here." Before she asked, he explained. "Frank is my seventeen-year-old Taggert cousin—knows more about cars than anybody else alive." He was holding Aria's hand as he strode down the long library then out into the corridor. "Last I heard Frank was mad because his father refused to let him join up. Frank in a good mood is difficult enough but Frank in a bad mood is not something I'd like to see."

"And you're going to invite him here?"

"We need him. If you had ships, I'd be able to help, but cars I don't know too much about." He stopped and asked one of the guardsmen where the radio was. Of course the guardsman knew and Aria led J.T. down to the northeast chamber of the vaulted cellars.

Chapter Twenty

ARIA came awake slowly, rubbing her eyes and yawning. She had been up late last night with J.T. and the man who she found out was the Royal Herald. His predecessors had cried the news throughout the towns but now he radioed his news. It was the first Aria had heard of him.

It took two hours to get through to Maine in the U.S., then they had to wait while someone drove to J.T.'s father's house and got him. Aria got to speak to Mr. Montgomery for a moment to ask him to say hello to Mrs. Montgomery.

Later, J.T. had mumbled something about his parents making his life miserable when this was over.

Mr. Montgomery said he would send young Frank out as soon as possible.

It was midnight before J.T. walked Aria to her bedroom. He glanced at the two guards flanking the doors and abruptly left her standing alone.

Now she stretched and wondered what he had

341

planned for today. She knew that at ten A.M. she had to be sixty miles south of Escalon at a vineyard for the blessing of the harvest. She wondered what J.T. would do and say today, how he would make the day interesting.

Her dressers drew her hair back into a perfectly neat and tight chignon. They snapped the steel fasteners of the long Merry Widow and dressed her in a somber black suit with a big diamond brooch on the left shoulder. For a moment, Aria considered exchanging the brooch for the gaudy enameled parrot she had bought in Key West on a shopping spree with Dolly, but she didn't have enough courage to carry out her idea.

Outside her room, J.T. was not waiting for her and he wasn't in the dining room. She was beginning to learn to ask a guardsmen if she wanted to know anything. J.T. had left the palace before six A.M. and had given no hint as to when he would return.

She waited until the last minute but she had to reach the Blessing Festival on time. She tried not to let her face fall when she saw Count Julian standing by the car door. His expression was stern.

"I thought perhaps you were going to discard your obligations again today," he said in reproach.

She didn't answer him because she felt too guilty about yesterday. She had had a good time yesterday. But princesses weren't supposed to have fun. They were to fulfill obligations, not play with the peasants' babies and exchange gossip about American movie stars.

"Aria, people are beginning to talk," Julian began once they were in the long black car. A Royal Guardsman sat beside the chauffeur behind the glass partition, and a carful of guardsmen followed them. "The king is too ill to take the firm hand with you that he should so I am left with the duty. You are behaving like a . . . a woman of the streets with that crude, vulgar American. You spent every waking moment with him yesterday and it is all anyone could speak of this morning. If you care nothing for your own family, think of what the servants say. They do not want a princess who is one of them—they want a *princess*. I hear you even dared to invade the Royal Guard's training ground. Have you no respect for the privacy of those men?"

Aria sat in the seat, her hands tightly clasped in her lap, feeling more awful with his every word. Then, to her utter astonishment, the guardsman in the front seat turned and *winked* at her! She came very close to giggling. What especially surprised her was that he had obviously heard every word Julian had said—and she had always believed the partition to be sound-proof.

Julian kept fussing and Aria kept listening, but she wasn't worried any longer. Maybe her family was ashamed of her, but it didn't look as if her people were.

Meeting the people today was very different from yesterday. The people were in their Sunday best and were using their best formal manners. They smiled at her, but no one laughed and they just asked her questions. It was really quite tedious for her.

The people seemed pleased to see Count Julian and repeatedly asked when the wedding was going to be. "But I'm already married," she wanted to tell them.

It was one o'clock before they were on their way back to the car and over the heads of the people Aria could smell food. There was a break in the crowd, and some distance away, at the side of a tiny house, a woman was ladling something into a piece of bread and handing it to a little boy. Aria knew what it was; she'd had one as a child. A piece of thick Lanconian bread, still warm from the oven, with a thick, chewy crust, was split and inside was ladled a generous scoop of spicy chicken stew made with grapes. Fresh goat cheese was sprinkled on top.

Aria wasn't even aware of what she was doing, but she turned away from where Julian waited by the open car door, started saying, "Excuse me," and made her way through the crowd to the woman's house. "May I have one?" she asked the astonished woman.

The old woman just stood there and stared.

"Gramma!" the little boy said loudly, bringing the woman to her senses. She spooned stew into the bread, sprinkled it with cheese, and held it out to Aria.

"Thank you very much," Aria said, biting into it. She suddenly became aware of the silent crowd behind her. She turned, a bit of sauce on her upper lip. "It's delicious," she said, and the crowd cheered.

A guardsman handed her a clean handkerchief to use as a napkin and she saw that there were four guardsmen near her. They had followed her as she went through the crowd.

"Princess," she heard, and looked down to see the little boy holding out a rough stoneware mug to her. "It's buttermilk."

Aria smiled and took the mug. "Thank you," she said.

The little boy grinned. "You're not like a real princess at all."

"Thank you again," she said, making the crowd laugh. The guardsmen parted the crowd as she made her way back to the car.

Julian was fuming. He lectured her all the way back to the palace as she greedily ate her sandwich and drank her buttermilk. He wanted to throw the mug out the window but she wouldn't let him.

When they arrived at the palace, the guardsman who had sat in the front seat opened the door for her and she handed him the mug. "I would like to thank that woman for her food. Would you please find out what she needs?"

"I saw an empty chicken coop," the guardsman said softly.

"Fill it," Aria said before Julian gave her a sharp look. "Do you know where Lieutenant Montgomery is?" she whispered.

"With the guards, Your Highness."

Aria turned her head so Julian wouldn't see her talking. "Would you please see that my horse is ready in twenty minutes?"

The guardsman merely nodded as they rounded the car and she was within earshot of Count Julian.

Aria had some difficulty escaping Julian and she saw a few other members of her family looking askance at her as she ran across the courtyard and made her way to the stables. Her horse was saddled and waiting for her and four Royal Guardsmen were ready to ride with her.

It was a matter of minutes before she reached the guardsmen's training field then halted her horse to watch the men. J.T. was with the guardsmen, wearing the white loincloth and battling with a stick against a guardsman. J.T. was as tall as the guardsmen but paler skinned and not as heavy. He wasn't very good with the stick either and the guardsman he was sparring with seemed to be toying with him.

"He will learn," said the guard beside Aria. "In another year or so he will be the best fighter in Lanconia."

Aria smiled at that, but then she remembered that in a year J.T. would probably be back in America and she would be married to Julian.

At that moment J.T. glanced at her, she waved, and the next moment J.T. was sent sprawling on the ground.

"Keep your mind on what you are doing," the guardsman standing over J.T. yelled.

Aria went running to J.T. "Are you hurt?" she asked as she knelt beside him. She glared up at the guardsman. "I'll have your head if you've hurt him."

J.T. smiled at her as he rubbed his bruised shoulder. "I may die of embarrassment but nothing else. Tell Rax you didn't mean what you said."

Aria was aware that many of the guardsmen were now watching them with curiosity. She genuinely wished she had not made such a fool of herself, but before she could say a word, Gena came running across the field. She was wearing practically nothing: a short-skirted, one-shoulder dress, a heavy gold bracelet on her right upper arm.

"J.T. darling," Gena said, falling to her knees by his side. "Are you all right? Have you been injured?"

Aria didn't speak but slowly rose with great dignity and walked away. She reached her horse before J.T. caught up with her. He grabbed her arm and pulled her into the trees. Aria squirmed to get away from him.

"Come on, baby, don't be mad," he coaxed, running his hands up her arms.

His bare skin was hot and sweaty and her face was inches from his chest.

"I had to do something with her. She was following me everywhere, so I gave her to the women to train. It's keeping her out of trouble."

"And *you* enjoy her. No doubt the sight of her in that little skirt—" She broke off as he kissed her.

She was breathless when he finished and she clung to him, her cheek against his damp chest.

"We shouldn't do this," he said after a long while. "This kind of thing will make our parting harder. Tell me what you did this morning."

"Gena is so pretty," Aria said, holding on to him.

He pushed her away just enough to look at her. "Not as pretty as you. Not as smart as you. Not as much woman as you."

"Really?" she asked, beginning to smile.

"Really." He kissed her again, but lightly. "Now tell me what you did. Did the guard protect you? Were you safe? Come back to the field with me and I'll give you some beer and we can talk."

Aria ended by spending the afternoon at the guards' training ground. For the first time she met the guards-women and she saw Gena trying to learn to wrestle. The men were watching the event as if it were very serious, but Aria saw the light in their eyes. She was sorry she had been jealous of her little sister when she saw the way Gena looked up at her with such adoration in her eyes.

Aria leaned toward J.T. "This Frank who is to come, what is he like?" she asked.

J.T. looked at Gena and began to smile. "He may be exactly right for her, although I don't think he'll want to stay here. He won't fit any more than I do."

Aria felt like laughing because if anyone fit it was Jarl. He was dressed in a white robe, his big legs bare, sitting on one of the wooden chairs, drinking beer. He could have been one of the guardsmen. The captain of the guard caught her eye and smiled as if he knew what she was thinking.

Five minutes later all hell broke loose because Julian arrived in a long black limousine. He was horrified by Aria's common behavior and told her she was late for tea with the Ladies' Historical Guild.

Aria left with him, surrounded by guardsmen, before he saw Gena in her skimpy dress.

For four days Aria tried to behave herself. She rode with Julian and six guardsmen in the morning, then answered requests from people until midmorning, and at ten she left the palace to attend one function after another. She did not see Jarl. He did not come to dinner nor did he attend one evening's festivities when the Lanconian Opera Company performed. The soprano was not very good and the tenor kept stepping in front of her so the audience could not see her—which made the soprano angry and her singing worse. Aria was afraid she might nod off.

On the fifth morning, she was having breakfast when J.T. strode into the room. He looked tired. "Frank's plane is about to land. You coming?"

Aria gulped a cup of tea and left with him to the astonishment of her relatives at the table. He didn't speak until they were in the backseat of the car and on their way to the airport. He turned to her and his eyes seemed to eat her.

"I've missed you," he whispered, then took her hand in his and held it tightly. They were silent for a moment, then both began to speak at once.

J.T. told her how he had been working eighteen-hour days, traveling all over Lanconia, trying to educate the farmers about selling their grapes as raisins. He had twice been in radio contact with

President Roosevelt and it looked like America was going to buy raisins. "But not very many," J.T. said. "America has California with millions of raisins." He sighed. "There has to be something else we can do to help this country stand on its own feet."

"We," Aria whispered. "We."

The two American airplanes were just landing when they arrived at the airport. Out of the first plane came several older American men then a hundred soldiers. These were the men to mine the vanadium.

Off the second plane came a six-foot-tall man who could have been twenty or forty-five. He had dark hair, dark eyes, and a big, thick body that looked like it could carry a great deal more weight than it did and a handsome face set in a scowl.

"There's Frank," J.T. said, taking her hand and pulling her behind him.

"*He* is seventeen years old? Why is he angry?"

"He was born angry but don't let him scare you. He's a good kid."

Aria stood back while J.T. and Frank shook hands.

"This is Her Royal Highness, Princess Aria," J.T. said.

"Pleased," the boy said, holding out his hand to shake hers, and Aria accepted it. He seemed to dismiss her as he looked back at J.T. "When do we get to work? I brought crates of tools and I'm ready as soon as they unload them."

Aria looked back at the plane in time to see three children being helped down the stairs. She touched J.T.'s arm. "Who are they?"

J.T. looked at one of the pilots near him. "Who are the kids?"

"Orphans. Their relatives were killed in France and a couple of guys smuggled them on board. We're stuck with them until we get home where we hope we can get somebody to take them."

Aria had no idea she was speaking; the words might have been someone else's. "I'll take them," she said.

"But Your Highness . . ." Lady Werta had followed Aria and J.T. as soon as possible to the airport and now she was giving warning looks to Aria.

Aria looked at the pilot, her chin up, her voice clear and loud. "I will take these children and Lanconia will take all the orphaned children you can find."

The pilot smiled indulgently. "Lady, there's a war going on and there are thousands of orphans out there. This place doesn't look like it could feed them."

At that J.T. stepped forward. "If Her Royal Highness says she wants children, then she's gonna get them. We'll take any children of any country and don't worry about food, we'll feed them."

The pilot obviously didn't like J.T.'s attitude. "Okay, buddy, you're on. If it's kids you want, it's kids you'll get."

Feeling very pleased with herself and with her husband, Aria went to the frightened French children and began to talk to them. Lady Werta didn't want her to touch the dirty children but Aria waved her away.

In the car on the way back to the palace, Aria held the two-year-old on her lap, while the three- and four-year-olds sat on either side of her. J.T. and Frank talked about making pulleys for getting the grapes off the hills.

At the palace, Gena came running to greet them, as usual, a little late and more than a little flushed after her run down the stairs. Her cheeks were pink, a curl had escaped her careful coiffure—and she looked divine.

Aria turned to greet her sister but then Gena's eyes widened and she came to an abrupt halt. A second later she moved past Aria as if in a dream and stopped in front of Frank Taggert and just stood there staring. Frank's angry look left his face as he gaped at Gena, his lower jaw slightly dropped.

"I think they want an introduction," J.T. said, smiling. He lifted a hand of each teenager and put them together. "Gena, Frank. Frank, Gena. Now, Gena, take Frank outside to play."

As if sleepwalking, the two teenagers started down the hall.

"I'm not sure . . ." Aria began. "I mean, Gena is . . . And Frank is . . ."

"Young. Both of them are young. Come on, let's get something to eat. I bet these kids are starving."

With one more glance at the backs of Gena and Frank, Aria followed J.T. toward the dining room.

That night Aria bathed the children and had beds put in her bedroom. The next morning four couples begged to see her, said they had heard of the children, and asked to be allowed to raise them as their own.

Aria didn't want to part with the children, but she turned them over to the couple that spoke French.

Forty-eight hours later an American plane landed and it was filled with one hundred and seventeen children, mostly French but some Italian. They arrived just as the entire royal family was assembled to watch a ceremonial parade celebrating the defeat of the northern tribes in 1084 A.D.

The Royal Guard brought the children to the capital city on horseback, in jeeps, on motorcycles, and in goat carts. The parade came to a halt. J.T. began thrusting children into the arms of the royal family.

After some initial protests from the family members, the dirty, tired, scared children were taken back to the palace, where tub after tub was filled with hot water and the scrubbing began.

Freddie, Nickie, and Toby found they had a new audience for their stories of their bravery against ferocious fawns and demented doves. Lady Barbara chose three pretty little Italian girls and washed them herself. Great-Aunt Sophie bellowed orders to two big boys who had fought all the way on the plane and they obeyed her meekly. Aunt Bradley chose two handsome boys of about fourteen.

Aria and J.T. parceled out the other children to various retainers until everyone was scrubbing behind ears.

"That's it," J.T. said. He and Aria had personally bathed fourteen kids and sent them off with the ladies-in-waiting to be fed and dressed in whatever could be found for them.

They were sitting on the damp marble floor of her bathroom, alone in the suite.

"Why are you looking at me like that?" she asked.

"I was remembering the woman on the island who demanded everything. You wouldn't even let a commoner sit with you and now you wash these very common children."

"Lanconia needs children. Whatever I have done, I have done for my country."

"Have you?" His eyes were beginning to grow hot. "Has everything been for your country?"

He was on her in seconds and their hands tore at each other's wet, soapy clothes, their hunger making them urgent.

"Baby, oh baby, I've missed you," J.T. kept saying as his hands grabbed her breasts.

They made love on the cold marble floor, then J.T. lifted her and set her on the side of the tub and attacked her with a renewed, driving force until she fell backward into the dirty water. He didn't even pause but grabbed the plug chain and kept up his long, deep strokes as the water drained.

They finished together, wrapped inside the marble of the sunken tub.

J.T. was the first to move. Quite suddenly, he looked at her as if she were something horrible and got out of the tub. "I have to go. I have to get out of here," he mumbled as he began pulling on his uniform. He had to get out, had to get away from her as quickly as possible. He murmured good-bye to her then fled the room as if a thousand demons were on his heels.

He ignored the guardsmen standing at the door as he hurried down the corridor, down the stairs and out into the garden. He made it to the King's Garden before stopping. As he lit a cigarette, his hands were shaking.

Seduction, he thought. Everything about the country was seductive.

Whenever he wanted food, it was there waiting for him. He dropped his clothes wherever they fell and minutes later they were gone. There were always silent people standing nearby waiting to obey his merest wish. If he wanted a car, he merely had to ask and it was readied for him.

And the choices he had! He could drive or be driven. He could get up early or sleep late. He could do nothing or work twenty hours a day. He could swim, ride a horse, climb a mountain, train with athletes, walk through acres of beautiful gardens. The freedom of so many choices was intoxicating.

J.T. leaned against a tree and inhaled on the cigarette.

And there was Aria—the most seductive of all. He

had looked at her tonight, her dress damp from the children's bathwater, and he had remembered her on the island. The king had said she was a warm and kind person but J.T. hadn't believed it. She was, but she had covered it with her haughtiness, and her rules to live by.

He understood better now, understood how she had been trained to believe that the world was her servant. He wondered what he would be like if he had been raised like she had. Would he be like Toby and pout because there was a tiny bit of green on one of his strawberries? Would he get so used to cashmere sweaters that he would toss them on the floor like Gena did? Would he become so used to the servants that he would walk in and out of rooms and not see them? Would he believe he was someone else's superior by divine right?

He knew how bad the atmosphere of this place was, but he was also feeling seduced by it, sucked into the vortex of it. Ever since he was a child he had loved hot chocolate. He had never mentioned it because he knew that people—these unbelievably well-trained servants—watched what he ate and drank and made sure that what he liked was always near. Now Walters brought him a pot of hot chocolate as soon as J.T. woke and pulled the bell by his bed.

For the last several days, ever since he had felt confident that the Royal Guard could protect Aria, he had worked long hard hours. He had enlisted a couple of Aria's secretaries, both intelligent men who generally had too little to do, to help him find out who needed money or who would most benefit from Aria's death. Aria walked about the countryside as if there had never been an attempt on her life, but he never forgot for a moment. He had spent hours with the kitchen staff, much to the chagrin of Aria's butler,

354

who considered J.T. part of the royal family, trying to find out what gossip he could. But as far as he could tell, no one knew anything.

He was no closer to finding who had tried to murder Aria than he ever was.

He had tried his best to treat his time in Lanconia as a job and nothing else, but he wasn't succeeding. When he and Aria had parted the first time, he had been so angry he was almost glad to get rid of her. He still remembered his fury when he had found out that she had tricked him and he was to remain in Lanconia forever. At the time all he could think of was that he was a sailor and she was asking him to live inland. He had also been enraged that he had been tricked so easily. His temper hadn't been helped by her grandfather ordering him to remain in Lanconia.

But now, a few weeks later, he understood more of what it meant to be part of the royal family. He saw how much Aria meant to the people. He had been among them and heard the special tone of reverence they used when referring to her.

He finished his cigarette, crushed it under his foot, and smiled as he remembered the day they had gone to see the vineyard. She hadn't been a princess then, she had just been his girl, and he had been proud of her. He had watched the faces of the people, seen how wary they had been of Aria, then he had seen how much they had *liked* her. Ol'-fashioned *liked* her, not because they were supposed to, but because she was pleasant and amusing and interested in them.

It had been so very, very difficult to leave her that night. It would have been perfectly natural to climb into bed with her, just as every husband had a right to do. But he knew better than to touch her because he knew she was borrowed and he had to give her back.

He had stayed away from her after that day, deliberately trying to forget her and hoping that she would forget him. He had felt his chest tighten every time he saw her with her little count, but he had not interfered. Of course he had to admit, though, that some of the gossip had given him great pleasure. Aria had pushed through the crowds and eaten a sandwich made by a peasant woman—and later she had sent the woman a flock of chickens in gratitude. He doubted if she had any idea how such actions pleased the people of Lanconia.

So far, J.T. had been able to force himself to stay away from her but sometimes he couldn't control himself. When she had shown up at the guards' training ground and threatened a guard's life as if she were a warrior queen of old, he had been very pleased. And then her jealousy attack over Gena later! It had been a woman, not a crown princess, who had stormed off that field. Then he had had to sit back and watch her ushered away by that pompous little count. The twerp didn't understand that what Aria did outside her official duties was more important than having tea with a bunch of fat, pedigreed women.

The captain of the guard had put his hand on J.T.'s arm just as J.T. was about to nail the little overbearing fop.

So now, J.T. had done the worst thing he could have: he'd made love to her again. Not really the long, slow all-night lovemaking that he dreamed of at night, but he had attacked her with all the pent-up passion that he felt every time he saw her. And she had responded in just the way he remembered.

He had to stop! He had to keep his hands off of her and his mind on the work that needed doing. He had asked the guardsmen to be especially vigilant in the coming days because he felt that another attempt would soon be made on Aria's life. This time he was sure the murderer would be caught, and as soon as he was, J.T. meant to return to America.

He closed his eyes, smelled the pine trees and the soft mountain air blowing across the acres of flowers that were planted everywhere, and tried to remember the sea. He would marry some pretty little woman who liked the sea and after the war he would settle in Warbrooke, work in the family's shipyard, and raise a few kids. He wanted only the average things in life, nothing special. No kingdom to rule. No gold-plated throne to sit on. No crown to wear. No pretty princess to make him laugh.

"Damn!" he cursed aloud. Maybe he'd go wake up Frank and they could work on some more plans, or better yet, they could start rebuilding a few car engines. He had never seen people who knew as little about machine maintenance as these Lanconians. What they needed were a few good vocational schools to teach the young people how to maintain equipment. And why wasn't there a good agricultural college here? And why weren't the girls learning to be nurses and secretaries?

He stopped and took a deep breath. Lanconia wasn't his responsibility. In another few weeks he would be gone and what King Julian and Queen Aria did was their business.

As he passed the garage, he saw that all the lights were on and he heard Frank Taggert's deep, angry voice. "A *crescent* wrench, not a ratchet wrench."

"How am I supposed to know which is which?" J.T. heard Gena say with just as much anger. "I'm a princess, not an auto mechanic."

"You have yet to prove to me you're worth anything. *This* is a crescent wrench. Oh, honey, don't cry."

J.T. laughed in the darkness and thought it would

be better not to disturb the two of them. It looked like Gena wouldn't be following him anymore. Probably tomorrow she would be wondering what she ever saw in somebody as old as him.

Smiling, he went up to his lonely, empty bedroom. At least somebody somewhere was happy.

Chapter Twenty-one

SLOWLY, Aria got out of the car at her grandfather's hunting lodge. It was dusk and she was tired after a long day of meetings with the Americans, but she so badly wanted to talk to her grandfather. It had been a harrowing day trying to bargain with the Americans over the price of the vanadium. Julian had insisted that she sit back and allow him to handle the negotiations but Aria soon realized he knew no more about bargaining than she did. Unwisely, she suggested they ask Lieutenant Montgomery to attend the meeting. Julian turned furious eyes on her until she was quiet.

After two hours, Julian seemed satisfied but Aria was not. She sent for Lieutenant Montgomery. He arrived wearing a sweat-stained undershirt, and when he saw the contract the Americans were offering, he laughed. Thirty minutes later he had sold half as much of the vanadium for twice as much money. "We'll negotiate for the rest of it later," he said. To Aria's disbelief all the Americans seemed happy with the deal and very pleased with J.T., yet they gave looks of contempt to Julian. Aria didn't understand at all because she would have thought the Americans would have liked Julian better.

After the meeting she wanted to talk to J.T. but he brushed her aside, saying he had to get back to the engines. She had felt rejected, and worst of all, she felt lonely. The rest of the day she had performed her duties but her heart hadn't been in them. At four P.M. she told her secretary to call her grandfather and tell him she was coming to visit him.

Lady Werta had nearly died when she heard of Aria's planned visit but Aria was getting good at ignoring the woman.

And now she was here and Ned was opening the front door to her. "He is in the garden, Your Highness," Ned said, bowing to her. "I have presumed to prepare a supper for you and set it in the garden. His Majesty said you wanted to be alone."

"Yes," she said as she hurried forward. Now that she was this near, she desperately wanted to see her grandfather. He was standing under a big elm tree and waiting for her with open arms. To the world he was a king but to her he was her grandfather, someone who had held her on his lap and read her fairy tales. With her mother and the rest of the world she had had to be a princess but with her grandfather she could be a little girl.

He held her close, his big, heavy body enveloping her, and she felt safe and protected for the first time in a long while. She could feel tears gathering in her eyes. She who a few months ago never cried seemed to always be crying now.

Her grandfather held her at arm's length and studied her. "Sit down here and eat," he said gruffly.

"Ned's given us enough to feed Rowan's army. It's about time you came to see me."

Aria took a seat and gave him a guilty little smile. She could feel herself becoming a little girl again, especially when she saw a dishful of the tiny chocolate cakes Ned had made for her, just as he had done all her life. But she had no appetite.

"What's on your mind?" the king asked.

Aria hesitated. How could she burden her grandfather with her problems? He was an old man and not well. She took a seat across the table from him.

The king raised one eyebrow at her. "Turning coward on me, are you? Has someone shot at you again? Or tried to drown you? And how's that American husband of yours doing with the car engines?"

Aria choked, and while her eyes watered and she gulped hot tea, her grandfather smiled at her.

"Why is it that young people think age brings stupidity? We're smart enough to raise children and run our lives for fifty-odd years but when we turn sixty, young people assume we're senile. Aria, I know *everything*. I know you were kidnapped in America and I was told you were dead. I knew there would be a scandal if you were killed on American soil, so I sent Cissy in your place."

"But I thought—"

"That Cissy wanted to be queen? She's got too much sense for that."

Aria was silent for a moment. "I see."

Her grandfather reached across the table to take her hand. "No you don't see at all. You aren't easily replaced if that's what you're thinking. I went through hell when I thought you were dead." He squeezed her hand. "You can't imagine my joy when the American president radioed me that you were safe and well. Of course by that time you were already married. He apologized for that and offered to have the marriage annulled and you returned to me."

Aria's head came up. "But you didn't."

"For all I knew, it was a love match. After all, he had rescued you from being killed. I was very grateful to the man."

Aria was pushing a bit of thinly sliced beef about on her plate. "So you let me stay with the man and fall in love with him." There was bitterness in her voice.

The king speared a turkey leg. "Why don't you tell me about that place where you stayed? Awfully hot, wasn't it? And whatever was that photo in the newspaper? Was that actually your lieutenant's mother? Good-looking woman she looked to be. My sources said you cooked dinner *and* did the laundry. Not possible, Aria, really not possible."

Aria gave her grandfather one of her American grins and started talking. As much as listening to her, the king watched her, saw the way she relaxed her body when she talked about America and the friends she had made there. He laughed with her when she told of learning to dress herself, of getting the money confused and tipping taxi drivers hundred-dollar bills. She laughed at how obnoxious she was on the island and told how she had started to eat the shrimp raw. She talked of the glorious freedom of going shopping, then went into a ten-minute tirade about the monotony of doing housework.

And every other word was "Jarl." It was how Jarl reacted to everything, whether an action made him angry or happy, how astonished he had been when she had dressed as Carmen Miranda (Aria stood and did a quick rendition of "Chica Chica"), how furious he had been when he had found out he was supposed to remain married to her. She told how proud he had been of her when she took the orphaned children. She talked of how magnificent he was when he had saved her from being shot.

She spent thirty minutes telling of all the things Jarl had done in Lanconia. "He has sold the grapes to America and he's bringing them down from the mountains with engines. This morning at breakfast he talked of schools to teach the young people how to do things so they won't leave Lanconia. He says the country could move into the twentieth century with a lot of work. Jarl said that Lanconia has a great deal of potential, that all it takes is know-what—no, I mean, know-how. American slang is so difficult to remember. And Jarl dealt with the Americans for the vanadium. He only sold them the rights to mine one site because he said it might be worth more later. The Americans said he was a fool but I don't think so, and they didn't really look as if they thought so either. And this morning Freddie got very angry because there was no snow for his snow cream. The Exchequer says Jarl has cut fifteen percent off the palace's budget. And the Royal Guardsmen adore him. He wrestles with them and he says it's a shame that over the centuries they've been relegated to door openers." Suddenly she stopped, out of breath and a bit embarrassed. She took a deep drink of her tea.

"And how is Count Julian?" the king asked, looking at her over his beer mug.

To her disbelief, Aria put her face in her hands and burst into tears. "Oh, Grans, I love Jarl so much. Why doesn't he love me in return? He is so very, very good for Lanconia. We need him so much. What can I do to make him stay? How can I bear to give him up?"

The king was big and Aria was thin and light, so he had no trouble pulling her into his lap and holding her as he did when she was a little girl. "You are asking him to give up his country. You want to keep what you have, yet you ask that he make many sacrifices."

"But it's not the same," she sniffed. "He is merely one person in his country. He is not a king or a prince. His father has other sons to run his business. If I were not a crown princess, I would go with him to his country. I would follow him anywhere. I would give up . . . I would give up Lanconia for him."

The king was quiet for a moment. "Thinking of abdicating, are you?" he asked softly. "Then Gena would rule Lanconia. Perhaps she could bring Lanconia into the twentieth century."

"Gena will do only what she is told," Aria said in disgust. "If I were to abdicate, Julian would no doubt ask for her hand in marriage—or rather ask for her throne in marriage," she said bitterly.

"Ah," the king said. "Tell me about Julian. I thought his father trained him to be a king."

Aria sat up in her grandfather's lap, pulled a handkerchief from his shirt pocket, and blew her nose loudly. "He was trained to be what kings *used* to be. He stays in the palace all day, doing heaven knows what, while the people of Lanconia are leaving by the truck load because there are no jobs. He gets angry with me because I eat a peasant's meal—a meal prepared by one of my own people! He told me he desperately wanted to marry me, that he . . ."

"Desired you?" the king supplied.

"Yes, he said that but it was a lie. He will do anything to get my throne. But all he wants from Lanconia is the prestige of being a prince consort and the luxury of the palace. He is terrified of being poor. But poverty isn't so bad. I know."

The king's voice was very quiet. "Aria, do you think he would kill you if he thought he couldn't marry you?"

"Perhaps, but then the first attempt was when we were firmly engaged."

"Firmly? And you aren't now?"

Tears formed in her eyes again. "I am Mrs. Jarl Montgomery for as long as I can be. He may not want me, but I want him for as long as I can have him."

The king hugged her. "I doubt if he doesn't want you. In fact, my guess is that he is going through hell right now."

She pulled away from him and smiled. "Do you think so? Do you really think so?"

The king smiled back at her. "Agony. Torture. Excruciating pain."

Aria's smile broadened. "What can I do to make his pain worse? How can I make him love me so much that he will never leave me?"

The king took her chin in his hand. "I asked him to stay to protect you. Now he has the guard protecting you, so why is he still here? Why didn't he go home last week?"

Aria's eyes widened as she thought about this. "I think I'm hungry. I think I'll eat that whole plate of chocolates and do you think Ned could open a bottle of champagne? *Lanconian* champagne?"

The king laughed. "Go tell Ned to open two bottles and get off my leg before it dies and get me a clean handkerchief, you've soaked this one. Really, Aria, didn't anyone ever teach you any manners?"

She laughed as she got up. "I guess they didn't take." She turned and started running across the lawn toward the house.

The king crossed his hands on his belly and smiled contentedly.

J.T. woke instantly, at the first sound coming from behind the panel that led down to the concealed staircase. Silently, he left the bed and made his way toward the panel. His service revolver was in the drawer by the bed and he got it as he moved.

With the revolver held ready, he waited for the door to open. It creaked on its hinges, then whoever was opening it stopped until it was silent again and pushed the door further open.

"Freeze," J.T. said, lowering the pistol.

His answer was a hiccup.

"Gena?" he asked.

"Gena!" Aria said, her voice just a bit slurred. "Gena!"

J.T. backed away from her as if she were diseased and turned on a floor lamp. Aria was clutching a bottle of champagne and wearing a thin, clinging bathrobe that looked as if she wore nothing underneath. "Get out of here," he said under his breath.

She took a step forward. "But, Jarl, aren't you glad to see me?"

"Aria, are you drunk?"

"I believe I am, but since I have never been drunk before, I'm not sure if I am. How does one know?"

J.T. backed away from her until he was against the wardrobe. "Why did you come here? Someone might have seen you."

Aria advanced until she was just a few steps away from him. "I came to spend the night with you," she whispered.

He started to say something in protest but then Aria dropped her robe. She was not wearing anything underneath and the sight of her nude body made him forget his protests. He was wearing only his pajama bottoms and he opened his arms to her, feeling her bare breasts against his chest.

He kissed her neck and cheeks and lips hungrily. "You shouldn't be here," he said, his lips trailing hot kisses up and down her neck and shoulders. "You have a reputation to uphold. A royal princess cannot—"

She put her mouth on his. "I am your wife tonight, not Her Royal Highness."

He pulled back and looked at her. "I like that," he whispered. "I like that very much."

Bending, he picked her up in his arms and carried her to the big bed, laying her across the sheets and looking at her for a long while before touching her, and Aria thought he was looking at her as if he planned to remember her for always.

"What is it you Americans say? 'Aren't you going to offer a lady a drink?'" Aria said, holding up the bottle of champagne she still held.

J.T. was still looking at her, sitting on the edge of the bed and lightly running his fingers over her breasts and her ribs, down her arms.

Aria used her thumbs to open the champagne bottle and the cork flew out. The champagne spewed over her belly and down J.T.'s back. She laughed and started to brush the flood of liquid away but J.T. caught her hands and begin to drink it off her body, his head moving upward until his mouth settled on her breasts.

She was intoxicated, feeling wonderfully free, able to do anything. With a quick, strong move, she pulled J.T. to the bed then wriggled out from under him and began to drink the champagne droplets from his bare back. She straddled his legs, loving the feel of his strong, heavy thighs between her own as she ran her tongue up his spine, then began making nippling little kisses down his back. He lay absolutely still under her, as if, were he to move, she might stop. Her breasts against his skin felt so good that she raked the tips of them across his back, her stomach touching his buttocks. She stretched out on him, her legs straddling his, moving her body along his, savoring the sensation of his skin against hers. She rubbed her hair and face on his back again and again, feeling him, tasting him, smelling him.

She moved downward and began to kiss his buttocks, his legs, the backs of his knees, his calves, his feet. She pressed the soles of his feet to her face, breathed deeply, then moved upward again.

When she reached his neck, she took her kisses across his cheek to his lips, and when she kissed his mouth, he turned over. His eyes were on fire and his stillness was gone. His hands were rough and quick on her body as he picked her up and set her down on his manhood.

She gave a delighted scream of surprise then began to move with all the abandonment she felt, her legs strong and moving with hard strength until they tightened and began to ache. J.T. turned her over and slammed into her with a few deep, hard thrusts until they came together in one blinding explosion.

He held on to her tightly, holding her against his chest, her legs wrapped around him.

"I love you," she whispered. "And I want you to stay with me."

He was still for a moment, then he rolled off of her to sit on the side of the bed and pull on his pajama bottoms. "Is that what this is about? You climb into bed with me and then demand payment? We have a name for women like you." He moved across the room and picked up her fallen robe. He didn't look at her as he tossed it to her. "Get out of here."

Aria tried to react with dignity, but she was a little too drunk on champagne and lovemaking to be perfectly lucid. She got out of bed, tripping on her robe, and made her way to the panel door he held open for her. He kept his head turned away as he held out a flashlight to her and she went down the stairs. The sound of the door closing behind her was horrible.

She was halfway down the stairs when a hand closed over her mouth and a gun was stuck in her ribs.

She struggled against the person holding her.

"So this is how you move about in this moldering old castle" came a familiar voice. "Keep that flashlight still."

She scratched at the hand on her mouth. "Freddie!" she gasped.

"You say one more word and I'll break your neck here and now, Aria. Everyone I've sent has failed at the job of killing you, so I might as well do it myself." He was dragging her down the dark corridor away from the door leading to the garden. "They'll find your body in a few days, and when they do, I plan to make myself king. All I have to do is get rid of Gena and I figure the old king will die of grief. I am next in line to the throne."

She managed to move her head enough to speak. "Why do you want to be king?" she gasped out.

"Dear, stupid Aria. You only looked at the peasants, nothing else. This is a dying country. Better to sell it to the Germans than to try to keep its independence. Uranium, my dear. The country is riddled with it. I shall sell the whole place to the highest bidder and live in France. Damn, but you have been hard to kill, Aria."

"And she's going to be harder" came a voice from the darkness.

Aria had seen several American movies and she imitated a western now by ducking while Freddie was distracted. Her flashlight fell and went rolling as she flattened her body onto the filthy floor. Shots rang over her head, the stone walls of the tunnel echoing with the deafening sound. Dirt and bits of stone rained down on her head.

She lay still for a moment until the air cleared. "Jarl!" she screamed, and she was as loud as the shots.

"Here, baby," he said, and she ran to him in the darkness.

She held on to him with all her might.

"It's over," he whispered. "You're safe and I can go home."

It wasn't easy to do but she pulled away from him. "Yes, you must return to your country and I must remain in mine. It will be better this way. Will you get a guardsman to see to my cousin?"

"Yes, Your Royal Highness," he said mockingly as he turned away and left her in the darkness.

Chapter Twenty-two

ARIA walked erectly as she left the limousine and made her way to the field behind the Lanconian Academy of Sciences building. The white plastered walls glared in the sun and hurt her swollen eyes. Even though she wore a little veiled hat, she knew the redness of her eyes was still visible.

It had been two weeks since the encounter in the underground passage between Jarl and Freddie. Freddie had not been killed, only wounded, but the Royal Guard had given him time alone in the library with a loaded pistol and Freddie had taken the honorable way out by putting a bullet through his head. The official story had been that he had had an accident while cleaning his gun. Only Aunt Sophie had questioned that statement. *"Freddie* clean his own gun? Balderdash! I never heard of anything so ridiculous. What *really* killed him?" No one who knew answered her.

Lieutenant Montgomery had left Lanconia the next morning without a word of farewell to anyone.

Immediately after his departure, Julian had become so possessive that Aria had told him to leave Lanconia and her life. She wasn't sure if he wanted her kingdom or the uranium. He certainly hadn't wanted *her*.

Young Frank Taggert had remained in Lanconia to help with the engines, but for all his size, he was just a boy, and a sudden long rain had left many vineyards with moldering grapes and no way to get them down the mountains fast enough.

Hours after J.T. left, Aria was in her grandfather's house and raging at him for not telling her about the uranium. He said she was more angry about that cowardly husband of hers leaving than about any secrets he had kept. She had defended J.T. but not for long. She had gone back to the palace to hear the news of Freddie's suicide. She gave orders that a royal funeral be arranged for him.

She had met with the people involved in putting Kathy Montgomery in Princess Aria's place in the War Room. Not even the groveling and apologies of the Lord High Chamberlain had cheered her from her deep depression. Lady Werta had looked as if she might faint and had whispered that she would like to resign from Her Highness's service. Aria said that whatever her ladyship had done, she had done out of faithfulness to the true princess. She awarded the woman the Order of the Blue Shield for her patriotism.

She also met with her cousin Cissy and thanked her for what she had done for Lanconia. Cissy was glad Aria was alive and unhurt and all she asked in reward was a banquet. She had been put on a semifast by both the Lanconians who had switched her and later by the American government who had held her as prisoner. Everyone except Cissy believed she needed to lose weight. Aria ordered a feast that took Cissy three days to eat.

Then, as if Aria didn't have enough misery in her life, a committee of Lanconians presented her with a petition asking for the return of the American, Lieutenant Montgomery, so he could continue helping them with the grapes. She explained to them that his return was impossible, that his own country needed him. To her horror, they wrote to the American president and, somehow, the story got into the American newspapers. The short article made the Lanconians look like incompetent, backward peasants and said that they needed a red-blooded American to run their country for them. Aria crumpled the paper in disgust. She would find someone else to teach her people about dams and wells and vocational schools and car engines and whatever else needed doing. She just had to find someone who could figure out what needed doing and where to start looking for that person. If she only had someone to ask for help—if she weren't so completely alone.

Julian had been gone for three days now, Gena saw no one but her young American, and Aria had no one to talk to or laugh with. She had never felt lonely before she went to America and met that odious man, so what was wrong with her now?

She went about her duties without feeling. Now she was never tempted to break through crowds and drink goat's milk, and she accepted every engagement proposed to her so she never had a chance to be alone to think—and to remember. The people of Lanconia noticed her dreariness and attributed it to the loss of her fiancé, Count Julian.

Today Aria was to unveil yet another statue of Rowan the Mighty, a twenty-foot-high stone sculpture of a square-jawed man sitting on a chair with lions' heads for arms. She had not slept well last night or the night before, or the one before that for that matter, and her eyes were tired and red and her head ached.

There had been built a raised stand that held a podium with a microphone (newly imported to Lanconia) and six chairs containing the sculptor and his guests. Three hundred people stood in the audience.

Aria mounted the three steps up, opened her piece of paper, and began to read the prepared speech. She was halfway into the part about Rowan's magnificent accomplishments when a noise to her left distracted her.

J.T. slouched in a chair in the big living room of his parents' house on the coast of Maine. Outside he could hear the wind and not far off a ship's horn sounded, but he had no desire to go see what ship was docking. In fact, for the last ten days he hadn't had much interest in anything. He had caught a ride out of Lanconia on the first plane leaving with vanadium. He knew he was being cowardly in not saying good-bye to Aria, but he had said good-bye to her before and once was all he could bear.

He didn't really have orders from the navy as to where he was supposed to be, so after landing in Virginia, he had thumbed a ride to Key West. There he had found his Uncle Jason doing a better job than he ever could have. He saw Bill and Dolly that night, but they reminded him so much of Aria that they made him feel worse than he already did. Everything seemed to remind him of her, and Dolly's hundreds of questions about Aria didn't help any. He ended up leaving in the middle of dinner and walking along the beach all night.

The next morning Commander Davis received word J.T. was to report to General Brooks in D.C.

On the long train ride, J.T. stared out the window and thought of the things that could be done in Lanconia. With the money from the uranium, schools could be built—maybe even a university. The countryside was so beautiful that he was sure there was some way to attract tourists.

The more he thought, the more depressed he became. He wondered if Aria was having a good time with Count Julian.

In Washington, General Brooks said J.T. was a disappointment to America, that America needed him in Lanconia.

J.T. made a halfhearted attempt at explaining that Aria could not put an American on the throne beside her, that the people wouldn't accept an American. She would have to abdicate. "Unless the people asked for me," J.T. mumbled.

"And you didn't stay there to fight," the general said with disgust. General Brooks sent him home to Maine until he could find a "suitable" assignment for him—which J.T. guessed was going to be either the front line or the worst desk job in the military. J.T. didn't care which.

He went home but he wasn't glad to be home. Nothing seemed to cheer him, not seeing his family or the sea, not rowing out to an island alone, nothing.

"Get out of the way."

J.T. looked up to see his brother Adam wheeling his chair toward him, Adam's healing leg stuck out straight in front of him. He had very little sympathy for J.T.'s sulks and moodiness, especially since J.T. refused to talk about what was bothering him.

"There's a special delivery letter for you from

General Brooks," Adam said, tossing an envelope in J.T.'s lap.

"Orders," J.T. mumbled, not caring much, not looking at the letter.

Adam leaned over and snatched the envelope. *"I'm interested in where you're going.* Maybe they're sending you to hell to use your sunny disposition to further punish the occupants." He opened the envelope. "It's a clipping of a newspaper article. Hey! It's about you. It says the people of Lanconia petitioned President Roosevelt for your return to their country. I'm glad *somebody* wants you."

It took J.T. a moment to react. He snatched the paper from Adam's hands. "They *asked* for me," he said softly. "The people of Lanconia *asked* for me."

Adam knew the basics of what J.T. had been through in Lanconia. "It says they want you to tell them about raisins and cars. They did *not* say they wanted you for their king."

For the first time in many days there was life in J.T.'s eyes. "But maybe there's a loophole in their constitution, maybe there isn't a constitution, maybe the people wouldn't mind an American king." J.T. stood.

"I thought you didn't *want* to be king. Bill Frazier told Dad you hated the idea. *I* would. No freedom, always shaking hands, some tight-lipped queen for a wife, tea parties."

"You don't know *anything!"* J.T. shouted at his brother. "You don't know what it's like to be needed, to be necessary. That place needs me and"—he paused—"and I need Lanconia—and Aria." He started out of the room.

"Where are you going?"

"Home," J.T. shouted. "Home to my wife. They

may not let me be king, but I'm going to die fighting for the right."

Adam laughed and tried to scratch under his cast.

Aria turned to see Lieutenant Montgomery standing at the edge of the platform.

Anger filled her so she could barely speak, but she continued reading, a tremor in her voice.

He walked to the podium and put his head between her and the audience, his mouth close to the microphone.

"People of Lanconia," he said, ignoring Aria, "I want to make an announcement. A few weeks ago your princess went to America. She was gone a long time and you were told that she had been ill. She was not. What took her away from you so long was her marriage to me."

Aria tried to push him away but he didn't budge as the crowd began to murmur in disbelief.

"I know I'm an American," J.T. said, "and I know I'm not of royal blood, but if you'll have me, I'll be your king."

The crowd was so stunned that no one spoke until one man yelled, "What does Princess Aria say?"

"No!" Aria said, and J.T. looked at her. "You went off and left me. I could never trust you to—"

J.T. pulled her into his arms and kissed her and the crowd began to cheer. "I couldn't bear living without you," he shouted to her over the din the crowd was beginning to make. "And the people asked for me, so you don't have to abdicate. And have you ever heard of Warbrooke Shipping?"

She was a bit too dazed to understand. "No. Does it have to do with boats? Jarl, we don't *need* boats. We need schools and wells and—"

377

He kissed her again.

"Long live King Jarl," the crowd shouted.

"Prince!" Aria yelled into the microphone. *"Prince Jarl,"* she said, but no one heard her.

"Come on, baby, let's go home," J.T. yelled. "I brought some members of my family with me. We're going to bring this country of ours into the twentieth century."

She slipped her arm around him, forgetting she was in public and that she was a princess. "Ours," she said, smiling. *"Our* country."

The Temptress

Prologue

The tall, lean, dark-haired man left Del Mathison's office, shutting the door behind him. He stood there, muscles in his jaw working, as if he were contemplating what he'd just heard. After a moment, he left the hallway and went into Mathison's richly furnished parlor.

In that room a man was leaning against the mantel of the empty fireplace. He was also tall, but he had the soft, cared-for look of a man who'd lived inside a house all his life. His blond hair was perfectly trimmed, his suit of clothes perfectly cut.

"Ah," the blond man said, "you must be the man Del hired to take me to his daughter."

The dark man merely nodded. He looked a little uncomfortable and his eyes constantly strayed to corners of the room, as if he thought someone might be hiding there.

"I'm Asher Prescott," the blond man said. "Did Del tell you about my part in this mission?"

1

"No," the dark man said in a voice that was felt as much as heard.

Prescott removed a cigar from a box on the mantel and lit it before he spoke. "Del's daughter has a penchant,"—he stopped and gave the dark man a quick look up and down—"I mean, she has the capacity for getting herself in trouble. For the last few years, Del's allowed her to have her head and she's been in one scrape after another. I guess you've heard of Nola Dallas the reporter." He paused. "But then maybe you haven't."

He took a draw on the cigar, waiting, but the dark man didn't answer. "Well, her father is tired of it and he's decided to force her to come to her senses. She's north of here now, staying with some friends of friends." He made a grimace of disgust. "Poor girl is convinced that Hugh Lanier, the man whose family she's visiting, is inciting Indians to massacre missionaries. The charge is ridiculous and Del's right that it's time she ended this folly."

Prescott studied the dark man as he stood looking out the window. Del had said this man could guide them through any part of Washington Territory. In fact, Del had said he even knew how to get through the rain forest—a place that was said to be impenetrable.

"The plan," Prescott continued, "is to take Mathison's daughter from Lanier's house, by force if necessary, and return her to her father. You're to lead us through the rain forest so it'll give me time alone with Miss Mathison. I plan to be engaged to her by the time we return."

The dark man turned to stare at Prescott. "I don't force women."

"Force her?" Prescott gasped. "She's a twenty-eight-year-old old maid. She's traveled all over the world writing those ridiculous bleeding-heart stories of hers and no man has ever wanted her."

"But you do."

Prescott clamped the cigar between his teeth. "I want this," he said, looking about the room. "Del Mathison is a rich and powerful man and all he has to leave it to is one horse-faced, sexless daughter who thinks she can save the world from all its evils. Now, I want it straight between us from the beginning. Are you going to help me or fight me?"

The dark man took a while answering. "She's yours if she wants you."

Prescott smiled around his cigar. "Oh, she'll want me all right. At her age, she'll be glad to get any man she can."

Chapter One

Christiana Montgomery Mathison put her hand in the tub of water to check the temperature and then began to disrobe. It was going to feel good to bathe after a day of hard riding and hours of sitting huddled over a desk writing. She had her story finished now and tomorrow she'd start the arduous journey back home.

When she was nude, she realized that she didn't have her dressing gown and went to the big double-doored wardrobe to get it.

When she opened the right hand door, her heart seemed to skip a beat, for there was a man standing inside the cabinet, his eyes wide, his mouth open as he looked at Chris's pretty little body in its unclad state. Chris, alert from years as a reporter, slammed the door shut and turned the key in the lock. Softly, obviously not wanting to be discovered, the man began to pound on the inside of the cabinet door. Chris had one foot toward the bed where she planned to take the spread

4

off and cover herself, but then things happened too quickly for her to react.

The left side of the wardrobe opened behind her and out stepped another man, and he had her in his arms before she could even take a breath or see his face. Her face was buried in his chest, his arms around the back of her, one hand on her bare shoulders, the other resting just above the curve of her buttocks.

"Who are you? What do you want?" she asked and was appalled at the fear in her voice. The man was large and she knew she'd have no chance of success if she tried to escape him. "If it's money you want—" she began but his arms tightened on her and she didn't finish the sentence.

His left hand began to stroke her hair as it hung halfway down her back, gently tangling his fingers in its soft blondness, and even through her fear she found herself relaxing somewhat. She managed to turn her head sideways so she could breathe more easily, but he didn't allow her to move the rest of her body as he kept her pinned close and intimately to him.

"Let me out of here," hissed the man locked in the wardrobe.

The man holding Chris didn't react, he just kept stroking her hair, his right hand inching down her back toward her buttocks. She'd never had a man touch her bare skin before and his rough, calloused hands felt good.

She recovered herself and began to struggle against him, trying to get free, but he held her firmly, not hurting her, but showing no signs that he ever intended to release her.

"Who are you?" she repeated. "Tell me what you

5

want and I'll see if I can get it for you. I don't have much money, but I do have a bracelet that's worth something. Release me and I'll get it." When she again tried to move, he held her fast.

With a sigh of frustration, she relaxed against him again. "If you plan to take me by force, I warn you that I'll put up a struggle such as you've never seen before. I'll take some of your skin to replace what you take from me." She tried to twist her head to look up at him but he didn't allow her to see his face. Am I saying the wrong thing? she thought, wondering if what she'd just said were words that were inflammatory to a . . . a rapist, she finally said the word to herself. In spite of her brave words, she began to shiver and his arms tightened around her in a way that, had the circumstances been different, Chris might have found protective.

"We've come from your father," he said in a voice that Chris felt through her cheek. It was a very deep, very rich voice. "There are two of us and we've come to take you home."

"Yes, I'm ready to go home. But first I have to—"

"Ssssh," he whispered, snuggling her against him as if they were lovers and familiar with each other's bodies. "You have to go home now whether you want to or not," he said, obviously not listening to her. "You can fight it out with your father later, but now we take you home to him. Do you understand?"

"But there's a story that I—"

"Chris," he said and the way he said her name made her try to look up at him, but he still wouldn't allow her to see his face. "Chris, you have to return to your father. I'm going to release you and I want you to get

6

dressed, then I'll let Prescott out of the wardrobe. I'll meet you outside with the horses. Pack only what you'll need for the trip. We'll be going through the rain forest and it'll take a few days so take rain gear if you have it."

"Through the rain forest! But no one can travel through that."

"There's a way and I know how. Don't worry your lovely little self about that, just get ready to leave."

"I have to take my story to John Anderson," Chris said. She didn't seem to be in all that much of a hurry to move away from him and sometime during the past few minutes, her hands had moved to his waist. She wasn't exactly hugging him but she wasn't pushing him away either.

"Who is John Anderson?"

"My friend and the editor of a newspaper. He's the one who first suspected Hugh of selling rifles to the Indians."

He moved his head so that his face was buried in her hair and she could have sworn she felt his lips against her scalp. "We'll talk about that later, but now we have to go. We've taken too long as it is. You'll have to get dressed so we can leave."

Chris waited, but he just held her, his hand now stroking gently across her shoulder blades. "Are you going to release me or not?"

"You aren't cold, are you?"

"I am not in the least cold. What I am is being kidnapped by a man who may or may not be from my father, but knowing him, you probably are, and I am standing here in my birthday suit being smothered by a man I've never even seen, much less been introduced

7

to. Now, will you please let me go so I can put on some clothes?"

"Yes," he said in that voice of his, but he made no effort to release her.

Chris made a sound that was half a cry of rage and half a scream of protest.

"If you hurt her, Tynan, you'll answer to me," came the voice of the man in the wardrobe who had been surprisingly quiet for the last several minutes.

The man called Tynan held her for a few more minutes, then with what seemed to be a heartfelt sigh, he released her and turned away toward her bureau all in one motion.

Chris grabbed the corner of the spread on the bed but she didn't need it since he stood with his back to her, toying with the items on the bureau top. With the spread wrapped around her, she edged toward the wardrobe, opened the left side and withdrew a clean riding habit.

"I need my other garments from inside the chest," she said to the back of him. From what she could see of him she could tell that he was big, broad-shouldered, had dark hair and that his clothes were completely new. From his boots to the gun and holster slung low on his hip, to his brown leather vest and his blue chambray shirt, all of it was new. He hadn't spoken since he'd released her and now he merely stepped aside, staring at the wall as if it were of great interest.

Chris withdrew undergarments from a drawer, all the while trying to see his face but she couldn't, and when she moved back into the room to put on her clothes, he went back to the dresser. She dressed as quickly as possible, tightening her corset strings with such speed that she knotted them and had to spend extra minutes untangling the laces.

"All right," she said when she was dressed, expecting him to turn around.

But he didn't turn toward her, going instead to the wardrobe and unlocking it. Out stepped a tall blond man who did nothing but look at Chris.

"Help her get packed. I'll meet you outside," Tynan said and before Chris realized what he was doing, he was out the window and she was alone with the blond man.

It was an awkward moment, but the blond man stepped forward, smiling. He was very good-looking, with bright blue eyes that looked as if they were accustomed to laughing and a smile that Chris was sure had melted the hearts of many women.

"I'm Asher Prescott. I'm sorry about what happened there," he said, motioning toward the wardrobe, but he didn't look sorry at all. In fact, he looked quite happy about everything. "We really are from your father and our assignment is to bring you back no matter what excuse you give. He is very worried about you."

She gave him a weak smile. "That sounds just like my father. I'll go, I was ready to leave, but I do need to pack a few things," she said as she walked in front of Mr. Prescott to pick up the toilet articles on the bureau top. As she did so, she saw that one of the items Tynan had been toying with was her hand mirror. And, as she looked from the mirror to where she had been dressing, she realized that Tynan had been watching her while she dressed.

A quick surge of anger ran through her but then she smiled, dropped the mirror into the carpet bag she'd taken from the bottom of the wardrobe, and went to

the desk to take the papers of her story on Hugh
Lanier.

After a second's thought, she sat down and wrote
a quick letter to Hugh, explaining the purpose of
her visit, and telling him why she had to do what she
must.

Chapter Two

Chris followed Asher Prescott through the window, where, at the edge of the trees, two horses awaited them.

"Miss Mathison," Mr. Prescott began, "may I say what a pleasure it is to—"

"You can do your courting later," came a voice that Chris recognized instantly. She looked up at the man on horseback hidden in the shadows. "We have to get out of here, so let's ride."

Both Chris and Asher obeyed that voice without delay.

Chris and Asher rode close to each other all night and all the next day, through trees as big around as horses, past small villages, both Indian and white, past logger camps, past saw mills. Always, they stayed away from people, moving southeast and allowing as few people as possible to see them. They traveled across

11

paths that were so narrow that they had to lead the horses. Tynan always stayed far ahead, leading them, scouting the trail, looking for places where too many people watched. Only once did they stop. Tynan gave a low whistle and Mr. Prescott put up his hand to halt Chris, then went ahead to see what Tynan wanted. He came back to say that ahead was a party of loggers taking their noon meal and so they had to rest until the men were gone.

Asher pulled jerky out of his saddle bags and a canteen and gave a piece of the dried meat to Chris.

Chris leaned back against the trunk of a tree, her body feeling weak with exhaustion. "I think there's something wrong with that Tynan of yours," she said to Asher, watching him from under her lashes. Sometimes the best way to get information from someone was to pretend to not want it. "I think he must be scarred or disfigured in some way or else he wouldn't be afraid to show his face."

"He's not *my* Tynan," Asher answered, looking affronted. "If he belongs to anyone, it's to your father. He hired him."

"Do you know why we're going through the rain forest?" Chris asked, trying a new tact. "It seems like such a long way around."

"It is," Asher answered, gazing off into the trees.

Chris had been a reporter for several years and she was used to interviewing people and she'd developed a sixth sense about when someone was lying. Perhaps this man wasn't exactly lying but he certainly wasn't telling the whole truth.

Before Chris could ask another question, there was a whistle from within the trees and, as obedient as a dog, Prescott rose from the ground and started packing.

"Tell me, does anyone ever *see* this Mr. Tynan?" Chris asked as she mounted her horse.

Asher looked startled. "Why are you so interested in him?"

Chris watched as Asher heaved himself into the saddle. He acted as if he were more used to the comfort of a buggy than being on horseback. "Professional curiosity. Do you know why my father hired this man? What are his qualifications for leading us through the forest?"

Asher shrugged as he mounted. "He's been there before, I guess, but he's an odd one. Doesn't seem to like people at all, always puts his bedroll outside the campsite, never wants to ride with anyone, and he doesn't like to talk. Ask him a question about himself and he refuses to answer. I'd like to know where your father got him too."

"Knowing my father, you probably don't want to learn the entire truth of whatever he's done," Chris said under her breath. When she got home, she was going to give her father a piece of her mind about this ridiculous kidnapping.

At sundown, they heard the whistle again and Asher halted her as he went ahead into the trees, returning minutes later with two fresh horses.

"Did you suggest to him that we might like to rest?" Chris asked as she mounted the horse.

"I most certainly did," Asher said. He looked more tired than Chris felt and she thought she was probably more accustomed to riding long hours than he was. "But we have to go on. Ty wants to get to the edge of the forest before we halt. But he says we'll have an entire day of rest when we get there."

"Ty," Chris murmured as she mounted. She spent

13

the next several hours as they jogged along wondering about this mysterious man who came into her room and held her, watched her dress, then disappeared to lead them through a forest that was said by the Indians to be haunted. And why had her father hired him? And who was Prescott? He didn't seem to know much more about traveling through this land than she did, but he'd been chosen as half of the rescue team. What in the world was her father up to?

Chris had plenty of time to puzzle over the facts since they continued riding all night. Her questions kept her mind alert and kept her from feeling the absolute exhaustion that ran through her. They'd had no sleep or rest for two days and two nights now.

When Chris was beginning to weave in the saddle and twice she had nearly fallen off, she thought she saw a light through the trees. Blinking several times to clear her vision, she began to be more sure of what she saw. Somehow, she knew it was a fire built for them. "Otherwise, Ty wouldn't let us get so near," she murmured to herself.

"Mr. Prescott," she called and succeeded in waking him from where he slumped forward in his saddle. "Look ahead."

There was renewed energy as they urged the horses on toward the fire and all Chris could think of was finally being allowed to stop and sleep. Even as she was still moving, she began to unfasten the straps at the back of the saddle that held her sleeping roll.

When they did halt, Chris dropped her bedroll onto the ground, then fell on top of it and was asleep in an instant.

She had no idea how long she slept before something woke her. She opened her heavy eyelids. It was still dark but there was a faint hint of early morning light and in it, she could see outlined a man wearing a wide brimmed hat moving almost silently as he unsaddled the horses and gave them food and water.

Chris half slept, half waked as she watched him and even when he began to walk toward her, she still didn't awaken fully.

He knelt by her and it seemed perfectly natural when he pulled her into his arms. Like a sleepy child, she just smiled and snuggled against him.

"You're on top of your blankets," he said in that voice that seemed to rumble through her. "You'll get cold."

She nodded once while he straightened the blanket under her, then put the other one on top. For just a moment, as he covered the far side of her, she thought his lips were near her forehead and she smiled, eyes closed. It was like a good-night kiss from her father. "Good night, Ty," she whispered and fell asleep again.

When she woke again, it was full daylight and at first she thought she must be dreaming, for around her was a place of fantasy. Tall, tall trees towered overhead, blocking the sun, everything covered with gray-green moss or ferns, everything so soft. It was as if she were at the end of the earth.

Near her, Mr. Prescott slept soundly. It felt to Chris that she was the only person alive on earth.

Slowly, she got up, stood and stretched. The eerie forest seemed to be utterly and totally silent. In front of her was what passed for a path, little more than a rut in the greenery. They'd come in from the right so now she took the left path.

She was no more than a few feet from the camp but, as soon as she turned a bend, she felt alone. She may as well have been a hundred miles away from another human. She kept walking, no more than a few yards on the springy forest floor, and she thought she heard water ahead of her.

Another few yards and she could see a rushing stream below and to her right, with big boulders in the water covered with patches of black moss. Suddenly, the only thought that Chris had was of the bath she'd missed two days ago. She thought with regret of the tub full of hot water that she'd had to leave behind. Why couldn't the men have stayed inside the closet until she'd finished bathing? Of course they might have if she hadn't opened the door to the wardrobe. Stayed in there and watched her, she thought with a grimace as she ran down to the water.

Now, all she could think of was getting clean again and she had her clothes off in a second and was wading into the water. It was icy and took her breath away but she wanted to be clean more than she wanted to be warm. She washed while standing behind a cluster of boulders so that if either of the men came from the camp, they wouldn't be able to see her, and she was close to the edge of the forest so she could make a run for it if necessary.

She was just finishing her bath and regretting her impulsiveness because she didn't have a towel with her when she thought she heard a man whistling and looked up to see Mr. Prescott coming down the trail. Quickly, she ran from the water, grabbed her clothes and ran into the forest—only to run smack into the hard chest of Tynan.

For a moment they were both too astonished to speak. The lush, abundant greenery of the forest deadened all sound and two people could walk into

16

each other without seeing or hearing anything before-hand.

Tynan's hands caught and held her, his fingers moving down her back as he stepped away from her just a bit so he could look at her naked body.

"Miss Mathison, I'd recognize you anywhere," he said with a smile.

Chris, with a cry, pushed away from him and ran a couple of feet to get behind a tree, where she began to dress with shaking hands.

"The water's really too cold to be taking a bath, Miss Mathison," he said and there was laughter in his voice. "Not that I haven't enjoyed all your baths, but next time, I think you should ask me first. I wouldn't want you to catch cold."

Chris could think of nothing to say as she dressed. All day yesterday, during that long ride, she'd fantasized about this mysterious man and had begun to believe what she'd asked Asher about, that he was probably deformed or disfigured in some way and that's why he didn't want anyone to see him. But even in the few seconds that she'd had to look at him, she'd known he was the most beautiful man she'd ever seen. He was very masculine, with generous features, perfectly formed lips, eyes of a brilliant blue, a big, square jaw, and black hair that curled about the collar of a shirt that repeated the color of his eyes.

When she was dressed, Chris stepped from behind the tree. He was sitting on the ground, his back to her.

She'd had such a different idea of what he looked like, she'd begun to think that he was even fatherly after the way he'd tucked her in last night. But there was nothing fatherly about this man.

She walked toward him and when he didn't turn

around, she moved to stand in front of him. He didn't look up, keeping his face concealed by the broad-brimmed hat. Boldly, Chris sat down across from him.

He kept his head down. "I want to apologize, Miss Mathison," he said softly. "I seem to keep embarrassing you and I haven't meant to. It's just that we keep meeting under very unusual circumstances. I don't want you to have the wrong impression of me. I was hired by your father to rescue you and take you back to him. And that's *all* I mean to do."

Chapter Three

Chris sat there looking at the top of his hat and thought how utterly bizarre the situation was. This man had made her look like a fool twice, he'd held her in his arms three times—not to mention that two of those times she'd had no clothes on—he had kidnapped her, telling her that it didn't matter at all what she wanted, yet here she was feeling as if she should comfort him. She put out her hand to touch his and as she did so, she saw a red, raw place on his wrist, just barely visible beneath his shirt cuff.

"You've hurt yourself," she said, immediately concerned.

He was on his feet instantly, and before Chris could say another word, he walked, half ran actually, to the edge of the stream and called to Prescott.

Chris was left sitting on the moss and wondering what she had said to offend him.

"Here she is," she heard Tynan saying before he reappeared, leading the man as if he were herding a

19

maverick. As little as she knew of Tynan, she was sure that the voice he was using was a false one. "You've introduced yourselves, haven't you, Miss Mathison? This is Asher Prescott. He's a friend of your father and will be with us while we slowly make our way through this forest. Ash, why don't you take Miss Mathison fishing? We'll need fresh food. And later, you two can gather firewood." He gave Ash a little push in Chris's direction.

Asher smiled down at Chris and offered her his hand to help her stand. "Shall we go fishing, Miss Mathison? I hear there are salmon in these waters."

Chris was confused by what was happening. She didn't want to spend the day with Mr. Prescott but it didn't seem as if she had any choice. It seemed to be already arranged. She glanced at Tynan but he had his head turned so that she couldn't see his face.

"Why, yes, fishing sounds like a delightful pastime," she answered as she accepted Mr. Prescott's hand. By the time she stood, Tynan had disappeared into the trees.

She and Asher walked back to the camp together to find that there were supplies and two mules that Chris had not seen before and Mr. Prescott was already handing her a fishing pole.

"Shall we go, Miss Mathison?"

He led her back the way she'd gone that morning, over rocks, past the place she'd bathed, but not far from the camp. "I think this will be a good place to try," he said.

"Is that your idea or Mr. Tynan's?"

He smiled at her. "I don't think he's *Mr.* Tynan. I'm not sure he has but the one name. But let's not talk about him. I hear you worked on a newspaper. Is it true that you're the infamous Nola Dallas?"

"Nola Dallas is my pen name," she said stiffly, as she expertly tossed the fishing line into the water. She'd always lived in Washington and she'd fished since she was a child.

Asher looked stricken. "I didn't mean to give offense, it's just that, having read your articles, I thought you'd be a much older woman—or maybe even a man. Did you really do those things you wrote about?"

"Every one of them."

"Even appearing as a chorus girl? Wearing pink tights on stage?"

Chris smiled at the memory. "And getting myself thrown out during the second act. I'm not much of a dancer."

"But then who cares about dancing when you can implement the reforms that you have?"

Smiling, she felt herself warming to him. "Tell me, Mr. Prescott, why did my father choose you to help in this rescue mission? I would have thought he'd choose a man who knew this forest."

"That's Tynan's job. He's to take care of the animals and the food and look after our safety."

"And what are you to do?"

Ash smiled at her in a very pleasant way. "My only job is to make your trip enjoyable."

"I see," Chris said as she looked back at the water. But she didn't see at all. "What do you do for a living, Mr. Prescott?"

"Please call me Ash. It's not as if we first met in a drawing room."

Chris tried to control the redness in her cheeks as she

remembered the first time she'd seen this man inside the wardrobe in Hugh's house.

"Until last year I had my own lumber mill south of here but there was a fire and I lost everything."

She glanced at him quickly and saw the way the muscles in his jaw twitched. Having lost his business, he was obviously not over the hurt of it. "But you've started another business?" she said with much sympathy in her voice.

"Everything I had was tied up in the mill and when it went, I had nothing left." His voice lowered. "Not even credit." After a moment, he turned to her and gave a little smile. "But I have every hope that my fortunes will change for the better very soon. Look! I think you have a fish on the end of your line. Shall I bring it in for you?"

"I can manage," she said as she began pulling and reeling in the line. There was indeed a salmon on the end and within another hour she'd brought in half a dozen good-sized fish, while Ash had two small ones.

He laughed good-naturedly about her being the breadwinner and they walked companionably back to the camp.

There was a small fire going, built for them by Tynan, Chris thought, but the man was nowhere to be seen.

"I'd like to discuss something with you, Mr. . . . Ash," Chris said as she expertly cleaned the fish and spitted them with a stick. "I wanted to talk to both you and Mr. Tynan but I can't seem to get you together. The reason I was at Hugh Lanier's house was that I was investigating a rumor that Mr. Lanier was involved in something quite evil and—"

"Evil?" Asher said, leaning back against a tree. "Perhaps evil is too harsh a word."

22

"I don't think so and I don't believe my readers will think so. Hugh Lanier wanted some land that had been settled by eight missionaries. But they wouldn't sell so he bought guns and hired white men to dress as Indians and massacre the missionaries. If that isn't evil, I don't know what is." As always, when she thought of injustice of this magnitude, her temper began to rise.

"But if it's only a rumor—"

"It *was* only a rumor. I have proof that he did it. Among other things, I have a bill of sale for rifles. I even heard him talking to one of the 'Indians' and—"

"Heard him?" Asher said. "Do you mean you eavesdropped?"

"Of course I did. I wore a green dress and hid among the cornstalks. But the point is, I have to get my evidence to the newsman who sent me on this mission and, by my calculations, we're due west of John's office. We need to leave tomorrow morning."

She watched Asher as he held his hat in his lap and played with the hatband. "Chris, I don't believe your father would want you traipsing across the country accusing men of . . . of what you're accusing Lanier of. Perhaps when we return to your father's house, he can send your information to this newsman. Until then I think it best that you stay here in safety."

Chris just looked at him for a moment. She'd grown up with a man like this one, and she'd worked with men like him. He was perfectly sure she was wrong and nothing she said or did was going to change his mind. "I think the fish are done," she said softly, then watched as he smiled at her in a way that men who'd just won always smiled at women. She returned his smile but it didn't reach her eyes.

She made light, ladylike conversation with Asher

while they ate, not once referring to her plans for getting her story to John Anderson. But as soon as they were finished, she stood.

"I think I'll go and see if I can find Mr. Tynan," she said absently as she started down the path toward the river.

"I wouldn't do that if I were you, Chris," Asher said. "I'm sure the man would be here if he wanted to be and I'm quite sure that he can feed himself. I think you should sit down and share your lovely company with me."

Chris didn't know what she hated more in life than being told what she *should* do. It was the source of all her problems with her father. He never tried to reason with her, but just told her what was best for her and expected blind obedience.

She smiled sweetly at Asher. "I think I'll look for our host," she said and moved so quickly down the path that she didn't give him time to voice a protest. Within seconds, she heard him thrashing about through the forest as he searched for her. Thanking her mother and her ancestors that she was small, she jumped over a fallen log and hid in the ferns until she saw him go by. When she could hear him no more, she walked a short way through the underbrush before finding that it was impossible to go any further due to the fallen logs and the heavy curtain of moss hanging from every possible surface. She went back to the trail again and started toward the water, essentially following Asher. At the top of the little ridge that overlooked the water, she could see him below, frowning and looking annoyed. Smiling to herself, she continued down the trail.

She'd only gone a few feet when all sound was gone. The rain forest gave one the oddest feeling of being

24

totally alone. All around her was green—gray-green, blue-green, green that was almost black, a lime-green, hundreds of shades of the color. And everything was soft. She ran her hand over a fallen log that was covered with a forest of its own in miniature and smiled at its softness.

Ahead were odd formations created of moss and rotted tree trunks. She couldn't hear her own footsteps as she walked.

As she rounded a curve, she gasped, for lying just inches off the path was Tynan, fast asleep. There was a pack near his head and a rumpled blanket under him. He slept as bonelessly as a child and he looked very young. Again, Chris was amazed at the sheer beauty of the man and she had an enormous desire to just sit down and look at him—a desire which she indulged.

She had been sitting there for just moments when he stirred and opened his eyes.

"Chris," he said with a little smile, then closed his eyes again. A fraction of a second later he sat bolt upright, grabbed his hat and put it low down over his face and looked at her. "Miss Mathison, I thought you were fishing with Prescott."

"I was until I caught so many more fish than he that he suggested we return to the camp. After that I managed to escape down the path and I found you. Did you enjoy your nap? You certainly deserved it after the way you stayed awake and took care of us."

Looking like a sleepy boy, he began to rub his eyes and this time, Chris saw that both his wrists were sore. There was also a bruise under his right cheekbone and a half-healed cut above one eye.

"Why don't you come back to the camp and join us? We have more than enough fish. Have you eaten?"

"Yes, thank you, but you ought to go back to the camp. Prescott's probably worried about you." He stood. "Besides, I need to get to work. I have to scout the trail ahead. I'm sure there're logs that have fallen across it since the last time I was through here."

"And when was that, Mr. Tynan?"

"Just Tynan, nothing else and certainly no mister," he said as if he'd said it a hundred times.

Chris rose and moved to stand closer to him. He turned his back to her, removed his hat and ran his hand through his hair, which looked to be damp. She wondered if he'd been bathing. His shirt cuff was unbuttoned and as it fell back, she saw that all the muscles in his forearm, along with the veins, were prominent under his skin. He looked as if he had been starved for a while.

"I don't want to be a troublemaker because I know that you're only doing what my father has hired you to do, but . . ." She hesitated over using his name. "But, Tynan, I think you could use a few good meals and I insist that you return with me. If you don't, I promise to make this journey very uncomfortable."

He opened his mouth to speak but then closed it and grinned instead—and Chris felt her knees go weak. His entire face lit up and it flashed through her mind that he could get *any* woman anywhere to do whatever he wanted.

"I can't resist an invitation like that. I'll follow you."

"No, we shall go together. Tell me, why were you in the forest before? Who made this path?"

"Did you enjoy your fishing expedition with Ash? He seems to be a pleasant man. All the way here he was a great help, nothing was too much for him to do. And

26

he's great with horses and everyone we met liked him. I guess you did too."

"Well, yes," she said hesitantly. "How did you meet my father?"

"Ash has known your father for years. It's a wonder you never met him. Ash's father worked his way up and made a lot of money in the east. I'm sure Ash is the same kind of man."

Chris looked up at Tynan in bewilderment. What in the world was he talking about? But he just smiled at her and, this time, instead of being dazzled, she wondered if he often used that smile to get women to stop talking about whatever he didn't want to hear—or from asking questions that he didn't want to answer.

She smiled back at him but, if he'd known Chris better, he would have known that her glittering eyes showed that she'd just accepted a challenge. She was going to find out who this Tynan—no last name, no first name—was.

Chapter Four

"I need to talk to you," Chris said as soon as Tynan was seated in the camp and eating one of the fish she'd cooked. She told him just what she'd told Asher, about Lanier being responsible for killing the missionaries, but Tynan didn't interrupt her, didn't say a word, in fact.

When she'd finished speaking, he licked his fingers. "Now tell me what you've left out," he said.

Chris was startled for a moment. "All right," she said, smiling. "The truth is, Mr. Lanier was very good to me while I was his guest and his wife is very sweet, so I've felt some twinge of conscience about telling the world what Mr. Lanier did. Of course every word of it's true, but, when the story comes out in print, I'm afraid Mr. Lanier's life could be . . . ah, changed."

"Not to mention the length of his neck," Tynan said, looking at her.

"So I left him a letter telling him what I planned to do."

There was a long moment of silence from Tynan. "So, if we step out of this forest, no doubt Lanier's men will be waiting for us with rifles, or maybe cannons, anything to prevent that story from going to press."

She gave him a weak smile. "Yes, I guess so." Her face changed. "But they are things I *had* to do. I *had* to give Mr. Lanier a chance to flee and I *have* to give this story to the press. Don't you understand?"

Tynan stood. "I understand that a man has to do what he must, but you, Miss Mathison, need help and I'm not in a position to give it. Prescott's in charge of this expedition. I'm just the guide. I follow orders and that's all. Thank you for the fish, ma'am, and now I need to go scout the trail ahead." He turned back.

"And I wouldn't consider going alone if I were you," he said as he picked up a piece of wood and tossed it to the right of her head onto what looked to be solid ground. The log fell through vines and hit the ground a full second later. He didn't have to say another word. One could leave the trail and walk into deep holes that were concealed by a tangle of greenery.

With that, he left Chris alone.

She stood there for a moment cursing all men everywhere. "*Women* must do what they must, also, Mr. Tynan," she said to no one and set about gathering wood for the fire.

Chris stayed in the camp, talked to Asher when he returned, and didn't mention Hugh Lanier again. When Tynan returned, she glanced at him, but he didn't look at her. Chris kept her head turned toward Asher, pretending to find every word he said fascinating. But in truth, she was planning how she'd escape these two men. John Anderson's newspaper office was on the edge of the rain forest, not four miles from where they'd entered the forest last night. If she could get a horse, ride like blazes down the trail, then into town, she could be there and back by sundown. If luck were with her, she could be back before she was missed.

She stood. "I think I'll take a walk," she said to Asher.

"I'll go with you."

"No thank you," she said, giving him her prettiest smile. "I have things I have to do." She widened her eyes. "Female things." The mysteries of womanhood always stopped men like Asher Prescott.

"Of course," he said politely.

She walked away from him, past Tynan, then hid in the undergrowth until both men had left camp. Nobody ever slapped a saddle on a horse faster than she did. The poor animal pranced around, lifting its legs. "Be a good boy now," she coaxed. "We're going to have a good run."

"And where would that be, Miss Mathison?"

Chris whirled on her heel to face Tynan, her jaw set. "I'm going to take my story to John Anderson and if you plan to stop me you'll have to tie me here—and you'll have to watch me night and day. You'll have to give up sleep and—"

"I understand," he said and Chris saw amusement in his eyes. "How far away is this Anderson?"

Chris held her breath. "With hard riding, I can be back by sundown."

"And what did you plan to do about Lanier's men? What if they're waiting on the edge of the forest?"

"Run just as fast as I can and pray I don't get shot."

He stood there looking at her for a while, then withdrew his gun from its holster, making sure it was loaded. "Maybe I can help some. Which way is this town?"

Chris mounted her horse. "Southeast from the edge of the forest. John's office is the third building on the right."

Tynan saddled his horse. "As soon as we drop it off, Lanier pulls a gun and takes it. You got more paper? Why don't you drop a package off at the freight line—if there is one—then stop and say hello to Mrs. Anderson?"

"Why . . . yes, that might work," she said, looking at him in wonder. "There is no Mrs. Anderson but his sister is married to the town doctor."

"Even better," Ty said, mounting. "You know how to ride?"

"I can go anywhere you can," Chris said arrogantly but soon wondered if she were telling the truth. Tynan led a pace that scared her—and her horse. She had to use all the muscles in her arms to control the animal as they ran through the dangerous forest.

At the edge of the trees, Ty didn't slow down but kept pounding down the road. Chris half expected gunshots over her head but all was quiet. When no one shot at them, Ty halted his horse and turned back to her. "We're going in the back way. No doubt they're waiting for us in town. I'm going to drop you off at the freight office and I want you to stay there until you see me. I'll take the story to the doctor's wife and leave your horse in back of the freight office. When you see me ride past the front, run out the back and get on the horse and ride like hell. I'll be right behind you. Think you can do that?"

"Yes," Chris answered, controlling her horse. "But if they catch you with the story—"

"Don't worry about me, worry about obeying my orders. My temper's worse than Lanier's bullets."

"Yes, sir," she said, smiling and he winked at her as he turned his horse and continued southeast.

They paused outside the new, rough little town, the single main street a rutted tract. Tynan sat still for a moment, looking at the town, then turned to her. "I think they're here."

"How could you know that?"

"Too many men doing nothing but looking, their hands on their guns. They're watching for somebody. Give me your story," he said, and when he had tucked it inside his shirt he looked at her. "You ready? You remember what you're to do?"

"It's not exactly complicated."

"But vital. Come on."

He led her through the back of the town, skirting in and out of shadows, staying close to the buildings, keeping her inside as he rode protectively on the outside. Once, a wagon came around a building and instantly Tynan pulled her halfway across his saddle into his arms. "You still sick, honey?" he asked loudly. "It's always that way with the first baby."

As soon as the wagon was gone, he pushed Chris back. He certainly is a fast thinker, she thought.

"Wait here," he said as they came to the freight building. There was a big loading platform and ramp in back and a hook suspended over the doorway. Chris sat on her horse and waited, jumping at every little sound. With Tynan gone, she suddenly didn't feel so brave.

"Here she is," she heard Tynan say, as he walked up on the dock with another man beside him. "She just can't go another step." Before she could speak, Ty pulled her up from the saddle onto the dock. "It's her first one and she's not used to the sickness yet, so mind if I leave her here while I fetch the doctor?"

"Sure thing. I got eight of my own, but I don't know what the doc can do. She'll just have to wait it out."

Tynan practically smothered Chris in his protective embrace. "If it'll help her rest easier having the doctor, then I'll do it."

"Sure. Here, little lady, just sit right here."

"How about by the window so she can watch for me? It'll make her feel better."

"Sure," the man said.

Ty escorted Chris to a chair in front of a window looking out onto the main street. "Don't forget to look sick and give him something to deliver for you."

Chris nodded as she looked up into Tynan's beautiful blue eyes. He hesitated for a moment then kissed her forehead. "I'll be back in a minute, honey."

When he was gone, Chris lounged against the chair, trying not to show how intently she was watching the street. Across the road were two men, both holding rifles, both wearing guns, their right hands resting on the handles as if they meant to draw at any moment. Chris saw that her hand was shaking as she withdrew from her pocket a sealed letter addressed to her father. She didn't have to do any pretending to the freightman as she was sure she looked as scared as she felt. And she realized that at least half of her fear was for Tynan. He wasn't involved in this, had no reason to risk his life on her behalf, but he was.

The minutes passed and Chris began to grow anxious. What was taking him so long? Maybe John's sister wasn't there. Maybe—

Her thoughts stopped as she heard gunshots from the end of town where Tynan had gone. She stood.

"There's no need for you to get upset," said the freightman from behind his big desk. "Somebody's always shootin' at somebody in this town. You just sit there and rest."

But Chris couldn't rest as she leaned toward the window to see farther out.

Her breath stopped as she saw what she feared: Tynan was riding hell bent for leather down the street, two men on horseback chasing him, their guns blazing. With wide eyes, she watched him approach, then turned to the freightman. "May I borrow this?" she asked, taking a rifle from a cabinet on the wall.

Before the man could grasp what she was doing, Chris walked out the door, fell to one knee on the porch, propped her left arm on her raised knee and took aim. She dropped the first man behind Tynan with a shot in his shoulder, and was aiming for the second when Ty turned his horse and rode straight for her. There was a ramp in front of the freight office for rolling barrels and now Ty rode his horse straight up it.

Chris stood, stepped back a bit and when Ty bent and stretched his arm out to her, she caught it, put her foot on his in the stirrup and hauled herself up into the saddle behind him. Ty didn't slow his pace as he went thundering through the freight office, past open mouthed workers, and out the back, down the ramp.

It took longer for the men following to go around the freight office, and Chris heard the scream of the horse as the one man who tried to follow them misjudged the distance and went flying off the side of the freight dock.

Chris hung onto Tynan with all her might, her hair coming unpinned and flying out behind her, her body plastered to his. He leaned forward on his horse and

34

she went with him. There were bullets coming at them but they were traveling too fast to be in range—and the men were shooting from the back of horses so their aim wasn't that good—or at least Chris hoped it wasn't.

When they reached the edge of the rain forest, Tynan didn't slow down, but kept on at a breakneck speed for a few hundred yards. Suddenly, he halted the horse, turned, grabbed Chris and lowered her to the ground. He dismounted behind her.

"Now we disappear," he said, taking the horse's reins and Chris's hand. He motioned for her to climb down into a tangle of vines. She clambered down so fast, she skidded half the way. "Persuading" the horse was another matter and Ty did it with a series of quiet-voiced threats that made Chris's eyes widen. No sooner had he gotten the animal into the ravine and pulled vines over their heads to cover them than three men came down the trail after them.

Ty held his hand on the horse's nose to keep it from making a sound while Chris stood close to him, both of them looking up through the vines at the men.

"We've lost them," one of the men said.

"Yeah and we lost four of our men on the way in. Lanier's not gonna like this."

"Let's get out of here. This place gives me the creeps. If they went in here, they won't come out alive. Ain't nothin' but ghosts in this place."

The first man snorted. "Lanier pays you to shoot ghosts. Come on, let's go back to the freight office. Maybe the girl left somethin' there."

Chris held her breath as the men left and only released it when she could hear them no more. With a sigh, she leaned against the bank and looked at Ty. "How did they know you?"

35

"Somebody saw us leaving Lanier's house and she recognized me."

"She?"

"I think she's a maid of Lanier's. Anyway, she told Lanier I was the one who took you, so when he found your letter, he was looking for me too. But I did get the story to the doc's wife."

Chris grinned. Now that they were safe, she was beginning to feel euphoric. "I wonder if those freight men have closed their mouths yet? I couldn't believe it when I realized you were bringing that horse straight on through the building."

Ty's eyes twinkled. "I could have taken a paddle to you when you walked out there and started shooting. You should have stayed inside, then when I was out of town, with everybody following me, you could have ridden away, safe and sound. Where'd you learn to shoot like that, anyway?"

"My father. That poor freight man. One minute I'm so ill I can barely sit up and the next—"

"And the next you're leaping onto a horse behind me. Chris, you were great!" He laughed, taking her shoulders and giving her a hard kiss of joy on her mouth.

Blinking, wide-eyed, Chris looked up at him. When he'd kissed her, a spark of pure, undiluted fire had run through her. "Oh," she whispered and moved toward him.

He released her shoulders as if they burned him, then turned his back on her. "I got to get this horse out of here and we'd better get back before Prescott misses us," he mumbled.

Chris felt a little lost, not sure what she'd done wrong. He'd seemed so pleased with her, so happy a

36

moment ago, and he'd kissed her. Not a kiss of passion, but one of friendship, between two people who'd shared a great deal, but when she'd shown interest in him, he'd moved away.

Glancing down at her body, she wondered if maybe she wasn't appealing to him. All her life she'd been told she was pretty, but her curves were subtle, not exaggerated as was the fashion.

"The maid at Mr. Lanier's who recognized you, was her name Elsie?"

"Yeah," he said under his breath, his back still to her. "You leave first and I'll come later."

With a sigh, Chris began climbing the steep bank, pushing vines away as she climbed. Elsie was the same height as Chris but weighed thirty pounds more—and all of it equally distributed above and below a twenty-inch waist. If that's the kind of woman he liked, no wonder he moved away from Chris.

She sighed all the way back to camp, fastening buttons that had come undone in the fracas.

"Are you all right?" Asher greeted her. "You were gone an awfully long time."

"I'm fine," she said, pouring herself a cup of coffee. "And you?"

"I'm all right and I'm glad you got some rest. Tomorrow will probably be another hard day of riding."

"Yes," she said, looking at him over her cup. "I am glad to rest. Is there anything to eat? Long afternoon naps make me ravenously hungry."

Chris didn't see Tynan until the next morning. Twice, she tried to catch his eye, to smile at him, but he wouldn't look at her. It was as if he wanted to pretend yesterday hadn't happened.

Yet, the more he ignored her, the more she watched him. They stopped to make camp in the afternoon and Tynan immediately put Asher and Chris together. Chris sat and watched Ty as he took care of the horses and as he walked past her, she was sure that once she saw him limp. Could he have hurt himself yesterday? He kept that blasted hat pulled down over his face so far that she couldn't really see his face, but as she watched, she saw him grimace as he lifted one arm to take the reins of the horse. Asher looked annoyed once, but Chris kept on watching every move Tynan made—and the more she saw, the more she was convinced that he was in constant pain.

Chris gave a big yawn. "I think I'm rather tired and if no one minds, I'll go down the trail and take a nap."

Tynan turned around and, briefly, his eyes met Chris's, but he looked away almost instantly. "Don't go too far," he mumbled as he passed her and went down the trail into the forest.

"Are you sure you wouldn't rather take a walk with me, Chris?" Asher asked. "I would so like to hear more about your newspaper work."

"I really am very tired. Perhaps another time," she said as she took up her sleeping roll and carpet bag, and, acting as if she could barely move, she started down the trail behind Tynan.

As soon as she was out of Asher's sight, she opened her carpet bag, removed her medical kit and started running down the path, hoping she could catch Tynan before he disappeared.

She seemed to have gone a long way and there was no sign of him when she thought she heard a horse neigh. Doing what she knew she shouldn't, she left the

38

trail to walk to a place where she hoped she could see what was below her.

The area off the trail was frightening to her, she was afraid of the covered drop-offs that Ty had shown them, and who knew what lurked beneath the layers of greenery?

She made it to the base of an enormous tree, parted the hanging moss and looked below. Tynan was standing several feet below in a rocky clearing, his shirt off, rubbing down one of the horses. When he turned and she saw his back, she let out a little gasp. She had been horribly right when she thought he moved as if he were in pain. Even from several feet away, she could see that the gashes that crisscrossed his back were only half healed. And she was sure the wounds had been made by a whip. What he'd done yesterday, tearing about on his horse, hauling her up, her clutching his back, must have caused him untold amounts of pain.

She waited until he'd turned again, so that he was facing her, and then she moved back into the forest, acting as if she were just coming out of it. She made a lot of noise and called his name.

When she emerged and could see him, he'd put his shirt on and was just pulling on his boots.

"Here," he called up to her.

"How do I get down there?"

"You don't. Go back to the camp."

She smiled at him and took a tentative step forward, as if she meant to go straight down the side of the drop off.

"No!" Tynan yelled, but it was too late.

Chris had meant to only pretend to go down that way but, what she'd thought was ground wasn't and she went sliding down the hill on her back.

Tynan ran across the clearing and leaped on top of her to keep her from sliding any farther.

Instinctively, Chris's arms went around him, clutching him close to her. When he lifted his head and looked at her, she was aware of his body on top of hers with every fiber of her being. For a moment, she thought he was going to kiss her—and she welcomed him.

He was a half inch from her lips before he jumped up, leaving her lying on the steep bank. For just a moment, he turned away from her and she had the distinct impression that he was trying to control his emotions. When he turned back, his eyes were alight, but he seemed calm otherwise. "I told you to go back to the camp. And I thought you were too tired to go anywhere and needed to rest."

"I lied," she said with a smile.

"And do you often lie, Miss Mathison?"

"Not nearly as often as the other people in this party," she said, blinking her eyes innocently. "You tell me the truth and I'll tell you the truth. I think that's fair."

He seemed to start to say something, but changed his mind because he turned away from her and went back to the horse. "There's a trail over there. You can use it to get back to the path that takes you to the camp."

She stood, straightened her skirt and retrieved the medical kit that had come down with her. "Actually, I was searching for you because I wanted to have a look at your back."

"My what?!" he said, turning toward her with a face full of fury. "Look, Miss Mathison, I don't know what you're after but I've had about all I can take." He was moving forward, pointing the horse brush at her, and

Chris was backing up. "Maybe you think I'm going to be one of those people in one of your stories but you've got another think coming. I was hired by your father to take you and Prescott through this forest and to take you home to him. I did *not* bargain for you following me everywhere I go nor did I expect for you to keep leaping out at me without a stitch of clothes on. Under different circumstances, I'd enjoy your entertainment, but on this trip I got a job to do and I plan to do it no matter what you do to tempt me. You, lady, are Satan in one beautiful package. Now get out of here and leave me alone. I don't want to see you until I wake you in the morning—and I might even get somebody else to do that."

He closed his mouth abruptly, turned his back on her and went back to the horse.

"All right," Chris said. "I'll return to camp and tell Mr. Prescott that your back is a mass of lacerations that look as if they may become infected and also tell him that something is wrong with your feet. I'm sure the mutiny will be over and done with in no time and you will no longer be our leader and you can return to wherever it is that you refuse to tell anyone. Good day, Mr. Tynan," she said as she started toward the path he'd pointed out.

She'd gone no more than three feet before she heard a muttered oath behind her and what sounded like the horse brush being thrown down with some force.

"All right," he said loudly and Chris turned toward him. "What am I supposed to do?"

"Remove your shirt and boots and lie down on your stomach there on that patch of moss."

"I guess I should be glad you don't want anything else," he mumbled sulkily but did as she asked.

41

As Chris knelt beside him and looked at his back, she saw that the wounds were worse than she'd thought when she'd seen them from a distance. Most of them were healing well but a few had broken open yesterday. She imagined that they were very, very painful. Taking a deep breath, she opened her case and withdrew some salve.

"This will help ease the pain," she said softly and began to soothe it on his skin. His back was broad and he was quite muscular but there was little more than skin covering his muscles, hardly any fat. He looked as if he'd been worked very hard and fed very little.

When she felt him begin to relax under her fingers, she said, "How long were you in prison?"

"Two years," he answered quickly, then whispered, "Damn!"

"Mr. Tynan, I am a newspaper reporter and I work hard at observing. I don't know anywhere else that a man can be worked at hard labor, starved and beaten—at least not in America."

"And if there was such a place you'd get yourself thrown in there so you could write a story about it, right? Am I going to be your next story? 'I went through the rain forest with an escaped prisoner.' Something to that effect?"

"*Did* you escape? Somehow, I thought my father had you released."

When he didn't reply, she knew she'd hit close to home. "You see, Mr. Tynan, I know my father quite well. If he wanted someone to take me through an impenetrable forest, he wouldn't hesitate when people said it couldn't be done. He'd just find out how to do it. My guess is that he found that you'd been through the

42

forest and it wouldn't matter to him if you were on your way to the gallows. He has enough money and power to cut any ropes, even if they're hanging around someone's neck."

"He'd trust his daughter to a murderer?" Tynan asked, turning his head to look at her.

She was thoughtful for a moment. "No, I don't think he would. I believe that my mother and I are the only people he's ever really loved. I wasn't sure he was going to recover after my mother died, but I think he decided he still had me."

"But you're saying that he put you under the care of a criminal, someone rescued from the hangman's noose."

She paused in rubbing the cream into his wounds. "Mr. Tynan, you must be an innocent man. You're perfectly right that my father would never entrust my care to a villain. Yes, of course, that's it. You're either innocent or you did something that wasn't violent. Breach of promise perhaps." Smiling, she resumed smoothing the cream on his back. By now, she was as much massaging his muscles as doctoring him.

"How close am I to the truth?" she asked and when he didn't answer, she laughed. "You see, Mr. Tynan, we all give clues to ourselves, no matter how hard we try to conceal them. I'm sure Mr. Prescott has no idea that you are in pain every time you move, but if you watch, you begin to see things about people."

She kept rubbing his back, greasing her hands and running them over the curves of muscle in his arms, massaging until she felt him relaxing completely. His breathing was soft and deep, as if he were asleep. All Chris's motherly instincts rose within her. How she'd like to take this man home and feed him and see that he rested. She wondered if her father's housekeeper, Mrs. Sunberry, had met him. If she had, Chris was willing to bet she liked Tynan.

Smiling, Chris lifted one of Ty's hands and began to massage it, being careful of his scarred, raw wrist.

"I'm not hurt there," he murmured sleepily but made no attempt to move.

"I was thinking about Mrs. Sunberry."

"Blackberry cobbler," Ty said. "With cinnamon in the crust."

Chris laughed. "So you did meet her. I thought she'd like you."

"Like adopting a stray dog?"

"You're a stray perhaps, but certainly not a dog. Ty, where were you born?"

He moved as if he meant to get up but she pushed him back down.

"All right, no more questions, but please don't get angry again. It's too nice a day to ruin with anger." She ran her hands in his hair and began to massage his scalp.

"Do you like being a newspaper reporter?" he asked.

"Yes, at least I did, but I think I'm getting tired of it. I'm twenty-eight years old and I started when I was eighteen. That's a long time. I think I want . . . I don't know what I want but it's something more."

"A home and kids?"

She laughed. "You've been talking to my father. Did he tell you how he got me back to Washington? How he lied to me? I was working in New York and he sent me a telegram saying he was at death's door. I cried from one end of the country to the other thinking he was dying and when I arrived home, filthy, tired and terrified, there he was atop a bucking bronco having the time of his life."

"You're lucky to have a father."

"You don't?"

"Not that I know of."

"Or mother?"

"She's dead."

"Ah," Chris said. "How long have you been alone?"

"Always. Are you going to look at my feet and get this over with? I need to check the trail ahead to see what's happened to it over the years."

Reluctantly, Chris removed her hands from his skin as he turned and sat up. For a moment their eyes locked and held. Chris never wanted to look away but Ty broke the gaze.

"I was safer in jail," he mumbled. "Here! Take a look at my feet. That should keep you busy for a while."

With a sigh, Chris turned away from his face to look at his feet—then gasped. There were blisters, and blisters that had been worn away to bloody patches and what wasn't actually blistered was about to. "New boots and no socks," she said, taking one foot in her hand. "Did you just put them on and wear them without breaking them in first?"

"I had to. I'd ruined my dancing slippers the night before," he said solemnly.

She laughed. "I'll bandage these places and then I'll see if Mr. Prescott has an extra pair of socks."

"No!" Ty said quickly. "I don't take charity."

Chris looked at him in astonishment. "All right," she

said after a moment. "No charity. But the first town we come to, we buy you socks. My father did pay you for rescuing me, didn't he?"

"Yes," he said, watching her as she began to bandage his foot. She ran her hands over his ankles which were as raw as his wrists. "Chains?" she asked.

He acted as if she hadn't asked. "What made you go after Lanier anyway?"

"I don't know. Somebody has to. John Anderson will have that story in print by now. People hate the Indians even more than they already do whenever they hear of them killing missionaries. This time they didn't do it, Hugh Lanier did, and I didn't think it was fair for the Indians to get the blame."

"Even though it meant that a white man, a man you knew, would probably lose everything?"

"The missionaries lost everything," she said softly.

"I've never seen a woman who handled being shot at as well as you did yesterday. Had some practice?"

"Some," she answered.

"I thought women like you wanted to stay home and raise babies."

"What does that mean, women like me? Besides, I've never been in love. Have you?" She held his ankle in her hands and had no idea how her fingers were tightening.

"A few times. Hey! Your little nails are sharp."

"Sorry," she mumbled, her head down.

"What does it matter to you if I've ever been in love?"

"It doesn't, of course," she said stiffly, easing the pressure on his foot. "I ask questions of everyone."

"Look, Miss Mathison, believe me when I say I'm not your type. I'm a drifter and if there isn't any trouble

46

I seem to make it. You ought to learn something from Elsie. She turned me in because she can't stand me."

Chris smiled at him. "You probably didn't pay enough attention to her."

Ty leaned back on his elbows and watched a bird overhead. "A man can't spend two years in jail and then not give something like Elsie every ounce of his attention."

She yanked on the bandage she was wrapping around his foot. "If you like women like her, that is. I doubt if you've seen a woman like her without her corsets."

Ty looked back at her, his eyes dancing with laughter. "Fat, are they?"

"Twenty-seven-inch waists at least and maybe they do have a lot on top but by the time they're twenty-two, they'll all be sagging and—" Chris stopped, aghast at what she was saying. "Put your boots on," she said rigidly. "Maybe you can get a fat woman to change the bandages in a day or two since you obviously like well padded women and I'm sure I'm too skinny for you."

She started to stand but he caught her arm, grinning at her, but she kept her head down. He was making her so *angry!*

He put his finger under her chin. "You don't think you'll be sagging in a year or two? As old as you are?" There was laughter in his voice. "You don't think I like skinny little girls who follow me around and ask me questions?"

"I don't know," Chris whispered and felt exactly like a little girl. She'd never wanted anything as much as she wanted this man to like her.

"Slim, pretty little blondes are my favorite," he whispered.

Chris looked up at him with eyes sparkling with tears

47

and, as he moved his head toward her, she knew he was going to kiss her, so she closed her eyes and parted her lips in anticipation.

"What the hell am I doing?" he said and pushed Chris so that she landed on her seat a foot away from him. "Get out of here right now! You hear me? Don't come near me again. You're right that I like a different type woman. Virginal nurses who follow me around are the type I like *least*. Now go back to camp and don't even get near me again!"

Chris, a little frightened by his temper, ran up the trail to the path back to camp.

Chapter Five

When Chris reached the camp, out of breath from running, Asher was sitting by a cheery fire, smiling up at her. He began to talk to her about the forest, but Chris was barely listening. She was wondering why Tynan had been sent to jail.

"Chris! Are you listening to me?" Asher asked.

"Yes, of course," she said, looking at him but not listening.

Later, when she was snuggled inside her blankets, she lay awake for a long time. She could barely see the stars through the trees but she watched the leaves and the blackness above. At night this forest was a frightening place.

She'd been awake for over an hour when she heard a soft sound to her right. She knew it was Tynan come to see that they were all right. She'd never seen a man take his responsibilities more seriously.

Her eyes were fully open as she watched him walk

49

about the camp, checking that Asher was covered, that the horses were properly tethered, that the food was covered and that the fire was out. When he came to Chris he started slightly to see her eyes open.

"You should be asleep," he said, standing over her. "You have to get up early tomorrow."

"How is the trail ahead?"

Asher stirred in his bedroll and Ty knelt beside Chris, lowering his voice. She raised on one elbow.

"It's all right, just some brush across it, but I cleared most of it."

"Did you get anything to eat?"

She saw the whiteness of his teeth as he grinned at her. "You are going to make some man a wonderful mother. Yes, I ate. Now go to sleep and I'll see you in the morning."

She lay down on the hard bedroll but he didn't leave.

"Miss Mathison, I'm sorry about this afternoon. I shouldn't have lost my temper. It's just that I think we should keep this trip on an employee, employer basis. As I pointed out to you, I haven't been around women for a while and there are things that are difficult for me."

"Do I make things difficult for you?" she whispered in such a way that there was no doubt of her meaning. She hoped he'd say she was making his life hell.

He rocked back on his heels and grinned at her again. "Not anything that I can't handle. Now, be a good girl and go to sleep."

"No good-night kisses?" she asked, a little angry at his laughing at her.

"Not from me," he said and she smiled because there was horror in his voice. As he walked away, she turned over on her stomach and went to sleep.

The first thing that greeted Chris the next morning was the sight of Tynan bending over the fire. His hair was damp and there were fresh fish frying in a skillet.

"Did you go fishing?" she asked, smiling at him.

He mumbled something but she couldn't hear what it was before he stood and walked to the horses.

All morning Tynan stayed away from her and the three of them rode in silence on the trail.

When they stopped at noon to eat, Tynan quickly told Asher to take Chris with him to gather firewood.

Asher took Chris's elbow and half propelled her toward the path they'd just traveled.

"I hear your father is in shipping, too," Asher said for the second time before Chris heard him.

"Yes, he is," she said distractedly. "Canning, shipping, cattle, a couple of saw mills, anything he can get his hands on."

"Yet you left it all to run away to New York to become a newspaper reporter. But now you're back."

"Not by choice. I plan to return to New York as soon as I get back to my father's house."

"Ah, I see. Somehow, I thought you had other plans."

"Such as?" she asked, turning to look at him. "Did my father tell you that I had other plans?"

"Only that you were ready to settle down, that you were still young enough and he had hopes that you—"

"Young enough for what?" she interrupted.

"Why, to start a family I would imagine."

Chris bit her lower lip to keep from replying hastily. "No, I don't think I'm over the hill yet, even at my advanced age. I assume women can still bear children at my age."

"I didn't mean to give offense."

51

Quickly, Chris looked at him and a wave of guilt ran through her. Here she was walking in the forest with a handsome young man who was trying to be polite and she, because of some imagined infatuation with a man she barely knew, was being almost rude to him. She smiled at Asher. "I'm sure that you didn't, Mr. Prescott. How did you meet my father?"

Asher returned her smile. "He and my father were friends and did some business together. I saw you once when you were a little girl. You were with your mother. I thought she was the prettiest woman I'd ever seen."

"So did I."

He began to gather firewood from the ground, making a stack of it at her feet.

"And why did my father choose you to go on this rescue mission?" She also picked up a few pieces of wood and added them to the pile.

"I think he took who he could get. There aren't many men my age who have no business, and, after working for myself for so many years, I can't seem to settle down to just being an employee."

"I know how you feel. My father continues to tell me what to do and how to do it, even sending men after me when I don't obey him."

"Yes, but you're a—" Asher took one look at Chris's sparkling eyes and stopped. "I almost put my foot in it that time, didn't I?"

She cocked her head to one side. "Would it matter if you alienated me?"

Asher gave her a big grin. He really was quite pleasant-looking, not anything like Tynan, of course, but very handsome. "I'm alone in the woods with a beautiful woman and you ask if it would make any difference if she's angry with me? Why, Miss Mathison, this time and place is a dream come true and I would as soon die as ruin it."

She laughed at his pretty speech as he picked a tiny purple flower from a bank of moss and gave it to her with a little bow. Chris stuck the flower behind her ear and smiled at him.

"Well," he said slowly, "I guess we'd better get back." He picked up an enormous pile of wood. "Put the rest on top of this."

"No, I'll carry my share."

"Miss Mathison, while I am around, no woman shall ever carry firewood. Now do as I say and put the rest of that on this pile."

"You sound just like my father," she said with a sigh.

"Thank you very much. I admire and respect your father and I take it as a high compliment that you consider me like him in any respect. Now, lead the way because I can't see a thing."

Laughing, pleased that he'd said that he liked her father and didn't complain about him as most people did, Chris led him back to camp. Asher said that not only could he not see but he couldn't understand her directions, so Chris "had" to hold two fingers of his left hand to guide him back to camp.

When they entered the camp, Tynan was bending over the fire frying fish dipped in cornmeal. He looked up when a laughing Chris and a laden Asher arrived, but put his head down again quickly.

Chris suddenly felt ridiculously happy. Holding the divided skirt of her habit out, she began to hum.

"I don't guess you'd care to dance, Mr. Prescott," she said, holding out her arms. Out of the corner of her eye, she watched Tynan but he didn't even look up.

With obvious happiness, Asher took Chris's extended hands and began a quick dance about the little clearing. It was a cross between the Virginia Reel and a square dance that was exuberant and happy. Chris followed his lead and no matter how fast he led her in the dance, even when her feet barely touched the ground, she stayed with him.

"Watch out!" she heard Tynan shout just before she and Asher tumbled into a foot-deep depression filled with ferns.

They lay there together, Asher's arms around her protectively, Chris's skirts around his legs, while Tynan stood looming over them. "Are you two all right?" he asked, his brows drawn together in a scowl.

"Never been better in my life," Asher said, then planted a hearty kiss on Chris's cheek.

Still grinning, she turned to see Tynan looking at her oddly.

"I think we can eat now," Tynan said before turning away to return to the campfire. "That is, Miss Mathison, if you are finished with your dancing."

"For the moment," Chris said and went to take a place by the fire.

Chapter Six

Asher was in rollicking good spirits after their impromptu dance and he did his best to entertain Chris, even singing to her. She joined in and they made an enthusiastic duo.

Tynan sat to one side of them, head down, whittling on a stick, not participating but not leaving them either. Once, as she was singing with her cheek close to Asher's, it occurred to her that maybe Tynan didn't know how to participate.

It was midafternoon before anyone thought of leaving and then it was Chris who stopped the laughter and suggested that they clear up and go.

Tynan tossed his stick away, put his knife in his pocket and slowly started toward the horses. As Chris was tightening the straps on her bedroll, he stopped beside her.

"That was nice," he said. "Real nice."

"Where did you grow up?" she asked quickly.

"Not where people sang," he answered just as fast. "You like the man?"

"Of course. You've pointed out what a fine man he is, haven't you? And you've told me to stay away from you so I should be pleasing you now."

He looked at her in a way no man had ever looked at her before. His eyes seemed as if they could burn her. "You do please me." Abruptly, he turned on his heel and walked away, almost crashing into Asher.

"What was that about? He looked angry. Is something going on that I don't know about?"

"Mr. Prescott, I have no idea what you know and what you don't."

"Chris, I must give you some advice. Tynan isn't the sort of man . . . well, I mean, a girl like you . . . I don't like the interest he's taking in you."

"Interest in me?"

"Your father told him you were a Montgomery and he asked what that meant."

"And did you know to tell him?"

"No, I didn't, except that they are your mother's people. People like him don't have relatives, they don't even have names."

"Mr. Prescott," she said icily. "You and I will get along a great deal better if you keep your opinions about Mr. Tynan to yourself. After all, I've known the both of you an equal length of time so I see no reason to trust you over him." With that she mounted her horse, and all the rest of the day, she felt Asher Prescott's eyes looking at her thoughtfully.

For two days they traveled hard. Three times the men had to cut away small logs across the trail, and once Tynan and Asher had to lead the horses across a log as wide as some boardwalks. Another time they spent hours on either end of a crosscut saw hacking a way through a tree down across the trail. At night they fell into their blankets and slept hard—at least Chris assumed Tynan did too since he slept apart from the camp.

On the evening of the second day, Asher kissed her again. They'd ridden together for a while during the day and he'd asked her more questions about her newspaper career. He also apologized for what he'd said about Tynan, saying he was only concerned about her safety. That evening he asked her to walk with him and, when they were a few yards from the camp, he told her how pretty she was and asked permission to kiss her. Chris said yes.

She'd kissed very few men in her life and wasn't exactly sure how to do it. Asher's arms went around her, holding her pleasantly and his kiss was warm and dry and comforting but nothing like the quick, happy kiss of Tynan's. No fire ran through her body. Nothing made her lean toward him wanting more.

"What the hell are you doing, Prescott?" came Tynan's outraged voice, making Asher release Chris. "I came out here thinking you'd gotten lost and here you are mauling Miss Mathison."

"I was not mauling. I asked permission—" Asher halted, his face angry. "What's it any of your business anyway?"

"My business is to return Miss Mathison to her father."

"And I don't believe that's *all* you've been hired to do either," Asher said.

"Go back to camp," Tynan ordered Chris. "Now!"

She scurried to obey him, leaving the two men alone. Later, Asher returned to camp by himself and grinned at Chris. "Sometimes employees forget their places and have to be reminded," he said with a wink.

Tynan didn't return to camp that night and in the morning he was quiet, always keeping his distance from Chris.

A part of her wanted to scream with frustration over the mystery of what was going on. What was her father's original reason for having her taken through the rain forest? He couldn't have known Hugh Lanier would be chasing them. Why had her father hired a man who barely knew how to build a fire outdoors to help in a place like a rain forest? Why was Tynan one minute pushing her toward Asher and the next acting like a jealous lover?

The day after Asher kissed Chris, Ty allowed them to stop in the late afternoon. As Chris helped Ty unpack, she tried to make converstaion but he only mumbled answers to her questions.

"What is wrong with you?" she hissed under her breath. "You haven't spoken to me since last night. Are you angry with me about Asher?"

"What you do is your own business," he said, unsaddling a horse. "I've been hired as your guide and nothing more."

"It's *you* who keeps pushing me off to be alone with him. It's 'Miss Mathison, go with Prescott and fetch wood,' and 'Miss Mathison, why don't you and Prescott go fishing?' Every minute you're pushing me toward him. So if I kiss him, isn't that what you had in mind?"

"Nothing's in my mind. Look, why don't you go over there and sit down? Why are you always following me? Can't you ever give a man a moment of peace?"

Quick tears came to Chris's eyes as she turned

toward the fire. He called her name but she didn't look back.

Once, she felt that Ty was trying to catch her eye but she didn't look up at him, and after a while she heard him leave the camp.

"I'm going to take a walk and write in my journal," Chris said to Asher, removing her notebook, pen and ink from her saddlebag. "I'll be back in an hour or so." She then went down the path in the opposite direction of Tynan.

Chris walked for longer than she meant to. Tynan's sharp, angry words had hurt her and she wanted to think about what she had been doing and what she wanted to do in the future.

It was odd how this man attracted her. Never before had she made such a fool of herself over a man.

After a while, the light began to fade and she moved just off the trail to sit on a log and write in her journal. Maybe if she put in all the facts of this odd trip, she could figure out what was going on. She wrote a good deal about the one man who was so kind to her as opposed to the man who seemed to hope that she'd fall into a deep hole.

She was sheltered under the tree branches and a particularly heavy umbrella of moss and didn't at first feel the cold drops of rain begin to fall. One minute she was warm and dry and the next she was sitting under what seemed to be a waterfall that began in the sky.

Gathering her things with haste, she dropped her pen. She was leaning over the log to get it, searching in the plants, when the entire side of the trail suddenly gave way and Chris went tumbling down. The log rolled out from under her and she caught at a tree root as she went flying down the side of the forest wall.

Hanging there, suspended, the icy rain coming down on top of her, her feet touching nothing and not being able to see anything below or above her, she prayed for help. "Tynan," she whispered, not able to hear herself above the rain crashing down.

"Tynan!" she shouted.

Her hands were beginning to slip. She tried to keep a cool head about where she was and how she could get out of this mess. If she could only see how far it was to the bottom of the drop. For all she knew, she could be six inches from the ground.

Twisting, she tried to look below her, but the rising mist made it impossible to see anything. One of her hands slipped.

After several long minutes of struggle, she got both hands back on the tree root. She could feel the skin begin to tear away. She tried to swing forward, hoping to get her foot into the mud and rocks of the bank.

"Curse all the Montgomery women for being short," she said when she couldn't reach the bank.

Suddenly, she stopped as she thought she heard a sound above her.

"Tynan," she yelled with all her might. "Tynan. Tynan. Tynan."

She hadn't finished her last scream before he was there beside her, his back sunk into the mud of the bank, his long arms reaching for her and pulling her to him.

She clung to him like a monkey to a tree, wrapping her body around his, her arms around his neck, her legs around his waist.

He began to go down the side of the bank, scooting along, pushing debris out of the way as he moved. Chris held to him, her face buried in his neck. Even when he started walking, she didn't let go.

"Here," he said at last, peeling her off of him.

When he stood her on the ground, she found that her legs were weak. Both their bodies were covered in mud.

"Sit there for a while and rest." He pointed to an outcropping of rock behind her, and, gratefully, she sat down, out of the pelting rain.

As she looked up at Ty, the misty, cold rain coming down behind his head, she knew she'd never seen anything as welcome in her life. Quite naturally, she put up her arms to him.

He came to her, holding her so tightly she could barely breath. "I knew it was going to rain," he said. "I was getting the tents up when you walked off. I thought you'd have sense enough to come back when it started. God, Chris, you're going to be the death of me. It's a wonder I found you."

Chris was so happy that she was safe and that he was here that she began kissing his neck exuberantly. "I knew you'd find me. I knew it from the moment the ground fell away. One minute I was sitting there and the next I was falling. I wasn't even sure it was raining."

Ty forcibly pulled her arms from around his neck—and he looked like a man in great pain. "Chris," he said in a pleading voice, "have you ever seen a grown man cry? I mean really cry? Like a brokenhearted two-year-old?"

"No, I don't believe I have or that I want to." She was reaching for him again. "Ty," she said.

He caught her hands in his, holding them together in front of him. "Then please stop this," he said. "Please

61

leave me alone. Don't follow me, don't touch me, don't mother me, don't put salve on my back, don't cry when I get mad at you. Don't do anything. I'm begging you, please."

Chris leaned toward him. "It doesn't matter to me that you were in prison. You may think that I'm of a different class than you but I'm not. Ty, I think I may be in love—"

He put his hand over her mouth. "Don't say it. Don't ever say it. I couldn't bear to hear it. We've only known each other for a few days and in a few more we'll never see each other again."

"The number of days doesn't matter. Do you know how many men have asked me to marry them? I receive proposals in the mail. I've been to dinner parties and had two proposals by the end of the meal, but I've never even been tempted—not by marriage or by their attempts at seduction. But you, Tynan, you're the man I want."

Ty's face went through one contortion after another and for just a moment, he leaned toward her as if he meant to kiss her. But the next second, he ran from the dry rock cropping, out into the rain.

"Don't you understand that I CAN'T? I *can't* make love to you. Now get up! We're going back to camp and don't come near me again." He grabbed her wrist and pulled her out into the rain with him, then half pushed her up the steep bank. Once on the trail again, he didn't touch her, just pointed the way back to the camp.

Chris knew that some of the water on her face was a deluge of tears but she didn't know how much until she reached the camp. There were three tents set up, one for each of them. Under a tree, its opening facing away from the other two tents, was a tarpaulin that she knew was Tynan's.

Ty stood back, arms folded over his chest while she went into the tent he pointed to.

It took Chris an hour to change into dry clothes, because her tears kept running down her cheeks. She cried all night long. The first man she'd ever loved and this had to happen.

When morning came, her face was red and swollen, her nose half again its usual size and her head was aching. When Tynan came to tell her that they'd stay in the tents until the rain stopped, she couldn't look at him, but just kept her head down and nodded.

By noon, Chris was exhausted from so many hours of crying and thinking, but she'd made some decisions. Slowly, she built a little fire under the dry leaves of the tent and heated some soup left from the day before.

She took her rain gear from the pile of garments in a corner. There was no furniture in the little tent, just a sleeping roll, a few clothes and now the little fire under the flap outside.

With her back rigid, Chris left the tent. The rain was coming down very hard and when it hit the hot kettle, it gave off wisps of steam.

Tynan had rigged himself a piece of canvas supported by two poles in the front. It left the sides and the front open and, as long as the wind didn't blow the rain about, the occupant could stay dry. Ty was stretched out, his head on his saddle, a book in his hand when Chris arrived.

"I brought you some soup," she said above the rain.

Sitting up, he reached out and took the pot from her as she withdrew biscuits from under her slicker. "May I sit down?"

63

"I don't think that . . . yes, of course," he said at last, looking at her hard. No one could miss the fact that she'd been crying for many hours.

"I've been awake all night and I've been thinking about what you told me and I've come to some decisions." She took a deep breath. There was no use stalling. "First, I'd like to say that I thank you for telling me what you did. I'm sure it's not something that you tell everyone."

She lowered her head and didn't look at him as he stared in open-mouthed astonishment. "I think the best way to say this is just to get it out. I don't know very much about love, never having experienced it before, at least not love between a man and a woman, but I think I have sense enough to recognize it when I see it. I don't know how or why, but I've fallen in love with you and I want to spend the rest of my life with you. I know your secret now and, after much thought—I don't want you to think that I say this lightly—I know it doesn't matter. I've never made love to a man before so I'll never have any idea what it is that I'm missing and, as for children, I have some contacts in New York and if it's all right with you, we can take in an orphan or two."

Chris stopped and looked up at a sound from Tynan. For a moment, she was astonished because he seemed to be having a sort of fit. Was epilepsy what was wrong with him?

"Tynan," she said, moving toward him.

He had his hands on his stomach, his legs drawn up, his mouth open and he didn't seem to be breathing.

She was ready to call for help when she suddenly realized that he was *laughing*.

She sat back on her heels, watching him as he finally

caught his breath and began to laugh as she'd never seen anyone laugh before.

"An orphan or two!" he gasped. "I don't know what I'm missing. I'll take you anyway." With each word, he doubled over harder and laughed more deeply—and Chris's backbone grew more rigid.

"I am certainly glad that I am a source of amusement for you, Mr. Tynan. May we pretend that this conversation never took place?" With that she moved out of his shelter and started back to her own tent.

Ty caught her skirt hem. He was still laughing and weak from the effort. "Don't be mad, Chris, it's just that I—" He broke off and went into fresh peals of laughter at a new memory and Chris wondered how she could ever have thought she loved this idiot of a man. At the moment she wished the earth would open and swallow him.

"Come in out of the rain," he said, making a valiant effort to control himself, but his lips were twitching and his eyes watery.

"No thank you. Please release my skirt so I can get back to my own tent. I don't think we have anything to say to one another."

He began to sober somewhat, although he seemed too weak to stand as he reached up, took her by the waist and pulled her into the shelter. It was like trying to manipulate a stone statue.

"Chris," he began and, again, he gave a little laugh.

Chris tried to get away but he pulled her into his lap and held her there, her hands held firmly against her sides.

He took a full minute trying to calm himself. "Chris," he said at last. "As long as I live I will remember this . . . ah, proposition of yours. I have certainly never been offered anything like it nor have I even heard of something like this being offered to anyone else. It is kind and generous of you."

"May I go now?" she asked, making a move to get off his lap.

"Not until you let me explain. When I said that I *couldn't* make love to you, I didn't mean that I—" He stopped for a moment and worked to control his smirking lips. Chris stiffened even more in his lap. "I didn't mean that physically I couldn't, I meant that there were other reasons as to why I can't touch you."

"You seem to have been doing enough of that," she said through tight lips.

"Sometimes I can't help myself. By 'touch' you I mean to make love to you. That I *can't* do."

"It's me, isn't it? If I were like Mr. Lanier's maid with her big bosom and hips you wouldn't have any problem at all, would you?"

"Damn it! It isn't physical! It's—"

Her nose was almost touching his. "I thought that if the woman was willing then the man *always* was. That's what my mother told me. I've been fighting off men all my adult life and now I offer myself to one and he *can't*. If it's not me and it's not you and it's not fat ladies, what is it?"

Tynan ran his hands up her arms. "Oh Chris, you are killing me. I had it easy in prison compared with this. Why did you pick me and not Prescott?"

Chris started to get off his lap but he pulled her back down. "I won't bother you again, I assure you."

He moved so that his face was near her neck and she could feel his soft, warm breath on her skin. "You'll always bother me. Every time you take a breath, you

66

bother me. And I can't stand to see you with Prescott. Chris, I've never wanted anything so badly in my life as I've wanted you since that first night I held you. I have nearly gone insane in the last few days. I think about you all the time. I can't even stay in the camp when you're there because I'm afraid that I'll do something like throw you on my horse and take you away with me."

"But I offer myself to you and you laugh at me. You've done nothing but yell at me to get away from you since I first met you. I don't understand! *Can* you make love? You're not physically impaired?"

"If you weren't so innocent, you'd know the answer to that right now from where you're sitting on my lap." He began to bite her earlobe and Chris just about melted into him. "If I make love to you," he said, moving down her neck, "I . . ."

"Yes," she whispered, her head back so she could enjoy his touch more.

"If I make love to you, your father will send me back to prison."

"Oh," Chris murmured, not really hearing him. Then she sat up and looked at him. "My father will *what?*"

"He'll send me back to jail. Look, Chris, I didn't want to tell you this and I really tried to get around it, but the truth is, you have been declared off limits to me."

She drew back from him, moving off his lap. "I want to hear the whole story."

With a sigh, Ty leaned back on his arm and looked at her. "I was in jail on a life sentence but your father got me out to rescue his daughter. When you said that he had enough money and power to get what he wanted,

67

you were right. He got me out but he holds the papers and he's made the rules: I touch you and I go back to prison."

"Well, we shall see about that," Chris said. "My father has been giving me orders all my life and I've only obeyed half of them—if that. We'll just go back to him and tell him that he can't do that to us."

Ty took her hands in his. "Chris, he's right. He doesn't want his only child to marry somebody like me. I don't even know how to treat a good girl like you. I don't know how to live in a house like that big one of your father's or even how to stay in one place for very long at a time. I'm not husband material and your father knew it. He didn't want me doing anything to his daughter short of marriage and we both knew I wasn't the marrying kind. Do you understand?"

"No," she said softly, looking into his eyes. "I love you and—"

"No you don't. You've just been too busy with your newspaper over the years to notice men and now you're worried that you're getting old and you think you're in love with the first man you see."

"Then why aren't I in love with Mr. Prescott?"

He leaned back, winked and grinned at her. "I'm better looking. There's no competition."

"I think you're right," she said, moving out of the shelter. "I believe I *have* made an error."

He caught her shoulder and pulled her back inside. "Don't get angry, Chris. Under other circumstances, I'd love to climb into bed with you, but I don't want to go back to that hellhole and I don't want to be unfair to you. You deserve a man who's husband material. I'm not. I hope you can understand."

"I think I understand better than you think," she said

coolly. "I want to apologize for my forwardness, for following you, as you've asked me not to do, and for imposing myself on you. I will try to do better in the future and not give you cause to fear that you will have to return to prison because I have put you in an impossible situation. Is that what you wanted to hear? May I go now?"

"I think you're angry with me. I didn't mean—"

"I am angry with myself," she interrupted. "And deeply embarrassed. I've never thrown myself at a man before and I can assure you that I will never do it again. You won't have any more problems from me, Mr. Tynan. Now, I'd like to go back to my tent and take a nap, if that's all right with you."

He frowned. "Yes, of course. Chris, I really do appreciate the offer, I mean when you thought that physically I couldn't—"

"We shall never know, will we?" she said as she left the shelter.

Chapter Seven

By the time they entered the little town at the edge of the rain forest, Chris had cried all the tears she could cry. She had done a marvelous job of staying away from Tynan. No matter what he said to entice her to stop and talk, she'd ignored him.

Nor did she spend much time with Asher. She did what work was required to keep the camp running and nothing else.

Tynan, after a day of attempting to talk to her, began to stay away from the camp more and more often until, at the last, he was the shadowy figure he had been at the beginning of the trip.

"This has not become the joyous trip I'd hoped for," Asher said with sadness and confusion in his voice. Chris didn't say anything. All she wanted was to get away from the place where she'd made such a fool of herself.

It was still morning when they pulled into the little

town at the foot of the rain forest. The place was busy with shoppers, wagons being loaded, cowboys strolling about, and a few women stopping and talking to each other. Most people halted when they saw the strangers come into town.

At least that's what Chris first thought was the cause of their staring. For the first time in days she came out of her dejection and began to take an interest in her surroundings.

As she watched the people, she became aware that they were actually stopping to stare at Tynan.

He was in front of her, his back held as straight as a piece of steel, eyes ahead, looking at no one. As they passed the sheriff's office, a man ran inside and the sheriff came out within seconds.

"I don't want no trouble," the sheriff called, directing his plea in Tynan's direction.

Tynan didn't acknowledge the man's presence but kept riding in a slow, steady pace.

As they passed a saloon, a garishly dressed woman came out, did a double take when she saw Tynan, then began running through the dirty streets. As they neared a place called the Pink Garter, the double doors swung open and out stepped a tall, older woman with hair an extraordinary shade of red—not natural-looking at all, Chris thought.

"Tynan!" the woman shouted.

Ty put his hand up for them to halt while he went to the woman.

Chris had never strained her ears so hard in her life as she did to hear what the woman had to say.

"You shouldn't have come back here," the red-haired woman said. "You're askin' for trouble."

Chris couldn't hear Ty's answer. With his low voice he could make the sound disappear when he wanted to.

After a moment of listening to the woman, he reined his horse away and motioned to the others to follow him as he led them to a hotel.

"You'll stay here tonight and tomorrow we'll ride out early."

"And where will you be staying?" They were the first words Chris had spoken directly to him in days.

He looked at her a long moment. "I have friends here. Go inside and ask them for a bath," he said before turning on his heel and leaving them.

"What do you think that was all about?" Chris asked Asher.

"The bath? I agree, Miss Mathison, that it's been so long since I had one that I'm close to forgetting what they are too, but you'll remember as soon as you see the hot water."

Chris ignored his attempt at humor. "No, I mean out there in the street," she said, following Asher into the hotel. "Why were all the people staring at Tynan? And why did that woman warn him?"

"I have no interest in anything except a hot bath, a hot meal and a cool, soft bed. I am not interested in any mysteries and as far as I can tell, our guide is one long mystery. Chris, will you please sign the register so we can get a room?"

At the moment, Chris couldn't have told anyone why she had been depressed for the last few days. All she could think of now was that there was a good story at her fingertips. Why was this entire town glaring at one man? Of course it had to do with Tynan's having been in jail but what had he done that made the whole town watch him?

"Miss," the desk clerk said, "would you like to register?"

"Yes," she said absently. She started to write Christiana, but suddenly changed her mind and wrote Nola Dallas.

The clerk, bored, turned the big book around and then his eyes bugged. *The* Nola Dallas? The one that went to Mexico?"

"Yes." Chris smiled as sweetly as she could manage.

"But I thought you were really a man."

"Many people do." She kept smiling at the man. Once, she'd persuaded a guard to open a cell for her with just that smile.

Asher looked annoyed. "We're just here for a little rest," he told the clerk. "Please don't tell anyone she's here."

"I wouldn't think of it," the clerk said, his eyes wide. "I wouldn't tell a soul."

Still frowning, Asher took Chris's arm and led her up the stairs as Chris kept looking over her shoulder and smiling at the desk clerk. "I wish you hadn't done that," Asher said when they were at the door of her room. "Your father was worried about some trouble from Lanier. Of course you didn't actually publish anything about him, but just the same . . ."

Chris smiled at him. "I just wondered if people this far west had heard of me, that's all."

"Oh well, I guess that's all right. You'd better rest now, Chris. I'll have a bath sent up."

Once inside the room, she looked in the mirror. Not bad, she thought, a wash and a comb should make her presentable.

"If you tell people who you are," she said aloud to the mirror, "and they feel that they know you, there's a good chance they'll be willing to tell you what you want to know."

It was an hour later that Chris was washed and she hoped the desk clerk had had time to tell the people who'd just arrived. When she walked into the lobby, people stopped and looked at her and she could hear them whispering, "Is that her?"

Smiling to herself, Chris went out into the bright sunlight. She seemed to remember a ladies' dress shop on the main street. If there was anywhere to hear gossip, that would be the place.

"May I help you?" the clerk asked, but before Chris could answer, the shop door opened and in walked three ladies. The door hadn't closed before two more walked in followed by four more. The little shop was packed with people as Chris made her way to a corner to try on a hat or two.

"You'll never believe who came into town," one of the women said loudly, directing her voice toward Chris. "Of course I couldn't believe it when Jimmy told me, but he said that Nola Dallas was in town."

"You know, the lady who got herself put into an insane asylum to report on what it was like."

"And she wrote that it wasn't safe for decent women to walk the streets alone at night."

"And she almost got herself killed in Mexico for what she wrote about the government," said a third woman.

"How very, very much I'd like to meet her," sighed another woman.

There followed a long, expectant pause and Chris knew they were waiting for her to make the next move.

As if she weren't aware of what they'd been saying, she tried on another hat, then removed it and started for the door. She had her hand on the knob before she looked back at the women who were unabashedly staring at her. "I am Nola Dallas," she said softly.

The flood gates burst after that. Chris was bodily hauled back into the store and asked thousands of questions.

"Did you really write that series on divorce?"

"Did you really spend three days in jail?"

"Weren't you frightened when you got that lobbyist and all those politicians arrested?"

Chris tried to answer all of them at once. All the while she was waiting to hear what she'd come to find out.

"I'm sure that it's none of our business but we think you should look more carefully to your traveling companions," said one woman with her nose in the air.

There was a hush on the crowd. "Oh?" Chris said with all the innocence she could muster. "They seem like such nice men."

"Perhaps one of them is but that Tynan . . ." The women looked at each other and were silent.

Chris modestly studied her hands. "I really know so little about him."

The women began to fall all over themselves in their rush to tell her all that they knew about the man— which, unfortunately, wasn't much. Tynan had been arrested for murder, tried the same afternoon and sentenced to hang that night.

"That seems awfully quick," Chris said.

"It was an open and shut case. He was guilty, everyone could see that."

"But he went to jail instead," Chris prompted.

The women exchanged looks. "During the night, some of the men decided not to wait to hang him—not that I believe in that sort of thing—but the way they rescued him, well . . ."

Chris waited patiently.

One of the women leaned forward in conspiracy. "The ah, ah . . ."

"What Ellen's trying to say is that the harlots of this town banded together and, carrying rifles, they protected this Mr. Tynan until the federal marshal could get here."

"They also demanded a new trial and the marshal said there wasn't any proof that he'd actually fired the gun that had killed the man—there were lots of guns being fired that day—so the marshal gave him life imprisonment instead of hanging."

Chris took a deep breath. "Who is the red-haired woman?"

The women stiffened, showing their goodness and virtue. "Just one of *them*. That Tynan stays in her saloon when he's in town."

"He really can be very nice," said a pretty young girl at the back of the group.

A woman who had to be the girl's mother looked shocked. She turned to Chris. "Some of the girls here have no sense. He's a no-good waster, travels around and makes the girls fall in love with him, then leaves them crying. You're best to stay away from the likes of him, Miss Dallas."

Chris moved toward the door. "I can't thank you ladies enough for telling me this, but now I have a story to research." She looked at the women and smiled.

"I've always wanted to know what the inside of a house of prostitution looks like, haven't you?"

For a moment, the women were too stunned to speak, but they considered Chris to be one of them. They'd read her articles for years and they felt as if they knew her.

"Yes," one of the women in the back sighed and the others began to laugh.

"Wish me luck," she called over her shoulder as she left the dress shop and made her way to the red-haired woman's saloon. Behind her, she heard murmurs of how brave she was.

There were only two cowboys in the saloon when she entered, sitting at a table listlessly playing cards. A big, aproned bartender was sweeping the floor.

"I'm looking for someone, a tall woman with red hair," Chris said. "Is she here?"

"Not to ladies, she ain't."

"Joe," came a voice from the head of the stairs and Chris looked up to see the red-haired woman. "This here little lady is Nola Dallas, the one that dressed up as a showgirl, remember?"

The faces of the bartender and the two cowboys changed as they looked at Chris. "Come on up," the woman called and Chris went up the stairs.

The woman led her to a large room that was very pretty if a bit loud in color for Chris's taste.

"I'm Red," the woman said, motioning Chris to a horsehair sofa. "You wanta drink? I ain't got any tea."

"Red?" Chris asked.

"On account of the hair. I gave up trying to have a name because everybody called me Red anyway, so why fight it? Now, what can I do for you?"

Chris withdrew a notebook and a pencil from her handbag and tried to look professional. "I believe you know Mr. Tynan. Do you know where he is now?"

Red laughed. "If I know Ty, right now he's in a bathtub with three of my best girls."

Chris was so shocked that she dropped her notebook and pencil and bent quickly to retrieve them, trying to cover her distress.

Red sat on the other end of the sofa. "Oh, dear, it's like that, is it? How long did you spend with him?"

"Just a few days," Chris said, smoothing her skirt, not lifting her red face.

"And you fell in love with him," Red said flatly.

"More or less," Chris mumbled then lifted her head, started to say something then stood. "The man is driving me crazy!" she said with passion. "I thought you might know something about him. He seemed to talk to you as if he knew you."

"I guess I know him as well as anyone. I helped raise him. Look, honey, women fall in love with Ty on a daily basis. He's so damned good lookin' and that voice of his can talk a woman into anything. But I can tell you that, as far as I know, he never has anything to do with good girls like you."

"That's just what he said. Oh, Miss Red," she said, moving back to the sofa. "I've never been in love in my life and I don't even know if I am now, but there's something intriguing about this man and I want to know all I can find out about him."

Red looked at her a while. "He deserves more than what he got dealt in life. He's a good boy and he ain't never had a chance at nothin' but bad. If I tell you about Ty, will you tell me how come he's out of jail?"

"My father got him out. Have you ever heard of Delbert J. Mathison?"

"About as often as I've heard of beer. Tynan ain't got hisself mixed up with the likes of him, has he? That man will eat Ty alive."

"He's my father," Chris said, then waved her hand in protest as Red started to apologize. "I know him better than anyone. For some reason, he got Ty out of jail to kidnap me from where I was visiting and take me home. Tynan said that it was because he knew the rain forest, but I don't think that's all of it. I think my father had another reason and I have no idea what it is."

Chris lowered her head. "I never met anyone like Ty and I like him a great deal. I sense that there is more to him than one can see right away. I . . . I'm afraid I threw myself at him. He told me that if he touched me my father would send him back to jail. Needless to say, I stayed away from him for the last few days of the trip."

"I told you that Ty never touches innocent girls. The last time he did, he got thrown in jail and would be dead now if some of us girls hadn't stepped in."

With an expectant look on her face, Chris waited for the woman to speak. She was older than Chris had originally thought, but her skin was well cared for and soft looking.

Red got up to get another drink of well watered whiskey. "I don't usually drink this time of day but seein' Ty again and havin' him to worry about makes me wanta get drunk and stay that way. You were right when you said that I seemed to know him. I'm one of four women that are the closest thing to a mother that boy ever had."

She sat down across from Chris. "He wouldn't like me tellin' you this but you give me a lot of pleasure in them articles of yours and I wanta do somethin' for you. About twenty-nine years ago when I was just startin' out in this business—and I was little more than a kid myself—a miner brought a newborn baby to the house where I was workin' and left him to us girls to take care of. That old man was as bad as they come, nobody could stand him. He'd cheat cripples if he could. Well, he brought this baby in and he hadn't even cleaned it, it still had the birth filth on it and it was weak from hunger. We ran around real fast and found a woman to feed the baby and we took care of him as best we could for as long as we had him."

"And that was Tynan? How had the miner come by him?"

"He wouldn't tell us until we'd given him free whiskey, but he said he'd found a pregnant woman wandering in the forest, out of her head. She stopped in front of him—I'm sure he didn't volunteer to help her—and delivered the baby herself. She whispered the single word of Tynan, then died. Knowing the miner, it's a wonder he didn't just walk away and leave the dead woman and the baby. But I guess he had plans to get what he could so he wrapped the boy up and brought him to us."

Red stood, her back to Chris. "We did the best we could but a whore house ain't no place to raise a kid. All the girls adored him and I'm sure we spoiled him rotten, but we had problems we couldn't help. When Ty was about two, we dressed him up in a little suit and escorted him to Sunday School. The ladies of the congregation ran us off. They wouldn't believe that Ty wasn't one of our byblows."

Red paused a moment. "He stayed with me until he was six years old. I never loved anybody more than I loved that boy. He was all that I had."

"What happened when he was six?"

Red gave a resigned sigh and looked back at Chris. "The miner that'd found him came back with a lawyer, said Tynan was legally his and took him away. Two towns away, he stood Ty on a table and auctioned him off to the highest bidder."

Chris sat still for a moment as she let this sink in. A little boy stood on a table and auctioned off as if he were an animal. Slavery had been abolished years ago. "Who, ah, bought him?"

"Some farmer on his way east. I didn't see or hear from Ty for twelve years. By then he was the strappin' big, good-lookin' thing that he is now, but he'd changed. I got him to tell me some of what had happened after he left the farmer's." She paused to smile. "I don't think the farmer was too happy with Ty's leavin' 'cause Ty had a couple of scars on his legs and when I asked him where he got 'em, he said it was caused by differin' opinions about whether he should leave the farmer's or not. I think the man worked Ty like a draft horse. After he left, at twelve, he was on his own. He traveled around, took odd jobs, got into a bad crowd a couple of times, learned how to use a gun, all the things a boy does. Then for a while he seemed to be headed for real trouble but something changed him. I don't know what it was or if it was anything special. A friend of his, an outlaw, got hisself hanged and that may have had an effect on Ty, I don't know, but whatever it was, somethin' made him go straight."

Red closed her eyes for a minute. "Goin' straight just about killed him. He took all the jobs nobody wanted or was too afraid to take on. He'd even go into towns run by outlaws and clean them up. But, since he always left dead bodies behind him, one after another, the good townspeople would always ask him to please leave."

"But that's not fair," Chris said.

"Honey, we ain't even come to unfair yet. Like I said, Ty never did fool around with clean girls, he always had sense enough to stay away from 'em. But that didn't keep the girls from swarmin' around him. They like the way he ignores 'em. Well, one of 'em, a real pretty little thing used to twitch her tail around Ty till he was about to break. Then one day she come into the saloon to get him. I saw her cryin' and he was holdin' her. He's always been a sucker for tears, couldn't stand 'em on a woman. Next thing I knew he was saddlin' a horse and takin' rifles out of a cabinet. This girl said that a big rancher around here was attackin' her father and could Ty help."

Red took a drink of her whiskey. "I told him not to go, that it wasn't his fight, but he wouldn't listen. There was a gun battle and when the dust and gunpowder settled, the big rancher's son was dead and Ty was being hauled off to jail."

"And that's when you rescued him."

"Heard about that, did you? Yeah, we rescued him. He didn't kill that man's son, that girl did and he was gonna hang for it rather than turn her in. It seems that she'd been sneakin' out to see the boy and had only been usin' Ty to make him jealous. But, even knowin' that, he wouldn't turn her in. I got to thinkin' that maybe he didn't mind dyin'. Sometimes he acts like he don't think he's worth much."

"He said he wasn't good enough for me," Chris said

softly. "He said I deserved more than somebody like him."

"Don't you believe it, honey, there ain't *nobody* better 'n him."

"That's exactly what I thought too," Chris said with a grin. "Do you think there's any way I can tempt him into giving me what I want?"

"And what you want is Tynan?"

"With all my heart and soul."

For a long while, Red stared at Chris. "You know, you may be just what he needs." She stopped and narrowed her eyes. "I feel like I know you from years of readin' your stories, but I'm warnin' you that if you think Ty's just one of those cases of yours and you get rid of him after a little while I'll—"

Chris burst out laughing. "This is a turn of events, isn't it? Isn't it usually the father who warns the prospective young man?"

Red returned her smile. "I ain't too good at bein' a mother."

"It seems to me that you've done a fine job. At least *I* like what you've done. My problem is that Ty doesn't like me. At least not the way I like him. How can I get past the threat of prison and the memory of how another so called 'good' girl treated him? And, besides, I think he really likes another type of woman better than me." Chris looked down at her own slight curves.

Red didn't get to answer because of the voice at the door.

"Red, you awake?"

There was no question of whose voice that was.

"Just a minute, Ty, baby," Red called. "You come with me," she said, taking Chris's arm in her hand as she opened a closet door. "This is a place for men that can't but like to watch. You stay in here and listen. I'll find out how much Ty does or doesn't like you. You game?"

It was on the tip of Chris's tongue to ask questions about the closet, but she suppressed herself. "Yes," she whispered, then Red half shoved her into a chair and closed the door.

"I'm just comin', Ty honey," she called and went across the room to open the door.

Chapter Eight

Ty's hair was wet and he was just buttoning his shirt.

"Don't even put it back on," Red said, holding the door open for him. "I want to look at that back of yours."

"It's fine," Tynan said but removed his shirt obediently.

Red ran her hands over his skin, turned him toward the light—and the closet—so she could see better. "It's all right but it'll be weeks before it's fully healed. And you're skin and bones. We need to fatten you up."

He put his shirt back on. "You sound like Chris."

"She that little blonde rode in with you? The one everybody's sayin' is Nola Dallas?"

Ty poured himself a whiskey and sat down on the sofa. "God, that's good. The thing you miss most in prison isn't freedom but the small pleasures of life like good food and drink, a clean bed,"—he grinned—"and women. You ought to pay that Leora more. Whatever you're paying her, it's not enough."

85

"You're not answerin' my question. Is that little blonde Nola Dallas?"

"Yeah," he said, looking at his whiskey. "Tell me what's been going on the last couple of years. Business good? You seem to have more girls than usual."

"I think some of the girls in the tub with you weren't mine," Red said heavily. "Tynan, stop dancin' around me. What are you doin' back here? Are you free from jail permanently or what?"

He smiled at her. "With a few hitches, I am more or less free."

"Hitches? Such as what?"

"One pretty little blonde that's about to send me back, that's what."

"Oh?" Red asked, eyebrows raised.

"Don't play innocent with me. Even in the tub the girls were giggling about this famous Nola Dallas being here. Is she really all that famous? I mean I know what she's done, her father gave me a stack of newspaper articles to read about her or by her, but I thought that out here . . ."

"Honey, she's what every woman dreams of being: brave, courageous, a fighter, and she's made it in a man's profession."

"More than I've done," Tynan muttered.

"Was it really bad in jail?" Red asked, sitting across from him.

"I think old man Dickerson had friends. I guess he figured that if he couldn't kill me with a rope, he'd have it done with whip and chains."

Red reached out, caressed his cheek and Ty kissed her palm. "But you're out now," she said.

"If I keep my hands off that pretty little daughter of Del Mathison's. And I've had easier jobs."

86

"You like her, huh?"

"Well enough, I guess. Any man would like a woman who put herself in his path the way she does. The first few times I met her she didn't even have her clothes on."

Red leaned back against the sofa. "Really? I can't imagine that someone of Nola Dallas's fame would have to pursue a man."

"Well, she damn well has pursued me. Said she wanted to spend the rest of her life with me."

"Would that be so bad? A home and kids?"

Tynan stood and refilled his glass. "Are you going to start on that again? Look, even if I did marry somebody, it couldn't be her. Her father holds the papers for my release. I take her back to him, leave her and I get a full pardon. I touch her and I go back to jail. And then there's the money, too."

"For taking her back?"

Ty looked at Red. "Did you see that city dude that rode in behind me? He's a fine, upstanding citizen, born with parents and a silver spoon in his mouth, and Mathison wants his daughter to marry him. I get ten thousand dollars if I bring his daughter back in love with Mr. Asher Prescott. Course she had to go and fall for me."

"How inconvenient for you."

Tynan grinned at her. "It wasn't my fault. I told you she followed me everywhere. I tried to stay away from her but there she'd be—usually stark naked. I'm only human, you know."

"More human than the rest of us. Did you ever think that maybe she *liked* you?"

"A girl like her? All she wanted was a fling before going back to her rich daddy. I'd have one night in the hay, then the rest of my life in jail regretting it. No thanks. Deliver me from good girls. I think I'll just stick with Leora and her kind."

"Oh Ty," Red said, standing, putting her arms round the back of him. "What are you going to do with your life?"

"*Not* spend anymore time in jail. I thought I'd take the ten thousand and buy some land with it."

"The money you get for matchmaking Miss Mathison with that man? You're sure you can do that?"

Ty walked to the window and looked out into the street below. "I admit it's not easy, not with what Mathison gave me to work with. That man has no . . . force, I guess you'd call it. He doesn't even know how to win a girl."

"Not like you do?"

He looked back at her. "Are you mad at me about something? You seem awfully short tempered."

Red sat down. "Ty, honey, I'm gettin' old and you're the closest thing to a son I'll ever have. I'd like to see you married and settled down with half a dozen kids. I'd like to think there's an empty room in your house that's for me if I ever wanta retire."

Ty took her in his arms and kissed her forehead. "Wherever I am there'll always be room for you, but I can't see me with a wife and kids."

She pushed away from him. "That's because you've never been in love."

"Why, an hour ago I was so in love with Leora that—"

"Hush! You know what I mean. Have you ever even asked a girl to a church social? Taken a girl out for a buggy ride and a picnic?"

"Sounds mighty boring to me."

"Well, it *ain't*," she said, glaring at him.

He looked out the window again. "You know, one day Chris and Prescott were singing and it looked like it might be an all right way to pass the time."

"You have a beautiful singing voice. Why didn't you join in?"

He shrugged. "I don't know. I just don't fit in with people like them. Hey! You got any pork in this place? I'd love four or five pork chops tonight."

"We got pork. Ty, are you gonna try to match Chris with that man?"

He took a while to answer, turning back and looking at his drink. "It's my job."

"But you're reluctant?"

"She deserves a lot better than him. She's got spunk. She liked the rain forest and wasn't scared to death of the place. She walked around while he huddled beside the fire. And she pulled her weight in work too. He treated me like a servant hired to wait on him but Chris always helped me unpack the mules." He smiled. "Except for that first night."

He put the whiskey down. "Oh, hell, she's not for me."

Red put her hands on his arms. "Why isn't she? Isn't she Mathison's only kid? I bet if he thought she wanted you, he wouldn't put you back in jail."

"It's my neck if you're wrong, isn't it? Besides, she doesn't want me. It was just that she thought I was the leader and the forest can make you feel as if there's nobody else on earth. It was the time and the place. And the fact that there was no competition."

"So now that you're out of the forest, she won't be interested in you, is that it?"

"I'm sure of it."

Red turned away for a moment. "You know something? I have more faith in this young lady. From reading her articles I think she's not at all flighty. If she said she loved you, I think she does."

"For how long?" Ty asked in disgust. "Deliver me from the faithful love of a good woman."

"How about putting her to a test?"

"Such as?"

"Rory Sayers."

Tynan didn't speak for a moment. "Is *he* here?"

"At the hotel. Want to introduce your Chris to him?"

"She's not mine."

Red smiled at him. "You know what your problem is, Tynan? You've never had to work to get any female. Did you know that there are other things to do with a woman besides take her to bed? You've probably never spent five minutes talking to a woman who wasn't a whore. I'll bet that you don't even know what to do with a girl outside the bedroom."

"I talked to Chris one afternoon in the forest." He narrowed his eyes at her. "Red, what are you trying to do?"

"I want you to do something that's not so easy for you. I think you're half in love with this Chris. Why don't you take her out a few times, talk to her, get to know what she's like? It'll be practice for when you're lookin' for a wife."

"And what if she keeps saying she loves me? I'm not going back to jail for her or anybody else. And I'll not be cheated out of the ten grand."

"There, you see, you can organize a few socials yourself. Take Chris and Prescott for a ride in the country. *Help* him court her. You'll learn from him and he'll learn from you."

90

"And what about Sayers? What has he got to do with all this?"

"Don't you think Rory would be a perfect match for your Chris? He's rich, established, owns all that lovely timberland and Rory certainly doesn't lack force. Maybe you could get Chris to marry him. I'm sure Mathison would approve and you'd get your ten thousand dollars."

Ty didn't say anything but picked up his empty whiskey glass and refilled it. "I can't see Chris and Sayers together."

"Oh, I can. Rory has so much personality and the women all adore him. You could take Chris and Rory and the handsome young man Mathison chose out in the country for the afternoon and just sit back and think about your ten thousand dollars. It'll be the easiest money anyone ever made."

"Chris may not like Sayers. She's got taste. She's a real lady. All her underclothes have her initials on them, not big and gaudy like Susie used to wear, but tiny initials done in white on white cloth. And Chris asks a lot of questions. She finds out about people. If Sayers tries a line on her, she'll see through him."

"But you'll be there to smooth things over and help Rory over the rough spots, won't you?"

"Chris isn't all that easy to fool. You know that she figured out I was in pain? Even guessed that my feet were blistered from the damn new boots. And she put it all together and figured out about my being in jail."

"Not like other women you've known, is she?" Red said softly.

Abruptly, Ty put his half full whiskey glass down. "Look, I got things to do. I'll see you tonight for supper."

91

"Yes, honey, you do that. Let's eat at the hotel and invite your friends. Maybe I can help you get the money. I'll make your Chris see what a charming gentleman has been chosen for her. And maybe we can invite Rory. He always livens up any gathering."

"Yeah, well, maybe. Chris won't like him, though. He's all hot air." He put his hand on the door. "And she's not *my* Chris."

"She is until you sell her to someone else."

"Why do I feel like I've been run over by a twenty-car train? I'll see you tonight."

"At six at the hotel," she called after him.

As Chris was dressing that evening, she noticed her underwear, looking at the initials on all of it and wondering when in the world Ty had had a chance to see it. He's seen what's under it, so what's the difference in seeing the underwear, she wondered.

As she examined the lovely blue velvet gown Red had loaned her, with its tight waist, the skirt fitting snugly around her slim hips, and a little bustle in back, she thought about what she'd heard from Tynan that afternoon. He seemed such an odd contradiction of confidence and insecurity, she mused as she left the room.

At the foot of the hotel stairs waited Asher and another man who stepped forward instantly and introduced himself as Rory Sayers—and Chris felt that she knew all about him at once. He was the type of man her father had paraded before her for the first eighteen years of her life. He was handsome in a sharp sort of way: sharp nose, sharp chin, eyes a snapping blue. And he had more confidence than any six other men, confidence that Chris knew came from having had money all his life.

There was coolness behind her smile as she took his arm and allowed him to lead her into the dining room.

Dinner was a disaster. Rory dominated the meal, talking about everything that had been happening in the country in the last two years—the years that Ty had been in prison. And Tynan looked like a sulky little boy who was being punished by having to eat with the grownups.

For just a moment, Chris closed her eyes and prayed for strength.

"Of course you wouldn't know about that, would you old man?" Rory said to Tynan who had his head bent over a plate heaped with pork chops. "You were a bit too busy over the last two years to read the papers, weren't you?"

Before Tynan could reply, Chris said, "I beg to differ with you, Mr. Sayers. Mr. Tynan has read all *my* articles. Perhaps he was selective in his reading."

"Not *Mr.* Tynan," Rory said with a smile. "I don't believe he has another name."

Chris could take no more. She couldn't stand the man's smugness or his catty remarks. She stood. "I'm afraid you'll have to excuse me as I have a splitting headache. Mr. Tynan, would you please escort me out into the fresh air? I think a walk will help clear my head."

Rory Sayers rose, presumptuously taking Chris's arm. "*I'll* take you, Miss Mathison."

With all the haughtiness she could muster, she jerked her arm from his grasp. "Sir, I only met you tonight. I do not entrust my safety to men I do not know. Mr. Tynan, would you mind?"

Rory was aghast. "I'm afraid," he said with emphasized tolerance for her ignorance, "that you don't know this man. He's—"

Chris hadn't traveled all over the United States on her own and not learned how to handle all types of men. "I have just spent a great deal of time alone with this man and I know all I need to know about him. I am especially aware of the fact that he has the manners of a gentleman."

She turned away to see Tynan standing beside her, an enormous grin on his face, his arm extended. "The lady has taste," he said to Rory. "Sit back down and finish your meal. I'll take good care of her."

With that, he led Chris out of the hotel and into the moonlit street. But as soon as they were outside, he released her arm.

"Why did you do that?"

"Because I can't stand that type of man," she said with feeling.

"Type? But I thought all women liked that kind of man. Most all of them I've ever known do."

"But then you've never met a woman who could run away from home at the age of eighteen and become a newspaper reporter either, have you?"

"No," he said with a grin. "I haven't. Do you really have a headache? Do you want me to take you back inside?"

She stopped and looked at him. "If I promise not to be forward, will you take me for a walk?"

"Forward?"

"Such as pursuing you and asking too many questions and, in general, making a nuisance of myself."

He gave her a startled look, then grabbed her arm and pulled her into an alleyway. Before Chris could speak, he had her in his arms, holding her head against his chest. "Chris, you don't understand, do you? Thank you for what you did in there tonight. If four men came up to me aiming guns at my head, I'd know how to handle them, but give me one spoiled rich boy and I'm at a loss. But you made me feel . . ."

"Like a winner?" she supplied and tried to look up at him but he held her head against him. "Deja vu," she whispered.

"What?"

"I have a feeling that I've been here before, in just this situation. Remember our first meeting?"

"No man could ever forget a meeting like that. Chris, you have to go back inside. I can't go walking with you in the dark."

Chris wanted to stay with him always and, had he asked, she would have climbed on a horse and ridden away with him—to live in the rain forest for all she cared. But she knew she had to obey him. He didn't know how he felt about her and she wasn't about to pursue him.

"All right," she whispered with great reluctance in her voice. "Let's go."

He moved away from her slowly, not looking at her, and allowed her to go first back onto the street. Chris took one step around the corner and saw Rory with Asher coming toward them, and they had the look of a vigilante committee out to rid the world of whatever they considered vermin. She turned back to Tynan. "Kiss me," she whispered urgently.

Ty looked astonished for a split second then he lost no time obeying her, taking her in his arms and kissing her with a passion Chris had never before known existed. She completely forgot about the reason she'd asked Ty to kiss her but returned his passion, her arms going around his neck and pulling him closer—not that he could get closer as he wedged his thigh between hers.

"Unhand her!" came Rory's voice as he pulled Tynan away from Chris.

For a moment, Chris was too stunned to even open her eyes, much less try to speak.

"I should call you out for this," Rory was saying.

Chris was leaning against a building wall and was in such a state of euphoria that someone could have told her a bomb was about to explode under her feet and she wouldn't have been able to move.

"I'm ready when you are, Sayers," she heard Tynan say in a voice deep with threat.

Reluctantly, Chris began to surface because she sensed that this was an argument that she had to stop. But as she moved away from the wall, her eyes opened wide for a moment. The entire back of her dress was unbuttoned.

Standing as straight as she could, not allowing the loose dress to fall forward, she confronted Rory Sayers with his backup of Mr. Prescott.

"Mr. Sayers," she said angrily. "I do not know you and, after tonight, I don't believe I want to. You have no right to interfere in my life and I kindly wish you'd stay out of it."

"Chris," Tynan said. "Stay out of this. This has been coming for a long time."

"I most certainly will *not* stay out of this," she said with so much feeling that the front of her dress fell forward, but she caught it and hoped the men hadn't noticed. If she ever got out of this, she was going to give Tynan a piece of her mind. Of all the audacious things any man had ever done to her, this was one of the worst. She was tempted to let Mr. Sayers have him.

"Miss Mathison, I have to take offense at this. I have met your father several times and I cannot believe that he'd want his daughter pawed by a man of this sort in an alleyway."

Tynan took a step forward, and Chris put herself between the two men. "My father hired this man to protect me and he is doing just that. You, Mr. Sayers, are the unwanted person. As it happens, Mr. Tynan has just asked me to marry him and I have, quite happily, accepted. Now, I do believe that a man has a right to kiss his intended without being molested by the local bully."

Rory Sayers stepped back at that. "Bully? Pardon me, Miss, I had thought you were a lady of higher ideals than to take up with this . . . this criminal. I can only think that you know nothing about him."

"I know that he was put into jail for two years without any evidence." Holding her dress, her back to Tynan, she advanced on Rory. "I know that he's never known who his parents are and that he's never had the advantages of money that you have had. And even though he's not had a formal education, he speaks like a gentleman, reads Voltaire in his spare time, and he constantly puts his life on the line to help other people. Can you say the same thing, Mr. Sayers?"

Rory straightened his back. "You are not the lady I took you for," he said and after one look at Tynan, turned, Asher on his heels, and went down the street.

"He can't say those things about you," Tynan said and started after the men.

Chris planted herself in front of him. "Don't you *dare*," she said through her teeth. "Don't you dare even think of going after him." She began backing him into the dark alley. "Especially don't you think of avenging my 'honor'. What do you know of a ladies' honor?"

"Chris, I—"

"Look at this!" she gasped, turning her back to him and showing him the unbuttoned dress. "How dare you try to remove my clothing!"

"Oh," he said with a slight grin. "I guess it's just habit. I didn't even think about it."

"Habit!" she gasped. "Whenever you kiss a girl you unbutton her dress?"

"Well," he said slowly, still backing up. "Most girls I kiss *want* their dresses off. You seemed to like it well enough."

"Of all the vain—I should have allowed Mr. Sayers to shoot you. You certainly well deserved it." She began to fasten her dress, struggling with the many tiny buttons.

"He can't shoot at all. All he can do is push a pencil around and flap his gums. Here, let me do that. I can button them as fast as I can unbutton them."

"And I guess you've had practice at that often enough," she said as he turned her around and began to fasten her dress.

"Sometimes you need to get into clothes real fast. There now, all done. I'll pick you up tomorrow."

"Not on your life. Frankly, Mr. Tynan, this has gone far enough. You don't want to go to jail and I'd like to get home to my father. I think that tomorrow we should start south toward my home."

"We can wait one more day. Look, Chris, you're not going to make a fool of me in front of this town—and especially not in front of Sayers. You told him we were engaged and I want at least a day of acting like we're engaged. I'd like to show these people that I can . . ."

"Can get a 'good' girl like me?" she asked softly. She put her hand on his chest. "Tynan, perhaps I've misled you. Perhaps it was the rain forest, the feeling of being isolated, something that made me lose my sense of proportion, but now that we're back to civilization, I think we should stay away from each other. After all, you would have to go back to prison if you touched me."

He took her upper arm in his hand and bent his face close to hers. "Right now Sayers is in a saloon telling half the people in this town that Nola Dallas is going to marry the murderer. And *you're* the one who gave him that idea."

She smiled at him in such a way that he took a step backward. "Tomorrow is Sunday. How about church in the morning and I've been invited to the town picnic later. Shall we appear as an engaged couple? Just for the day, of course, and on Monday we can start the journey home. And then we'll no longer be engaged. Does that suit you?"

"Church?" he asked and even in the darkness, she could see his face turning pale.

"Church," she said firmly and slipped her arm through his. "We'd better get out of this alleyway or my reputation will be ruined, engaged or not. I'll see you the first thing in the morning." They were almost back at the hotel. "Cheer up, Mr. Tynan, I'll make sure that you enjoy the day. Goodnight, dear," she said to him as she smiled at a passerby. "You may kiss my cheek," she whispered, "and don't unbutton so much as a cuff, if you don't mind."

Still too stunned to speak, Ty bent and kissed her

cheek, then looked up to see three women standing in the hotel lobby looking at him with disapproving eyes. On impulse, he grabbed Chris about the waist and kissed her quite thoroughly.

When he released her, Chris had to catch a chair back to keep from falling.

"See you in the morning, sweetheart," Ty said with a wink, replaced his hat and left the hotel.

Chris tried to regain her composure. "Oh, my, but he does get carried away," she said, smoothing her dress front. "Goodnight," she said to the women who were watching her with their mouths hanging open.

Chris whistled all the way up the stairs.

Chapter Nine

Asher Prescott was waiting for her outside her room. His face was grim. "I feel I must talk to you."

"I am rather tired and I . . ." she began then stopped. When a man got it into his head that a woman needed lecturing, it was just better to let him get it out of his system. Chris had learned years ago that "teaching" a woman seemed to make a man feel much better. "Yes, what is it?" She stood there patiently and waited.

"I don't think you're conducting yourself properly and I believe you're losing your sense of proportion. I know you like to champion the underdog but sometimes the underdog isn't deserving of a champion. I believe, Chris, you should know something about the man whose cause you are fighting.

"When he was sixteen he was already known as a gunslinger. He killed not one but two men in a street shootout. By the time he was twenty, he had more enemies than most people have in a lifetime. Did you

101

know that for a while he rode with the Chanry Gang? Once, he was caught and sentenced to hang but the gang blew up the jail and got him out. He's taken on jobs that were suicidal, walking alone into towns against twenty outlaws."

Asher began to warm to his subject. "And the women, Chris! Hundreds of women! To somebody like him, a woman isn't someone to love, she's someone to bed, then leave. You talk of love for this man, well, he doesn't even know the meaning of the word. He's a no-good wastrel and he'll never be anything else."

Chris didn't say a word, just stood there and looked at him.

"You're talking of marrying him but I don't think you understand what marriage is. It's the day in day out of living together. This Tynan can be charming when he wants to but tonight he was morose and sullen. He can't talk, he knows nothing about civilized society, and that woman who everyone says is probably his mother. . . . Well, Chris, I can't believe you even agreed to eat at the same table with her. I for one—"

He stopped himself then smiled at her fondly. "You know what I think? I think this Tynan is interesting because he's a mystery. You solve the mystery and you'll find he's just another run-of-the-mill, cheap gunslinger. What you need, Chris," he said softly, taking a step toward her, "is a husband from your own background. A husband and children."

She gave him a wide-eyed look. "Someone like you, Mr. Prescott?"

"I find you a *very* attractive woman, Chris."

As he leaned forward, his eyelids closing as if to kiss her, Chris opened the bedroom door and slipped inside, closing it firmly behind her. "Kiss *that*, Mr. Paid-to-Marry-Me Prescott."

She went to bed thinking of the coming picnic.

The next morning, Tynan was waiting for her in the hotel lobby wearing a clean suit, leaning against a window frame reading a newspaper.

"Good morning," she said, smiling up at him.

He smiled too when he looked at her, but he looked as if he were smiling through adversity.

Chris pulled on her gloves. "Are you ready to go?"

Ty only nodded, offered his arm to her, and led her out of the hotel onto the street.

There were several other couples also on their way to church and each one of them stopped to stare openly at Tynan and Chris.

In church, Chris pulled Tynan to the third pew, away from the back row where he started to sit. Throughout the service, he was silent, listening to the preacher with attention. During the singing, he seemed familiar with the songs and, as Red had said, he did indeed have an excellent voice.

As they left the church, he seemed relieved that it was over and had gone well. Standing at the door, the minister made an effort to shake his hand and tell him he was welcome.

As they went down the stairs, they saw Red waiting for them in a beautiful big-wheeled carriage, holding the reins to a sleek black gelding.

"I brought you baskets of food for the picnic," she said. "I didn't want you to go empty-handed. Here, Ty, help me down."

"You aren't going with us?" Chris asked.

"A church picnic ain't no place for the likes of me.

103

You two go and have a good time. And, Tynan, you start to look happier or I'll take a switch to you."

That made Ty laugh as he kissed her cheek. "Maybe I need *both* of you to protect me."

Chris slipped her arm in his. "One can handle you. We shall miss you, Red, but we'll see you tonight. Pray it doesn't rain."

"Honey, I ain't stopped prayin' since you came to town. Now get out of here."

Ty lifted Chris into the carriage and soon they were speeding down the dirt road with the other couples. Chris moved close to him on the seat and held his arm. "Who are the Chanrys?"

"Been snooping again?"

"Of course. Who are they?"

"A bunch of two-bit crooks. Most of them are either dead now or locked away."

"Were you part of them?"

"They wanted me to be. Even told people I was."

"But I thought they broke you out of jail. Tynan, how many times have you been in jail?"

"Total?" he asked seriously. "Even for being drunk?"

"Never mind, don't answer. How did your name get linked with those criminals?"

"I told you. They wanted me to join and when I wouldn't, they got angry. They didn't break me out of jail, a U.S. marshal did."

"Explain, please," she said over the sound of the carriage.

"The Chanrys didn't like the way I told them I wouldn't join their gang no matter what they offered me. You see, they needed a fast gun since their best man had been killed. As revenge, they robbed a bank and kept calling one of the men Tynan. The local sheriff came after me. Only problem was that I was laid up with a broken leg, but he didn't seem to think that was proof that I was innocent. One of the women where I was staying got in touch with a marshal and he came up to investigate. When he couldn't persuade the sheriff not to hang me, the marshal blew up the jail. The sheriff told everybody it was the Chanrys—proof that he should have hanged me."

"Tynan, you are full of the most awful stories."

"When a man lives by the gun, he should expect to be faced with other guns. Here we are. Why don't you take the baskets over there and I'll—"

"No, you have to carry the big one and I have to introduce you to everyone."

"But I already know most of these people. They're the ones—"

"They are the ones who know nothing about you. Now come along."

"Yes, ma'am," he said, grinning. "You do tie them apron strings to a man, don't you?"

"Sometimes, apron strings give a man purpose in life. And they're a lot less violent than guns."

"Hmph! Strangulation is a slow way to die."

She ignored his remark as they walked toward the others. The men and women were separating, the women spreading food on bleached and ironed table-cloths, the men walking together toward the river.

Chris set down a basket of food. "I believe you've met my fiancé, Mr. Tynan, haven't you?" she said. "I'd introduce you by name but I'm afraid I've been in town so short a time that I haven't met you all."

Looking as if they'd just been introduced to a coiled rattlesnake, most of the women nodded tentatively in Tynan's direction.

"Ty, dear, would you please put the other basket there? Thank you so much." She gave him a little signal with her eyes, motioning him toward the men.

He removed his hat. "It's very pleasant to meet you ladies again after all these years." He picked up a roll from the table, winked at Chris and left.

"Miss Dallas!" the women started as soon as he was out of earshot. "You don't know what you're doing. You couldn't know anything about him or you wouldn't—"

"You should talk to Betty Mitchell, after what he did to her, and poor Mr. Dickerson—"

"Mitchell?" Chris said, unpacking one of the baskets. "Wasn't she the girl who was in love with the boy who was killed?"

"Well, she *had* been," one woman said. "Thank heaven it was all over when he was killed."

"Oh, yes," Chris said. "By then she was visiting Tynan in the saloon and seeking him out wherever she could. Why did she and the Dickerson boy end their involvement?"

The women fell all over themselves answering.

"Betty didn't exactly pursue Tynan. . . . Maybe she did go to the saloon but I'm sure he enticed her."

"Billy started seeing a girl who was visiting from Seattle, but I'm sure it would have blown over if that Tynan hadn't interfered."

"Tynan killed Billy, we know that," one woman insisted.

Chris put an apple pie in place. "Billy Dickerson started seeing another girl. Betty started pursuing

Tynan, then Mr. Dickerson went after Betty's father and—"

"No!" one of the women said, then stopped.

Another woman leaned forward. "Betty was in the family way and Billy wouldn't marry her."

"Ah," Chris said. "So Tynan stepped in to help a young girl get the man who was refusing to marry her. And he *killed* this young man? Tynan must have loved Betty to do something like that for her."

The women began shifting the food on the table.

"Betty only loved Billy and after his death she went back east somewhere."

"But I thought she and Tynan were so in love that he killed a man for her," Chris asked, wide-eyed.

The women didn't say anything for a while.

"I do believe my son is pestering your young man," a woman said, looking toward the river.

Four young boys were encircling Tynan, looking up at him with eager faces.

"He won't . . . . do anything, will he?" a woman asked hesitantly.

"No," Chris said with confidence. "He is a very good man. Now, shall we call all our good men to the table?"

The men were more tolerant than the women and they didn't seem to care one way or another that Tynan had been in and out of jail. They were more interested in corn on the cob and fried chicken.

Rory Sayers tried his best to make Tynan feel out of place.

"Better than prison food, isn't it, old man?" Rory asked, sitting across from Ty. "But then, over the years you must've gotten used to it."

As Rory reached for a piece of chicken, a woman, the one whose son had been talking to Ty, smacked

Rory's hand sharply with a wooden spoon. Everyone at that end of the table looked up at her as the woman's face turned red.

"I can't teach the children not to reach if the adults do," she said at last, then looked up at Chris who was smiling broadly at her. The woman also smiled. "More beans, Mr. Tynan?" she asked sweetly.

"Why, yes, please," Tynan said, looking at the woman in surprise.

"Tell us what it's like to take a man's life," Rory said as the woman was heaping beans on Tynan's plate.

At that moment, one of the other women overturned a cup of coffee into Rory's lap. As Rory jumped up, one of the men began to laugh.

"Boy, you get married and you'll learn that women have ways of fightin' that cause you to lose the war before you even know it's been declared."

Another man began to laugh and before long, they'd all joined in. Tynan sat there grinning.

"Sit down, boy," someone called to Rory. "You'll dry. Martha, give Sayers some of that cherry cake of yours. That'll make him forget everything else, even pretty little blondes."

Chris became very interested in the inside of a pitcher of milk but she could feel her ears growing warm.

An hour later the food was packed away, the younger children were being put to sleep under shade trees, the adults were gathering in groups and the young ones with the energy were laughing and planning ways to be on their own.

"Will you come with us?" a pretty, dark-eyed girl asked Chris. "We're going canoeing on the river. It'll be a lot of fun."

"We'd love to," she said, holding onto Tynan's arm.

"They're kids. I don't want to—" Tynan began but Chris didn't look at him.

"They want to talk to us. Don't you realize we're almost celebrities to them? You, the notorious gunslinger and me . . ."

"The lady who gets herself into trouble on purpose." He held her back as the others got into the three canoes. They were out of sight of the picnic area. Just as Chris was about to step into a canoe, Tynan gave her a little push, causing her to stumble back against him.

"Chris," he said and there was great concern in his voice. "You've hurt your ankle. Is it sprained? Here, don't walk on it, let me help you."

Before Chris could say a word, he had her in his arms and was carrying her toward the trees.

"She'll be all right," he called over his shoulder to the others. "I'll take care of her."

Chris could hear giggling behind her and knew he hadn't fooled anyone.

"Now that you have me, what do you plan to do with me?" He smiled at her in such a way that Chris said, "You most certainly will *not*. And if you put me down and so much as one button is unfastened, I'll never speak to you again."

"No one has to say a word."

"Tynan!" she gasped.

"Chris, enough is enough. I don't mind adults but spending the afternoon with adolescents looking at me as if I might do something deadly at any moment is more than I can take. I thought maybe we'd go in the woods and . . ."

"And what?" she asked, eyebrows raised.

"I don't know," he said quite honestly. "What does a

couple do if they don't—" Again, a look from Chris stopped him.

"Talk, get to know each other. You may put me down now."

Tynan kept walking with her. "Who are the Montgomerys? Your father mentioned them."

"And what did he say? No, you can tell me the truth."

He stood her on an overturned log so that her face was about even with his. "Let me see if I get this correct. He said you were related to them and a more headstrong, stubborn, stupidly fearless lot of people had never been born. Does that sound right?"

"Perfect. They're my mother's relatives, a very old family that came to America during Henry the Eighth's reign."

"Sixteenth century?"

"Yes," she said, smiling at him and holding out her hand. He took it and Chris began walking along the narrow top of the log. "Tell me more about your meeting with my father. What else did he say? What did they say when they released you from jail?"

"Nothing much. They don't do much explaining in jail, they just pull your chains and you follow."

"Whenever I ask you about how you got into prison, whichever time you've been in, you were always falsely accused. Have you ever done anything illegal?" She turned on the log and started back in the other direction.

"Why do you have to know a man's secrets? As a matter of fact I have done my share of outlawing, but I was never caught at it, which is why I keep getting accused when I'm innocent. I guess they figure they can hang me for one crime as well as another."

"And when did you quit and start earning your way in a proper manner?"

Tynan snorted. "I think Red's been opening her big mouth. I've been straight since I was twenty-two."

"Seven years," she said.

"Red *has* been talking. Get down, you're making me dizzy. I know some things about you, too, Mary Christiana," he said as he lifted her down from the log.

"Not as much as you think," she said with eyes twinkling. "It's not Mary Christiana. At birth, I was given the name of Mary Ellen after my paternal grandmother, but my name was changed when I was six."

"All right, it's your turn to tell a story. Sit down here, away from me and don't come too close."

Still smiling, and feeling like the most desirable woman in the world, she sat on the grass and leaned against the log. "I have second sight," she said simply. "I've only had two visions but even one was enough to get my name changed. It seems that it's a tradition with the Montgomerys to name all the women with second sight Christiana."

"So what happened when you were six?"

"My parents and I were in church and I don't really remember how I felt beforehand, but one moment I was standing beside my mother and the next I was in the aisle screaming that everybody had to go outside. My mother said the congregation was too stunned to move, but she knew the traditions of her family and knew that every third or so generation a girl was born with second sight. So my mother yelled the single word that was guaranteed to clear the building."

"Fire," Ty said.

"Yes, except that after the people ran out of the

111

building in a state of panic, and one of them broke a stained glass window with a chair, they saw that there was no fire. I will always remember the looks on the faces of the people as they advanced on my mother and me. I thought they were going to kill us and I tried to hide in my mother's skirts.''

She took a breath. "They had just about reached us when the sky opened up and a bolt of lightning hit the church and the back half of it collapsed. When the dust cleared, the people looked at my mother and me as if we were witches. I'll never forget my mother's look that day. One of the men said, 'How did Mary Ellen know?' My mother put her nose in the air, took my hand and said, 'My daughter's name is Christiana.' And it has been ever since. Of course my father wasn't exactly delighted since I'd been named after his mother, but Mother promised him more children and he could name them what he wanted.''

"But there weren't any more.''

"No, just me. Some branches of the Montgomerys are very fertile and some are almost barren. There doesn't seem to be any middle ground.''

Tynan leaned back on the grass, stretching full length, his feet toward Chris. "She sounds like a wonderful mother. Do you miss her?''

Chris looked away. "Every day of my life. She was strong and soft, sensible and intelligent, wise and. . . . She was all anyone could hope to be.''

"I think you may be like her, what I've seen, that is.''

Chris grinned broadly at him. "For that, you may turn around here and put your head in my lap.''

"That is an honor," he said as he did as she offered. "This is nice," he said as Chris smoothed his hair back from his forehead. "You're not like any other women I've met."

"Good. Ty, what are you going to do now that you're free?"

"I'm not yet. I have to get you back to your father."

"Yes, but what can you do besides shoot a gun and sit a horse well? Or get drunk and land in jail?"

With his eyes closed, he smiled. "Doesn't sound like much, does it? Well, let's see, what can I do? I guess women don't count, do they?"

"Most definitely not."

"I know," he said, opening his eyes. "I can run four whore houses at once."

Chris let out a gasp. "Somehow I don't think that is a good—"

"No, not the women. I let Red handle that, except if there's a fight, then I separate the women, but one time Red's bookkeeper got killed in the crossfire of a shootout—one I wasn't involved in, I might add—and she asked me to look into the accounts because the bank was about to foreclose on one of the houses."

"Did the bank foreclose?"

"Hell, no. Oh, excuse me. It turned out that little weasel had been embezzling her money. I found it buried under the front porch of his house. And I had to learn to do bookkeeping and straighten the whole mess out. Now, every time I see Red I go over her accounts."

"What a marvelous ability. My father says that half his empire is nothing but book work. You could be of great use to him."

"I'm sure that your father would entrust his accounts to a gunslinger."

113

"He entrusted his daughter to one," she said softly.

"I guess he did at that," he said, smiling at her and beginning to run his hand up her arm. "Chris, do you really think he meant that about not touching you? Do you think he had any idea what he was asking?" His hand was at her neck.

"Maybe he'd heard about your reputation with women and he wanted to protect his daughter's chastity."

"Of course if neither of us told anyone what had happened, there'd be no way he'd know." He was pulling her head down to his.

"But my husband would know on my wedding night."

"What husband?" His lips were a breath away from hers.

"The man I marry. The man I plan to spend all my nights with."

He was pulling her closer but she was resisting. "But just the other day you were offering yourself to me."

"But then I thought you couldn't and that I was safe. I think we'd better go back to the others."

"In a minute," he said, pulling her to him.

Chris's lips parted for him and again she was amazed at the feeling that passed through her at Tynan's touch. It was as if her bones were disintegrating and she fell down across him.

He was expert at maneuvering her body so that soon she was stretched full out beside him and it was what she wanted when he moved one of his heavy legs on top of hers. Her body arched upwards toward his.

Later, she wondered what would have happened if he hadn't heard voices and moved away from her. Chris just lay there, eyes closed, too stunned to move.

"They're coming back," Ty whispered, lifting her off the ground into his arms. "Get dressed." As if she were a doll, he leaned her against his shoulder and began to button the back of her dress.

"What happens if I wear a dress that buttons down the front?" she murmured huskily.

"Don't. Save my sanity and your virginity and don't tempt me more than you have already. There, stand up and get that dopey look off your face. They're coming."

"Yes, Tynan," she said, allowing him to pull her upright.

Chapter Ten

Chris and Ty were swept away together with the crowd
of returning young people. People were getting restless
and wanting to eat again and play games. The women
took Chris with them so they could ask her questions
about some of the stories she'd written and they left
Tynan with the men and the boys—who constantly
begged Ty for stories of the gunfights he'd been in.

Chris and the women were on very friendly terms.
They believed in her so much that they were willing to
look differently at a man they'd been so sure was
wrong. One of the women bravely asked Chris what a
house of ill repute looked like inside and she had a good
time entertaining them with stories of red wallpaper
and highly polished brass lamps and women who
looked very bored. They were all laughing when the
shot rang out.

Chris hoped she was wrong, but somehow, she knew
that Tynan was involved with that single gunshot.

Grabbing her skirts, she started running, the women

behind her. On the ground, surrounded by men, lay Rory Sayers, a derringer in his hand, blood spreading over his shoulder—and standing over him was Tynan. Chris looked at Ty with disbelief on her face.

"I'm afraid I'm going to have to take you in," said a young man who Chris had seen wearing a deputy's badge. "The sheriff will have to deal with this."

Chris's eyes were still locked with Tynan's and it was only after a long moment that she turned away. The face of every woman around her had a look of "I told you so" on it.

Chris lifted her skirt and began walking back to the tables.

"Chris," Tynan called softly from behind her but she didn't look back.

At the tables she began packing food away, trying to stay calm while the others put the injured Rory on a wagon bed and started back toward town. Since Rory was yelling that they were going to kill him and also he was raging that he was going to kill Tynan, Chris assumed that he was going to live.

Minutes later, Tynan walked past her, stopping within a few feet of her, but she didn't turn around, instead, busying herself in putting the food away.

The women came to help her, working in total silence as they gave her looks from under their lashes. After a few minutes, Chris could stand no more. She put down the food, turned toward the road and began walking back to town. She didn't care about Red's buggy that she left behind or about anything else for that matter.

It was miles back to town but Chris walked all the way, shaking her head no at the people who stopped their carriages and offered her a ride.

In the hotel, people were watching her in such a way that she ran up the stairs and into her room, slamming the door behind her. She was so ashamed of herself that she wanted to climb into bed, pull the covers over her head and never come out again. For the last two days, she'd strutted around this town and, in essence, told them they were all fools, that they didn't know a man who'd lived among them most of his life. She'd used the love she'd earned as Nola Dallas to tell them that they knew much less than she did after spending only a few days with the man.

Slowly, Chris began to undress, taking off the dress that Red had loaned her.

How vain I was, she thought, to think that I knew more than they did. And how conceited I was to think that I could reform a man who has chosen a life of crime and violence. How right my father was when he introduced me to men from my own background, men I could understand, not men who went to picnics and shot people who disagreed with them.

She packed her small bundle, put her riding habit back on and took the two dresses downstairs to the clerk. His eyes were different now. No longer was he looking at her with interest, wanting to know more about the young woman who worked for a big city newspaper. Now she was just one of many women who'd fallen for a cheap drifter.

She didn't look at the others in the hotel lobby who were watching her with interest, waiting until she'd gone upstairs again so they could tell others what had happened at the picnic.

"Miss," said a young man behind her, "I have a message for you."

With her eyes downcast, Chris took the piece of

paper, crumbled it in her hand and went up the stairs. Chris sat on the bed and thought for some time. She felt that she owed him this one last visit, to say goodbye, to tell him that she was returning to her father and that she would see that he was given his pardon.

She wrote a note to Asher telling him that she planned to start the journey home tomorrow.

With her shoulders squared, she went downstairs, leaving the note to Asher with the desk clerk, and went outside. As soon as she started toward the jail, she had a following of curious people, some of them snickering. So, the big city girl thought she could come to this town and tell us about someone we already knew, she could almost hear them saying.

Once, a man blocked her passage, and she had to look up at him, giving him her most withering look to make him step aside. He spit a big wad of tobacco juice at her feet, barely missing her.

One thing about people who made a fuss about someone they thought was better than they were, when their idol came to earth, they were very angry about it.

"May I see your prisoner?" she said to the deputy sitting at the desk.

"Oh sure, Miss Dallas," he said, getting the ring of keys from a nail on the wall. "I'm real sorry about what happened. The sheriff should be here tomorrow and this thing will be cleared up. There's someone to see you," the boy said to Tynan as he let Chris into the cell.

Tynan turned around quickly, looking at her with eyes that examined and searched. He didn't seem to like what he saw because he turned away again.

"I got your message," she said, looking down at her hands.

"I've seen what I wanted to, you can go now."

119

The coldness in his voice made her head come up—and her anger surface. "Tell me, are you innocent again? Like with the Chanry Gang? Were you perhaps protecting children from Rory? What was it this time that got you involved in a shooting?"

"Get out of here, Chris," he said softly. "I don't want to fight with you."

"Because I don't have a gun? Oh yes, I know the code of the West. You'd never draw on an unarmed man—or woman. How could you do that to me? Those people *trusted* me! They told me their secrets and I asked them to trust me more. I asked them to give you another chance, to let you start fresh. And they *did!* But what did you do but show them just what you really are, what I was too stupid to see?"

He just stood there with his back to her, his arm up, pressing against the stone wall, looking out the cell window.

"Look at me when I talk to you. If you have no conscience, at least you can pretend to have manners."

Slowly, he turned toward her and he seemed to be a man Chris had never seen before, one of coolness, as if he were far away and not there at all.

"I never lied to you about what I was. I always told you I wasn't for you. But you never listened to anything I said. You were so busy showing the world that you could reform the criminal that you never thought about who I really was."

"I guess I've learned now." She walked toward the cell door. "I won't bother you again. I just came to tell you that I, and probably Mr. Prescott, will be leaving early in the morning. I'll make sure, though, that you will be given your pardon by my father. Deputy," she called.

Tynan was across the room in seconds, barring her exit. "You will not leave without me. I swore to your father that I'd deliver you and I plan to."

"Of course, the Western man always keeps his word. He may kill people on a daily basis, prison may be a way of life to him but he *always* keeps his word. Deputy, you may let me out now."

Tynan slammed the door shut, startling the boy against the wall. "You can't leave tomorrow morning. You can't go across this country with just that man, he doesn't know anything about surviving."

"I have to agree that he doesn't know how to shoot innocent men at church picnics."

"He didn't shoot Sayers," the deputy said. "Sayers attacked him from behind."

"I knew you were innocent," Chris said. "A man like you doesn't get caught when he does something illegal. Deputy, please open this door."

Ty held it shut. "Chris, you can't leave until I get out of here. You need—"

"Mr. Tynan, if I waited for you to get out of one jail after another, I'd never get home. Let me make myself clear. I am going to leave tomorrow morning and start home to my father. You will have your precious pardon and you will get rid of me in the bargain." She grabbed the door and jerked, stepping outside quickly. "When you make your way to my father's, via the jails of Washington, however falsely accused you are, he may even have the ten thousand dollars you've worked so hard for. Good-bye, sir, and I hope we never meet again."

Chapter Eleven

Asher led the way out of town the next morning before the sun was up. She'd mumbled answers to his many questions on the night before, saying her engagement to Tynan had been a farce, something to save him from Rory's barbs. Asher seemed satisfied that she was properly contrite.

As they passed the jail, Chris saw the dark shadowy outline of Tynan standing in his cell watching them. She kept her head up high and didn't return his stare. By the time he got out of prison, she'd be far away.

Neither she nor Asher had much to say as they rode, not really running, but not giving themselves time to enjoy the scenery either. At noon they stopped to rest the horses and eat the stale biscuits they'd brought.

As the sound of thundering hooves came down the narrow little road, Chris's heart nearly stopped beating. But it wasn't Tynan or anyone else interested in them. Three big men on scraggy horses went tearing past them, their heads down, their faces hidden under their hat brims.

"I'm glad they aren't looking for us," Asher said when they'd passed.

Asher didn't talk to Chris much and she remembered how she'd sometimes been rude to him. As he helped her onto her horse, she took every opportunity to smile at him. Now that Tynan was gone, and Chris was no longer blinded by that man's light, she could look at Asher with new eyes. This was a man her father *wanted* her to marry. This man wasn't likely to pull a gun and kill for the smallest offense.

It was nearly sundown before they saw the overturned wagon, and even then they wouldn't have seen it except for Chris having noticed the way the ground had been torn up. There were deep, fresh gouges in the earth, leading off into the underbrush.

"Let's stop here for a moment," she called, dismounting and running down into the bushes. She hadn't gone but a few feet when she saw the big old wagon on its side, and what looked to be a woman's hand protruding from under it.

She ran back up the bank, shouting for Asher to come and help her. "Under there," she pointed. "We have to get the wagon up and get her out."

He only hesitated for a second, then ran forward.

When they got to the far side of the wagon, they could see only part of the woman's arm. Her head and the rest of her body were buried under the wagon.

"Can you lift that?" Chris asked, pointing to a broken part of the wagon. "I'll try to pull the woman out."

Asher used most of the strength he had as he

123

propped himself against the side of the wagon then squatted until his legs could work to lift the weight.

"Now!" he shouted and the wagon moved.

Chris lost not a second pulling the woman out to safety.

Asher, kneeling, lit a match because the evening was growing very dim, and studied the woman. She seemed to be covered in blood. "She's been shot at least three times," he said quietly.

"But she's still breathing." Chris took the woman's bloodied head into her lap. "We'll get you to a doctor," she whispered to the woman as she began to thrash about.

"My husband," she gasped. "Where is my husband?"

Chris looked up at Asher but he was already searching the surrounding area. Chris could see where he stopped. Turning, he shook his head.

"Your husband is fine. He's sleeping now."

"Can you tell us who did this to you?" Asher asked when he came back.

The woman was having great difficulty talking, and blood was seeping steadily from her wounds. "Three men," she whispered at last. "They wanted us dead because we know about Lionel. We were going to save Lionel."

Suddenly the woman looked at Chris with eyes as red as the blood that was washing from her body. "Help him. Help Lionel. Promise me that."

"Yes, of course I will. As soon as you're better we'll both—" She stopped because the woman's head had fallen to one side and she was dead.

Asher sat back on his heels. "We have to get the

124

sheriff out here. We'll leave the bodies here for now while I bring the sheriff back.''

"Chris," he said sharply because she'd begun to look through the packages that had fallen from the wagon. "What in the world are you doing?"

"Looking for something that will tell who Lionel is."

He caught her shoulders and turned her toward him. "I don't think we should look for the trouble that got that woman killed. We're going home and we're stopping for no one or nothing. This Lionel will have to take care of himself. Now, we're going to a town."

"We can't leave them here like this," Chris said.

He seemed to want to protest, but he stopped, then went to the man's body, and carried it up the bank.

Chris went to the woman, smoothed her hair, crossed her hands over her breast. Even in the darkness, she could see how young the woman was, that her hair, under the blood that stained it, was the color of wheat. She was much too young to have died, especially to have been murdered.

Standing, Chris looked at the bundles around her, a meager lot of women's clothing in a carpet bag, another little sewing bag, one bag of the man's clothes. These had scattered across the ground when the wagon had tumbled down the side of the hill. Something shining in the moonlight caught Chris's eye. When she went to it, she saw that it was a little leather bound book with a brass clasp.

Quickly searching the man's bag, she found a box of matches, lit one and scanned a page of the book. As she hoped, it was a diary and, before Asher saw her, she made out the words, "We must help him" and "Lionel's life may be in danger. He's only a child and he has no one but us."

When she heard Asher behind her, she slammed the book shut and slipped it into the pocket of her habit.

They left the wagon and the bundles where they were for the sheriff to examine, mounted their horses and rode south.

They got to the inn, and, vaguely she heard Asher murmuring complaints and apologies about the food and the dirt of the place, but Chris wasn't really listening. Over a dinner of burned beans, all she could think of was the diary.

When Chris was finally alone in her room, she sat in the bed and began to read the diary. It started three years ago when Diana Hamilton had married the man she'd thought was the wisest, cleverest man on earth, Whitman Eskridge. It hadn't taken her but a few months to find out that he'd married her for her money. Within six months he'd spent everything she brought to the marriage and wanted more.

Chris read how this man had wheedled his way into the Hamilton business—and it wasn't until after Diana's father's suicide that she found out that Whitman had been embezzling funds.

The company went bankrupt, but Diana stood by her husband through all the scandal and the public auction of their belongings. When he said he wanted to go live with her rich relatives in Washington Territory, Diana had reluctantly agreed. She wrote her cousin, Owen Hamilton, a man she'd never met, and begged him for mercy and kindness—and for a roof over their heads.

There were several days when Diana didn't write in the diary, then she took it up again with the news that Whitman had told her that Owen was stealing from Lionel. Chris found this confusing until she'd read a few pages more. As far as she could tell, Lionel was

126

really the owner of the Hamilton holdings in Washington. He was a boy of about eleven, and everything had been left to him in care of his uncle, the man who was Diana's cousin. And Whitman Eskridge had produced some type of proof that Owen Hamilton was cheating his nephew out of his inheritance. Unfortunately, the diary didn't tell what that proof was.

It was hours later when she finished reading and fell asleep, the book across her lap. She had a dream that she was Diana Eskridge.

"Chris, wake up," Asher was saying, shaking her awake. "I pounded on the door but no one answered. Did you stay awake all night reading that book?"

Yawning, Chris nodded.

"Well, whatever it is, I hope it was worth it. I just rode in and I wanted to tell you that the sheriff has the bodies. I'm going to sleep now. I'll see you at dinner."

Chris was tired but she could sleep only fitfully. She kept thinking and dreaming about what she'd read. It was so unfair that the pretty young woman had had such a terrible life. And what would happen now to that poor little boy whose inheritance she was trying to save? Lionel now had no other relatives except his dishonest uncle.

By evening, she was convinced that she should do something about this young woman who had died. She couldn't let her die in vain, couldn't let her agony and pain be for nothing.

At dinner, she asked Asher many questions about the looks of the young woman who'd died.

"Chris, how can you be so morbid?"

"Do you think she was built like me? Was she anything like me at all?"

When he saw she wasn't going to cease, he began to

answer her. "Why don't you tell me what you have on your mind," he said softly.

Chris nearly choked from trying to tell too much too quickly. When she'd calmed herself, she began again. First, she told him about the diary and Diana Eskridge's miserable marriage. "She never had a chance for happiness. And she was on her way to do something very good. She was going to save her cousin whose estate was being stolen from him by a wicked uncle when she was killed."

Asher looked at his plate of food. "Did it ever occur to you that the wicked uncle might have been the one who killed her?"

"Of course it did. But her dying request was that I help by protecting Lionel."

"And just how do you propose to do that? Walk up to this uncle and say, 'Excuse me, but are you stealing from your nephew? If so, would you please turn yourself in and go to jail for the rest of your life?' Really, Chris! This is too absurd."

Chris took a deep breath. "I thought that since this man has never seen his cousin, I might be able to pose as her."

Asher's jaw dropped as he gaped at her. "But if he's the one who has had her killed, don't you think he'll be a little suspicious when you walk in the door?"

"I don't guess he can say that he thought I was dead, can he?"

"Not *you*, Chris, Diana Eskridge. You couldn't possibly get away with this. There's too much that you don't know about her. How are the two of them related? Maybe this Diana has a birthmark that's a family trait. There are a thousand things that you don't know. Why has she never met this man before? No, you couldn't possibly do it."

Chris looked down at her plate and she tried to control herself but she felt the tears coming.

"What's the matter, Chris?" Asher asked, reaching for her hand.

"Tynan," was all Chris could sob. She heard Asher's sharp intake of breath and she realized it was the first time she'd admitted that there was actually anything between her and the guide. But right now, secrecy didn't matter to her. All she thought about was Tynan.

Asher kept holding her hand. "If you went to visit Diana Eskridge's cousin, what about her husband? Surely Owen Hamilton would be expecting the two of them? You can't exactly say that you lost him on the way out west."

"I hadn't thought about him," Chris said, wiping her eyes with her hand. "Maybe I could appear as a widow. Smallpox got him or a rabid dog or maybe Indians on the plains or—"

"What if you appeared *with* him?" Asher interrupted. "What if you came with your husband?"

"You mean get Tynan to pretend to be my husband? After the things he said to me about marriage? He'd probably take after Owen with a gun the first day. He'd no doubt—"

"Could you get that man out of your mind for a moment?" Asher asked angrily. "I was thinking about myself."

"You as my husband?" Chris asked, her mouth open in disbelief.

Asher gave her a look of disgust for a moment. "Do you *really* want to help Lionel or not?"

"I do but . . . besides, Mr. Prescott, you can't do this. I'm sure you have somewhere else you have to be and the last place you want to be is risking your life to save someone you don't even know. No, I'll just have to do this by myself. I'll say that my husband was killed under a stampede of horses when the train stopped for water. Or maybe the water pipe fell on him, knocked him unconscious and he drowned in the middle of the desert. I'd like something awful to have happened to Mr. Whitman Eskridge. He deserves it for the way he treated Diana."

"Chris, if I don't go along on this to take care of you, I'll tell your father where you are and what you're up to this time."

"You wouldn't," Chris gasped.

"Try me," he answered, narrowing his eyes at her.

Chris leaned away from him and suddenly felt his intensity. He'd made several attempts at showing how much he liked her, but now she felt that he sincerely wanted to help her.

Asher smiled at her. "Of course I'll have to read the diary before we go to see just what kind of a son of a—oh, excuse me." He grinned. "Think you can play the dutiful little wife who agrees with her husband no matter what he does?"

Chris's lips tightened into a line. "I can play whatever role is needed. How would Owen Hamilton know what I was like?"

"I'm sure that if he's a man like you think he is, to take away a child's inheritance, to have his relatives killed, then he's the type who would investigate a person. Surely he knows about Diana's father's suicide and he must have heard about the funds I"—he winked at her—"was embezzling."

"You're willing to risk your life for something that's none of your business?" She still couldn't believe he *wanted* to do this. Did he like her that much? Or was it her father's money?

"If you hadn't risked your life so many times as Nola Dallas, there would be fewer reforms in our laws. Chris, I'd be honored to be your husband whether for a night or forever."

"Oh," Chris said, blinking.

"Now, shall we start making plans?" Asher asked. "I think we should stay here today and maybe tomorrow, and read that diary aloud and find out everything we can about Diana Eskridge and her husband. You'll walk into this as prepared as you can be. Agreed?"

Chris looked up from under her lashes at Asher who was smiling as if he were extremely pleased about something. This time tomorrow this man would be her husband—sort of.

When he turned and looked at her, she noticed for the first time how thick his lashes were and now he was looking at her in a way that was decidedly making her uncomfortable. She shifted in her chair while listening to him make plans.

131

Chapter Twelve

Owen Hamilton's house was a three-story mansion not
far from the sea on Washington's west coast. It had
taken them three days of preparing for the trip, before
Chris and Asher had climbed into a buggy that had to
be fifteen years old and ridden west.

Asher and she hadn't spoken a great deal on the way
to the Hamilton house, both of them going over what
they needed to know to carry off this escapade. They
spent the night at an inn, taking separate rooms, and
started in the early morning.

They were within a few miles of the house when
Asher turned to her. "This is your last chance, Chris,"
he said. "If you want to back out, now's the time."

"Not unless you do."

Ash chuckled. "This is a man's dream. I get to spend
nights and days with a beautiful young lady, I get to do
something constructive with my time besides beg banks
for loans they won't give and I might get some of the
satisfaction you get from helping people. What more

132

can I ask?" He looked at her out of the corner of his eye. "By the way, Chris, I mean to use this time to win you over. By the time we leave here, I plan to have you in love with me."

"Me or my money?" she asked, one eyebrow cocked.

"Did your gunslinger tell you that?"

"No," she said honestly. "But isn't it true that my father sent you on the rescue mission in the hopes that I'd fall in love with you? My father badly wants me to marry, stay home and have babies."

He smiled at her, snapping the reins to make the horse go faster. "It started out that way. I think I was to the point that I would have married a three-headed ostrich if I thought I could have a chance at getting my self-respect back. But the truth is, Chris, it's come to mean more to me. You're the most courageous woman I've ever met. You're the most . . . most interesting woman I've ever met. If we lived together for ninety years, I don't think I'd get bored with you."

Chris had to laugh. "I think that may be one of the nicest compliments I've ever received."

"And now that that strutting criminal is out of the way, I think I'll have a chance. I'll never understand why you ladies fall for that type."

As Chris watched, he shrugged. Was Tynan just a type? she wondered. Was that all he was and nothing more? He had seemed so special, so unique. Maybe she'd been blinded by his extraordinary exterior beauty. A horse pounding along the road beside them made her heart nearly skip a beat, but it was just a cowboy. She relaxed against the back of the seat—relaxed as much as she could in the springless carriage. "You have my permission to try, Mr. Prescott," she said. "You may try."

Two hours later, they arrived at the Hamilton house. "Now remember that you are Diana Eskridge, a meek, mild-mannered woman and not the notorious Nola Dallas. If you step out of place, I may have to reprimand you."

Chris, with eyes wide, looked up at him and started to speak, but the front door was opened by a fat, aproned woman and Chris put her head down. She'd chosen clothes she thought Diana would wear, simple little calicos, all insipid colors, all hint of stylishness gone. They were the clothes of a woman who'd allow her husband to make her life miserable.

"You must be the Eskridges," the heavy woman with the broad face said. "We've been expecting you for days. Was beginnin' to worry about you. Just set those bags down and I'll get Mr. Owen." She went straight ahead, up some stairs. "By the way, I'm Unity," she called over her shoulder.

Chris stepped farther into the room. They were standing in an entryway, with a music room to the right, a parlor to the left, and to the right, farther down the hall a dining room. She looked up as a man came down the stairs. He was tall, broad-shouldered, with a small mustache over full lips. The last thing in the world that he looked like was anyone's idea of a villain. He was smiling in such a pleasant way that Chris wanted to tell him the truth of who she was.

"You must be Diana," he said and he had a deep voice that instantly made a person relax. "We meet at last."

She offered him her hand. "Yes, finally," she murmured. "May I introduce my husband, Whitman? We can't thank you enough for inviting us to your lovely home."

He smiled at both of them with genuine warmth. "Think nothing of it. I'll be glad for the company and Unity will be pleased to have someone to fuss over. Now, you must be tired. Let me take you to your room. We'll eat in about an hour and until then I'm afraid you'll have to excuse me as I have mountains of paperwork to do. Quite unexpectedly, I have a buyer coming in from the East day after tomorrow and I have to be ready for him. Make yourself at home. There's a garden in back that you might like. Here we are." He opened the door to a large, spacious room with a big, double, four-postered bed, a closet and a little bay-window seat in the corner. Chris was grateful to see a fainting couch along one wall. Ash followed her eyes and winked at her, making her face turn pink.

"This is more than adequate," Ash said. "Thank you very much."

"If you need anything, just let out a holler. We're not formal here. Unity is usually in the kitchen below or sometimes you can find me upstairs. I have a billiards table up there and a complete bar. One of my great luxuries in life. I'll see you in the dining room at twelve-thirty." He closed the door behind him and was gone.

Asher sat on the bed, bouncing a bit to test the springs. "I wouldn't want this to squeak. More marriages are ruined by loud mattresses than any other—"

"He didn't say a word about Lionel," Chris said, cutting Ash off. "Do you think he's here? You don't think he's already done something to him, do you?"

"Buried him in the rosebushes? Owen doesn't look like a man who'd do anyone a bad turn. I never met anyone who welcomed his destitute relatives with such open arms before. How about a nap before dinner?"

"I sincerely hope that you aren't going to persist in talking of the . . . the intimacies of married couples. I think I'll see this garden Owen mentioned. An eleven-year-old boy might be there playing."

Chris went down the stairs to the kitchen. Unity wasn't in the room but the smells of the food cooking were delicious. She felt as if it had been years since she'd had a decent meal.

The garden outside was beautiful, full of azaleas, wildflowers from the mountains, bulb plants. It was obviously the great love of someone and she guessed it was Owen Hamilton. There was a curved stone bench under a big Douglas fir and she sat on it, leaning back against the tree and closing her eyes. At the moment she'd never been so homesick in her life. Her mother used to have a garden like this but since she'd died, her father had not taken care of it. Now, when she visited, she almost cried to see the weeds overtaking it. "You should stay home and see to it yourself," her father kept saying to her.

"You will not be allowed to sit there. That is *my* bench."

Chris opened her eyes to see a boy standing in front of her. He looked a little like Owen except where Owen's face was pleasant, this boy's was scowling.

"You must be Lionel," she said, smiling. "I'm—"

"I know who you are. You're the poor relatives who've come to live off me. Now get up and go away."

Chris just sat there looking at him.

Lionel's face began to turn red. "I told you to get up. That is *my* seat. This is *my* garden. This is *my* house. Do I have to call my uncle to get rid of you?"

"Why, yes, I do believe you'll have to do just that," she said, wondering what Owen would do if he were summoned away from his paperwork to tell a guest to give her seat to a rude little boy.

Lionel's face began to lose its redness but she could see that his anger was just beneath the surface. "You have to obey me."

"Why is that?"

"Because I own everything here and you are at my mercy."

Chris smiled at him, repressing a laugh. "It doesn't look like you own this seat at the moment. Nor do you seem to own any manners. Shall we begin again? I'm your cousin, Diana Eskridge."

Lionel took a step back from her, then, in a split second, he grabbed a handful of mud from a flower bed and threw it onto the front of her clean dress. Before Chris could speak, he ran out of sight.

Standing, Chris looked down at the front of her dress, then started back to the house.

Unity, taking a pan of cornbread from the oven, looked up. "I take it you met Lionel. Here, honey, sit down and we'll get you cleaned up. That boy is gonna be the death of us all."

"I'm sure it's none of my business, but does anyone ever discipline that child?" She took the wet cloth Unity gave her.

"Till their hands near fell off. When you get as old as I am, you learn that kids are as different as night and day. Some of 'em you can discipline with a look, most of 'em you can discipline with a birch rod—and then there's Lionel. *Nothin'* has any effect on him. Believe me, his uncle's tried ever'thing."

"How about gentleness?" Chris asked, wiping at the mud on her dress. "I mean he is an orphan."

"You ain't been here long, but you'll see. Mr. Owen

is the gentlest man alive. It breaks his heart when he has to take a rod to that boy. For years, he wouldn't do it. He kept sayin' he wanted the boy to feel at home here but I've known him since he was a baby."

Chris wasn't sure how much Diana was supposed to know, but she had to chance it. "You were with Lionel before his uncle was?"

"I keep forgettin' that you don't know about us."

"If you'll hand me that bowl of peas I'll shell them for you," Chris said.

"Now this ain't to be usual. You're family, but for today I'll let you help. Now, where was I? Oh yes. I worked for Mr. Owen's brother and sister-in-law; I was there the night Mrs. Laura had little Lionel. That was a happy night. But it wasn't but a few months later that they was killed in that fire. Lionel was only six months old. Of course everything was left to him, with Mr. Owen to take care of the property until Lionel reached twenty-one. He's done the best he could, but that boy . . ." She trailed off, leaving the rest to the imagination.

Chris couldn't get anymore from the woman and Unity spent the rest of their time together talking about what a wonderful man Owen was and how she was fortunate to be able to work for him. Chris thought that this was every homeowner's dream, to find a dedicated servant.

At dinner, Lionel came to the table late, his mouth set into a sulky pout. Owen greeted him and introduced him to his cousins, Diana and Whitman, but Lionel just gave them a sullen look and began to push the food about on his plate. Twice, Chris caught him looking at her with especially hostile looks. Both times she smiled at him.

"What a brat of a kid," Ash said when they were alone in their room. "Has anyone taken a switch to him? And why was he eating with adults anyway?"

"Probably because he owns the place," Chris said as she hung up her meager wardrobe.

Asher ran his hand along the edge of the wardrobe. "I never thought I could come to love a piece of furniture. Remember the first time I saw you? I told Tynan we shouldn't be hiding in a lady's bedroom but he said we had to get to you without your making any noise. We thought you'd be asleep but the bed was empty and we jumped into the wardrobe when we heard you coming back into the room."

"I don't want to talk about him."

"Him? Who? You don't mean that two-bit gunslinger, do you? I thought you were over him. After what he did at that picnic, I'd think you'd never want to see him again."

"I don't. Could we talk about something else? Such as how we're going to find out what's going on in this house? What is making that child so miserable?"

"Being spoiled rotten is all that's wrong with him and if you had any children of your own, you'd know that."

"And you do have children? So many that you're an authority on the subject?"

"I know enough to be sure of what I see. He's been given everything and he expects more. Chris, let's not argue. Let's enjoy this time together." He reached out his arms to her, his hands almost catching her, but she sidestepped him.

"I'm going outside to the garden. I'll see you later. See if you can make yourself useful to Owen and find out something. We're here for a story and that's what I plan to look into."

Chris left the room with a sigh of relief. She hadn't given much thought to actually living with a man, of being in the same room with him night after night. But already, she could see the problems that it was going to involve.

Downstairs, she found Owen and Unity looking perplexed. "I'll take care of it," Unity was saying. "You just go back to work where you belong."

Chris bit her tongue to keep from asking what Lionel had done now, but, instead, she politely murmured that she would like to help with whatever was the problem.

"It's merely one of those household complications that can't be helped," Owen said. "But today I do need to get work done before the buyer arrives and I don't have time to—"

"May I be of help?" Chris asked. "I've run my father's house for years."

"We can't ask you . . ." Owen began, then halted. "Diana, I'd be eternally grateful if you'd help. Unity has her hands full and doesn't have the time. Five minutes ago, my gardener said he has to go to San Francisco to take care of a sick sister and he's hired his cousin to run my gardens, only I don't know this man and it'll take me days to tell him how I want things kept."

"Leave it to me," Chris said. "I'll take care of everything. Where are the gardeners? The old one and the new one? I'll get instructions from the old one and give them to the cousin—and I'll ask for references."

Owen was looking at her with his head cocked to one side and Chris thought maybe she'd made a mistake. Diana Eskridge was supposed to be a mouse of a woman, not one who took over someone else's household. But then, men rarely thought anything about housework. A woman could run an army of servants yet a man'd think she didn't have sense enough to handle a twenty-dollar bill.

"Diana, I'd appreciate it very much if you'd help me with this. Domestic responsibilities are my downfall."

Chris gave him a demure smile. "I'd like to help all that I can."

"Al is waiting in the garden for me with his cousin. I give it all to you."

Chris was glad for something to do and she went to the garden with a smile. Maybe she'd be able to find out something if she had access to some of Owen's time. He'd be more likely to tell her something if she were helping him in whatever way she could.

She was walking around a corner when she came face to face with the one man she did not want to see. "You!" she gasped. "Get out of here!" She turned on her heel and started back toward the house.

Tynan caught her arm. "Is that how you treat the new gardener? Will you tell Hamilton that you can't hire me?"

She stopped and glared at him. "I told you that I never wanted to see you again."

"And I told you that you were my responsibility until I returned you to your father. I'm not leaving you alone until you're in his care."

"You were also to bring me back in love with Asher. I can do that on my own. I'm staying here with Ash and I plan to fall in love with him."

"Good. Great. Glad to hear it. I wish you both the best in the world, but you're staying near me too until I personally hand you over to your father."

"That may be what you think but I'm going right now and tell Owen that you are unsuitable as a gardener. I'll tell him that you are untrustworthy, that you may use a gun to do the weeding."

"I hope you do," he said, starting to walk beside her. "I never wanted to be a gardener anyway. I'll just tell Hamilton the truth about who you are and we can go back to your father and we never have to see each other again. And I can get my pardon and you can have your wedding to the illustrious Mr. Prescott and I can get my money for playing Cupid. This suits me fine."

She stopped. "I want to stay here and find out about Lionel. I made a promise to a dying woman."

"Ah, I see, your promise to someone you don't know is sacred but my promise to your father isn't worth anything, is that it?"

"No, you're twisting my words. You have self-interest in this, I don't."

"Enhancing the reputation of Nola Dallas with a story that will break the readers' hearts isn't self-interest?"

"Get away from me," she said but she didn't walk toward the house any longer. "I am perfectly safe and I don't plan to get into any trouble. I'll write a letter to my father saying that you've fulfilled your obligations and he's to give you your pardon and the money. I'll even pay the money from my mother's estate. Now, will you go?"

"And leave you here to take care of yourself? If Hamilton is doing something illegal, do you think he'll stop at violence when he's been discovered? Someone has to protect you from yourself."

"Asher can protect me."

Tynan gave a sound that bordered on a laugh. "And who'll take care of him? You have a choice: either I stay here as the gardener and keep an eye on you, or we both leave now."

Chris hid her fists in the folds of her skirt. "How did you find out where I was?"

He moved his face closer to hers. "Through wearing out three horses and two saddles. Lady, I have done nothing for the last few days but follow you and try to find out where you were. I finally got the sheriff to tell me something about it."

"And what could he know?" Chris asked, glaring at him.

"More than you could guess. He's heard of Owen Hamilton. The man does some big business dealings, controls a lot of money. You're not dealing with a simpleton like Prescott who you can wrap around your little finger."

"I can't wrap Asher—" She stopped because, walking through the trees, was an utterly beautiful woman with dark hair and eyes, a perfect figure, and a graceful walk that emanated sexuality. "Who is that?"

"My bodyguard. I thought since you could make up a new identity, I could too. Pilar has agreed to be my wife for the duration of this fiasco. I figured with your living with the brave Mr. Prescott, and me with Pilar, there wouldn't be anymore of what happened in the rain forest. I don't plan to go back to jail."

"Wife," Chris whispered. "Wife?"

Tynan narrowed his eyes at her. "Yeah, the gardener has a wife. Pilar will be helping out in the house and I'll be out here. Between the two of us, we should be able to watch out for you."

"Where will you live?"

"In the gardener's house, of course. Look, Chris, if

we're going to play this until you get your story, we'd better get started. Are you supposed to tell me what to do?"

"I would love to tell you what to do, Mr. Tynan," she said with a false smile, turning away from him and starting back to the house.

"Don't you want to meet Pilar?" he called after her, laughter in his voice.

Chris kept walking.

144

Chapter Thirteen

"Diana!" Asher said sharply. "Your cousin was speaking to you."

Chris looked up from her plate of food to gaze blankly at Owen Hamilton, for a moment not knowing who he was.

"You can see what a time I have with her," Asher was saying. "She can be most exasperating at times."

"Yes, well . . ." Owen said hesitantly. "How did you get on with the new gardener, Diana?"

Unity set a large bowl of carrots on the table. "Anybody that looks like him can get along with any woman. I'm not sure I ever wanta see Al's ugly ol' face again."

Owen gave his housekeeper a look of reproach.

"He seems to know what he's doing," Chris murmured. "I think he's worked on a farm."

"*I* don't think he's a farmer," Lionel said. "I think he's a robber. I think he robs banks and kills people."

"There are worse ways to go," Unity muttered before leaving the room.

Asher was watching Chris intently, while she just looked at her food. Thirty minutes later, as everyone was leaving the table, he grabbed her arm. "Come outside with me, I want to talk to you."

Asher practically dragged her into the garden, out of hearing distance of the house. "All right, who is this robber–farmer? Is it who I think it is?"

"Yes," she said, "but I had no idea he was coming here. He says I am his responsibility until he turns me over to my father."

"So now I have to deal with him again. Chris, I hope you aren't going to make a fool of yourself over him this time. I don't think it would fit meek little Diana's image to be seen following the gardener about."

She was glad for the darkness to hide her red face. "No, I am not going to make a fool of myself again. Besides, he brought a woman with him. He doesn't want to have any more to do with me than I with him. Now, does that soothe your jealousy? Could we go in now? I'm awfully tired."

Asher looked at something over her head and then he quite suddenly grabbed her and pressed his mouth to hers. Chris thought it was meant to be a kiss, but it didn't feel like one. Her eyes were open and his were staring at something behind her. She began to push away from him, but just then she heard someone whistling from behind her and she knew who it was. She grabbed Asher closer to her, trying to put some passion into the kiss. It seemed to work for Ash because his eyes closed and he began to pull her to him, but Chris was only aware of where Tynan was.

"Ah, newlyweds," Tynan said as he passed them. "It's so good to see people in love."

Chris pushed Asher away with some force, put her chin in the air and walked past Ty without a backward glance.

When Asher got to their room, she was slinging sheets onto the narrow fainting couch. "I *hate* that man! Absolutely, totally, completely hate that man. I wish he'd go back to jail and stay there forever. I'd like to think of him rotting away somewhere."

"It didn't look to me as if you hated him," Asher said stiffly. "It seemed to me that you were trying to use me to make him jealous."

"Jealous! He said he couldn't stand to see me with other men, but he didn't really care. All he cares about is getting that money."

"Maybe he was jealous after he'd just gotten out of prison and before he'd visited a . . . a place like Red's."

Chris's eyes widened. "And before he'd moved in with the luscious Pilar." She pounded a pillow with her fist. "I truly, sincerely hate that man. I wish I'd never seen him before in my life. I wish I never had to see him again. I wish—"

Asher caught her by the shoulders and turned her to face him. "Chris, you're protesting too much. I know a way to put him out of your mind." He began to lower his head to hers. "You're obsessed with him because you have nothing else to replace him." He touched her neck with his lips. "Spend the night with me. I'll make you forget him. I'll make you forget everything except us. We'll be a real married couple and when we leave here, we can go to your father and have a legal ceremony."

147

Chris tried to enjoy the lovely way he was kissing her neck. He was a handsome man, he smelled good, there was absolutely nothing at all wrong with him—except that there was no spark. She could have fallen asleep standing up while he was kissing her. As it was, she suppressed a yawn.

"Please, Ash, don't rush things. I . . . I'm not sure of myself yet. I've just been through something awful with one man and I don't feel as if I can trust myself with anyone else. Please understand."

He pulled away from her with a hurt look that made a thread of guilt run through her. She so hated lying for any reason whatever, and she especially hated lying to Ash who'd been so nice to her.

He stepped back. "All right, but I won't give up trying."

"I hope you don't," she said with a smile. There was no screen in the room, so she opened the wardrobe door and undressed behind it, all too aware that Asher was lying in the bed watching her. It made her nervous and a little frightened—but it did not make her want to climb into bed with him. She began to imagine how she'd feel if Tynan were lying in that bed, his shirt off, his hands behind his head, waiting for her. Even the thought seemed to make her skin glow.

She took a few deep breaths before she walked out from behind the door. Ash had on a long nightgown and he was watching her like a cat with a mouse. Chris said a soft good-night, blew out the lantern, and climbed onto the little couch. It was hard and uncomfortable, but it was better than the alternative.

She woke the next morning to Asher kissing her face and neck. For a moment, she enjoyed it until she remembered who he was. "For heaven's sake!" she said, pushing him away. "Really, Mr. Prescott, you must control yourself. I won't be able to stand this sort of thing every minute of the day."

"I told you I planned to make you fall in love with me."

"And you think this is the way? By mauling me at every opportunity?"

Asher stood. He was wearing a robe over his gown and his hair was tousled from sleep. "That's just what your gunslinger called it: mauling." He turned away. "Well, today you won't have to stand my company because your cousin has asked me to drive twenty miles into town to pick up some supplies. You know, Chris, I think the man plans to get all the work he can out of us."

"And what's wrong with that?" she asked, putting on her robe before removing the covers from her body. "We are asking him to support us. The least we can do is help."

"You help in the garden with your outlaw and I get out of the picture. That should suit you just fine."

"He's not mine. I didn't ask him here and I volunteered to help in the garden before I knew he was the gardener. You can't blame me for any of it. Can't we have an ordinary conversation? One minute you're asking me to marry you and the next you're accusing me of carrying on with another man."

Asher didn't answer her but started dressing— behind the wardrobe door. Chris wasn't sure if he was modest or he was saving her delicate sensibilities. She chastised herself for criticizing every move he made. When he was dressed, he left the room.

Downstairs at breakfast, she began to see another Owen. Until now, he'd been the epitome of cordiality,

149

but now he was giving instructions to Chris and Asher with the authority of a general.

"I want the north acre reseeded," Owen was saying. "And I want all two hundred of those bulbs I ordered set by the end of the day. And, Whit, I'll give you a list of what I want from town. You're to take the wagon directly to the saw mill. You can do it all in a day if you don't dawdle. Lionel, eat those eggs. Unity, have you shown the new housemaid what to do? I want the ceilings upstairs washed."

No one else at the table said much. Later, Asher escorted Chris outside. "You don't have to do this. Remember who you are and that we can go home any time you want. I don't want you working as a field hand."

"How kind of you, but I don't mind working at all."

Suddenly, Ash moved away from her. "Diana, even you aren't too stupid to do a little work. Now get over there and act like the woman you aren't."

Chris turned to see Owen approaching with Tynan, both men seemingly unaware of what Asher was saying but she knew that, just as Asher had planned, they'd heard.

Owen said a few more words to Tynan, which she couldn't hear, then gave Ash an appraising look. "Come with me," he said and Asher followed, leaving Chris with Tynan.

"I don't guess you could have volunteered to help with the washing, could you?" Ty said. "Or the horses? It had to be with the garden."

She turned on her heel to glare at him. "If I'd known you were to be in charge of the garden, I would have shoveled coal first. Shall we get started and stop wasting time? I have more to do with my life than spend it listening to you insult me."

"It seems to me that the man you claim as your husband was insulting you worse than I ever could."

"It's part of the charade. Diana Eskridge was a woman who allowed her husband to bully her, so Ash and I are acting out a part."

"You'd better work on it then, because you don't look like the type to take bullying from anybody. Every time he speaks to you in that tone, you look like you're about to set his hair on fire. Here, take this," he said, handing her a box of bulbs. "You know how to plant?"

"You'd think he'd hire more than one gardener to do this. My father's garden isn't half this size and, when it was kept, he had four men taking care of it."

"Ah, but he paid them a salary, they lived on his ranch and he fed them. Hamilton only has to give his poor grateful relatives a roof and food."

"But he seems like such a nice man."

"People aren't what they seem," Ty said with a cold voice.

"Is that supposed to refer to anyone I know?" she asked, setting down the box of bulbs.

"Not unless you claim it. I thought I'd met a good girl who was different, but she wasn't. You're just like all the rest of them. You're excited by the reputation of a man with a gun, and you'll use him however you want, but in the end, when the chips are down, you'll side against him. No more good girls for me. You and Prescott were made for each other."

"I didn't side with anyone else against you. You betrayed me! I trusted you and then at the picnic you shot a man. Do you know how I felt with all those people against me? They were looking at me as if I were a piece of vermin. A man on the street spit at my feet."

Tynan looked at her for a long moment. "Yeah, I know how it feels. I've known all my life. Wait until a man spits in your face and then draws a gun on you."

"Is that what Rory Sayers did?" Chris whispered.

"I twisted his arm to keep him from shooting me and the gun went off."

"But why did the deputy take you to jail if it was all Rory's fault?"

He narrowed his eyes at her. "For the same reason you condemned me without any facts. By reputation. Because I'm not one of the 'good' people like they are—like you are."

Chris took a bulb planter from a tool box by Tynan's feet and began to dig in the soft earth to set the first bulb. "I think I was wrong."

"No you weren't," he said, kneeling beside her. "You were right. People like you and me don't mix. You deserve somebody like Prescott, not a nameless nobody like me."

"I don't think I deserve anyone at all after betraying a friend," she whispered, mostly to herself. "Tynan, do you think you could ever forgive me for not trusting you?"

He looked at her. "No," he said simply. "It may take me a while to learn a lesson, but I do eventually learn it. I think that from now on I'll stay even farther away from girls like you."

He moved away from her, leaving her to do the planting on that side of the plowed field by herself. The sun came out, making her perspire and the soil that was getting on her made her itch, but she didn't notice as she went over the events of the past few weeks. Since Tynan had popped out of the cabinet and held her nude body in his arms, she'd not been the same. She'd changed from a sensible young woman interested only in a story to an Amazon who pursued a man without shame. She'd thrown herself at him in the rain forest; she'd sworn to a woman who trusted her, Red, that she'd not betray him—yet at the first opportunity, that's what she'd done. She was acting like a spoiled little girl: one minute she hated him and the next minute she loved him.

Sitting back on her heels for a moment, she wiped her forehead and looked across at Tynan as he used a scythe to clear some underbrush. His shirt was drenched with sweat and she could see his muscles working under the thin cloth. He looked as if he'd gained some weight in the last few weeks. Against her will, she remembered the raw stripes on his back where he'd been whipped.

She thought of the way the townspeople had turned against her after she'd made one error of trying to help a man who looked as if he were guilty. How people everywhere must have treated a man who was always being accused of wrongdoing! How impossible all the "good" people made it for a man to stop doing wrong.

She turned back to the planting with a vengeance. And she'd been just like them. One time she'd been doing a story on women who worked under the hideous conditions of the sweatshops and she was being very sympathetic when one woman said, "But you can afford to give sympathy because you've never had to be where we are." It hadn't made much of an impression on her at the time, but now she was beginning to understand what the woman meant. It was easy to

153

judge, to say what you'd do in a situation if you weren't faced with that situation.

She had wanted to be Tynan's friend, even his lover, when the only person she had to stand up against was a man who admitted he'd wanted to marry her even before he'd met her. But when she had to face the ridicule of an entire town and risk the reputation of Nola Dallas, she didn't stand up so well. She'd walked away from him at the first sign of trouble.

Chris was sure that she'd never felt so rotten in her life. She had almost earned the trust of a man who didn't give his trust very often and then she'd betrayed him. She was no better than that girl who'd been willing to see Ty hang rather than tell the truth.

And now she'd lost him. He was gone from her as if the few days they'd spent together had never been. The fragile beginnings were broken forever.

Standing, easing her back against her hand, she went to the pump and filled the water bucket. She took a drink from the dipper, shaded her eyes against the sun and looked for Tynan. He was still chopping weeds, clearing the brush away for a new area of garden.

She put the dipper into the bucket and carried it to him. "Thirsty?" she asked.

He turned, smiling at her before he caught himself and the smile disappeared. He didn't speak as he took the dipper from her.

"You look awfully hot. Why don't you sit a while?"

"No thanks, and this is nothing compared to what I've been doing the last few years of my life."

"In prison?"

"Where they put all bad men like me. Move back so I don't hit you."

Chris stepped back and as she did so, she could see

154

the sweat rolling off his face and dripping into his soaked shirt collar. On impulse, she picked up the bucket of water, cold from the underground well, and threw the contents on the back of his head.

Tynan gasped at the shock of the water, then turned on her in anger.

Chris backed away from him with a little giggle. "I thought you needed cooling off."

"Not from you I don't. I don't need anything from you." He began to advance on her.

Chris put her hands behind her back, a big smile on her face and started moving away from him into the trees. "I didn't mean anything, Ty. Truly I didn't."

"You never mean anything, do you? You didn't mean anything in the forest either, did you, when you nearly drove me crazy?"

"Did I?" she asked innocently. "But last night you didn't seem too upset when you saw me with another man."

"That weakling? I'll worry when I see you with a *man*." There was a hint of a smile on his lips as he moved toward her, deeper into the shadowy forest.

Chris found herself up against a tree and she made no effort to move as Tynan came nearer her, but she had a look of mock fearfulness.

He caught her about the waist and began to rub his sweaty face against hers. He hadn't shaved that morning and the sharp whiskers were scratching her skin. She squealed for him to stop, tried to get away from him, but he held her tight. Still struggling, she managed to get out from between him and the tree and start running. She took only a few steps before he caught her, pushing her down on the ground and continuing to rub his face about her neck and cheeks.

Chris was squealing with delight when he suddenly stopped.

She looked up at him, smiling, as he got off of her, his face solemn. "Get up," he said.

She held up her hand for him to help her and, reluctantly, he did so. She tried to stand close to him for a moment but he didn't allow that. Silently, she turned her back to him so he could button her dress.

"Stay away from me, Chris," he said. "You're playing with my life and I don't like it."

She turned to face him so that his hands were on her shoulders. "I was wrong to go off and leave you. I should have stayed by you at the picnic. I was wrong and I want you to please forgive me."

He stepped back from her. "It's better that we stay apart. In fact, I think it's better that we call off this entire masquerade. I thought it might be all right since you've done this sort of thing before, but I don't like it. Tomorrow I want to take you back to your father. After I deliver you to him, you can come back if you want. It won't matter to me because you'll no longer be my responsibility, but I can see right now that this won't work. Go back to the house now and get cleaned up and pack. I'll do what has to be done here." With that he turned and went back into the sun to slash at the weeds.

Silently, Chris started walking back to the house.

Chapter Fourteen

As Chris neared the house, she saw Owen getting into a carriage and driving away. Lionel was attacking a young tree with a dull axe, Unity and the luscious Pilar were hanging clothes on the line and, with Asher away for the day, Chris was alone in the house.

She washed and changed her dirty dress and began to think about the fact that tomorrow she'd be going home. She wasn't even going to argue with Tynan about staying at the Hamilton house. Perhaps it wasn't any of her business to try to find out what Owen was doing to his nephew—if he was doing anything at all.

As she struggled with the buttons on her dress, she remembered that she was alone in the house and it occurred to her that now she had the chance to look into Owen's office.

She went up the stairs outside her bedroom and opened three doors before she found Owen's office. It was packed with papers, and there was a big oak filing

157

cabinet in the corner. She had no idea what she was looking for but perhaps she could find it in there, or maybe she could at least find out what Owen knew about the Eskridges.

She had just opened the filing cabinet and seen a fat folder with the name of Diana Eskridge on it when she heard voices on the stairs—and one of them was the voice of Owen Hamilton.

Chris's heart began pounding as she looked for an escape route. There was only one window in the office and it was open. Without even looking outside, she stuck her leg over the casement and climbed out. The door to the office opened just as she pulled her skirt out of view.

She was standing on the smallest of ledges, about the width of a drain pipe, and below her was nothing for three stories.

She flattened her back against the wall of the dormer that contained the window to Owen's study and held on with her hands behind her.

"That trip was particularly foul," a voice Chris didn't recognize, coming from inside the office, was saying. "Are you sure you have all the information? It's him?"

"Without a doubt. When I tell you all the trouble I had getting this, you'll believe me. Samuel Dysan is the name, isn't it?"

Chris leaned toward the window. There was something about the way they were talking that made her want to hear what they were saying.

"What about Lionel?" the stranger asked. "Did you get the little bastard's name on the papers?"

"Wait a minute, let me close this window. There are too many people living in this house for me to keep up with the whereabouts of all of them."

Chris pulled back as he shut the window and locked it. Now she was stuck on the roof, with no way to get back inside.

The men stayed in the room an hour—the longest hour of her life. Behind her, she could hear the muffled voices of Owen and the stranger but she couldn't make out what they were saying. She heard drawers slammed, doors creaking open, then shut again, and all the while she could do nothing but stand there and try to keep her skirt from blowing across the window.

When at last the men left the room, Chris immediately tried to open the window but it was firmly locked.

"Now I've done it," she murmured. Whatever excuse could she give for being outside this window? If Owen was stealing from his nephew, it could be quite dangerous to let him know that she was interested in what he was doing in his office.

With a big sigh, she turned back around, and as she did so, she slipped. She managed to catch herself before she actually fell, but she could feel her hand being scraped. Wincing at the pain, she grabbed for the casement ledge and pulled herself up. She was breathing quite hard by the time she reached her perch again, and she stood there, clutching the wood behind her, and was glad for her safety.

She stood there for quite some time, too fearful to move, when, below her, she began to hear sounds. Within minutes, she saw the top poles of a ladder appear, leaning against the roof line. Holding her breath, she watched to see who was coming to her rescue—or to her trial.

The relief she felt when she saw Tynan was great. "How did you know?" she asked.

He put a finger to his lips to silence her, then

motioned for her to give him her hand. He led her down the roof of the second story, then guided her feet onto the ladder, his arms always surrounding her as he backed down first.

When they were at last on the ground, she clung to him for a moment. "I was so frightened."

"You'll be more frightened if Hamilton finds out you were spying on him," he said, peeling her arms away from him. "Let's get out of here before he sees us."

Chris turned away just in time to see a shadow disappear around the edge of the house. "Ty! Someone was there."

"It's only Lionel. He told me where you were. Come on!"

She ran behind him, down a path she'd not seen before, to a small cottage hidden amid the trees. As Ty hooked the ladder beneath the eaves of the house, she saw blood on the back of his shirt.

"Ty! You're bleeding."

"No, you are," he said, taking her wrist and turning her palm upward, looking at where the skin was scraped away. "Come inside and I'll clean it and I want you to explain what you were doing on that roof."

"Listening," she said as he pulled her inside. The cottage had only one room, half of it kitchen, the other half holding a big double bed. "Is this where you live with Pilar?" she asked quietly.

"Yes," he said as he held her hand over a basin of water and began to clean it.

"Have you known her long?"

"Years."

"And she doesn't ever betray you?"

"I've never found out. We're on the same side. Hold still so I can see this."

160

"On the same side?" Chris's eyes widened. "You mean she's a lady outlaw?"

"Sure. She can outdraw anybody."

"Oh. You're teasing me, aren't you?"

He looked at her as his head was bowed over her hand. "Climbing out the window was pretty stupid of you. If Hamilton had found you—"

"It was worth it. I heard Owen's visitor asking about Lionel. He said—pardon me, but this is a quote—'Has the little bastard signed the papers yet?' Doesn't that sound as if they're into something dreadful?"

Ty opened a tin box on a shelf by the fireplace and withdrew clean bandages. "No, it sounds like he's met Lionel. The kid *is* a little bastard."

"Then why was he helping you? Ouch!"

"If you'd hold still, I wouldn't hurt you. Lionel and I have an understanding."

"He says he thinks you're a bank robber."

"Now and then. Shrewd kid. Sit down and I'll get you some milk and cookies. I need a drink."

"Did I scare you? Why didn't Lionel give me away and why did he come to you? Who made the cookies?"

"Pilar made the cookies," he said, sitting down across from her at the rough table. "And Lionel has been the soul of helpfulness ever since I cracked a whip around his neck."

Chris took a cookie but put it back on the plate. She realized that her hands were shaking and reached for Tynan's glass of whiskey. In exchange, he took her milk and began eating the cookies.

"We're going home tomorrow," Ty said, not looking at her.

"And leaving Lionel to his own fate, I guess."

"He's not your problem."

"Have you ever heard of Samuel Dysan?"

"No and don't change the subject. Tomorrow we leave."

"What if Asher doesn't agree? That'll be two against one."

"Prescott can stay here for all I care, but tomorrow you and I leave for your father's house."

"Just the two of us?" she asked, running her finger along the whiskey glass.

He took the glass from her and drained it. "It's time for you to go back to the house. You can say you hurt your hand on a sharp rock and couldn't work anymore."

Chris made no effort to move but picked up a cookie. When she was with him, she never wanted to leave. "How is your back?"

"Healing quite well thanks to Pilar's gentle attentions. Chris, go away."

She looked up at him with sad eyes. "I was wrong when I left you alone. I should have gone with you to the jail."

"The world is full of should haves." He stood. "I'm going back to work and I want you to go back to the house and stay out of trouble."

"Maybe I should lock myself inside the bedroom with Asher."

"If you can stand the boredom," he said, slamming his hat on his head and leaving her alone in the cottage.

Reluctantly, Chris left the little cottage and started back to the main house. The sun was gone and the air was beginning to feel like rain.

"It's gonna come a storm," Unity was saying as Chris entered the kitchen. "What'd you do to your hand?"

Chris looked up—and into the dark, pretty eyes of Pilar.

"I cut it," Chris managed to say after a while. No wonder Ty liked her; she was utterly lovely.

"Would you like a cool drink?" Pilar asked in a soft voice. "We've just made an herb tea. It's quite good."

"No," Chris said, wishing the woman wouldn't be nice to her.

"You look a little pale," Unity said. "I told Mr. Owen you shouldn't work outside. You're too little to be able to stand the outdoors."

Chris had no idea what being small had to do with sunshine, but it was the type of comment she'd heard all her life. "Yes, I would like something to drink."

"Pilar made cookies. Have some."

"No, thank you, I already did," Chris said without thinking, then looked at Pilar. There was understanding in her eyes. "On second thought, I think I'll lie down a while. Maybe the loss of blood is making me weak."

Chris left the kitchen and was on her way upstairs when Owen called to her.

"Diana, could you come in here? There's someone I'd like you to meet," Owen called from the parlor.

Chris knew it was the visitor she'd heard earlier and she wanted to meet this man, but as soon as she saw him, she stood still, unable to move. It wasn't that the man was ugly nor was there anything outwardly repulsive about him, but she knew he was a bad person. He was tall, dark, and his face had probably once been quite handsome, but somewhere along the way his nose had been broken and there was a scar that parted one eyebrow. In spite of the slight disfigurements, he was

163

still good-looking—but Chris didn't want to walk inside the same room with him.

"Diana, don't be shy," Owen was saying. "This is a friend of mine, Mr. Beynard Dysan. He's come to stay a while."

"How . . . how do you do?" she managed to whisper, holding out her hand to him, although she very much didn't want him to touch her.

"It's a pleasure to meet you. Owen told me of your father's unfortunate death. I'm sorry."

She backed away from him. "Yes," she murmured. "I cut my hand this morning," she said, showing her bandaged hand, "and I'm feeling a little weak. If you'll excuse me, I must go upstairs." She fled before either of the men could protest.

Upstairs, she stood with her back to the door for a few minutes. Until now she'd not been sure there was anything wrong going on in this house. But after meeting Beynard Dysan, she knew he was involved in something evil.

She almost jumped when she heard the men on the stairs outside her room. Listening, she heard them walking up toward Owen's office. She opened the door a bit.

"I'll be ready to ride in about half an hour," she heard Dysan say. "That way we'll be sure of privacy."

Chris closed the door. They were going to go somewhere to talk and if she wanted to find out what was going on, now was her only chance, because tomorrow Tynan planned to take her home.

She quickly dressed in her riding habit, then tiptoed down the stairs and left the house through the narrow door in the music room. She didn't want anyone to see her. In the stables, she saw that the boy was busy saddling two horses and she slipped inside, chose a sleek black mare, saddled it and managed to get out the side door without encountering anyone.

It was easy to hide in the trees until she saw Owen and Dysan come out and mount, and it wasn't difficult to follow them at a distance. They were traveling slowly, talking, Owen pointing at things now and then.

She followed them for about four miles, across a bridge over a deep stream, down a narrow road, when they turned right onto a path and disappeared. Chris waited several minutes at the crossroad then cautiously went after them. The trees were too dense for her to see very far ahead and her heart began pounding. It would be too easy to ride into them.

With her head bent forward, she listened as intently as she could over the mare's noisy steps. Suddenly, she stopped because close ahead, she heard a loud laugh. Dismounting quickly, she tied her horse and began to move through the underbrush toward the sound of the laughter.

She'd only gone a few feet when she crouched low. Ahead of her, standing on a ridge, were Owen and Beynard Dysan.

"When do I meet Sam?" Beynard was saying.

"Soon now. I don't want any trouble near my place."

Beynard gave Owen a smirk. "So you can save your trouble for your nephew? I never met a more repulsive kid."

Owen smiled. "Isn't he? No one will mind when he meets his fate. See that timberland? This time next year it'll all be mine."

"How do you plan to do it?"

"That cousin of his will. Eskridge has already embezzled, driven a man to suicide, and he beats that little wife of his. It should be easy to prove he'd murder too."

"What about the wife?"

Owen and Beynard exchanged looks. "She's served her purpose. Shall we get on with this? I'd like to get out of here before this storm breaks."

To Chris's utter disbelief, the men turned in unison and started toward her. It was almost as if they knew where she was. Of course that couldn't be but she crouched lower—and the men kept coming.

Then suddenly came the sound of a man whistling and both of them stopped—the men less than a yard from Chris's hiding place.

"Hello!" came Tynan's voice and Chris could have cried in relief. "I guess those horses belong to you, Mr. Hamilton."

"What are you doing here?" Owen snapped.

Chris put her head up enough to see Ty. Over his shoulder was slung a couple of rabbits.

"Unity sent me out for rabbits."

Chris wiped away the first drops of rain that fell on her face.

"And I wanted you in the garden," Owen said.

Chris saw that Dysan, who'd been looking across the valley while Ty and Owen talked, turned to look at Tynan.

"And I expect you back there as soon as possible."

"And withstand Unity's wrath?" Tynan said cheerfully, blinking against the rain that was coming down steadily. "No thanks, I'll stay here and get all three rabbits, just as I was ordered." He paused as lightning lit the valley below them. "You gentlemen are sure gettin' your fine clothes wet," he said in a drawl.

166

For a moment, Chris held her breath, for the three of them looked for all the world as if they were going to shoot each other. Why? she wondered.

Dysan backed down first. "Let's go," he said, and, quietly, Owen followed him.

Chris crouched low in the bushes, trying to keep the rain out of her face and to keep Tynan from finding her.

There was no hiding to be done. Two minutes after the men left, he grabbed her arm and hauled her up before him. "I ought to take you over my knees. Do you know you could have been killed?"

Water was running off his hat onto her face. "How did you know where I was?"

"Pilar saw you going off and told me." He had a nasty grip on her upper arm. "Now come with me."

"But my horse, it's—"

"You think they just left it?" He started down the hill the opposite way she'd come, pulling her behind him.

She kept her head down against the pelting rain, tripping along behind him. "Where are we going?"

"Home! To your father. You've taken twenty years off my life already and I don't have many more left."

"But what about Asher? They're going to kill Lionel and blame it on Asher."

"That's his worry. You're mine." He stopped at a saddled horse and helped her up, then mounted behind her.

"Can we get back this way?"

"We can get to your father's this way."

"Tynan," she said, turning in the saddle and putting her arms around his chest. "We can't leave Asher there. We have to go back and warn him. Please." She looked up at him with pleading eyes.

He studied her for a moment. "All right, damn it. We'll warn him but then you go."

"Yes, Tynan," she said, still holding onto him as they rode. His muscles under her cheek completely blotted out the thrashing of the rain and the slash of the lightning.

He was traveling as fast as the laden horse would go when its front hooves suddenly came off the ground and Ty fought to control the horse and hold Chris in the saddle.

"Damn!" he said in a way that made Chris twist around to look. Lightning had struck the bridge, and the swollen stream was far too violent to cross.

"We'll have to go back the other way," Chris said, looking up at him.

"There is no bridge on the other side."

He was holding the reins of the horse tightly, both of them drenched with rain, lightning all around them—yet Tynan made no effort to move.

"Hadn't we better go?" Chris asked, wiping water out of her eyes. "This storm is getting worse."

"There's nowhere to go," Tynan said. "We're cut off from the main road and there's only virgin forest north of us."

"Ty! It's getting dark. We can't stay here all night. Is there any shelter nearby? The water will recede after the storm's over."

Ty didn't answer, just sat there looking at the raging, deep stream.

"Tynan!" Chris yelled up at him. "Let's go back into the trees. Maybe we can find a rock overhanging or something."

"There's a logger's cabin near here."

168

"Then let's go."

The horse was dancing about nervously and the rain was coming down harder, but Ty didn't move.

"What is *wrong* with you?" she shouted.

"*You* are what's wrong with me," he yelled back at her, then turned the horse and started north.

Chapter Fifteen

The cabin had originally been for a surveying crew that
had worked in the area and, since then, it had been
maintained by someone, probably Owen since it was on
his land—or Lionel's as Chris insisted. It was one tiny
room, completely bare except for a fireplace and a stack
of wood. There was no furniture. Shortly after arriving,
Ty had the horse stabled in a lean-to in the back and a
fire going in the crude stone fireplace and the rabbits
skinned, spitted and roasting. There was an abundant
supply of dry firewood along one wall. Ty had removed
the saddle and the bedroll and flung it into the cabin for
Chris to take care of while he saw to the horse.

She removed the blanket from the bedroll and was
pleased to see that it was relatively dry. Shaking it out,
shivering against the wetness of her clothes, she began
to be aware of just why Tynan had been so reluctant to
stay in the cabin. With the rain coming down hard
outside, the fire crackling warm inside, and with the
prospect of removing her clothing and putting on the

single, loose blanket, she had an idea of what was going to happen.

With a whoosh of a sigh, she sat down on the saddle, the blanket clutched against her. What would her mother say if she knew what her only child was contemplating? Would she be horrified? Would Judith Montgomery have liked Tynan, this one-name gun-fighter who didn't even know what the word "home" meant?

Chris turned the rabbits over the fire and tried to think as calmly and rationally as possible. She'd never even considered the idea of seducing a man before. Sometimes she thought it was ironic that all a girl's life she fought off men, starting when she was a child with her mother warning her against taking candy from strangers, and saying no until the very wedding day. Women were trained to say no, so how did she say yes now? Even more important, how did she say yes to a question that was never going to be asked of her?

She stood for a moment and gazed into the fire. Maybe Tynan didn't want her and that was why he was able to resist all her advances. Maybe the beautiful Pilar was enough for him.

She shivered once against her wet clothes and began to peel them off, still staring into the fire and wondering what she was going to do—and if she should do it—when Tynan came back into the room.

Instinctively, she pulled the blanket up to cover her nude body.

Ty, after one quick glance, looked away from her to hang the bridle on a nail by the door, then removed his hat to pour the water out of the brim. "It looks like it'll keep up all night. Are the rabbits ready?"

Chris wrapped the blanket around her and went to

the fireplace to test the meat. "I think so but I'm not sure."

She looked up to see Tynan staring at her and she realized that the blanket she wore was gaping open at both top and bottom. Ducking her head so he couldn't see her smile, she looked back at the rabbits. At least she had some effect on him, if only to make him look.

"I'll test them," Ty said and that buttermilk voice of his was even richer.

She looked up at him through her lashes.

"Get back," he said with force. "Go stand by the wall. No, not on this side, on the far side. Now stay there while I look."

"Tynan," she said, exasperated, "you act as if I have a contagious disease. I can assure you that I'm quite clean and free from all illness."

"Hmph!" he grunted, tearing off a succulent, hot rabbit leg. His clothes were wet and they clung to his muscular body, outlining every hill and valley of his back. She could see where the whip marks had left some scars. "You are worse than disease, lady, you are poison."

"Was prison that bad?" she asked softly.

"Unfortunately, the memory is fading. Here, take this," he said as he removed the rabbits from the skewers. "On second thought, I'll put it here and you can come and get it."

"For heaven's sake, Tynan! I'm not going to harm you. You act as if I were holding a rifle on you."

He looked her up and down for a brief second. "I'd rather deal with twenty rifles. Eat that and then lay down over there and go to sleep. We'll leave very early in the morning so I can get you back as soon as possible. Then, as soon as you get Prescott, we'll leave again. I don't want you near Hamilton."

Chris stretched out on the hard plank floor, chewing on the meat while trying to get comfortable, but not succeeding. The blanket was small and her legs remained uncovered from the knee down. She tried to put them under her but had no success. If she covered her legs, her shoulders were exposed to the cold, and if she covered her shoulders, her legs got cold.

"Will you hold still!" Tynan suddenly shouted.

She looked up at him in surprise. He was sitting on the saddle, chewing on a piece of rabbit and looking into the fire. "Well, Tynan, I'm just trying to get comfortable and not freeze to death."

"It was your idea to come to this cabin so make the best of it and stop complaining—and go to sleep."

"How am I supposed to sleep when I'm freezing to death? And why are you still wearing your wet clothes?" She sat up. "Look at your skin! It's turning blue with cold. Is there anything that we can use for a coffee pot? I'll make you something to warm you up."

He didn't bother to answer her or even acknowledge her presence, but just sat there glaring into the fire and chewing.

Chris moved to sit in front of him, and when he continued to look over her head, she took his hands in hers. "Is something wrong? Does this cabin remind you of something bad that happened to you? Maybe one of the outlaw gangs you've ridden with? Or the man who was your friend who was hanged?"

Ty looked down at her with an expression that asked if she'd completely lost her mind.

His hands were as cold as a piece of metal left in

snow. She began to rub them between her own, blowing on them, trying to warm him.

"Chris," he said in a husky whisper. "I don't think I can take too much more. Please go over there and leave me alone."

"You'll never get warm if you sit there in your wet clothes. You'd better take them off." She looked up at him and she knew that what she felt for him was in her eyes, yet he didn't seem to react at all. He just sat there looking at her, and if there was anything in his eyes, it was sadness.

She was about to say something else when suddenly he reacted. He grabbed her in his arms and pulled her up to put his lips on hers. If Tynan was good with buttons, he was even better with blankets. Before his face was touching hers, the blanket was off, flung somewhere across the room. Chris gasped when Ty's cold clothes touched her warm, bare skin, but her arms went around his neck and pulled him closer.

"Tynan," she whispered as he began to hungrily kiss her neck, his hands running up and down her back, his fingers curving over her buttocks.

He took her head in his hands and looked at her. "Chris," he murmured, "I've never wanted anything as badly as I want you at this moment. This is your last chance to say no because from now on I won't be able to help myself."

Their noses were touching so she turned slightly so she could give him a quick kiss. "Yes," she said joyously. "Yes and yes and yes." She punctuated each word with a kiss.

He began to smile then, a warm, seductive smile that

174

made Chris's skin tingle. So, she thought, this was the face of Tynan the lover.

With a broader grin, he ruffled her damp hair, leaned forward and began to use his teeth to nibble at her bottom lip. Chris was taken by surprise. She knew the basics of how humans mate, but this had nothing to do with what she'd heard.

"Come here, you tempting little imp," he said, pulling her up higher. She was between his legs, his wet trousers pressed against her ribs, holding her in place while he kissed and nibbled on her ears, her neck, across her shoulder, down her arm.

Chris's neck began to weaken. "Oh, my, but I do like that," she murmured, eyes closed. Tynan's hands began to rub on her body, warming her. He seemed to be able to reach all of her, from the soles of her feet, up her calves, lingering on her buttocks and then his fingertips massaging up her spine.

After a moment, she no longer felt his cold clothes, felt, instead, only his hot hands on her skin, felt only his lips moving over her body—a body which had never known a man's lips before.

He was as smooth at moving her about as he was at unbuttoning her dresses. She had no idea when he changed her to a prone position—but she was aware when his lips first touched her breasts. Her eyes flew open, startled, and she looked at him.

The dark room with only the firelight from behind Tynan made him better-looking than usual and Chris suddenly thought that perhaps Apollo, the god of the sun, was making love to her. She put her hand in his dark hair, pulling his head up to hers so she could kiss him. "I love you, Tynan," she said, putting her arms around him and kissing him. She wasn't even surprised to find that his shirt was gone. No doubt he was as skillful at removing his own clothing as he was with women's.

His hands kept moving up and down her body in a sensual, caressing way, roaming over her stomach, down her thighs, up to her breasts. He felt so good to her, his big, wide shoulders, the way his muscles moved under her hands as he moved, the way his hips were gently undulating against the side of her hips.

Chris's heart was rising in her throat, pounding, as his hands began to caress the soft inner flesh of her thigh, kneading on the skin, touching soft, quiescent muscle. Of her own accord, her legs began to open.

"Ty," she whispered. "My lovely Tynan."

He didn't say a word, but began to move his lips downward as Chris arched her neck back in anticipation of what was to come. His hot, wet mouth closed on her breast, causing a groan to escape her lips. He continued to make love to her breast as his hands roamed over her legs.

When he moved on top of her, she clutched him to her, wrapping her legs about him instinctively. Gently, he disengaged her legs and moved them so they were bent, knees up, by his side.

When he entered her, Chris gasped, opening her eyes to look at him. He lay still on top of her, smiling at her, seeming to be at ease, but there were great drops of sweat on his forehead.

She had expected pain but there was none, only surprise at how lovemaking actually felt. Blinking a few times, she moved her hips slightly upward, toward his, and she saw Ty's eyes close, his head lean back and he entered her fully.

Chris thought her heart was going to leap from her breast as he began to move inside her, so gently, so slowly at first—and the sensation was absolutely heavenly. Slowly, deeply, rhythmically, he moved, touching her in a way that seemed to consume her, to make her grow bigger, to expand until she felt as if she might explode.

"Tynan?" she said and there was some fear in her voice because she didn't know what was about to happen.

He caught her legs, moved them back around his waist then lifted her hips upward so that half of her body weight was supported by his hips. He began to move more quickly and, if possible, more deeply. Chris put her hands up to touch the heavy muscles of his chest, clutching at him, digging her fingers into the thick muscles, wanting to claw him. Her head began to turn back and forth and there were little sounds coming from her.

Tynan's movements quickened until Chris thought she might explode.

Afterward, she lay still, clinging to him, not wanting to let him go.

"You can, can't you?" she said at last.

With a chuckle, Ty moved off of her, but held her close, one arm under her head, one thigh across hers.

"That was lovely," she said, stretching. "Did I do all right? You weren't disappointed?"

"No," he murmured.

"You aren't falling asleep, are you?"

"Not if you keep jabbering. Chris, we have to get up early tomorrow, this has been one hell of a day, what with you climbing across roofs, so I'd like to get some sleep."

"Sleep?" She moved so she could look at him. "But I'm starving and we have so much to discuss. I want to know how you found out about my following Owen and when we'll be married and what we'll do about Lionel and Pilar has to go and—"

"Wait a minute!" His eyes flew open. "Married? Who said anything about marriage?"

"But I thought . . . I mean, after what we did . . ."

He rolled away from her, pulling on his pants.

She watched, the blanket clutched to her, as he built up the fire then lifted the cooked rabbits and began to reheat them. At long last, he handed her a big chunk of meat before he went to stand by the door.

"I never wanted this to happen," he said, turning to look at her. "I meant to keep my hands off of you, just like your father demanded."

"If you're worried about the pardon," she said, mouth full, "I'll see that you get it. My father won't send you back to jail."

"Don't you have sense enough to understand that it's deeper than that?" he asked angrily. "Somebody like me can't marry somebody like you, and besides, I don't *want* to get married."

Chris paused in eating. "Oh, Tynan, you have such a low opinion of yourself."

"So do you when the chips are down."

Chris tried to keep the meat from choking in her throat. "I made a mistake and I apologize. It won't happen again. Especially if you're my husband."

"Well, I'm not going to be!" he said, moving away from the door. "If I *married* every woman I've—"

"Never mind, thank you!" she said quickly. "But, Tynan, I love you."

"You think you're in love with what you see. Chris,

I'm trying to be kind to you. What happened tonight was just what always happens when a man and a woman spend a night in a cabin alone. It was inevitable."

Chris threw the bone in the fire, then stood, wrapping the blanket around her. "Maybe in your world it's inevitable, but not in mine. When I was investigating the Mexican government, I spent three nights alone with a Mexican guard and he never touched me."

"How many guns were you holding on him?"

"One very small pistol," she said with a smile. "Tynan, I—"

"There's no more to be said. I want you to lay down and sleep. It's best if we forget what happened here tonight."

"Forget, but—"

"What do you want from me? Do you want me to tell you the *truth*? The *truth* is that all you are to me is one hot little morsel and I finally took a bite. You're no more or less to me except a way to get a pardon from prison. You're more trouble than a corral full of sheriffs and half the time you're not even as much fun, what with your do-gooder attitude of wanting to save the world. All I want is to turn you over to your father, get my pardon—if he'll give it to me after violating his pure daughter—and get the hell away from you and your kind. Now, have I made myself clear?"

Chris straightened her spine. "Perfectly," she said through a throat that was swelling shut. "And you'll get your pardon. I'll see to that."

She didn't want him to see how horrible she was feeling. Slowly, she turned her back to him, dropped the blanket and began to dress in her damp under clothing.

"What are you doing?"

"Nothing that will interfere with your pardon."

"Chris, wait . . ."

She didn't look at him. "You've had your say, and, if you don't mind, I'd rather not hear anymore. You may have your blanket back. I wouldn't want to cause you more inconvenience. I shall stay here in this corner until morning."

She didn't look at him again as she sat down with her back to the wall.

Chapter Sixteen

Morning came much too soon. Chris had slept very little and her head and eyes ached. Twice Tynan tried to talk to her but she turned away. The rain had stopped and, without a word between them, they left the cabin. Tynan put out his hand to help her mount but she moved away from him and mounted by herself.

They had to ride quite far to find a fordable place in the stream, and all the while, Chris did her best to keep from touching Tynan, and she never once spoke to him.

When they finally reached the Hamilton house, she was never so glad to see anything in her life.

"We're going to leave in one hour," Tynan said but she refused to look at him. He caught her arm as she started to walk away. "Did you hear me? I'm taking you out of this place and back to your father where you belong."

Chris jerked away from him. "I've heard *every* word that you've had to say," she said as she turned away and started back to the house. She hesitated for a moment on the outskirts of the garden, wondering what her reception would be, if Owen knew where she was or if anyone had been looking for her. Idly, she picked a tall daisy, twirled it in her hands before putting her chin back and moving forward. As she entered the garden at the back of the house, she saw Owen, and Asher with his back to her.

Owen stopped talking, his eyes widened and the next minute, Asher turned, saw her, and was running toward her with his arms outstretched. He caught her in an exuberant hug, lifting her off the ground, twirling her about.

"Chris," he said with his face buried in her neck. "I was worried to death. Are you all right? You aren't hurt?"

She hugged him back with enthusiasm. It was so very, very good to feel wanted. "Yes," she managed to whisper because her throat was overcome with tears.

But the next moment her tears disappeared because a shot rang out. She could feel the hot rush of the bullet as it went tearing past the back of Ash's head. Chris looked down at the suddenly headless flower in her hand then at Tynan standing a few feet away, a smoking gun in his hand. He'd shot the flower, which she'd held as she'd hugged Asher, away.

Unity came running from the house. "What's goin' on? I heard a shot."

Tynan was looking at Chris and she was glaring back at him in return, her arms still around Ash.

"Just doin' some weedin', ma'am," he drawled before turning away.

"What was that all about?" Asher asked.

Chris threw the headless flower down on the ground

182

as if it were poison. "Nothing. Absolutely nothing."
She looked up as Owen came toward them.

"Diana, we were very worried about you. No one
knew where you were. We've been out all night looking
for you."

For the first time, she looked at the two men, saw the
way they were dirty and tired-looking, with unshaved
cheeks.

"I saddled my own horse when I left," she mumbled.
"We found shelter from the rain. Could I see you for a
moment?" she asked, turning to the man who was
playing her husband.

"Of course, dear, you must be very tired." Like a
concerned husband, Ash escorted her into the house
and up the stairs to the room they shared.

"All right," he said as soon as they were alone, "I
want to know where you've been and what was going
on outside. Has that man done anything to you?"

"Not anymore than I've asked for. Turn your head; I
want to change out of this. I followed Owen and that
dreadful man, Beynard Dysan, out into the forest."

"What makes him dreadful? He was looking for you
as hard as any of us were."

"Keep looking out the window, if you don't mind. I
don't know what it was that made me dislike him in the
first place, but after what I heard, I know I was right.
He and Owen are planning to murder Lionel and blame
it on you."

"Me? But what do I have to do with the brat?"

"Not you, but Whitman Eskridge, the one who
embezzled and beats his wife and—"

"Beats his wife?" Ash said with a smile in his voice.
"I didn't know about that."

"Well, I hope you never find out," she said quickly.

"But that's where I was: hiding in the bushes and listening to Owen talk to that man."

"You rode up there and they never saw or heard you?"

Chris thought about the few moments before Tynan had appeared, then it had seemed that the men had known of her whereabouts and were coming after her. But of course that had been her imagination. "The storm was just beginning and they didn't hear me over the rain and thunder. The only problem now is that that . . . man is insisting that we leave here now. In fact, he wanted us to leave directly from the forest and not even come back here to warn you."

Asher didn't say anything.

"Well?" Chris said. "You see that we can't leave now, don't you? We have to protect Lionel." She was dressed and she went to stand before him.

Ash looked down at her. "How did Tynan find you?"

"I don't know. Followed me, I guess."

Asher put both his hands on her arms. "Chris, I think Ty's right. You should be on your way back to your father's right now. If you hadn't come back, I would have looked for you for another couple of days, then I'd have left and gone back to your father's, too. Then everyone would have been safe. It wasn't very smart of you to come back here knowing that there might be a murderer."

She moved away from him. "But what about Lionel? Doesn't anyone care that he might lose his life?"

"All we have to do is alert the local sheriff. If he questions Hamilton, that'll put Owen on his guard."

"So he'll kill Lionel in a very, very secretive way. I'm sure it'll look like an accident and Owen will be no where in the vicinity."

"That's not my concern. My concern is you. I think we should get out of here as soon as possible. Today." He moved toward the wardrobe and withdrew her carpet bag. "I want you to pack right now. I'll tell Owen that the dangers of this place are too great for a lady like you and that I've decided to take you back East where you belong."

"I won't go," she said, glaring up at him.

"Then I shall tell him who you really are. I don't think we'll be welcome after that. Get packed, rest, and I'll be back in an hour or so. I want to talk to Tynan first."

"Don't talk to him!" Chris said angrily. "He wants to get rid of me as soon as he can."

Asher paused at the door. "On the trail back, I want you to tell me what went on when the two of you were gone all night. But now, to discourage you from trying to do something brave and stupid, I'm going to lock this door. I'll see you in an hour."

Before Chris could say another word, he was out the door and she heard the key turn in the lock. For a moment, she leaned against the door and cursed all men everywhere, but then she looked at the soft bed, spread with clean, fragrant sheets, and she walked toward it as if she were in a trance. She was asleep almost before she landed.

The sunlight was coming into the room and Chris was deeply asleep when she felt the hand on her mouth. Her eyes flew open in alarm—only to see a man with a black cloth hood over his face.

"Be quiet, missy, and you won't get hurt. You're gonna take a little ride with us."

She didn't recognize the voice nor the shape of the body. She tried to struggle but the man held her easily

185

as he tied a tight gag about her mouth and then tied her hands. Even when she tried to kick him, he clamped down on her ankles with big, hamlike hands.

He tied her with what seemed to be yards of fine, flexible rope that cut into her when she tried to make any movement, tied her as if she were a corpse bound for burial at sea. When he was finished, little more than Chris's eyes were visible, even her hair, loose down her back, was fastened to her body.

He easily lifted her body and slung it over one wide shoulder and carried her toward the window. A ladder stood ready and, as if she were a rolled-up carpet, he carried her to the ground.

Chris tried to turn her head to see if there was anyone about, but her bindings made movement impossible. A horse awaited him in the trees and he tossed her across the saddle and mounted behind her, then took off quietly so no one could hear him. Chris thought that everywhere she went she was seen by someone, but now that she needed help, no one was near.

She didn't think any more because her captor had speeded their progress and the saddle was pounding into her soft stomach. For the next few hours, she did nothing but try to keep from being sick.

It was nearly nightfall when she became aware that there was another rider beside them. She didn't know when he'd joined them but, when at last the horse she was on came to a stop, she heard the man who'd taken her speak.

"She give you any trouble?"

"No. Yours?"

"Not in the least. Untie her. They'll not last long like this."

186

The man pulled Chris from the horse and put her on the ground. Out of the corner of her eye, she could see another bundle, completely immobile like she was, being removed from another horse. The other man put the semi-corpse next to her but Chris couldn't turn her head to see who it was. It was only when the man began to unwind her and he freed her head so that she could see, that she looked—and gasped.

Pilar lay beside her and looked as surprised to see Chris.

The man removed her gag. "What are you doing here?" she managed to gasp. "What is this?"

"Cut the noise," the big man said. The other captor was tall and thin. "We don't want to hear you. You want some water or not?"

Greedily, Chris's shaky hands took the dirty tin mug the man offered.

"Who are you?" she asked the man. "What do you want?"

"You want the ropes on you again?"

Chris started to reply but she felt Pilar's hand on her arm. Looking at the dark woman, she saw Pilar shake her head slightly. Chris turned away but she said nothing more. Minutes later, the big man hauled Chris to her feet and tossed her into the saddle.

"I don't like talkative women," he said into her ear. "You keep your mouth shut and we'll get along fine. You open it and I'll have to shut it. You understand?"

She saw him throw the hood on the ground but she didn't twist around to look at him; she was too busy trying to keep her seat on the horse and to avoid the man's hands that were beginning to creep over her body.

* * *

"Chris and I are leaving in less than an hour," Tynan said to Asher, his mouth in a straight line, his eyes angry.

"Wait a minute, I want to talk to you."

"I don't have time," Tynan said, starting to walk away. "You can come with us or not, your choice."

Asher caught his arm. "I want to know what happened last night. Where were you two all night? And what do you mean by shooting so close to my head? I ought to—"

"What, Prescott? You ought to what?"

Asher took a step backward. "Look, I'm in this as much as you are. Mathison hired you to take me to Chris, and you were to help me win her for my wife. So far all you've done is keep her to yourself. And now you spend the night with her doing only God knows what."

"That's right, only God knows because I'm sure as hell not going to tell you. Now I'll tell you again: Chris and I are leaving in one hour and you can go or stay, it's up to you."

"I'll be there," Asher said, "don't you worry about that."

With anger on his face, Asher made his way back up the stairs to the room he shared with Chris. Damn! but that man could be highhanded. He was a good man to have on a trail but there were times when he overstepped himself.

He tried to regain his composure before he went to Chris. He'd hated locking her inside, but he knew it was the only way he could keep her from doing something stupid.

Very quietly, he unlocked the door to the bedroom. She'd damn well *better* marry him after all she'd put him through—and all he'd done in an attempt to please her. Right away, he saw that she wasn't there. His first thought was that she'd climbed out the window, but one glance out there, at the impossibly small ledge, showed him that she couldn't have gone out that way.

He didn't even think about his argument or his anger with Tynan, but he ran down the stairs, out through the garden and to the little cottage where Tynan was staying. The dark man was removing tools from a shed at the back of the cottage.

"She's gone. I was afraid she'd do something stupid so I locked her in the room, but she got out. She was really worried about that kid."

Even as Asher was talking, Tynan was pushing past him and heading for the house, stopping only long enough to strap on his gun. He took the stairs two at a time.

"I wish she wouldn't do things like this," Asher was saying. "It's bad enough that she spends the entire night with a—" He broke off as he realized what he was saying. Tynan was now examining the window ledge. "Do you see anything? How could she have gone out there?"

"Believe me, she could have. There's been a ladder here recently, the paint's scraped." He walked back toward the bed, looking at the covers thoughtfully. The sheets were torn off the bed, the spread was on the floor. "Where's Hamilton?"

"I'm not sure. I think he's upstairs. Do you think he's seen Chris? I would imagine that she's the last person he'd want to see." He was following Ty out the door. "Did she tell you what she overheard, that Hamilton was going to kill his nephew? Not that I believed her, I mean, I just came along on this so I could pretend to be her husband. I think a man should take advantage of what he can."

Tynan stopped on the staircase. "If you keep flapping your gums, I'm going to apply some force to that spot." He turned on his heel and started up again.

Owen Hamilton was sitting in his office looking over papers on his desk. Tynan shut the door behind him, locked it, then very calmly walked to the window and tossed the key to the ground below.

Asher plastered his back to the door and held his breath but Owen just looked up with eyebrows raised. "To what do I owe this little charade? Have the aphids been too much for you?"

"Where is she?" Tynan asked in a low, husky voice.

"I have no idea who you mean," Owen answered, a study in unconcern as he shuffled the papers on his desk. "If you think that wife of yours and I—"

He didn't finish the sentence because Ty grabbed him by the collar and pulled him up across the desk. "I want to know where she is and I don't want to play games. Either you tell me right now or you start losing parts of your body, bit by slow bit."

"I have no idea what you're talking about."

"Chris!" Asher said. "I mean, Diana. Where is she? She isn't in her room where I left her."

"Who's Chris?" Owen asked.

Tynan slapped the man across the face. "I don't know how much you know but I suspect it's a great deal. I've already turned that extra set of books of yours over to an accountant friend of mine. I think he'll find out how much you've stolen from that nephew of yours."

"Books, what books?"

Tynan hit him again, this time making the corner of

his mouth bleed. "I'm tired of your lies. I didn't much care what you did within your own family but that little girl is my responsibility and I want to know where she is."

"Who is she? Diana Eskridge was killed."

Ty's grip on his throat tightened. "By you, no doubt, but I'll leave that up to the law. Where is Chris?"

When Hamilton didn't answer, Ty struck him again, then drew his gun and held it to the man's head. "What do you want to lose first? A hand or a foot? I think I can keep you from bleeding to death long enough for you to answer me. Now, one last time, where is she?"

"Dysan took her."

Tynan was obviously surprised by this, so much so that his grip on Hamilton lessened. "What does Dysan want with her?"

"I don't know. He came here because of a cousin of his"—Owen's eyes shifted to one side—"and he decided he wanted the woman pretending to be Diana." He looked back at Tynan. "He had your wife taken too."

"Pilar?" Ty asked. "Who is this man?"

Ty's grip had relaxed so much that Owen was able to pull away and begin rubbing his bruised throat while applying a handkerchief to his bleeding mouth. "He's somebody you don't want to deal with. I don't know much about him. He's very mysterious about where he lives, who he is or anything else about himself. He comes here once a year and buys lumber and horses from me, then disappears. I've never dared ask him much about himself."

"Yet he took Chris," Asher said. "Do you think he plans to hold her for ransom?"

"Ransom?" Hamilton exploded. "Who *is* she?"

"Del Mathison's daughter," Tynan said under his breath.

"Oh Lord," Owen gasped and sat down heavily in the chair. "I thought she was a two-bit actress trying to get what she could." He looked at Ty. "How did you find my other books?"

Tynan didn't bother answering him. "I want to know all there is to tell about Dysan. I want to know where to find him."

"I told you that I know nothing. He just appears and disappears. He said he wanted the two women and it was all right with me. All of you were trying to play me for a fool anyway, following me, searching my office, pretending to be related to me. What did I care what he did to the women? If he wanted them, it was fine with me. I had no idea she was Mathison's daughter. If that man finds out . . ." He trailed off.

"Open the cash box," Ty said. "We're going after them and we'll need capital."

"I don't intend to be part of a robbery," Asher said.

"No one asked you to be. Hamilton, I wouldn't try my patience if I were you. Get the cash."

Owen hurried to obey him, unlocking a small safe behind a picture behind the desk. "You'll never be able to find him. You aren't in Dysan's league. He chews cheap outlaws like you up for breakfast."

Ty took the thick stack of cash. "Then he'll get the worst case of indigestion he's ever had. Now, take off your belt."

Tynan took the handkerchief from the desk and tied it around Hamilton's mouth, then wrapped the belt about his hands, using the holed end to suspend him from a hook he drove into the ceiling. "That should keep you for a few hours. The accountant will report to the attorneys handling Lionel's affairs. I have a feeling that the books you show to them aren't the same ones that I found. And, too, there's the small matter of the murder of the Eskridges."

Owen struggled against the leather that was holding him, his feet barely touching the floor.

"I'm also having Unity take the boy down to Mathison's until this is cleared up. I thought I was going with her but it doesn't look like I will be. I sure do hope that somebody comes along soon to let you out of there. You could be in real pain in a couple of hours if they don't."

Asher stepped away from the door as Tynan started toward it and, to the blond man's surprise, Tynan took a key from his pocket and unlocked the door, locking it again when they were on the other side.

"But I thought that—"

"Don't always believe what you see or hear," Ty said as he went down the stairs and into the kitchen.

Unity, her face white, her eyes filled with fear, was sitting in the kitchen, Lionel standing beside her.

"I don't want to go," Lionel said. "This is my place and I plan to stay here. You cannot make me leave."

Ty didn't say a word but took the boy about the waist and carried him outside to where a wagon and two horses waited. "You'll go and, what's more, you'll help Unity. Prescott will go with you and see that you're safe on the journey. I'm sorry but I can't go with you."

Asher touched Ty's arm. "I want to go with you."

"Absolutely not. I don't need someone fighting me and, besides," he said with contempt, "I need someone who knows which end of a gun to point."

"May I?" Asher said, nodding toward Ty's gun.

Ty handed it to him.

Asher took the weapon and, in the flash of an eye, turned and removed a thin tree branch by half inches, using all the bullets in Ty's gun. He handed the firearm back to Tynan. "There are other reasons I was hired by Mathison to go after his daughter. I've handled every gun made today. I can shoot tail feathers off sparrows with a rifle. I may not have the experience you have but I *do* know how to shoot."

Tynan very calmly reloaded his gun then looked up at Unity. Lionel was sitting on the wagon seat with his mouth hanging open. "Prescott is going with me. Is there anyone else who can travel with you?"

"I . . . I don't know who I can trust anymore," she said, on the verge of tears. "But my brother lives about ten miles from here. Maybe he can—" She stopped as Ty took a wad of bills from his pocket.

"Hire him. When you get to Mathison, tell him all of it. He may want to send someone back here but leave it up to him. Tell him I've gone after his daughter and if I don't return with her it'll be because I'm dead—nothing else will stop me. And tell him to worry about her, to worry plenty." He looked at Lionel. "And if I so much as hear a word of complaint about you, you'll answer to me. When you get to Mathison's you can act up all you want. Mathison will take care of you. Now, get out of here." He slapped a horse on the rump and they were gone.

Ty turned and looked at Asher, shaking his head for a moment. "I hope I haven't made a mistake. If you have a gun, go get it. I'll meet you by the stables with two of Hamilton's best horses."

Chapter Seventeen

For three days, the men dragged Chris and Pilar across the country. They were fed little, given no privacy, and allowed no rest. At night the men tied the women's hands, raised them above their heads and fastened the ropes around trees, making it impossible to sleep. Nor were the women allowed to talk to each other. Each morning, they continued to head northeast, the women still bound and now riding together on a horse one of the men had suddenly appeared with—Chris wondered if he'd stolen it.

In spite of her weariness, she tried to keep the direction they were traveling in her head. But on the second day, the men blindfolded her, leaving Pilar to watch the direction, seeing when the horse was about to step into a hole so she could hold Chris into the saddle. Then they removed Chris's blindfold and covered Pilar's eyes.

Although the women never talked to each other, they began to depend upon one another for protection.

At first Chris was very hostile to Pilar, not wanting her help, resenting her touch, resenting her very presence.

Pilar seemed to understand and left Chris alone—until once Chris nearly fell off the horse and had to grab the other woman to keep steady.

"We'll fare better if we're not enemies," Pilar whispered and was struck across the face by one of the men for daring to speak.

After that, Chris's hostility began to leave her. What did she have to be angry about anyway? Tynan was the only common bond she had with this woman and he'd made it abundantly clear that he wanted nothing to do with Chris. If Tynan wanted Pilar, then he was free to choose.

It was late on the third night when the men finally stopped the horses and pulled the two exhausted women to the ground, grabbing their wrists and leading them inside the doorway of a dark house that Chris couldn't see. The men pulled them upstairs and when Pilar's arm knocked against the bannister, they just jerked her harder.

"We can walk!" Chris said, putting out her hand to steady Pilar.

The man holding her didn't say a word, just shoved her up three flights of stairs to the fourth floor. Pilar's captor grabbed a ring of keys off the wall, opened a door that looked to be constructed of several inches of solid oak and pushed the two women inside.

There wasn't any light in the room, but Chris's eyes adjusted to the darkness fairly soon after she heard the heavy door slam behind them. She began to make out the outlines of a large, soft bed in the middle of the floor.

With a gasp of disbelief and tears in her eyes, she stumbled forward, Pilar close behind her, and fell onto the bed. She was asleep instantly.

The sun was already low in the sky when Chris woke the next day, showing that it was afternoon. For a moment, she lay there, looking out one of the tiny windows, flexing each muscle, trying to ascertain what was sore and what seemed to be damaged beyond repair. Holding her arms up, she saw that they were scratched, some of the wounds scabbing, some covered with dried blood, and there were several fierce mosquito bites on them as well.

She moved her head and looked at Pilar who was still sleeping, on her stomach, and Chris wondered if she looked as bad. Pilar was dirty, there were deep dark circles beneath her eyes, and what could be seen of her body protruding from her filthy clothes was disgustingly scratched and raw-looking.

Pilar opened one eye. "Go away," she muttered and turned over.

Chris lay still, waited and, a moment later, Pilar turned to face her again.

"It can't be true," she said. "I thought it was all a terrible dream." Pilar tried to raise herself on her arms but groaned at the pain and collapsed back on the bed. "Where are we? More important, *why* are we wherever we are? And do you think there's a chamber pot around here?"

Chris sat up on her arms, then moved her head in a circle, trying to relieve the cramped muscles. "There's a screen over there, maybe it's behind that."

"I guess this is something I have to do for myself," she said, moving slowly to get out of bed.

Chris also got out, taking moments to steady herself enough to stand up. "I don't think I'll ever be the same."

It was a round room, with three windows along the wall across from the bed, a door to the right, a screen to the left and no other furniture in the room.

Chris slowly made her way over to one of the windows. Outside, she saw nothing but thick forest, trees that had never been cut. Looking down, she could see that the room was at least four stories above the ground.

"I can tell this is going to be easy to escape," Pilar said with a grimace, coming around the screen and looking at the treetops outside the windows. She stopped at the window next to Chris, then turned her head. "Do I look as bad as you?"

"Much worse," Chris said quite seriously.

Pilar gave a sigh of resignation and went back to bed, pulling a pillow under her head. "Do you have any idea what's going on?"

"None," Chris called from behind the screen. "I was hoping you'd know something. Did anyone say anything when they took you?"

Pilar waited until Chris was back in the center of the room. "I think you know more than I do. Tynan had some reason for being Hamilton's gardener and I was never told what it was."

"Oh? You just moved in with him when he crooked his little finger?"

"I owed him a favor, several favors if it comes to that. Look, are we going to play cat games or are we going to work together on this? I'd like to figure out what's going on but if you want to fight over a man, let me know so I can bow out."

"I have no reason to fight over Mr. Tynan. He is dead to me. He's yours."

Chris ignored the way Pilar lifted one eyebrow and gazed at her archly. "I am a newspaper reporter and I write under the name of Nola Dallas. I went to—"

"*The* Nola Dallas? The one that gets herself in trouble just so she can write about it?"

"I'm afraid so," Chris said.

Pilar put out her hand to shake. "I'm glad to meet you. Are we in one of your escapades and someone's going to show up to rescue us at any minute?"

Chris gave her a weak smile. "I think I better tell you all of it." She told Pilar everything, from finding Diana and Whitman Eskridge's bodies to when Tynan said they were going to leave Hamilton's house.

Pilar sat up, hugging her knees to her chest. "I think Ty found out something. He kept leaving the house in the middle of the night and one night he came back with a big book under his arm. He sat up all night reading it, but in the morning it was gone and I never saw it again."

"What was it a book of?"

"Numbers. You know, like Red has."

"Red?" Chris asked. "You mean the woman Tynan knows, in the . . ."

"Yeah, in the whore house." She narrowed her eyes at Chris. "The place where I worked."

"Oh," was all Chris could say. Of course Tynan would want that kind of woman for his wife, or pretend wife, or whatever she was. She put her mind back on the current subject. "Maybe that's why we were kidnapped, because Tynan stole a ledger from Hamilton or maybe . . . Have you ever heard of Del Mathison?"

Pilar gave a little smile. "He's a little before my time

but I've heard stories about him. One house threw a wake on the day of his wedding."

Chris's mouth became a narrow line. "He's my father."

"Sorry," Pilar said, but she didn't look sorry. Her head came up sharply. "If you're Mathison's daughter, then you must be rich. Maybe you're being held for ransom."

"That's what I thought. My father always had a horror of my being kidnapped. One of the ranch hands said it was because he had so many enemies, but, whatever the reason, it's something I've been prepared for."

"So why am I here? You think he brought me along to serve as your handmaiden?" Pilar said archly.

"I don't know, but I hope this kidnapper plans to feed us."

"And give us some hot water. I have three inches of dirt on me now."

As Pilar stopped talking, there was a sound at the door and the next moment, the heavy door was thrown open and the two men who'd taken the women were standing in the doorway. Behind them were two women, who looked to be scared to death, bearing trays of food. The men motioned for Chris and Pilar to stand back while the women set the trays on the floor. Next came big ewers of hot water and basins, then two dresses were tossed on the bed. A sewing box was placed by the bed.

One of the women backed against the doorjamb. "You're to wear the dresses tonight. If they don't fit, you can alter them." With that, they were out the door, the men behind them, and Chris could hear the lock being turned.

"Food first or hot water?" Chris asked Pilar when they were alone.

"Both at the same time," Pilar answered and the women did indeed dive into both at the same time, washing with one hand, eating with the other.

"It is possible that our captor has no idea who I am," Chris said with her mouth full as she washed her left arm. "Maybe he thinks I'm Diana Eskridge and this all has something to do with Owen Hamilton trying to kill Lionel. Maybe Owen wants time alone to do his dirty work."

"That still doesn't explain why I'm here," Pilar said. "I didn't know any of what was going on."

"But whoever took us doesn't know that. If Tynan was stealing things from the house at night, it would look as if you knew everything since you two spent every night together." Chris had a difficult time with the last part of that sentence. It wasn't that she any longer had any feeling for Tynan, he'd killed that the night in the cabin, but she did hate losing.

"If that's true," Pilar said thoughtfully, "then he probably took Tynan too. Do you think he's here with that young man of yours?"

"Asher? I can't imagine what he'd want with Asher. He only came along because I needed a husband."

"Whatever has happened, I don't understand it. I rather think that you've been kidnapped for ransom and the men brought me along because. . . . Truthfully, I don't know why I'm here. I have nothing anyone would want."

Pilar was standing in the light, mostly unclothed, her long black hair down her back, her body firm and well rounded, and Chris thought that she had something that any man would want. "I'm here for money and

201

you're here because our captor probably fell in love with you," Chris said under her breath, trying not to let her envy and hurt show.

Pilar said nothing but continued to wash.

When at last the women were clean and fed, they looked at the dresses on the bed.

"Not exactly my style," Chris said, holding a dress up. There wasn't a whole lot of fabric above the waist.

"Well, don't look at me, I haven't worn anything like this in years. Yours is too long and I think it might be too big in a few places."

Chris sighed because Pilar was right. "Maybe you were brought along because you fit the dress."

"Come on, let's get started altering it."

"The bust alone will take hours," Chris muttered.

They sewed until the sun went down, then dressed in the moonlight coming in through the windows. They had no candle, no combs to free their hair of tangles, no jewelry, and no idea where they were being taken.

When the oak door was thrown open, they were ready as best they could prepare themselves. Chris wasn't aware that she was shaking until Pilar slipped her hand in hers, giving her fingers a tight squeeze of confidence.

One of the men pushed Chris forward, Pilar after her, and the two women headed down the stairs.

"How do you even know which way to go?" Asher was shouting to Tynan as the men rode at full speed.

Tynan didn't bother to answer as he led them southeast, not stopping until they came to a dirty little patch of ground covered with tents. The place didn't deserve the name of "town." The streets were deep in half a foot of mud from the recent rain and, as they rode past a tent with a big sign outside that read simply "women," there were two men fighting, wrestling about in the mud. Asher's horse jumped sideways as the fighting men, locked together, lurched toward him. He had to struggle a moment to control the animal and when he could get away, he saw Tynan disappearing into one of the larger tents. Asher dismounted into the mud and followed.

Tynan was at the bar, leaning against it as if he had all the time in the world. There were several tables set up with men gambling. Ty was watching a man who looked clean compared to the rest of the men in the tent, with his gold embroidered vest and two guns with pearl handles.

Asher ordered a beer and had just taken a long drink when the game broke up. Immediately, the gambling man looked up at Tynan.

"I thought you were in jail for some reason or other."

"I got out for the same reason," Ty said. "And now I'm coming to you to collect a debt."

The man gave a curt nod, then walked to stand by Ty at the bar. "Two whiskeys," he said, then lowered his voice. "What is it you want?"

"Information."

"That comes high."

"I've already paid," Tynan said. "Have you ever heard of a man named Beynard Dysan?"

The gambling man choked on his whiskey. When he'd cleared his throat, he looked at Tynan. "Stay away from him. He's bad, real bad."

"He has something that belongs to me and I mean to have it back. Where can I find him?"

"Let him have it. Whatever it is, it isn't worth it. If

all you had to lose to him was your life, you'd be all right, but that man can take more than your life. Stay away from him."

Tynan didn't say a word for a moment. "Are you going to answer me or pretend to be my mother?"

"It's been real nice knowing you, Tynan. I'll send flowers to your grave. I don't know much about him at all except what I've heard in whispers. He has a place up north of here. There's a town up there called Sequona, if anybody knows anything about him, someone there will. And you might ask a few questions about him on the way, but you risk a bullet in your head—probably in the back of your head. This man likes to stay private. He doesn't like anybody looking into his business."

The man finished his drink. "What's he got of yours?"

"Del Mathison's daughter."

The man gave a low whistle. "Mathison's power against Dysan's. That may be a war to end all wars. Tynan, watch your back. Dysan has his hand in everything and he hires people to kill whoever interferes with what he wants. You ought to let Mathison get his own daughter back."

"He's hired me. Thanks a lot, Frank. Consider your debt to me cleared." With that, Ty turned and left the tent, Asher taking a last swallow of his beer and following him.

Tynan paused a moment outside the tent, not looking at Asher. "You heard what Frank said and you can back out now. If you don't lose your life in this you may not be the same afterward."

"And lose out on Mathison's daughter?" Asher said

just before a bullet went whizzing past Tynan's head. Ty fell to the mud, his arm coming out and pulling Asher down with him. Asher, not being prepared for the movement, hit the mud face down. He came up spitting. Another bullet came at them and his face went down again. Behind them was the sound of tables being overturned and men shouting as the two bullets had come into the tent.

Asher looked at Tynan, at the man's clean face as he held it above the mud and at the pistol in his hand. Behind them came a voice.

"I'd be willing to bet it's Dysan."

Asher turned to see the gambler, Frank, crouched in the tent opening, a gun in his hand.

"Hang on and I'll see if I can help."

A minute later, Asher could hear the man shout, "They just brought in a load of whores across the street. All of them virgins."

Tynan shouted at Asher to roll out of the way and Ash was glad he did because within seconds, a stampede of men came charging out of the tent. "Now!" Asher heard Tynan shout and Ash, fighting against the resistance of the mud, moved to the back of the tent. He was a little confused as to what he was to do next when Tynan appeared with the horses. "Let's ride," was all Ty said before mounting and leaving the muddy town and what sounded to be a riot behind them.

Tynan led them north, riding so hard that the drying mud began to flake off and fly about them. Toward afternoon, he pulled into the trees, onto a path that Asher didn't see until they were on it, and led them up a hill. It began to rain and both men pulled their hats low over their faces.

It was almost dark when Tynan stopped and dismounted. "There's a cave of sorts over there. We'll spend the night in it," he shouted over the rain.

A few minutes later, they had a tiny fire going, beans and coffee boiling and their clothes were almost dry on their bodies.

"You think we'll be able to find her?" Ash asked, poking at the fire with a stick.

"I plan to," Tynan said. He was leaning back against his saddle, his hat over his face.

"If Dysan just wants money then he surely won't hurt Chris, will he?"

"Or Pilar."

"Oh yes," Ash said. "I remember seeing her in the kitchen. She cleans, doesn't she?"

Tynan pushed his hat back and after one look at the back of Asher's head, took the beans from the fire and began dividing them onto plates.

Ash took the plates and a cup of coffee from Ty. "I guess you have a plan in mind, don't you? I mean, you *do* have a way to rescue Chris. Her father will be furious if you let anything happen to her."

"And you'll lose her money," Tynan said.

"Chris is a very attractive young lady, perhaps a bit headstrong at times, but attractive nonetheless. And I really don't see what's wrong in my taking over the management of her father's estates. He doesn't have a son and Chris obviously isn't interested in finding someone to take over." He gave Tynan a sharp look. "You aren't thinking of marrying her yourself, are you? Mathison's money would be quite a—"

"We'll get along a lot better if you keep your opinions to yourself. Now, put out that fire and get some sleep. We ride in the morning."

It wasn't morning—far from it—when Tynan woke Asher by putting his hand over his mouth. There was warning in Ty's eyes as he motioned for Asher to follow him out of the shallow cave. They carried their saddles and packs and led the horses, as quietly as possible, down the hill. It was still drizzling rain.

"What time is it?" Asher asked, yawning.

"Our last day on earth if we don't get out of here. There was someone outside the cave."

"I didn't hear anyone."

"All right, then you stay but I'm leaving."

Asher took one look about the dark forest, then mounted his horse and followed Tynan.

They rode all day and into the following night, with Asher half asleep in the saddle. When at last Tynan did stop, Asher didn't even recognize the stable for what it was.

"Unsaddle your horse," Ty ordered. "Or do you plan to stand there all night?"

Slowly, Asher obeyed him, shoveling hay and oats into the stall with the horse, then blindly following Ty out into the night and up the stairs at the back of a house. He didn't even ask any questions when Ty levered himself onto the roof, then, crouching low, ran across the roof and jumped onto the next roof. Asher was glad it was dark so he couldn't see how far it was to the ground. After they'd crossed three roofs, Tynan withdrew a key, opened a trapdoor and went down what was obviously an attic stairs. Once inside the building, he silently walked down a long corridor and opened the third door on the left.

A young woman turned over in the bed and looked up sleepily. "Alice, this is Asher and he needs a place to sleep."

The woman pulled the covers back then turned over on her side and went back to sleep. Tynan pushed Asher into the room and shut the door behind him. Two doors down, Ty opened another door.

Red was just getting out of bed, pulling a robe around her. "I thought I heard someone."

"Why is it so quiet?" Ty asked, pouring himself a whiskey.

"Four men rode in and shot the place up. I closed it down after that. Ty, they were lookin' for you."

He downed the whiskey in one gulp. "They've been on my trail for two days. You have anything to eat?"

Red opened a cabinet and withdrew bread and cheese. "I thought you'd come here, but you can't stay." She sat down on the sofa. "Oh, Ty, what have you done now? I thought you'd go straight for a while."

"They're not after me, except to keep me from finding Chris," he said, mouth full.

"Chris!" Red's head came up. "That two-timing little liar? I trusted her and she went off and left you to rot in jail when you were innocent."

"Yeah, well, that's true love for you. Whatever she's done, it's my responsibility to get her back to her father."

"At the risk of your own life?"

Ty just kept eating and didn't answer her. "You have an extra bed somewhere? I put Prescott in with Alice," he said after a while.

"You can have my bed," Red said heavily. "I've had all the sleep I'm gonna get tonight. Who do you want? Leora and you seemed to hit it off last time."

"Just sleep," Ty said, refilling his glass with whiskey. "No women."

He wasn't aware of the way Red just stood there opening and closing her mouth. "All right," she said after a moment. "Just give me your clothes and I'll have 'em washed."

She stood by silently while he undressed down to his underwear and watched as he slipped into bed. She sat by him, smoothing his hair back while he fell asleep, and when he was asleep, she kissed his forehead and tiptoed from the room.

"Tynan!" Red called urgently as she ran into the bedroom. "They've come for you."

Ty threw back the covers and put his feet on the floor. "Where the hell are my pants?"

"Wet. You've only been asleep three hours, but you've got to get out of here. There're half a dozen men downstairs askin' about you."

Tynan ran his hand through his hair. "Three whole hours, huh? Dysan doesn't leave any stone unturned."

"Dysan?" Red said. "You're after Beynard Dysan?"

"I don't need mothering now but I do need a pair of pants. Get me something to wear."

"I ought to refuse. I ought to get the sheriff to lock you up and save you from yourself."

Before Ty could speak, a woman barged into the room. "He's dead," she said with disgust in her voice. "I told you he couldn't take all three of us at once." She stopped talking, her eyes widening. "Why, Tynan, I didn't know you were here."

"And he isn't gonna be for long," Red said, pushing the woman out the door and closing it. "Now everyone'll know you're here and—" Her eyes brightened. "Sit there. Don't move. I have an idea." She left the room immediately while Ty began to search for something to wear.

Minutes later, Red returned with a pile of white leather and fringe over her arm. "That man that just died was from a wild west show and he won't be needin' this anymore." She held up the gaudiest, flashiest garment anyone had ever seen: white leather with three foot beaded fringe hanging from shoulder to wrist. There were also matching pants with silver medallions down the legs and a hat with a band of fake diamonds as big as pennies.

Tynan barely looked at the outfit. "If you don't get me some pants I'm—"

"Here!" Red said, tossing him the leather pants.

"Not on your life," Ty answered, letting them fall where they landed. "I need—"

"Wait a minute, Ty. There are six of them and one of you, and they have this place surrounded. Rachel said she saw a rifle on a roof so maybe there's more than six of them. You walk out of here and they'll never give you a chance. But they're expectin' what they know you look like. They ain't expectin' some fat, drunken ol' snake oil dealer."

Tynan sat down on the bed. "I won't wear that."

"You'd rather die than wear this?" Red gasped.

"With my boots on and my own pants on. What if I was to get buried in that?"

Red rolled her eyes toward the ceiling. "Of all the fool things I ever heard, that's the worst. Look, Ty honey, how are you gonna save that girl if you're dead? And that's what you'll be if you walk out of here wearin' your own clothes. With this on, you can walk right out the front door. Ever'body will be so blinded by the diamonds and silver they'll never even look at your face. And you ain't even seen all of it yet, there's white boots and silver guns with white handles and even silver bullets. It's a real wingdinger of an outfit."

Ty sat on the bed, his jaw rigid.

"You get yourself killed out there and I'll see to it that you're buried in this," Red said.

Ty shook his head. "I hope Mathison appreciates what I've gone through to get him his daughter back."

"Come on, let's get busy. We gotta pad you to make this fit."

An hour later, Tynan stood surrounded by giggling females. Asher, smoking a one-inch diameter cigar, sat in a chair with Alice on his lap.

"It suits you, Tynan," Asher said. "It really suits you."

Red put her hand over Tynan's, which was on his gun handle, as she checked his hair which was whitened with talcum powder.

The women had sewn pillows in the long johns of the dead showman so that Ty could fill out the voluminous suit. He now had a belly that hung over his silver buckled belt, and they'd adjusted the pants so they hung down low, the crotch half way to his knees.

"Too bad to cover that up," Leora said, running her hand over his buttocks.

"Now," Red said, "you look ready, but you gotta get in the mood. That man come in here with pistols blazin'. You gotta go out the same way."

"*I* like to see you with pistols blazin'," Leora said in Tynan's ear.

"He don't have time for that now," Red said. "You ready, Mr. Prescott?"

"Any time."

"Then you can help him out, 'cause Ty, you're too drunk to get out by yourself. You got that?"

Tynan nodded silently.

"The horse ready?" Red asked.

"What horse?" Ty asked.

"You'll know it when you see it," Asher laughed. "Believe me, you'll know it."

Red clasped her arm firmly through Tynan's. "Honey, I wanta see you again and this is the only way. Now, give me a kiss and go."

Ty held her for a minute, kissed her cheek then left the room, long, ornate spurs clinking on the wooden floor. At the top of the stairs, he halted, drew both the silver pistols and fired into the ceiling. The next minute he was down the stairs, women hanging onto him.

"I'm meaner 'n a snake and twice as quick," he bellowed, lurching forward, then he grabbed a woman and kissed her while firing a pistol into the ceiling and one at a table full of men. He hit two glasses of beer and narrowly missed a big cowboy.

The cowboy got up and started toward Tynan, but Asher interposed his own body.

"He's drunk," Asher said. "It was an accident."

"You'd better get him out a here," the man growled, still standing, his gun hand loose.

"I'm strong as a grizzly and as eagle-eyed as a hawk," Ty yelled.

"Come on, hawk, let's get out of here," Asher said, pushing Ty toward the door.

"I can outride, outshoot, out—"

Asher, seeing that Ty again had his pistol aimed toward the table of watching cowboys—probably Dysan's men—knocked Ty's arm upward so the shot hit the painting over the bar, making a hole in the plump buttocks of the nude woman in the painting.

"I'm as tall as a fir tree and as ugly as a mule but the girls love me best 'cause I'm as hard and big as a ship's oar," Ty yelled as Ash pulled him out of the saloon.

"Get on the damn horse," Ash said, "before you get us killed."

Standing before them was a white skinned, pink eyed stallion wearing a white leather saddle. Ty didn't even hesitate before jumping into the saddle, wrapping the reins about the pommel, then withdrawing a rifle from the sheath on the side. While standing in the stirrups, fringe flowing behind him, the horse galloping north out of town, Tynan began firing along the edges of the roofs. Some of the men hiding there stood to see what was going on and Ty shot within inches of them.

Asher, on a horse following Ty, was sure he was as white as Tynan's leather suit, but the men on the roof seemed to think they were being treated to a free show, and a couple even fired their rifles skyward in appreciation.

Asher only began to breathe again when they were miles from the town, and abruptly, Tynan disappeared behind some trees. When Asher got to him, he was frantically searching through the white saddlebags.

"What is it?" Asher asked, dismounting.

"I was hoping there were some other clothes in here. Damn! But Red didn't give me any."

"You seemed to do well enough with those. Did you realize you almost shot one of Dysan's men?"

"I counted eleven in all. How many did you get?"

"How many what?"

"Why did you think I made so much noise? I wanted them all to come see what the ruckus was. There were four inside, five on the roofs and two came around from back. I think there may be a couple more south of town. I give them two hours before they realize it was me wearing this thing. So we got two hours to get me all new duds and to get rid of this." He looked at the pink-eyed horse in disbelief. "It'll be like trying to hide a mountain in a dollhouse. I wish we could get somebody else to wear this. Then Dysan's men could follow him and give us some time."

Asher snorted. "Oh yeah, and where are we going to find such a fool? I don't know anybody who could be paid enough money to wear that and if you try to give it to somebody he'll ask why. They're sure to be suspicious. The best thing is to burn it. We've no hope of finding somebody stupid enough to wear it."

"I don't know," Ty said as he mounted, cursing as he had to pull fringe out from under him, "the world is full of all sorts of people."

Chapter Eighteen

Tynan stood plastered up against the white wall of the building as if he hoped he could disappear. Asher was certainly taking his time in finding clothes to replace the white suit. There'd been a few minutes when Ty thought he was going to have to do something about Asher's mouth—maybe shove it down his throat—but Ty had been able to persuade him that it was in his own best interests to help find new clothes.

Slowly, Ty put his head around the building and looked to see if anyone was near. When he was sure the street was empty, he walked the two feet to the horse trough and put his head under. Asher'd had several comments to make on the smell of the French Lilac talcum powder Red had used to turn his hair white.

Just as he was lifting his head from the water, he felt the unmistakable coldness of a gun barrel on his neck.

"Say your prayers," the man said, "cause this is your last minute alive."

"Lester Chanry," Tynan said, drawing back and

looking at him. He was a tall bean pole of a man with red hair that reached his scrawny shoulders. His face was covered with freckles, those being the only color on his face since his eyebrows and lashes were so light as to appear nonexistent. He was wearing a bright red shirt with a four-inch-wide row of Indian beading across the shoulders and in his hair were three silver conchos. "Lester, it's good to see you again. In fact, I was just talking about you."

"I'll bet you were. Were you talking about how you killed my brother?"

"That was an accident."

Lester pushed Tynan against the wall. "You killed him and now you're gonna pay for it."

"It wasn't me and you know it."

"That sheriff was chasin' you and you might as well have killed him. You're the one that's gonna pay for it. Are you ready to die?"

"Just so long as you promise to bury me in my new suit."

For the first time, Lester looked down at the gaudy garment Ty was wearing, and Tynan watched his face. "You'll promise me that you'll bury me in it, won't you, Lester? It's my dying wish and a man should have his last wish honored."

"Where'd you get duds like them?" Lester asked with awe in his voice.

"A man had to give up his life before I could have these," Tynan said. "You'll promise me, won't you?"

"Well. . . . Maybe you'd sell 'em to me. I sure like those things."

"Sell them! What would I do with the money if I'm dead? What if I make you a deal? I'll *give* them to you if you let me go free."

216

Lester pushed Ty back against the wall. "I'll just shoot you and take 'em."

"I bleed real bad. If I cut myself shaving I get blood all over everything. It'd stain the suit so bad it wouldn't be fit to wear and, besides, you'd miss out on the matching horse."

"Horse?" Lester asked. "Are you lyin' to me, Tynan? If you are, I'll—"

"Lester, I'm fighting for my life. You don't kill me and I'll give you this white suit and a white horse with a white saddle."

"White saddle?" Lester gasped. "I ain't never seen no white saddle. Tynan, if you're havin' me on I'll—"

"Just ease up on that pistol and I'll take you to where the horse is hidden and I'll give it to you, with a bill of sale. It'll all be legal. But if you shoot me you'll get a bloody suit—and you know how blood makes leather so stiff—and you'll never find that horse. Some farmer's kid'll find it and have the one and only white saddle in existence. Did I tell you that it has little silver roundels on the bridle?"

Lester took several minutes to consider what Tynan was saying while Ty lifted one arm to show off the dangling fringe.

"All right, I'll do it, but if you try to trick me I'll—"

"Try to trick one of the Chanrys? Lester, I didn't get this old by being a fool. Come on, let's go. It'll be easier to part with my suit if we don't take too long at this," Ty said with a sigh.

As Chris descended the stairs, she tried to pull the top of the dress higher over her breasts, but there wasn't enough fabric to cover what needed to be covered. With one glance at Pilar, she saw that the other woman was hanging out more than Chris ever hoped to be able to expose.

At the bottom of the stairs, the two men stopped, abruptly leaving the women alone in a large room with brick floors and heavy furniture that was covered with silk scarves. It was a rich room with a few chairs, a small table against one wall and little else.

There was a door to the left with a window next to it. Immediately, Chris went to the door and tried it but it was locked. Just as she was starting toward the window, a voice came from behind her.

"You'll find all the exits are locked, Miss Eskridge."

It was a voice she recognized. "You!" she said, turning on her heel.

"I thought you would have guessed by now," said Beynard Dysan. "After the way you followed me around the house and the forest land, I thought you'd know right away that I was the one who had you taken."

"I was following Owen," she said in a half whisper. "Not you."

"I wasn't to know that, was I? Will you ladies join me for dinner?"

Involuntarily, Chris took a step backward, moving away from him.

"We would be delighted," Pilar said, taking Chris's hand and pulling her forward as she took Dysan's arm in her other hand. "We are starving."

Chris let Pilar talk as Dysan led them into a dining room because she wanted to regather her equilibrium. She had to get over her instinctive dislike of this man if she was to find out anything. By the time Dysan pulled a chair out for her, she was calm enough that she didn't cringe away from him.

When they were all seated and food was set before them, Dysan looked at Chris, at the foot of the long table, across from him, Pilar next to him, and said, "Now, what was that all about at Hamilton's? What were you trying to find out?"

Chris took her time in answering. She didn't want to give away too much to this man without finding out what he knew. "My father . . ." she said, then filled her mouth full of food, taking her time in chewing.

"Yes," Dysan said, "I know your father committed suicide, but then that husband of yours had something to do with that, didn't he?"

Chris was sure now that Dysan didn't know who she really was, that he thought she was actually Diana Eskridge. "Whit and I have . . ." She looked down at her food and managed to squeeze a tear from her eye. "I really do love him, but my father . . ."

She looked up at Dysan through damp eyelashes and saw that he was looking at her with great impatience and a lip curled in distaste. Good, Chris thought, let him think that she was a meek, cowardly little thing. Pilar, after a few looks of disbelief at Chris, kept her eyes on the food.

"What did you hope to find at Hamilton's?" Dysan persisted, sounding as if her timidity repulsed him.

"My cousin, Lionel, was in danger. I only meant to help. Why were we taken? What do you plan to do with us? I was only trying to help Lionel. And Pilar has nothing to do with this."

Dysan began to eat. "Consider yourself my guests. I fear that I cannot allow you the freedom of my house but you will have every comfort while you are here."

"But *why* are we here?" Chris said, leaning forward.

Dysan merely looked at her and said nothing more.

"They will come after us, you know," Pilar said softly into the silence.

"Do you mean that husband of yours? Do you think he'll come and rescue you? Shall he threaten me with a garden rake?"

"With a—" Chris said but cut herself off. "Someone will come to find us."

Dysan put down his fork and leaned back in his chair. "I have sent out over a hundred men to patrol the area between here and Hamilton's. They are to shoot to kill anyone who even asks a question about one of you ladies or about me. I assure you that no one will come for you."

"Then it's ransom you want?" Chris asked without thinking.

"And how can I ransom you?" he asked as if the answer greatly interested him. "Who will pay for either of you?"

"No one will pay money," Pilar said quietly, "but someone might be willing to pay with his life. We will be found."

Dysan took a while to study Pilar, looking her up and down in a hot, insulting way. "Perhaps you're right, but we shall see, won't we? Now, I'm afraid that this is all the time I can spare you. You will be taken back to your room and you will wait there."

"Wait for what?" Chris said.

"For when I decide what's to be done with you," Dysan said, then stood and left the room. Chris quickly wrapped some slices of beef in a napkin, and slipped the small package into her pocket. Seconds later, the two men who'd first kidnapped the women came into the room and escorted them back through the entryway and up the stairs to their room.

"So what did we find out except that if we make him angry we don't get to finish our meal?" Pilar asked when they were alone in the room. "Do you *really* think he sent a hundred men to guard the trail behind us or do you think he was bragging?"

Chris was looking out the window, considering how far it was to the ground. "I think that man is capable of any evil. *Why* are we here?" she half cried. "He doesn't know who my father is so we're not being held for ransom. I thought maybe, with these dresses, he'd decided he wanted one of us—physically, I mean—but that doesn't seem to interest him. So what does he want?"

"Do you know something that he doesn't, something that he might want to know?"

"Sure," Chris said. "He thinks I know where the lost Inca treasure is. If he wanted to know something, why didn't he ask us?"

"But all he asked us was if we thought Tynan was coming after us," Pilar said thoughtfully. "Do you think he's after Ty?"

Chris's mouth set in a line. "It seems that the only people who take a great interest in Tynan are those on the side of law and order. I don't think Dysan wants to arrest Tynan for whatever crime he's committed this week."

Pilar looked at Chris for a while. "You certainly are angry at him, aren't you? What's he done to you?"

"Made a fool of me, that's all." She sat down on the bed. "I don't think Dysan wants Tynan. If he did, he could have had him in a much easier way than in this elaborate scheme. He could have taken him on a picnic and Tynan would have gladly shot it out with him. No, there's something else. I think Dysan *does* know who

221

my father is and we're being held for ransom. Then the hundred guns makes sense because Dysan wouldn't want anyone to interfere with his holding of us."

"Us?" Pilar said. "You've never explained why I'm here."

"Who knows? Pilar, do you think that if we tied those sheets together, they'd reach down to the ground?"

"Are you out of your mind?" Pilar said, moving to look out the window. "Can't you see those men with rifles out there? Do you think they'll just wave at you as you climb down?"

"Not if I do it at night."

"Chris," Pilar said with great patience in her voice. "Let's just wait here until your father pays the ransom and then we'll be free."

Chris looked at the dark woman for a long moment. "Free us so we can identify Dysan as a kidnapper? So we can go to a federal marshal and tell who held us captive? No, I don't think that's going to happen. Dysan may get the ransom, but he can't risk freeing us to tell anyone who took us." She paused a moment, her eyes locked with Pilar's. "I think he'll kill us as soon as he receives the money from my father. He has to keep us alive until then in case my father demands proof that I'm alive."

Pilar went back to sit on the bed. "So how long do you think we have?"

"My father will move heaven and earth to get however much money Dysan demands and . . ." She paused a moment since tears were coming to her eyes. Maybe she'd never see her father again, maybe she'd never see anything again except the inside of this room.

"He'll get the money here as fast as horse and rider can travel. If Dysan sent a ransom note south while we were being taken north, I figure we have about two days before the money's here."

"Two days?" Pilar gasped then her head came up. "So that means that Tynan could be here tonight."

"We can't risk it," Chris said, putting her hand on Pilar's. "Do you want to go with me or wait here and hope I make it back with help?"

"I want us both to remain here," Pilar said, then sighed. "All right, I'll stay here. Maybe I can hide the fact that you're gone for a while."

"If Dysan finds out that I'm gone, tell him that you're Christiana Mathison, then he'll want to keep you safe until my father gets the money to him. Now, will you help me get these sheets torn and tied?"

"If I must," Pilar said and found, to her consternation, that her hands were shaking. "I'll help if I must."

Tynan put his hand up to halt Asher as they entered the little town of Sequona. "I want you to go in first. Go to that big saloon there, about halfway down the street, and take a corner table. Do nothing but order a beer and wait for me. Don't talk to a single person, you understand?"

"Don't you worry about me, I can handle myself."

"Take your gun out, put it under your hat and wait. I want you ready when the shooting starts."

"Shooting?" Asher whispered. "How can you be sure there'll be any shooting?"

"How can you be as old as you are and not be sure? You ready?"

Asher just nodded as he reined his horse forward,

down the long, dusty street and stopped in front of the saloon. As he entered, a body came flying out, barely missing him and landing in the street.

"And stay out!" said a man wearing an apron, his big arms flexed, the muscles outstanding.

Asher waited until the entrance was clear, then went inside. He had to stand at the bar for a moment until the back table had cleared of a group of men playing poker, then he took his beer and sat down. As inconspicuously as he could, he removed his gun from his holster and placed it on the table, hidden under his hat.

He was leaning back in his chair, his eyes half closed when Tynan walked in—and immediately he could feel several eyes turn toward the man. So, Ash thought, Ty was right and there were people waiting for them.

Tynan ordered a double whiskey, and, as he was drinking it, a woman sidled up to him, putting her arm about his waist and running her hand over his back.

"How about buyin' a lady a drink?" she said.

Asher straightened his chair, trying to look as if he were interested in his beer, but he was actually trying to watch the men around him. There was one fat, dirty cowboy to his right whose hand was inching toward his gun belt. Get out of the way, lady, he thought with all of his might.

Tynan moved away from the woman just a bit. "Honey, I'd like to share more than a drink with you. You think that could be arranged?"

The woman's smile made her eyes disappear.

"Why don't you go on upstairs and wait for me? I need to wet my throat a little bit and I'll be right up."

The woman, in her dirty red-and-black dress, gave a look of triumph to the few other women in the saloon then started up the stairs. When she was halfway up, Ty turned to the bartender and said loudly, "What I really want is some information. You know the whereabouts of Beynard Dysan?"

There was a split second pause before the first gun was fired. Tynan, obviously watching the room in the mirror over the bar, spun on his heel, crouched low and fired into the belly of the fat cowboy across from Asher. Jumping up, Ash brought his gun up and shot another man on the balcony overlooking the main room of the saloon. As a bullet whizzed inches past his ear, Ash fell to the floor, knocked the round table over and got behind it.

As he was firing, he tried to see where Tynan was so he could protect him. Ty was backing toward an outside door, dodging bullets as he went.

Just as Ty was about to reach the door, Asher saw a man's head in a window to Ty's left. Standing, Asher bellowed, "Tynan!"

Ty turned and fired, the man at the window fell back, and Ty left the saloon just as Asher felt a searing pain in his leg before he could again reach the safety of the table.

Now Asher was alone in the saloon, all guns blazing at him, pinned down behind a little round table, the front door several feet away. He sat down to reload, watching the blood seep from his wounded leg, when he heard the softer more deadly sound of rifle fire in the saloon.

Looking around the table, he saw Tynan standing in the doorway, a rifle at his shoulder. "The next one that moves gets it. Get over here, Prescott," he commanded.

As Asher moved from the table, Tynan shot at a man in the corner and a gun dropped from his hand.

"I'm looking for Beynard Dysan and I want to know where he is. Watch my back," he said under his breath to Asher.

There were only four men left in the saloon now—and five bodies. The others who had been there had either run when the shooting started or were dead now.

"You!" Ty said to a tall man with a scar over his eye. "You'll be the first. I'll take a few inches off your left foot in about two seconds if you don't tell me what I want to know. Where is Dysan's place?"

Tynan put the rifle deeper into his shoulder.

"He has a big place ten miles due north of here," the man said. "But it's guarded and no man that he don't want in there can get in."

"That's my problem." Ty began to back up, Asher in front of him watching the crowd that was gathering in the street. Their saddled horses were waiting.

"Ride like you never rode before," Tynan called to Asher as they made their way north out of town.

Asher followed Ty as they thundered down the road and headed for the forest. For a while, Asher thought Ty knew where he was going but as they left the road and went into the trees he saw Ty stop several times and look around him. "You don't know this country, do you?" Ash asked.

"If I did, I'd have known where Dysan lived. Get down, I think this is it."

"What's it? Where are we?"

"Someone's to meet us here."

"Who?" Ash asked but received no answer as Ty dismounted, removing his saddle bags from his horse. Wincing with pain, Asher dismounted also.

"Let me look at that leg," Ty said as Ash lowered himself to the ground. After a rough, but thorough examination, Ty took a bottle of whiskey from his saddle bag. "This'll sting but it'll kill any lead poisoning. It's not a bad place, more a burn than a real bullet wound. You'll be fine in no time, even if you are a little sore."

Ash nearly screamed when Ty poured the whiskey on the raw, open cut, but he managed to control himself.

"First gunshot wound?" Ty asked, amused.

"The first this week," Ash answered as he tried to get his breath.

An hour later, both men were stretched beneath trees, when Ash heard a sound coming from behind Tynan. He looked at Ty but there was warning in Ty's eyes, telling Ash to be quiet. Pretending to be asleep, Ash watched in fascination as a woman, not quite young, but not old either, came sneaking up behind Ty, making as little noise as a human can make in a forest.

Just as she reached Tynan, who seemed to be asleep, with his hat pulled down over his eyes, Ty reached out, grabbed her and pulled her into his lap.

"Let me go!" she yelled at him.

"Come on, Belle, you're not still mad at me, are you?"

"I'd take a knife to you if I could."

Tynan held her easily in his arms, struggling only with her hands, with which she meant to claw him. "You know I never meant to hurt you, but that girl was only thirteen years old. I couldn't let you sell her to that old man."

"You didn't have to shoot up my place to save her. I lost everything in that. I had to go back on the streets to get enough money to pay for what you did."

Tynan began nuzzling her neck. "I'll bet you made a fortune."

"I did not!" she yelled at him, then began to relax. "Well, maybe I did make some at that. What are you doing here? And askin' about Dysan! You must wanta stop livin'."

"I just want to find him. You know anything about him?"

"Not enough that I want to lose my life by tellin' you. What's he done to you?"

"Taken Chris Mathison," Asher said. "Allow me to introduce myself. Asher Prescott at your service, ma'am," Ash said, removing his hat.

The woman tried to free her hands from Tynan's grip but he still held her. "All right, what do you want from me?" she said with a sigh. "Tynan, one of these days, you're gonna ask for one too many favors."

"What I like about women is that they always know how to give."

Suddenly, the woman stiffened in Ty's lap. "Chris? Is that a woman? Tynan, if you got me out here to help you find another woman, so help me I'll—"

Ty kissed her to keep her quiet. "It's strictly business. I've been hired by her father to take her to him and Dysan has her."

"Then you'd be better off leaving her where she is. She won't be worth much when Dysan finishes with her."

Tynan frowned. "Are you speaking from first-hand knowledge?"

"I saw a girl after he got through with her. He doesn't like women; he doesn't like anybody for that matter. He has a place not far from here, but I don't think he stays there much, I think he goes back East pretty often, and, for the life of me, I can't figure out why he even comes to this godforsaken hole. He has money enough that he can live anywhere he wants to."

Tynan released her hands but she still stayed in his lap. "I heard he has business around here."

"There are rumors that he's involved in whatever evil trick has been pulled lately, but no one's been able to prove anything yet. The law's terrified of him."

Tynan was quiet for a moment. "You said this place of his was guarded. How well guarded?"

"An army post could learn from him. He has men patrolling his big house night and day—and they have dogs on leashes at night. Anybody even gets close and the dogs are let loose. They say those dogs can really take you apart."

"Has *anyone* ever made it inside?" Asher asked.

"Why would anybody be stupid enough to want to try?" the woman asked, looking from one man to the other.

"Belle, you know anybody who's been in the place? Somebody we could ask questions?"

Belle looked down at her hands. "To tell you the truth, I was in there last year. I went with some other girls and. . . . Tynan, I don't like to think about what happened that night."

Tynan pulled the woman to him, hiding her face in his shoulder. "Dysan has a young woman now and he's holding her captive. Prescott and I plan to get her out so I need all the help I can get. If you could tell me anything that you remember about the place, a way in, the floor plan of the house, whatever you can remember, I'd sure appreciate it."

Belle moved away from his shoulder. "You don't deserve my help, not after the way you tore up my place, but I'll do what I can." She looked at him in a seductive way. "I'll do it in memory of that time down in San Antonio. You remember that?"

"Every day of my life," Ty said, smiling. "I use it to judge everything else by. Prescott, you got any paper? Belle's going to draw us a plan."

Ty pushed her off his lap while Asher managed to move his stiffening leg so he could get to his horse. Minutes later, the three of them were hunched over a map Belle was making, and an hour later, the two men were mounting their horses again.

Belle looked up at Tynan. "By the way, Ty, there was some guy through town yesterday lookin' for you."

"What'd he look like?"

"Tall, skinny, long red hair. His arm was in a sling and he walked with a limp. Seemed real anxious to see you."

Tynan leaned down from the horse and kissed her lingeringly. "You tell him you saw me about forty miles south of here."

She smiled at him. "Maybe. I might consider it if you come back through here and make it up to me about what you did to my saloon."

"I might do that." Ty smiled at her, then was off, heading north toward Dysan's house.

Chapter Nineteen

Pilar was sitting on the floor, leaning against the foot of the bed, and, in spite of her good intentions, she was asleep and didn't hear anyone in the room until a hand covered her mouth, startling her awake.

"Tynan?" she asked in disbelief. "Is that you?"

"Where's Chris?" he asked at once.

Pilar sat up straighter. "I don't know. She's been gone for hours and I heard the dogs and men yelling but I didn't hear anything from her. Ty, I'm worried about her."

Tynan's face showed what he thought of Chris leaving the room. "How did she get out?"

Pilar started to stand. "We tore the bed sheets into strips and she went down through the window. Ty! You're injured. Here, sit down."

"I don't have time. I have to find her and soon. Leave that alone, it's not bad, just a couple of dog bites. Why in the hell did you let her go? I don't expect

231

her to have any sense, but you, Pilar, I expected more from you. I told you to watch her."

"How was I supposed to stop her? Dysan said that he'd sent out over a hundred men to stop anyone from finding us. You could have been dead for all we knew and then Chris said Dysan wasn't going to release us since we could identify him."

"Has he contacted Mathison yet?"

"That's what's strange, Ty, I'm not sure Dysan knows who Chris is. He talked about her father committing suicide and about her husband being an embezzler. If he doesn't know that Chris is wealthy, then why has he taken us?"

"I'll worry about what's on the man's mind later. Right now, I'm more concerned about his guns. Did you see what Chris did when she reached the ground? Did she try leaving the grounds or did she go back into the house? She just loves snooping in people's private papers."

"I didn't see because I was pulling the rope up, but I think she probably had to go into the house because the dogs came around minutes after she touched the ground. She wrapped her shoes in pieces of sheet and rubbed them with some meat fat. She was planning to throw the cloth away when she reached the edge of the forest."

"Well, it doesn't look like it worked because she's nowhere to be seen outside. Now, I want you to listen to me and do exactly what I say. Prescott, the man from Hamilton's place, will be here in a minute and I want you to let him help you get out of here. He'll take you over the roof."

"And where will you be?"

"Searching for Chris." With that statement, he went

232

to the window and proceeded to climb up a rope toward the roof. Pilar could hear him walking softly overhead and then all was silent.

Tynan gave a signal to Asher who crouched behind a dormer on the tall house, then tied his rope about a far chimney and started down. Thanks to Belle, he knew most of the layout of the house and he was heading now toward Dysan's office. This would be the room that Chris most likely would want to explore.

The room was dark and there wasn't a sign of any activity in it—no papers, only a few books, no ledgers with their revealing account numbers, no pretty little blonde snooping through things.

Cautiously, Tynan made his way out the door and into the dark hallway. Listening carefully, he heard voices downstairs, but they didn't seem particularly upset about anything, as they might be if they'd just found Chris haunting the rooms. With his back to the wall, he began to ease his way down the stairs, stopping constantly to listen to whatever he could hear.

According to Belle, the house was a big one and Ty wasn't sure where he should begin searching, but the library seemed like a good bet—not because he thought Dysan might have something there but because Chris would want to search a place like that.

He stopped twice at the foot of the stairs to listen but he heard nothing, so he went across the empty dining room to the closed door that he knew led to the hallway. Still listening and, as quietly as a cat, he made his way through the door and into the hall. The first door on the right was the library.

Once inside the library, he paused, pressed his back against the door and waited. He wasn't sure what it was, but something was wrong. He stood so still that he became part of the shadows, fading into his surroundings so that he disappeared.

The sound of a match being struck made him turn his head—and he saw Beynard Dysan sitting in a chair before him, bringing the lit match up to his cigar tip.

"Bravo," Dysan said. "You were almost silent." He bent forward to touch the match to a lantern on the table before him.

In the light, Tynan could see Chris in a chair beside Dysan, her hands and feet tied, her mouth gagged. Her eyes were wild and she looked as if she'd seen something awful.

"I wouldn't try it," Dysan said as Ty took a step forward. "I have a gun on her and I wouldn't hesitate to shoot her."

Tynan stood where he was, not moving a muscle but trying to look about the room.

Dysan smiled. "I can assure you that there is no way to escape. You got in because I allowed you to enter." He took the cigar from his mouth and looked at it. "I wondered which one of the women you'd go after first."

Dysan stood and walked to stand behind Chris, putting a gun to her head, running his hand along her throat and pulling her head back. "Why do I get the feeling that she's not what she seems? Hamilton said she was his cousin, a mousey little thing that allowed her husband to beat her, but here she is, having escaped down the side of a four-story building, and I somehow sense that she isn't what she appears."

"What do you want? If it's money, you'll be paid. All you have to do is release her."

"Money?" Dysan sounded genuinely surprised. "And do you have money to pay for her ransom?"

"I can get it."

Dysan walked away from Chris but not far enough that he couldn't have hurt her if Tynan tried anything. "And what do you have that you can sell? Do some of the prostitutes you know have money? Will they sell their diseased bodies to get money for you? Or has that miner of yours finally found gold?"

Tynan just looked at the man, not saying a word.

"Ah, the rescuing hero doesn't want to tell what he knows. What can I do to loosen your tongue? Remove pieces of this little lady?"

Still, Tynan didn't move.

Dysan moved closer to Chris and began to run his hands down her arms. "Do you mind that other men touch her? Do you insist that this one is yours alone?"

"Do what you want with her," Tynan said. "She's just a job to me. I get paid to take her back to her father."

"And who is her father that he would pay for her?"

Tynan took his time in answering. "Del Mathison," he said into the silence.

The only sign Dysan gave that he heard was that his cigar shook just once as he held it in his hand.

There was a long silence in the room as Dysan stared at Tynan. "I think I have underestimated you. I thought you only went in for whores."

"I do. I want nothing to do with girls like her. She's been nothing but trouble so if you have some grudge with me, you can leave her out of it."

Dysan ran his hand along Chris's neck. "Shall I test your words? Shall I see how little you care about her?"

"Mathison won't take kindly to his daughter being mistreated and I don't think you're big enough to buck a man like him."

Dysan seemed to be considering this, but, after a moment, he walked toward the door, his gun aimed at Chris and looked out. Immediately, two men appeared. "Take them to the cellar and lock them in."

Tynan stood back as he watched Chris being untied, and when she was released, she fell forward. One of the men caught her arm roughly and jerked her upright. Ty still stood where he was as she looked up at him as she was being pulled along.

Without any protest, he followed behind her, in front of a man bearing a rifle.

They were led downstairs into a deep basement. There was a door against one wall and one of the men took a key and opened it, throwing Chris into the dark, dank little room. Tynan entered of his own accord, standing by the door until the men closed and locked it behind them.

Instantly, he was across the room to Chris, groping for her in the darkness. "Chris, Chris," he whispered repeatedly while running his hands over her body as if he were inspecting her. "Are you hurt?"

Chris clung to him as if she were drowning. "He's a horrible man," she gasped, then choked over her tears. "He told me about three women who'd been here. He told me about using a riding crop and—"

"Sssh," Ty said, holding her, stroking her back. "It's over now."

Chris hiccupped. "The woman *died*. He killed her. He told me in florid detail what he did and how he made the other women watch. The woman bled to death."

"Chris, stop crying. He won't do anything to you now."

236

"But how could one human do something like that to another? He told me about it and he wasn't sorry. Why wasn't he punished?"

"I don't know, just so long as he didn't hurt you."

It took Chris several minutes more to control herself. "What does it matter to you?" she asked, pushing away from him and moving back against the wall. "I'm well enough to get back to my father if that's what's worrying you." She sniffed.

Ty's hands moved away from her and there was resignation in his voice. "I'll see if I can find a light."

She leaned against the wall and listened to him rummaging around the room. Her head ached, there were rope burns on her ankles and wrists and along with Dysan's hideous stories, her ears were ringing with Tynan's words that she was nothing to him.

She watched as he struck a match and lit a candle. It was a dreary little room, dirt walls on three sides, the heavy wooden door on the other. There was a crude wooden cabinet against one wall, the door hanging off its leather hinges, exposing a few jars of canned fruit and a couple of half-burned candles on the shelves. Except for a few plants trying to grow out of the walls, the room was bare—and cold.

"Let me look at you," Tynan said, his voice cool, his face set.

Chris jerked away from his approaching hands. "Don't touch me. I am perfectly all right," she said. "You don't need to concern yourself with me."

Ty rocked back on his heels. "We'll get along a lot better if we work together. As long as you fight me, we'll never get anything done."

"So you can get me back to my father and you can

237

get your money? Maybe Dysan will let you go free now that you've told him who I am. Maybe you two can share the money from my father."

"Of all the ungrateful—I ought to leave you here."

"Go ahead. There's the door."

Tynan opened his mouth to speak but closed it again, then stood and walked to the door and began looking at it.

"You have on new clothes again," Chris said after a while.

Tynan didn't answer her but kept looking at the door.

Chris tried to stand up, using the wall for support. "I guess you got Pilar out safely."

"If you'd stayed in your room, you'd be out now, too."

"He knew when you were inside the house so what makes you think he didn't know when you were in the upstairs room?"

Ty didn't look back at her but kept searching the room, inspecting the ceiling which looked as if it were always wet, and the floor which was nothing but hardened mud.

"Dysan said he'd sent out a hundred men to stop anyone from finding us, so how did you get here?"

"Your father's money was a powerful incentive. It got me through clouds of gunfire."

Chris leaned against the damp wall, flexing her sore ankles. "All right, maybe I was rude and I apologize. I thank you for trying to rescue me and I'm sorry that I'm going to cause your . . . that I'm going to cause whatever will happen to us."

He turned back to her. "I think that finding out that you're Mathison's daughter will curtail whatever Dysan planned. Now, I suggest that you sit down and get what rest you can because, come morning, I think he'll take us out of here."

Chris sat down on the floor and was silent for a moment. "You could have gotten away in there. You could have overtaken those two men. Why didn't you?"

Tynan stretched out with his back against the door, his eyes half closed. "Maybe, maybe not. Why don't you get some sleep now? You might need to do some running in the morning."

Chris couldn't sleep, but she was quiet as she sat and watched Tynan across from her. Since that awful night in the cabin, she'd done her best not to think of him, not to remember what he looked like, how he smelled, how he'd touched her, but now, with him so near, it was impossible not to recall every bit of it.

And with the pleasant memories came his words: he only wanted to get her back to her father, that all she was to him was a possibility of a pardon, that she was just one of hundreds of women he'd bedded, no more, no less. Chris remembered with shame the way she'd tried to talk him into marriage. In the flickering darkness, she could feel her face turning red. How childish she'd been, how immature.

And how childish she was acting now, she thought. She kept thinking that he'd betrayed her when the truth was, he'd been more than honest with her, never had he insinuated that he wanted any more from her than a job and a good time.

As she watched him, he opened his eyes and looked at her, and for a moment, Chris almost threw herself into his arms. Whatever she felt for him was not returned and she'd better get used to that fact. He

239

didn't love her and she was going to stop loving him—even if it killed her.

"Would you like to see what I found?" she asked.

He gave a nod, but said nothing, just sat there looking at her with hot eyes.

Probably thinks that since we've made love once, we will again. Not on your life, cowboy! she thought.

Turning away from him, she unbuttoned her blouse and withdrew a long narrow belt of what looked to be silver links. "It's mine," she said, caressing the belt and taking her time before handing it to him.

"It's worn out and it looks old. Where was it? In your carpet bag?"

"No, of course not," she said, taking it back. "I found it here, when I was looking through Dysan's things. He had several treasures in a little cabinet. I think he found them in the sea—salvage. But I knew right away that this was mine so I took it."

Tynan looked at her in confusion for a moment. "You mean that you've never seen this thing before but you think it's yours?"

She looked up at him with a stubborn expression on her face.

"Is this your second sight again?" he said and there was laughter in his voice.

Chris merely kept her jaw set and put the belt back into her blouse.

"What is the thing anyway?"

"I think I'll get some sleep now," Chris said with her nose in the air.

"I didn't mean—" Ty began but he stopped himself. "You want to hear why I have on new clothes again?" he said after a moment.

Chris tried to control her curiosity but couldn't. She

was a reporter to the tip of her toes and she was not capable of resisting a story. Reluctantly, she nodded.

He started with entering Red's place secretly and then went on to tell of the men waiting outside for him. He told of his reluctance to wear the sideshow man's white leather outfit, and of at last agreeing.

Chris listened with held breath, in awe of what he wasn't telling her: of how difficult it had been to get to her. She didn't laugh until he started telling her about Chanry and how the man had loved the suit.

"But won't the men chase him when he's wearing the white suit, and won't they think they're chasing you?"

Tynan grinned at her. "That's the idea."

"Oh, Ty, that's dreadful of you. That man could get killed."

"Hmph! You'd rather I'd have worn the suit and let myself get killed?"

"That isn't what I meant and you know it."

"Then you'll be happy to know that I've already heard that Chanry escaped, a little dented maybe, but he's alive."

"And looking for you, no doubt."

"I seem to be a popular fellow," Ty said.

"Do you have any idea why Dysan wants you? He seemed to be very interested in you."

"I doubt it. He just wanted to see who could get through that gauntlet he set up. Chris, seeing as this might be our last night alive, would you like to—"

He didn't get to finish. "Of all the audacious, disgusting things I have ever heard, that's the worst. After the things you said to me! How dare you ask me something like that! What kind of woman do you think I am?"

"But in the cabin—"

"In the cabin I thought I was in love with you and I

241

thought you were going to marry me. That was *before* I found out what kind of low-life scum you really are, that you have no more feelings for a woman than what you can get out of her. But I can tell you that you will never, *ever* get anything out of me again."

"I just thought I'd ask," he said and there was a hint of a smile in his voice. "Let's get some sleep now."

Chris didn't say anymore but she didn't sleep either as she sat there, her blood boiling. How dare he? How dare dare *dare* he?

She was still angry when the door was unlocked and opened.

Chapter Twenty

A man grabbed Chris's arm before she was out the door, roughly pushing her toward the stairs.

"You're ours once he's through with you," the man whispered in her ear as she stumbled up the stairs. "And after he's killed the pretty boy," he added, meaning Tynan who was walking behind them. Another man, holding a rifle, brought up the rear.

At the top of the stairs, they were shoved into the dining room where Dysan waited for them. Dysan didn't say a word as the men tied Tynan to a chair, then left the room.

Dysan lit a cigar, looking at Chris standing at the end of the dining table and at Tynan as he sat immobilized in a chair by the window.

"I have waited a long time for this," he said at last. "I've spent years planning this, what I would do, how I would do it. I had no idea that you'd drop the answer into my hands so easily."

243

As Dysan was speaking, he was looking at Tynan, it was as if Chris weren't even in the room, but she got the impression that she was the answer to which Dysan was referring. She was what Dysan was going to use to do what he wanted to Tynan.

"Before we . . . die," Chris said, "could you tell us why? What have we done?"

Dysan took a long draw on his cigar. "I have no intention of telling you anything. By tomorrow, this house will be a pile of cinders and in the ashes will be the bodies of two people. No one will even be able to identify the bodies. Your father will never know what happened to his little daughter."

"What about the world? Won't they want to know what happened to Nola Dallas?"

Dysan didn't speak for a moment. "You are certainly full of surprises." He turned to Tynan who was still and silent in the chair. "As well as yourself. She isn't like your usual women."

"What is it you have against Tynan? And if you think he wants me for anything, you're wrong. I'm nothing to him, absolutely nothing."

Dysan gave a little smile of delight. "Of course you're not. Now, come here."

Chris stiffened. "I will not."

"For every order of mine that you disobey, I will take an hour from his life. You obey me and he lives longer."

"I can't . . ." Chris began but she stopped at the look on Dysan's face. She didn't look at Tynan because she was beginning to feel her first anger at him. Why didn't he at least make some form of protest? Did he care so little about her that he'd allow whatever happened to just happen to her?

244

Chris tried to clear her mind. Tynan wasn't going to help, wasn't going to even say anything that might discourage Dysan so it was up to her. What would she do if she were alone in the room with an aggressive man?

She tried to look about the room without seeming to do so and she saw that on the sideboard were two built-in silverware holders. Inside one of them had to be a table knife. If she could lead Dysan that way . . .

She began moving toward Dysan, and his eyes never left hers. "What makes you think that I care anything about him? He's only a cowboy who was hired by my father to take me through the rain forest. Did you know that he'd been in jail? My father had to get him out of prison to lead the expedition. He's not my type of man at all."

Dysan watched her and Chris was glad to see that his eyes went down to her hips a couple of times, from the way she was swaying them, he could hardly miss them.

"I like a man with power." She was standing close to him now, both of them in front of the sideboard. "Do you have any idea how very wealthy my father is? Can you imagine what an empire you'd have if you were to merge your kingdom with his?"

Dysan looked amused. "Are you trying to seduce me? Do you think you can make me forget what I really want? You are a bystander who got caught in the crossfire."

Chris was inches away from him now, her face just below his. "I'm trying to save my own neck. If you and I merge, so to speak, we can have control of a great deal. If you murder me, my father will pursue you to the ends of the earth. Your life will be hell."

"And what about him?"

"What does he matter? Let him go. We don't need him."

Dysan smiled down at her. "Nice try, princess, but it won't work. The both of you die. Mathison would never let someone who'd once threatened his little girl into his kingdom."

Suddenly, he grabbed Chris about the waist and pulled her to him, grinding her mouth with his, forcing her lips open and thrusting his tongue inside.

When he released her, her revulsion showed on her face.

He thrust her away from him. "And you think you could pretend to *want* me," he said between closed lips. "I don't like to be thought a fool. Now come here."

Chris was really afraid of him now. He wasn't going to fall for anything she'd planned, he was going to torture her in front of Tynan, then kill Tynan in an equally disgusting way—and she wasn't even going to be told why she was dying.

Hesitantly, she walked toward him, and when she was in front of him, she voluntarily put her arms up to go about his neck. She began to kiss his neck, moving over his lips, trying to shift his interest entirely onto her—and while she was kissing him, she was trying to reach the box of silverware behind him.

Feigning passion as he again put his tongue in her mouth, she managed to get the box open, and with one eye open, she saw that there was a set of six table knifes, handles up, in the box. Now, if she could only reach one of them. She was almost there when Dysan suddenly turned and grabbed her hand, her fingertips held an inch above the handle.

"Going to stab me in the back, my dear?" he said before he slapped her across the face.

Chris hit the floor, her hand going to the corner of her bleeding mouth.

Dysan advanced on her, and Chris scooted backward on the floor.

It was just as Dysan reached her and had his hand raised to strike her again that Tynan sprang from his chair and grabbed Dysan about the neck, a small knife held to the evil man's throat. "I think it's time that you pick on someone your own size," Tynan said.

With that, Ty spun the man around and slammed a right fist into his face.

Dysan went down on the nearest chair and hit the floor next to Chris. Tynan didn't give him time to regain his breath before he was on him again. "You coward!" Tynan said under his breath as he grabbed Dysan and began to beat him.

Chris got up and tried to stop Tynan from killing the man, but Tynan was so angry that she couldn't make him hear her. She kept watching the door, fearing that any minute, one of the guards would come in and take them back to the cellar. They had to get out now while they had the chance.

She jumped on Tynan's back, hoping that her weight would have some effect on him.

Tynan shrugged her off and, again, Chris went skidding across the floor. It was a long moment before Tynan realized what he'd done. He dropped Dysan, allowing the man to slide down the wall to the floor in a bloody heap while he went after Chris.

"That was a fool thing to do," he said, lifting her up from the floor.

Chris shook her head to clear it. "We have to get out of here while we can. What took you so long to get loose?"

"Have you ever sawed through half-inch ropes with a pen knife? And you didn't look like you were in any misery. Maybe you want to stay here with Dysan rather than escaping with me? Maybe you two can still merge empires once you get rid of the cowboy."

"Could you go into a jealous rage later? I'd like to get out of here and we still have to get past the guards and the dogs outside."

After helping her to stand, Tynan went to Dysan and hauled him up. "You're going with us and if the dogs get too near, I'll throw you to them. Chris, hand me that piece of rope."

As Tynan tied Dysan, Chris looked out the window. "What do you think our chances are? There are guards everywhere."

"I'm hoping that Pilar and Prescott got away."

"They didn't. They're in the cellar now," Dysan said before Tynan put a dirty handkerchief from his back pocket across Dysan's mouth.

"Then we have to get them out," Chris said, heading toward the door which led to the stairs into the cellar.

Tynan shoved Dysan against the wall and grabbed Chris's arm. "What makes you believe him? If they're locked up, then after I get you out safely, I'll come back for them—alone. You understand me?"

"Because you'll go back to jail if I'm not safe? Pilar and Asher don't matter to you, do they?"

Tynan closed his eyes a moment, then turned back to Dysan and began to search him, removing a small derringer from inside his coat pocket. "All right, let's go. Chris, I'm taking him out the window first, then I want you to follow us when it's safe." He paused a moment, looking at her. "And I want you to swear to me that you won't do anything stupid like try to get back into the house to find the others. You understand?"

Chris nodded, but she was thinking about Pilar and Asher hidden away in the cellar. Wouldn't it be better if the two of them tried to get them out, instead of Tynan coming back alone later?

"Chris!" Tynan hissed at her as he stood outside the window. Dysan was giving him trouble so Tynan cuffed him once on the side of the head.

There was a low brick wall in the back of the house, a place for flowers and kitchen herbs. Ty crouched down behind the wall, forcing Dysan down in front of him. He kept turning to look at Chris, as if he expected her to disappear and he wanted to be able to go after her as quickly as possible.

They were at the end of the wall when Ty stopped and put his head up. The forest was several yards away and Chris could hear men talking nearby on the other side of the wall and the dogs in the distance. It would probably be only minutes before the guards found them.

Tynan leaned back against the wall and checked Dysan's derringer to make sure it was loaded. "Chris, I want you to stay behind us. I'm going to use Dysan as a shield and get us to the forest. You think you can do that? I don't want any more trouble than I already have. No going back for the others."

It was obvious that he hadn't believed her when she'd said that she would obey him.

Tynan looked toward the forest for a moment then back at Dysan. "And you give me any trouble and I'll blow your head off."

"All right, let's go," he said, grabbing Dysan and pulling him upright.

They left the safety of the wall and stepped into the open ground—but they stopped there because no one was even interested in them. They could see about a dozen guards, one with four dogs on a leash, but not one eye was turned in their direction. The guards were frozen where they stood, staring at something around the corner of the house.

Chris could hear bells in the distance.

"Get back!" Tynan said to Chris, shoving Dysan back toward the wall.

"What is it?" Chris asked.

"I think it's a peddler's wagon," Ty said. "Pilar used to work on one. If it is them, then we'll do better to leave with them. The dogs will smell our trail in the forest in no time."

"But how do we get out? We can't just walk to the wagon. And what do we do with him?"

"We leave him here, then we make our way toward the front of the house. We'll figure out a way to make Prescott see us."

Chris watched as Tynan tied one of Dysan's ankles to a spike in the top of the brick wall, allowing the rope to fall only enough so that Dysan wasn't dangling, but he was very uncomfortable. "Something tells me that I ought to kill you now," Ty said under his breath. "I think you're going to be nothing but trouble and there'll come a time when I'll regret having missed my chance." He looked up at Chris. "You ready?"

"Ty, are you sure it's Asher and Pilar? Maybe it's really a peddler's wagon and they're actually locked in the cellar."

Ty didn't answer but grabbed her arm and pushed her back toward the house. Looking inside the window, he made sure no one was about then climbed inside and helped Chris after him.

She followed him as he led her through the house, keeping her back to the walls as he instructed her, while he checked each room they passed for signs of a guard. Once, he slipped inside a room and Chris heard a dull thud, as if a body were hitting the floor, then he returned to the hall and motioned for her to follow him.

Chris didn't question how he came to know the plan of the house so well, but just trusted him. He stopped in a bedroom at the far end of the house.

"It's Pilar, all right," he said after looking out the window. "She's on top of the wagon dancing, and Prescott is driving. I don't know how much longer we have before they get tired of watching her. On second thought, considering what Pilar's wearing, we may have the rest of the week."

He turned back to Chris. "How fast can you run?"

"I . . . I don't know. If someone's chasing me, I guess I can run rather quickly."

"I'm going to create a diversion and I want you to climb out the window and run to the wagon and get in the back. Think you can do that?"

"But what about you? I can't go off and leave you."

"After the way you were kissing Dysan, what do you care about me?"

"Dysan?" she asked, bewildered. "I was trying to get a knife from the box. I had to divert him. Tynan, are you jealous?"

"Definitely not. Now, are you going to get out there or are you going to waste time and maybe get us all killed?"

She nodded at him, but she didn't like it. She hoped he wasn't going to do something that would get him caught again. She didn't think Dysan would be so easy to overpower the second time.

"Good girl," he said and started to turn away, but then abruptly turned back and pulled her into his arms. His kiss was hard and quick, so quick, in fact, he only undid three buttons, but it was a kiss filled with feeling. He released her as abruptly as he'd taken her. "I'll be all right," he said over his shoulder. "You just get yourself out of here when you hear the gunshots."

It seemed to Chris that it was the longest few minutes of her life while she waited for Tynan to begin firing. She crouched below the window and peeped out to see the tall, gaudily painted peddler's wagon surrounded by men with rifles over their shoulders. On top of the wagon was Pilar, dressed in odd, voluminous trousers of pale blue silk and a tiny top of matching silk. It was apparent that the costume hadn't been made for someone of Pilar's dimensions because the fabric strained everywhere, threatening to split apart at any moment. Chris guessed that that was half of the men's fascination with her—the hope that the garment would give way while they were watching.

While Chris was watching Pilar undulate, there suddenly came the sound of gunfire from the back of the house and the guards' reaction was instantaneous. They all took off running toward the sound.

Chris lost no time climbing out the window and running across the lawn to open the back of the wagon and climb inside. She heard Pilar yell down to Asher, on the wagon's seat, "She's in," then the wagon started off at a breakneck speed.

Chris grabbed the side of the wagon and tried to hold her balance. The wagon was full of merchandise, from bolts of cloth to pots and pans to farm tools, nearly all of it fastened down so it couldn't fly about when the wagon moved.

The back door of the wagon flew open just as Chris regained her balance. As she reached forward to close it, she saw that they were traveling away from Dysan's big house.

"No!" she gasped, but there was no one in the back of the wagon to hear her.

If she was to get Asher to turn around, she had to do something and do it fast. Fighting the rocking of the wagon, she began to climb over the boxes that were stacked toward the front, grabbing a small handled axe off the wall as she moved.

It took three swings before the axe went through the front partition and came out uncomfortably close to Asher's right ear.

He turned to look at her in disbelief as she used her feet to kick the rest of the way through the thin wood. "You have to go back," she yelled at Asher. "You can't leave Tynan back there."

Pilar hung down from the top. "She's right," she shouted over the sound of the horses. "We have to get Tynan out."

"Then I'll go back but you two women stay here," Asher said even as he was halting the horses.

"No!" the women screamed at him in unison.

Asher didn't say another word as he flicked the whip over the horses and headed back toward Dysan's house.

Chapter Twenty-one

Chris held on for her life while Asher drove the wagon back over the ground they'd just covered. Their only hope of rescuing Tynan was that Dysan hadn't been discovered yet and his men didn't know that the peddler's wagon was involved in the escape.

Above her head, she could hear Pilar singing and making noise to attract attention.

"Cover this hole," Asher yelled as he whipped the horses harder.

With unsteady feet, falling several times, Chris managed to hang a piece of cloth over the hole she'd made in the front of the wagon. Just as she'd caught the edges of the cloth on a piece of splintered wood, Asher called, "I see him and he's running toward us. Oh Lord. Get down! Both of you women get down," he yelled as the first shots rang out.

Chris, with her heart pounding, flattened herself on the floor of the wagon—or as close to the floor as she could get with all the merchandise scattered about.

Overhead, she heard Pilar hit the roof very hard, almost as if she'd fallen. Immediately the gunfire increased to a torrent.

Inching forward on her belly, she pushed one of the wagon doors open. Tynan was running down the road with men and dogs on his heels, the men firing their rifles as they ran. The bullets were hitting the back of the wagon at a regular rate, some of them whizzing inches over Chris's head.

She moved closer to the door and stretched her hand out toward Tynan. "Come on," she yelled. "Come on."

Ty yelled something back to her but the blood was pounding so hard in her ears that she didn't understand what he was saying.

"You'll never get out of jail," she screamed at him.

It was then that one of the bullets hit Ty in the leg. He faltered and she thought he was going to fall but he kept on coming.

Chris made a dive through the merchandise, one box that was sliding across the space hit her hard in the side, but she continued until she reached the front and stuck her head out to Asher and bellowed for him to slow down, that Tynan had been shot and couldn't run.

Then she went back to the rear of the wagon to put her hand out to Ty. Asher couldn't slow down much or Dysan's men would catch them.

Tynan reached the wagon and Chris's hand just as the dogs reached Ty's heels. She helped to pull him into the wagon as Ty yelled to Asher to get the hell out of there. Ty had to shake one dog off his ankle even as the wagon bounded forward, leaving Dysan's men standing where they were.

Immediately, Chris started examining the gunshot wound on Ty's right thigh.

"Do you know if Prescott has horses ready?" he shouted to her over the noise of the wagon.

"I don't know anything. Ty, you're bleeding a lot."

"There's a place we can go. How is Pilar? Is she still on top?"

"Yes and I haven't heard a sound from her since the first shot."

Tynan frowned. "Have you got something to tie around this to stop the bleeding? It'll take us a good four hours to get where we can rest."

"Yes, of course I can, but, Ty, you need a doctor."

"About three of Dysan's men need an undertaker. Why did you come back? Why didn't you get out of here while you could?"

"We came back to save your ungrateful hide," she said as she tore off a long strip of her petticoat and began to bind his leg.

She'd barely finished tying his wound when Asher brought them to a halt that nearly sent Chris and Ty flying out the back door. Within seconds, Ash was at the back door.

"I have horses waiting. Pilar said there was an old man you knew who had a camp near here and you could lead us to him."

"How is she?" Ty asked.

Asher climbed to the top of the wagon and after a long, long moment of suspense, yelled down that she had been shot.

Ty, his wounded leg stiff in front of him, maneuvered himself out of the wagon. "How bad?" he asked quietly as he stood on the ground.

"She's alive but she's bleeding a great deal."

Chris was already climbing the little ladder that was attached to the side of the wagon and making her way up to Pilar. She gasped when she saw the woman. Pilar looked to be laying in a pool of blood, and her face was completely white.

"Ty," Chris called down, "she's wounded in her shoulder and she's unconscious. Her heartbeat is strong but she's weak. Can you help us get her down?"

"Yes," he said impatiently.

Chris worked as quickly as she could, wadding cloth against the wound and trying to tie it, but the location made a tourniquet impossible. The thud Chris heard on the roof must have been Pilar falling after she'd been shot. The guards had taken aim at the easiest target: the woman on the top of the wagon.

"We'll get her down to Ty," Chris said to Asher when she had Pilar taken care of as best she could. "Help him all you can as he's wounded too," she whispered.

Ty caught Pilar and held her then began walking with her to the waiting horses, the blood seeping from his leg, his forehead covered with sweat.

"Give her to me," Asher said, taking Pilar in his arms. "You lead."

Tynan merely nodded as he handed Pilar's inert body to Asher and started toward the horses. "There's some rough terrain ahead of us, but I don't think they'll be able to follow us. I don't want any heroics, you understand, Chris? If I tell you to go on ahead, I expect you to do it, you understand?"

"I can follow sensible orders. Shall we ride before Dysan's men find us standing here?"

Asher mounted, then Ty put Pilar in the saddle before him, so that he was holding her in place. "You think you can hold her?" Ty asked and there was a sadness in his voice that Chris was sure came from not being able to take care of her himself.

Within seconds, both she and Ty were mounted and they started to ride.

He was right when he'd said that it would be a difficult trip. They went straight up for a while, then across a boggy area that sucked at the horses' feet, then across several of Washington's cold, swift streams. For about a mile, they walked the horses through the water, hiding their trail from their pursuers.

Chris kept looking back at Pilar, whose eyes were still closed as Asher held onto her. She looked even paler.

"Watch where you're going," Tynan said in a tight-lipped way that told how much he was worried.

Once, they heard the dogs on a ridge above them and they moved their horses into the shelter of trees near a sharp rapids in the water. Chris's horse slipped but Tynan caught the reins and pulled her back to safety.

When the men and dogs were gone, they rode down the stream into the forest, going the opposite direction of their hunters.

It was nearly dark when Tynan stopped his horse and stiffly dismounted. "Wait here for me. He won't want any visitors."

"Who won't?" Chris asked but Tynan had already slipped into the trees and didn't answer her.

"The old man." It was a ragged whisper from Pilar. "Could I have some water?"

Quickly, Chris dismounted and removed her canteen from the back of the horse. Asher held it to Pilar's lips while Chris examined Pilar's wound. The bleeding had stopped, but she didn't look as if she had much strength left.

Chris's head came up as she heard the blast of a shotgun from somewhere close.

Pilar leaned back against Asher. "It's the old man," she said. "It's the man that found Tynan when he was born."

"The miner?" Chris asked.

"Whatever he calls himself. Mostly he sells whatever comes his way."

"Like six-year-old little boys," Chris said with disgust as she recapped the canteen.

Pilar didn't answer as she continued leaning against Asher, while Ash gave Chris a look that told her they needed to rest soon.

Tynan came back, moving silently through the trees, appearing almost as if from nowhere. "We have a place for a couple of days but no more," he said as he watched Chris remount and looked at Pilar with concern. He stayed back and let Asher go first, then started out beside Chris. "He's not like other people," he said to her, his eyes on the narrow trail ahead of them. "Don't turn your back on him and don't trust him. Don't tell him who your father is and don't think there's anything good about him. And don't ask him questions."

"You really hate him, don't you?" she whispered.

"Yeah, I really hate him," Ty said as he moved his horse forward to lead them up the steep hillside to the miner's cabin.

It was a nasty little building, filthy beyond belief, clinging to the side of a rock wall that fell down into a ravine below. Chris thought that the rock probably wanted to rid itself of something so dirty. There were half rotted carcasses around the doorway and the flies were so thick that they were like a black, moving curtain. Nearby were piles of animal skins and a pot of rancid meat. A scrawny dog that Chris had at first thought was dead was tied to the front wall.

"We'll leave Pilar out here while we clean this place up," Ty said as he yanked away the rope that held the starving dog in place. The poor animal limped to a pot of water with scum on it and began to lap greedily.

Ty helped Pilar off the horse while Chris stood and stared at the place, brushing away flies, trying to cover her nose at the smell.

"I ain't givin' no charity," came a voice from behind her. "You pay for what you take. I never asked for you to come here. What'd you let that dog loose for? He'll eat ever'thin' in sight."

Chris turned to see a gnarled little man with black, rotten teeth, his face twisted into an agony of misery as he saw that Tynan had begun to throw the rotten meat carcasses into the canyon below.

The old man ran toward Ty. "What are you doin'?" he whined. "That's my *food*. You're tryin' to kill me, just like you done your own mother. You wanta starve me."

Tynan ignored the old man's hands clutching at his arm and looked over his shoulder at Chris who was staring dumbfoundedly. "See to Pilar," he commanded, "and, Prescott, see if you can shoot us some fresh game. Chris, take that pot and scrub it out with sand and go up that hill to the stream and get some fresh water."

"Take, that's all you ever do. Took a woman's life

before you took your first breath. Now you want to take what's mine."

Tynan took a tool that had once been a shovel and began to use it to remove a half foot of debris from in front of the cabin, throwing it into the crevasse far below. At one animal carcass, he stopped to examine it, then tossed it to the dog that was cowering a few feet away, its breath coming quickly against its ribs.

The old miner made a lunge toward the dog to grab the meat from the starving animal, and the dog, reverting to instinct, began to fight for its life. As Chris watched, the old man took an ancient pistol from inside the layers of filthy clothes he wore and shot the dog in the leg. The animal began to whimper.

With a look of triumph, the old man took the half-rotten meat from the dog, put it under his arm, and started back toward the shack.

Tynan, with unhurried steps, walked to the old man, took the meat from him and went back to the dog. "Chris," he said as he examined the dog, "can you look at this? I don't think it's bad. He never could shoot."

It took Chris a moment to react and move from Pilar's side. With eyes wide, she went to where Ty kneeled by the dog.

"Put a bandage on its leg and, here." He handed her his gun. "If he bothers the dog again, shoot him. It won't be any great loss to the world."

Chris watched, with her mouth open, as Ty gave the dog the meat and the wounded animal began to eat.

Ty put his hand under her chin and shut her mouth. "With this many flies around here, you can't afford to be astonished. Fix the dog then go get us some water. And then there's the cabin to be cleaned. You think this place is bad, wait till you step inside."

261

"Does he have a name?" she asked, nodding toward the old man.

"Not any that he ever gave anybody. Of course, I never tried paying him for it."

"You mean, you've been around him since you were born and you don't know his name?"

"That's right."

"You came after my gold, didn't you?" the old man wailed. "You want everything I have."

"All I want is shelter in a place that's hard to find," Ty said as he went back to cleaning the area. "I sure as hell don't want anything else from you."

Chris saw that the dog was indeed only grazed then she went to get the water bucket. It was slippery with slime. "Ty, your leg," she said, looking back at him. The tourniquet was gone and there was dried blood about the wound but now, with this new activity, it was beginning to bleed again.

"I can't stop now," he said. "Go get the water."

As Chris took the bucket and started up the hill, the old man stopped in front of her. The foul smell that rose from him took her breath away. "He don't have a mother. He killed her."

Chris moved away from him as she'd moved away from the piles of rotting meat.

By the time she returned with the newly clean bucket and fresh water, Asher was back with a deer he'd shot and Tynan had cleaned a place under a lean-to for Pilar. Chris saw that his leg was bleeding steadily.

Asher prepared a fire and began to roast the meat while the old man crouched on the outside of the group watching them suspiciously.

Tynan eased himself down onto the ground near

where Pilar rested on a blanket covered pile of hay. For just a moment, Chris saw pain register on his face. It was growing dark now and the only light was from the fire.

"We have to make some plans," Ty said and he sounded very tired. "Prescott, we'll have to take turns keeping watch."

"Watch?" Chris asked. "But surely Dysan's men won't be able to find us here. The dogs won't be able to track us after the number of streams we crossed, and, Ty, you need to rest."

"I thank you for your concern, but it's not Dysan who needs watching. It's him." He nodded his head toward the old miner. "If he thinks there's a reward for us, he'll find whoever wants us and bring them here. We have to stay awake to make sure he doesn't leave."

"Oh," Chris said, taking meat from Asher and moving to lift Pilar. Tomorrow she'd try to make a broth but for now this would have to do. "Then as long as we stay here someone has to stay awake and watch him."

"If we want to stay alive," Ty said.

Asher cut off chunks of the roasted meat. "Pilar needs a doctor and she needs to rest. And you're in worse shape than you let on."

"I'll be all right," Ty said. "But I agree that we have to take care of Pilar, it's just that I don't know anywhere else that's as safe as this—or it would be safe if he weren't here."

Asher threw the old man a piece of meat as if he were a dog, and the man grabbed it, hiding it from the others, eating it with watchful eyes. "What we need is some help," Asher said as he looked at Chris. "If we could get a message to your father, he could send an army of men to escort us back to his place. I don't think even Dysan wants to take on Mathison's men."

Chris drew her knees to her chest and gave a little smile. "Yes, my father could defeat him. But he's there and we're here."

"You have to go get him, Prescott," Tynan said. "You have to leave the women and me here and travel as fast as you can and bring Mathison back."

"And leave you to the mercies of that?" Asher asked, motioning toward the old man. "Do you have any idea how many people are looking for you?"

Tynan looked toward the dark sky for a moment. "About half a dozen Chanrys, a hundred or so of Dysan's men and . . ."

"And Rory Sayers would probably like a piece of your skin," Chris added.

"And what was the name of that man on the far side of the rain forest?"

"Ah, yes," Chris smiled. "Hugh Lanier. I don't imagine he's over his anger at what I wrote." She smiled at Tynan, remembering the way he'd helped her that day.

Tynan leaned back against a post. "So half the world is looking for us, two of us are damaged, and we have a traitor—if he were given the chance to be—in our midst. It doesn't make for a secure, healthful future."

"I'll take him with me," Asher said softly. "I'll take the old man with me and leave the three of you here alone and I'll bring back Mathison with every man he can spare."

"He'll slit your throat the first time you turn your back on him or the first time you sleep."

"I'll not turn my back on him and if I sleep, I'll tie

him up. It's our only chance and you know it. You can't take care of him here and all I have to do is get him fifty miles south of here and then Mathison can have him. It's our only chance. One man might make it out of here, but not two women and a wounded man."

Chris could see the way Tynan was considering Asher's words. She could see how much he hated them, how much he hated being put in such a position. And she also realized that he must be hurt more than he was allowing them to know if he were so much as considering what Asher proposed.

"Ty, it's the only way," Chris whispered. "We can't move Pilar and we can't leave her here. Dysan is out there and someone has to go for help." She arched one eyebrow at him. "Are you afraid you won't get your pardon if someone else brings my father to me?"

Tynan looked at her for a long time before he spoke. "Prescott, you'll leave early in the morning. I'll stay awake tonight and watch the old man and you sleep. I want you rested in the morning. Now, the both of you go to bed."

Chapter Twenty-two

Once Tynan sat down, he didn't seem able to get up again. Chris rebandaged the wound in his leg, finding that the bullet wasn't in it as she'd feared. While she worked on him, he lay still, leaning back against the post, his eyes closed, seemingly unaware of Chris's hands on his thigh. She tried to touch him as little as possible, tried to not show how the sight of his torn flesh upset her.

"I don't think Prescott can handle the old man. Prescott's not mean enough. He's too trusting."

"Ty, how long did you spend with that man? Did you really have to live with him?"

"Off and on until I was six, but kids learn fast. It didn't take me long to learn that I had to take care of myself."

"As independent as you are, why didn't you run away when he . . . when he sold you? Couldn't you have gone back to Red's?"

Tynan opened his eyes and looked at her. "I was

266

drunk, and he kept me that way for two days before the"—Ty grimaced—"sale."

"But you were only six years old."

"I've never met a little kid yet that didn't like beer. You ought to get some sleep now. You'll need rest for tomorrow."

Standing, she took the bucket of bloody water and moved away from him, watching him as he leaned against the pole. He looked as if he were asleep but she could see the dark light of his eyes between his lashes. He planned to stay awake all night to protect them from the old man—but he didn't tie the man or incapacitate him, and she wondered why.

She moved away from Ty to go back to the spring to get fresh water.

"Chris."

She was startled to hear Asher's voice so near.

"May I speak to you?"

"You should be asleep. You have a hard ride ahead of you tomorrow and Ty says—"

"Ty says! That's all I hear, that Tynan says this and Tynan says that."

"He is the leader of this group," Chris said, "and it's been his decisions that have kept us from getting killed." She continued on her way to the spring.

He caught her arm. "I didn't mean to be angry. I guess I'm just jealous. Chris, the real reason I wanted to talk to you is . . ."

"Yes," she said, looking up at him in the moonlight. "What did you want to say to me?"

"I wanted to ask you to marry me."

Chris was taken aback for a moment. All she'd been able to think about for the last few days was getting away from Dysan. "Isn't this rather sudden?"

"You know it isn't. Chris, I've fallen in love with you, with your spirit and your courage. Any woman who'd chop through the back of a wagon to make herself heard is the woman I want to spend my life with, no milksop women for me."

"And it's not my father's money? Or the fact that he's offered you a position in his business? That doesn't make me more attractive to you?"

Asher opened his mouth to speak but nothing came out. Instead, he drew Chris to him and kissed her softly and gently. "At one time, I thought that I'd have married Del Mathison's daughter if she were as ugly as my father's favorite mule, but then I met you and everything changed. Chris, you're like no other woman I've ever met. I wish with all my heart that you'd marry me. And if it's your money you think I'm after, I'll give up all claim to it. I think that with you at my side, I could start over again, and this time I wouldn't fail."

Still holding her in his arms, he smiled down at her. "I don't think you'd allow any failure on my part. I think if there were a setback in my finances, you'd crack a whip over my head, and not allow me to give up."

She smiled back. "No, I don't guess I do give up, not if I want something badly enough." Suddenly, she thought of Tynan. "Unless I have to give up," she murmured.

"I think we'd make a good pair," he said. "We'd have my level-headedness and your spirit. I could keep your feet on the earth and you could prevent me from giving up when the going gets rough."

She laughed. "You make us sound like a merger."

He snuggled her closer. "Some mergers can be quite good. Chris, please say you'll think about it. I'll do whatever you want. If you want me to renounce your father's money, I'll do so. Whatever you say."

"That seems rather drastic and my father does want someone to help him run the place."

"Are you saying you'll marry me?" he asked, his eyes alight.

"Like hell she will," came Tynan's voice from behind them. "Get your hands off her, Prescott. And if you don't, I'll shoot them off."

Chris moved away from Asher. "You're supposed to be asleep."

"Is that what you were hoping? That I was asleep so you could meet him behind my back?"

"Now just one minute, Tynan," Asher said. "I have every right to do whatever Miss Mathison wants. After all, you were hired to help me win her. Oh, Chris," he said as he realized what he'd revealed.

"It's all right, I knew. Tynan, you have no right to interfere in what I do. Now, I want you to go back to—".

She didn't finish the sentence because Tynan grabbed her arm and pulled her to him. He couldn't walk very well as his leg was stiffening, but he could force her closer to him. "Prescott, go back to the camp and see to Pilar and watch the old man. I'll be there in a minute."

Asher started to protest, but one look at Tynan made him decide against it and he turned back toward the cabin.

"Get your hands off of me!" Chris said, trying to jerk away from him, but not succeeding. "You have no right to interfere in this. Besides, I believe my father hired you to *help* him fall in love with me."

"I don't even want to know how you found that out, but that was before . . ."

269

"Yes? That was before what?" She was looking up at him with anger flashing in her eyes.

He grabbed her to him, burying her face in his shoulder for a moment, then kissing her as if he were starving.

"Please don't, Ty," she said, her voice sounding as if she were in agony. "Please leave me alone." She tried to push away from him, but he wouldn't release her.

"Chris, I can't stand to see him touching you. I just can't stand it." His hands were going up and down her back, caressing her, touching her neck, his thumbs toying with her ears.

She managed to push away far enough to look at him. "*You* can't stand it? What right do you have to prevent me from doing anything? What right do you have to even voice an opinion? I made an absolute fool of myself over you and you threw everything in my face and now you stand here and tell me I can't talk to a man who has the most honorable of intentions."

"My intentions toward you are honorable. I've always been fair and honest with you. And now I'm saying that if Prescott touches you again, I'll shoot him. I can't be more honest than that."

"You!" she gasped and gave a lunge that separated her from him. "What you want from me isn't honorable. All you want is a . . . is for me to . . ." She was glad the darkness covered her red face.

"So what's wrong with that? You didn't seem to mind the last time. Ah, Chris, I don't want to fight. We had a good time that night and, besides, I haven't had any women since then."

Chris was sure that her anger was about to make her explode. "You haven't had any *women*—plural—since

270

then? Am I supposed to feel sympathy for you? Am I supposed to do what you want merely because you've been on the run and haven't had time to—"

"I had time," he said. "I just didn't want any that were offered."

Chris sputtered for a moment. Was he actually asking her for sympathy? "So now you're . . . and I'm supposed to . . . of all the dastardly, disgusting, repulsive things—I want you to know that Asher asked me to *marry* him. He didn't ask for a quick assignation, he wanted to marry me, to live with me forever."

"He wants to live with your father's money forever."

"So what's the difference between you two? He wants my money and you want my body. Neither of you seem to want *me*. Well, let me tell you, Mr. Tynan," she advanced on him, "I'm not sure I want either one of you. I certainly don't want what you offer."

He caught her arm. "Chris, you do want me. I know it. I can see it in your eyes. And I want you, so why not?"

She gave him a serious look, the muscles in her jaw working. "And do you plan to include marriage in your offer?" she asked softly.

He took a step back from her as if she'd just contracted a contagious disease. "Marriage? Chris, you know that's impossible. Your father would send me back to jail on a life sentence and then you'd have no husband. I couldn't do that to you."

"Men!" she gasped. "What convenient memories you have. My father said that you'd return to prison if you *touched* me, yet you were more than willing to risk that because it was something you wanted. But now you hold it up to me when the matter of marriage is

271

mentioned. Listen to me, Tynan, and listen good. I am *not* going to go to bed with you again and you can believe me." She turned on her heel and started up the hill toward the spring, grabbing the bucket in anger.

"You'll give in," Ty said after her, "and you'd better not let Prescott touch you."

"You hardheaded, vain . . . cowboy, I'm never going to let you touch me again!" She dug the bucket into the spring water, then, on impulse, stuck her face under the cold water. She wasn't sure whether she needed cooling off from her temper or from Tynan's kisses, but, whichever it was, her blood was steaming.

She stayed at the stream for a while before returning to the cabin and settling down beside Pilar to sleep. She woke repeatedly during the night, sometimes sitting up with a jolt and looking around her. Each time she woke, she saw that Tynan was still leaning against the post, still watching the old man.

By the time morning came, she felt as if she'd not been asleep at all. She sat up, rubbing her aching back and looked around her. Ty was gone from his post and Asher was in the yard in front of the cabin saddling his horse. She walked toward him.

"The old man's giving Ty trouble," Ash said in the way of a greeting. "We may have to tie him on his horse just to get him out of here."

Chris stifled a yawn. "I hope he ties him face down over the saddle."

Asher caught her arm and pulled her close to him. "This is the last time I'll see you for a while. I hope you'll miss me. I hope you'll think about my proposal. I hope you'll . . ." He began to kiss her neck. "I hope you'll say yes."

The next minute, Asher was on the ground as Tynan

jerked him away from Chris. Ty stood over him, feet apart, fists ready.

"Come on, Prescott, get up. You've been asking for this for a long time. Or aren't you man enough to maul somebody your own size? Do you only pick on women?"

"For heaven's sake!" Chris said, going to Asher to help him up.

Tynan advanced on the man.

"If you touch him again," she said, "so help me, I'll ride out of here with him. What in the world is wrong with you?"

Tynan lowered his fists and there was a bewildered expression on his face. "I don't know," he said in wonder. "Prescott, you better go now so you can use all the daylight. The old man will go with you but you'll have to watch him every minute. I think he understands now that we're hiding out so he'll do what he can to make money off that knowledge."

As Asher stood, Tynan looked a bit sheepish for a moment, then he turned back toward Chris. "You wouldn't go, would you? I mean, I'd have to bring you back and someone needs to stay with Pilar."

Chris looked at him for a long moment. "No," she said at last, "I won't leave. Not if you don't hit Asher again. Now, could you leave us alone? I'd like to say good-bye."

Tynan didn't move a step. "You can say good-bye right now. He has to leave."

"If you think—" Chris began, ready to give him a piece of her mind, but a call from Pilar stopped her. "Yes, I'm coming," she answered, then deliberately turned and put her arms around Asher, meaning to kiss him good-bye, and show Tynan that he had no right to give her orders. But her lips never reached Asher's because Tynan pulled her away from him and held her to him, her back against his front.

"Get on your horse, Prescott," he said in a deadly voice.

Asher hesitated for a moment, but, then, with a sigh, he put his foot in the stirrup. "We'll settle this later," he said, glancing back to the old man who was sitting atop Tynan's horse and ready to leave.

Tynan, still holding Chris, stepped back. "Make sure you watch him night and day. Don't give him a minute or he'll take all you have and maybe your life with it."

"Yeah," Asher muttered and, with one quick look at Chris, reined his horse away. "Come on, old man," he called over his shoulder and then was gone from sight.

Chris pushed away from Tynan. "Release me, you oaf!"

She turned to look at him, anger in her eyes. "What right do you think you have to tell me what to do? Just who do you think you are?"

Tynan looked completely confused, seemed to want to say something but, instead, turned on his heel and went up the hill toward the spring.

Chris stood there for a moment, glaring after him, before she went to Pilar.

"I thought there was going to be a fight there for a moment," Pilar said as Chris handed her a full canteen.

"I'd like to take a club to his head," Chris said. "He doesn't want me but then he hits anyone else who *does* want me."

Pilar leaned back against the hay as Chris began unbandaging her shoulder. "Oh, he wants you all right. He wants you badly."

"And I know exactly how he wants me." Pilar

smiled. "I've never seen him like this. Even that time with that rancher's daughter, he wasn't like this. We all hoped then that he was going to settle down, but it didn't work out."

"Was that when he ended up in prison?"

"Red tell you about it?"

"Most of it. Pilar, how do you know Tynan? Why were you living with him at Owen Hamilton's?"

"He saved my husband's life."

Chris stopped cleaning Pilar's wound. "Your husband?"

"I used to work with Red when I was younger. Tynan was there, the prettiest, sweetest little boy you ever met, and we all adored him. After the old man took him away when he was six, I hardly ever saw him again. And when I did see him, I'd see that he'd grown harder. He'd seen a lot in his short life and it'd made him cynical. But by then I'd married a rancher and we had a couple of kids of our own and I wanted to forget where I'd known Ty."

"Children?" Chris whispered.

Pilar smiled. "Two little boys. They're nine and seven now." She paused a moment. "One day I was in town and I saw Tynan on the street. He grinned at me and started toward me, and all I could think of was that he was going to let the 'good' townspeople know where I came from and they were going to see that I wasn't the respectable rancher's wife they thought I was. I hate to say it, but I ducked into a store and acted as if I didn't know him. Ty was the perfect gentleman and two days later when I ran into him again, he acted as if he'd never seen me before in his life."

"So how did he save your husband's life?"

"I don't like what I did then. I wouldn't speak to Ty

275

on the street but a week later, when my husband was being threatened by a big rancher trying to drive us off our little place, I didn't hesitate to ask Ty for help—and Tynan didn't hesitate to come to my aid."

"But later, when he asked you to help him get into Hamilton's house, you agreed."

"I didn't even ask what he wanted. I just kissed my family good-bye and went with him. Jimmy didn't ask what he wanted either, because he knew he could trust Ty."

Chris's hands paused in rebandaging Pilar's shoulder. "Why *did* he want you to come and pretend to be his wife?"

Pilar smiled. "He wouldn't say, wouldn't answer me when I asked him. But one day, he muttered something about a curvy little blonde who was trying to tempt him out of his soul."

"Hmph!" Chris said. "Some tempting I've done! I made the fatal error of liking him, just plain liking him. I liked the way he took on responsibility when he was leading us through the rain forest. And he helped me when I needed him."

"And then he also happens to be the most beautiful man alive," Pilar added.

"That had nothing to do with it. He was so quiet. With most men who are silent, I usually find that they just plain don't have anything to say, but I thought that maybe Tynan did have something to say, but he was repressing it. I'm not sure what it was, but I was certainly drawn to him."

"Was?" Pilar asked. "You aren't any longer?"

Chris rocked back on her heels. "He isn't any different from other men. He only wants one thing. I thought he felt the same way about me that I did about

276

him, but he told me he wanted nothing to do with me, that I was wrong about him. He told me to leave him alone—except of course I was free to . . ."

"To go to bed with him?"

Chris nodded, her head down. "I'm not any different from a hundred other women to him."

"I've never seen him act like he did a few minutes ago with another woman. I've never seen even the slightest sign of jealousy before. Are you sure you aren't different?"

Chris stood, taking the bowl of dirty water with her. "I'm quite sure. He's made it clear what he wants from me and he just doesn't want anyone else to have what he's being denied. Tynan doesn't love me any more than he loves . . . than he loves that old dog. Now, I want you to rest and I'm going to cook something, if I can find anything around here that's edible."

"Anything will be all right," Pilar said thoughtfully. "Ty will help you. He is quite capable of handling anything."

"He can't handle love," Chris said softly. "He can't find love at the end of a gun or by using his fists, so he runs away from it. Go to sleep now."

Chapter Twenty-three

Chris spend an hour trying to make a stew with the few ingredients from around the cabin and from the saddle bags. There hadn't been much time to pack when they'd been escaping Dysan and now they were feeling the lack of provisions. She looked at the cabin and decided to see if there was anything inside it. So far, the smell of the place had kept her from getting too close to it.

Holding her breath, she went to the door and looked inside. This looked as if it were the old man's treasure trove. He seemed to have kept everything he'd ever owned. No matter how worn out it was, how deteriorated, how many bugs infested it, the old man had kept it.

Chris glanced over her shoulder toward where Pilar was resting and she felt a renewal of courage. What was a little unpleasant smell or a few crawly things compared to a human's comfort?

She took the shovel that Tynan had leaned against the outside wall of the cabin and began to carve a way into the interior.

Two hours later, she had made a huge pile outside by the edge of the cliff. She wasn't going to push anything over until she'd had a chance to inspect it in the daylight, but, mostly, there seemed to be improperly cured hides and hardened pieces of food that were covered with ants.

In the back corner of the single room, she found a little wooden crate, the kind used to ship fragile items across the sea. Lifting it, she carried it outside into the sunlight.

It had a big lock on it, but, like everything else in the cabin, the lock was rusting away, so, after a few minutes of work, she managed to open it. There were a few dollars inside, with mold growing on the bills, a big rock that looked as if it were solid gold, and in the bottom was a photograph of a young, pretty woman. Chris held it to the light, wiped the mold off a corner, and studied the woman. She looked happy and pleased about something and ready to take on the world. With a smile, Chris put the photo in her pocket and began to close the box.

"Anything interesting?" came Ty's voice from behind her.

"You should be sleeping," she said. "You were awake all night."

"I got enough. What are you doing? I never saw a woman who liked to snoop more than you do."

"I wasn't snooping, I was cleaning."

With an infuriatingly knowing little smile, he sat down beside her. "Cleaning inside locked boxes?" he asked, nodding toward the big, rusty lock on the ground beside her. "Find anything interesting?"

"Only about two pounds of gold," she said smugly, holding out the big rock to him. "This is why your miner doesn't want to leave this place."

Ty took the rock, leaned back on one elbow and looked at it. "Fool's gold," he said. "The old man doesn't know gold when he sees it. Up on the side of the hill, there's a place where he's been digging for years. He was digging it when I was a kid."

Chris took the rock from Tynan. "If there's no gold, why does he stay here? Why does he live like this?"

"He believes there is gold and facts have nothing to do with this man's beliefs. As for why he lives like this, he's just afraid to let anything go. If he can't sell it today, he'll keep it until it's worth something."

"Like babies. They're not worth much as newborns, but strong little boys can work." Tynan didn't reply to her, just gazed at a bird overhead, seeming to be content to lie still for the moment. "How has he lived up here? He must have had money for food from somewhere. Has he always stolen things and sold them?"

Tynan took a while to answer. "He used to steal but now I send him money when I can."

"You? But why? After what he did to you and the way you hate him, I'd have thought you'd do nothing for him."

"That old man is the closest thing to a father I've ever had. Besides, I didn't want him selling any more children."

"I wonder how someone like him got to be the way he is. I wonder what awful things happened to him. I bet he was in love once. Maybe he lost her and never recovered."

Ty was looking at her as if she'd lost her mind. "What makes you think that old man ever loved anybody?"

"I found a picture of the woman he loved."

"Let me see it," Ty said softly and Chris gave him the photograph. He looked at it a long while before handing it back to her. "He said he threw it over the side and I believed him."

"You've seen this?"

"It was my most treasured possession for most of my life."

She hesitated. "Who is this woman?"

"I've been told she's my mother."

"Your mother? But, Ty, don't you realize that if you have this maybe you can find out who she is? Find out who you are?"

"I know who I am," he said with a set jaw.

Chris looked at the picture for a while. "What's her name?"

"I have no idea."

"But didn't you ask?"

He looked at her. "Who was I going to ask? The old man told me she said one word before she died and that was, 'Tynan.' "

"Did you show the photo to the women in . . . to Red and the others?"

"Sure, they saw it, but no one knew who she was. They thought it was all real romantic and they kept buying frames for the picture, then the old man'd come and take the frame and sell it. It was a great source of income to him for years."

Chris turned the picture over. "It says something on the back, but I can't make it out."

"Sa. It has the letters Sa on the back and the rest is faded. I used to imagine that my mother's name was Sarah."

"You've spent a lot of time looking at this, haven't you?"

Tynan didn't answer her, but lay on his back and looked at the sky. "I missed seeing the sky while I was in prison. What you can see is covered by iron bars. And I didn't like the noise either."

Chris wanted to hear more about the photo. "How did the old man get this picture? If she had this, she must have had other things too."

"He sold everything else, even her clothes and her underwear. I imagine he threw her naked body off the side there. Or else it's still around here."

"Tynan! How can you be so crass? The woman was your mother, and she died giving birth to you."

He sat up. "She died from three bullet wounds in her back."

"But who wanted to kill her? Why?"

"Is there anything to eat around here? Maybe I could scout up some game."

"Are you going to answer me? Do you have any idea why someone would shoot a woman who was carrying a child?"

He looked down at her. "Why do men cheat at cards? Why do men get drunk and try to kill each other? I don't know. She wandered in here with three big holes in her back, lay down, gave birth to me, said 'Tynan,' then died. That's the sum of all I know. The miner watched her give birth, planned to leave both her and the kid, but then he thought he could sell what clothes she hadn't bled on and the screaming brat, so he stripped her and carried me down the mountain. That's it, Chris, that's all there is to tell. He sold everything except the picture. Nobody wanted a photo of a woman they didn't know, so I took it one summer when he had me up here working. Now, can I eat?"

Chris sat on the ground and looked at the picture. "She's a very pretty woman."

"Was. She *was* pretty. She's been dead for a long time. Chris, why are you so all-fired interested in my mother?"

"I'm interested in—" She stopped abruptly. She'd almost said that she was interested in him. "I'm a reporter," she said, rising. "I'm curious, that's all. I'm curious about everything."

"Well, I'm curious about what's cooking in that pot." He moved closer to her. "Maybe you could go hunting with me."

"I can't leave Pilar."

"She can go with us. It'll do her good to walk around some."

"I don't think so. I need to clean up around here and . . ."

Ty moved even closer to her, then put his hand to the side of her face. "Chris, please go with me. I promise I'll behave. I won't do anything you don't want me to."

She took a step away from him. He could use that voice of his to make a person's resolve melt. "I shouldn't. I should . . ."

"Should what?" he asked, following her as she backed away.

"Chris!" Pilar called. "I'd love to get some exercise. Could you go with Ty for my sake?"

"I . . . I guess so," she began, looking into Tynan's

smiling eyes. "But don't you try anything," she warned. "I'm not going to give into you."

His eyelids lowered. "Sweetheart, I haven't even *asked* you yet."

After Tynan had eaten most of the stew Chris had cooked, he took his rifle, helped Pilar to stand and started up the little trail behind the cabin. Chris complained twice about his walking on his injured leg, but he just grinned at her.

"Remember the time you and the Chanry boys robbed that bank down in Texas and—" Pilar began.

"Robbed the bank?" Chris gasped. "Robbed a bank!"

Ty winked at Pilar. "She thinks I'm as clean as a new snow, that I'm innocent on all counts."

"I've seen you shoot people. I took him to a picnic and he got into a fight with a man and the man got shot. On a church picnic, mind you."

"Rory Sayers," Ty said to Pilar as if that were answer enough.

"I never met anyone who was asking for it more," Pilar said. "Ty, didn't you have a garden up here when you were a boy?"

Chris trailed along behind the two of them and felt as if she'd just entered a party and she was the only one who didn't know everyone. Pilar and Ty talked easily about things that were meaningless to her. They exchanged names of people and places, fantastic happenings such as repeated brushes with the law, shootouts, the names of outlaws she'd only read about.

At the top of the hill, Tynan moved some underbrush about until they saw a little clearing. "It was here," he said, "and I planted carrots and potatoes and strawberries. The strawberries didn't make it and the rabbits kept eating the tops of the carrots as soon as they grew above the ground. Look at this," he said, holding up a rusty can that had been flattened. "One of my first targets. I used to practice up here for hours."

"Not much else to do," Pilar said. "Is the old man's gold mine near here?"

"Not far, just along that trail."

Pilar turned and started walking but Chris held back. Tynan went to her, and, before she could stop him, he put his arms around her. "Feeling a little lost?"

She pushed at him but he still held her. "Of course not."

"We could tell Pilar to go away and you and I could go into the bushes. I know a place that was made for making love. It's quiet, secluded, near a little stream and flowers grow there all summer long. Would you like to make love on a bed of flowers?"

"No I wouldn't," she said, but there wasn't much conviction in her voice. "I don't want to be any man's woman of no morals."

"Morals? What do morals have to do with making love? Chris, honey, I could make you feel so good. We could make each other feel good."

She twisted away from him. "Leave me alone, Tynan. I'm not going to be one of your women and you'd better get used to the idea. I'm going to go home to my father and I just might stay there and marry some rancher and have a dozen or so children."

"Who do you have in mind?" he asked angrily. "Prescott?"

"I'm sure Asher would make a fine husband and he has asked me and I just might say yes. What does it matter to you, anyway? You don't want to be saddled with a wife and kids. You've made your choice and I've made mine, so what do you have to complain about?"

She could see the anger in his eyes.

"You call yourself a woman of morals, but what's the difference between selling yourself for a few bucks and selling yourself for a piece of paper and a gold ring?"

She glared up at him. "At least *I* get to choose what the price will be—not you." She swept past him and continued up the trail after Pilar.

She found Pilar standing outside a dark hole that seemed to be the mine entrance, holding a rock like the one Chris had found in the chest in the cabin.

"It's full of this stuff. I guess he thinks it's gold and everybody is just too stupid to know that it is." Pilar looked up at Chris. "Uh-oh, it looks like you two have been at it again."

"No, we haven't. He is the most stubborn man. He can't seem to get it through his thick skull that when I say no, I mean no. Hasn't *any* woman ever said no to him before?"

"I doubt it," Pilar said seriously. "But then I've never seen him pursue a woman before you either. He usually just sits down and that face of his does the rest. At worst, he has to open his mouth and speak and if there's one woman who hasn't yet thawed, she will when she hears that voice of his."

"I expect more from a man than just beauty and a nice voice. And Tynan doesn't seem capable of giving that."

In the distance, they heard the sound of a rifle shot. "I think he got us something to eat. Let's go and meet him," Pilar said.

When Chris seemed determined to stay where she

was, Pilar took her arm. "In a few days your father will be here and you'll never have to see Ty again. This is the first rest any of us have had in ages, so let's make the most of it, all right?"

Reluctantly, Chris allowed Pilar to pull her forward. She wasn't about to show anyone how the thought of never seeing Ty again made her heart jump into her throat.

When they found Tynan he was already skinning a small deer and Chris built a fire. Soon the smell of roasting venison filled the air.

"Nice place, isn't it?" Ty asked, handing Chris a piece of meat.

She looked around and realized that this was the place he'd just described—the place where he'd wanted to make love to her. "It's all right," she said coolly. "Pilar, why don't you tell us about the joys of married life? And about your children? How old are they?"

She ignored Tynan's heartfelt groan as she turned her head and began listening to a homesick Pilar as she told about her husband and children. She didn't gloss over the hardship of their lives, or dismiss the constant poverty and struggle, but there was a lovely sense of togetherness that Chris knew she wanted in her life. In turn, Pilar asked Chris about her newspaper stories and said how exciting all that must be.

"It was, but I'm ready to settle down."

"She's been ready ever since a certain party jumped out of a clothes wardrobe," Tynan said from behind her, his voice heavy with sarcasm. "She thinks that if a man touches her, he has to marry her."

"That's not true at all!" Chris said, turning on him. "I don't know why I ever thought I was in love with you. You are insufferably vain and are too used to

287

getting your own way. I doubt if I'd marry you now if you were to beg me."

"Don't hold your breath. A week from now, I'm going to be free. I won't have the responsibility of taking care of some spoiled little rich girl who thinks she can have whatever—or whoever—she wants merely by asking. I'm going to be *free,* you hear me? Not you or anybody else is going to take away my freedom."

"Stop it, both of you," Pilar said. "You sound like my two boys. Look, we have to spend the next few days together so why don't we try to get along? Ty, you're probably angry because you haven't had any sleep and your leg hurts. Why don't you lay your head in Chris's lap and she'll tell us a story? I'd offer my lap but I plan to stretch out here and sleep myself."

Chris didn't look at Tynan and there was a long moment of silence. "All right," she said at last. "Maybe we do need some rest. You may use my lap."

"Only if you swear this won't be taken as a marriage proposal."

"If you were one of my children," Pilar said, "I'd smack you for that. Now lay down there and behave yourself."

Chris leaned back against a tree and Tynan lay his head in her lap. For a moment, they were very stiff, touching as little as possible.

"I read a book in French last year, *Le Comte de Monte Cristo,* I could tell that story," Chris said.

"Only if the people don't get married and live happily ever after," Tynan said, his head turned, his eyes closed.

"It's a story about greed, betrayal, infidelity, murder and revenge. I think it might be your autobiography."

"Sounds all right," he said, snuggling his head in her lap.

"I'm sure the French nation will be pleased that you approve." She started her story, telling of the revenge that began over two men in love with the same woman.

"Figures," Ty grunted, but said nothing else while Chris's voice began to soften as she told the story.

Within minutes, she heard the soft sounds of Pilar's breathing as she slept in the drowsy afternoon. Tynan also seemed to be asleep, and, feeling safe, she began to stroke his hair back from his face. He looked so young with his face relaxed. There was a dirty bandage on his leg, dirty from his constant moving about the forest, showing through the hole in his trousers that the bullet had made.

She kept on with her story, even though she knew that both her listeners were asleep, but she liked stories and she liked to tell them. At the tragic end of the story, she stopped, her hand on the side of Tynan's face, her fingers buried in the curls of his dark hair, and listened to the birds.

"I liked that," he said softly into the stillness.

"I thought you were asleep," she said and started to move her hand away.

He caught it in his own. "No, I wanted to hear the story. A store clerk told me that at about the time I was born, the miner sold him a book. I always wondered if it was a book from my mother and, if it was, what it was. I've always liked stories." Idly, he began to kiss her fingertips, as if it were the most natural thing in the world to do.

"Will you stop that?"

"Chris, if I were going to get married, I swear, you'd

289

be the first woman I'd consider. In fact, thinking about living with you is the most tempting offer I've ever had. You're pretty, enthusiastic in bed—"

She gave a sharp look at Pilar but she seemed to be sound asleep.

"And you're the most interesting woman I've ever met. I've talked to you and told you things I've never told anybody, but, the truth is, I'm just not marriage material. I don't think I could stay in one place for very long—that is, if I ever get out of jail where your father would throw me if I dared think I was going to marry his precious daughter. Don't you see that it just wouldn't work?"

Chris didn't let the anger she felt show. It seemed that men could rationalize anything. He didn't want to get married—was probably terrified of the idea—so he tried to tell her that he couldn't because he was only thinking of her. "I understand completely," she said with sympathy in her voice. "You don't want to get married and I refuse to sleep with a man who won't marry me. We'll leave it at that."

He turned his head to look up at her. "But, Chris, shouldn't we take what happiness we can find? When we can find it? Before we're separated forever and never see each other again?"

She gave him her sweetest smile. "Not on your life."

For a moment, she thought he was going to start yelling at her again, but there was just the hint of a smile on his full lips. "You can't blame a man for trying." He turned his head again and resumed kissing her fingertips. "By my calculations, we have at least four more days before Prescott returns with your father. Who knows what will happen in that time?"

"I know what will *not* happen," she said smugly, but

Tynan didn't seem to believe her as he began applying his teeth to her sensitive palm.

"There you are, old man," Asher Prescott said as he readjusted the smelly man's bindings for the third time. There was a part of Asher that was bothered by what they'd done: they'd taken the man from his home and now he was being bound hand and foot, yet the old man had done nothing to merit such abuse. So, when the old man had complained that the ropes were too tight, Asher had had pity on him and loosened them.

"I'm going to get some sleep now," Asher said, rubbing his eyes. He'd been in the saddle for almost two days and he knew that if he didn't rest, he'd never make it to Del Mathison's house.

With one last look of sympathy at the old man who huddled against a tree, his little dark eyes looking suspicious, Asher settled down to sleep, using his saddle as a pillow.

The old man seemed as if he too slept, until he heard the soft snores from Asher, then he wiggled his hands and the ropes fell away. "Fool," he muttered, looking at Asher's sleeping form with contempt as he untied his feet. "Fool."

He stood, making no noise at all, looked around a bit until he saw a large rock nearby then picked it up and crept toward Asher. He brought the rock crashing down on Asher's head as he slept.

The old man stood over Ash for a moment, looking at the unconscious form before ransacking his pockets. It took him only fifteen minutes before he'd taken everything of value from Asher, leaving him lying there in his underwear only, his saddle and gun gone, no money, no boots. For a moment, the old man contemplated taking his underwear or at least cutting the buttons off, but he heard a horse in the distance and decided to get out of there.

As he mounted one horse, leading the other one, he began to mutter, "You think you're so smart, Mr. Mother-Killer Tynan, but I know somebody that'll pay to know where you are. I know somebody. I'll show you." He cursed and muttered as he traveled north toward the Dysan estate.

Chapter Twenty-four

Chris tried her best to stay away from Tynan for the next two days, but it was almost impossible to do. If she went for water, there he was. If she stopped for a moment to look at the scenery, there he was, his eyes on her in invitation. Once, she jumped when she heard something in the underbrush and Ty was there to put his arms around her and hold her. They heard shots in the distance on the morning of the second day and her heart was in her throat as Tynan, with rifle in hand, crept down the steep path to see who it was. She nearly cried with relief when he came back to tell her that it was only hunters and they were far away.

"Worried about me?" he asked, his eyes hot and showing his desire for her.

Chris picked up her skirts and fled from him.

"Anything wrong?" Pilar asked innocently. She'd taken over the cooking ever since Chris had ruined some of their precious flour trying to make biscuits.

"That man is the worst!" she said, her heart pounding.

"He certainly does like you."

"Well, I don't like him."

Pilar snorted. "Didn't your mother teach you not to lie?"

"I think there were many things my mother didn't teach me," Chris said softly. "Such as how to say no to persuasive gunslingers. Pilar, I think I'm weakening. Two more days of this and I won't be able to say no to anything he asks of me."

"I have an idea Ty knows that."

"Well, I have to be strong. I am *not* going to give into him and that's final. No matter what he says to me, no matter how he looks at me, I'm not going to give into him." She looked at Pilar with great sadness and worry in her eyes. "But if he kisses the back of my neck one more time, I'm lost."

Pilar turned back to her biscuits with a smile on her face.

Chris succeeded in staying away from Ty for the rest of the day but that night he asked her to take a walk with him.

"I didn't ask you to run off with me, Chris, just take a walk," he said when he saw her lips form the word 'no.' "I swear I won't touch you since I know you can't trust yourself with me, but at least—"

"Can't trust myself with you! I most certainly can trust myself with you. I could spend the rest of my life on a tropical island with you and still resist you," she lied.

"That's great," he said with a grin. "Then you can go with me into the moonlight right now."

Chris knew she'd talked herself into a corner and so

she appealed to Pilar for help, but Pilar refused to go with them, saying that her arm hurt too much. Of course it hadn't hurt while she'd pounded dough, but now it was too painful for her to even move.

Reluctantly, Chris started walking up the little trail toward the spring, Tynan behind her.

"Are we competing in a road race or are you afraid to walk beside me?" he asked.

She stopped and turned toward him. "Of course I'm not afraid to walk with you. It's just that you don't realize how slow your sore leg makes you."

"Is that it?" he said, smiling in a knowing way. He took her arm in his. "Then maybe you should help poor little invalid me," he said.

They walked together for a few moments, Chris trying to stay away from him in spite of their locked arms.

"A few weeks ago, I couldn't get rid of you. Every time I turned around, there you were, demanding that I take off my shirt or shoes, and the first few times I saw you, you weren't wearing a stitch of clothing. Now, you'll hardly get near me."

"That was before," she said, looking straight ahead.

"Before the night in the logger's cabin? Before the night we made love and had such a wonderful time?"

"It wasn't such a wonderful time to you. You told me you wanted nothing to do with me, that I was just one of many women to you."

"Maybe I was a little hard on you that night, but you scared me to death with your talk of marriage and kids. Can't you forget that and we could start over? We were getting on so well until you decided you just had to put that noose around my neck."

She pulled her arm away from his. "I don't want to

put a noose around your neck. Marriage is different. It's for two people who love each other and I stupidly thought that's what we did that night—made love. I was in love with you or I wouldn't have done that . . . I wouldn't have let you touch me. But it wasn't love to you. You don't love me, you never have. You got what you wanted, but I didn't."

She turned away to hide her tears.

He pulled her to him, turning her so that her face was buried in his chest. "Chris, I don't think I've ever had a woman in love with me before, and I have no idea what it means to be in love. I'm sorry, I don't mean to hurt you. Maybe you just think you're in love with me because I can handle a gun and I'm not like anyone you ever met before and—"

She looked up at him. "I've met hundreds of gun-slingers and hundreds of outlaw criminals and I resent your telling me that I don't know my own mind. I can tell you that—"

She stopped because Tynan kissed her, hungrily drinking from her lips, caressing her back, pushing her hips into his, trying to envelop her with his hard, hot body. Chris knew she wouldn't last long if he continued touching her.

"Please don't," she whispered when his lips moved to her neck. "Please don't touch me. I can't bear it. I can't resist you."

"I don't want you to," he said as his teeth took her earlobe.

It was when his lips touched the corner of her eye and he tasted a salty tear that he stopped. Abruptly, he drew away from her. "Go on then," he said with suppressed anger in his voice. "Go back to your cold bed and stay there alone."

Chris's tears began in earnest then and she fled down the steep, dark path to the cabin. Pilar didn't say a word as Chris fell down onto the pallet beside her.

Chris cried for a long time before she made a decision. She didn't care whether he married her or not, and she didn't care if he loved her or not. Right now all she felt for him was desire and she wanted it to be the way it was that night in the logger's cabin. She wanted to feel his hands on her body, wanted him to make love to her again.

Sniffing, but feeling better now that there was no more indecision, she got up and left the lean-to shelter. She knew that Tynan slept not far from them, a little way into the trees so that, should anyone come to the cabin during the night, he'd not be seen. She went to his sleeping place but he wasn't there.

Slowly, with deliberation, she removed all her clothing, stretched out on his blankets and waited for him. When he didn't come, she went to sleep, smiling at the thought of how he'd waken her.

"Chris," Tynan said, pulling her into his arms. "Oh my beautiful, lovely Chris."

Sleepily, she opened her eyes. It was daylight, the birds were singing, the smell of the early morning forest was all around them—and Tynan's hands were on her body, pushing away the covers and caressing her skin. His hands ran over her hips with the eagerness of a boy's with his first puppy.

"You came to me," he whispered. "You came to me. I didn't sleep last night. I just wandered in the forest. Oh Chris, you're driving me crazy. My beautiful, beautiful Chris, you are making me more miserable than when I was in prison."

Chris could feel her skin glowing with the joy of his

words. She sincerely hoped that she was making him miserable—at least as miserable as he was making her.

He brought her head up to his and kissed her as if he never meant to let her go, his hands in her hair.

Her arms went around his neck to pull him close. This is what she'd wanted for so long, but what she'd been fighting against for what seemed to be forever.

He stretched her out on the blankets and moved to lay beside her, touching her gently, while, at the same time, removing his own shirt.

With his leg between hers, he rubbed his rough clad skin against hers while kissing her.

Abruptly, he pulled away from her and put his head up as if he were listening. "I have to go. Someone's out there."

"It's just Pilar," she said, trying to pull him back down to her. "She won't come here."

Tynan moved away from her and pulled his shirt back on. "Someone's coming up the trail." He gave Chris a look of resignation. "It's my luck that it's your father here all ready." Chris thought he looked on the verge of tears. "You'd better get dressed. If it's not him, we can continue this later and if it is, he might not stop to ask questions if he found his little daughter kissing the hired hand." When she opened her mouth to speak, he stopped her. "Don't give me any argument, and don't make this harder for me, just please get dressed and let me see who this is."

Tynan moved away from her, standing and watching her with eyes that bore an expression of sadness, desire and pain. When she was dressed, he grabbed her arm and pulled her to him. "I've aged twenty years since I met you. I hope with all my might that this is *anybody* except your father." After a quick kiss, he released her, took her hand and led her into the cabin clearing.

Chris could see Pilar's sleeping form under the lean-to.

"Go look in my saddle bags and you'll find a pair of field glasses. Bring them to me."

Chris ran to do what he asked. Pilar raised on one elbow to look at her.

"Happy this morning?" Pilar asked.

"I've been happier," Chris said, searching inside the saddle bags. "I would be extremely happy if Tynan'd bothered to return to his sleeping roll last night."

Pilar groaned, then asked, "What's going on now?"

"Ty says he hears someone coming up the trail. I haven't yet heard anything but he's gone to see. Ah, here they are."

"I'm coming with you," Pilar said and was out of her sleeping pallet in a second and was soon running down the hill behind Chris.

Tynan was stretched out on a rock, as flat and as unnoticeable as a lizard and he had to call to the women before they saw him. "It's them," he said with great sadness in his voice. "I knew it would be." He reached out his hand to Chris for the glasses.

Chris and Pilar climbed on the rock beside him. "You're sure it's my father?" Chris asked, excited.

"Whoever it is, I hope they've brought us some supplies," Pilar said.

"From the size of the group, I think Mathison's brought his entire ranch."

Chris took the glasses from him. Her father was unmistakable, sitting on top of the horse that looked too small for him, riding with his back as straight as a railroad tie—and even at this distance he looked angry. She put the glasses down and saw that Ty was looking at her with a teasing smile on his face.

"Want to borrow my gun to protect yourself?" he asked, one eyebrow raised.

"Who's the man with him?" Pilar asked, looking through the glasses.

"Never saw him before," Ty answered.

Chris heaved herself up from the rock. "I guess I better get this over with. If either of you have delicate sensibilities, you'd better leave now. My father's temper is . . ." She couldn't think of anything that would adequately describe it.

She took a deep breath for courage, then started down the hill toward her father and the men who rode with him. She was hesitant at first, but as he came more clearly into view, she began to pick up speed until he saw her.

Del Mathison spurred his horse forward in a burst of speed that left the others standing.

Chris lifted her skirts and took off running as fast as her legs would carry her—and Del's horse came charging toward her. When he reached her, he didn't slow, but extended his arm and hauled her up to toss her in the saddle behind him. It was a trick he'd taught her when she was a child, and it'd come in handy in her life, such as the time Tynan had run his horse through the freight office.

As Chris held onto her father, she saw that Ty had followed her down the hillside, gun drawn, protecting her as she'd run away from the shelter of the camp. She turned to see the man who'd been riding beside her father stop and help Tynan mount behind him.

Del didn't waste any time when he reached the cabin. Before he even dismounted, he began yelling at Chris.

"Of all the damn fool, stupid things you've ever done, this is the worst. So help me, I'm never going to let you out of my sight again. You and your mother's whole family, none of you ever had a lick of sense."

Chris stood on tiptoe and put her arms around his neck. She was glad to see that he looked as good as he always did: big, handsome, with the head of a lion, thick gray hair spreading out like a mane around his handsome face.

He hugged her back for a moment, then pushed her away. "Do you know what hell you've put me through? Do you have any idea the number of people that've come to me and told me you were within inches of being killed?"

"How many?" she asked solemnly.

"Don't you get smart with me, young lady, I'll do what these men *should* have done with you. Where is that young pup I sent after you? He was supposed to *protect* you."

Tynan stepped forward. The area in front of the cabin was filling with men and their horses. "Are you asking for me?"

Del looked Tynan up and down, took in the dirty bandage on his thigh. "I see she's about done you in, too."

Tynan straightened. "I take full responsibility for everything that's happened. There were several times when I had the opportunity to get her back safely."

"Hmph!" Del snorted. "You couldn't very well control her when you were in jail. And what's this I hear about you two being engaged?"

Chris held her breath as she looked from her father to Tynan. It looked as if Ty weren't going to say anything, and Chris suddenly realized the seriousness of this moment. If she said they were engaged, her father could send him back to jail. She thought of Ty's back as it'd been in the rain forest. She thought she could control her father, but she wasn't positive. What if she were wrong? If she were, then Ty would be returned to prison.

"We're not engaged," she said softly. "I just said that to prevent a fight. He's been a perfect gentleman at all times and he did everything he could to protect me. He even saved me from Dysan."

Chris watched her father as he continued to study Tynan and after a moment, he grunted, but made no other comment.

"I'm hoping that Chris will accept my proposal," said someone behind her and she turned to see Asher standing there. There was a bandage across his forehead. With a smile of possession, he put his arm around Chris's shoulders. Her father looked at her as he had when she was a child, and she knew he was trying to figure out if she was telling the truth or making up one of her highly imaginative stories. Chris couldn't meet his eyes, so she looked down at her hands clasped in front of her.

Pilar broke the silence. "Let me introduce myself," she said, moving toward Del, hand outstretched. "I'm Pilar Ellery. We've never met, but I've certainly heard a great deal about you. You wouldn't happen to have some food in those saddle bags, would you? We're all starving."

Del shook her hand, but he didn't smile at her, and

Chris knew that he was upset, deeply upset, if he didn't smile at a pretty woman.

She moved away from Asher's proprietary grasp and slipped her arm through her father's. "I'm sorry I caused you so much trouble. I didn't mean to."

Del looked at her for a long moment and she saw a sadness in his eyes. Was something troubling him besides her being in danger?

"Miss Mathison, may I introduce myself?"

Before her stood the man who'd ridden beside her father. He was about the same age as her father, a tall, slim man with black hair that was graying at the temples. He had the lean, hard look of a man who was used to physical exercise, but at the same time, he had an elegance that could only have come from generations of selective breeding. Even though he looked at home with a gun slung around his hip, she could easily imagine him on a dance floor or holding a wine glass.

"I am Samuel Dysan," he said in a deep, rich voice.

"Samuel Dysan?" She looked behind him toward Tynan, then back at the older man. "You're the one Beynard . . ."

"He is seeking me?" The man looked surprised.

"I heard him saying that he'd searched for years for Samuel Dysan."

Sam and Del exchanged looks. "Oh yes, I see. And when did he tell you this?"

"I, ah . . . he didn't really tell me, he, ah . . ."

Tynan stepped forward. "She hid in the bushes and listened."

"It was for a good cause!" she snapped at him. "Lionel was—"

"Lionel?" Del said. "You mean you did something

for that brat you sent to me? I turned that kid over my knee three times in one day."

"You *beat* Lionel?" she gasped. "He's just a little boy."

"I should have taken my hand to you more often, but, no, I had a soft heart and thought that little girls were different. I'll not make a mistake like that again. I mean to raise this boy right, so he has some sense and doesn't go off to big cities and write stories that get him shot at. Do you have any idea how many people have said to me in the last few days, 'Yeah, she was here, left three dead bodies behind her'?" He looked up at Tynan. "Between the two of you, there're about a hundred fewer people in this world."

"I don't think that's fair," Chris said. "Tynan did what he had to do. He—"

"Except when I shot Rory Sayers," Ty said in all seriousness.

She turned on him. "And what were you supposed to do? Stand there and let him shoot you? You saw the way all those people were egging you on, trying to make you do something exciting. There was nothing else you *could* do. You *had* to protect yourself."

Suddenly, she stopped as she realized what she'd said. She'd told him she was wrong to have left him alone in jail but she'd thought that out logically. This time there was passion in her belief in him.

Tynan stood there looking at her for a moment, an angelic smile on his face, then he turned toward Del. "Sir, she only gets into trouble because she wants to right all the world's wrongs. I think you've done a damn fine job of raising her. Now, would anybody like to eat?" He held out his arm. "Miss Mathison, may I escort you in to dinner?"

Chris felt a little weak-kneed as she took Ty's arm. She'd never been around a man who didn't cower in the presence of her father. Every other man did just what Asher was doing now: standing back and looking on quietly.

They joined the others—Del had brought about fifty men with him—and ate the first decent meal they'd had in days. Chris kept smiling at her father as he glowered at her as she tried to answer all his questions without telling the truth about the danger she'd been in. She didn't want to upset him more than she had already. She never really lied but then she didn't tell him all of it either.

"You went to Hamilton's knowing that he'd had his cousin killed?"

"I wasn't sure of that. I mean, it was an awful wagon accident. I'm sure the fall could have killed any number of people and all I wanted to do was help a little boy. Besides, I had the two big, strong men you sent to me to help me. What could possibly have gone wrong?" She didn't dare meet the eyes of Tynan or Asher or Pilar.

Del leaned toward her. "What went wrong was Dysan. Do you have any idea what that man's like?"

"Yes, I do," she said softly. "Papa, do you think you should talk about him like that now?" She gave a pointed look toward Samuel Dysan.

Mr. Dysan put his plate down. "You can't offend me. I know more than anyone what my grandnephew is like. I have had the misfortune of watching him grow up."

Chris's curiosity came to the surface. "Then why did

305

he say he'd been searching for you for years? Didn't he know where to find you?"

Del began to tell his daughter to mind her own business, but Chris kept her eyes on Samuel. The man was watching Tynan, looking at him with such interest that Chris began to look from one man to the other. Samuel caught himself.

"I have never understood the workings of the boy's mind," Samuel said. "His mother married my nephew because she thought he was the heir to my holdings, and when she found out he wasn't, she turned her son against me."

"And who is your heir?"

"Christiana!" Del yelled at her. "I will not stand for your lack of manners."

"I apologize, Mr. Dysan. It's just the reporter in me. I thought there might be some doubt about who was your heir if the woman thought her husband was going to be."

Samuel put his hand on Del's arm. "It's all right, I don't mind the questions. I have a son but he disappeared at sea many years ago. Perhaps I'm a fool but I have always had hopes of finding him again. But, even if I never found him, I would never leave a penny to my grandnephew."

"He seems to have enough money as it is."

Samuel's face turned hard. "Whatever he has, he has obtained by stealing, cheating, lying, killing."

"Oh," Chris said and looked down at her plate.

"Mr. Tynan," Samuel said, "I have had some experience with wounds. May I take a look at your leg?"

Tynan looked surprised. "If you'll look at Pilar first."

"Yes, of course," he said, smiling at Tynan.

306

"You know . . ." Chris began, looking from one man to the other.

"And what was that you wrote about Hugh Lanier? You accused that poor man of some of the worst crimes of this century," Del yelled at her.

Chris gave her attention back to defending herself to her father.

Chapter Twenty-five

Chris couldn't get away from her father for even a minute all that night. She wanted to talk to Tynan alone, but he seemed to always be busy. And then there was Asher. He obviously wanted to prove to Del that he'd done his duty and Chris was planning to marry him, because he was never two feet from Chris's side. He kept saying things like, "Have another biscuit, Chris, I know how much you love them." He made it seem as if they were on intimate terms.

Tynan, on the other hand, kept calling her Miss Mathison and tipping his hat to her in the most formal way.

"He treat you all right?" Del asked her when she was frowning at Ty's back because he'd again acted as if he'd never met her before tonight.

"How'd you get him out of jail?"

Del Mathison gave a little snort. "I don't plan to start telling you all my secrets. I got him out, that's all you need to know. He tell you he was in jail?"

"I guessed it and he answered my questions. Who do you plan to tell your secrets to? The man you picked out for me to marry?"

"You have been asking a lot of questions. You and Prescott get along?"

"Well enough," she answered. "He's asked me to marry him, if that's what you had planned."

Del looked at her for a while. "It's time you settled down and gave me some grandkids."

"Yes," she said softly. "That's just what I want to do."

They didn't speak any more as they prepared for bed. Del went to the foreman of the small army of men he'd brought and set up watches all night. Chris, wrapped in a blanket, watched as her father stood in the moonlight and talked to Tynan for a few minutes.

"He seems like a sensible young man," Samuel said from near her. "Del said he was in prison for murder."

"Yes, but he didn't kill the man—at least not the man he was imprisoned for killing, and, yes, he is the most competent of men."

"You weren't . . . frightened of him, of being alone with him?"

Chris turned to give the man a look of disbelief. "I'd trust Ty with my life, with the life of anyone I loved. He's a good, kind, intelligent man who has never been given a chance in his life. Yet, in spite of that, he's trustworthy and has the highest of ideals." She stopped, feeling a bit embarrassed. "No," she whispered, "I was never afraid of him."

Samuel Dysan smiled at her in the darkness. "I see. Well, good night, Miss Mathison. I'll see you in the morning." He went away from her whistling.

The next day, Del woke the entire camp long before

309

sun-up. Sleepily, Chris looked out of the covers and saw that Tynan was already loading a couple of the pack horses. She threw back the blanket and went to him.

"Good morning," she said, smiling at him.

He didn't look at her, but moved to the far side of the horse. She followed him.

"Go get the coffee ready," he said under his breath. "We'll need a few gallons of it."

"Ty . . ." she began.

He turned on her. "Look, Chris, it's over. You go back to your world and I go back to mine. You become the little rich girl and I'm the ex-convict. It's over. Now, go get the coffee ready."

Quick tears came to her eyes. "It's not over, Ty. You know how I feel about you."

He put his hands on her shoulders. They were hidden from the others by the horses. "Chris, I told you it wouldn't work. I told you that from the beginning. Right now you think you . . . that you're in love with me, but you're not. You love the adventure and the excitement, but you also love the luxury of your father's house. You wait, you'll see. Two weeks in your father's house, after you give a few parties, after you've had a few baths and bought a couple of new dresses, you won't even remember me. If I walked into the parlor, you'd worry that my clothes were going to get the furniture dirty. And you won't even believe that you once thought you were in love with somebody like me."

She looked at him for a long minute. "I hope you make yourself believe that. I hope you can sleep at night. I hope you . . ." Her anger left her. "I hope that someday you realize that you love me just as much as I love you." She jerked away from him. "I have to make coffee. When you're man enough to tell yourself the truth, let me know, I'll be waiting."

She ran away from him, stumbling over Samuel Dysan, but she didn't look at him either. She kept her head down and helped the camp cook prepare breakfast for the many cowboys who were preparing to ride.

When they mounted, ready to ride, she saw that all around her the men had their guns ready. She was encircled by her father, Sam, Tynan and three of her father's hired men. Asher and Pilar were likewise guarded. "Do you think Dysan's out there?" she asked Samuel beside her.

"I think he's out there," he answered grimly. "We have something he thinks belongs to him."

Her father called for them to ride before she could ask another question.

They rode south for two hours before they encountered Beynard Dysan's men. He approached them with all the confidence in the world, as if he knew the outcome of what was about to happen.

Del called a halt to the group behind him, and Tynan put his horse directly in front of Chris. He, Del and Sam were in the front of the army facing Dysan's hundred or so men.

"You were looking for me?" Samuel said and there was such coldness, such hatred in his voice, that Chris shivered.

"Not you," Dysan answered. "You know what I want. I want what's rightfully mine."

"No," was all Samuel said.

"Then I'll take it," Beynard answered. "And I'll take all of you with me."

Samuel reined his horse forward, snatching the reins

from Del's hand when Del tried to stop him. Sam rode up to Beynard. Behind her, Chris could hear rifles being cocked, barrels of six-guns being rolled to check that all the chambers were loaded.

While Sam and Beynard talked, Ty moved his horse back to stand by Chris. "If I give you the order, I want you to ride like hell toward those trees," he said under his breath. "You understand me? No heroics."

Chris looked up to see her father turned around in his saddle and he was nodding to her that she was to do what Tynan said.

"Pilar?" Ty said over his shoulder. "Be ready to ride."

Chris, a lump of fear in her throat, watched as Tynan moved back into place beside her father. The two men she loved most in the world in front of her, the first ones to be killed if Dysan's men began firing. She was sure her heart was going to break her ribs as she strained to see Samuel talking to Dysan.

It seemed an eternity before Sam turned back toward Del.

"This fight is between the two of us," Samuel said. "Winner takes all."

Del nodded at Sam while Tynan looked on with eyes that were dark.

Chris reined her horse forward. "What's going on?"

"Nothing for you to concern yourself with," Del said, his eyes on Samuel's back.

"The two of them are going to settle it," Tynan said. "Whoever wins gets the spoils of war."

"But Samuel is an old man," Chris said. "He can't possibly have the reflexes of the younger man. And, besides, he has a right to leave his estate to whoever he wants."

Del gave her one of his looks that told her he wanted her to shut up. "I am the executor of his estate. If Sam loses, I'll see that the right person gets his money."

"But then Dysan will be after you and—"

"Chris," Tynan said softly. "Come over here and be quiet."

She ignored her father's look as she obeyed Tynan and moved her horse next to his. Her hands gripped the pommel until they were white as she watched Samuel and Beynard ride down the trail and into the trees. It seemed forever until they heard the first shot.

Chris gasped and held her breath and waited. And waited.

There was a second shot, then nothing.

She looked at Tynan, saw that the muscles in his jaw were working, then he kicked his horse forward and tore past the hundred gun-bearing men who had been hired by Dysan. He galloped into the trees to where Samuel and Beynard had disappeared.

Chris watched his cloud of dust for a moment, then she too kicked her horse and went after Ty. Behind her, she could hear her father shouting at her, then at his men, but she didn't stop, just kept following Tynan into the trees.

She reached the clearing just as Ty was dismounting.

Samuel and Beynard were lying on the ground, both of them bloody. She jumped off her horse while it was still running, skidding to a halt just as Tynan was lifting Samuel.

The older man smiled up at Tynan. "It's just a scratch. I can get up."

Tynan turned to look at Chris. "What the hell are you doing here? Get back to your father."

"I came to see if you were all right," she answered angrily. "I thought you might need help."

"Not from a half pint girl, I don't. Now, get back to—"

Sam struggled to sit up, using Tynan's help. He was smiling broadly. "As much as I like hearing the love play between the two of you, I think I'm bleeding to death."

Chris smiled at Tynan with an I-told-you-so look, while he opened and closed his mouth twice, with nothing coming out.

Just then Del Mathison came riding into the clearing amid rocks and dust and a flurry of anger—all of it directed at his daughter.

"What happened here?" Tynan said in a half yell that was obviously meant to stop Del's tirade.

Sam struggled to sit up while Chris ran to get bandages from her saddle bags. "We drew and I won. I thought he was dead but I went to him. He was my brother's child, I knew him since he was a boy. There were times when I thought there was some hope for him, but his mother never allowed him to forget who she thought he was. No matter who he hurt, she was there behind him, telling him he had every right to do whatever he wanted. She hated me."

"And made him hate you," Chris said, handing Tynan the bandages. Ty cut the man's shirt away. The wound was in the fleshy part of his upper arm, not bad, but painful. Chris moved so that Sam could rest against her while Ty bandaged him.

"Yes, he hated me. Said he wanted to show me he could make as much as me." He paused. "It's over now."

"How'd you get shot?" Ty asked.

"I went to him after I'd shot him. He had a derringer up his sleeve. He used his last breath to shoot me with it."

Chris leaned forward and kissed the man's forehead. "It's over now and we can all go home."

Samuel took Chris's hand and, while holding it, he looked up at Del. "This is what I wanted," he said quietly.

Chris started to ask what he meant, but Del interrupted her with orders of what to do to get the place cleared up.

They buried Beynard where he fell, putting up a crude cross to mark the place. The men who'd come with him disappeared into the trees quietly, and, after Samuel had had a few minutes alone at the grave, they began to ride south.

Chris knew she should have been relieved that now they were more or less free, that now it was safe to return home, but the closer they got, the worse she felt. As soon as they reached her father's house, Tynan would leave her life forever.

Asher came forward and began to talk to her about the scenery and recounted all their experiences since they'd first met. He talked abnormally loudly when he recalled the way he'd first seen her—stark naked, and Chris thought that, for some reason, he wanted her father to hear the story. And he'd only ridden toward the front after all the danger was over. It was difficult for her to give her attention to what he was saying.

On the second day, Tynan called a halt to the group, telling Del that they were near Pilar's home and he wanted to return her.

"I'll leave you now that you have your daughter back safely," Ty said, his side turned toward Chris.

"We'll wait for you, or we'll all go to see that the lady is returned safely, and then you can go back with us," Del said.

"No, sir, my job was to get your daughter back and I've done that. I think I'd like to go now."

Del took a while to answer him.

"Del," Samuel said, "doesn't he have a pardon coming?"

"Yes, of course. It's right here in my pocket." It took him some minutes before he could get it out to hand it to Tynan.

"Thank you, sir. I hope I did a satisfactory job for you."

"The money, Del," Samuel prompted.

Chris sat on her horse rigidly. With each passing moment, she expected Ty to say that he couldn't leave her, that she meant more to him than all the money in the world and that he'd risk jail if it meant he could have her. But he never even looked at her. Del took a long time opening his saddle bag and withdrawing a leather pouch.

"There's ten thousand dollars in there. That's what we agreed on, isn't it?"

"Yes, sir." Tynan put out his hand to shake Del's. "If you have anymore need of me, I'll be around. Mr. Dysan." He tipped his hat to the older man.

Chris didn't breathe as he turned toward her—but he didn't look at her, just nodded in her direction, gave one of his infuriating hat tippings, mumbled, "Goodbye, Miss Mathison," then turned away, Pilar beside him.

Chris sat there for a moment, barely aware of Pilar waving to her, then she leaned across her horse and grabbed her father's pistol from his holster and aimed it at the back of Tynan's head.

"What do you think you're doing?" Del shouted as he knocked her hand skyward.

The pistol rang out, the bullet flying a foot over Tynan's head, but he still didn't turn around.

Del took his pistol from his daughter. "Of all the fool things—"

He stopped because Chris had buried her face in her hands and began to cry. She *had* been only a job to him, a job to make money and, in the end, he hadn't cared anything at all about her.

As always, Del was at a loss as to what to do when a female cried, but Sam moved his horse closer to her and pulled her into his arms.

Chris recovered herself quickly, then moved away from Samuel and, with clear eyes, looked back at her father. "Forgive me. I'm ready to go now." She was very aware of the men around her, all of them embarrassed.

"Look, if you want to stay here . . ." Del was awkward in trying to comfort her.

"She's fine now, aren't you?" Sam said. "I think we ought to go."

Chris looked at him with gratitude and minutes later they were on their way toward home.

Chapter Twenty-six

Chris put down her book and leaned back against the tree that grew behind the little stone bench. She'd been in her father's house for three weeks now and she knew that she wasn't going to leave it again. She wasn't going back to New York, wasn't going to write any more stories about what was wrong in the world. Instead, she was going to marry Asher Prescott and live in her father's house forever.

With a sigh, she closed the book. She'd already told Asher and now all that was left was to tell her father. For some reason, she hated telling him. Of course he'd be utterly delighted that she'd at last done something that he wanted her to do, but still, Chris hesitated.

"Might as well get it over with," she murmured to herself as she stood. "A lifetime of being Mrs. Prescott and I think this will 'get it over with,' " she muttered.

She straightened her shoulders and started walking back to the house, passing Samuel Dysan on the way. The man had stayed on after the rescue and had become part of the family. Twice, Chris had considered telling him her problems, but each time, something held her back.

She knocked on the door to her father's study.

"Come in," he called and, as usual, he sounded angry. Since they'd returned, he always seemed to be angry, sometimes not talking to Chris—as if he were furious with her about something.

He looked up at her. "What is it?" he asked coolly.

"I have something to tell you. Something that will please you, I'm sure."

He didn't say anything, just looked at her with one eyebrow raised.

"I have accepted Asher Prescott's marriage proposal. We're to be married one week from today."

She expected a burst of happiness from her father, but his face blackened. Wasn't she doing what he wanted?

"You never could do anything to please me, could you?" he began, coming up from his chair behind the desk. "I wanted you to stay home, but you wouldn't. I wanted you to marry and have babies, but you wouldn't. I wanted you to marry a *man* but you won't even do that, will you?"

Chris stood there blinking for a moment. "I'm going to marry the man you sent to me, the man you *wanted* me to marry."

"Like hell you are! I sent Tynan to you. I wanted you to marry *him*."

"Tynan?" Chris said as if she'd never heard the name before. "But you said that if he touched me, you'd send him back to prison."

Del heaved a sigh, went to a bookcase, opened a door, and withdrew a glass and a bottle of whiskey. He

319

poured out a healthy shot and downed it. When he looked back at his daughter, he seemed to have gained control of himself.

"I know that you've never done anything I've ever wanted you to do, so I thought I'd be able to get you to do what you thought I didn't want you to do. I sent you two men: one a weakling that could barely sit on a horse and the other one a . . . a man in every sense of the word. I thought you'd have sense enough to choose the right one. All I did was put a few obstacles in your way to make it more interesting."

Chris wasn't Del's daughter without having inherited some of his temper. "Of all the lowdown, rotten tricks, this is the worst. Do you mean that you created that entire story just to make me more interested in him?"

"It doesn't matter what I did since it obviously backfired. You chose that . . . that . . . don't you know that he only wants your money?"

Chris took a moment to control her rising temper. "I most certainly *do* know what he wants from me. But for your information, it was your hand-picked Tynan who turned me down, not the other way around. Your precious *man* refuses to have anything to do with me."

"And what did you do to him to make him dislike you?"

For a moment, Chris closed her eyes in an attempt to keep from screaming at her father. "I did nothing to make him dislike me," she said softly. "In fact, the reason I am marrying Prescott is because I'm carrying Tynan's child."

That successfully closed Del's mouth. "I'll go after him and bring him back here. I'll—"

"You will do no such thing. I'll not marry a man who doesn't want me."

320

Del sat down in his chair heavily. "But Prescott—"

Chris sat in the chair on the other side of the desk. "Asher wants my money and I want my child to have a name. I think it's a perfect arrangement."

Del seemed to age before her eyes. "Sam and I thought we'd planned everything so carefully. I didn't see any loopholes. We couldn't have been more wrong."

"What has Mr. Dysan to do with all of this?"

"Sam is Tynan's grandfather. In fact, Tynan's real name is Samuel James Dysan the third."

Chris couldn't speak for a moment. "He's who? What in the world are you saying? Tynan knows nothing about who he is."

"Sam hasn't known it all that long himself."

"Would you mind explaining what you're talking about? How long have you known about Tynan? Did you know when you got him out of prison?"

"Of course. You don't think I'd trust my only child to an outlaw, do you? I've always known who he was."

He leaned back in his chair. "I don't guess it'll matter that I tell you now, now that all Sam's and my plans have fallen through. Sam has hopes that Tynan will return, but I think I gave up last week."

"And decided that he didn't return through some fault of mine," she said with disgust. "How did you first learn about Tynan?"

"You're too young to remember, but Sam and I knew each other many years ago. He was a suitor of your mother's." Del smiled. "Now there was a woman with sense. She knew which man to choose. Anyway, Sam married soon after I did and he and his wife had a son right away, named him Sam after himself. There wouldn't have been any problems except for that hellion Sam's brother married. Sam made all his money on his own, but whatever his brother touched, failed. Sam's sister-in-law screamed night and day at her husband, then at her son who was just like him. Both men died young. It was when her grandson was born that she saw some hope of ever achieving what she wanted."

"And that was Beynard," Chris said.

"Yes, the woman thought for years that Beynard was going to be Sam's heir because Sam the second didn't produce any children. But then he and his wife decided to go to Washington to see about buying some timberland and they never returned."

"They were killed," Chris said softly. "Ty said that his mother had three bullet wounds in her back."

"All Sam could do was guess what had happened. He heard that his son and daughter-in-law had been killed in a boating accident and never made it to the coast of Washington. For years, he thought that he was going to have to make Beynard his heir, even though he disliked the boy. But six years ago, a friend of his daughter-in-law's came to visit and asked Sam what had happened to Lilian's child. Until then, Sam hadn't even known she was going to have a baby." Del gave Chris a hard look. "Sometimes fathers are the last to know what's going on in their children's lives."

Del folded his hands on the desk. "So, for six years, Sam's moved heaven and earth to find out if she had a child and if it lived. He found him three years ago. He's your Tynan. We think his mother must have said, 'Dysan,' and the old miner misheard it as 'Tynan.' "

"Who killed Tynan's parents?"

"Sam could only guess that his sister-in-law hired

someone to do it. Maybe she found out there was going to be a rival for her grandson's place as Sam's heir."

"So this is why Beynard wanted us. On the hill that day, at Hamilton's, he was talking about Tynan when he mentioned Sam, wasn't he?"

"Probably, but Beynard never had a chance. His grandmother was crazy and she poisoned his mind against Sam's family. She made him as crazy as she was. Sam made the mistake of telling the boy that he thought he'd at last found his grandson. Beynard broke into Sam's office, stole the papers on Tynan and came to Washington to find him. Several of the things that happened to Tynan over the last few years were caused by Beynard."

"So, actually, he kidnapped Pilar and me to get to Tynan?"

"We have no way of knowing for sure, but Sam and I think he knew Tynan . . . cared for one of you but he didn't know which one, so he took both of you."

Chris was silent for a few minutes as she digested this information. "So why did you come up with this elaborate scheme with Tynan and me? Why didn't Mr. Dysan just get his grandson released from prison and take him home? What did I have to do with this?"

"Sam only knew of his grandson by reputation. He'd heard of every gunfight, every time he got thrown in jail, the banks he robbed when he was a boy, all the scrapes he got himself into, and all the women." Del was watching Chris but she didn't say anything. "Sam wanted to know what his grandson was like. He was afraid he was like Beynard. And, too, we both hoped for an alliance between our families."

"So you used me," she said, her jaw set. "You used me in your matchmaking experiment."

Del's voice rose. "I thought maybe you could benefit by meeting a man, something besides those city slickers you'd met in New York. Give a job to a woman! Of all the stupid—"

"I don't think we'd better start this again," Chris said. "If you'd wanted me to meet him, you should have invited him to the house and introduced him to me. But no, you had to concoct an absurd farce to get us together. You had to threaten him with a return to prison if he so much as came near me and you also had to send that man Prescott who was drooling over me at every opportunity."

"And now you're going to marry him."

"I *have* to! That *man* you chose for me won't have anything to do with marriage. He's scared to death of the idea. And he'd rather do anything than go back to jail."

"Is that what he told you?"

"Yes, he did. I begged him to marry me, but he refused. You'll be happy to know that your little scheme worked on my part. I fell in love with Tynan— or Sam, whatever his name is—practically from the moment I saw him. But all he wanted from me was . . . what he got, so now I'm carrying the consequences of having fallen in love with him."

"He walked out on a woman carrying his child?"

"I most certainly did not tell him."

Del stood. "Well, we'll find him and make him marry you. He can't do this to my daughter."

"You do that and I'll walk out of this house and you'll never see me or your grandchild again. I'll not force myself on a man who doesn't want me. I've talked to Asher and told him about the baby and he's agreed to marry me and raise the child as his own. I think it'll work out nicely."

"Nicely," Del mocked. "I never would have thought this of Sam's grandson. I thought he had more guts than this."

"He said he was doing this for me and I think some of him believes what he's saying. He says he's not husband material and that I'll be better off with some man who's housebroken."

"But he could learn. *I* learned, didn't I?"

Chris looked at the floor. "I don't want to talk about this anymore. Tynan didn't love me. As much as you and Mr. Dysan wanted it to happen, it didn't. I'm going to marry Asher in a week and I'm going to stay here and raise my child and I'll probably never even see Tynan again. Besides, with his propensity for trouble, he'll probably be back in prison by the time of the wedding. Now, I think I'll go lie down and rest."

With that, she left the room.

Chapter Twenty-seven

"Do you really think you have the right to wear white?" Asher asked Chris as she sat in her father's garden. "I mean, isn't that asking for gossip?"

Chris didn't answer him. Since she'd, in essence, asked him to marry her, he'd started showing what he was really like. He was deeply angry that she'd spent a night with "someone like that gunfighter," and never lost a minute telling her so. They'd agreed that the child was to be known as his, so he could act proudly modest when the baby came three months too early. He didn't mind people thinking he'd seduced the rich Nola Dallas, but he refused to let anyone know that there'd been another man. He'd been angry when she'd told her father the truth.

"Won't you be showing soon?" he continued.

Chris closed her eyes for a moment. "How would I know? I've never had a baby. Doesn't my father have some work for you to do? I thought you were going to learn some of his business so you could help him."

"I can't this morning. There's a divine mare being put up for sale at Frederikson's and I need one more look at her before I buy her."

"But you've bought two horses already this week."

He stood back and looked at her and Chris knew what he was thinking. He'd taken Del Mathison's pregnant daughter off the man's hands and, because of this noble deed, he expected to be given the keys to the kingdom. He did no work and Chris suspected that he never planned to, that he was quite willing to go on living there, taking all her father had worked for and contributing nothing in return. And her father couldn't have cared less what Asher did. He was too angry at Chris to think of anything else. And Samuel kept looking at her with the saddest eyes.

"I thought maybe I'd buy this horse for you," Asher said. "You'll need a horse after his child is born."

She tightened her lips. In public, the child might be theirs, but in private, it was only "his."

"Yes, of course," she mumbled. "Of course I'll need a horse." She knew she'd say anything to get rid of him. As she watched him leave, she thought that after the baby was born, she'd probably leave Washington and return East. Her baby'd have a name, and she wouldn't have to deal with Asher every day.

She tried to bury herself in her book, but nothing could keep the tears from coming. She ran back to the house, tears pouring down her face, ran past Samuel, and up to her room where she spent yet another day crying.

The day of the wedding was overcast and looked as if it would rain. Mrs. Sunberry helped Chris to dress and there was never a more dismal dressing of a bride in history. Mrs. Sunberry kept crying, letting out little statements like, "He's not the man your mother would have wanted for you," and "He's already spent twice as much as your father does in a year," and "It's not too late to change your mind."

Chris had to grit her teeth each time the woman spoke. She had taken an instant dislike to Asher because he'd started giving orders the minute Chris told him about the baby.

Chris smoothed the white dress, put her chin in the air and left the room, Mrs. Sunberry sniffling behind her.

Her father was waiting for her at the foot of the stairs, and he managed to offer her his arm without so much as looking at her. His anger at her showed in every line in his face. Samuel walked behind them and he tried to put on a smiling countenance, but Chris thought he looked miserably unhappy.

It was on the tip of her tongue to scream at both of them that if they hadn't interfered, maybe this wouldn't be happening. If they hadn't told Tynan he'd have to return to prison where he would be beaten and starved, maybe he'd have considered marriage.

Quick tears came to Chris's eyes, because she didn't believe that for one minute. It wasn't the threat of prison that was keeping Tynan from marrying her, it was the fact that he didn't love her.

The church was packed with people she hadn't seen since she was a girl, and many people she'd never met before. There were some of her mother's relatives, the Montgomerys, standing there and watching her as she slowly walked down the aisle on her father's arm. Asher waited for her at the altar, smiling triumphantly.

"Probably thinking of the herd of thoroughbreds he's

going to buy tomorrow," Del said under his breath to her. "Do you know why that business of his failed?"

"I don't want to know," she hissed at him. "He's the man *you* chose."

"As contrast. I thought you were smart enough to know that."

"I was. Tynan wasn't."

"You could have—"

"Borne him twins?" she asked, glaring up at him as she reached the altar.

It was only as the preacher started the ceremony that Chris realized the full extent of what she was doing. She was promising to love, honor and cherish this man for the rest of her life. Tears welled up in her throat and closed it so that the pastor had to ask her three times for her answer. She was aware of Asher looking at her as if he meant to strike her if she didn't give her answer soon. Behind her, she could hear the people beginning to get restless.

It was then, while she was trying to answer, that all hell broke loose. A shot was fired outside the church and, suddenly, the building was overrun with men bearing arms. Men came in the windows, through the back door, from the door behind the altar. Two men must have been hiding in the balcony and they now rose, rifles aimed and ready.

"I wouldn't try it if I were you, mister," said a man with a pistol pointed toward one of Chris's Montgomery uncles who had his hand to his vest.

Everyone stood still, looking at the twenty or so men who surrounded the interior of the church. The big double doors in the back were open, three men guarding the entrance.

Chris watched with widened eyes as she heard a

horse approach the back doors. The rider seemed as if he had all day.

Through the doors rode Tynan on top of a big chestnut stallion, his gun sheathed, looking for all the world as if he were out on a Sunday stroll. He halted about halfway down the aisle, then, with everyone watching in open-mouthed astonishment, with twenty guns aimed at the guests, he took the makings of a cigarette out of his pocket and began to roll one.

"I don't guess I can let you do this, Chris," he said softly, licking the paper to stick it around the tobacco.

Chris took a step forward, but her father was there before her.

"You aren't taking my daughter without being married to her," Del said. "You're not going to make a whore of her."

"I never meant to. That's why I came to church." He hadn't yet looked at Chris, but kept looking down at that cigarette that was taking a long time to roll.

Del stepped back. "You can get on with it. The boy's marrying my daughter."

"But—" Asher began but Del grabbed him by the ear as if he were a little boy and pulled him to a pew.

"You can all sit down," Del bellowed out to the congregation as if it were the most normal thing in the world that the bridegroom was sitting on top of a horse in the middle of the church. "And you men," he said to the gunmen around the periphery of the room, "take off your hats."

They did as they were bid.

Chris heard chuckles from the congregation, then they sat down. She turned back to the pastor who looked a little pale and didn't seem to know what to do.

"Perhaps you should hurry before the horse spoils the church," she whispered. "His name is Samuel James Dysan III, also known as Tynan."

"Yes," the preacher said and cleared his throat.

This time, Chris didn't have any trouble answering his questions. Her hearty "I do," caused the congregation to laugh. When the preacher got to Tynan's part, she turned back toward him. She wanted to watch his expression when his name was said.

Tynan blinked a few times, and hesitated, and glanced at Samuel, saw the man nod once, then looked back at Chris—for the first time. "I do," he said and the congregation broke into applause.

Chris let out a yell of "hallelujah," tore off her veil, sent it flying toward Asher and ran toward Tynan on his horse. He caught her arm, heaved her behind him and backed the horse out of the church amid cheers and yells and guns being fired in jubilation.

She held onto him with all her might as he thundered across the countryside.

It was twenty minutes later that he stopped and hauled her around to the front of him and started kissing her. Her dress was unbuttoned to her waist after the first kiss.

"Wait a minute," he said, drawing back. "Is anybody going to come after us? I mean, is your father planning to send a posse out after us?"

"Maybe to send his thanks," she said, trying to continue kissing him.

"What was all that back there? Why did that man say my name was Dysan?"

"Because it is. Oh, Tynan, I have so very much to tell you. I know who you are and about your mother and

331

father and Sam is your grandfather and I'm going to have your baby and what made you come back for me?"

He sat there looking at her for a moment, not able to take in all of it. "Is your father going to have me sent back to jail?"

"Only if you desert me."

"Ow," he said as she ran her hands along his ribs. "Stop that."

"You've been hurt. What happened?"

He grinned at her. "Lester Chanry found me again."

"And what did you do to that poor man this time?"

"I gave him a piece of the old miner's gold and told him where the mine was."

"So poor Lester will go up there and be met by that old man?" she asked, smiling.

"They deserve each other." He began kissing her neck again. "If nobody's chasing us and we just got married, does that mean we can go somewhere and start the wedding night?"

"This early in the day?" she asked in mock alarm. "Shouldn't we wait until night?"

"It'll be night by the time I get through kissing your pretty little body."

"Oh, well, that's all right then."

"Tomorrow you can tell me all about my—" he grinned, "grandfather, but now I have more important things to think about."

Holding her onto the horse, he kicked it forward and started down the road at a breathtaking speed.

Three minutes later the countryside rang with Tynan's shout of, "A BABY!?" Chris's laughter followed close behind.

Raider.

Dear Readers,
I have had the plot of my next book, THE RAIDER, in
my head for many years, and while I was writing the
TWIN OF ICE and TWIN OF FIRE, now and then I'd
come up with an idea for my masked-man-story and
toss it in a folder. I knew from the beginning that I
would use a Montgomery for the hero. But after I
finished the TWINS, I was so in love with Kane Taggert
that I knew I wanted to keep the Taggert family also.
So, I decided to marry a Taggert to a Montgomery.

I had no idea what I was getting myself into when I put
a Taggert and a Montgomery together. Two more
stubborn, hard-headed people I have never met. And
what a joy they were to write about.

Alexander Montgomery dresses in black and rides
against the English, who are invading the colonies in
1768. But he gets shot, and, to cover his wounds, wears
an enormous gaudy coat and pretends to be fat and
wimpy. He believes everyone in his hometown in
Maine will see through his disguise even though they
haven't seen him for years. But he hadn't counted on
Jessica Taggert. She believes just what she sees, laughs

333

at him, and tells everyone she always knew Alexander would grow up to be less than a man.

Alexander decides to keep his disguise and become the Raider.

The book gets complicated when the Raider falls in love with Jessica but Alexander can't stand her.

This book was a complete pleasure for me. And I hope you enjoy reading it as much as I enjoyed writing it.

Jude Deveraux
Santa Fe, New Mexico
February 1986

334

The Raider

Alexander Montgomery opened his eyes to see the familiar swing of a lamp as it swayed to the rhythm of the sea.

"Well, it looks like you may live after all."

Alex moved his head just a bit to see Nick sitting beside him, his coat off, his shirt dirty with blood on the front. "What time is it?" Alex asked as he started to sit up but was dizzy with the effort so he lay back down.

"It's almost dawn," Nicholas Ivonovitch said, getting up to move to a basin of water and wash his hands. "You almost died last night. It took a while to get the bullet out."

Alex closed his eyes for a moment and thought about his foolish stunt of being the Raider. "I hope you don't mind my imposing on your hospitality a while longer, but I think it will be a day or so before I can travel to Warbrooke."

Nick dried his hands on a towel. "You can't step onto the street without hearing about the exploits of the Raider."

Alex gave a groan of disgust.

"That's the least of it. The English have sent every soldier at their disposal to look for you. There are already posters out for your arrest. You are to be shot on sight. They've been here twice this morning and demanded to search my ship."

"I'll go then," Alex said. He sat up despite the pain in his shoulder.

"I've kept them away by threatening them with war with my country. Alex, if you stepped onto that gangplank you'd be shot within minutes. They are looking for someone tall and slim, with black hair." Nick's eyes burned into Alex's. "And they know you're wounded."

"I see," Alex said, still sitting on the edge of the bed, and he did see. He knew that he was facing the end of his life, but he could not stay here and risk getting his friend involved. He tried to stand, leaning heavily on the chair in front of him.

"I have a plan," Nick said. "I have no wish to be pursued by the English Navy, so I'd like to allow them to search."

"Yes, of course. At least that way I won't have to walk down the gangplank. I was dreading that." Alex tried to smile.

Nicholas ignored his attempt at levity. "I have sent for some of my cousin's clothes. He is a fat man and a gaudy dresser."

Alex raised an eyebrow at that. To his taste, Nick's clothes put even peacocks to shame, so what must this cousin's be like?

Nick continued. "I think that if we pad you to fill the clothes, fortify you with a little whiskey, and put a powdered wig on over that mass of black hair, you'll pass the soldiers' inspection."

336

"Why don't I put on the disguise and just walk off the ship?"

"And then do what? You will need help and whoever gives it to you will be putting his life in danger. And how many of your poor Americans could resist the five hundred pound reward that is being offered for your head? No, you will stay here on my ship with me and we will sail for this town of yours. Will there be someone there to take care of you?"

Alex leaned back against the wall, feeling even weaker than when he woke. He thought of the town of Warbrooke, the town his grandfather had settled and most of which his father now owned. There were people there who were his friends, people who, from what his sister had written, needed his help, and he was a product of those people. If he was brave, then they were twice as brave. No English soldiers were going to frighten the townsmen of Warbrooke.

"Yes, there are people there who will help me," Alex said at last.

"Then let's get you dressed." Nick threw open the cabin door and called for a servant to bring the clothes he needed.

"Alex," Nick said gently. "We're here. We're in Warbrooke." He looked at his friend with sympathy. For the last week Alex had been running a high fever and now he looked as if he'd been on a week long drunk: his eyes were sunken, his skin dry and red, his muscles weak and rubbery.

"Alex, we're going to have to dress you in my cousin's clothes again. The soldiers are still searching for the Raider and I'm afraid they've come this far north. Do you understand me?"

"Yeah, sure," Alex mumbled. "They'll take care of me in Warbrooke. You'll see."

"I hope you're right," Nick said. "I'm afraid that they may believe what they see." He was referring to the ridiculous sight Alex made in his fat padding, brocade coat and powdered wig. He certainly didn't look like a handsome young man come home to save a town from a dastardly brother-in-law.

"You'll see," Alex slurred, since Nick had been giving him brandy to help him face the coming exertion. "They know me. They'll laugh when they see me like this. They'll know that something has happened. They'll take care of me until this damned shoulder heals. I just pray they don't give me away in front of the soldiers. You'll see, they'll know that no Montgomery ever dressed like a peacock. They'll know there's a reason for this."

"Yes, Alexander," Nicholas said soothingly. "I hope you are right."

"I am. You'll see. I know these people."

"I don't know why *I* have to be there to meet him," Jessica Taggert said for the thousandth time to her sister Eleanor. "Alexander was never anything to me—nothing good, that is."

Eleanor tightened her sister's corset strings. Eleanor, by herself, was considered a pretty woman, but when Jessica was present, she was overshadowed—as was every other woman in town. "You have to go because the Montgomery family has been very good to us. Get down from there, Sally," she said to her four-year-old sister.

The Taggert house was little more than a shack, small

338

and only as clean as two women with full time employment and the responsibility of taking care of six young brothers and sisters could make it. The house was on the edge of town, set back in a tiny cove, with no close neighbors; not because they chose to be so isolated, but because eighteen years ago when the fifth loud, dirty Taggert had entered the world and there didn't seem to be an end in sight to their increasing numbers, people had stopped building near them.

"Nathaniel!" Jessica shouted to her nine-year-old brother who was dangling three, fat, angry spiders on a string in front of his little sister's face. "If I have to come over there you'll be sorry."

"At least you wouldn't have to see Alexander," Nathaniel taunted before wisely scurrying from the house just after he tossed the spiders onto his sister.

"Hold still, Jess," Eleanor said. "How do you expect me to lace you into this dress if you're wiggling about?"

"I don't particularly want you to lace me into it. I really don't see why I have to go. We don't need charity from the likes of Alexander Montgomery."

Eleanor gave a heartfelt sigh. "You haven't seen him since you were both children. Maybe he's changed."

"Hah!" Jess said, moving away from her sister and lifting two-year-old Samuel off the floor where he was trying to eat some unidentifiable substance. She saw he had one of Nathaniel's spiders in his fat, dirty little hand. "No one as bad as Alexander changes. He was a pompous know-it-all ten years ago and I'm sure he hasn't changed. If Marianna was going to get one of her

339

brothers to come and help her get away from that man she was fool enough to marry, why couldn't she have asked one of the older boys? One of the *good* Montgomerys?"

"I think she wrote each of them and Alex received his letter first. Sit still while I get some of the tangles out of your hair." Eleanor took her sister's hair in her hands and couldn't help feeling a little jealous. Other women spent untold hours trying to do what they could with their hair to make it look good, while Jessica exposed hers to sun, salt air, sea water and her own sweat—and it was more beautiful than anyone else's. It was a thick, soft chestnut that looked red in the sunlight and matched her mahogany colored eyes perfectly.

"Oh, Jess, if you just tried, you could get any man—"

Her sister cut her off. "Please don't start on me again. Why don't *you* get a husband? A rich one who'll support us and all the kids?"

"From this town?" Eleanor sniffed. "From a town that's afraid of one man? From a town that lets a man like Pitman run it?"

Jessica stood and pulled her hair back from her face. There were few women pretty enough to be able to scrape their hair back that tightly and still be beautiful, but Jessica succeeded. "I don't want one of those cowards any more than you do." She put baby Samuel down on the floor again. "But at least I'm not fool enough to think that one man, especially somebody like Alexander, is going to save us. I think all of you remember the Montgomerys as a group, not as individuals. I couldn't agree more that there was never a more magnificent group of men than Sayer and his two oldest

340

sons and I cried as hard as any of you when the boys went off to sea—but I didn't cry when Alexander left."

"Jessica, I don't think you're being fair. What in the world did Alex do to you that's made you dislike him so much? And you can't count the schoolboy pranks he pulled. If they counted, Nathaniel would have been hanged four years ago."

"It's his attitude. He always thought he was so much better than anyone else. His brothers and father would work with everyone else, but Alexander thought of himself as too good. His family was the richest one in town, but he was the only Montgomery who made sure we all knew it."

"Are you talking about his charity? The time you threw the lobsters he'd brought us in his face? I never understood that, since the whole town was always giving us things."

"Well, they don't now!" Jessica spat in anger. "Yes, I mean the charity, living from hand to mouth every day, never having anything, always wanting. And Pa coming home every nine months, just in time to get Mama—" She paused to calm down. "Alexander was the worst. The way he smirked every time he brought a bag of cornmeal. The superior way he looked at all of us each time he saw us. He used to wipe his trousers every time a Taggert baby got near him."

Eleanor smiled. "Jess, it was necessary to wipe your trousers—or your skirt or your hair—every time a Taggert baby got near you. I don't think you're being fair. Alexander was no better or worse than the other men in his family. It's just that you two are only two years apart in age and therefore you felt more kinship with him."

341

"I'd rather be kin to a shark than to him."

Eleanor rolled her eyes. "He did help Patrick get the post as cabin boy on the *Fair Maiden*."

"He would have done anything to get rid of one more Taggert. Are you ready to go?"

"I've been ready for some time. I'll make a deal with you. If Alexander turns out to be the pompous spend-thrift you seem to think he is, I'll bake you three apple pies next week."

"I'll win this without trying. With his arrogance, he'll probably be expecting us to kiss his hand. I hear he was in Italy. Probably met the Pope and learned some things from him. Think he'll wear scented lace under-wear?"

Eleanor ignored her sister. "If I win, you have to wear a dress all week and be nice to Mr. Clymer."

"That old fish-breath? Oh, well, it doesn't matter. I'm going to win. This town's going to see that, when Alexander is alone and not surrounded by his brothers and father, he's a lazy, vain, condescending, pom-pous—" She stopped because Eleanor was pushing her out the door.

"And, Nathaniel, if you don't watch after those kids, you'll hear from me," Eleanor called over her shoul-der.

By the time they got to the dock, Eleanor was having to drag Jessica. Jess kept enumerating all the things that needed doing: the fishing nets that needed repairing, and the sails that had to be mended.

"Well, Jessica," said Abigail Wentworth as the Tag-gert sisters stepped onto the dock, "I see that you couldn't wait to see Alexander again."

Jessica was torn between wanting to smack the woman and turning to leave the dock. Abigail was the second prettiest girl in town, and she hated being second to Jessica's first. Therefore, she loved to remind Jessica that she was a ripe and ready sixteen while Jess was drying on the vine at the grand old age of twenty-two.

Jessica gave Abby her sweetest smile and prepared to tell her what she thought of her when Eleanor grabbed her arm and pulled her away.

"I don't want you two to get into a fight today. I want this to be a good day for the Montgomerys without Sayer having to get you out of the stocks. Good morning, Mistress Goody," she said sweetly. "There it is, that's the ship Alex is on."

Jessica gaped at the ship. "But that beam is too narrow. I'm sure that's against statutes. Has Pitman seen that yet? He'll probably confiscate the ship, and then where will your precious Alexander be?"

"He's not mine. If he were anybody's, Abigail wouldn't be here waiting for him."

"How true," Jess sighed. "Wouldn't she just love to get her hands on the Montgomerys' eight thousand feet of dock space? What are those people looking at?"

Eleanor turned to see a group of townspeople standing stock still and gaping. As Jessica and Eleanor waited, the crowd began to part, their mouths open, but no sound came forth.

As the sisters stood there and waited, a man came toward them. He was wearing a jacket of canary yellow, with a wide border of embroidered flowers and leaves about the edge and hem. Because the jacket had to stick out so far to cover his enormous belly, the sunlight flashed off the many colors of the silk embroidery. The breeches covering his fat legs were emerald green, and he wore a full wig that hung down in curls past his shoulders. He walked across the dock, stumbling now and then from what was obviously too much drink.

The townspeople seemed to think he was another official from England, but Jessica recognized him right away. No amount of weight or wig could completely cover that imperious Montgomery expression. In spite of being about a hundred pounds overweight, she could still see those cheekbones that Alexander had inherited from his grandfather.

Jessica walked forward, swishing her skirts and letting everyone see her.

"Good morning, Alexander," she said loudly and with laughter in her voice. "Welcome home. You haven't changed a bit."

He stood there and looked at her, blinking uncomprehendingly. His eyes were red, from drink she assumed, and he swayed so badly that a dark, burly man had to catch him.

Jessica stepped back, looked Alex up and down, then put her hands on her hips and started to laugh.

The Enchanted Land

~ *Chapter One* ~

MORGAN stared at the ugly brown dress spread across the bed. She shivered. Remembering again what she must do tonight, she turned slowly and gazed wistfully into the mirror, seeing without interest her pale hair and blue eyes. She tried cocking her head and smiling. But no . . . she wasn't pretty, and she was sure she never would be.

She turned quickly as a knock sounded and her uncle strode in. He was a short, portly man, given to excess at the table. He smiled at her and reached out to touch her chin. She turned her head away.

"What do you want?" she asked coldly.

"Is everything all right? How is your packing coming?"

"Fine." She kept her face averted.

He looked around the room at the closed trunks and, finally, at the brown silk dress on the bed. He touched the silk lightly.

"Why don't you rest before we leave for the ball? You have a few hours yet."

She didn't answer, and he turned and left the room, closing the door behind him quietly.

Morgan removed her dress and replaced it with a plain dressing gown. She lay down but she couldn't sleep. Instead, she found herself going over it all yet again.

The problems had started before she was born. Both her father and her mother had been brought up to the

1

life of wealthy plantation owners in southern Kentucky. But her father had wanted to venture out, to seek the hardships and challenges of the frontier.

After her parents' marriage, the young couple had moved to New Mexico. Morgan was born there. Her mother had nearly died in childbirth. The baby was early, and it was a full eighteen hours before her husband could bring a midwife to his wife. Morgan had heard many times from her mother of the horror and pain she went through all alone. Being a lady, she would not allow any of the ranch hands in the room.

When Morgan was a year old, her mother and she returned to Kentucky. Her mother had refused to bring up her daughter in savage New Mexico. There had been many an argument between her parents, and her father had said that if his wife took their child and left him, he never wanted to see either of them again. And that's the way it had been: she had not seen her father in seventeen years.

Her mouth hardened as she realized that he had his revenge now. In death, he was punishing his wife through his daughter.

She tried to keep her mind off the reading of the will, just two weeks ago, that horrible will that had led to her decision about tonight.

She turned her head toward the door when she heard a light knock, smiling at her aunt's voice.

As Lacey entered, Morgan couldn't help but think how well the older woman's name fit her. Lacey was small and frail, as if she might break. She reminded Morgan of a starched and crocheted doily.

"Hello, dear. Are you feeling all right? I imagine you're excited about tonight."

Aunt Lacey was always so sweet. She assumed that, since Morgan was young, she must be excited about going to the ball. And Morgan would have been, too, if the circumstances were different. She gazed at the non-

2

descript brown dress, which she had pushed to one side of the bed, and Lacey's eyes followed hers.

Lacey walked around the bed, touched the silk, and said gently, "Brown isn't really your color, is it, my dear?"

Morgan fought the urge to throw back her head and laugh hysterically. "It's all right, Aunt Lacey. I don't mind. I could have a Paris gown and it wouldn't matter. Nothing could make me pretty, just as Uncle Horace says."

Lacey's eyes were sad. She moved around the room to sit beside Morgan on the bed. She looked at her niece closely. "I know Horace says you're not pretty."

"My mother said so too."

"But I can't help thinking that if you wore brighter clothes and didn't hide your hair . . . you know you have lovely hair." She ran a finger down Morgan's cheek. "And such lovely skin." She paused. "I really feel, dear, that if you smiled more, you would be much more attractive."

Morgan grimaced. Her aunt had often told her that if she looked happier and were a little bit livelier, she would be pretty. Morgan smiled faintly at what her mother would say about her aunt's encouraging Morgan to make herself more "attractive." Attractive indeed— like a flower enticing bees.

Seeing Morgan smile, Lacey patted her hand. "That's better, dear." She rose to leave, pausing with her hand on the door. "Could I help you dress, or help with your hair?"

"No, thank you, Aunt Lacey. I think I may sleep awhile."

"Good. I'll wake you in an hour."

The door closed, and Morgan was alone again. She lay back and slept. An hour later, Lacey returned to waken her, then went back to her own room to complete her toilette.

3

Morgan lifted the brown silk dress, stared at it a moment, and tossed it back on the bed. She had to fight the urge to tear it to shreds. Again, she thought of her father. This was all his fault. In all her eighteen years, she had never had to worry about her appearance.

She and her mother had lived alone for fifteen years in Trahern House. *Trahern House.* The very name made her homesick. Trahern House was one hundred seventy-five acres of green, rolling countryside with a duck pond, bridle paths, and woods. Her mother had indulged Morgan's every desire. She longingly recalled her pretty little mare, Cassandra.

Her mother had told her she was plain, but she knew her mother had wanted her to be plain. Her mother had never allowed male visitors at the house. She had told Morgan that men cared only for pretty faces, and that Morgan was better off plain. If she were plain, she could live her life in peace, at Trahern House. And Morgan had never wanted to live anywhere else.

Yet her mother's unexpected, early death two years ago had cast Morgan into her uncle's house. And the will had been a second, terrible blow. Why hadn't her mother told her that her father really owned everything? She knew that Trahern House had belonged to Morgan Trahern, her maternal grandfather, so she assumed her mother had inherited it. What had happened, that the house and lands were given to Grandfather Morgan Trahern's son-in-law rather than to his own daughter?

Morgan looked back at the mirror. Her eyes were cold as she said, aloud, "You may have been my father, Charles Wakefield, but you have not treated me like a daughter. You took away the only thing I had—Trahern House. And you have required an ugly thing of me to secure it." She drew closer to the mirror and her voice was hard, a deep whisper. "But you never knew your daughter. She is strong. I vow here and now that

4

neither you nor any other man," and here her mind touched briefly on her Uncle Horace, "will ever stop me from getting what I want."

She stared at herself for a few seconds and was startled to see her normally blue eyes turn a deep green. What did it matter that she didn't have physical beauty? As her mother had told her many times, she had inner beauty. And that was what mattered. Physical beauty was for silly women who wanted only to catch a man. And the last thing Morgan wanted was a man.

She turned again to the bed and the dress, thinking that tonight, for just this one night, she would like to be pretty. Because tonight, Morgan was going to have to do the very thing she had never wanted to do. She was going to have to catch a man.

She sighed and began to dress, pulling her hair back from her face and slipping into the loose, plain dress.

"You look lovely, my dear," Uncle Horace said as he entered and extended his arm to her.

But Morgan saw the complacency in his eyes, the satisfaction. Of course, he is pleased, she thought If I were beautiful, in a low-cut, red satin dress, some man would carry me off to New Mexico and he'd lose all the money. But she knew her uncle had no reason to worry about that tonight.

They arrived early. Few others were there yet. Morgan was glad. She would have a chance to appraise the people as they arrived. She must consider them all carefully: she could not afford to make a mistake. Her spine stiffened.

As they entered the glittering ballroom, Horace led Lacey and Morgan over to their host and hostess, Matthew and Caroline Ferguson. Morgan had met the Fergusons several times before.

"Morgan, I'm so glad you are here. You get out much too seldom." Caroline Ferguson smiled.

"Well," said Horace, "our little Morgan much prefers the solitary life, with her books and her walks through the garden."

Morgan shrank as Horace's hand touched her shoulder, but she managed a smile for the Fergusons.

As the little party was walking away, Cynthia Ferguson made her appearance. Cynthia was beautiful, knew it, and made sure everybody noticed it.

"Why, Morgan," she drawled, "you dear thing. I'm so glad you could come to our little party. My, what a . . . charming little dress."

Morgan thought she might strike Cynthia. Cynthia had on a low-cut gown of mauve watered silk, set off by tiny jet beads around the bodice and hem. Morgan bit her tongue and held her pride. "Thank you, Cynthia. I am glad to be here."

"You just make yourself at home. I know all the boys are going to fill your card and I'll never get another moment to speak with you again all evening."

As Morgan walked away, she heard Cynthia murmur to her mother, "I had no idea silk could look like *that*." Morgan did not hear Mrs. Ferguson's reply.

Horace seated Lacey and Morgan and went to speak to some men friends in a corner of the room. Then Lacey saw some of her friends, and after Morgan assured her she would be all right, Lacey left.

Morgan sat back, enjoying the quiet and the chance to survey the guests. She moved slightly, sitting so that she was in the shadow of a curtained doorway.

As each man entered, she looked him over carefully. It had been strange to learn that an entirely different world existed outside Trahern House, a world which included men. In this new world, Morgan felt awkward and out of place. It was incredible that her personal value could be assessed by such things as clothing, physical beauty, and whether or not she made a good match.

She saw Brian Ferguson enter and considered him

for a moment. Tall, slim, handsome, he was about twenty years old. He would probably not want to leave his comfortable home and travel to the wilds of New Mexico. He was an only son and would inherit his father's plantation. She must look for a second or third son, one who would need money, and who would lose little or nothing by moving to New Mexico.

The music started and couples began to dance. Morgan sat in the shadows, wishing she were back at Trahern House and not sitting here, awkward and lonely. Older women began to take the chairs near Morgan. They paid little attentoin to her, except for occasional glances of pity.

Morgan listened carefully as the women pointed out various people to one another and exchanged gossip about them.

"That Cynthia Ferguson—whatever can her mama be thinking by letting her daughter wear a dress cut so low?" asked a gray-haired woman dressed in black.

"Her mama is thinking very carefully of trying to get that handsome Mr. Seth Colter for her son-in-law," explained another.

Morgan's eyes followed their glances. She saw him standing not too far from her, and her eyes widened at the sight of him. Seth Colter certainly was good looking, but, somehow, he was not conventionally handsome. For one thing, he was too big. He was probably one or two inches under six feet, but the width of his shoulders and the thickness of his chest made him look terribly powerful. His chest tapered to slim hips and legs, but the muscles in his thighs bulged under snug pants. Morgan blushed and looked away. What in the world was she doing, staring at a man's thighs? She smiled as she thought of what her mother would say!

The women beside her kept talking and she forced her eyes around the room again. She considered every man, most of whom she knew nothing about. She began

7

to listen more attentively to the women. Again, she found they were talking about the man her eyes had so carefully avoided for the last fifteen minutes.

"Well, I don't understand it, either. He has everything. Nora and William Colter have given their lives to that plantation, and everything will be his someday." The lady in black was talking.

"And I don't blame William at all for refusing to give him the money for that place of his. Where is it?"

"New Mexico, I believe the territory is called."

Morgan nearly jumped. She considered what she had heard: Seth Colter needed money and he had a place in New Mexico.

Seth was talking to Cynthia now, and a wave of anger crossed Morgan. He was looking down at Cynthia with a sort of mocking expression, as if he were amused by her.

As Morgan studied Seth's face, she felt eyes on her and looked to see Cynthia staring at her. Seth, following Cynthia's gaze, turned to look at Morgan. He looked at her thoroughly, seeming to look at every part of her. He smiled slightly, but showed no real interest in her.

"Morgan, you dear thing, sitting all alone here in the shadows. No one can even see you. Has anyone asked you to dance yet?" Cynthia obviously wanted to show Seth the difference between her own popular self and this rather plain girl in the ill-fitting dress.

"No," said Morgan timidly, "I haven't danced. But then, we haven't been here very long." She felt she had to save some pride. Why did that man have to keep *staring* at her? Why did she feel so warm under his gaze?

Cynthia's eyes darted from Morgan to Seth. She seemed to enjoy Morgan's obvious embarrassment. "Seth, dearest, why don't you dance with our little Morgan?"

"No—" Morgan began, looking up at the man who seemed to be enjoying her confusion.

"Seth, I promised the next dance to Paul Davis, and if you could just keep Morgan company, I'll come right back to you." Her lashes fluttered, and she gazed up at him with promise in her eyes. Morgan's mouth tightened as she realized that Cynthia thought her thoroughly safe company. She'd be no threat to Cynthia!

Seth Colter looked down at the young woman that Cynthia was pushing at him. Poor Cynthia, he thought, just like my sisters. She thinks that if she flutters her lashes at a man and he dances with her twice, then the next step is an engagement.

Somehow, this Morgan interested him. She kept her eyes lowered, and he looked at the top of her head. He saw hair that was both blond and brown, not evenly mixed, but streaked, with parts very light and parts the color of dry piñon needles. He could tell very little about her body under that horrible brown bag of a dress, but he knew she was small. He doubted she reached five feet.

Seth knew Cynthia considered Morgan no temptation. Certainly the girl knew it too. She wasn't pretty— or was she? He wondered how she would look with her long pale hair loose, cascading across her shoulders and down her back, with no clothes on.

Seth assured Cynthia that he would very much like to dance with Morgan. Doubt crossed Cynthia's face, but only for a moment.

"But would you please introduce us first?" he said.

The introduction completed, Morgan extended her hand and found it totally engulfed by his. His hand was warm, the palm calloused and hard.

"I am pleased to make your acquaintance, Miss Wakefield." His eyes smiled. He showed much more interest in her than he had a few minutes before. He turned to Cynthia. "Please excuse us. A waltz has begun, and I am interested in knowing how Miss Wakefield came by a first name like Morgan." He led Morgan to the dance floor. She could feel the warmth of his body through his coat sleeve.

He took her in his arms and they began to dance. She was glad now that Aunt Lacey had arranged for her dancing lessons. She wanted to glide, to enjoy herself, but she remembered the job that had to be done.

"Mr. Colter, I heard it mentioned that you have a place in New Mexico."

He paused before answering. What game was she playing? "Yes, I do . . . a small cattle ranch."

How to go on? How do you lead up to asking a total stranger to marry you? "My father lived in New Mexico for a number of years. I was born there." When he didn't reply, she said, "His name was Charles Wakefield."

He tilted his head. "I've heard of your father. A very wealthy man, with a large spread just south of Albuquerque."

She looked straight into his eyes and said it plainly. "Yes, a very wealthy man."

He laughed aloud. He thought he saw her game. He knew her father had died within the year. She probably was an heiress. Since she couldn't flirt with looks, like Cynthia, she was going to dangle her money as bait. It was incredible what a woman would do to get a husband.

Morgan took a deep breath. "I shall be honest, Mr. Colter. I'd like to make a business deal with you. As you say, my father was a very wealthy man. And now he has left that money to me, on a condition.

"In compliance with that condition," she continued, "I'd like to offer you a job. It would be no more than a job," she emphasized. "The job would last one year, you would not have to leave your ranch in New Mexico, and I would pay you twenty-five thousand dollars for your services during that year."

He was about to speak when the music stopped. They both looked up to see Cynthia rapidly making her way toward them. She doesn't waste any time, thought Morgan.

"Miss Wakefield," he said, taking her arm, "your job interests me. Shall we go somewhere where we can talk?"

Much to Cynthia's chagrin, Seth led Morgan away. Of course, he couldn't have seen me coming or he would never have turned his back, thought Cynthia. Yet there was just a seed of doubt.

"Cynthia! What a lovely dress!" someone called. Cynthia turned to accept the compliment and missed seeing Seth lead Morgan into the garden.

Morgan and Seth sat side by side on a stone bench under a copse of trees.

"Now, Miss Wakefield, just what is this job that is so important that you are willing to pay twenty-five thousand dollars for it?" He leaned against a tree, and smiled a half-smile.

Morgan thought quickly. She sensed that if she burst out that the job was to marry her and live with her for one year, he would leave. No, she must explain it all from the beginning and gradually lead up to his part in her life.

She looked at her hands and took a deep breath. "Mr. Colter, this is an unusual story, and before I tell you of the job, I must explain some of its background.

"I have said that I was born in New Mexico. My mother and father lived there, together, for two years, including the year after I was born. My mother hated the heat and the dryness and the lack of comfort. She had been accustomed to much better in her father's house here in Kentucky.

"She left him, took me, and returned to her home. I lived alone with my mother, in the country, until I was sixteen. Then she passed away. For the past two years I have lived with my aunt and uncle here in Louisville." Morgan felt the anger rise in her as she arrived at this point in her story. She rose and stood by the bougainvillea vine at the corner of the bench.

Without looking at him, she continued. "My life was peaceful until six months ago. I had planned to live with my aunt and uncle until such time as my uncle gave his consent for my return to Trahern House, the home of my childhood. I must digress a moment and tell you, Mr. Colter," she met his eyes, "that I do not feel at ease around large numbers of people. My major goal in life has been to live alone at Trahern House. You must understand that."

Seth recalled his home in the mountains of New Mexico, the isolation of it, the peace of it. "I do understand that," he said.

Morgan sensed that he did.

"Please continue, Miss Wakefield. You were saying that everything changed six months ago?"

"Six months ago my father died. He left his money to me, but with a stipulation, which is what puts me here at this exact moment."

"Come now, Miss Wakefield, you do not flatter me. I trust that our friend, Cynthia, would not find being here with me so distasteful."

Morgan stiffened. "I am not at all like Cynthia Ferguson. If I had my wish, I would be at home at Trahern House."

"I am sorry. I did not wish to arouse your hostility. I am still waiting for my part in this."

"My father had always wanted my mother to send me to New Mexico, but she refused. So my father decided to see to it that I went to New Mexico after his death." She paused to draw a breath, and looked directly at Seth. "If I am to collect my inheritance, I must marry a man and live with him in New Mexico for one year."

12

She watched him intently. But in the dim light, she could see no change in his expression.

"I must do this before I am twenty-five years old or else everything goes to my uncle." Her voice changed. "And of course my uncle is planning everything in his power to keep me from marrying. You can see the way I am forced to dress. In two days, he plans to take my aunt and me to Europe for an extended trip. My bags are already packed."

She sat back down on the bench, feeling spent. She did not like having to pour out her troubles to a stranger. She could not look at Seth.

There was a long pause. Morgan began to feel that she had lost.

Finally, he spoke. "Well, then . . . am I to be the man who fulfills your father's wish?"

Her head came up. "I offer you a business deal, sir. I will pay you twenty-five thousand dollars for the use of your name and for a year's room and board in your house in New Mexico."

He said quietly, "What do you plan to do at the end of the year? How do you plan to dissolve the marriage?"

Once Morgan had heard her Aunt Lacey and some friends gossiping about an elopement that had been annulled. "It will be annulled."

"Annulled?"

She could hear the amusement in his voice and wasn't sure that he understood. "Yes. Annulled—as the elopement of Kevin and Alice Fulton was annulled last spring."

He laughed aloud, actually more of a snort than a laugh. "Oh, I see. I believe that brief marriage was annulled on the grounds of lack of consummation. Are those the grounds you would choose for the annulment?"

Morgan was not sure about the meaning of the word, but she had heard whispers. She wanted no closeness with this or any other man. She wanted to be free to return to Trahern House at the end of the year. "Yes," she answered him, meeting his eyes, "this will be a marriage in name only."

Seth looked at her charming, honest face, bathed in moonlight, and smiled to himself. He thought about the isolation of his house in the New Mexico mountains and the coldness of the winters. He wondered whether, after the two of them had lived together all winter long, they would qualify for an annulment. He hoped not.

~ *Chapter Two* ~

"MORGAN, Morgan!" Uncle Horace's voice reached them in the garden.

"I must go in, or he will send every person in the ballroom to find me." She turned to Seth with questioning eyes, reluctant to go without a firm agreement between them.

He understood her hesitancy and said, "I accept your offer. You said you were to leave day after tomorrow?"

"Yes."

"There are arrangements to be made. I will come for you tomorrow, but it may be late in the day." As he took her arm and they returned to the ballroom, Morgan begged him to keep their arrangement a secret. She feared her Uncle Horace would take her away if he knew.

As they returned, Morgan noticed a few faces turned toward them.

Cynthia moved quickly to them. "Why, Seth, you are such a dear to make Morgan feel welcome." Her words were confident, but her eyes betrayed her. She touched Seth's arm and fluttered her lashes at him. "Seth, dear, I believe this is our dance."

Morgan saw the frown crease Seth's broad forehead, and guessed that he did not like Cynthia's possessiveness. She spoke loudly, "There is my Aunt Lacey. If you would escort me to her, I'd like to sit down."

15

He turned to Cynthia. "If you will excuse us, I will take Miss Wakefield to her aunt."

They left, arm in arm, Cynthia glaring.

As they approached Aunt Lacey and the other women, a hush fell over the women's talk. Morgan seated herself, and Seth said in a low voice. "I will see you tomorrow." His smile held the same mocking quality that she had seen before.

"My dear," asked the lady next to Aunt Lacey, after Seth had gone, "do you know who that is?"

"His name is Seth Colter." She was curious to find out what the women knew.

"Have you heard of the Colter plantation outside Louisville?" At Morgan's silence, she continued. "It is one of the largest and richest in the state, and it is all to be his some day. Yet he is throwing it away to live in some unholy place out west."

Yes, Morgan knew this. She wanted to know more of this man who would be her husband in another day. She smiled when she thought how this overweight woman in damp, green satin would react to the news: "Do you mean that that dowdy little thing, Lacey's niece, married rich, handsome Seth Colter?" Morgan caught herself before she laughed aloud.

She looked at the Green Lady and said innocently, eyes wide, "But I thought he and Cynthia Ferguson were practically engaged. Surely Cynthia wouldn't go out west to live?"

"No," said another woman, the lady in black whom Morgan had heard earlier. "That's just what Caroline Ferguson would like to think. But that daugher of hers hasn't snared him yet."

"She'd just like everyone to assume they're engaged," echoed the Green Lady.

Morgan saw her Uncle Horace approach then, and she rose, knowing he and Aunt Lacey probably wanted to depart.

The three of them took their leave of Mr. and Mrs. Ferguson, and Morgan searched the crowd to find Seth. She needed some reassurance from him. She saw his broad back far across the room, next to a pretty young woman, and she felt a wave of anger. Then she told herself that was silly.

All the way home in the plush-lined carriage, Morgan thought and planned. She would secretly rearrange her baggage so she'd be ready to leave when Seth came the next night.

With a start she remembered that she had not told him which window was hers. She would leave a light, and hope he would find it.

They arrived home after the short journey. After goodnights, she was at last alone in her room.

She took off the ugly brown dress and tossed it across the settee, unfastened her blond hair, and sighed. On impulse, she removed all her undergarments and looked at her nude body in the mirror. She looked at firm, round breasts, tapering to a small waist and flat stomach and then rounding out again to full hips and thighs. She ran her hand down the smooth skin of her waist, onto her hip. She shivered, shocked by what she was doing. No decent woman ever looked at her own naked body, much less at a mirror reflection.

Quickly, she turned from the mirror and slipped her nightgown over her head. But still, she remembered the image of her body. And she thought maybe she wouldn't be so plain if she left her hair in curls.

Morgan climbed into bed and snuggled deep into the warm covers. Soon she was asleep.

She was up the next morning before the rest of the household. She had always liked the early morning and was at her best then. If she were at Trahern House, she could go to the stable, saddle Cassandra, and ride across the dew-covered fields.

17

Instead, she quietly went to the kitchen and made her own breakfast. One of the many indulgences her mother had given her was cooking lessons from a French chef. Her mother had been appalled when she had first found her little daughter in the kitchen helping Cook. She and Morgan had argued long over that, but in the end, her mother had given in. A month later, Jean-Paul arrived. He planned to stay six weeks, but had instead become a member of the family and stayed for a little over a year, until he had to return to Marseilles.

She remembered the many happy hours with Jean-Paul in the sunny, spacious kitchen at Trahern House, and she was glad that Jean-Paul had taught her so much about cooking. He had made her churn her own butter when she first started. Soon, she could make delicate preserves and jellies, and learned a light touch with breads and pastries.

"Morgan, dear," came Aunt Lacey's voice, "are you up so early?"

"Come in, Aunt Lacey, and I'll make you some breakfast." Morgan knew this might be their last breakfast together. She would miss Aunt Lacey's gentleness.

Over fluffy omelets, oozing cheese, Morgan and Lacey discussed the ball. Or, rather, Lacey talked and Morgan listened.

After breakfast, each woman went to her own room to continue packing for the next day's journey, the start of their long trip to Europe.

In the privacy of her room, Morgan began arranging things in the luggage. She packed a small trunk and one bag to be carried by hand, for the trip to New Mexico.

She had only the plain, too-large clothing that her uncle had commissioned a seamstress to sew for her. He had had her clothing from Trahern House taken away. The last item she packed was her recipe book.

At seven o'clock that evening, as they were sitting

18

down to dinner, the Wakefields' old servant announced, "A Mr. Colter to see you, sir."

Morgan gasped audibly, and Horace and Lacey's eyes turned on her, but she said nothing.

"Show him into the library, please, Roy. If you ladies will excuse me." He turned one last puzzled glance to Morgan, then left the room.

"Is that the nice Mr. Colter you danced with last night?" At Morgan's silence, Lacey continued, "I thought he was taken with you. I wouldn't doubt but that he is here to ask permission to court you."

"In Europe?"

Lacey looked down at her hands and was silent. She had been at the reading of the will. She knew why Horace was taking them to Europe.

Morgan regretted her comment and walked to Lacey's side and patted her shoulder. "I'm sorry, Aunt Lacey. You're probably right. Maybe he is here to speak to Uncle Horace about courtship."

Lacey smiled and resumed her chattering. Morgan paced the room and watched the clock, hardly aware of Lacey's words.

Forty-five minutes later, the door opened and Horace entered with Şeth. Seth had a slight smile on his face, but Horace was grim and his voice cold.

"Get your things and go."

It was Lacey's turn to gasp. "Horace . . ." she protested weakly.

At the sound of his wife's voice, Horace turned. His face lost some of its hatred, and his voice became softer. "It seems that Mr. Colter has come to take our Morgan away." He paused. "They are to be married tonight at Judge Stevenson's."

Morgan's eyes widened. What in the world had Seth done to get Uncle Horace to consent to the marriage?

Lacey hugged the stunned Morgan. "Oh, Morgan!

An elopement! How very romantic. What ever will you wear? We must pack. There is so much to do."

Seth stepped forward and took Morgan's arm. "We must hurry, my dear." He led Morgan into the hall. He dropped her arm and his manner changed. He stepped back and looked her up and down with a mocking expression. "If the two articles of clothing I have seen are a correct indication of your wardrobe, leave it all here. I will purchase more suitable clothing for you—at least something that fits."

Morgan was about to forget her good sense and tell him what she thought of his manners, when Horace and Lacey came into the entryway. Morgan turned on her heel and went up the stairs to her room.

She returned in a few minutes with only her small bag. In it were a few pieces of jewelry, her cookbook, her nightgown, and a few toilet articles. She would leave her carefully packed trunk upstairs.

After a tearful farewell to Lacey and a cold goodbye to Horace, she and Seth entered the waiting carriage.

They rode in silence for a few minutes. Then Morgan spoke. "How did you do it?" she asked.

"How did I do what?" He turned toward her.

"What did you do to get Uncle Horace to allow me to leave?"

He smiled. "I just mentioned a few names and asked if he thought it was quite ethical to spirit you away, not allowing you to try to find a husband who could help you to fulfill your father's will."

She waited for him to say more, but he turned his head again and seemed to be occupied with his own thoughts. As they rode in silence, Morgan began to feel uncomfortable. She had never been alone with a man before, at least not with a man so near her own age.

"It just happened so differently than I imagined."

He turned, startled, seeming for the first time to realize her presence. "And how did you imagine it?" His tone was condescending.

She felt like a child about to be reprimanded. "I . . ." she started, "left a light in my window . . ."

His face brightened, showing dancing lights in his eyes. "Did you imagine that I'd come in the middle of the night and steal you away?"

She did not answer, but her tightened mouth gave her away. He laughed loudly, and she wanted to hit him.

He sobered somewhat when he saw the hurt in her eyes. He reached over and placed his hand on hers and said quietly, "Did you really think I'd climb a ladder like a schoolboy?"

The appeal in his eyes made her see the humor. No, she could not imagine this enormous man climbing a ladder in the middle of the night to spirit his bride away. She smiled back at him.

They rode on, again in silence, but there was no more hostility between them. Morgan was no longer nervous.

They had been riding for what seemed hours, each occupied with his own thoughts, when the coach stopped, and Seth said, "Are you sure you don't want to change your mind?"

She shook her head slightly. "Yes, I'm sure."

"Good." His eyes danced. "I guess that means you think you can stand me for a whole year."

He got out of the carriage, helped Morgan out, and led her to the front of a large, pleasant, whitewashed house. Morgan looked around. She knew they had been heading south, toward Lexington, but she wasn't sure where they were now.

Finally a servant answered the door and Morgan preceded Seth into the hallway.

"The judge is waiting for you, Mr. Colter," he said.

"Thanks, Elijah."

The servant led them to a door off the hallway into a cozy drawing room.

A large man came toward them swiftly, hand extended. "Well, well, well! I never thought I'd have the honor of this day—I mean night. It's good to see you are finally going to get married, Seth."

Seth smiled. "May I present Miss Morgan Wakefield."

"I am very glad to meet the lady who has been chosen by this young man. Why, I've known his father for years."

"And his mother, too." A small woman entered the room. "Nora Colter is my dearest friend."

"This is my wife, Sara, and if this man of yours hasn't told you, I am Judge Samuel Stevenson."

Morgan extended her hand, which he shook robustly. "I am very happy to meet you."

"Let's begin, shall we?" said Judge Stevenson.

The service was over so quickly that Morgan hardly realized it had taken place. The silence at the end was awkward. Finally, Judge Stevenson laughed and said, "Go ahead and kiss the bride, Seth."

He turned to Morgan with a winning smile and bent down to kiss her, gently taking hold of her shoulders.

At first she was astonished. Then, just as his lips were very close to hers, she turned her head quickly and his kiss landed on her ear, just above the earlobe. His breath was soft and warm in her ear, his kiss moist, and she felt chills on her arms.

Morgan kept her eyes from Seth's and accepted the congratulations from the Judge and Mrs. Stevenson. In spite of their entreaties to stay, the young couple left immediately after the ceremony. They were soon on their way again in the coach.

Morgan had just snuggled into a corner of the coach when she felt it lurch. She looked up to see Seth's broad shoulders leaning toward the window.

"Well, my little bride, we are here." He stepped out of the coach and turned to help Morgan down the two steps.

She saw before her, shining in the moonlight, an enormous white mansion. What was it the woman had said last night? The Colter plantation was one of the largest and richest in the state.

The house had two stories, with massive, white columns extending the full height. There was a deep veranda with several large oak chairs and rockers scattered about. On either side of the veranda were two large old willows, moving slightly in the night breeze.

On the second story there was a balcony, with a delicate, white-painted railing. She could see one pair of double doors leading onto the balcony and guessed there were others.

Seth carried Morgan's bag and led her into the house and up a massive staircase to the second floor. She followed him silently down the thickly carpeted hallway and into his bedroom.

Seth lit the lamp, and Morgan could see that the room was very large. All the furniture was walnut: dark, rich, and heavy. The prominent feature of the room was an enormous four-poster bed. Morgan stood staring at it, thinking that it was just the sort of bed that a man like Seth should have.

Seth had come up behind her and stood quietly as Morgan was staring at the bed. "It's just as comfortable as it looks," he whispered.

Morgan jumped and turned toward him, their faces inches apart. He bent toward her. "Come, *mi querida*, and I'll show you what it's like to be a real bride." His voice was low and soft and persuasive. But Morgan, unused to the presence of a man, was frightened by his large body and took a step backwards.

Her face betrayed her fear, and Seth laughed. "Don't be afraid, little rabbit, I won't hurt you. Where is that look of fire I saw you flash at Cynthia Ferguson? Anyone who can give such a look shouldn't be afraid of a mere man."

Morgan smiled.

"That's better. You may take the bed and I'll sleep on the couch. Does that ease your fears?"

Morgan hastily took her bag and went to the adjoining dressing room. She was nervous as she removed her dress and put on the plain, white nightgown. As she took the pins from her hair and brushed the mass into fat, shiny curls that reached her waist, she tried not to think about Seth.

When she returned to the room and self-consciously walked across to the bed, she saw that Seth had turned down the covers. He was already wrapped in a blanket on the couch, his head away from her. He appeared to be sleeping. Somehow she felt a tinge of anger that he could ignore her so completely.

As she blew out the lamp and snuggled under the covers, she heard Seth say sleepily, "Goodnight, *mi querida.*"

Morgan smiled and said, "Goodnight."

The next morning, Morgan was awakened by a knock on the door. "Mr. Seth, are you up yet?"

Morgan sat up just in time to see Seth striding across the room towards her. Morgan's eyes opened very wide in astonishment at the sight of him. He was completely naked. Morgan had not seen many men, even clothed, and had never seen a man without his shirt. She glimpsed a broad, heavy chest covered with thick, curling hair, large arms and shoulders, all tapering to a hard, flat stomach. He climbed into bed with her before she could complete her survey.

"Close your mouth, little one. You don't want Bessie to think a newly wedded couple would spend their wedding night apart, do you?" He moved close to Morgan so that their thighs touched. Louder he said, "Come in, Bessie."

A very large woman entered the room carrying a tray

24

of coffee. As she saw Morgan in the enormous bed sitting beside Seth, she stopped and stared. Seth moved even closer to Morgan and put his arm around her shoulders. "Bessie, I'd like you to meet my wife, Morgan."

It didn't take Bessie long to recover her voice. "I declare, Mr. Seth, you didn't give nobody word that you were bringing a bride. I bet even your mama don't know."

Seth grinned and hugged Morgan closer, idly taking a curl in one hand and rubbing it between his fingers. "No, Mother doesn't know, but then it was a rather hurried marriage. Morgan and I just met the night before last."

"An elopement! Your sisters are just going to love that." Bessie had a twinkle in her eye. "Well, I must mind my manners. It's nice to meet you," she said to the still-silent bride.

Morgan managed to murmur, "Thank you."

Bessie smiled broadly and said, "Well, Mr. Seth, I'll just leave you two. You come down whenever you're ready." The twinkle deepened and she winked at Seth. He returned the wink. Morgan looked down at her hands and blushed.

Bessie put the tray on the bedside table and turned to leave. As she did so, she stopped for a second and looked at the couch with the rumpled quilt and pillow, still dented where Seth's head had been. She frowned for a second, then left, closing the door behind her.

The room seemed too quiet, and Morgan was acutely aware that Seth was making no attempt to leave her side or even to take his arm from around her shoulders. She continued to study her hands.

Seth put his other hand beneath her chin and turned her head. Without a word, he tipped her head back and gently touched his lips to hers. Morgan felt she had

25

never experienced anything so sweet and gentle as his lips.

Seth withdrew his lips and looked down at her. The sunlight filtered through the curtains, capturing the brilliance of her long, golden hair. He decided he'd like very much to find out what lay under that billowing nightgown. He smiled at the thought and Morgan opened her eyes to find him smiling.

"Do you always find me amusing?" she asked in a cold voice. Her body stiffened under his arm.

Seth removed the arm. "Quite often. But I also find it astonishing that you can hide all that hair away in such a tight little knot." He lifted his hand to play with a fat curl.

Morgan's voice was cold. "May I remind you, Mr. Colter, that our arrangement is a business one. The way I arrange my hair is of no concern to you."

Morgan saw his jaw muscles flex as he ground his teeth together. "You are right, madam. Your looks, or lack of them, is of no concern to me." Morgan winced. Why did people *always* have to remind her of her plainness?

"Now if you do not want to be shocked, you had better look the other way."

Morgan did not understand his meaning until he threw back the covers. She turned her head, but could not keep her eyes averted. She looked up to see a broad back with a deeply grooved backbone, leading to roundly curving buttocks and firm thighs. The thighs were covered with golden hair. At the sound of Seth's laughter, she looked up to meet his eyes in the mirror over the dressing table.

"So! My shy little bride is not so shy when my back is turned."

Morgan kept her eyes on his. In what she hoped was a cool voice, she said, "Only curious."

Seth roared. He continued laughing as he began to dress. Morgan carefully kept her eyes averted.

He left, telling Morgan to come down when she was ready, that his family would be anxious to meet her.

As Morgan dressed, she had time to think. She did not like the way things were going. Already she and Seth had had one quarrel, and they had been married just a few hours. If they were to live together for a full year, they must come to terms. They could not go on this way, with stolen kisses and angry words.

His three sisters were waiting at the foot of the stairs. "Hello. You must be Seth's wife," the tallest one called. "This is Jennifer, the youngest, Eleanor, the middle, and I am Austine, the oldest."

"Austine and Eleanor are engaged!" Jennifer chirped.

"Let's go into the drawing room and get acquainted. Bessie says you two have only known one another for a day and a half!" Austine looked at Morgan questioningly.

"Yes, that's true."

"Love at first sight! I would never have guessed that Seth could be so romantic," Eleanor added.

Jennifer smiled, "We're so glad it was you and not that Cynthia Ferguson."

"Jennifer!" Austine's anger did not seem real. "What Jennifer means is . . ."

"Just what she said," Eleanor supplied. "You're our sister now, and we can tell you what we think."

Austine seemed suddenly to notice Morgan's unfashionable, baggy dress. "Did you bring much luggage?"

Morgan blushed. "No, I . . . Seth wanted me to buy new clothes before we left for New Mexico."

"New Mexico!" Eleanor cried. "I thought he'd stay at home now that he had a wife." She looked close to tears.

"Hush, Elly. Seth and Morgan will decide what they want to do. Now we must have time to think about your clothes. Papa will take us to Louisville, and we can buy lots of fabric."

"And ribbons and lace."

"This is so exciting! Why, Morgan, we'll make you the most fashionable young lady in the entire West."

"Girls! Please allow your mother to meet her new daughter." Morgan looked to the door to see a tall, slim woman with an abundance of thick, dark blond hair coiled around the back of her head. She was so different from her plump, pink-and-white daughters. In fact, there was something about her that reminded Morgan very much of Seth.

"Oh, Mama, Seth told her that she was to get new clothes before they left. They are going to New Mexico." Eleanor said this with a hint of disbelief.

The girls' mother smiled at Morgan, and Morgan felt relieved. Here was someone she could talk to—these chattering girls were difficult to comprehend.

"Morgan, my name is Nora. Let's go to the morning room so that we may talk." She ushered Morgan out of the drawing room, down the large entry hallway, and into a small room decorated in green and white. A large window faced the east, and the sun was streaming in. Nora motioned Morgan to be seated.

"I watched you for a few moments with my daughters. You did not seem to take an active part in their chatter."

Morgan immediately liked this woman. She felt she could be honest. "No, I am not used to talk of clothes and lace and romance."

Nora did not change her expression. She continued looking at Morgan directly. "Why did you marry my son?" Nora hesitated for only seconds and then continued. "I know that one of you slept on the couch last night, and I also know my son. He does not fall in love at first sight." She looked steadily at Morgan.

Morgan decided to tell her the truth.

"I will tell you. My one goal in life is to live in my childhood home, Trahern House. I am a quiet person. I am uncomfortable around many people, and I plan to live alone there.

"Two years ago, my mother died. Since I was not of age, I was sent to live with my aunt and uncle. My parents had separated when I was one year old, and my father still lived in New Mexico."

Nora's brows lifted at the mention of New Mexico.

"A month ago, my uncle told me of my father's death. I never knew him so I could feel little grief. Two weeks ago his will was read. It was a great shock to me. It seems that everything—the business in Kentucky, the land in Kentucky, the large ranch in New Mexico, and Trahern House—all belonged to him. He left everything to me, but he stated that everything would be mine only if I married and lived with my husband for one year in New Mexico. If I did not fulfill this contract, everything would go to my uncle. As you can see," her hand swept across her dress, "my uncle did everything he could to keep men from noticing me."

Morgan paused and looked carefully at Nora.

"I went to a ball two nights before my uncle planned to take me out of the country. I heard some women mention that your son had a place in New Mexico. I offered him twenty-five thousand dollars if he would marry me and take me to live with him in New Mexico. He accepted."

Nora said simply, "Good."

It was too much for Morgan. She rose from the chair and came to stand before Nora, her eyes blazing. "Good? Good that a father would make his own daughter stoop to buying a man's name, to living with a man she doesn't even know?"

Nora waited an entire minute before answering, and her calm encompassed Morgan. "I meant that I was glad you are sensible. You were faced with an impos-

29

sible situation, and you decided to fight for what you wanted."

Nora rose now and walked to the sunlit window, looked out for a second, and then turned to face Morgan. "Let me tell you about my son. My son believes all women are like his sisters. Don't misunderstand me. I love my daughters. But, as you can see, they are very young and have little else in their heads but dreams. Their father loves this and indulges them. My son does not see women as people."

Nora returned to her chair. "So, I say 'good' to your story, because my son needs a sensible wife, one he can like as well as love. Seth is a very strong man, and when you two learn to love one another, you will make an excellent couple."

Morgan stared at Nora. Didn't she understand? "Mrs. Colter—Nora—you do not seem to understand. This is a marriage to fulfill a business contract. I do not intend to love your son."

Nora looked at Morgan with what was very close to a smirk, and Morgan realized that she had seen the same expression on Seth's face. "Do you really believe that you can spend twelve full months alone with a man, and at the end of that time feel nothing for him? Do you really believe that you'll be able to leave easily and return to your solitary life?"

"I loved my aunt dearly, and I lived with her for two years, yet I left her."

Nora then threw back her head and laughed. "How old are you, Morgan?"

Morgan tilted her head up and said, "Eighteen."

"The love a woman has for another woman is very different from her love for a man."

There was an awkward pause, and Nora could see the anger in Morgan's eyes. "I am sorry. This is not happening as I meant it to. I asked you in here mainly to welcome you to the family, and to tell you that, from

30

what I've seen, I like you. You are sensible, and I believe you will be a good wife for Seth."

Morgan opened her mouth to protest, but instead let out a sigh of exasperation.

Nora walked to her, patted her shoulder, and said, "Please allow a mother to believe that her son has found a good partner."

Morgan smiled and they walked to the door together. "About the clothes," Nora said. "There won't be time to get but a few things made, but my daughters would love to send yards of fabric with you."

Morgan knew that Nora was her friend, and she felt good about their talk.

Morgan spent the day with Seth's sisters. It wasn't too difficult to feel at ease with them. Their chatter required little response and no deep thought. Austine and Eleanor talked of their fiancés. Morgan gathered that Austine's beau was an older man and very sensible, but that Eleanor's was quite the opposite. Eleanor's intended was Jackson Brenner, and he was the oldest son of an old, very wealthy family. Austine's fiancé was James Emerson, a widower with a young child.

Just before dinner, Morgan went upstairs to wash, and as she left the room to return downstairs, she heard Seth talking with another man. She paused at the top of the stairs to look at her father-in-law.

She had seen some of Seth's expressions in his mother's face, but looking at William Colter was like seeing Seth in twenty years' time. He was a large man. The two of them seemed to fill the room. The older man still had an abundance of hair. And they had the same indulgent, patronizing looks on their faces as they watched the three sisters.

Seth looked up and saw her first. For a second she wished he had looked at her the same way she had seen some men look at their brides, but she buried the desire.

31

"Well, well, well, I have another daughter, and such a pretty one, too." William Colter extended his arms.

Morgan took both his hands in hers, and said, "I am indeed your daughter, but you certainly must not be seeing me correctly!" She said this with a smile.

William took her arm through his, patted her hand, and smiled. "All women are pretty to me. Shall we eat? I'm starved."

They all entered the dining room, and sat at a large mahogany table. Morgan was seated between William and Seth, with Nora across from her. Austine and Eleanor sat beside Nora, and Jennifer was beside Seth. It was easy to see that Jennifer, especially, adored Seth.

"Papa," Eleanor started, "Morgan needs some new clothes and we must have them made before they leave. Could you take us to Louisville tomorrow to purchase fabric?"

William turned to Morgan, and for the first time noticed her dress.

"May we, Papa?" Jennifer continued.

"Yes, of course. I need to make some purchases myself."

Nora looked at Morgan, aware of her stress. She knew enough about her new daughter-in-law to know that she would not like a day shopping with the three giggling girls.

"Girls, you forget that Morgan is a new bride. I am sure she'd like to spend the day with her husband."

Morgan sent Nora a grateful look. "Do you ride, Morgan?" Nora asked calmly.

"Yes, but I haven't been on a horse in two years."

"All right then. Seth, you must take your wife on a tour of the Colter plantation."

Seth said, "Why, of course." He took Morgan's hand from where it lay on the tablecloth and raised it to his lips. His eyes were mocking as he said, "I'd love to take my little bride for a day in the country. Is that all right, *mi querida*?"

"Oh, Seth," Jennifer breathed, "you are so romantic!"

Morgan turned to see the entire family watching. Eleanor and Austine had rather dreamy expressions, but Nora and William looked like two fat, contented hens. They were pleased that their son had finally married.

Again, Jennifer was the first to break the silence. "But how will we know what to buy for Morgan? She must go with us."

Morgan calmly said, "As you can see, I know little about clothes. Whatever pleases you will please me."

Nora said, "No. My daughters tend toward flounces and laces. You are too small for those. And also," she seemed to inventory Morgan's face, "their dimpled, round, good looks tend toward pastels. You need clear, bright colors—reds, greens, black, and bright blues." Nora spotted the bored look on her son's face. She laughed. "Yes, dear. I will stop talking of clothes."

"Just make sure all the material is sturdy," Seth added.

The rest of the meal was filled with talk of the plantation.

After the meal, Morgan retired to their room upstairs. The last two days had been exhausting. She entered the room to find Bessie filling a large, white bathtub.

"I knew you'd be too tired to stay up very late, so it's all ready for you."

"Thank you so much, Bessie. You don't know how much I'm going to enjoy this." She reached up to unpin her hair.

"Here, young 'un, you just sit down and let old Bessie help you. I've done this more times 'an you can count, what with three little girls to raise."

As Morgan's hair tumbled from the hard knot at the back of her head, Bessie drew in her breath. "Land sakes, child! Why do you want to keep all that beautiful stuff hidden?" She grabbed an armful of it and piled it on top of Morgan's head. "You should let me fix it up for you, like this," she said, as she pinned it loosely on top of Morgan's head.

Morgan laughed and stood up as Bessie unfastened the tiny buttons on the dress. As she stepped out of it, and then her undergarments, Bessie exclaimed, "Why, I thought you were kind of thick-waisted and that you had no bosom at all. But just look at you."

Morgan felt an urge to cover herself. She had never been nude before anyone except her mother and her nurse, and not since she was a child. She stepped into the tub, leaned back, and closed her eyes. She lay there, dreaming, and did not hear the door close behind Bessie, or open again.

Seth stood for some minutes, looking down at his little wife. The blond hair was piled on her head, a few curls falling down her back and a few clinging to her steam-dampened face. Her skin was flawless, glistening over smooth shoulders, its creamy texture leading to the two round swellings just glimpsed above the cloudy water. One slim arm was on each side of the tub. He was looking at these when he realized her eyes were open.

They looked at one another for a second, and Seth grinned. "My sisters sent me to ask you if you have any preference for a style of clothing. That seems to have a good deal of bearing on what fabric they choose."

Morgan, still holding his eyes, said evenly, "No. I know nothing about it."

Seth turned to go and then looked back, his eyes mischievous. "May I tell them that I prefer the style you have on now? That bathtub is by far the most becoming thing I have seen you wear."

"*You!*" Morgan glanced around for something to throw.

34

Seth laughed. "Careful, or I'll see more than just the bathtub." He turned and left the room, chuckling.

She tried to return to her dreaming, but Seth had ruined it for her. She finished bathing, stepped from the tub, and dried. Then she climbed into the big bed. As she drifted off to sleep, she remembered Seth's eyes. Why had his gaze made her feel so warm?

She was asleep when Seth returned to their room. He undressed quietly, and settled onto the couch.

"Wake up. I thought you wanted to see the plantation." Seth was shaking her gently.

She stretched and smiled up at him. God! he thought. She looked like a cat, all grace in the early-morning light. As he looked at her, he began to feel his desire for her growing. "Either you get out of that bed, or I'm getting in with you."

She was startled by his tone and her eyes flew open. She rolled across the bed and climbed out the side farthest from him. As she ran toward the dressing room, she heard him mumble something about being a bull in the mornings. She couldn't stifle a giggle as she slipped into the same gown she had worn the day before.

She saw Seth's frown as she stepped back into the bedroom. "If you will remember, it was you who told me to leave my clothes behind. This and my nightgown are my only articles of clothing."

He left the room and returned in a few minutes with a riding habit. "This is Jennifer's. Try it on."

She returned in moments in the light-green whipcord habit. Jennifer was taller than Morgan, and weighed a great deal more. The outfit fit as poorly as the one her uncle had bought for her.

Seth grimaced. "I guess it will have to do."

No one was up yet, even in the stables. Seth handed her a thick slice of bread covered with butter, and saddled the two horses for them. Morgan's mare was gentle, and she was glad, because she did not feel up to fighting a horse.

They rode in silence, both of them enjoying the cool March morning. After they had ridden for an hour, Seth slowed his horse. "This stream is the boundary of the Colter plantation. Let's get down and I'll show you a place where I used to play as a child." He helped Morgan down, seemingly unaware of his hands on her waist.

"Give me your hand and we'll cross over these rocks." His hand was large, warm, and dry. After they had crossed the stream, he continued to hold her hand as they walked across the meadow. "I used to come here a lot. It seemed exciting, because it wasn't on Colter land."

"Didn't your sisters come?"

"They were afraid to get dirty."

"At Trahern House there was a special place for me. It was a big, old, sycamore tree, set in a large open meadow. I trampled all the grasses down and made a large area under the tree, but no one could see me from a distance, because the grasses were above my head." Her eyes shone.

"I think I would have liked your place."

She laughed. "I never had brothers or sisters, so I never had anyone to show it to. Maybe I would have shown it to you." She stopped, putting her hand over her mouth.

"What is it?" He seemed alarmed.

"Well, I just realized that when I was a child, you were a great, grown man already."

He laughed with her. "Yes, I guess I was. I'm fourteen years older than you, after all. I think I forget that you are the same age as my baby sister."

Morgan looked up at him, smiling, and squeezed his hand tighter. "I take that as a compliment."

Seth was overcome with an urge to kiss her, but the

moment was lost as she saw a great black and orange butterfly and skipped ahead, pulling Seth with her.

Damn it! Women were for kissing and dressing up like dolls, he thought, not for running around the wood together and talking about your childhood.

He forgot his moment's doubt as he saw the tree. It had at one time stood well away from the creek, but the water had washed the soil away, so that it now stood at the creek's edge. The branches hanging over the stream made a roof above the clear water.

"There it is."

Morgan saw the tree, and before he could say any more, she had dropped his hand and was scrambling down the bank to sit beneath the tree. She looked up at him cheerfully.

He stood looking at her. There was dirt on the enormous skirt, and a smudge on her cheek.

She realized what he was looking at. "I thought you already knew. I'm not a lady, and I never plan to be one. I am much happier here than at Cynthia Ferguson's ball."

He laughed. "I like it better here, too." He climbed down the bank to sit beside her.

She seized the opportunity to clear things up. "Seth, I want to talk to you. Yesterday morning we quarreled about the way I wear my hair, and last night I was angry when I was taking a bath." She paused, but he said nothing. She could feel him looking at her.

"I want to keep our relationship on a friendship level. I don't want us to quarrel. What I mean to say is that I want it clear between us that this is a marriage for convenience, a business arrangement."

"I understand. You do not want to share a bed with me." His eyes were cold. "All right." He looked at the tight hair, the baggy dress. "I believe I can refrain from molesting you. Is that what you are worried about?"

She was hurt by his anger. "Yes, I guess it is."

"Then I give you my word that I will not at any time force my attention on you. Does that satisfy you?"

She sighed. "Yes."

For Seth, the high mood of the day was broken. But for Morgan, it seemed an even brighter day. She was relieved. It seemed there would be no more fights between them.

Seth's gruff voice broke the silence. "Let's go back." He started toward the tethered horses.

"Seth, wait!"

He stopped, an impatient expression on his face.

"Seth—" She put her hand on his forearm. "I didn't mean to make you angry. I was trying to say that I want to be your friend. I don't want to fight. Somehow, I seem to have made everything worse."

His anger left him and he smiled. "You're right, little wife. I do have a quick temper. I apologize for my rudeness." He removed his hat and made a bow.

Morgan laughed. "I forgive you, sir."

"And to show my repentance, I shall ask Cook to prepare a picnic basket tomorrow, and we will go to my cabin—a pretty little place much farther upstream. Does that please you, my lady?"

"Well, good sir, it does, except for one part."

A slight frown replaced Seth's smile. "What part is that?"

Morgan's smile was winning. "That you allow me to prepare the picnic basket."

"You! You can cook?"

"I'll let you judge that tomorrow."

Seth returned Morgan's smile. "It seems I got more than I bargained for. A wife who can cook! I hope Lupita doesn't get jealous."

"Lupita?"

"She's my cook at the ranch in New Mexico."

"Tomorrow I want you to tell me about your ranch. I like being with animals."

38

They smiled at one another, returned to their horses, and rode back to the big house in a companionable silence.

Just before dinner, Morgan heard the voices of her sisters-in-law.

"Morgan, come look!" Jennifer's plump face had broken into a very large smile. She pushed Morgan toward a table heaped with fabrics and trimmings. In spite of what Nora had told her daughters, all the fabrics were creams, pink, and pale blues. Nora was examining the things.

"But, girls, I told you to get bright, clear colors. Morgan is too fair to wear these."

The three young women looked dismayed. Eleanor said timidly, "But, Mother, they are such beautiful colors."

Morgan felt the thin silks and satins. They would be totally unsuitable for New Mexico.

"Well, I can see my little sisters have chosen well for a grueling trip to the New Mexico mountains."

Everyone turned to Seth. Jennifer tilted her head toward him. "Just because a lady has to travel to a forsaken land doesn't mean she has to stop being a lady."

"Jennifer's right," Austine added. "When a lady wears silk, then she always remembers she is a lady."

"If a woman is a lady, then she is a lady no matter what she wears, including men's trousers."

"Trousers!" Eleanor's voice reflected disbelief. Deep down, she wasn't sure her own plump legs would fit properly into a pair of men's pants. The idea was appalling.

The joking tone left Seth's voice. "All right, sisters, since you have chosen completely inappropriate clothing for Morgan, then you must keep these fabrics for yourselves and supply her with some more suitable

39

garments from your own wardrobes. She will need the sturdiest fabrics you can obtain."

Morgan could readily see that the idea of several new dresses did not displease the girls.

Austine was the first to speak. "Morgan, let's go upstairs and we'll go through the chifforobe."

As the three sisters ushered Morgan upstairs, she turned a backward glance to Seth. He was looking at the pile of silks and brocade with an air of disgust. No wonder he thinks all women are silly, she thought.

Two hours later, Morgan emerged from the girls' bedrooms, totally exhausted. She had tried on dress after dress. No matter what she tried, it was huge on her. The sisters had wanted to start immediately on taking things in, adjusting them so they fit her snugly. Morgan had considered this for only a second. She knew that Seth gave her those special glances only when she had her hair down and she sensed that she would have an easier time holding him to his promise of the morning if her dresses fit loosely. She made excuses to her sisters-in-law, saying anything she could think of to persuade them not to alter the dresses.

At the dinner table, Austine tried to enlist Seth's help in getting Morgan to change her mind about taking in the dresses. But, much to her chagrin, Seth sided with Morgan.

"I think my little wife is right. Tight dresses with heavy corsets"—the girls' eyes widened; they wondered how their brother knew of ladies' corsets—"are not suitable wear for long hours in the sun, sitting on a jolting wagon seat."

The matter seemed to be settled, and the conversation turned to other matters.

After dinner, the family retired to the drawing room. As they began to occupy themselves, a groom came in to tell Seth and William that Susan was about to foal.

Seth was on his feet in seconds. "No, Pa, this is mine. You stay and enjoy your brandy." He looked at

Morgan and hesitated, but only for a second. "Come on."

Her face showed her joy as she took his hand and they went quickly and silently to the barn.

The mare, Susan, was lying down in the sweet-smelling straw, her breath heavy and rapid. As Seth assisted with the already-emerging colt, Morgan held the horse's head and soothed her, speaking quietly and evenly.

The birth was an easy one, but still the tension was great. Morgan knew Seth loved the pretty little mare, and that this colt was to be his. Seth helped the mare clean her colt and, within minutes, the little stallion was trying to stand.

Morgan and Seth stood by and watched, laughing together at the colt's clumsiness. When the colt began to nurse, they decided it was time to leave.

As they stepped out of the warm barn into the cool night air, Morgan shivered. Without thinking, Seth put his arm around her shoulders and drew her to him, so that the sides of their bodies touched. Morgan started to draw away, but something in the casual way Seth had put his arm around her was reassuring.

"You were good with the mare."

"Thank you."

"I think you'll do well in New Mexico. There are many jobs like that one."

"I like being outside. Could we walk a few minutes before we go in?"

Without a word, he led her around the barn and toward a grove of trees. "It's been a long day, hasn't it?"

"Yes."

"How were my sisters this afternoon? Did their chattering bother you?"

Morgan laughed. "Yes. They seemed very upset because clothing is not my passion."

Seth halted and swung Morgan around till she was in

41

his arms. His voice was low. "Tell me something, Morgan. What *is* your all-consuming passion?"

Without hesitation, she answered simply, "Trahern House."

Seth continued smiling at her. "I like your honesty. It's unusual in a woman."

"Unusual in the women you've known, maybe, but I assure you there are things besides men that are important to some of us!"

Seth laughed loudly, his whole body shaking with merriment. Morgan moved from within the circle of his arms and repressed an urge to slap his smirking face. Her mother had been right! It was impossible to carry on an intelligent conversation with a man. They were always so sure that you, a woman, were an inferior being. She turned and ran toward the house, her strides filled with anger.

Before she had reached the house, Seth had her by the arm.

"Now wait a minute, Morgan!" His voice was stern. "Think about what you said and answer me this question: How many of the unmarried women you have met in the last two years cared about *anything* except getting a husband? And how many mothers with marriageable daughters cared about anything except getting that daughter married?" He paused a few seconds and then continued in a lower voice. "When women change their attitudes toward men, see a man as something besides a prize to be won, then, and only then, will men change their attitudes toward women!"

Morgan looked at the ground. He was right. Most women were like Cynthia Ferguson and Seth's sisters. She looked up at Seth and smiled. "You're right. But *I'm* different!"

A teasing look was in Seth's eyes. His voice was low, almost a whisper as he moved his face very near hers. "I can see you don't care about frivolous things . . . but what about men? I think maybe you haven't had a chance to learn about that." His lips moved to her ear and his breath was soft and warm. "Any time you want to find out about men, let me know. I'd be happy to help you in your . . . explorations."

His huge body made Morgan nervous. She quickly moved from him and ran for the safety of the house.

~~ *Chapter Three* ~~

"MORGAN." Seth's voice was close to her ear. "Get dressed and let's go. It's nearly sunup." He paused and looked at her drowsy face. "Better yet, don't get dressed. I like you that way."

Morgan opened her eyes and smiled up at him. His voice, his always-teasing manner, and his open, generous smile were becoming very familiar to her. They had been married only four days, and had known one another for only five, but already the sight of him was familiar. She wondered how she could ever have been afraid of men. Seth was reasonable, kind, and considerate. The next year would be a pleasant one if their friendship continued to grow.

"Well?"

"I'm getting up." She went into the adjoining dressing room and quickly put on the large green riding habit that had once been Jennifer's. Her hair was still flowing down her back as she returned to the bedroom and crossed to the mirror. She started brushing it in preparation of pulling it back into its tight little knot at the nape of her neck.

"Don't." Seth's voice startled her as his large hand loosely clasped her wrist. "Leave it down. I like to see it." She opened her mouth to protest, but he placed two warm fingers over her lips. "Don't give me a lecture about how your hair doesn't matter. Just leave it loose. Please."

Morgan didn't want to start the day with an argument, so she dropped her hands and left her hair to curl softly past her waist. As they left the room to tiptoe downstairs to the kitchen, she could still feel Seth's fingers on her lips.

"It's even earlier than I thought, if Cook, that old tiger, isn't up," Seth whispered as they entered the large, still-dark kitchen.

"She was very nice to me when I was in here yesterday afternoon, preparing the picnic basket."

"Nice? Cook nice to a lady? She doesn't think a lady is worth a handful of salt."

"Maybe she doesn't consider me a lady. After all, I was cooking. I don't believe cooking is a ladylike occupation."

"Oh, yes. I had forgotten that my little wife cooks. I don't guess there is a lady in five counties that can cook. Wife!"

Morgan was startled at his exclamation.

"Where's my breakfast?"

Morgan bristled at his tone. "I cook only when I want to. No man commands me to do anything."

Seth groaned and turned his eyes upward. "Oh God! Am I going to be cursed with a year of this? A woman without a sense of humor? If I tell her her hair is pretty, she tells me it is none of my business. If I tell her I need food, she tells me she doesn't take orders. Tell me, Lord, what is this poor man to do?" Seth tilted his head down slightly till he could see Morgan out of one eye. She had her hand over her mouth, trying to hide her smile.

Thus encouraged, Seth returned to his prayer. "What's that? You think the lass needs some persuasion? A what? A kiss? Ah, yes, that could bring her 'round. Thanks, Lord."

Seth bent toward Morgan, who now stood staring at him, eyes wide. "Seth—"

"You heard Him. I have nothing to do with it." He began walking purposefully toward her.

Morgan ran quickly to the other side of the big oak table. "Seth . . . don't." As she went to one side of the table and as he pursued her, they both began to laugh.

"I have orders to kiss the cook—to gentle her into making my breakfast." His smile was infectious.

"I'll make breakfast. I don't need persuasion," Morgan said between peals of laughter.

"Enough of this play, lass." Seth leaped up and bounded across the top of the table toward Morgan. She stopped where she was, stunned by the sight of his massive body leaping with such agility.

Before she had regained her senses, his arms were around her. "Now," he began, still laughing. But as his lips moved towards her, all at once both of them were serious.

"What is this? Sounds like the old bull got loose in my kitchen. What are you two doing in here, sparkin' in my kitchen before the sun's even up?"

Cook's querulous voice broke the spell. Morgan was embarrassed and looked down at the floor, but none of it seemed to have affected Seth.

"Good morning, Cook. We were making noise so you'd get up. We knew that if you got up, you'd bring sunshine with you."

"Go on with you." Cook tried to hide it, but Seth's flattery obviously pleased her.

"Look." Morgan pointed to the floor, at the first, tiny sunbeam. It lay at Cook's feet. "Seth's right, Carolyn. You have brought the sun."

The young couple passed the day riding and exploring Seth's boyhood haunts. It was a day of easy companionship and warm good humor.

By the time they arrived back at the Colter house, Seth and Morgan were good friends.

47

"Morgan, I had a wonderful time today. Thank you."

She smiled brilliantly. "So did I, Seth."

He moved closer, but she shouted for him to catch her, and ran toward the house.

Nora heard their laughter before she saw them. To her delight, she saw them race past the parlor window, both laughing. She turned to Cynthia Ferguson and said in what she hoped was a smug voice, "It looks as if my son and new daughter had an enjoyable ride."

She put down her teacup and rose to go to the door to greet Seth and Morgan. But before she could get to the door, Austine was there. Nora turned and smiled at Cynthia, who was sitting so calmly with her two admirers, Nora's daughters. The girls were almost fawning over the coldly beautiful Cynthia.

As Nora closed the parlor door behind her, she heard Austine's excited, breathless voice telling Seth and Morgan, "It's Cynthia Ferguson. She's come to pay her respects to you. I don't think she really believes you eloped. She says she just can't imagine the two of you together."

"Hush, Austine." Nora looked carefully at Morgan. Morgan's face was just slightly sunburned, and it made her eyes radiant. And her hair! Nora hadn't imagined Morgan could have so much of it. Her daughter-in-law was very close to being beautiful. She looked as if she had just left her lover's arms. Nora truly hoped this was the case.

Seth also had an unusual glow about him. He was smiling now, not that awful, patronizing leer he had so often, but a smile of real joy.

"I must change. I can't very well greet Cynthia in a riding habit and with my hair like this."

"I'll help you, but we must hurry. Cynthia has already been waiting for half an hour." Austine took Morgan's arm.

"Yes. Morgan should go right in," said Nora.

"But, Nora, at least let me tie my hair back."

"No, dear, I definitely do not think you should tie your hair back. If Miss Cynthia Ferguson can appear unannounced, then she must be prepared to view her hostess and host"—she glanced up at Seth—"in whatever state she finds them."

She started toward the parlor door with Morgan, but Seth took Nora's arm and whispered to her, "What are you up to?"

Nora looked at her son with widened eyes. "I declare, I have no idea what you mean."

"Morgan, Cynthia has come to see you." Eleanor called, awe in her tone. Wasn't Cynthia Ferguson a renowned beauty? And here she was, making a long drive just to pay her respects to Morgan.

"Hello, Cynthia." Morgan couldn't help but feel somewhat intimidated by Cynthia's presence.

"Why, you dear little thing, what an . . . interesting dress." She languidly extended her hand. Morgan wondered wryly whether she was expected to kiss it. "Sit here by me." Cynthia patted the love seat. Then she turned her eyes to Seth. "Hello, Seth. Your mother tells me you've been out riding. Isn't it a little cool for riding?"

Seth smiled warmly at Cynthia. "There are things to help warm a man." He looked meaningfully at Morgan.

Morgan had to hold her laughter. There was an awkward silence in the room.

"Your sisters have been telling me of your elopement. I find it difficult to believe that I introduced you two the night of my party. Were you, by chance, pretending? Did you actually know one another before that night?" Her question was addressed to Seth. She seemed unaware of anyone else.

"No, Cynthia." He accepted the cup of tea that Austine handed him. "I guess you'll have to say it was love at first sight. We met that night and I did not see my little wife until the next day when I talked to her uncle. A few hours after that, we were married."

Jennifer could not restrain herself. "I hope I fall in love just like that."

Morgan sat quietly. The way Seth told the story, it did sound romantic. She didn't like to remember the night of Cynthia's ball, when she had asked Seth to marry her. She took in Cynthia's dark beauty, the exquisite gown, the intricate yet soft arrangement of her hair. Maybe Seth would marry her in a year, when they had their annulment.

Nora interrupted the silence. "Seth, you and Morgan seem to have had a good time today. Where did you ride?"

"A little past Johnson's meadow."

Nora walked to the love seat to stand by Morgan. "Well, I'm glad you had a good time." She ostentatiously removed a leaf from Morgan's hair, studying it for a second before placing it on the table.

Cynthia spoke. "Riding horses around in the woods is not my idea of a good time." She looked at Morgan's dishevelment with open contempt. "It's a little too dirty for me."

Seth and Morgan immediately exchanged looks and then laughed aloud. Just the day before, Seth had mentioned that ladies did not like to get dirty. Morgan had replied that she was not a lady. The exchange of laughter over what was obviously a lovers' joke made for another embarrassing silence.

Nora, reassured that Morgan could handle herself with Cynthia, gathered her daughters and left.

When Nora left, Seth was the first to speak. "Cynthia, may I say that you look lovely, as always."

Cynthia tittered. "Why, Seth, dear, you may say it as often as you like. You know . . . no matter how many times you have said it, I still love to hear it." She turned slightly toward Morgan to make sure she heard every word. "Morgan, has Seth told you what old friends we are?" Her voice had a cutting edge.

Morgan returned the sweet smile with one of her own. She reached over and patted Cynthia's hand. "My dear Cynthia, you shouldn't consider yourself such an *old* friend."

Cynthia's features hardened and her eyes blazed. They both turned at a sound from Seth. He was choking on a cookie. "Excuse me, ladies." He struggled to regain his composure. "Won't you stay for dinner, Cynthia?" There was laughter just beneath his voice. Or was there? Cynthia could not be sure.

"No, I must be going." Cynthia rose, as did Seth and Morgan. Suddenly, Cynthia's face brightened. She purred. "What I really came for was to kiss the groom." She moved very close to Seth and placed a lace-covered hand on his chest. She turned her head toward Morgan. "You don't mind . . . do you, dear?"

Without waiting for an answer, her arms slid up and around Seth's neck in what Morgan knew was a much-practiced gesture. Cynthia pulled Seth's mouth to hers, her body melting to meet his as his arms encircled her. Morgan turned away.

"Well, I must say, Seth, you haven't changed." Cynthia then turned to Morgan, as if startled to find her there. "I really *must* be going. You'll visit me before too long, won't you?" She addressed this to Seth, but then turned slowly to Morgan. "And you must come, too, of course."

Seth moved to Morgan and put his arm around her shoulders. "My wife would love to come visit, on one of our return trips from New Mexico."

"New Mexico! I thought a . . . wife would change your mind about that desolate place."

"No, my little wife is just as anxious to go to New Mexico as I am."

Morgan smiled at Cynthia and extended her hand, very aware of Seth's arm around her. "You must come again. Do you know your way out? But of course you do." Morgan's voice held a trace of venom.

Cynthia turned and left, nearly slamming the door behind her. Morgan stood and stared at the door, seething with rage. How dare Cynthia! She was totally unaware that Seth had drawn back from her and was now grinning broadly.

"Be careful. That door is made of wood and your look just might set it on fire."

She turned on him. "And just what are you grinning about? You certainly enjoyed her visit!" Morgan mimicked holding a teacup, her little finger extended. In a falsetto voice, she said, "Didn't Seth tell you we were *very* old and *very* dear friends?" Morgan's anger mounted. "And then, 'May I kiss the groom?' It looked to me as though she had done *that* several times."

Seth's laughter rang through the room. "Calm down, little one. You'll make me think you are jealous!"

"Jealous!" Her voice grew more calm. "I'm not jealous—I just don't like being insulted. She had no right to insult me."

Seth moved close to her and pulled her to him. "Were you insulted? You noticed that she looked familiar with kissing. Were you that interested?"

"No." She was still very angry. "It looked like she was familiar with kissing *you*."

"So you were interested."

"No . . . I . . ."

"I told you that any time you were interested in trying out kissing—or anything else for that matter—I'm ready."

"Seth, you promised."

"I promised I wouldn't force you, but I didn't promise I wouldn't try to persuade you."

52

Her anger was slowly receding. How she had hated seeing him kiss Cynthia!

She tilted her head back, and molded her body to his as he started to kiss her.

"Oh, excuse me." Nora had quietly entered the room, and Morgan quickly moved to free herself from Seth's arms. Seth refused to remove them, holding her tightly to him.

Seth told his mother, "Cynthia's gone. She saw what she came to see, and then she left."

Nora was beaming. She had known that nature would take its course.

Morgan, embarrassed at being found in Seth's arms, brought an elbow sharply into his stomach. He didn't flinch. She turned and glared at him, whispering through clenched teeth, "Let me go."

Seth chuckled and, relenting, released her.

"Dinner will be in an hour. Maybe you two would like to rest before dinner?"

Seth immediately grabbed Morgan's hand and led her across the room. "That's a good idea, Mother." He led her quickly up the stairs to their room. "Now, let's start where we left off." He turned to her, but she moved from him.

"No, Seth, I was angry before." Her voice was pleading. "I want to be friends—no more."

Seth smiled. "All right. I have a long time. I'll wait. Why don't you rest? Bessie could bring you a bath."

"I'd love that." As Seth turned to leave, Morgan said quietly, "Thank you for understanding, Seth."

Morgan sat in the hot water for a long time. She tried not to think about the day, the long ride with Seth, how she had felt when Cynthia kissed him. Everything was moving too quickly! She lay back in the tub and thought about Trahern House.

Life had been so simple, so quiet and gentle there.

She had always done exactly as she pleased. Her days had been filled with riding, cooking, embroidery, and caring for her flowers. She had been very happy. There had been so few people in her life then. She had been left in peace.

She thought about Seth's family. Nora was so kind, and always close to laughter. William was always easy to be with. And the sisters—it was funny how a person always thought of them together. They, too, were always smiling. Everyone seemed to enjoy life so much. Morgan slid deeper into the tub, thinking that if she ever did leave Trahern House, the Colter family would be pleasant to live with. But, of course, she never would leave Trahern House. What had made her think such a thing?

She was just finishing dressing when Seth came to the room to change for dinner. He nodded toward the tub, still full of water. "I should have come up earlier."

Morgan smiled at him as she adjusted the tight knot of hair on her neck. Seth strode towards her, touched the knot, and said, "I like it better the other way. But at least this way you're no temptation."

Morgan swung around to meet his eyes, "Good! Now maybe you'll not embarrass me in front of your family."

After dinner, Seth disappeared to the library, and the rest of the family retired to the large drawing room. William read, smoking a large cigar. The three sisters asked Morgan if she'd like to help embroider Austine's linens for her trousseau.

"Eleanor's wedding dress is a light blue silk and Austine's is a pink satin," Jennifer chattered. "They are going to be married together, this summer. I wish you could stay for the wedding."

"That would be nice, Morgan. You could be our matron of honor. It would be wonderful if you would stay. Do you think you could?" Austine looked at Morgan expectantly, but Morgan sat quietly, unresponding, absorbed in her stitching.

"Morgan." Nora's voice was clear in the silence.

Morgan immediately looked up and realized what had happened. "I'm sorry, I guess I was thinking of something else."

Nora turned to her husband. "William, do you know where Seth went?"

"He's in the library, reading those old journals of his." Then, as if taking the hint from his wife, he said, "Why don't you go join him, daughter? I'm sure he'd like to show them to you. When he was a little boy, he used to read those by the hour. And he'd read them to anyone who'd listen, too."

"I promised Austine and Eleanor I'd help with the linens."

"Don't be silly, Morgan. This is your honeymoon. Go spend the evening with your husband." Nora's eyes were dancing. She knew that Morgan could hardly say no to her suggestion.

"If I had just been married, I'd spend every minute with my husband." Jennifer was always the romantic.

Morgan left the room, went down the hall, and quietly opened the door of the library. Seth was sitting in a large leather chair behind a massive, carved walnut desk. He was smoking a large cigar and seemed totally engrossed in an enormous book. Thinking he hadn't heard her come in, she moved noiselessly to his side. His voice startled her.

"Look at this." He pointed to a yellowed page with angular, faded handwriting.

We have waited eight days for the flood waters to recede. The sun is merciless. There are no trees for shade. Ahead of us lies nothing but flat grassland. There is much tension among us because of the Indians we have seen.

55

"Who wrote it?"

"I don't know. When I was very young, my grandfather bought it from a Frenchman he met in Louisville. This is only the center section of the journal. As far as I can guess, and I've read it several times, this was one of the earliest American parties to try to make it to Santa Fe."

"What happened to them?"

"I don't know that either. But as far as I can gather, before Santa Fe gained independence from Spain, all Americans in Santa Fe were either killed or imprisoned."

Morgan was quiet.

"Morgan, what we have ahead of us is not pleasant. The journey takes about three months, and we go through some rugged country. Sit over here, and I'll read to you."

They moved to a small leather couch beneath the shuttered window. A small fire burned in the fireplace to their left. Morgan curled up on one end of the couch and listened as Seth read. His deep voice was calming even as he read of the horrors of traveling on the Santa Fe Trail. He read of their joy at seeing the Cimarron Spring, of the lack of water in places, and of flooded rivers in others. Morgan tried to imagine herself experiencing these things, but could not do so. She lazily watched the fire and listened to Seth's deep, resonant voice.

Seth stopped reading to look at his little wife. She was sleeping peacefully, her legs drawn up under the voluminous skirt. She looked about ten years old. Of course, he mused, she really wasn't so very much older than that. He blew out the lamp and moved closer to her. In sleep, she nuzzled against his warm body. He put his arm around her shoulders and drew her even closer. Her head rested on his chest.

An hour later, when Nora came in to say goodnight,

that was how she found them. She watched the scene for a couple of minutes, feeling slightly guilty about intruding.

Morgan awoke at the sound of the door closing.

"Well, little girl, are you ready to go to bed?"

Morgan was embarrassed by her position and stood up quickly, hurrying toward their room. She undressed rapidly in the dressing room and was soon in bed.

Seth came up the stairs, after she was in bed, and undressed in the moonlit room. Morgan made herself look away as he removed his clothing. She shivered and then snuggled deeper under the covers. It's only curiosity, she told herself. At last she fell asleep.

The sun was high when Morgan awoke the next morning. She stretched lazily. It had been good to sleep late. The last few days had been very wearing. Just six days ago she had been dressing for Cynthia's ball.

She looked toward the foot of the bed and saw that Seth had gone. Immediately, she jumped out of bed, dressed, pulled her hair back, and ran downstairs to the kitchen.

"Good morning, Cook."

"Morning! I've been up for four hours!"

"I'm just lazy. Where is everyone?"

"Who knows? Them gals are out pickin' flowers, I reckon, and the Missus is in her room. Master and Mr. Seth rode out hours ago. You want some breakfast?"

"I'll get it." She paused. "You say Seth rode out? Do you know where?" She tried to sound nonchalant.

"I knowed you'd want to know. He's got every other girl in the countryside after him, why not his own wife?"

Morgan decided it was best not to talk about Seth anymore, so she finished her breakfast as quickly as possible and left the kitchen.

She met Nora in the front hallway. "Seth is planning to take some good furniture back with him to Santa Fe.

He told me this morning that I was to let you pick out what you wanted."

Morgan was very pleased by this, and she and Nora went upstairs to begin their search. The master bedroom was enormous, with oak paneling and oak floors. The bed was even larger than the one in Seth's room, and the headboard was intricately carved.

"I couldn't choose any furniture from these rooms."

"Morgan, you may have anything in this house except William's bed. I want you and Seth to have a good start in New Mexico."

"Nora . . . you know about our arrangement. I will return after one year."

As they left the master bedroom and continued down the hall, Nora said lightly, "Who knows? You may like New Mexico."

Morgan smiled. "I may like New Mexico, but you don't know how much I need Kentucky . . . and Trahern House."

"A house and a piece of land are no replacement for love."

"How is love involved?"

"I've watched you two, the way you tease and the way you laugh together. Friendship is the very best basis for a good love."

Morgan considered this for a few minutes. "Yes, I think you are right. I believe I will love Seth at the end of a year."

Nora stopped abruptly to turn to stare in triumph at Morgan.

"As a sister loves a brother," Morgan added hastily, feeling she had won the joust.

Seth and William joined Nora and Morgan for lunch. The sisters had been invited to a neighbor's, where they would probably stay till dinnertime.

"Well, did my little wife choose every piece of furniture in the house?"

Morgan did not like his patronizing tone at all. "The only thing I really wanted was the carved bed in the large bedroom at the head of the stairs." She watched both Seth and his father as their eyes widened.

Seth nearly choked as he said, "But it would take an entire wagon just for that bed. And besides, that bed has always been in this house."

Nora couldn't help laughing. "Morgan's only teasing, Seth." She saw the two men relax. "And you deserve it, too, when you talk to your wife the way you do to Jennifer."

Seth looked sheepish and returned to eating. William asked Morgan if she did find any furniture. Then, hesitantly at first, she talked of her idea about New Mexico, of her certainty that this beautiful furniture would not fit in there.

She gained courage as she saw Seth looking at her with respect. "That's just what I told Mother and the girls when I first came back. I wanted to take some furniture back, but Chippendale does not fit into an adobe house."

"Nora, did you show them the attic?" William addressed his wife.

"I had forgotten all about it. Morgan will love the furniture."

After lunch, Seth returned to the fields with his father, while Nora and Morgan went back to their explorations.

A great deal of the furniture that had been in the Colter home before Nora came was stored in the attic. It had been made in America, and was much plainer than the Chippendale. Here were things that other people had stored in wagons as they came to the Kentucky wilderness. The prize was a sturdy bride's chest with birds and the year 1784 painted on it, all enclosed in a heart.

There were several sturdy oak tables with chairs to match. This was furniture that had been made with love, and although it was old, it was strong. It had been carried across the country before, and it would stand up to that again.

~ *Chapter Four* ~

THERE was one more day before they left. Morgan regretted leaving Seth's family—they had been so kind. She was also afraid of the long trek across the country where she'd be alone with Seth. The day passed in a frenzy of packing and preparation for the trip.

After the noon meal, Jake arrived. He was a short, wiry man. Morgan judged him to be about sixty. Jake and Seth hugged one another in greeting.

"You little polecat! I can see by your size that you haven't been eatin' right. You get any littler, and I won't be able to see you," said the small man as Seth's massive frame nearly smothered him. He grinned up at Seth with a nearly toothless grin.

"Well, Jake, I miss your cookin'. A few pieces of your shoeleather steaks and I'll be near as big as you."

They turned toward the house, their arms around one another. Then they saw Morgan. Seth seemed embarrassed, and stammered, "Jake, meet Morgan. She's my . . . er . . . wife."

Jake turned startled eyes to Seth, dropped his arm, and began to howl with laughter. Seth stared at his feet. Morgan could not help smiling, infected by Jake's laughter. With tears in his eyes he choked, "I told you, I knew it." Then, sobering, "No offense, ma'am, we jist had us a little bet, and I reckon I won." He offered his hand. "Glad to meet you."

Jake turned out to be a born story-teller. He kept

61

everyone entertained during dinner. After dinner, the women went to the sitting room, and Jake and Seth's father went to the library.

Seth took the opportunity to add a last-minute package to the loaded wagons. He put in a small music box that he intended to be a Christmas present to Morgan. He stood in the moonlight, wondering what would be between them at Christmastime. At last he returned to the house.

Jake had retired, and William and Seth were left alone. The two were close, and they had much to share. By ten o'clock they had drunk a great deal of brandy. They both rose to greet Nora, the girls, and Morgan as they came to say goodnight.

As the women turned to leave, Seth called, "Stay with us a little while, Morgan."

Seth smiled, showing his dimples, and offered her a glass of brandy.

"A toast to my new daughter." William's smile was just as impish as his son's.

The liquid was warming, making Morgan feel very relaxed.

"Seth, my son, I want to congratulate you on your choice of a wife." William's words were just slightly slurred.

Seth moved to the back of Morgan's chair and began to knead the back of her neck with his fingertips, feeling the silky hair and the warmth of her scalp. Seth and William were talking, but she heard nothing, feeling only the warmth of the brandy and the touch of Seth's hand. She leaned back and closed her eyes.

She was startled from her reverie by silence, and opened her eyes to find the men looking at her. Seth smiled. "I think you're tired. Why don't you go to bed?" His eyes were bright with liquor, and somehow Morgan found him very appealing.

She rose, silently, and went toward the door. She

heard William mutter under his breath, "I'd never let my new bride go to bed alone." He added, "At least you can kiss her."

Perhaps it was the unaccustomed liquor, but Morgan's heart began to pound. Her hand was on the doorknob before she felt Seth's hand on hers. The warmth of him, the size, and the smell of him made her tremble. He turned the knob and followed her out the door. They were in the empty moonlit hallway.

He touched her arm, and she turned. Very gently, his arm went around her waist while his other hand tipped her head up to face him. The moonlight made his hair silver, and the height and width of him made her seem small and delicate. His lips touched hers very gently, very softly. Morgan swayed against him, unthinking, now only feeling, wanting his warmth to touch her. Her arms went out, encircling his neck and drawing him closer to her. Her head was swimming, and she had no idea whether or not she was breathing.

His lips began to move over hers. Her lips parted as he began to be more demanding. They pulled one another closer and Seth leaned forward until Morgan's back was bent into a bow shape. She heard herself moan as she felt Seth's hips move slightly.

Seth lifted his head and looked at her with startled eyes—and with another expression Morgan did not recognize. Silently, he lifted her in his arms and carried her up the stairs to their bedroom. Morgan put her face into his neck, feeling the soft, warm flesh. He made her feel so safe, so protected. Nothing existed but Seth. She moved her face deeper into his neck, touching with her lips the tender spot where the neck joined the shoulder. She felt Seth's breath quicken as he opened the door to their bedroom.

Closing it with his foot, he again turned to Morgan to kiss her. The kiss was searching, and she clung to him as he carefully laid her on the bed and stretched out beside her. His hand caressed her hair, her shoulder, as it found its way to the buttons on her dress. He kissed her throat, and each area of flesh as it was exposed by the unfastened buttons. She felt Seth's leg across her own.

Seth sat up on an elbow and looked at her in the firelight. His eyes were tender. He slowly unbuttoned his shirt and removed it. The hair on his chest was thick and curly, the skin such a delicate, golden brown. She stretched out a tentative finger and touched his shoulder. God! but he was beautiful. His arms made her think of the muscles on horses.

"Seth . . ." His kisses, his gentleness, made the idea of stopping him seem cruel.

"Don't talk, my love, just enjoy," he murmured.

"Seth, you have to stop . . . please don't." Her voice was barely a whisper. "Please . . ."

It was several minutes before Seth began to hear her. Her voice was so soft. As the sounds penetrated his senses, he began to feel anger rising in him. He did not know why. Abruptly, he dropped her onto the bed.

His jaw was clenched. "No, madam, I will not force you. I will not have a woman who says no to me." He stood up and grabbed his shirt, angrily thrusting his arms into it. "There is a name for women like you—women who kiss a man like you kissed me in the hall, who allow a man to get worked up and then refuse him." His eyes were very angry. "You've said no to me several times, but this will be the last time. I'll not ask you again."

Now it was Morgan's turn to get angry. "I made you a business offer, nothing more. I made that clear from the beginning. I've not wanted your advances, so what right do you have to be angry with me? I have kept my part in our bargain."

Seth's face softened. His eyes, though, were still angry, his voice a harsh whisper. "You are right, you have kept your part." There was a look of sadness about him now. "As old as I am, I never learn—there are two kinds of women, my silly sisters and the calculating Cynthia. Somehow I thought you were different, but now I know just where you fit." His voice lowered. "I will see that you get your beloved Trahern House, and I will bother you no more."

Her hair was loose, her dress unbuttoned, showing the shadow of a breast. Abruptly, he turned and left the room.

Morgan stared at the door, tears gathering strength.

Nora was disturbed the next morning to see the coolness between Seth and Morgan. Jake noticed it too, but neither said anything.

Tearful goodbyes were said, and both Nora and William forced money on the reluctant Morgan.

At last Morgan sat on the wagon beside Jake, while Seth rode ahead on his horse. Jake talked incessantly about New Mexico, about Kansas City, about anything that came to his head. Morgan listened and bounced on the wagon seat, and watched Seth's broad back. Morgan realized that no matter how big the horse was, Seth would probably make it look like a pony. "It would probably take a draft horse to look big in proportion," she muttered.

"What was that?" Jake looked toward her.

"I was looking at Seth," she answered, blushing.

Jake smiled, showing his three teeth, and began to talk about Seth. "Sure glad that boy got married. Tired of running that ranch myself while he keeps going into town for a woman." Then it was his turn to be embarrassed, "Uh, sorry, Mrs., uh, Morgan."

Morgan hadn't thought about the possibility of another Cynthia waiting for him in New Mexico. "Jake, does Seth have a girl in New Mexico?"

"Well, there is one that seems to have set her cap for

him. A young lady whose father owns quite a bit of Santa Fe." Jake looked at Morgan and grinned. "She'd fill out that big dress of yourn and half of another one like it. You sure are a mighty *little* thing."

Jake was so natural that Morgan felt no resentment. "I guess Seth likes women like that—big, I mean."

The smile vanished from his face. "I can't say as he *likes* any women. He seems more to use them than anything. Oh, he's nice to them, and they sure like him, but he never seems to think anything about any of them after he leaves them." He paused. "Now me," and his grin returned, "I've been in love so many times." He laughed and slapped his thigh. "I remember a gal in Louisville once, had black hair and eyes. I was so in love with her that I couldn't eat for three weeks. Thought I'd die without her." He seemed to enjoy just thinking about the woman.

"What happened?" Morgan asked.

"Oh . . . she left me for some rich guy, but she'll never forget me, that much I know."

Morgan was quiet awhile.

"You don't think Seth's ever been in love?"

"Well, I used to work for his daddy, and I've been around Seth since he was about nine years old, and as far as I know, he ain't never been in love. Too bad, too. You miss a lot in life when you don't fall madly in love at least once a year."

Morgan was quiet after that, just sitting, listening to Jake and watching Seth move to the rhythm of his horse.

The first days were easy. At night they stopped at local inns where a hot meal and warm, clean beds awaited them. Seth always made sure Morgan had her own room, while he and Jake had another.

Seth and Morgan stayed away from one another as much as possible, speaking only when necessary.

A few days before they reached Kansas City, Jake

began to tell Morgan about someone named Frank. Jake seemed to have a lot of respect for Frank and was glad Frank would be traveling with them.

"Will anyone else be going with us?"

It was a minute before she could understand Jake's answer.

"Joaquín. What a nice name."

Jake muttered something unintelligible.

Kansas City was much more rustic than Louisville, and Morgan liked it. The people all seemed to be dressed for necessity rather than for fashion.

"Seth!" A man as big as Seth came up behind him as Seth was tying his horse in front of the hotel. They shook hands vigorously, obviously glad to see one another. "And Jake, you little old toad, you're still as ugly as ever." His eyes stopped at Morgan.

Seth followed his eyes. "This is my wife, Morgan." Seth's voice held no warmth.

Frank reacted immediately to Seth's voice. He knew something was wrong. Frank held out a tentative hand and helped Morgan from the wagon. "I am pleased to meet you, Mrs. Colter."

Morgan smiled, lighting up her face. "Jake has told me a lot about you—everything except your last name."

He smiled back at Morgan. "It's Greyson, but everyone calls me Frank."

"If you call me Morgan, it's a deal."

Smiling, they started into the hotel. As they were signing in, Seth said to Morgan, "My shy little wife sometimes loses her shyness. Do you think she saves it just for her husband?"

Morgan was startled by the hostility in his voice, but before she could say anything, he had turned to talk to the hotel manager.

Jake had overheard Seth and whispered to Morgan,

67

"He's jealous," and then followed Frank up the stairs.

Seth turned back to Morgan, taking her arm and leading her away from the desk. "They have no adjoining rooms. In fact, they have only one room left in the hotel. I could bunk with Frank and Jake."

Morgan's eyes went to Seth's. Somehow, she did not want everyone knowing the truth about her relationship with Seth. She would rather people thought theirs was a normal marriage.

Seth was talking. "Jake already knows. But if you'd rather Frank didn't, just say so and I'll arrange something."

Morgan lowered her eyes. "I'd rather he didn't know." Maybe it was her imagination, but she thought she saw relief on Seth's face.

Seth escorted her to a small but clean room with one rather narrow bed which took up most of the space.

Morgan sat on the bed, as there was nowhere else to sit. She watched Seth. He ignored her and began to undress.

"Seth, what are you doing?"

"I am planning to wash some of this trail dust off me before dinner." He turned toward her. "You don't have to watch if you don't want to, you know."

She moved to the other side of the bed and looked out at the busy street, but she had difficulty concentrating.

He had hardly spoken to her since the last night at his parents' house. She tried to picture Trahern House, but saw only Seth's angry eyes. She heard Nora's voice saying that Morgan would fall in love with Seth.

"Morgan?"

She turned. Seth was standing so close to her. She felt like crying. Unwanted tears gathered in her eyes.

Seth dropped to his knees beside her. She was such a child. "What's the matter, little one? If you don't want me to stay here, I won't. I'll find someplace else."

His voice was so gentle . . . She *couldn't* be in love

68

with him! She'd known him less than a month. Why was Seth's image so clear, and the image of Trahern House so blurred?

The tears started, and she couldn't stop them. She turned and buried her head in the pillow and began to let out the tears that had been locked inside for so long.

Seth knelt by the bed. After one puzzled look, he lifted Morgan into his arms and sat on the bed, leaning back against the headboard. He just held her and stroked her hair while she cried. After a while, as the sobs began to subside, Morgan began to hear Seth's voice.

"Shh, *mi querida*, be still. You are safe. No one will harm you. I won't bother you again. You have nothing to fear."

Morgan raised her head to look at him, but he gently forced her head back onto his chest and began to hum a tune. It felt so warm, so sweet to be near him, to be protected. Maybe, if she loved him, he would love her in return one day?

When Morgan awoke it was daylight, and she was in the bed, fully clothed, with a blanket over her. The last thing she remembered was lying in Seth's arms hearing him sing to her.

As she washed her face and combed her hair, she realized she was ravenously hungry.

Jake knocked on her door, and they started down the stairs together for breakfast. She wanted to know where Seth was, where he had slept, what he was doing.

At the foot of the stairs was one of the handsomest men Morgan had ever seen. His blue-black hair was perfectly ordered. His clothes were impeccable and in the best of taste. He looked like a picture Morgan had once seen in a magazine of Aunt Lacey's, a picture of a man for whom a young woman had left her husband and children. Of course, the man in the magazine had turned out to be bad. But this man was smiling up at her and was now extending his hand to her.

"Ah, this must be the lovely bride."

Morgan felt Jake's arm stiffen under her hand.

Ignoring Jake, the handsome man took Morgan's arm as if they had known one another for years.

"Allow me, Morgan. I may call you that, seeing that we are to be such close companions."

"I . . . uh," Morgan stammered. The man certainly was charming. Morgan found herself standing a little straighter.

He laughed slightly, showing perfect white teeth. "Excuse me, I am Antonio Joaquín Santiago de Montoya y García, at your service. You may call me Joaquín." He took her hand from his arm, just as they were entering the dining room, and held it to his lips, his eyes never once leaving hers.

Morgan had not yet said a word. The man's eyes had a hypnotic effect. A loud laugh that she recognized as Frank's reached her, and she turned toward the sound quickly. Seth looked at her with malice. Why was Seth looking at her like that? She moved to the table and seated herself.

Frank laughed again. "Well, Joaquín, it looks like you won another of the ladies. But I reckon you better stay away from this one. If you don't, you'll be tangling with ol' Seth here."

Seth looked at his empty plate. They had waited for Morgan before ordering. "I don't put chains on my wife."

Joaquín was very calm, showing no awareness of the tension at the table. He looked at the four other faces. Seth and Jake were angry, Frank laughing, and Morgan was looking at Seth's bent head with an expression of puzzlement and helplessness. Joaquín thought, "So that is how it is. For some reason, there is a very willing wife but a not-so-willing husband."

A keen observer of people, Joaquín liked to file bits of information away for future reference. Right now, he needed to know more about Seth.

"Seth, you must tell me where you met such a pretty young woman. Ah, but then you have always had such incredible luck."

Seth seemed to regain his composure, but he lost none of his furious look. Morgan did not know whether his anger was directed at her or at Joaquín.

"Morgan's father lived in New Mexico for years." Seth deliberately turned the conversation to a safer topic.

The three other men all turned interested eyes on Morgan.

"I haven't seen my father since I was a baby. I only heard recently that he had died."

"It's too bad he had to go before seeing his lovely daughter again." Joaquín raised Morgan's hand to his lips once more. "May I offer my sincere sympathy?"

Jake, who had been quiet through the whole awkward scene, nearly jumped at Seth. "What's the matter with you, boy!"

Seth leaned back against his chair and smiled at Morgan. It was a cold smile, and it did not spread to his eyes. "My little wife is quite capable of saying no to a man when she chooses to."

Morgan rose, very slowly and steadily, avoiding Seth's eyes. "Excuse me. I don't think I am hungry after all." She turned and left the room after assuring Joaquín that she needed no escort.

By the time she reached her room, she was so angry that her entire body was shaking. She sat on the bed. There was a great deal of thinking to do. Nothing was going as she had planned.

Morgan spent the day in the shops while the men loaded the wagons. She paused before a window, taken by a shiny dress that caught the sunlight. She was drawn inside, hypnotized, her eyes never leaving the dress.

"May I help you with anything?" a soft voice asked.

Morgan was startled, embarrassed at having been caught staring. The dress was scarlet, the neckline was cut very low, and there was an inch and a half of very fine burgundy lace across the bodice. What wasn't entirely revealed by the low neck would be just barely covered by the openwork lace. Above the waist, just under the lace bodice, was a satin ribbon that tied in the back in the Empire style. The thin fabric was tightly fitted below the ribbon until it reached the waist, where it tapered into a long, flowing, bell skirt. The sleeves were puffy and reached only to the middle of the upper arms.

The woman followed Morgan's eyes and began to visualize how the blond young woman would look in the elegant red dress. It would suit her perfectly. The woman continued staring at Morgan for another moment. "I am Miss Satterfield. That dress was made for you."

Morgan heard the earnestness in her voice. "Yes," Morgan whispered, "yes."

Recovering herself, Miss Satterfield said, "That dress has the strangest history. Last year a young woman came in here and asked for a job as a needlewoman. Of course, I couldn't hire her without seeing some of her work, and I told her that. She seemed really excited when she left, and came back in a couple of hours with this dress. I could see her needlework was excellent, even if the dress was forty years out of fashion. She said she had copied the style from a book. I never did understand where she got such fabric as that, but I do know she tatted the lace herself."

Both women stared at the dress for a moment. "Would you like to try it on?" Her eyes gleamed.

Morgan, who had never cared much about clothing, remembered wondering, on the night of Cynthia Ferguson's ball, how she would look in red satin. She was certain the dress would fit.

"No, I don't think I'll try it on. But I would like it wrapped, please, very plainly. I'm leaving on a wagon tomorrow, and the package can't be too large."

"All right."

As Morgan left the store, she wondered what had caused her to do such a thing. She could never wear the dress. All the way back to the hotel, she told herself she should return the dress at once.

Morgan had lunch with Frank and Jake. Seth and Joaquín were busy in town. She was glad, as she didn't want to see either one of them.

At dinner, Seth avoided her eyes, and she was kept busy trying to avoid Joaquín. He was so charming, and seemed so concerned with her welfare.

Seth didn't come to their room that night. She lay awake, gazing out the window at the stars, wondering where he was sleeping.

~ *Chapter Five* ~

EVERYONE told Morgan that the first part of the trip was the easiest, but to her it was unbelievably difficult. The days were long and hot, and the nights were too short. The first week she was so tired she could hardly speak. Always, someone made a bed for her under the wagon. She never knew who it was. She was usually too tired to eat, even to wash. She wanted only to lie down and be still, to quiet her body after the jolting of the wagon. But the hard, cold ground gave her no relief.

By the eighth day she began to become aware of her surroundings. She became used to the long days and the hard bed. For the first time, she sat by the fire and drank a cup of Jake's coffee.

"Well, it's nice to see you back with us." Frank smiled down at Morgan.

Morgan returned his smile.

"It is always nice to have a beautiful woman near, no matter where one is."

Joaquín's flattery made Morgan uneasy. She couldn't help being pleased, but Seth always seemed to be scowling in the background. As Seth tossed down a load of firewood, he growled, "Well, maybe my wife will be able to help with some of the work around here now rather than letting the men wait on her."

Morgan gave him what she hoped was a very sweet smile and said, "Of course, Seth, I'd like very much to

75

help." She wasn't going to allow his gruffness to upset her.

Seth tossed the blankets at her. "Then you make the beds tonight."

At her puzzled look, he motioned her to the wagon. He showed her how to make the blankets into a passable bed. This was her place. She knew it was because she had crawled under the wagon between the blankets to sleep for the last several nights. She watched silently as Seth spread another bed under the wagon hardly a foot from her own sleeping place.

"What—?" she started.

Seth grinned at her. "That is your husband's bed. You have been asleep each night when I came to bed, but you've slept very close to me every night." Suddenly his grin faded, and he left her abruptly.

That night, Morgan was very aware of Seth's big body spread out so close to her own. She could hear his slow, deep breathing. The sound made her feel safe.

The days began to form into a pleasant routine. Seth was still cool to Morgan, but his hostility had lessened. Joaquín always seemed to be near Morgan. Whenever she needed anything, there he was.

They stopped early one night at a place called Council Grove.

"Can you shoot a rifle, Morgan?" Seth asked her.

"No."

"You're going to learn. You may need to know how later on."

They made their way through the trees to a little clearing. Seth marked a target on the tree, and then stepped back.

"Now, put the rifle into your shoulder like this," he demonstrated.

"I didn't realize it was so heavy."

"Here, I'll show you." Seth stood in back of her and his powerful arms encircled her, his hands covering hers.

His body felt good to her. He had not touched her since they had left Kentucky. Feeling his warmth, she snuggled against him.

Seth bent his head next to hers to show her how to sight the rifle. Her hair was sweet, her neck was slightly damp from the heat of the day. As he looked from the rifle to her, he felt her move against him and involuntarily he felt his breath quicken. Her small, round bottom pressed against his groin caused his manhood to stir.

"Damn you!" He abruptly dropped his arms and stepped away, turning his back to her.

"Seth?" She had no idea what had made him so angry. She went to him, put her hand on his arm. He jerked away from her touch.

Angrily, she turned from him. "My mother was right. Men are incomprehensible creatures. One minute I think we can be friends, and the next minute you're cursing me." She started back to the camp, each step quicker than the last, each step angrier than the one before.

Seth, recovering himself, reached her in a few long strides. His eyes and voice were as angry as hers. The hand on her arm hurt her as he swung her around to face him, the sun blazing behind him.

"Your mother! If your mother had been any kind of mother at all, she wouldn't have poisoned your mind. If she'd had your interests in mind, she would have taught you about men and women, rather than imprisoning you in that big house like a nun."

She jerked her arm from his grasp. "How dare you!" She spat her fury at him. "And your behavior proves she was right in everything she told me about men. I can't talk to you, I can't even be near you without you becoming angry with me for no reason." She started quickly down the path toward the wagons.

Again Seth was next to her, even more angry. He stood in front of her. Through clenched teeth he said,

"You're damn right I can't be near you. What do you expect when you wiggle against me?"

"Wiggle? What are you talking about?" She looked at him with hatred.

Quickly, his big hands reached out and encircled the back of her head, pulling her lips to his. His kiss was gentle and searching. Morgan had the drowning sensation again. She felt her body go limp and at the same time she could feel every part of her react. She reached out, her hands touching his waist, feeling the firm, hard muscles of his stomach with her thumbs.

Gently, he drew back from her and looked down at her closed eyes, the delicate blue veins showing through the lids. Her eyelashes were long and thick. His voice was a whisper. "Your mother should have explained about men being very sensitive. That's why I can't be near you without being angry at not being able to have you."

Her anger was gone now, but many years of training by her mother cried out in her head. The anger was replaced by a look of determination and arrogance. "My mother was correct when she told me that men could not love, that they cared only for horses and business and that they used women. Since I have met you, Mr. Colter, you have shown me less consideration and friendliness than you show your horse. Now, if you'll excuse me, I have some work to do at the wagons."

She left him standing alone.

"What is it, my pretty little dove?" Joaquín's voice was soft and very close.

Morgan was leaning against a tree, trying to fight the tears that threatened.

She sniffed and smiled nervously up at Joaquín. "I guess I don't understand men."

"Ah, but men are very easy to understand. It is

78

women who are mysterious. It is women who control men."

"*Control* men! I don't even seem to be able to talk to one."

"A lover's tiff. Soon you will make up, and then you will be happy again."

She took Joaquín's arm and he escorted her back to the wagons.

The next day Frank took over Morgan's shooting lessons. Seth avoided her.

One day as Joaquín and Morgan returned from a spring, both laughing, Seth met them on the pathway. His eyes showed amusement.

"My little wife seems to enjoy your company, Joaquín. She is usually not so friendly with men."

Joaquín looked from one to another. "Morgan is an enjoyable person. I envy any man with such a wife. Excuse me, I have some things I need to do before our journey tomorrow."

Silently, Morgan started down the path. Seth walked beside her.

"Look at that!" Seth pointed to the trees.

"I don't see anything."

Seth moved behind her, his hands on her shoulders, and turned her to see a brilliant, red cardinal sitting quietly on a branch. They both smiled.

"I was just going for a walk. After all day on a horse, it feels good to stretch my legs. Want to come?"

She smiled up at him. He stretched his hand to her and she took it.

"Come on, then." They ran, Morgan stumbling along behind to keep up with him.

"This greenness reminds me of Kentucky. But we'll leave it behind soon enough."

"Tell me more about New Mexico. Is it really flat and barren?"

"It's not flat at all. To some people it seems barren, but I don't think of it that way. The deserts and the mountains have always seemed like enchanted places to me."

They rounded a curve in the stream to a secluded area where the trees overhung the banks.

"That water looks good after the dust of the trail. I think I'll take a swim. Like to join me?" His eyes twinkled.

Before she could answer, Seth had removed his boots and shirt. His muscles were enormous and stood out easily. Morgan watched, fascinated.

As he started to remove his pants, she gasped, "Seth . . ." He smiled, "Remember, *mi querida*, we are married. I see nothing wrong in undressing in front of one's wife. Anyway, you could turn your head."

She turned to stare at a tree trunk behind her until she heard a loud splash.

"The water's so warm. Sure you won't join me?"

She longed to get into the water, to get rid of the trail dust. Sponge baths in the wagon never got her really clean.

"No, I'll just sit on the bank and put my feet in." She watched as Seth swam a ways down the creek. His back and arms were powerful in the water. She could see him clearly as he glided across the water: his arms and back, and then tapering to his buttocks and the tops of his thighs. Morgan shivered as she watched. She did not go in. Seth returned a bit later, and she walked ahead as he dressed.

"It's all right. You can come back now. I won't shock you any longer." His hand reached out for hers. "Sit down a minute—I'd like to dry off." He had not put his shirt back on but was using it to towel his wet hair.

She sat down, leaning against a tree. Seth sat beside

her, then turned and lay his head in her lap. He closed his eyes.

"Seth, talk to me about you. You know so much about me. Jake has told me about you, but I want you to tell me about yourself."

His hands were crossed on his chest. She moved a hand to remove a leaf from his stomach and then left her hand there. His skin was so warm. Her other hand twisted a curl of his hair, now very gray in the sunlight.

"What did Jake tell you about me?" Seth was keenly aware of Morgan's hands.

"He said he didn't think you had ever been in love, that you only used women." She paused. "And he said there were lots of women who wanted you to marry them."

Seth smiled. "I guess that's true. But I figure most women want to get married. I just happened to be single." He snuggled his head deeper into her lap, and his hands covered hers, both pairs of hands lying on his chest.

"What about the other part—*have* you ever been in love?"

He took a minute to answer. "I guess not. At least I've never met a woman I wanted to be with for the rest of my life. I usually grow tired of a woman after a very short time." He raised her hand to kiss her palm, his eyes still closed. He felt Morgan jump slightly at the touch of his lips.

"What about your girl in New Mexico?" He looked at her, then closed his eyes again. His cheeks showed long dimples from trying to suppress his laughter.

"Jake told you a lot, didn't he? Marilyn's very pretty and very . . . uh . . . obliging, but no, I'm not in love with her."

Morgan leaned her head against the tree and smiled, feeling very happy.

"Seth, you said my mother was wrong—that she

should have taught me about men and women." She paused. Seth remained silent, but listened closely. "I don't understand about men. And I don't understand you at all. You are sometimes so kind, and then sometimes you look like you hate me. Then again, there are times, like now, when I feel I've known you all my life.'

Seth's eyes were serious. "Yes, little one, sometimes I don't understand myself. Sometimes I hate you, and sometimes I want to pick you up and toss you in the air. Right now, I just want to be still." He closed his eyes again.

Morgan relaxed against the tree again and then she whispered, "Do you ever want to toss Marilyn into the air?"

Seth roared. "It would take a bigger man than me to toss Marilyn Wilson in the air. I can see you're not going to let me rest. Let's go and see what Jake has for supper."

He turned over and studied her for a minute. "God, I hate the way you hide your hair." He reached behind her, unfastened the knot of hair, and pulled it forward over her shoulders. "That's better."

He stood up, took Morgan's hand, and pulled her up beside him. She gazed up at him with complete trust

"Oh, Morgan," he groaned, "how am I going to keep my hands off you for a whole year?"

Morgan smiled. "That's easy—if you can't catch me, you can't touch me!" she called over her shoulder as she ran down the trail.

Seth paused to grab his shirt, stuffing it into his belt, and took off after her.

Just before they reached the wagons, Seth sent one long arm shooting out to encircle Morgan's waist She struggled, kicking and hitting against him while laughing uncontrollably. "Can't catch you? You're no bigger than a mosquito," he teased.

He lifted her above his head and turned her around

in the air several times. Morgan screamed, "No, no," repeatedly, choking with laughter.

Seth then threw her over his shoulder, slapping her firmly on the behind when she struggled. He walked into the camp carrying her this way.

Jake and Frank looked up from the fire.

"I thought maybe we was being attacked by Indians." Jake frowned. Seth just grinned.

Embarrassed now, Morgan whispered into Seth's back, "Seth, put me down."

As Seth crossed in front of them, going toward the wagon, Morgan heard Jake tell Frank, "At least that boy knows how women ought to be handled."

No one saw Joaquín standing in the shadows, a scowl on his face.

Seth put Morgan down on the far side of the wagon, away from the campfire. Her back was against the wagon, and one of his arms was on each side of her, closing her in.

"Seth, that was awful. What will Jake and Frank think of me?" She tried to scold, but she was too close to laughter to sound sincere.

He moved his face closer to hers. "Keep looking at me like that, and I may do more than throw you over my shoulder."

She hadn't realized how she had been looking at his bare chest, the soft, curling hair on the bronze skin. She blushed and looked away. As she did so, he bent and kissed her on the ear. His lips, so moist, so sweet, caused her to turn toward him again.

"Morgan, sweet one," he whispered. His arms closed around her shoulders, and she put her arms around his waist. He held her, without speaking, for some minutes.

Morgan could feel his skin against the side of her face, could feel his hand gently stroking her head and tangling into her hair Her mind was blank, she felt only security and contentment while being so close to this man.

He was the first to pull away. "You're a witch, you know that?" His voice was husky. "Go out there and get me something to eat, like a good little wife."

"Aren't you coming?" She didn't want to leave him.

"Morgan, you have a lot to learn about men. I'll stay back here a minute or so until I'm more presentable for company." He glanced downward.

Morgan followed his eyes to the large bulge in his pants. "Oh," she murmured, unnerved, and turned and walked quickly to the campfire.

Joaquín was very quiet that night. He usually managed to sit close to Morgan and always found ways of slipping compliments to her. But tonight Morgan had no ears for Joaquín. He noticed that every look, every gesture, was directed toward Seth.

Once, Seth glanced at Joaquín and was startled to see a look of undisguised hatred. At Seth's glance, Joaquín quickly recovered his countenance. For a few seconds, Seth puzzled over what he had seen on Joaquín's face, but soon dismissed it. Many things about the Spaniard were strange to him.

Joaquín Montoya was the head of a very wealthy ranch south of Seth's more modest ranch. Seth seldom thought about Joaquín except for an occasional feeling of distaste for his too-smooth manners. Of course, Joaquín's beautiful sister, Lena, was another matter. The first time Seth kissed her, she bit his lip nearly through, and then threw back her head and laughed. Making love to her was like making love to a wildcat. His back had been sore for a week, and her teeth had made a wound on his shoulder that had taken two weeks to heal. Seth did not think about the Montoyas very often.

Seth stayed around the campfire to talk of plans for the trip, while Morgan went to her bed under the wagon. She lay with her hands behind her head and looked up at the underpinnings of the wagon. She thought of the day, and the remembrance of Seth, laughing with him, touching him, being so near all day, made her skin glow and her breath come deeper and quicker.

When Seth came to his bed, so near to hers, she stretched out a hand to touch him.

"Oh, no, *mi querida*," he whispered. He kissed her fingertips, and put her hand by her side. "I don't think I could stand any more kissing and touching today. I am only human. Go to sleep now, and don't test me anymore." He turned onto his stomach, and before long Morgan heard his quiet, even breathing.

The next night they camped at Diamond Springs. Seth took Morgan's hand and led her to see the spring flowing from a large, hollow rock. The water was clear and cool. They lugged the heavy water barrels back to camp, laughing at one another.

Morgan washed her hair in buckets of the clear, cool, spring water. As she sat in front of the fire, turning so her hair would dry, the four men watched.

"I never saw hair like that in my life," Jake murmured.

"My little girl has hair almost that color, but not so much of it," Frank added.

Seth grabbed a handful of the hair, jerking Morgan around. "I think I should get you out of here before I have to fight for you." Seth pulled Morgan to her feet.

"Seth, you're hurting me."

"If I didn't know better, I'd think you weren't a lady. That's a nice trick—to sit by a fire and spread all this around you." His hands were buried in her hair.

He led her into the dark woods, away from the camp.

"Seth," she said angrily, "I don't know what you're talking about."

"I don't either. I guess it's just that you look better to me every day. I'm beginning to think about you a lot. I can't even take a trip to the bushes without wishing you were with me."

Morgan felt her heart beat harder. "Seth . . ." She lifted her arms to him, and their lips met. He set off a fire in her. Her lips moved with his, feeling his tongue touch her own. Her arms pulled him closer. One of his legs parted her own, and she could feel his thigh, so hard and so exciting.

He kissed her neck, and she could feel his teeth making small nibbling bites on her skin. Chills went up her spine and down the backs of her thighs.

From a long way off, she heard Frank calling for Seth. Neither of them wanted to hear it.

"Damn him!" Seth muttered in her ear. "I have to go, sweet. Maybe Frank is your guardian angel."

"Maybe he's the devil," Morgan whispered under her breath.

Seth drew back, surprised. Then he chuckled. "I think I'm going to like spending a year with you." He kissed her on the forehead and left.

Morgan walked closer to the camp and stood, watching Seth as he talked to Frank. She didn't want to think, but she knew she wanted him to come back to her in the cool forest. Maybe I do love him, she thought. I wonder if it is possible to fall in love so quickly.

After waiting some minutes, she gradually became aware of the chill in the air and returned to camp.

A rider had come to their camp, and Seth was leaving that night with him to scout the area ahead, to find the best way of crossing Cottonwood Creek.

As he packed his gear, he told Morgan he'd see her at the crossing in two days.

He held her in his arms a few moments before leaving, and kissed her gently. "Think about me while I'm gone?" His eyes were laughing.

"Maybe." They smiled happily at one another, and then he was gone.

At supper that night, Joaquín was especially attentive. "Possibly you would walk with me after supper. I'm sure my old friend Seth would want me to make sure his wife was entertained."

"Morgan needs to help me clear up the camp," Jake snapped.

Joaquín turned cold eyes on Jake, "I don't believe Morgan usually does that, and I don't see why she should now. May I escort you?" He offered his arm to Morgan.

They walked silently in the moonlight for awhile. "How did you come to marry Seth, Morgan?"

Morgan was startled. She had hoped that no one other than Jake knew of the marriage arrangement.

Before she could answer, Joaquín continued. "I ask because I am an observer of people, and I see that there is something wrong between the two of you. I know that each night Seth sleeps away from his little bride." He touched Morgan's cheek. "If I had a bride so lovely, I would not have ridden away from her, no matter how many creeks were in danger of flooding."

She jerked away from his touch. "Don't say anything about Seth! I owe him a great deal and he is good to me."

"I am sorry. I only meant to be your friend, to tell you that if you need someone to talk to, I will listen."

She looked at him closely. His slim, smooth handsomeness was so different from Seth's huge maleness. "I'm sorry for getting angry, Joaquín. Thank you for the offer. I will remember it."

Seth rode all that night, thinking of Morgan's softness, her eager returning of his kisses. He shook himself out of his reverie and spurred his horse on. He wanted to get back to Morgan.

Joaquín was never far from Morgan's side for those two days. He asked no more questions about Morgan and Seth's relationship. Instead, he concentrated on being a pleasant companion and on making Morgan forget Seth.

Joaquín and Morgan went to gather water. Morgan gazed into the water and remembered the day before, when she had sat by the stream and held Seth's head in her lap.

Joaquín laughed quietly. "You look like a nymph by the water, looking for her lover. Tell me, little Morgan, what is on your mind?"

"I was just thinking about the water and its coolness." She smiled and looked away from him. "Joaquín, have you ever been in love?"

He scrutinized her carefully before answering. "Yes. Once when I was very young."

"Did it change you a lot? I mean . . . did you seem to forget everything and everyone else except the one you loved?"

"Yes. It was like that." His eyes clouded as he looked away.

They were silent a moment. "But Jake said you weren't married."

"No." His voice was low. "She was killed in a riding accident a few days before our marriage." His voice had hardened. In a whisper, he said, "I died with her."

Morgan was embarrassed by something in Joaquín's voice, and remained silent.

"Morgan, we are too serious. It is a beautiful sunset, and I am alone with a beautiful woman, and yet I talk of serious things."

"Joaquín, I'm not beautiful. Surely you can see that." Her voice was teasing and light.

"I have seen many women, and I know you could be beautiful. The last few days I have seen a look in your eyes that has changed you. Too often you are sad, and you try to hide it."

Seth had ridden most of two nights to return to Morgan. He was not used to the feeling he had. He longed to see her, to hold her in his arms, to see her run to him.

He thundered into the camp and jumped off his horse, throwing the reins to Jake. "Where is she?"

"At the stream." Seth ran down the path toward the stream as Jake watched. Jake had never seen such a look on Seth's face. "That young 'un has finally fallen in love," he muttered and grinned. Then his smile changed to a frown. "God, I hope that Montoya isn't up to some of his tricks with that little girl."

As Joaquín was telling Morgan that she could be beautiful, he put his fingertips under her chin, lifting her lips to his, and bent his head to hers.

Seth entered the clearing just as Joaquín kissed Morgan. It took a second for him to take in the scene. He turned and left.

Morgan turned to see Seth's broad back retreating into the woods. She forgot Joaquín.

"Seth!" She was surprised when he did not respond. She gathered up her long skirts and ran after him. Again he did not turn when she called. She caught up to him, grabbed his arm and planted herself in front of him.

For a second Seth nearly grabbed her to him. Then he jerked his arm from her grasp and angrily started down the path.

Morgan did not see Joaquín looking on with an amused smile.

"Seth! What's wrong with you?"

He turned toward her with a look of hate. His voice was low as if he were controlling a great rage. "What's wrong with me! I rode for two nights to be here with you and what do I see?" He jerked his head toward the stream. He paused and took a deep breath. His outward anger seemed to recede, but his eyes still blazed.

"I am sorry. It is my fault. I should have expected nothing. You offered nothing more than any other woman." He extended a hand and cupped her breast, hidden under so much fabric. He was momentarily surprised at its fullness.

She inhaled quickly and jerked back from his touch.

"Isn't that what you want, my dear, if not from me then from your handsome friend back there? It's such a shame that I found you out—you are such an accomplished actress. You almost had me believing in your innocence."

He turned and left her then. Morgan was totally bewildered. An actress? She remembered how she had run to him, eager for him. And then she remembered Joaquín's kiss. Was *that* what had made him so angry? She must go to Seth, reassure him that Joaquín meant nothing to her.

Seth was unsaddling his horse.

"Seth . . ." her voice was gentle, "let me talk to you."

"We have nothing to say to one another."

"No, Seth. I realize why you are angry. You saw Joaquín and me, didn't you?" Her voice had a pleading note. "It meant nothing, Seth. Not like when you kiss me."

He turned to her, his lips snarling, his eyes cold. "As I have said before, I have no chains on you. You may kiss whomever you wish. As for comparing my kisses to Joaquín's, that is the trick of a whore." His laugh was ugly. "Stay away from me. I want no more part in any of your games."

~ *Chapter Six* ~

"JAKE, what's a whore?"

Jake nearly dropped the skillet of bacon. "What . . . ?" he stammered.

"I've heard the word before, and I wondered what it meant." It had been two days since Seth had called her that. Having lived alone with her mother and then in the very sheltered company of her Aunt Lacey and Uncle Horace, she had never before been exposed to such talk.

"Well . . . it's a woman who gives her . . . uh . . . favors to a lot of men," was Jake's embarrassed reply. "Why'd you want to ask me that?"

Morgan couldn't tell him about Seth's remark. "I just heard it somewhere and wondered." She sat by the fire mending a tear in Seth's shirt. She had seen very little of him in the last two days. He and Frank had spent a lot of time fishing for catfish, and Morgan had begun to gather buffalo chips for the fire. There were no more trees now, only the plains. Morgan found the country-side ugly and hoped New Mexico wasn't as flat or as barren as the prairie was.

The next day they crossed Turkey Creek. Morgan watched as Seth removed his shirt and struggled with the horses to get them up the steep, muddy bank. She was fascinated by the magnificence of his enormous body. She remembered his arms around her, the way he

91

had so easily lifted her and spun her around. She trembled, remembering.

That afternoon the rain started. It came down so hard that Jake could hardly see to drive the horses. Morgan sat on the wagon seat, drenched.

"Get inside the wagon, you little fool!" Seth's shout could hardly be heard. Water dripped down his hat and across his poncho.

"No!"

He lunged at her, and she quickly went through the opening into the dry wagon. She could see drops of water that had formed on the underside of the canvas.

Now that she was inside the wagon, she was very glad that Seth had made her come in. She removed the big dress and dried herself. It felt good to rub her skin until it glowed. She looked for something warm to put on and found a robe of Seth's in the bottom of a trunk. The robe was enormous on her but very soft and warm. She stretched out on the narrow wagon cot and was soon asleep.

Voices awakened her. It was night, and the wagon had stopped rolling, but the rain was coming down as hard as ever. She heard Seth's voice shouting, very close to the mouth of the wagon. The end of the wagon canvas was opened, and Seth climbed inside.

"Get up, wife, and perform some of your wifely duties." His voice had a leer in it.

She hurried to obey, nearly tripping on the long robe as she did so.

"What do you have on?" he demanded.

"It's your robe. I hope you don't mind, but it was cold."

He looked at her, his blue eyes clear in the lantern light. "Help me out of these wet clothes. I'm so tired I'm not sure I could get them off by myself."

She was glad to be near him, glad to have him speaking to her again. As she removed his boots and then his wet socks, she kept asking herself where her pride was.

She dried his feet briskly, massaging the toes until some warmth returned to them. She unbuttoned his shirt.

Seth leaned back on his hands and suffered her ministrations as if he were a small boy. The front of the robe gaped open and he saw the rounding and the cleavage of her breasts. Her hair fell now, cascading around her shoulders and down her back. It glowed in the dim light.

As she finished unbuttoning his shirt, she put her arms around his waist so she could pull the shirt free of his pants. He looked down at the top of her head.

When she had removed his shirt, she began rubbing him with the towel, briskly so that he was warmed by the action.

Morgan was trying not to think of what she was doing, trying not to look at Seth's massive arms and the mass of dark gold, curly hair on his chest. She rubbed the towel over his hard, flat, stomach muscles and on his back.

As she finished, Seth began unbuckling his belt to remove his pants.

"Seth," she said hesitantly.

He grinned at her, knowing what she was about to say. "All right." He took the towel from her.

Morgan sat on the bed as Seth removed his pants and began to dry off. His back was to her, and she tried not to look, but his body was beautiful, like the Greek statues of athletes she had seen in a Louisville museum. But Seth was about twice the size of the statues.

As she looked him over, he turned toward her, and she found herself staring at his manhood, something she had never seen before. She quickly looked away.

"My innocent little bride is quickly losing her innocence. Since you've told me whose kisses you like better, tell me—whose body do you like better?"

She had always tried to be friends with him. A few days ago she had thought maybe she could be in love with him. Now, because of one silly, accidental little kiss, he taunted her cruelly. All right, she could hate too.

"I like a gentleman better than an animal who can't even be civil," she spat.

"Well, the little girl drops her cloak of shyness. Tell me, miss, is there twenty-five thousand dollars to be collected for this marriage, or is that just another one of your stories? Possibly it was a ploy to get me to give a name to someone else's bastard?"

"I don't know what you're talking about!"

"It seems to me that ever since I met you, you have been teasing me, leading me slowly to your bed. You profess innocence, yet your kisses have a passion that belies innocence. It just occurred to me that maybe you are carrying a child, and that this little whore's game of yours is a way to convince me that I am the father."

Morgan listened in total astonishment. She said softly, "You have been around women like that too long. I will tell you this again, and if you do not believe me, then I cannot help it. I asked you to marry me so I could collect my inheritance, and for no other reason. I kissed you with such passion because, for a while, I thought I could love you. I am sorry I was such a fool. At the end of this year you will get your twenty-five thousand dollars, and I never want to see you again. Until that time, I suggest we stay away from one another as much as possible." She turned from him.

"You are right. I don't believe you. I think there is another reason why you trapped me into marrying you." He took a step toward her, a towel about his hips. He grabbed her hair in his hand and jerked her head back. "From now on you will perform your wifely duties for me."

She stared at him with hate and not a little fear. "Keep your hands off me."

He laughed and released her head. "I wouldn't touch you if you were the last woman on earth, but you are my property, and for the next year you will obey me. Now lie down."

He laughed again at the fear in her eyes, but not as viciously as the last time. "Did you think I planned to sleep outside in this rain?"

She lay down, as far on the side of the cot as was possible. He removed his towel and stretched out beside her, naked. He pulled the blankets over them, and soon the rain lulled them to sleep.

Seth woke first in the morning. As he looked at her sleeping figure he smiled, and then remembered all he had said the night before. He wanted to kiss her, to hold her close, to make love to her. Then he remembered her with Joaquín. Feeling Morgan snuggle closer to him in her sleep, he slipped out of bed and dressed quickly.

Outside the air was wet and the ground muddy after the heavy rains. After a cold breakfast, they started the day's miserable journey. Morgan gathered chips for the fire.

Joaquín met her in the twilight. "Ah, Morgan, I have been noticing that you look sadder than ever today. Is something wrong?"

Joaquín made her feel good. He noticed her, and cared about her moods.

"Here, let me help you with that." He took the bucket of chips from her. "Remember, I am your friend."

She looked at him and smiled. "Thank you. Everyone has been so kind, you and Jake and Frank and . . ." She finished uncertainly.

"Your husband is a man of many conflicts. I'm not sure he knows how to love."

"Montoya!"

They both turned to see Seth standing a few feet away.

95

"If you want to keep that dapper little body of yours in one piece, then you'll stay away from my wife!"

Joaquín's eyes flashed hatred for an instant, and then they cleared to hold amusement. "Goodnight, señor, señora." He smiled at Morgan and left.

Seth glared at Morgan. "It seems I can't leave you alone even for seconds." He extended a hand and caressed the back of her neck.

His touch made her skin come alive. She closed her eyes and leaned into his touch. Seth groaned softly and removed his hand. "Let's eat. Tomorrow we come to the Arkansas River, and we'll need plenty of rest before crossing it."

Seth told her that there were beginning to be signs of Indians, and he thought she'd be safer in the wagon. They'd all start taking turns soon with night watches.

Morgan undressed hurriedly and slipped into the voluminous nightgown. Seth walked in and caught a glimpse of his wife in front of the lantern, the light from which made the gown transparent. He had a sight of slim legs and a small waist, and then she slipped beneath the covers. He frowned and looked away. "Someday I'm going to tear off her damn clothes and see what she looks like," he muttered under his breath.

"Did you say something?" Morgan asked from under the quilt.

"Just go to sleep." His voice was gruff.

The Arkansas River was wide and shallow with no trees on either side. Yet there was an island in the middle covered with cottonwood trees.

They stopped early that night, ready to cross the river the next morning. Morgan began to think of a bath and washing her hair. She visualized herself in the water, feeling thoroughly clean for once.

Seth and Frank had gone ahead to look for signs of Indians. Only Jake and Joaquín were left with the wagons. If she hurried, she could have her bath before Seth returned.

Quickly she got soap and a towel together and then told Jake where she was gonig. She saddled a horse and left.

Seth and Frank returned to the camp some time later.

"No sign of Indians, yet," Frank said in answer to Jake's question, "but a lot of buffalo trails. You'd better get your frying pan ready for some buffalo steaks."

"Where's Morgan?" Seth stepped from behind their wagon.

Jake looked up from his cup of coffee. "She went over to that little island to take a bath." He returned to his conversation with Frank.

Seth quickly made sure that Joaquín was in the camp. He was sitting a little aside from the fire, polishing the silver on his ornate saddle. When their eyes met, Joaquín gave Seth a knowing look.

Quickly, Seth straddled his horse and started toward the island. He made his way across the water slowly. He knew there wasn't any danger now, but the idea of his little wife being alone so far from camp made him uneasy.

He led his horse across the sandy island to the far side and tied him near a clump of sweet grass. Morgan's horse was closer to the shoreline. He smiled as he looked down and saw her clothes in a heap on the shore. He saw her a few feet away, standing waist-deep in the water, her back to him. Her hair was full of soap suds. He stepped back into the trees, in a shadow of the fading sunlight.

The sunlight glowed on her skin. It was the color of pale honey. He could hear her humming as she lathered her hair. She turned quickly and extended her arms to the water, and then went below the surface. Seth jerked upright from leaning against the tree, and his breath caught at his first glimpse of Morgan's nude body.

No clothes on earth could hide a body like that. It must be a trick of the setting sun. Morgan had said herself that she had a boy's body. That's just the way she looked sometimes, too, like a young boy in a woman's clothes. How could this lovely creature be his plain Morgan?

Seth stopped thinking when he realized he had not seen Morgan surface. Quickly he ran into the water toward the spot where he had last seen her. He saw one small hand above the surface. He dived under the water and caught her small body in his arms. Her foot was entangled between two logs. He twisted it and it came free.

He carried her to the beach and stretched her out on the sand. As she coughed up the water she had swallowed, she lay in his arms with her eyes closed, half-conscious and breathing jerkily.

She began to awaken, and found herself lying in Seth's arms. It seemed to her, in that moment, that every time she needed help, Seth was there. She smiled up at him and snuggled her head closer to his chest. Seth was too astonished to smile back.

Something in Seth's manner made her realize her situation. She sat up, trying to cover her breasts with her arms. "What happened? Seth, go away!" Her voice was frantic.

"Little wife, you need not try to cover anything—there's nothing I haven't seen." Then, releasing her, he said, "I think you had better get dressed now, because you are very close to losing something other than your life."

They slept in the wagon again that night.

Morgan remembered how she had felt today, awakening beside the water in Seth's arms. For an instant she had felt warm and safe. But she realized now that all he had cared about was seeing her without her clothes. As she drifted off to sleep, she wondered what Seth had thought when he saw her nude. "Probably thought I looked like a boy compared to Cynthia Ferguson," she murmured, before she fell asleep.

In sleep, his arms enfolded her and held her close to him. Morgan was getting used to having his body near hers, to feeling his breath close to her ear.

Joaquín was the first to notice Seth's and Morgan's new attitude toward one another. He had seen several changes in them already. At one time they had looked at one another with an expression akin to love. Now they never seemed to look at one another at all, though Joaquín had noticed Seth staring wistfully at Morgan a few times.

From the moment Joaquín saw Morgan on the stairs of the hotel in Kansas City, he had known she was beautiful. He had been surprised that it was not treated as a fact, and generally accepted by everyone. It amazed him that all men couldn't see her beauty just because of ill-fitting clothes, and that rather sad look about her. There were times when that expression left her face, and she held her head up, and her shoulders didn't drop. Ah! Then she really was beautiful.

Colter, thought Joaquín, you've had everything all your life, but you won't have it all much longer. No, Nuevo Mexico will soon belong to us again. His lips curled. He lifted his coffee cup to Seth in a simulated toast.

After crossing the Arkansas, the group had taken on a tension that hadn't been there before. Seth or Frank constantly rode ahead to check for signs of Indians. Each night the campfires were smaller, and there was little conversation. At the snap of a twig, someone jumped toward the sound with a rifle or gun.

They were over halfway there now, and Morgan longed for the jolting days to stop.

"Morgan, I'm glad to see you holding up so well under the strain," Frank told her one night.

She managed a smile. "My father seemed to think New Mexico was worth all this." Her hand swept toward the blackness outside the little camp.

"Oh, yes, Seth mentioned your father. What was his name? Maybe I knew him."

"Charles Wakefield. He had a ranch somewhere around Albuquerque, I believe."

Joaquín listened carefully. Seth was on watch, and Jake was on the other side of the wagons.

"Charley Wakefield!" Frank nearly shouted, and then quieted his voice. "I knew your father—no wonder I liked you from the moment I saw you. Your father was a hell of a man. It really made me sad to hear he'd left us. Seems like a lot of the good ones die young." He looked at Morgan with a puzzled expression. "I always wondered why Charley never married."

Morgan had never heard her father mentioned in favorable terms before, and she wanted to hear more. She stared at the fire. "Tell me what he was like."

"He was a good man and a hard worker. I didn't know him until he'd been around for some time, but I heard he built up his ranch from practically nothing. It'd take a man a week to ride the borders of his land." Frank smiled. "I worked as a hand for him some years ago. Charley wasn't like most of those rich boys; he joined right in and worked alongside us. He could rope a steer with the best of 'em." Frank stared at the fire in silence. Then he added, "Sure never heard him mention a wife or little girl, though."

"My mother took me back to Kentucky when I was very young." Morgan's response was stiff. It was difficult to feel kinship with a man who had made her marry and leave her home against her will.

Frank sensed Morgan's hostility and wondered about it. "You sure missed a lot by not living out here. This country's got more excitement in one day than the East has in a year."

A bit later on that night, she slipped to the side of camp to sit on a rock and stare at the stars. Joaquín's voice startled her.

"There are no stars in the East like there are out here, are there?"

"No, I guess not. But it seems a high price to pay for stars."

Joaquín smiled, his teeth white in the moonlight.

"I was raised out here. To me the East is too unchanging. There is no surprise, no adventure."

"You have a ranch, too, like Seth's?"

Joaquín chuckled, and there was a tone of contempt in his voice. "I have a ranch, yes, but not like the Colter one. The Montoya ranch is several times larger than his, and it has been in my family for generations."

"Do you live there alone?"

"No," Joaquín answered, "I live with my sister, Lena." When one of his riders had told him about Lena and Colter, he had wanted to kill her. All she had done was laugh at him. He had vowed then to avenge himself on Colter one day.

"Tell me, Morgan, do you hate our West so much?" His voice had a slyness that Morgan missed.

"Yes!" was her vehement answer. "I hate this dust and the constant danger and . . . and . . ." Her eyes involuntarily went to the west where she knew Seth was on watch.

"And your husband?" Joaquín's voice was very low.

"Yes." Her voice was resigned, and Joaquín realized that she was close to tears.

"Morgan, I told you once that I was your friend. If you want to tell me anything—if you want a shoulder to cry on, I am here."

A tear rolled down Morgan's cheek and then another. She sobbed into her hands. Joaquín waited. Her first words were almost inaudible. "I don't know why he hates me. I wanted to be friends. I wanted to be like we were in Kentucky. We rode together and talked and laughed together. Then he kissed me." She shivered as she remembered Seth's kisses.

"Sweet Morgan, I am your friend." Joaquín's hand caressed the back of her head, but he did not try to touch her beyond that. "Why did he ask you to marry him?"

Morgan's sobs shook her body even more. "He didn't. I asked him to marry me. I didn't want to. My father willed that all the money went to my uncle unless I married and lived in New Mexico for a year. I offered Seth money to marry me." She continued crying softly and Joaquín sat back to digest this.

This explains a lot, he thought. Yet, he knew that as soon as both of them got over their anger, they would realize that they cared for one another a great deal. Joaquín had seen the way Seth protected Morgan, and the way her eyes followed him around the camp. He smiled in the darkness, very glad to have heard what he had been told.

"Not all men understand a woman's gentler feelings. Some men only use women. I am afraid you have married a man who may be like that." He changed his voice to a seductive tone. "I wish you had asked me to marry you. I would gladly have done so, without money. It would be a pleasure to be in the company of so beautiful a woman." He raised her hand to his lips and looked into her tear-filled eyes.

"I'm not beautiful, Joaquín," she whispered.

His smile was soft and knowing. "But you are, and someday you will know it. It would have given me great pleasure to show you how beautiful you are. I would like to dress you in satins and silks."

102

Morgan felt herself blush at Joaquín's words.

"Little Morgan, when you know you are beautiful, then you will be beautiful."

They sat together in silence awhile, thinking of different things. Then Joaquín said, "Let's go back now before people start wondering where we are." He took her arm and led her back to the wagon. "Goodnight, my fair princess," he kissed her hand again. "Sleep well."

Joaquín left Morgan at her wagon and turned to be met by the hostile stares of Frank and Jake. He smiled and bowed toward them, then went to his own wagon.

"Somebody ought to do something about that little dandy," Jake muttered.

"Yeah, and I know who ought to do it." Frank looked toward where Seth was standing.

Crossing the Cimarron River was a nightmare for Morgan. The area around the river was crawling with rattlesnakes. The men kept shooting at them to keep them away from the horses. By the end of the day, everyone was tense and exhausted.

The next few days after crossing the river were just as tiring as the first days of the journey had been. At Middle Spring, Morgan had her first glimpse of tarantulas. She had not minded the rattlers as much as these huge, hairy spiders. Willow Bar was a welcome relief with its sand and willows.

Another relief was that Morgan had almost become used to undressing in front of Seth. And their attitudes toward one another were softening. Several times she had caught him smiling at her, and she had found herself smiling happily back!

Early one morning Seth rode ahead of the wagon train. "I'll meet you at Rock Creek in two days with some fresh game," he told Morgan as he packed his saddlebags.

103

Both of them remembered the last time he had gone away. The memory brought tears to Morgan's eyes, and she kept her head lowered so he couldn't see.

"What's this, little one?" his tone was mocking, "Will you actually miss your husband?"

She kept her eyes on the ground.

He said quietly, "It seems you and I always say the wrong things to one another, doesn't it? Let's try to start over again, when I get back. All right?" He smiled at her and made her smile back. "Could you spare a kiss for a lone knight?"

Before Morgan could think, she was in his arms. "Seth . . ." she whispered. His lips touched hers gently at first, and then they both felt the longing of the last weeks. Morgan drew him closer while kneading the muscles in his broad back and sides.

"No, sweet, we're going to go *slowly* this time. Both of us need time to learn to trust. I'll see you again soon, and we can start all over."

He touched her cheek briefly and then leaped into the saddle and was gone.

～ Chapter Seven ～

THAT night Morgan lay in the wagon, half asleep, pictures of Seth floating through her mind.

"Lookee here what I found, Ben." A stranger was climbing into her wagon! She pulled the blanket close to her chin in fear. "Lotsa yella hair, too."

Another man appeared at the end of the wagon. "Bring her out here, Joe." His voice had a strange, rough quality.

"Ah, let me get her now. She's no good to us. Let me have her." He was pleading.

"You get out of here and let me see if she's worth anything or not." The first man left the wagon, and the second entered.

"What are you doing here? What do you want?" Morgan's voice shook with fear.

"Nobody's going to hurt you. Just get up and let me see you." His voice gave Morgan chills. It was rough, but at the same time it was a sly voice, the voice of a person who could not be trusted. "Come on now, get up."

Morgan obeyed.

"Now, I'll just stand here, while you find a lantern and make some light in here." Morgan was shaking as she found the lantern and the tinder box. If a snake could talk, she thought, its voice would sound like that.

"Cat Man!" The voice came from outside the tent. "What we gonna do with these two?"

105

Morgan jumped—a cat! Yes, that's what his voice reminded her of.

"I'll be there in a minute. Just hold on and don't bother me again."

Morgan heard low, throaty guffaws from the men outside the wagon. There seemed to be at least two others besides the creature in the wagon with her.

Cat Man sat on the cot. "Now," he said when she had the lantern lit, "let me look at you. Come close to me."

With her first glance at Cat Man, she let out an involuntary gasp. His face fit his voice. His eyes were an exaggerated almond shape, long and thin, and his nose was wide and flat. His mouth was small, thin-lipped, practically nonexistent. She almost expected to see long whiskers above his upper lip.

Cat Man smiled at her, a knowing smile that made his eyes even more catlike. "Come here," he repeated.

Morgan inched slowly toward him. He seemed to enjoy her fear. When she was close to him, and while still holding her eyes with his own, one long, thin arm darted out and tore her nightgown from her.

Morgan covered her body with her arms.

"No." His one word conveyed his meaning, and she dropped her arms, staring off to the side of the wagon.

"Ah, yes, you'll do. Nice. Get some clothes on and come outside." He left the wagon.

Without hesitation, Morgan did as she was told. She didn't feel that Cat Man was usually disobeyed.

"What happened to all that purty hair I seen? Did she cut it off?"

"No, it's still there. Now you two get them tied up, and then let's get out of here."

"What about her? We gonna take her?" This was from another man.

"Yeah. Now get busy!"

Morgan saw the other two men, both rather tall but

thin, pulling Jake and Joaquín from the side of the wagon.

"What you goin' to do with her?" Jake's voice was angry. "Her husband'll come after you. Don't take her, she's just a little girl." One of the two men hit Jake across the head with the butt of his revolver.

"No!" Morgan gasped and started toward the fallen Jake, but Cat Man's grasp on her shoulder, his thin, steely fingers biting into her flesh, halted her.

"He is a foolish old man. Now look at your other friend there. He's more sensible." She followed Cat Man's slanted eyes to Joaquín, who was, as always, slightly smiling! He nodded his head faintly toward Cat Man. They seemed to understand one another.

In that one second Morgan had an insight into Joaquín. She realized that his only friend was himself, and that he didn't care any more about her than about the dirt under his feet. Her face must have betrayed her feelings, because his smile widened and he tipped his hat to her. She shivered. Any hope of being saved from these men was lost.

"Did you go through all the wagons?"

"Yeah," said one of the men. "And there ain't nothin' here. Just some old furniture, no money or nothin'."

"Well, we're not going away completely empty-handed," Cat Man stroked Morgan's neck. When she pulled away from him, he let out a low, throaty sound.

"Get her horse saddled, Ben, before this husband of hers returns."

Morgan wished more than anything in the world to see Seth riding in now, to get her away from this awful Cat Man and the two tall, thin men who came with him.

"Get on the horse."

Morgan's skirt caught under her leg as she straddled the horse, exposing a large expanse of calf.

107

"Woowee, gonna like that!" Joe nudged Ben in the ribs as they leered at Morgan's smooth leg. The party started away.

"What happened?" Jake held his head in his hands and looked up to see the four riders go off into the moonlight. "I've got to go after them," he began.

"Untie me first," Joaquín's voice floated up to Jake, and he stumbled toward the dark man and slowly untied the ropes binding his arms. Jake stumbled, still stunned from the heavy blow to his head.

"Careful, old man, you get too excited and we'll never find anyone." Joaquín put a helping hand under Jake's elbow.

Jake jerked from Joaquín's grasp and straightened his aching body. "It'll be a long time before I need help from the likes of you."

Joaquín watched, amused, as Jake painfully made his way to Frank's body.

"Well, you ain't dead yet, so I guess you're too mean to kill." Jake's voice showed his relief as he held Frank's head in his arms. "You!" his voice held the contempt he felt for Joaquín, "help me get him back to the wagons."

As Jake cleaned Frank's head wound and his own, Joaquín began gathering the horses that the bandits had dispersed.

"What happened, Jake?" Frank moaned.

"They took the little girl."

Frank started up from the cot. "I've got to go get her. You know what they'll do to her?" His voice cracked with the effort of talking.

Jake pushed him back down. "You couldn't swat a fly, and I can't see well enough anymore to go trackin' them, and that heathen out there ain't gonna help. So that leaves the boy." To Jake, Seth would always remain a boy, the closest thing he had to a son. "I'm gonna go now and find him."

"Jake, you can't go. Send Joaquín."

Jake spat on the wagon floor. "I wouldn't trust him not to spend his time staring at the stars. No, this is a man's job, and I'm sending a man I can trust—me. I'll see you as soon as I can manage."

He turned and left the wagon, saddled one of the horses, and left the camp, his destination unknown.

It took Jake all that night and into the next before he saw Seth's campfire. He called into the camp before he entered. "Seth, it's me, Jake. Are you there, Seth?"

Jake was nearly exhausted and Seth helped him from his horse. "What's wrong, Jake?" he demanded.

"It's Morgan," he gasped out. "They took her."

"Morgan! What do you mean, old man? Who took her?" He grabbed Jake's shoulders.

"Three men, one they called Cat Man . . . looked and sounded like a cat, too. They came to rob us. Frank was on guard, but they knocked him out—bad wound, too. Then they got me and Joaquín. They took the little girl with them and headed due west."

"When? When did they leave?"

"Last night about this time. I been lookin' for you ever since. Frank was too bad hurt to go after her, and I figured my old bones wouldn't hold up. So I came straight to you instead."

Seth began saddling his horse and packing his saddlebags.

"There's game strung up in that tree. Take it back with you. Then when Frank's better, take the wagons and go on to the ranch. I'll get Morgan, and then I'll meet you at the ranch." His voice was grim. As he straddled his horse, he looked into the horizon and then back to Jake. "I'll get her, Jake, and they better not have hurt her." His eyes were cold.

He rode off toward the west and was soon out of sight. "I hope for their sakes that they haven't hurt her," Jake muttered before he turned back to the fire. He had been without sleep for thirty-six hours, and he collapsed onto the ground.

Morgan had been on the horse for two days and two nights before they stopped and made camp. Until then, they had stopped for only brief periods to rest their horses. They had eaten pieces of dried beef while traveling. She had become proficient at sleeping on her horse. Cat Man held the reins while she slept.

At first Morgan wasn't even fully aware that they had stopped. She sat on her horse while the three men began to build a fire.

"Gonna enjoy this night." Joe motioned toward Morgan. "Sure am gonna have a good time."

Morgan, still on her horse, her head drooping with exhaustion, felt someone near her. "Get down," Cat Man's voice was low. Obediently, she moved one painfully aching leg across the saddle and slid to the ground. She saw a bedroll spread out by the small fire. Cat Man's long finger extended in a gesture toward the blankets. Morgan stumbled toward the skimpy covers, dropped to her knees, and then lay down, so very grateful to be able to stretch out. She was asleep instantly.

Voices woke her and she heard them through a haze, as if they were a long way off.

"I seen her first! She's mine!"

"It don't matter who seen her first. She's mine, 'cause I got the gun out." Morgan heard a click.

"You ain't gonna shoot me, 'cause I'm gonna shoot you first."

"You and who else?"

"Stop it!" This was the cat voice that Morgan had grown to hate. "Nobody's gonna have her. Now make something to eat." His voice was calm and assured. Morgan had her eyes closed, but Cat Man must have walked out of the camp, because she heard the crackle of underbrush and rocks.

There was silence around her, and she began to drift back into sleep. Then the whispering seemed louder than the arguing of a few moments ago.

"It'll take him a while out in the woods. If we're quick, we can both get it done before he gets back, and he'll never even know."

"What if she tells him?"

"She won't. We'll just tell her she better not."

"I'm with ya. Who goes first?"

"Let's flip for it."

Morgan heard a low chuckle and then, "Damn!"

"You hold her and I'll stick her." The voices were very near.

Morgan turned over quickly to look into the two leering faces. She managed a gasp, before a hand closed over her mouth and then another held her two hands. She began to kick as she felt other hands on her ankles, then sliding up her legs to her thighs.

"Skinny little thing, ain't she?" Both men chuckled greedily.

Then, just as her skirts were tossed over her head, her legs were released and she felt something heavy fall across her right leg, below the knees.

"You didn't have no call to hurt Ben," whined one of the men. "We was just gonna have a little fun. We wasn't hurtin' nobody."

"Let her go."

Morgan was humiliated to her soul. Why was she lying here, pinned to the ground, her body exposed to men she hated?

When Joe released her, she immediately pulled her skirts from her face and covered her legs.

Joe grabbed Ben and dragged him away from her. As Ben began to recover his senses, Cat Man jerked both of them in front of him by the fire. Although Cat Man was very slim, he had a great deal of power in his spare frame.

"Now listen to me, you two, and listen good. This woman is a present to Boss, and Boss doesn't want leavings. I want her untouched and I want her treated with respect. If I leave her here for you to guard, that's what I expect you to do. Is that clear to you two thickheads?"

"Yes, Cat Man." Their voices were contrite. "We didn't know she was a present. You didn't tell us."

Cat Man's lithe body relaxed, and he smiled that strange, malignant smile of his. "Well, boys, now that you know, don't forget it. Now get me somethin' to eat."

"Yes, Cat Man, yes." They stumbled against one another in their attempts to obey.

Cat Man walked to Morgan. "They won't bother you now."

Morgan was beside herself with rage. "What gives you the right to give me as a 'present' to anyone? I'm not something you can own." She kept her teeth clenched, trying to control her anger.

Cat Man looked at her in puzzlement for a few seconds and then laughed his peculiar laugh. It flashed through her mind that he worked at it, that he tried to look and sound like a cat.

He said quietly, "You are a woman—something to be owned, something to be bought and used. You'll make a pretty little ornament for Boss." He turned and left her before she could reply. "Give her some beans, Joe."

Joe brought her a plate of pinto beans, but she could hardly eat, because anger had made a lump in her throat. She climbed back under the covers to resume her sleep.

The next thing she felt was a hand on her shoulder, shaking her awake. She smiled as she thought of Seth

112

and snuggled under the covers again. It wasn't even morning yet, so why was Seth trying to wake her? A hand on the side of her breast made her eyes fly open, and she looked into Ben's grinning, vacant face. His eyes were glittering. She shivered and jerked away from him.

As she sat up, she realized that the shoulder of her dress was torn at the seam, and as she looked at it she remembered the previous night's happenings. Joe and Ben watched her as she rolled up her blankets, as Seth had taught her, and strapped them to her horse.

I must keep my sanity through this, she thought. I must remember Trahern House and Kentucky and . . . Seth. Yes, Seth. She clung to her image of him.

They rode hard all day, stopping only once to water and rest the horses. Morgan splashed her face and hands. The water was so cool and good after the long, hot days. She was less sore than she had been the day before, but the insides of her thighs were raw from the saddle.

"Let's go."

"Ah, Cat Man, why do we have to keep runnin'? There ain't nobody followin' us."

"Yeah, I'm gettin' tired. What you say me or Ben go back a ways and see if we see anybody, and then if we do, we'll kill 'em?"

Morgan gasped and put the back of her hand to her mouth.

"Looks like the woman thinks somebody is following us." They all turned to stare at her standing by the water. "Who do you think is following us? Couldn't be that old man, and the young one didn't seem to care if we took you or not. Ben, here, near killed the one on watch, or did you finish the job, Ben?"

"I don't know, didn't look to find out." Ben smiled at Cat Man.

"Well, then the only one left is this husband of yours.

113

He was away, but I don't think there were other men with him—too small a train. If someone had taken my woman, I don't think I'd go miles in the opposite direction trying to get help. No, I guess I'd ride out for her myself. Is that what you'd do, boys?"

Ben and Joe grinned idiot smiles at him.

"So, little lady, I figure there's only one man following us, and I reckon the three of us can take him on. You agree, boys? Tonight we'll stop early, and one of you can ride back a ways and see if you can find this husband of hers."

When she again mounted her horse, Morgan had something to worry about besides her own problems. She prayed that they wouldn't be able to find Seth. She never even questioned her certainty that Seth was following.

In the late afternoon they rode over a ridge to see a little adobe house nestled against the back of a hill. It was the first adobe house Morgan had ever seen, and she wondered at the flat roof. In Kentucky, the rain and snow would eat through the roof in a few years. Yet this house had the look of having been there for a long time.

As they stopped to look down at the house, a woman came out the side door, gathered an armload of wood from a pile, and carried it back inside the house.

"Cat Man! Maybe we can have a little fun with that one, huh?"

Cat Man smiled at Joe. "Let's go see if maybe they'll give us something to eat."

Ben grinned. "Yeah . . . and then the woman."

As they started their horses down the steep hill, Cat Man turned toward Morgan and gave her a malevolent look that she knew was a warning.

"Good afternoon, ma'am." Cat Man's voice seemed kind as he called out to the other woman, and Morgan looked at her with wonder when she showed no fear of the four strangers.

114

The woman *was* usually more cautious of strangers, but since they had a woman with them, she relaxed.

"Afternoon." She smiled at them timidly.

"Who is it, Meg?" A man came to the door. He also showed fear for a few seconds, until he saw Morgan. Then he smiled. "We don't get many visitors up here, so we have to be pretty cautious." Morgan saw the rifle in his hand. She glanced at Ben, who had moved his hand to his sidearm.

"Won't you come in and set a spell? Meg can rustle up some grub, and you can tell us any news. We don't get out of here very often."

"Well, that's right neighborly of you. We sure appreciate that." Cat Man's voice sounded sincere. He got off his horse, and then helped Morgan from hers. Again he flashed her a warning look.

After the four of them had washed at a small stream, they sat down at a large table covered with the strangest food Morgan had ever seen. She wondered how anyone could have prepared so much food so fast, until she realized that each dish had the same basis—a red sauce and pinto beans.

In spite of her situation, she enjoyed the food. Her favorite was a roll made of a kind of corn bread, but very flat and thin, wrapped around a mound of mashed pinto beans. It was covered with onions and the thick, hot, chili sauce, and then sprinkled with white cheese.

"This is very good," she murmured.

Cat Man laughed. "My wife," he watched her intently lest she contradict him, "is new to this country and our food."

Don't trust him! she wanted to scream to these people, these generous people who offered him hospitality.

"You sure can cook good, ma'am," Ben said. He pushed his plate away, having filled it three times.

Morgan helped the woman clear the table, and as they went to the end of the room where the washtub stood, she tried to manage a way to warn the woman. But she constantly felt Cat Man's eye on her. Maybe they'll just go away, maybe they won't hurt them, she offered a silent prayer.

When the dishes were done, she returned to where the others were sitting and smoking home-rolled cigarettes. Cat Man pulled a chair close to his own, smiled at Morgan, and patted the seat of the chair. To all the world it must have looked like a loving gesture between a husband and wife. With her back to the others, she allowed her face to show all the hate she felt for him. That secretive, catlike smile never faltered.

"Where was it you said you was headed?" the man asked Cat Man.

Before Cat Man could answer, Morgan saw Ben look at him with questioning brows. Cat Man nodded slightly toward him, and Morgan gripped the arms of the chair until her knuckles were white. If it was going to start, it would be now.

In an instant, Ben's arm reached out and grabbed the woman, Meg, around her ample waist. She was a large, strong woman, and she began to fight Ben with success.

Her husband reacted instantly, quickly crossing the room to his rifle. The second his fingertips touched the rifle barrel, a shot exploded beside Morgan, and she saw him crumple. Ben and Joe stopped to stare at the man lying in the corner. Meg jerked free and ran to him.

"John, John," she whimpered.

"I'm all right, Meg." His eyes caught hers, and motioned to the rifle at his side.

"Touch the rifle, and he won't live another minute." Cat Man had dropped the fake-sincere voice and returned to the lower, sly voice Morgan knew so well. "I didn't mean to kill him. I thought he might like to watch the boys here in action."

Both John and Meg looked at Cat Man with horrified eyes. Morgan whispered, "No, no."

Cat Man turned to her. "Sit!" he ordered, "unless you want to see them both dead."

Shaking with fear, she sat down again, turning her head to the wall.

"She's yours, boys," Cat Man said with a sneer.

As Joe and Ben advanced on Meg, she began to scream. John raised himself up, holding his bleeding thigh, and started again for the rifle.

Ben kicked the rifle away and then started to kick John.

"No!" Cat Man told him. "Tie him up and gag him —so he can watch."

At the sound of tearing cloth, Morgan jerked her head around to see Meg's large body exposed. Ben held her arms, while Joe fondled her large, sagging breasts and turned to grin at Cat Man.

John writhed under the ropes and gag, but his eyes remained fixed on his wife. Meg stopped fighting and stood as if she were made of stone, staring at the ceiling.

Morgan couldn't stand it any longer. "No," she screamed, "you can't do this! You're animals! Stop it!"

Cat Man slapped her hard against the mouth. "Shut up, or I'll let them have you," he growled.

He sat down and pulled Morgan into his lap, putting a thin hand across her forehead, holding her head toward the sight of Ben and Joe holding the woman. "Look," his voice was soft. "Look at what I'm saving you from."

Ben roughly lowered the woman onto a rag rug. Morgan looked away, but it was difficult with Cat Man holding her head in his steely grip.

Joe pulled his pants down and mounted the woman. Morgan closed her eyes and ears to the sight. She tried not to think, but Cat Man's rapid breath in her ear made it impossible for her to escape the reality.

"Me next." Ben's voice was as excited as a five-year-old's.

As Joe left the woman and Ben removed his pants, Morgan looked at Meg, her head turned away from her husband, staring at the wall by Cat Man's feet. Her eyes were glazed, like a dead person's.

When Ben gleefully climbed on top of the prostrate woman, Cat Man's hand stole to Morgan's right breast and began to fondle and knead it. She tried to pull away, but his iron grip held her.

"Like a rabbit! You finished faster'n a rabbit," Joe laughed at Ben.

Joe's ugly jeer made Cat Man drop his hand. His breathing returned to normal. Morgan jumped from his lap. He grabbed at her, catching her skirt and tearing it at the waist. He smiled at her, narrowing his eyes.

"Ben, look for any money and pack some food."

"I was thinkin' about goin' agin." He looked down at the nude woman on the floor. She hadn't moved since they had put her there. Ben turned at a sound from John, and Morgan saw his eyes were pleading. She knew that John's look of entreaty was more likely to encourage their cruelty than to stop it.

Morgan grabbed a quilt from the back of a chair and covered Meg, and then put her arms under Meg's shoulders to lift her up. It was like holding a rag doll. Tears sprang to Morgan's eyes. "I'm sorry, I'm sorry," she whispered to the unresponding woman.

"Leave her alone. We got to go. Ben, you find any clothes to fit . . ." He looked at Morgan and grinned. "I don't even know your name."

She wanted these people to know their names, his name as well as hers. In a cold voice, she said, "It's Morgan, Cat Man." Perhaps this would help Seth to find her.

His eyes shifted to the man on the floor at his feet. He knew why Morgan has used his name. It didn't matter to him. He liked people to know who he was. He liked it when his name caused fear in people's eyes.

"Find some clothes for Morgan," he called, his eyes never leaving hers.

"What about these?" Ben held up a pair of boy's jeans and a plaid shirt. Joe held a pair of boots.

"Good, I think they'll do real well. Now go outside and get the horses ready. I'll be out in a minute."

"Can't we see the little girl put the clothes on?" Ben whined.

"No! Now go do as I say." The two men hurried to obey.

When they were gone, Cat Man turned back to Morgan. "Now get dressed."

Reading her reluctance correctly, Cat Man quickly drew his gun and shot close to the head of the man against the wall. He hardly even looked where he was shooting. Meg, at Morgan's feet, turned her head to look at her husband, but she did not move otherwise.

Morgan began to remove her clothes. When she was totally naked, she stood straight up to stare at Cat Man, who was holding the clothes she was to put on.

Cat Man had seen her nude before, but now that he saw her body in daylight, he began to regret his decision to give her to Boss Martin. Her skin was flawless, her waist so small, and the curve of her hips made him ache to touch her.

Cat Man tossed the clothes to Morgan. "Put these on—fast."

The pants and shirt were made for a young boy, and were too small on Morgan's curvaceous body. The pants fit over her hips and legs like a second skin, and the shirt strained across her breasts. It was one more cause for misery. How much longer could she bear this?

Seth had been tracking them for three days. He knew they were traveling fast, because he had found only one campfire in the three days. For a while he seemed to have lost their trail. Now he looked down on a cabin

119

nestled against a hill. There were animals in pens around the place, but no sign of human life. Cautiously, Seth made his way down the hill toward the adobe house.

A rifle shot rang out, and Seth felt it whiz by, close to his left ear. Quickly, he turned his horse and was soon out of sight of the house.

He had followed the trail of Cat Man and Morgan to this cabin, and he meant to find out what they knew about his wife. He decided to wait until dark before going to the cabin again. He found a circle of piñon trees that gave privacy and shelter, and he stretched out on the fragrant needles to obtain some long-needed sleep.

When he awoke, the moon was high, and gave eerie shadows to the trees and shrubs around him. Quietly and stealthily, he made his way down the ridge to the back of the little house. About fifty yards from the woodpile, he tied his horse and then approached the house. He didn't know how many people were in the cabin, and he didn't want to take the chance of walking into a hostile group.

As he ran to the woodpile, he heard a noise from the door and watched to see a tall, slim man open the door slightly and look out. Holding a rifle in front of him, he limped slowly to the woodpile, looking around constantly.

When he seemed satisfied that he was alone, he propped the rifle against the stack of wood and began to fill his arms.

Seth sprang over the mound of cut logs, and before the man could even turn, Seth had a gun in his ribs and one powerful arm around the man's neck.

"Don't hurt us, mister. We been hurt enough," the man pleaded.

"I have no cause to hurt you. I just want to ask some

questions. Did three men come by here just recently, with a woman?"

Before the man could answer, the door to the cabin opened. Both men turned toward the sound.

"John . . . John, are you all right?" Her voice was full of fear.

When she made out her husband's form in the moonlight, and then Seth's much larger form holding him, she screamed and began crying hysterically, incoherently.

"Let me go to her. I'll answer your questions, but just let me go to her."

Seth released the man, and he went to comfort his wife. As he held her in his arms, he looked up at Seth, his face sad.

"I don't mean you any harm," Seth said quietly. "I'm just trying to find my wife."

John nodded his head. "The little blond woman?"

"Have you seen her?" Seth's voice was jubilant.

"Meg, it's all right." John's hand stroked his wife's hair. "He's not here to hurt us. Why don't you go inside, and I'll be in in a minute?"

Sobbing, Meg went back into the house, and John shut the door behind her.

"Yesterday, about sundown, three men rode up. They had the woman with them." His hands were clenched into fists at his sides.

"Did they give you any idea where they were going?"

"No." Seth could not help but wonder at the hatred in the man's voice.

"Had they hurt her?"

John remembered Morgan standing nude, but he also remembered that Cat Man had not touched her, and that he had forbidden the others to bother her.

"No, they hadn't hurt her, but that Cat Man is evil."

"Did they do that to your leg?" Seth motioned to a wound that still seeped blood onto John's pants.

"This is the least of what they did to us." Seth's eyes followed John's to the cabin, and understanding passed between the two men. "If you catch them, mister, I hope you kill them."

"I plan to."

Seth returned to his horse and mounted to leave.

"They dressed her in boy's clothes," John said. "But she'll still be easy to find when it's known that she's riding with that Cat Man." Quickly, he described the men and their horses.

As Seth prepared to leave, they shook hands and exchanged names. "I hope you get 'em," John called after Seth.

"I sure as hell do too," he whispered into the darkness.

Days later, as they came over a ridge and looked down at the little town, Morgan knew it was a mistake to even call the place a town. There were only five or six buildings, each looking as if it might fall down at any minute. A little apart from the other buildings stood a large white house. They started down the hill before she could see any more.

"Cat Man! Good to see you again."

"Joe, honey, where you been so long?"

Morgan looked around. The woman who had called to Joe was lounging in the doorway of a derelict, faded building. Her reddish hair was matted and filthy. Her dress revealed most of her sagging breasts. Morgan guessed that at one time the dress had been red and gold, but now stains and several unmended rips obscured the material. The woman returned Morgan's stare boldly.

"What you got here, Cat Man? Pretty little thing. Can I have her when you're done?"

Morgan felt a rubbery palm on her leg, and looked down to see a short, fat man, with a large nose and

122

thick, protruding lips, staring at her. His greasy hand was caressing her thigh. Quickly she jerked her leg up and out to kick him hard in the chest, just at the base of the neck.

Unprepared for the blow, he landed sitting in the dust and refuse of the street. In front of her she heard Cat Man's low chuckling.

"That serves you right, Luke. Keep your hands off from now on. She's the Boss's woman."

Morgan heard laughter from the other people as they watched the fat man pick himself up from the dirt. She shuddered at the hate-filled look he sent her.

Several people had come out to see the little procession, and they all seemed to know the three men. There was much interest in Morgan.

"You say she's for Boss? I bet Boss's Nancy ain't gonna like that."

The four riders rode out of the tiny town to the white house that Morgan had glimpsed briefly from the hill. The townspeople did not follow them to this house.

It was two stories high and very well kept. A porch ran around two sides of the house, and the second story had a large, round turret on one corner, with a conical roof. Everything was trimmed in brilliant green, making a sharp contrast with the stark surroundings.

At a motion from Cat Man, Morgan threw one leg over the saddle and slid to the ground. She was so tired that it seemed as if none of this were really happening to her. She moved automatically, and felt very little.

The front door was unlocked, and Cat Man led Morgan into a spacious entryway and up a wide, carpeted stairway. She had a brief sight of carved furniture and lush red curtains.

To the right at the top of the stairs was a door, and Cat Man opened it to reveal a large, bright room. Against one wall was a spacious fourposter bed, draped in a silky, white fabric. There were sprigs of sea-green flowers all over it. The carpet, walls, and the rest of the room echoed the colors of the pale green and white. The room was refreshing and inviting.

At Cat Man's hand on her arm, she stiffened. His cat-laugh sounded low in her ear, and he jerked her to a mirror over a chintz-covered dresser. She was startled by the sight of herself. She was as dirty and unkempt as the woman she had seen in the town. Her face was smudged, and her eyelids drooped. But what caused her to gasp was the sight of her own body in the tight pants and shirt. Her breasts strained against the fabric, and her nipples stood out taut and rigid. There was a gap between two buttons exposing the curve and roundness of her breasts. The pants fitted sleekly over her thighs, and the belt showed off the roundness of her hips.

"Like yourself, don't you?" Could Cat Man read her mind? His hand caressed her thigh. "Too bad I said I'd give you to Boss," he murmured. "But he's not too happy with me now, and I know what he likes." His hand lightly cupped her breast, and the thumb moved over the already taut peak. "I think he'll be real grateful to me."

He moved his face close to hers as if to kiss her, and she turned her face away. She heard his warning growl in her ear.

"That's all right, little princess. You think you're so good now, but a few months with Boss Martin will change your mind."

He moved away from her. "We'll stay here two days. Then we leave. I want you to get some sleep. Tomorrow you'll have a bath. If I took you to Boss now, he'd think you were a polecat."

She looked for something to throw at him.

"Don't." His voice was deadly, and after the last spurt of energy, Morgan realized how tired she was. She had been insulted too much to let another taunt hurt her.

"Now get some sleep, and don't try anything." His eyes went to the open window. "If you should get out, you'd be facing Luke, and I don't think he'd treat you with respect."

Morgan felt chills on her back as she remembered the fat, dirty man pawing her leg. Cat Man had made his point.

When Cat Man left the room, all ideas of flight left Morgan. The room was cool, and the green-and-white bed beckoned. She removed her boots, her pants, and then the tight shirt. As she crawled into bed, she marveled at the difference between men's and women's clothing. Women had to wear so much more than men.

The sheets were cool and clean, and felt good to her bruised and chapped body. She was so tired that she didn't even mind the dirt on her body. Cat Man was right—she did smell terrible. Just before she drifted into an exhausted sleep, she saw Seth's smiling face, saw him standing with his arms extended to her.

When she first awoke to the sounds of Ben and Joe's voices just outside her door, she thought she had been asleep only a few minutes. The sun was low in the sky and slanting across the thick, green carpet.

"Watch where you're goin'! You hit me in the leg with this thing."

"I don't see why we have to carry this up here anyway. Who the hell wants to take a bath?"

Morgan still wasn't awake when the door opened to admit Joe and Ben carrying a large copper bathtub. Morgan turned over on her side, pulling the sprigged sheet to her neck.

They put the tub down in the center of the room and turned toward her. At the sight of Morgan's lush curves, covered only by a sheet, the frowns left their faces.

"I sure would like to climb in there with that little

girl." Joe took a step toward the bed, but Ben grabbed his arm.

"Let's go get the water."

In a few minutes they came back with four large buckets of hot water, and poured it into the tub. When the two men left, Morgan nearly ran to step into the steaming water. She lay perfectly still for several minutes, allowing her body to luxuriate in the hot water. Gradually, she became aware of her surroundings again, and began to scour her body and hair. As she scrubbed, she noticed that clean, fluffy towels had been placed in the room, and that her shirt and pants were clean, and had been draped across the end of the bed.

Now she realized that she must have slept for twenty-four hours, an entire night and day! Her mind was less cloudy. She began to think.

Somehow, she must escape. What would Seth want her to do? He would probably tell her to stay where she was until he could come for her. But she wasn't really sure that he could find her.

The door opened, and Morgan turned quickly toward the sound. An old woman came in and stood with bowed head at the foot of the tub.

"What do you want?"

The little woman kept her head lowered. Her dark hair was greasy, her dress torn and unwashed.

"What do you want?" Morgan asked again. When the woman didn't answer, Morgan shrugged, stepped out of the tub, and wrapped herself in a large, white towel. Silently, the old woman began filling buckets with the bath water. After several trips downstairs, she had emptied the tub.

Morgan sat in front of the mirror over the dressing table and combed the tangles out of her clean hair. "Seth, please come," she whispered to her reflection.

Quickly she dressed in the clean shirt and pants. The soft cotton fabric felt good against her skin. As she looked at herself in the full-length mirror, she wondered what Seth would think of her in the shape-hugging clothes. She ran her hands down her body, watching the points of her breasts come alive.

The sound of the door opening startled her. "Ben'd be real good to you, honey."

Morgan jerked the door open wider and stepped past Ben into the corridor. One dirty hand caressed her hip as she hurried past him.

"You look so much better now, little Morgan." Cat Man smiled at her. "Now my gift will be appreciated." His slanted eyes devoured her body, and Morgan felt her face growing hot. He ran a thin finger down her cheek. She turned her face away.

"Why don't you let me go? I've never harmed you. Let me go." Her voice was pleading.

Cat Man was dressed in black, and the color emphasized his yellow eyes. He took her hand and led her into the dining room, where a table was set with a large meal. He pulled out a chair for Morgan, and when she was seated, he took a chair beside her.

"You will find, Morgan, that often beautiful women's lives are ruled by their faces and their figures more than by their own minds. You are a woman to be owned—a woman to love, a woman to fight for, possibly to die for."

"You talk nonsense. I'm not beautiful, and I never will be. All my life people have told me how plain I am. Why do you talk this way?"

Cat Man's eyes widened for just a second. "It's difficult to imagine that anyone could be so blind." He reached for a buttered roll. "But then, I have seen you with a look of great sadness. Possibly your expression, the dress you wore at first, and the way you did your hair have all concealed your beauty. But it is difficult to believe, even so."

Cat Man continued eating. "The food is excellent.

127

Would you like some wine?" he asked, as he filled her glass. She realized she was ravenous. Without another word she began eating the largest meal she had ever consumed.

Seth watched the town from the ridge above it. He had been tracking Morgan's captors for seven days, and now that he knew he was so close, he decided to rest awhile before he attempted her rescue. He needed strength. He knew from the looks of it that he'd get no help from anyone there.

There were no riders coming into the town, and Seth knew that his appearance would cause some speculation. He had followed the outlaws to the town early that morning, and knew they could not have arrived much before the previous evening. As he pulled his hat over his eyes and went to sleep, Morgan also slept. It would be hours before she woke to a hot bath and dinner with Cat Man.

He awoke when the sun was low, and he quickly made his way down the hill into the town. As he had conjectured, his appearance caused a stir. Casually, he tied his horse to the post in front of the saloon. He ordered a beer, and made his way to the back of the dirty room to an even dirtier table.

After a few moments of staring, the group began to lose interest in the stranger and returned to their own talk. Seth leaned his chair against the wall, sipped his beer, and watched.

He listened carefully to a group in a corner near him. He heard the name "Boss" mentioned several times, and then "Boss's woman" and loud laughter.

"You mind if I sit down, or you savin' this seat?"

Seth looked up to see a woman with red hair staring at him. Her eyes and lips were heavily painted, and she smelled strongly of perfume over her unwashed body. She could have been thirty or fifty. She eyed Seth with

128

wariness. Seth wondered what could have caused her such fear.

"I'd be pleased to have you." At the gentle tone of his voice, the woman's look of caution increased. "Could I buy you a beer?" Mutely, the woman nodded.

"Barkeep! A beer for the lady."

The others in the bar turned toward Seth. They laughed. "You sure are a stranger, mister. Janie's a lot of things, but she sure ain't no *lady*."

"You don't know nothin' about a lady, Luke. That one yesterday sure set you on your ass," the woman beside Seth answered.

"Why, you!" The fat man came out of his chair toward the woman. She rose also, hands and fingers made into claws.

"I'd hate to have to defend the lady's honor." Seth's eyes narrowed, and his voice was steel. The fat man stopped and appraised the stranger.

"Come on back, Luke. She ain't worth a fight."

Luke relaxed his shoulders and smiled. "You're right, boys. Sorry to have bothered you, mister." He didn't want to fight with the enormous stranger. He turned his back on Seth, and returned to his table. "You're right, that whore ain't worth anything," he tossed over his shoulder like a child who had lost an argument.

"Thanks a lot, mister." Her eyes were adoring now.

"I just don't like to see a lady's name maligned." He emphasized the "lady."

The bartender brought Janie's beer, and she drank half of it down in one noisy swallow. She wiped her mouth with the back of her hand and looked at Seth. "You stayin' here long?"

"That depends."

"On what?" Her eyes and voice were eager.

"I've been hearin' that there's a big outfit working out of here, and I might be interested."

129

"You a lawman?"

Seth laughed derisively, held out his hand, and ran a finger across the curves of her breasts. "Do I look like a lawman?"

Janie had had her first man when she was twelve years old, and had long ago lost any feeling about the things men had done to her body. Yet, once, when she was sixteen, there had been a boy, a big, strong, clean, farm boy who had been good to her. He had wanted to marry Janie. He would have, too, if his mother hadn't found out how Janie had been supporting herself for four years.

Janie remembered the boy with affection, and Seth's kindness to her made her feel a sensation she had thought long dead.

She gazed up at him, hunger apparent in her eyes. "I reckon you don't look like a lawman." She paused. "I sure do like big men."

Seth leaned closer to her, seeing more clearly the cracks in the heavy makeup she wore. "Well, I got me a partiality to women—all of 'em." She opened her mouth to speak, and Seth smelled the stale odor of her breath.

"Anything you want, mister, and it's yours. It'd be my pleasure." She fluttered skimpy eyelashes at him.

Seth smiled knowingly at her. "What about this Boss I keep hearin' about?" He motioned his head slightly at Luke and the other men nearby.

Janie looked around to make sure no one could hear. She leaned toward Seth. "Boss Martin's the leader. He don't come to town much, but when he does, he stays in that big white house at the end of the road."

"Well, Janie." He put his hand on her arm. "How could I get in touch with this Boss Martin?"

Janie put her hand over Seth's big one. "Cat Man rode in yesterday, and is stayin' at the Boss's house."

"Cat Man?"

130

Janie shivered. "Yeah, he looks like a cat—real slanty eyes. Walks like one, too. None of the girls like to go upstairs with him. I thought he was goin' to kill me one time." Janie smiled. "But this time he brought his own woman. Dressed her up like a boy and took her down to Boss's house. She's a real snooty bitch, but nobody deserves what Cat Man does to a woman."

Seth worked the muscles in his jaw. "This woman he brought—what'd she look like?"

Janie frowned and looked at Seth, but he was staring across the bar, away from her, his eyes seeing nothing. "Yella hair . . . little, like a kid. What you want to know for? You interested in her?" Janie's voice was hostile.

Seth turned to her and smiled, showing his even, white teeth, and the long dimples in his cheeks. "I was just wondering what somebody'd bring into town, when they already had so much here."

Janie smiled back at him, showing a broken tooth on the left side of her mouth.

Seth drained his beer. "I got to be goin' now."

"Don't go yet, mister. I don't even know your name." She followed him to the door, hanging onto his arm. "I told you I'd give you whatever you want." She smiled up at him, coquettishly. "Tell me, is all of you as big as your arm?"

"It sure is, honey." He pinched her earlobe and left her.

Seth rode out of town past the big, white house. There were two men on the porch, both drinking and arguing loudly. Neither fit the description of Cat Man.

Seth tied his horse not far from the back of the house, hidden halfway down the side of a deep arroyo. When it was completely dark, he made his way down to the house.

"I don't know why Cat Man has to take so goddamn

131

long, and why one of us ain't enough to stay with the little girl. What are you laughin' at?"

"I's just rememberin' that woman in the cabin—on the way here."

"Yeah, she warn't bad. Not bad at all."

Seth listened carefully. It seemed that there were only the two of them in the house. He listened a while longer to their bragging, and knew they were very drunk. Silently, he stepped through an open window. Through the open doorway across the hall, he could see both of the men in the lantern light. Remembering his promise to the raped woman's husband, he regretted not being able to kill the men now, but marked them well for a later fate.

Seth figured Morgan would be kept upstairs. He cautiously crossed the hall to the stairs and began making his way to the second floor.

"What was that?"

Seth froze on the stairway.

"I didn't hear nuthin'. Give me that bottle and quit worryin'. Ain't nobody goin' fool with Boss Martin's property."

Joe laughed. "You're right. Give me the bottle back."

Seth found only one door locked upstairs. He couldn't risk the noise of trying to break it open, so he entered the bedroom next to it. As he had hoped, there was an adjoining door, also locked, but a quick search of a night table revealed a key.

Quietly he entered Morgan's bedroom and saw her snuggled under the sheet, her long, golden hair spread around her, making a halo. He smiled his relief.

To keep her from crying out, he put his hand over her mouth. Instantly, her eyes flew open in terror. When he saw recognition reflected there, he removed his hand. Her arms flew around his neck, the sheet falling away from her nude body.

He held her close, burying his face in her clean, soft hair.

"I knew you'd come, Seth," she whispered tearfully. "I knew it. They said no one could find us, but I knew they were wrong." She pulled him closer. "I'm sorry for all the mean things I've ever said to you." She kissed him on the neck.

"Morgan, sweet, we've got to get out of here. Get dressed, and don't make a sound."

Her face showed her fear. "Seth, they're horrible. You don't know. They've done horrible things. I don't like to remember." Her eyes were full of tears.

"There's no time for that now! Get dressed!"

Quickly, she put on the tight pants and shirt.

"Let's go," he hurried her. "Follow me, and no noise."

Quietly and easily they made their way past the two drunken men and out of the house. Soon, they reached Seth's horse. He mounted and pulled her up to the saddle in front of him. He kissed the top of her head, murmuring a quick prayer of thanks for her safety. Then he nudged his horse up the hill.

~ *Chapter Eight* ~

THEY rode all night. Morgan snuggled against Seth and slept part of the way, safe with his enormous arms around her.

At dawn, Morgan awoke to a very different countryside than that surrounding Boss Martin's white house. The trees were tall here, straight, with white bark. They looked eerie, since they had markings that looked like eyes. The leaves were nearly round, and the gentle breeze made a rustling sound through the trees. It was quiet here, and cool, and somewhere in the distance she could hear the sound of running water.

"Where are we, Seth?"

"We're in the mountains of New Mexico. I came through here years ago and found the place where I'm going to leave you. There aren't many white men who have been there."

"Leave me?" She turned to look up at him. The sunlight shining through his hair made it seem very blond. His skin was tanned, and there were little lines at the corners of his eyes. "You're not going to leave me alone somewhere, are you?"

"I have to for a while. Cat Man and those two buffoons will be following us." He grimaced. "I don't believe he'll let you escape without trying to find you. I have to go back and find them first."

"No. They might hurt you. Please don't leave me. Let's just go on and get away from them."

"Little Morgan, how long do you think two of us can ride on one horse? We can't possibly lose them." At her worried look, he kissed her forehead. "Don't worry. I'll be back soon, and then I'll take you to my ranch."

She smiled up at him. "I want to see your ranch. Is it as pretty as this place?"

"No, it's not this high. There are no aspen trees there."

At the foot of a wall of growth, they dismounted. Seth tied the horse, then led Morgan between some trees. Now she could see an ancient trail, nearly overgrown with brush, spiraling upward. They climbed, Seth holding her hand and guiding her.

After several minutes, they came to a flat, worn place in a sheer rock face. There were several steps, and then they saw the village. There was an opening in the face of the rock about one hundred feet long and about forty feet high. Set back under the protection of the overhanging rock were ancient mud buildings. Some were crumbled, but others were still whole.

"What is it, Seth?" Morgan whispered, awed by the ghostlike city.

"It's an old Indian ruin. Frank, Jake, and I came down here years ago, and an old cowboy showed us this place. You'll be safe here."

Morgan left him to peer inside the nearest house. It was tiny. There was barely enough room for her to stand up. The ledge in front of the houses was bright and sunny, but the houses were cool and dark. She didn't feel as though she and Seth were alone. It seemed the spirits of people long dead were still there, watching. She smiled. She felt the spirits were protective.

"I like it here. The people are good."

Seth looked at her strangely, and then returned her smile. "You're right. They'll take care of you while I'm gone."

She ran to him, throwing her arms around his waist,

burying her head against his chest. "Seth, let's stay here. They can't find us here. We'll wait a while—a week—and then when they're gone we'll leave."

He lifted her chin. "I want no more tears. I am going back. That's it."

She smiled and wiped her tears away.

"Do you have any kisses left?" he asked.

She stood on her toes and her arms slipped around his neck. His kiss was gentle at first, and then they both gave in to their need for one another. He kissed her cheek and then her neck. "Sweet little Morgan. I hate to leave you."

Abruptly, he held her at arm's length. "I have to fill the canteens. I'll be back in a few minutes."

For a second, Morgan was startled by his brusque way of leaving her, but then she smiled and hugged herself. She wanted to dance and laugh and cry all at the same time. She began humming and whirled around the shaded courtyard doing a waltz step. She would buy beautiful clothes, and she'd wear her hair loose. Or any way Seth wanted. Anything her beautiful, darling Seth wanted was his.

"May I join in?" Seth took her in his arms, and they glided gracefully to the music in their heads. Laughing, they collapsed on the floor, and in an unconscious gesture, Seth put his arm around her shoulders and drew her head to his chest.

As they looked into one another's eyes, their smiles faded and their lips met in a quiet, searching kiss. Gently, Seth lowered Morgan to the floor and began caressing her body. Expertly he unfastened the buttons of her shirt and exposed her warm, full breasts to his touch.

She returned his kisses with ardor, her tongue and teeth gently massaging the muscles of his neck and the open part of his shirt. She began to writhe and arch against him in the ancient manner of women. She rubbed his lean, hard thighs, searching. Gently, she kneaded the bulge she found between his legs.

An animal sound broke from Seth's throat. He rolled off her, his heart pounding and his breath coming in gasps. He sat up quickly and held both her hands in front of her. His eyes were glazed and his hair was rumpled. Silently, he buttoned her shirt. "Not now, little one." His voice was low and husky. "When I make love to my bride, it won't be hurried, it'll be when there is plenty of time."

He took a deep breath. "Stand up and listen to me. I have quite a few things to tell you before I go."

She listened. She was not to leave the ruins for any reason, not even to sit in the sunlight in front of the houses. He left her food, water, and blankets.

"Now, if I don't return within three days, try to make it east. About four days from here is the cabin where Meg and John live." At the question in her eyes, he said, "Yes, I met them. They will help you."

She put her arms around his neck and held him, desperately. "Please stay, Seth. I don't want to lose you again."

"You'll have time to think. I want you to be sure about us."

She looked at him. "What about you, Seth? Do you want me?" Her eyes hardened as an ugly thought crossed her mind. "Maybe you don't want me. Maybe you just want to enjoy your year as a husband before collecting your reward money."

The words were out before she realized, and she was frightened. Seth's reaction astonished her. He threw back his head and laughed and then picked her up in his arms and twirled her around. "Sweet little Morgan. Do you know so little about me that you think I'd marry for money? I think I must have fallen in love with you when you flashed Cynthia Ferguson that first look of hate. You were so sad in that ugly brown dress.

The way you hung your head wrung my heart. But then, just for a second, your eyes lit up. And I was trapped." Laughing, he kissed her.

"Do you really mean that, Seth? You do love me?"

"Always."

She frowned slightly. "Then why didn't you tell me before?"

He laughed again. "And have you tell me off? You wouldn't have believed me if I had told you." He kissed her thoroughly. "I must go now, love. You'll do as I say and stay here?" At her nod, he continued. "I'll be back soon. Will you still love me . . . or will you have changed your mind again?"

"Oh, no! Seth, I won't. I do love you." She stopped, eyes narrowed. "You're laughing at me!"

He smiled and hugged her close, then set her on the ground. "I'll think of you every moment, my love." He turned, grinned, and was gone.

Morgan listened intently to the quiet sounds of Seth's horse trotting away. When it was silent once again, she turned to face the wall. It wasn't as warm now as it had been when Seth was there. She felt small and very alone.

The tears began to run down her cheeks. "No!" she said aloud. "I won't cry, because Seth will be back soon, and there's absolutely no reason to cry."

After a few moments she decided to explore the ruins, and thus fill up the long period of waiting for Seth. The back of the village seemed to have been a waste area, and she found many pieces of pottery and bones.

After two days she grew bored with the village and its great numbers of broken pots and scraps of ancient fabrics. Her clothes were dirty, and she had unwisely drunk nearly all of the water Seth had left her.

Cautiously she began to make her way down the

worn stone steps to the bottom of the canyon. She made sure that she was always hidden under trees or brush and never exposed to the full view of anyone in the canyon or on the ridge above.

She followed along the stream and found a little pool surrounded by cattails and boulders. She removed her clothing and stepped into the clear, cold water. After bathing, she washed her cotton pants and shirt, and spread them on a rock to dry. She lay down on a rock and dozed in the fading sunlight. The sensual pleasure of the heated sandstone against her bare flesh made her remember Seth even more vividly.

Smack! The sharp pain on her bare buttocks made her eyes fly open. Quickly turning over, she saw Seth towering above her, his eyes blazing.

"I told you to stay out of sight! What are you doing down here stretched out for the world to see?"

She frowned, becoming angry herself, and opened her mouth to speak.

"I don't want to hear one damn word from you. I heard you come down that path like a buffalo."

His eyes were furious. "Anyone on that ridge could have seen you taking a bath. And now here you are stretched out, inviting trouble."

The fury she had felt left her, and she barely suppressed a giggle.

"What the hell are you laughing at! I try to make sure you're safe, while I risk my life to keep you that way, and you lie there and laugh!"

She smiled up at him, falsely innocent. "If you heard me coming down the path, why didn't you come to me then? Why did you wait until I'd finished bathing?" She turned on her side, her nude body tantalizing him. "You said I was inviting trouble. What kind of trouble were you thinking of?"

The tension left his body, and he gathered her to him. "Damn you, Morgan! You shouldn't have left the ruins. You weren't safe coming down here." He was serious.

"But what could happen to me now that you are here?"

He laughed. "I ought to spank you here and now, but I'm afraid you'd enjoy it." His voice lowered, and he said flatly, "I worried about you a lot. Please don't take chances like that again."

She was sorry she had caused him worry. "No, I won't again. Seth, is everything . . . finished?"

He stroked her hair, her head on his shoulders. "Yes. It's done now, and we won't speak of it again. I sent a message on to the ranch, to let them know we're all right." He drew her head back to look at her, his eyes teasing. "I met a woman in the saloon, and she was very friendly. I got the idea that if I ever wanted to go back, I'd be welcome."

"What do you mean, go back? And who is this bitch anyway?"

"Bitch! My, my, you have certainly learned a lot in the last few months. I could almost think you're jealous."

She said coolly, "I don't think she would be so interested in you if she knew your wife of four months was still a virgin." She turned to look at the water, idly running her fingers through her damp hair. "Of course, we did have geldings back home. Maybe she'd understand."

Seth's quick intake of breath was audible. "Lord! You would think that at my age I'd learn not to try to tease a woman. Come here, viper." He kissed her and ran his hand freely over her nude flesh. "Tonight you are my bride."

"Seth . . ." she began.

"What's this? Fear? From someone who has just called me a gelding?" He laughed and crushed her to the granite hardness of his chest. "Don't worry, my

141

little one," he whispered. "I love you too much to hurt you."

He held her silently for a moment. "That water looks inviting. Help me out of these clothes, wife!"

In an instant they both were nude: two golden bodies drenched in the dappled sunlight. One body was big, strength showing in every contour, the other was small and delicate. Morgan stretched out a tentative hand to touch the steely muscles of his chest. "I like you like this," she whispered.

Seth smiled down at her, then quickly jumped in to bathe in the clear pool. This time Morgan watched him unabashedly, glorying in the way the water glistened on his magnificent back and arms. She sat on the edge of the pool and briefly wondered at the changes that had occurred in herself in the last few months. As Seth stood up, the water sliding over his glistening body, she thought, I'm in love now, and love changes everything! She stood up and ran to meet him, his arms enclosing her.

He led her to a grassy spot near the pool, sat down, and pulled Morgan beside him. At the nearness of her, and the sight of her perfect body, his manhood rose with an iron strength. He pulled her to him, and she felt his throbbing strength against her thigh. Her searching hand found him and held him in a firm grasp. Seth emitted the low moan that she had heard earlier. The size of him startled her, and she was afraid.

Seth sensed this. Gently, he kissed her lips, her neck, her breasts, teasing the pink tips with his tongue. His mouth traveled farther, while his hands stroked her inner thighs. Her legs separated of their own accord, as his tongue touched her most secret place.

His mouth found her lips again, and gently she felt him probing her. Slowly, he entered her, until she felt he filled her entirely. He lay still until the first, sharp pain faded and she began to move her hips. Following her lead, careful not to hurt her, Seth began to move with her, very slowly. Then, unable to contain himself, he moved more quickly until he lay quietly on top of her, supporting his weight on his elbows.

Morgan felt Seth's warm breath in her ear. What she had just experienced was so different from what she had imagined. It made her feel good to give pleasure to Seth, the man she loved. He hadn't hurt her, but neither had she felt the mounting excitement that he had, and then the quick relief.

"Did I hurt you, *mi querida*?" he whispered.

She hugged him closer, her arms not reaching across the broad expanse of his back. "No." She didn't want to tell him that she didn't find making love the joyous experience she had expected it to be.

Seth rolled off her, and rested his head on his elbow. He smiled at her. "Don't worry, little bride—it will get better."

She was startled by his understanding.

"What's there to eat around here? When a man changes from a gelding to a stallion in one day, it makes for hunger."

He laughed at Morgan's blush. Quickly she stood up and began to look for her clothes. "Here!" He tossed her his shirt. "I'm not ready to cover all that up, yet."

In minutes she returned from the cliff dwelling with Seth's saddlebags of food. He had started a fire in a sheltered copse of the canyon. Together they heated beans, and Morgan made baking-powder biscuits.

"If only Jean-Paul could see me now," she laughed. "We spent a week on white sauces, and now I am making crude biscuits over an open fire."

After the meal, Seth spread blankets. And as he held her close, she could feel his desire rising. As he kissed her and touched her body, she began to lose herself and feel a new urgency. Seth spent a long time with his love play, before he heard her soft moans and felt the movement of her body with his own.

When they made love the second time, she felt no

pain. Her body felt good. She wanted this new feeling to go on forever. She was surprised at Seth's mounting passion, and was disappointed when he rolled to her side, spent.

He held her close, and was soon asleep. Morgan stayed awake for a few minutes. For some reason, she felt like running until she dropped from exhaustion. But the soft call of an owl finally lulled her to sleep.

They awoke together in the dawn. "Seth," she whispered.

Seth was smiling. She held out her arms to him, and he came to her quickly, his needs meeting her own. He held back, until she clawed at his back and held his buttocks, pulling him deeper into her. Her desires met his, and they collapsed together in one another's arms, sated.

Morgan slowly recalled her abandonment of the moments before. She was embarrassed, and turned her head away from Seth. She had acted like an animal.

"What's this? Morgan, what's wrong?" He looked into her tear-filled eyes. "Tears, from my little wildcat?"

She began to cry more. "I'm not a wildcat. I'm a *woman*," she sobbed.

He laughed. "So that's it. It's that damned mother of yours. Sometimes I wish I could have met her. But I'd probably regret what I would say to her." He kissed Morgan's damp cheeks. "Your mother had some wrong ideas about what makes a lady. I love you, and you love me. What we do between us isn't wrong." His eyes twinkled. "Didn't you enjoy this morning?"

"Yes."

"Then that's all that matters." He stood up, took her hand, and pulled her up to him. "Come on."

"Where?"

"We're taking a bath. I've smelled buffalo more pleasant than the two of us."

She looked at his hair and noticed it was wet with sweat, as was her own. Seth was right. She had enjoyed their lovemaking . . . more than enjoyed it. She needed it. And she wasn't going to let anyone interfere.

"Race you," she called as she ran to the pool.

~ *Chapter Nine* ~

THEY spent four days in the canyon of the ancient ruins. Seth introduced Morgan to the joys of lovemaking, and after her initial fears were over, she learned to return his love with an abandonment that surprised them both.

"Morgan, sweet, it's time to go." Seth's voice was a whisper in the early-morning stillness.

"Go where?" She snuggled closer to him, still groggy with sleep.

"Today we have to start for home. We've been here long enough. I want to take my little bride back to my ranch."

It was a minute before Morgan reacted, and then she sat up, throwing the blanket from her body. The sight of her golden skin with the full curves of her breasts and hips always made Seth's body react. He reached out one large hand to caress her and pull her back to him, but with lightning quickness, she was already standing out of his reach.

"Hey," he called softly, "why don't you come back to me for a little while?"

She ran to him, pulling his head to her chest. "I want to go. I want to see your ranch, and I want to meet Lupita, and I want to be your wife."

"My wife? That's just what I want you to be right now." His hand reached inside her cotton shirt.

She laughed and pulled away from him. "Oh, no, Seth

147

Colter, I know you. We'll make love, and then we'll sleep, and then we'll make love, and before long the day will be gone. You'll never take me home until I'm old and ugly and you don't want me anymore."

Her reasoning made sense to him. "You're probably right. So why don't we just stay here for a few more years?" He made a grab for her. "I promise to take you home when I'm tired of you." At the look in her eye he said, "All right. I'm getting up." As he put his clothes on, Morgan heard him muttering something about being henpecked so soon.

The journey east and north to Seth's ranch took over three weeks. They stopped often to rest the horse, which was overburdened with the weight of two people. There had been places where they could have purchased a horse, but Morgan had protested. This was her honeymoon, and she liked the feeling of being so near Seth.

Seth had said that they would reach his home within the next two days. She twisted in the saddle and unbuttoned Seth's shirt to kiss the bronzed skin of his chest.

"Can't keep your hands off me, can you, wench?"

Morgan giggled and then sighed, her chest against his cool skin. "Seth, do you think I'll fit in? Do you think the people on your ranch will like me?"

He kissed the top of her head, warm from the sun. "As long as I like you, then that's all that matters. Besides there aren't many others. You know Jake, and Lupita will adore you. For years, she's been trying to marry me off to every female relative of hers from fourteen to fifty. Paul runs the place while I'm gone."

"You've never mentioned Paul."

"He's been with me about two years. Between Jake, Paul and me, we keep the place going. In the spring we hire a few men, but then they leave again in the fall. I hope you're not disappointed, sweet, but you are not married to a wealthy man."

"Seth," she leaned against him, enjoying the feel of his muscles against her back, "What will happen to your father's plantation? Wasn't he angry when you came out here to live, rather than run the plantation? You're his only son."

"He was at first, but then I think he envied me my freedom. He married and then I was born, when he was still very young. He had to support his family, and couldn't go off to new territory to start a life that offered no security. The plantation will go to my sisters and their husbands."

"It seems strange for a rich man's son to give up everything and start all over again, poor."

"But my ranch in New Mexico is mine, not handed to me. My son will be able to choose where he wants to live, too."

"Son!" Morgan murmured, and felt her belly. She would be glad to get home, to a home in this enchanted land for her, Seth, and their children.

It was late afternoon of the following day, when they saw the house. Even from a distance, it looked enormous to Morgan. "Well, when a house is built of adobe, I guess you can afford a big one."

It was low and sprawling, with fences and low walls surrounding areas off the rooms. In back were four other buildings, houses for Lupita, Jake, and Paul, and a sort of barn for horses and Lupita's dairy cow. There were several cottonwoods around the houses, and here and there chickens scratched in the dirt.

Other than the chickens, Morgan saw no signs of life. When they were about a hundred yards from the house, Seth dismounted, emitted three low whistles, and suddenly he was surrounded by dogs. They were glad to see their master, and leaped to greet him.

Smiling up at Morgan, still on the horse, Seth told

her, "They're the worst watchdogs in the world, but I couldn't possibly get rid of them."

"Señor Colter! You are home!" A short, plump woman ran to Seth and threw her arms around his waist. Seth picked her up, swung her around, and kissed her heartily on the cheek.

"You're so skinny!" she laughed, wiping away tears. "They have no *frijoles* in that place, no *tortillas*?" She stopped when she saw Morgan.

"This is my wife, Lupita," Seth announced proudly, as he lifted Morgan from the horse and held her in his arms like a child.

"Put me down," she whispered to him, embarrassed.

Lupita laughed happily. "Jake has been telling me about you. I am so happy to meet you. I have been telling this buffalo a long time it is no good to live alone."

"Well, Lupita, she's only second best." Seth could feel Morgan's eyes on him. "I wanted Lupita, but she wouldn't have me."

Seth ignored Morgan's struggles and pulled her closer. "I seem to remember an ancient Roman custom, where the husband carries his bride into the house."

Lupita glowed as she saw the obvious love between the two. She had not expected this, not after what Jake had told her about the constant bickering during the journey. She loved Seth as the son she never had, and she knew this tiny bit of a woman that he so easily held was going to be her daughter. Maybe soon there'd be lots of babies for her to take care of. She laughed aloud.

"See, Lupita approves of my carrying you." Morgan relaxed against her husband as he started walking toward the house.

"Seth!" Morgan turned her head to see Jake running toward them. "What the hell took you so long? Frank's been over twice to see if you were back yet." He grinned his toothless smile and took Seth's outstretched hand in both of his.

"Well, I see you got the little girl back."

Seth pulled her close and said, "I would have been back sooner, but this little wildcat kept me holed up in a canyon for a week. Wouldn't let me go."

"Seth!" Morgan hid her reddened face in Seth's shoulder. Through clenched teeth she issued threats against his life, but he happily continued carrying her and ignored her protests.

When he reached the house, he paused at the threshold and sought her lips. He kissed her as he carried her into the house.

Sensing their need for privacy, Jake and Lupita walked around the house, leaving the newlyweds alone.

Seth enjoyed showing Morgan his house, and she immediately fell in love with it. There were few rooms in the house, but each one was enormous. The kitchen was in the center, with an open porch on one side and a long, narrow room with many windows on the other side. The living area was L-shaped, and she saw that Jake had already set up the furniture Nora had given them.

The only other room was a huge bedroom with big double doors leading onto a little walled-in courtyard. The bed was set against one wall, and was encased in a crudely but ornately carved bedstead. There were several rugs on the floor, of boldly patterned designs in bright colors. Every room except the kitchen had an open fireplace shaped like a beehive.

Morgan sat on the bed. "I love it! It's a beautiful house—not at all like what you described."

"Well, I didn't want you to be disappointed. It's not exactly like Trahern House." He looked at Morgan sideways, watching her reaction.

She didn't turn, but replied nonchalantly, "Trahern House? I don't believe I've heard of that place." She turned to him and smiled invitingly. She tested the bed with her hands. "Nice bed," she murmured.

Seth embraced her. "I want this to be your home. I want you to be happy here."

"I could never be any happier than I am right now. I love you so much."

Seth tangled his hands in her hair and pulled her back with him on the bed. "You know, I've never made love to you on a bed before!" He kissed her lips and her throat as she moved her thigh between his legs.

The following week was blissful. Seth was gone during the day, and she was content to stay in their house and perform the many chores there. At noon she often rode out to Seth and took him a lunch. More often than not, they made love under the piñon trees.

Lupita had loaned Morgan some embroidered blouses and full, bright-colored skirts. These fit her as poorly as the clothes from Kentucky. Lupita had said she should go into Santa Fe and get clothes to fit her, but Morgan didn't want to leave the ranch even for a day.

But Lena changed things.

She came one morning, riding a beautiful black stallion. Morgan was outside feeding the chickens, dressed in a particularly drab dress, with one of Lupita's old aprons tied around her waist. She held the apron in front of her, filled with chicken feed.

The sight of Lena astonished Morgan. Never had she seen anyone so beautiful. Lena's riding suit was entirely black, with a small patch of white lace at the throat. Her legs were encased in tall boots of soft black leather. Lena's blue-black hair was intricately arranged in soft, lustrous curls on top of her head and gently flowing down her back to her waist. Cocked over one eye was a tiny little hat with a slim red feather curling around the brim.

"Señorita Montoya!" It was Lupita's happy voice behind her as Morgan stood as still as a statue. "Long time since you come. How have you been? Come and meet Señor Colter's wife. You will like one another."

Lena smiled down at Lupita and slowly, gracefully, dismounted. Lena kissed the older woman's plump cheek, and Morgan saw that Lena was small, like herself.

"Yes, I have heard about this little beauty of Seth's. Where is she?" At the question, Lena looked around and saw Morgan a few feet from them. She stared for a moment, and then confidently walked to Morgan and around her.

"Oh, yes . . . I can see what Joaquín meant. Yes. You do hide your beauty very well." She turned quickly to Lupita. "What do you mean, allowing the lady of the house to work like a *péon*?"

Lupita threw up her hands. "She does what she wants, and that husband of hers lets her. She cooks, she even scrubs floors, and no matter what I say, she does it. Maybe you can talk to her."

"Yes, I think I'll have to." She turned back to Morgan and possessively put her arm around Morgan's shoulders. "Now, drop that," she sneered at the chicken feed Morgan still held in her apron, "and let's go inside. By the way, I'm Lena."

Lena had always been spoiled, and she grew up believing she was the center of the world. She had never had any reason to suppose differently.

Morgan was shy around the beautiful woman who seemed so at home, so confident. Lena asked questions about their return trip to the ranch. Morgan briefly told the story of Cat Man.

"I think you were very brave and very smart to keep quiet and wait for Seth. Me—I would have killed the man myself."

Morgan shivered as she remembered Cat Man's eyes.

Lena, sensing her reluctance to talk further of the horrible episode, dropped the subject. "Well, Morgan, we have a lot to do to get ready."

"Ready?"

"Yes. Didn't I mention that the reason I came was to invite Seth and you to a party at the Montoya ranch in three days? No, I guess not. Joaquín said that there was some mixup in your clothing, that for some reason you had none of your own and had to take things from Seth's sisters."

"Yes, it was a . . ."

Lena watched Morgan carefully. "No matter. You and I will leave now for Santa Fe, and in two days Mrs. Sanchez can make you several dresses."

"Leave? Lena, I can't leave now. I still have too many things to do. The cow needs milking this evening, and I have bread that has to be kneaded and . . ." She couldn't bear the idea of being away from Seth for three whole days.

"*Qué tontería!* Bread and cows!"

"Seth. I don't want to leave Seth." Morgan's voice was quieter.

Lena's laughter rang out. "Ah! Now *that* I can understand. And Seth—such a beautiful man! I would not want to leave him either, if he were mine."

Morgan felt her jaw clench, and she shot Lena a look of fire.

"Morgan, let us be friends. Let us be honest with one another. I have been somewhat in love with that good-looking husband of yours for years, but he has turned me down." Lena did not mention that he had turned down her hints at a permanent relationship, but not her offers of lovemaking.

"Don't worry," Lena continued. "You and I will be friends. But tell me, honestly, would you like to go to my party in that dress?"

Morgan compared her own dress to Lena's elegant riding habit.

"I thought not. Now, I will ride out to tell Seth Colter myself. It will do him good not to see his little bride for a few days." She looked at Morgan critically. "When I get through with you, he will be even more in love with you than he is now."

Instantly, she was gone, and when Morgan heard the sound of the stallion's hooves, she collapsed in a chair. Lupita's laugh rang behind her. "That one! So full of fire. Do not worry, Señora Colter, she always gets her way. When Lena wants something, she lets nothing stand in her way."

"What about Seth? She wanted Seth. She's so beautiful, Lupita. What will Seth say when he sees the two of us together?"

"He will not even notice there is anyone else in the room except his wife. You had better pack some clothes, because if I know Señorita Montoya, you will be leaving very soon for Santa Fe."

Morgan knew she was right and went to the bedroom to get ready. For some reason, she was frightened at the idea of leaving the ranch. She looked around the room at the fireplace, the rugs, the big bed she and Seth had shared for so few nights.

"This is silly," she said aloud. "I'll be back in just a few days, and then Seth will be happy to see me and . . ." She shivered again. On impulse, she pulled a trunk from the corner of the room and dug deep into the bottom of it until she found the red dress. She held it up to the light and marveled again at its texture and the beautiful handmade lace across the bodice. She had never shown the dress to Seth because she had wanted to save it for a very special occasion. When she saw him again, after having been away from him for days, she'd wear the dress. Her eyes misted as she quickly packed the silky fabric beneath her other plain dresses.

"Morgan!" A thrill of joy ran through her. She ran to him and clung to him. It seemed much longer than three hours since she had last seen him.

155

"I missed you, too, little one." He kissed her hair, caressed her back and held her close. "What's this about your leaving me?"

"I don't want to go, Seth. I don't need any new clothes." Why did she feel such fright at leaving him?

Seth held her at arm's length and looked at her. "Lena convinced me. In fact, she's made me realize how selfish I've been, keeping you here all to myself." He smiled at her, and Morgan ached with love for him. "Don't look like that, it's only for a few days. In three days I'll come to the party, and then I'll take you home. I couldn't live without you longer than that."

Lena watched the two of them together. Such a fuss over being separated for three days! Then she looked at Seth's enormous back and shoulders and she remembered how he felt, close to her, her arms around him. For that one, perhaps I, too, would cry over three days' separation.

"All packed?" Seth asked as he saw the little case on the bedroom floor.

Morgan nodded.

"You won't forget me?" Seth teased.

Morgan looked at him pleadingly. "I love you, Seth. I love you more than life itself."

He held her close to him. "I love you, too. More than I thought possible." He kissed her, and she returned his kiss urgently.

"If we don't leave now, Lena may have a two-hour wait."

Quickly, he ushered Morgan outside, and Jake led her horse next to Lena's beautiful black stallion.

For miles, Morgan kept turning to look back to see if she could still see the house.

"Santa Fe is not what you have been used to in Kentucky, but it is a pretty little town, and Mrs. Sanchez is a magician with a needle. I just show her a picture, and she can make a copy of the gown." Lena did not seem to notice Morgan's silence. "Of course, now that they've discovered gold in California, everything is changing. I heard that they're opening a stage line all the way from St. Louis to San Francisco. Already, more and more goods are coming into Santa Fe as the traders stop here on their way to the coast."

Lena continued talking as they rode.

It was nearly sundown when they reached the town. The buildings were like Seth's ranch house, made of adobe with long poles protruding from under the roofs. There were few stores, but the town seemed busy as the people moved around under the broad porches.

Lena led them to the hotel. The room was large and comfortable. Lena ordered a bath for Morgan as she left to get Mrs. Sanchez and some of her own clothes, which she always kept in town at Mrs. Sanchez's house.

Morgan was luxuriating in the hot tub when they returned. Mrs. Sanchez was a stout woman, dressed in black. "Here she is," said Lena. "She'll take your measurements and start on some clothes. Here, dry off so we can get busy." Morgan smiled as she took the towel from Lena. She was getting used to the way Lena ordered everyone around.

Lena gasped as Morgan stood up. "My brother told me you were beautiful under your ugly clothes, but he could not have known how much of the truth he spoke!" Quickly, Mrs. Sanchez took Morgan's measurements. Then she and Lena discussed Morgan's new clothes. After the seamstress left, a waiter brought their dinner. Lena went to her own room, and Morgan sank into the empty bed. It was the first time in weeks she had slept without Seth's arms around her, and she had to exercise control to keep from crying herself to sleep.

By midmorning of the next day, Mrs. Sanchez returned with a completed dress. Morgan looked at the woman's red-rimmed eyes, and she knew she had worked on it all night.

As Morgan slipped on the dress and then looked into the full-length mirror, her spirits lifted. The dress was beautiful. It was a brilliant blue, the color of her eyes, and it fit her curves perfectly.

Lena was watching her in the mirror. "It is strange what a beautiful gown will do for a woman."

"Lena, it is beautiful. I've never had a dress like this before. Do you think Seth will like it?"

"A woman in love! How very tiresome they can be. Of course, he will like it, and the women will hate you."

Morgan smiled at her own reflection.

"Now we will fix your hair, and soon we will be ready to show Santa Fe its newest citizen."

An hour later, Morgan stood before the mirror again, hardly recognizing herself. The mirror told her she was beautiful, and she held her head high. She laughed.

"What amuses you?"

"I was thinking about an old girlfriend of Seth's. Cynthia thought she was going to marry Seth. I wish I could see her now."

Lena laughed also. "I knew there was more to you than what I first saw scattering feed for the chickens. You would like to show off in front of your husband's admirer, would you?" Her eyes danced mischievously. "I think we could take a trip to a certain store in Santa Fe before dinner. You might find something to interest you there."

On their way from the hotel to the store, people turned to stare. Lena was attired in a maroon dress with thin bands of ruby-red trim. Morgan began to enjoy the way the people looked at them, and as they reached the store, she realized she was happy she had come to Santa Fe.

"Good afternoon, Marilyn. We came to see some yardgoods. My friend would like to have some shirts made for her husband."

At the mention of Marilyn's name, Morgan knew

who the woman was. She was pretty, and her figure was generous, but Morgan guessed that in a few years she would be fat. This was Marilyn Wilson, the woman some people thought Seth might marry.

"Yes," Morgan said, "I would like some very fine cotton and silk, if you have it." She looked at Lena and acted as if she were suppressing laughter. "I will need several yards of each. You see, I'm very new at this and my husband is . . . a very large man." She gave an embarrassed laugh. "You know how it is, I'm sure, Mrs. . . . ?"

"Miss Wilson."

"Well, yes, you will learn in a short time, I am sure." Morgan patted Marilyn's hand. "Let me introduce myself. I am Mrs. Seth Colter. My husband and I have just journeyed all the way from Kentucky, and I find his wardrobe sorely depleted." Morgan walked to the counter, piled with bolts of fabric, pretending to be unaware of the woman's astonished stare.

Marilyn fairly exploded. "Seth!"

Morgan whirled to face her, her blue eyes wide in innocence. "Do you know my husband? But of course you would. My dear Seth is such a rogue, is he not? Why, even back home I sometimes had trouble with other women. Of course, Seth and I have been engaged practically since we were children."

"Engaged! You mean all the time he's been out here, he was engaged to you?"

"But of course. Didn't he mention me to you?" Morgan gave her a look of sympathy. "I'm so sorry, my dear. Seth has always been such a tease. I hope he hasn't caused you any distress? Lena, I think we should make our purchases some other time." She paused again to pat Marilyn's hand. "Why don't you come out to the ranch sometime for a visit? We'd love to have you."

Outside the store, Lena and Morgan walked together in silence for a while.

"Morgan, I am glad you and I are friends, because I would certainly hate to have you for an enemy."

Morgan smiled. She had only been protecting what was hers.

~ Chapter Ten ~

THE Montoya ranch was enormous. The main house itself could have housed a small army. In fact, the shape of the house suggested that it had been made to hold off an attack. The house enclosed all four sides of a large garden and courtyard.

Everywhere there were servants. There were always men working in the garden, and every room had one or two women cleaning and polishing. Lena had introduced Morgan to two young girls whose sole job it would be to take care of Morgan. Morgan soon found that she liked being pampered.

The party would start in a short time. Lena had already gone downstairs to stand beside her brother as they greeted their guests. Morgan had not seen Joaquín yet and had, in fact, given him very little thought.

Seth had not come yet.

"Señora Colter, he will be here soon. You are so beautiful that he will be very sorry he took so long."

"Thank you, Margarita."

The dress was of shimmering red silk. It was cut low in front and exposed Morgan's creamy shoulders. She was not used to the tight restrictions of the laced corset, but she liked the way it pushed her breasts above the restraining fabric. Her golden hair was piled on top of her head, with great masses of curls cascading down her back.

There was a knock, and Morgan, expecting Seth,

161

eagerly stepped toward the door as Margarita opened it. Her face fell as she saw it was Joaquín.

"My beautiful little Morgan, is your old friend such an unwelcome sight after all we have shared together?"

She smiled at him and took his extended hands. "No, Joaquín. I am glad to see you. It's just that I expected Seth."

"He was always lucky with beautiful women." Morgan missed the slight edge to his voice and the passing look of hatred that fired his eyes.

"But let me look at you." Still holding her hands, he appraised her every curve until she felt the blood rising to her face. "I knew you were beautiful, but I did not realize how beautiful." He dropped her hands and reached into his inside coat pocket. "Lena told me what you were wearing, and she thought I might lend you some of the Montoya jewels." He opened a small leather case to expose a sparkling chain of sapphires surrounded by tiny diamonds. There were earrings to match.

"Joaquín, they're beautiful! But I couldn't wear them."

"Why not? They are not a gift, only a loan for one night. Surely you would not turn down a loan between friends? If you would like, think of them as coming from my sister. I am merely her messenger."

Morgan laughed. "Joaquín, I believe you could charm butter into cream with just your words."

Joaquín smiled, his eyes devouring her. "I wish that were so, because there are some things I would like to have. Seth is a lucky man."

There was an embarrassed silence until Morgan broke it by asking the maid to help her with the jewels. Joaquín took them from her instead, and as he fastened them around her lovely neck, Morgan had the distinct impression that he was about to kiss her. Somehow the moments she spent with Joaquín always became awkward. She wished Seth would hurry.

"There! They are nearly as lovely as you are."

"Oh, *señora!* They are really beautiful on you. Your husband will know you are the most beautiful woman in all of *Nuevo Mexico!*"

"Do you really think so, Margarita? I hope he likes me."

"Likes you?" Joaquín smiled. He had heard from Lena how they had clung to one another in parting. He himself had seen only the way they had acted on the trip to New Mexico. As he looked at Morgan, breathtaking in the silken gown, he ached to take her in his arms. "Morgan, little one, no man will be able to resist you at all tonight. If that husband of yours does not fall at your feet, I will shoot him myself." Joaquín's roaring laughter at his own comment caused Morgan to look at him curiously.

"Since your husband does not seem to be here yet, may I have the honor of escorting you downstairs?"

She really wanted to wait for Seth, but since Joaquín had been so nice about the jewels, she took his extended arm and they went downstairs to the party.

"Morgan! There are so many people here who want to meet you." Lena lowered her voice. "There are going to be a lot of women here who will hate you." She laughed at Morgan's startled expression. "Seth has been the most eligible bachelor around here for years. He and Joaquín have been pursued by every woman with a marriageable daughter within two hundred miles of Santa Fe." She touched Morgan's silk dress. "Isn't silk nicer than chicken feed?" They laughed together.

Lena had been right in telling Morgan that she would feel hatred from some of the women. Morgan felt that some of the people had come only to see her, to judge Seth Colter's new wife. As she shook hands with seemingly endless numbers of people, she overheard remarks from all sides.

"No wonder Colter waited so long. He was holding out for the best."

"Of course, if I had allowed my Katherine to dress like that, she would have had several men around her, but I prefer modesty and a certain respectability."

Morgan turned at this remark, obviously intended for her hearing. She saw an overweight matron glaring at her. Close behind the woman was a tall, thin girl with protruding teeth and a sharp nose. Morgan smiled at the girl and remembered herself, shy at a ball, less than a year ago. That had been the most fortunate night of her life. She had met Seth that night. She looked again toward the door for the thousandth time.

"You don't look as if you are having a very good time."

She smiled at Joaquín. "I just wish Seth were here. I hope nothing has happened at the ranch."

"You are the talk of everyone here tonight. There isn't a woman at my house now who wouldn't sell her soul to be as beautiful as you are. Yet you stand here and worry about problems on the ranch. Smile, sweet Morgan. Laugh and enjoy yourself. Come, dance with me, and let's give them more to talk about."

"You're right, Joaquín. I'll have to stop worrying."

Joaquín led her onto the dance floor, and Morgan was again glad her Aunt Lacey had arranged for dancing lessons.

"Who would have thought you could be so beautiful? There is a woman making her way toward us who has the most incredible look of hatred directed right at you."

Morgan turned to see Marilyn Wilson staring at her. She was escorted by a slim man with a pencil-thin mustache. He seemed almost as young as Morgan.

"Why, Mrs. Colter! What a pleasant surprise."

"Hello, Miss Wilson. Are you enjoying Lena and Joaquín's party?"

"Oh, yes." She looked up at her partner and then at Joaquín. "But I would have thought a bride would be dancing with her husband." She smiled. "At least for the first few weeks."

Morgan smiled back sweetly. "My husband was detained tonight, but it is nice to be a bride, don't you agree, Miss Wilson? Oh—*pardon* me. Of course, you wouldn't know, would you? Joaquín, could we get some champagne? I seem to be suddenly very thirsty."

At the long table set against the wall, Joaquín gave Morgan a glass of chilled champagne. "You are deadly to your enemies, are you not?"

"Oh, yes, I guess," Morgan was distracted as she glanced toward the door again.

"Come little one, I am not used to women who find me boring."

"Oh, Joaquín, it's not you; I'm just worried about Seth."

"Come walk with me in the garden. The fountain is lovely in the moonlight."

She looked at him apprehensively.

"I promise not to molest you or even to kiss your lips."

She smiled at him, took his extended arm, and walked out through the open door with him into the moonlit garden.

Seth entered in time to see his wife, her body clad in red silk, smiling up at Joaquín. She took his arm and they stepped into the moonlight.

Seth's impulse was to run after her and knock the little Spaniard down. He'd like to have seen Joaquín on the floor, blood running from his nose. Damn her! I leave her alone a minute and she runs off with someone else.

"Seth! It's good to see you." Marilyn followed his eyes to the open door. She had also seen Joaquín and Morgan leave together. "Well, aren't you going to ask an old friend to dance?"

165

"Marilyn." He had just realized she was there.

"Seth, honey, would you like some refreshment? You look like you've just had a shock."

He allowed himself to be led to the table. After three straight shots of Joaquín's twelve-year-old bourbon, he felt stronger.

"Feel better now, honey?"

"Yes, I do." He looked at Marilyn. Her large breasts were nearly spilling over the top of her dress. In the last few months he hadn't looked at any woman other than Morgan. After another shot of whiskey, Marilyn began to look even better to him.

"Would you care to have this dance, Miss Wilson?" he asked sweepingly.

Marilyn felt good being in Seth's arms again. None of the other men she had ever had made her feel the way Seth did. Most men cared only about themselves, but when Seth made love to her, he made sure she enjoyed it, too.

"I met your wife a few days ago." She had his attention. "It seemed so strange to me that she was a new bride, yet running around the countryside with that Lena. You know what Lena's like. I thought it was odd then, and here she is tonight flirting like a . . . like a . . . Well, I'm sure you understand my distress." She cast him a sidelong glance to make sure he was listening. "And that Joaquín Montoya, of all people!" She smiled when she felt Seth's arm muscles tighten. "Yes, everyone is talking about them, about how they keep standing in dark corners, giggling and drinking champagne together. I'm sure if I had a husband, I wouldn't—"

Seth dropped his arms from around her and quickly left the room, out the same door Morgan and Joaquín had used a few minutes earlier.

A few people turned and stared, and Marilyn nearly laughed aloud with joy. Little bitch, she thought, I'll teach her to snub me.

The first thing Seth heard was Morgan's laughter.

"Well, it looks like my little wife is enjoying herself."

"Seth!" She ran to him and threw her arms around his waist. "I was so worried. You're so late."

He disengaged her arms, holding her from him. "Yes, I can see how worried you were."

"Seth! For Heaven's sake, you're not going to be jealous, are you? Joaquín and I walked out into the garden together for a few minutes. That's all. You are not going to spend our entire married life getting angry every time I speak to another man, are you?"

Seth looked at Joaquín. "No," he said quietly, "I don't think I'll spend all our married life getting angry, because we may have had all the married life we are going to have. Now, if you will excuse me, I believe I can find other things to occupy myself than trying to keep my wife from her lover—or is it lovers? Goodnight."

Seth was gone before she could react to his accusations. She started walking toward the house after Seth, but Joaquín caught her arm. "Morgan, you cannot think to pursue him after he has treated you as he has. No, you must wait for him to come to you, to apologize and to beg your forgiveness."

She stared at him. "I don't understand why he should be jealous. He's the only man I've ever cared about. How *could* he accuse me of the things he did?"

Joaquín put a comforting arm around her shoulders. "He was wrong, and soon he will know it. He'll come back to you and everything will be all right. Now, cheer up. A lover's quarrel is not the end of the world. We will go back inside, dance, and show the world we do not care."

She jerked from his arm, not seeing the frown on his face. "But I do care. I care more than you'll ever know. I love him more than my own life, and he must know that. I must find him."

Quietly, Joaquín agreed. "I will help you. We will go to my stables now, and we will find this ignorant husband of yours, and you may explain all night if you like."

"But, Joaquín, your guests."

"Pah! Lena is the one who loves parties. She will not even know I am gone, and she will be glad that your beauty is no longer there to compete with hers."

It seemed they had traveled for hours when Joaquín stopped at a little house Morgan had never seen before. Joaquín began to dismount in front of the house.

"Joaquín, what are you doing? Seth isn't here."

"We must rest the horses, and I, for one, am very thirsty."

It was very dark now, but she could see the look of determination on Joaquín's handsome face.

The interior of the house was unexpected. There were mirrors everywhere, and the walls were covered with crimson silk. In front was a tiny living room and then an enormous bedroom. The furniture was gold and white, while the bed was draped in a sheer version of the crimson silk.

"What is this place, Joaquín?"

"Can't you guess?" She turned quickly at the peculiar tone in his voice. His eyes were hard. He stared openly at her body. Involuntarily, her hand went to cover her breasts.

"Joaquín, why are you looking at me like that?"

He moved closer to her and took her hand, kissing it. "I have wanted you from the first moment I saw you. That husband of yours did not even see your beauty. I was glad when I saw how the two of you fought constantly and glad when he did not spend the night with you in the wagon."

She backed away from him, beginning to be very frightened. "But, Joaquín, I love Seth."

"Seth, Seth, Seth! That is what I hear from too many women—my own sister, and that cow of a woman, Marilyn Wilson. Do you think that one must be as big as Colter to be a man? I assure you, it is not so. Come, little Morgan, and I will show you tenderness. I will show you the fine art of lovemaking, not the crudeness of these Americans."

"Joaquín, I'd like to go now." She started firmly for the door.

"Oh, no." He grabbed her arm, pulling her to him, clasping her body close to his. "I've waited a long time for this." His lips on hers made her shudder. They were too soft, too moist. They didn't make her feel as Seth's lips did.

She twisted in his arms, pulling her mouth from his. "No, Joaquín." His lips moved down her throat leaving a damp trail, like a snail.

"No!" She fairly screamed the word and pushed against him with all her might, catching him off guard. He nearly fell. She looked into his eyes, and the hatred she saw there made her realize the danger she was in.

"So, you refuse me. You teased me on the wagon train, yet you meant nothing. You do not use a Montoya and get away with it. Now you will be punished."

She screamed when he came to her and tied the gag around her mouth. She fought him, but he was surprisingly strong and held her easily.

"Remember this, little one—you have chosen your fate. We could have been such lovers, but now—" He finished tying her hands and then her ankles and tossed her on the bed. "Now that husband of yours will die because of your teasing." He laughed as he saw Morgan's eyes widen in horror.

He walked to the doorway. "I will be back in a few hours, and then I have some plans for you."

After one last searching look at her, he turned abruptly and was gone.

~ *Chapter Eleven* ~

WHEN Seth left the Montoya party, he rode hard for an hour until he realized what he was doing to his horse. He stopped and rested. The first blind rage was gone, and the cool night air helped to clear his head of fury and liquor.

Gradually, he began to remember the way Morgan's face had lit up when she saw him, the way she had run to him. Damn that Montoya! Seth had played right into his hands, and Joaquín had enjoyed every moment of it.

Morgan, sweet little Morgan. She was so innocent that she probably didn't even realize what Montoya was like. He had been a fool to leave her there alone. He mounted his horse and started back to the Montoya ranch. He was so lost in his thoughts that he didn't hear the approaching rider. A shot rang out and the bullet slammed into his shoulder.

Before he could get to his own gun, the rider took it, then grabbed the reins of his horse. Silently, he led Seth back toward the Montoya ranch, blood dripping from his wound, each step increasing his pain.

When Joaquín returned to Morgan a few hours later and removed her gag, she tried to reason with him. He smiled at her, and she wondered why she had never understood the coldness of his smile before.

171

"It would do no good now to try to save yourself or your husband."

"What have you done with Seth? Where is he?"

"Ah, sweet little noble Morgan, would you like to save the life of your husband? If you could save his life, what would you do for me?"

Her eyes looked straight into his. "Anything," she whispered.

"Yes, I believe you would. Too bad Colter had such a woman as you and never realized it. But you can save his life, and very easily, too. All you have to do is write a letter."

"A letter?" A new fear was growing in her stomach.

"Yes. You see, I have been trying for a long time to get Colter to sell his ranch to me. I thought I had succeeded, but then he brought back a wife. A wife makes a man settle down."

"Why would you want Seth's small ranch when yours is so large?"

"A good question, my little pretty one, but your husband's ranch has the source of water for my ranch. At any time, he could cut off all the water to my home and my cattle."

"But Seth wouldn't do that."

"Who can say? I do not like to trust my fortune to someone else."

"So, you think Seth will sell the ranch to you if I am gone?"

"Yes. Exactly. But first I plan to make him never want to see the place again. That is important, and that is where your letter comes in."

The fear inside her increased.

"I want you to write a short note saying that you and I are going away together, that we had planned it for some time, ever since we were on the wagon train together."

Morgan's eyes widened in horror. "No," she whispered. She could not do this. If she ever did find Seth again, he would hate her. Even if she escaped, he wouldn't want her again. He'd believe the note. Joaquín must know that.

"No? A moment ago you said you'd do anything to save his life. I guess I'll tell the men to kill him." He turned toward the door.

"No! I'll do what you ask. Don't hurt him. Please."

"That's much better. Now I will get a pen and paper."

Morgan wrote the note with trembling hands. She knew she was writing the end to her marriage. Seth would never want her again.

Quickly, Joaquín took the note from her, retied her hands, and replaced the gag. As he removed the sapphire necklace and earrings, he kissed her neck and she flinched. His eyes hardened, and he raised a hand to strike her.

"No. I will not mar your lovely skin. I have plans for you. I am sure there will be many men who will do more to that lovely body than just strike your cheek."

Her eyes had gone dead. She didn't look at him, but held her eyes on the note he carried in his hand.

He left. Morgan felt that her life went with him.

Joaquín's two men led Seth west, away from the Montoya ranch. The pain in his shoulder had intensified, and the loss of blood was making him weak. Eventually they came to the walls of a crumbling adobe hut. Here the two men dismounted, and painfully Seth did also. It was close to dawn, and the sky was beginning to lighten. He stuffed a handkerchief against the wound to try to stop the blood.

The two men said nothing. They just watched him, pointing a revolver at him continually.

When he saw Montoya riding up in the faint morning light, he used his rapidly draining strength to rush at him.

"Where is she? What have you done with her?"

Roughly, the guards pulled Seth to the ground. One of them kicked him in the ribs. He raised his foot to strike again but Joaquín halted him.

Seth regained his breath and pulled himself into a sitting position, leaning against the mud wall.

"Such concern for your little wife. Too bad she does not return that feeling for you. You see, she and I have been planning this, er . . . meeting . . . for a long time."

"I don't believe you," Seth's voice was hoarse. Breathing hurt, and he knew his ribs were cracked.

"Somehow, I knew you wouldn't. So I brought you a little note from my beloved. Read it."

Seth winced. He read the note twice. It said very simply that she had always loved Joaquín and that she was leaving with him.

Seth remembered the time on the wagon train when he had seen her kissing Joaquín. Yet he also remembered the four days they had spent in the canyon, and the weeks since then. How could anyone have been such an actress? He had believed she loved him. He crumpled the note.

"I see you sense the truth of her note," Joaquín sneered. What fools these *gringos* are, he thought. Colter couldn't see that the woman lived only for him. She adored him and the dolt was blind to her devotion.

"Now I will take your horse and leave you."

Seth put his hand to his bleeding shoulder. As he did so, Joaquín noticed a ring on Seth's little finger. It was surely a woman's ring.

The three men mounted their horses. When they had ridden a few yards, Joaquín turned, aimed his pistol at Seth's head, and fired. Seth's head slumped forward onto his chest.

Joaquín turned to the man on his left. "He has a ring on the little finger of his left hand. Bring it to me."

When he had the ring, the three of them rode toward

the east. After Joaquín had given the two men exact instructions, he rode to the little house where Morgan was.

For hours, she had worked at the rough rope fastenings until her skin was raw and bleeding. The sound of the opening door set her heart pounding.

"Well, little one, I see you are still here." He removed the gag from her mouth. "It is too bad to have to cover up such a lovely mouth." He bent to kiss her and frowned when she turned her head away.

He slumped in a chair, ignoring the tight ropes that held her wrists and ankles together. "It's over," he sighed.

She turned fear-filled eyes toward him, too afraid to ask what he meant.

"Oh, yes, I have something for you." He rose and untied the bindings on her wrists. As she rubbed her numb wrists and hands, he held out the ring. Instantly, she knew what Joaquín meant. Her eyes flew to his.

"I believe you recognize the ring? I seem to remember seeing it on your lovely little hand when we were on the wagon train." He tossed it into her lap and returned to his chair.

Gingerly, she picked up the ring. Her mother had given it to her just before she had died. After she and Seth arrived at the ranch, Jake had taken it into Santa Fe and had it made to fit Seth's much larger finger. Seth had never taken it off since she had put it on his finger. That Joaquín had the ring meant that Seth had believed her note.

"He believed it," she whispered, more to herself than to Joaquín.

"More than that, sweet Morgan. It seems that your husband met with an unfortunate accident and is no longer a problem to anyone."

"Accident?" Morgan was uncomprehending. "Accident! What do you mean? You said if I wrote the note you wouldn't harm him—you'd let him live."

"Morgan, you must learn not to trust everyone." His voice was heavy with sarcasm. "I couldn't very well leave him alive when he knew I had taken his wife away, now could I? With the owner of the Colter ranch dead and his new little bride nowhere to be found, it should be easy to obtain his ranch. But even if I didn't want the ranch, I would have killed Seth Colter." His eyes gleamed with hatred. "I would like to kill all the Seth Colters."

Morgan screamed and lunged at him, her fingers curled into claws. She would kill him herself. As her bound feet caught her and made her fall helplessly to the floor, she screamed her rage and cursed him.

"Such language from such a pretty little bird." He caught her hands behind her. She twisted her head and sank her teeth into his arm. He groaned and hit her across the face, sending her head reeling. He retied her hands and the gag and set her back on the bed.

His teeth clenched as he looked at her. "My men are making arrangements for you now. I will return for one last visit in a few hours." Then he was gone.

Seth was dead. Joaquín had killed him after all. The world was full of Cat Men and Joaquíns. Even the nearly five precious weeks she had spent with Seth had been marred by his jealousy. Now he was dead, and he had died thinking she had betrayed him.

"That her?" The voice was deep with a heavy accent.

Morgan had lain there for hours, tears soaking the gag. There were no more tears now. She wasn't even aware of the numbness in her feet or the blood on her wrists. When Joaquín entered, she showed no interest in him or the men with him. He was startled at her expression. It was as if she were dead, she as well as her husband.

When he unfastened her bindings, she remained motionless. "I liked you better when you were raging at me, my love." She failed to respond and did not even rub her chafed wrists and ankles.

"*Trop petite.*" The man who had spoken first now made his contempt clear. He was a short man, very stocky, and his clothes were a mixture of rough cottons and animal skins. His hair was matted and reached past his shoulders. There was a gold earring in one ear.

"I do not like them so little. They do not last on the journey to the coast. And these blond ones—it is too much trouble to keep the Indians away from them. They like light hair." He grabbed a handful of Morgan's hair and jerked her face up to his. "This one—something has killed her spirit. It will be hard to keep this one from doing herself harm."

"All right, Jacques, what do you want? More money?"

"She will be a great deal of trouble."

"Here!" Joaquín thrust some bills into the Frenchman's calloused hand.

Jacques grabbed Morgan's hair again, pulling her to her feet. "She must have something else to wear." With a swift jerk, he tore the red silk down the front.

Joaquín heard his own sharp intake of breath. He took a step forward. Then he stopped himself.

"Skin and bones! This one will be much trouble, but if she survives the trip over the mountains, she will bring a good price at Madame Nicole's." He uttered something in a guttural language to a tall, sinewy man who was standing in the doorway. The man was the first Indian Morgan had ever seen. He had on a long tunic, once white, over leather leggings and high moccasins.

Morgan stared unfeelingly at the sight. She had made no effort to cover herself. Now she saw the Indian leave and quickly reappear with a bundle. He tossed it on the bed.

"Get into that!" he ordered Morgan. When she didn't respond, he slapped her. He thrust the bundle at her. Mutely, she rose and stepped out of her dress, and the Frenchman deftly used his knife to cut the bindings of her corset and the back of her chemise.

Morgan felt as if she were already dead. She paid no attention to Joaquín's avid interest in her body. Slowly, deliberately, she stepped into the leather shirt and pants. She pulled on moccasins that came to her knees. The clothes were too big for her, and hid her curves.

The group moved outside, and one of the Indians tossed her onto the saddle of a shaggy pony. The Frenchman took the reins of the little horse and led her away. Morgan did not think about where they were taking her.

They rode through the hot New Mexico sun for hours. Morgan's face was burned, and her back ached from the long hours on the horse. Only once did the Frenchman pass her a canteen of water.

Neither the Indians nor the Frenchman talked, and Morgan was left to dwell on Seth's death.

The sun was low when they arrived at a large camp. Morgan was vaguely aware of people around her and of dogs barking. She was pulled from her horse and dragged, stumbling, to a crude shelter of sticks and dried grasses—a wickiup.

She fell against the back wall of the hut, the tiredness in her body numbing her to the sharp sticks pressing into her skin. As her eyes adjusted to the dim light, she saw three other women in the hut. Two were watching her and one huddled in a corner, her face turned away from the others. The oldest of the women left the hut and returned with a dipper of water. Quietly, she held this to Morgan's lips, cautioning her to drink slowly. Then she spread a heavy blanket on the floor and gently guided Morgan to lie down on it. She covered her with another of the patterned blankets.

"You get some sleep now, honey. They'll be movin' tomorrow, and you'll need your rest." She stroked Morgan's forehead, and Morgan was soon asleep.

In the morning Morgan could hardly move for the stiffness in her body, but the woman who had helped her the night before told her she must cooperate or else Jacques would hurt them all. Morgan could not miss the pleading in her eyes.

Unspeaking, she followed the woman's directions for dismantling the wickiup and fastening the poles onto a travois that was then lashed to a horse. An Indian motioned for her to mount one of the scruffy little ponies.

They traveled in a long column for two days, stopping for only a few hours at night. The woman, continuing to befriend Morgan, rode beside her and urged her to eat the strips of dried meat she offered and to drink the water.

At the end of two days, they made camp again, hastily erecting the crude shelters. As Morgan was lashing some dried grass to the roof of the hut, Jacques stopped beside her.

"My scouts have just returned to tell me that no one is following us. The little Spaniard said he had killed your husband, but I would not trust such a one as him. *Eh, ma petite?*" She stared at the Frenchman as if seeing him for the first time. He was a short, thick man with a scar across one eyebrow and a belly that hung over his belt. He looked very old, as though every single event in his life had etched a line on his weather-beaten face. He stuck out a dirty hand and caressed Morgan's breast. Involuntarily, she jumped backwards.

"Ah, so—*la petite* comes alive. They usually do. You are lucky now. On other trips, I have let my Apache *amis* take their pleasure of the white women. But they are not gentle and one of the women died. I lose money when one of my women dies. Other women showed up at Madame Nicole's with Indian babies in their bellies. My old friend does not like this. She says the white men are such silly creatures that they do not like to go where a redskin has gone before." He cupped Morgan's chin in his hand and studied her. "Yes, Madame Nicole will like you." Morgan tried to move her head from his iron grasp, and the Frenchman laughed.

"Such spirit from one so little! Be careful, Golden Hair, or I may take special notice of you myself." He turned and was gone.

Morgan stood for a few seconds glaring at his back, her eyes blazing with hatred. Then she went into the hut and was soon asleep. For the first night since she had been taken from the Montoya ranch, she dreamed. She saw Seth in her dream, and she ran to him, her arms open. When she was close enough to see his eyes, they were sad and he turned his back on her and began to walk away. She called his name, pleadingly at first, and then her cries became more and more desperate.

She awoke, her body drenched in sweat, to feel a hand pressed firmly over her mouth. "You're all right now. I'll take care of you. Just be quiet or they'll hear you."

Morgan felt herself being cradled. It was good to have an older woman's comforting arms about her. In the three days she had been a prisoner, she had paid little attention to her surroundings or to her fellow captives. Now she felt she desperately needed this woman's comfort.

The woman talked to Morgan as she held her. "My husband and my little boy and me lived up on the side of a mountain, about three days east of where they picked you up. It wasn't an easy life. The winters were hard, and Bobby was always out with the sheep." Her voice was toneless.

"The three of us had just set down to eat when the door busted open and the Frenchman and two of his

Indians walked in. Without a word, they killed Bobby and little Jimmy. He was only three years old.

"They looked me over, like I was an animal. I made a jump for Bobby's gun, not to kill them but to kill myself. I didn't want to live after what they did to my baby. They caught me. So here I am."

"Why?" Morgan asked through her tears. "Who is this Madame Nicole? What does he want with us? Why doesn't he just kill us? If he killed us, then I could be with Seth."

"Seth is your husband?"

Morgan nodded.

"I'm not sure, but I believe he deals in white slavery. He doesn't keep all women." She shuddered. "Only the ones who pass his inspection."

"A slave?" Morgan asked. "I don't understand. You can't sell white women."

"Well, it seems he can and is going to. I heard them mention San Francisco."

"Just be glad you're little and pretty." Morgan turned to another woman. Although it was dark in the hut, she knew the woman was young, with bright red hair—pretty in a brassy way. Her mouth was too wide to be really beautiful. "Her mother wasn't so lucky." She inclined her head to the girl in the corner, quietly sobbing. "They raped her mother and then killed her. The girl had to watch." The girl in the corner was only about sixteen years old.

"My name's Jessica," said the red-haired woman, "but everyone calls me Jessy."

"And I'm Mary," said the woman who still held Morgan. It seemed understood that they would not use last names.

Morgan murmured her own name.

"Morgan? Strange name for a girl," Jessy said. When Morgan held her silence, Jessy continued. "The girl

181

over there is Alice." She turned again to Morgan. "How'd they get you? What happened?"

Mary interrupted Jessy's questions. "Don't bother her now, Jessy, she needs rest. It's too soon for her to talk about it."

Jessy continued, "I can guess how you feel, but I figure for me anything's better than my old man. They killed him, too, but I don't feel no regret. In fact, I'm almost glad to be goin' to San Francisco. Been itchin' to go ever since I heard about the gold."

"Let's go to sleep now." Mary put an end to Jessy's story. "They'll want us to start soon enough. Let's remember, though, that we're in this together."

The next night they set up camp again. Morgan was beginning to be adept at taking apart and setting up a wickiup. The three women felt a good deal closer, and for the most part, they worked well together. The girl Alice still spoke to no one, and went about her work awkwardly. Morgan joined the other women in covering Alice's errors and slowness.

Morgan set the last bundle on the ground by the wickiup. As she straightened, she felt a hand on her hair. She knew it was one of the Indians. She had seen them staring at her as she hastily braided her hair each morning. In spite of herself, she felt a scream rising in her throat. As her mouth opened, a hand closed over it, a hand tasting of smoke and horses.

Morgan felt her body shiver with fear. She did not like the Indians. They never showed any feeling.

Gently, the Apache unfastened her braid and held the blond silk up to form a curtain that caught the sunlight. He uttered some guttural words and seemed pleased as he rubbed his hand in the softness of the hair.

A shot rang out close to their feet. The Indian dropped his hands from Morgan and reached for his knife. She turned to see Jacques holding a rifle, aimed at the Apache behind her. The two men exchanged a few of the guttural sounds and the Apache turned and left, angrily.

Jacques went to Morgan, her body shaking with fright. The Frenchman grasped the uncoiled braid of her hair and let it twine around his fingers.

Her eyes holding his, she asked, "Where are you taking us? Why have you kidnapped me?"

Still holding her hair, the Frenchman laughed, a deep, rumbling laugh. "I don't like my women so thin, but with your eyes and hair a man could be tempted." He moved his face closer to Morgan's, and she instinctively moved back. "You ask me questions. I will answer them, *ma petite*. I dealt in furs for a while, but that is hard work. I met Madame Nicole and we worked out our business arrangement. I bring her pretty young women, and she pays me for them." He smiled at Morgan's shock.

"You can't *sell* people!"

"Oh, but I can, little one. Madame Nicole finds unwilling women often please her customers more than the ones who readily agree to their whims. Bah! There are no real men left in this new country. I do not need to fight a woman to prove I am a man.

"One thing . . . do not tempt me to anger, pretty one. Madame Nicole will pay me well for such a one as you. I would not like to lose the money." Abruptly, he left her alone to stare after him.

"I thought as much." Jessy was standing beside her. "I've heard of some of these houses in San Francisco. A girl can live in luxury there."

Morgan turned to stare at Jessy. The events of the last few days were suddenly too much for her. Blindly, she began to run. She stumbled over dogs that ripped at her, but she hardly noticed. There was only one thought in her mind, one overwhelming desire—to escape, to get away from her captors. Reason had left her.

She halted as Mary caught up to her, jerking her arm painfully. "Morgan! Stop it! Look around you. You can't escape—they'll kill you first." Mary's fingers bit into the flesh of Morgan's upper arms. "Look at me and listen. This is not the way to escape. How long do you think you could survive in this land?"

"I don't care. I just want to get away. Even if it means my death, I can't face going on without Seth. I can't face what they have planned for us. I cannot."

Mary's eyes were hard. "Of course, you can face it. No matter what they do, we are still alive, and we need to survive."

Morgan's eyes had a faraway look as the tears quietly rolled down her cheeks. "Do you know what they plan to do with us? They plan to sell us as whores. Whores! Did you know that a few months ago I didn't even know what that word meant? Now I am to become one! That's funny, isn't it?"

Her voice grew louder. "Five weeks ago I was a virgin. Now . . ." She began to laugh loudly.

Mary looked up to see the Indians surrounding them, pointing at Morgan. Behind them she saw Jacques making his way over to them, an angry scowl on his face. She began to shake Morgan. "Stop it! Stop it! You'll cause more trouble if you call attention to yourself. Now come into the wickiup."

Morgan followed Mary, and the older woman was relieved to see the Frenchman turn and walk away from them.

In the hut, Mary turned to Morgan. "Why don't you help her?" she asked, nodding toward the girl Alice. "Jessy and me can't seem to get through to her. Maybe if you help someone else a little, you won't be so wrapped up in yourself."

Quietly, Morgan sat by the unseeing girl. Mary was

right. She was not the only one here. She took Alice's limp hand into her lap.

"I sometimes think that if I cry enough or if I wish hard enough, I'll open my eyes and this'll all be gone. Then I'll be home with . . . Seth." The name brought fresh tears to Morgan's eyes.

"Do you know how I got here?" Morgan continued. "A neighbor, a friend, wanted me to sleep with him. I said no, so he killed my husband and paid Jacques to take me. All my life my mother told me men were horrible, wicked creatures who cared little about women. Then I met Seth. I fought my feelings for him for a long time, but then I realized how much I loved him. Seth is . . . was . . . the most handsome man imaginable. He was so gentle and so good. Everyone on the ranch loved him. He even had some old dogs who were so lazy they wouldn't even bark until a stranger was practically inside the house. Seth was too kind-hearted to get rid of them."

She stopped talking. Alice was staring at her, tears glistening in her soft brown eyes. Morgan put her arm around the girl and pulled her head to her shoulder.

There was only two years' difference in their ages, but Morgan felt old enough to be Alice's mother. They sat in silence for a while, and then Alice began to talk, very quietly.

"My father went to the gold fields and said he'd send for us when he struck it rich. But after he left, my mother said she couldn't live without him, so we packed up and started west. We were going to join a wagon train in Santa Fe, but we never got that far. There were four wagons. They . . . they killed everyone, all the men. They took Mother and me with them.

"When we got to the camp, Jacques tore our clothes off. He had an Indian hold me while they . . . while they . . ." She couldn't finish her sentence and buried her head against Morgan's soft shoulder. After a few minutes, she began again. "They made me watch. She told me she loved me just before she died."

Morgan stroked the girl's brown hair. "We must stay alive."

"Why? So they can do to us what they did to my mother?"

"I don't know, Alice. I thought I wanted to die, but my life must be worth something. I know Seth wouldn't want me to die. I know that if he were here, he'd tell me to live . . . no matter what."

The days turned into weeks. They traveled every day. The trip from Kentucky to Santa Fe had been luxurious compared to travel with the Indians. Morgan learned much about the Frenchman's Apache followers, a rugged group. The women took care of all the work on the trail, putting up the shabby grass huts each night and tending to the food. One of the Indian women, Little Flower, had a new baby strapped to her back, bound onto a cradle board.

After the one attempt to touch Morgan, the Indians left the four white captives alone. The captives were given dried meat and roots that the Indian women gathered on the long, grueling trip.

Morgan took over the cooking for the four of them. Little Flower, who was about the same age as Morgan, showed her how to grind corn and cook it on top of the stews made from the game the men caught. Gradually, they began to understand one another through signs and a few words exchanged in the two languages.

At the night camp, Little Flower took her son from his cradle board and let him play on a blanket while she cooked. Morgan gestured to Little Flower to ask if she could hold the child.

"What are you doing with that heathen child?"

Morgan turned to see Mary's angry face. "Don't you realize that it might have been his own pa that killed your precious Seth?"

Morgan was calm, looking at the baby who had extended a chubby hand toward her golden braid. She smiled at him and he gurgled in delight as he caught the soft hair in his fingers. "White men killed my husband, but it wouldn't have made any difference. Babies are innocent, no matter who their parents are."

"Not when they're Indians!" Furious, she turned on her heel and left Morgan and the baby.

"Don't mind her." It was Jessy. "She just can't bear to look at another kid since hers is gone. Now me, that's somethin' I hope I never have." She looked with contempt at the child in Morgan's arms, happily putting her braid in his ever-open mouth. "Either they're squalling or their other end needs attention." She cocked her head and stared at Morgan. "I reckon you'd like one though. Maybe you're carryin' one now?"

Morgan's head jerked up. The thought of Seth's baby made her body glow. Her face lit up. "Yes," she said quietly. "I'd like that. I'd like very much to have a baby . . . Seth's baby."

Jessy went back to the wickiup, and Morgan stayed with the baby. Morgan had hope now, and as the days passed, she began to pray fervently that she was really carrying a child and that, if she were, it would survive the trip.

~ *Chapter Twelve* ~

JAKE had been riding for three days when he first saw the circle of buzzards. He removed his hat, wiped the sweat from his brow, and spurred his tired horse forward. At the bottom of the arroyo he saw the ruin and next to it a large dark form. He shot at the birds, scattering them. Something inside of him knew it was Seth there, lying so still, the hot New Mexico sun beating down on him. He was unaware of the tears that began to roll down his cheeks. He had one goal, and even his blurring vision couldn't keep him from it.

Seth was on his stomach, blood forming a halo around his head and across his shoulders. Carefully, Jake turned the big man over, cradling his head in his arms. His sobs were louder now and he rubbed his sleeve across his nose.

"Seth, boy. You hear me? It's Jake. I come to take you home."

It seemed an hour before Jake could still his own heart's frantic beating long enough to listen for Seth's. When he felt a slight pulse, he raised his tear-filled eyes skyward and offered a prayer of thanks.

He lay the wounded man's head down on the ground and went to his horse for his canteen. Slowly, he poured a few drops of water onto Seth's parched, cracked lips. Seth rolled his head and groaned.

"Just be still now, boy. You'll be all right. Drink slow, now."

189

"Morgan." Seth's voice was a harsh whisper and his breathing was ragged.

"Don't talk none. Just let ol' Jake take care of you. Like I done since you was a little boy."

Jake wet his handkerchief and began to wipe Seth's face. There was no way at first to tell the extent of his wounds, because his entire body from the waist up was covered with patches of dried blood. Jake used nearly all the water he had in his two canteens cleaning the nasty wound on the side of Seth's head.

"Got to get you home now, so's we can take care of you." The older man smiled down at Seth's enormous body. "You always was too big for your own good. Now I bet you wish you was just ordinary size, something ol' Jake could handle."

Jake used his sleeve to wipe his tears. "Got me bawlin' like a baby. Always did care too much for you." Jake looked around at the scrawny trees on the side of the arroyo, judging them for size. He stroked Seth's forehead. He was flushed, showing signs of fever. "We're gonna get you out of here Injun-style."

The knowledge that Seth was still alive gave Jake new energy, even after the three long days in the saddle. Slowly, carefully, he fashioned a travois from two young trees and strips of blanket from his bedroll. It took several hours, because he needed to make it strong enough to carry Seth's enormous body without any mishap.

His horse was tired and protested loudly when Jake fastened the travois to the saddle. The sun was just setting, turning the horizon red and orange. Jake knew he and his horse should rest, but if he waited until morning, it would mean traveling under the hot sun.

It took all of Jake's strength to get Seth onto the travois. Seth made no sound, hardly even opened his eyes, yet Jake could see the pain on his face as he tried to move. He was still semiconscious, and Jake knew

Seth was using all the strength he had to control the pain. His shoulder wound reopened and began to bleed again. The ugly wound on the side of his head was puffy and looked as if it might be infected.

"That's good, boy. The hard part's over. Now we're going to take it real slow and get you home."

They traveled all night. Jake led the horse most of the time rather than riding it. That way he could see more clearly and lead the tired horse around rough spots and mesquite bushes. Jake stopped often and bathed Seth's face with cool water. Seth seemed to realize that he was being taken care of. He began to relax and let the pain take over.

The fever increased and he began to lose consciousness. He mumbled Morgan's name over and over.

"We'll find the little girl. Just as soon as we get back to the ranch, we'll find her for you. She's probably there now, worried sick about you."

When the sun began to rise, Jake started to look for a place to spend the hot part of the day. He didn't dare travel with Seth exposed to the sun.

He found a muddy-bottomed arroyo, and after digging a hole about two feet deep, he had enough water to bathe Seth's wounds. Under the shade of an old piñon tree, he cut away Seth's shirt and began to examine the wound. The bullet had gone through, making a large but clean hole.

For the first time since he had found Seth, his joy at finding him alive began to turn to anger. "Why would anyone want to hurt my boy?" Seth's breath whistled through his clenched teeth.

"I'll kill whoever did this. Shot a man and then left him to die in his own blood. They didn't even make sure he was dead, just left him to rot in the sun. A man wouldn't even treat a dog like that."

As he pulled Seth to one side to cut away the rest of his shirt, Seth's face blanched, and Jake saw the pain in

191

his glazed eyes. Carefully, Jake felt along Seth's side and knew the ribs were broken. He removed his own shirt and tied it around Seth's ribs, binding them.

Jake covered Seth's body from the drafts, and the big man slept. Jake didn't even have a shirt to cover his bony body from the sand burrs and needles of the ground, but he lay close to Seth's travois, and slept.

It was late afternoon when he awoke. Seth's breath was shallow and fast, and when Jake felt his forehead, it was cool and his fingers were cold. He was beginning to try to move, to kick the blankets off, but at the same time clutching them closer.

"Easy, boy. Quiet now."

"Morgan . . ."

"We're going to her. We'll find her. Just be quiet and she'll be with you soon."

They traveled many hours, and Jake became increasingly worried about Seth. Walking beside the tired horse, he began to piece together what he knew of the few days before Seth was hurt. And by the time he came to the Colter ranch, he knew that Joaquín Montoya was responsible for this.

Lupita hadn't slept much since Morgan had ridden to Santa Fe with Lena. Somehow she had known that things were going to turn out badly. When neither Seth nor Morgan returned the day after the party, she was sure that something was wrong. Paul had laughed at her, but Jake worried as much about Seth as she did. They had waited all that day and night, and early the second morning he had set out to find Seth.

"You'll be embarrassed when you find them nestled in some cabin somewhere. The way they act around here, they may not be back for weeks," Paul had teased Jake.

Jake's mouth had been set, clamped over near-toothless gums. "I'd rather be caught with my hand in the pot than be here when the boy needs me someplace else."

Paul doubled up with laughter. "Boy! Seth's gonna love this! You're half that boy's size, and I don't think he's gonna need any help with that little wife of his."

Jake had ignored him and finished saddling his horse.

Lupita had been nervous and on the alert ever since then, so when the first sounds came to her, she was ready in seconds. When she first saw the tired figure of Jake outlined in the moonlight, she started toward him. The sight of the travois stopped her. She turned and ran toward Paul's cabin.

Within minutes the young foreman was dressed and running ahead of Lupita toward Jake.

Jake motioned toward Seth, and Paul went to him. Now that Jake had brought his beloved boy home, his own strength was going.

Silently, the three of them carried Seth into the house and put him into the big double bed that he and Morgan had so recently shared. Lupita deftly began to cut away Jake's makeshift bandages, removed the rest of Seth's clothes, and began washing him. His body was hot now, and he moaned when the cool cloth touched his fevered skin. Lupita gradually became aware of loud voices in the next room.

"You can't go anywhere, old man. You wouldn't even make it to the corral."

"Just who the hell do you think you're callin' an old man? It was me that brought him back." Jake raised his fists toward Paul.

"What's going on here? Isn't there enough to worry us without you two fighting? And why are you still here? One of you should go . . . "

Jake lowered his fists and checked his gun. "That's just where I'm going—to kill that Montoya."

"Jake, you've got to let the sheriff handle this. You can't just ride into the Montoya ranch and kill Joaquín."

"Sheriff! Kill!" Lupita fairly screamed. "There's one man in there nearly dead, and you two talk of more killing! Before anyone kills anyone, I want a doctor here!"

Both Paul and Jake stared blankly at Lupita.

"Jake, I'll need your help here." She knew how tired the little man must be. "Paul, go into town and get the doctor, and then get the sheriff—but a doctor is what we need most." She turned toward the bedroom, took a few steps, and then turned back to the two men. "Does a man have to *die* to get you two to move?"

Quickly, Jake followed Lupita and Paul left the house.

In the hours that followed, Seth began to talk, mostly saying Morgan's name over and over. As Lupita continued to wash Seth, she noticed his left hand always clenched into a fist.

"Jake, what does he have in his hand?" It took the two of them to pry open his fist. Jake read the note from Morgan first to himself and then to Lupita.

Jake sat down in a chair heavily. "How could she have done this? How could she leave Seth for a man like Montoya?" He looked at Seth, the tears forming in his eyes again. "She did that to him, as much as if she'd pulled the trigger herself."

"No," Lupita's voice was a whisper, "I do not believe it. No." She looked up at Jake. "It is a trick of some sort. She loved him. She could not pretend so well."

"We have proof that she aimed to run off, and the proof involves Montoya, too."

Lupita's eyes held Jake's. "You may believe your little piece of paper, but I will believe what I know to be true. Señora Colter was very much in love with Seth, and she would not leave him of her own free will."

Jake turned his back on her. "We'll see what the sheriff says," he mumbled.

It was nearly daylight when Paul returned with the sheriff. Jake had finally dozed off in the big chair beside Seth, but he was quickly through the doorway, showing the sheriff the note.

"Hold on, Jake. I know how you feel, but I can't just shoot the man. We went to the Montoya ranch first and Señor Montoya had witnesses who said he was there all night. This note mentions Joaquín, but we can't even be sure when it was written."

"I don't care how many witnesses the little bastard has! He nearly killed my boy!"

"All right. We'll go again. We'll face him with the note. The doctor should be here any minute. He was out in Pecos, so it'll take him a while. Paul, you ready?"

Helplessly, Jake watched them go. An hour later the doctor came.

He complimented Jake for the care he had given Seth on the rough trail, and after he had examined him, said there was nothing else to do but wait and see if the fever broke. He wrapped the broken ribs tightly, to keep him from breathing too deeply and putting one through his lungs.

Seth's fever raged for days. Lupita and Jake took turns sponging his perspiring body and forcing broth down his throat. He talked a lot about Morgan, and how he loved her, how he wanted her. He kept calling for her, asking where she was, sensing even in his delirium that she wasn't there. With every mention of her name, Jake's hatred for Morgan grew.

After nearly a week, Paul and the sheriff returned to the Colter ranch. They had been searching for Joaquín and Lena Montoya all that time. They had returned to the Montoya ranch the morning after Jake had brought Seth back and found the servants closing down the house. Joaquín and Lena had left immediately after the sheriff's first visit.

"They didn't plan on Seth still being alive," Jake yelled in frustration.

"Someone should try to find the Señora Colter." The three men turned to stare at Lupita.

"But she's the one who caused all this. She and Montoya had their escape planned. It probably wasn't Montoya's sister who left with him at all."

"Jake's right." Paul's voice was calm and tired. "I think we should leave this up to Seth. When he's well, he'll decide whether he believes his wife's note or not." Paul's expression left in doubt none of his feelings toward Morgan.

With a sigh of resignation, Lupita went back to Seth.

It was two more weeks before the fever broke.

"Lupita?"

Lupita turned from gazing out of the window. She whirled toward him. "Señor Colter. You are well." Her voice held both joy and relief.

Seth grinned weakly at her. "I don't think I'm well of anything yet. Everything hurts. How long have I have been ill?"

"Three weeks now."

"Three weeks! Where is everyone? Where's Morgan and Jake and Paul and . . . food! I've never been so hungry in my life. Tell Morgan I want some of those little doughnuts of hers and one of those cheese and bacon things in the crust." He grinned as Lupita hurried from the room. "Tell Morgan I want her *now*!" he called toward the door.

He lifted himself up and grabbed a pillow to prop behind his head. He ran his hand over the welt on the side of his head and felt where the scar ran under his hair. His ribs and shoulder hurt, and his legs ached. "Three weeks!" he murmured. "I'll bet Morgan had her hands full, but I'll make up for lost time."

He grinned at himself. Smells from the kitchen

reached him and he wondered where the hell she was. What was taking her so long?

He put his hands out in front of him, stretching his muscles, easing some of the stiffness that three weeks in bed had caused. "Three weeks in bed," he laughed. "I bet I spend the next three weeks in bed, too, but not for the same reason. And not alone! Where is she?"

It was then that he noticed the white spot on his little finger. Morgan's ring! Where was it? And then, in a flash, he remembered everything, every ugly detail.

He put his hands over his eyes, rubbing the heels deep into the sockets, trying to block out the images . . . Joaquín and Morgan in the garden . . . Joaquín giving him the note . . . Joaquín aiming the pistol and firing. "No," he whispered. "Please, God, no!"

"Here is food and lots of it. Jake and Paul will be here in a minute. They will be so happy to see you well. They have both worried themselves sick over you." She bustled into the room with the tray of food, but the smile left her face when she saw Seth. She knew then that healing his body had been easy compared to what it was going to take to heal his spirit.

"It's all true . . . what I remember. Isn't it?"

Lupita would have sold her soul to be able to tell him that it all had been a dream, that his lovely wife was running to him, would be here in a moment. "I do not think it was true. The little *señora* would not do such a thing. I think someone should go and find her."

"Well, I don't." Seth and Lupita turned to see Jake in the doorway. "We found the note. I say let her go. If she wants to leave here, let her."

The pain in Seth's eyes was more than Lupita could bear. "She loves you. She loves you very much. She could not have acted like she did and not love you. The day Lena came for her, she did not want to go. She wanted to stay here in her home. She was so happy here."

"Stop it!" Seth fell back onto the pillows. "To me
. . . she is dead. I never want to hear her name again. We
will not refer to her again, in any way." His eyes were
cold, but both Jake and Lupita could see the pain behind them. "I think I'd like to sleep now."

"But your food! You need to eat."

"No, Lupita, I don't feel hungry now."

Jake silenced Lupita's protests with a stern look.
"That's right, boy, you just rest and get well. The
food'll be waitin' for you when you wake up."

Seth's recovery was slow. He didn't seem to mind
staying in bed, and he showed no interest in anything.
Jake tried to ask his opinion about what he and Paul
were doing on the ranch, but Seth hardly answered him.
Eventually, he began to move around the room a little,
going only from the bed to the chair. He sat and stared
at the walls. Lupita encouraged him to sit on the little
patio by the bedroom, but he didn't seem to care where
he was.

As the pain left Seth's body, the pain in his mind
increased. He was continually reminded of Morgan.

She seemed to be everywhere. He started sleeping on
the couch in the living room because he couldn't stand
the bed they had shared. One day he rode out with
Jake, and it seemed she was even outside. A clump of
trees recalled a time when she had brought his lunch to
him and then run from him, laughing, unfastening her
clothes as she went. Even the sunlight recalled her hair
and skin.

The snows began and he remembered how he had
planned on long snowy days of lovemaking. With
Christmas coming, Lupita decorated the house with
chilis and popcorn. Seth watched lethargically as Lupita,
Jake, and Paul decorated the little piñon tree.

On Christmas Eve, Seth remembered the music box
he had packed in Kentucky. It was to have been a

Christmas present for Morgan. It had been weeks since he had been in his own bedroom, but he went now and found the box. He wound it and listened to the tune. How she would have loved the delicate carving!

"Why, Morgan, why? He couldn't have offered you more love than I did. It isn't possible!" Tears blurred his eyes as he brought one powerful fist down on the little box and smashed it.

He glared at the broken little box, and through clenched teeth, he swore, "If I ever find you, Morgan, I'll kill you!" With one sweep of his arm, he knocked the remains of the box to the floor.

He left the room and announced to the others that in the spring he would leave the ranch for the California gold fields.

In March, 1850, when the snows were barely gone, Seth set out for California and the gold fields. After the heavy use of the previous year, the trail was well defined. He was only a few miles out of Santa Fe when he met the Chandlers' wagon train.

∽ *Chapter Thirteen* ∽

IT took the little band—the Indians, the Frenchman, and the four women captives—five weeks to reach the mountains. After a week of grueling travel, everyone's temper was short. The nights grew cooler, and the nip of autumn was in the air. Morgan figured it was somewhere around the first week of October, 1849, and she knew now that she was not carrying Seth's baby.

"I don't know why I always seem to do most of the work around here." The closer they got to San Francisco, the angrier Mary became. She took her fear and hatred out on everyone.

"What with Morgan doing all the cookin', I don't see how you can think you're doing most of the work." Jessy's happiness and excitement were obvious.

"Please, can't you two stop fighting?" Alice pleaded with them tearfully.

"It's just these Indians! They're always around. A body can't even step into the bushes without one of them watching. I'm always ready to scream."

Jessy looked across the camp at one of the Apache braves who returned her stare. "Indians ain't all that bad. That Yellow Hand's not a bad looker at all."

"You filthy little slut! I ought to tear your hair out!"

"You and who else?"

Mary raised clawlike hands and started for Jessy's face. Morgan quickly stepped between the two of them.

201

"Stop it, you two! They may decide we're not worth the trouble and kill us now."

"Death just may be better than the life they have planned for us." Mary's face was twisted as she sneered at Morgan and Jessy.

Alice's whimpering carried across the campfire.

"Oh, Lord! Is she going to start that again? That girl is afraid of her own shadow." Jessy rolled her eyes.

Alice's sobs increased, and Mary went to her to comfort her. "If you had any feelings, you'd realize she's just a child."

"Child, hell! It may interest you to know, Miss Mary-Know-Everything, that that 'child' and I are the same age."

Both Mary and Morgan turned startled eyes to Jessy. There was an ageless quality about Jessy that made her seem anywhere from fourteen to fifty. Neither of them had ever considered her true age. "That's right," she laughed. "I just turned sixteen on my last birthday, sometime in June. My pa never could remember the exact date." She turned and left the three staring after her.

"I'm older than her," Alice whispered.

Along the Gila River, the trail was so narrow that the horses were frightened and skittish. The nerves of the four captives were even further strained.

After the river, they came to a wooded area. Jacques told them to take advantage of the water, because it would be the last they'd see for a long time. In another couple of days they'd start the long trek across the desert.

"May we take a bath then, before we start?"

Jacques touched her cheek with a large, coarse hand. Morgan bravely met his eyes. She didn't even move away, as much as she wanted to. "You are a temptation, *ma petite*. Of course, you may bathe. All of you

202

may splash and play in the water all night." He smiled at her, and his eyes swept down over her buckskin-clad body. His hand dropped from her cheek to her shoulder to her arm, his thumb caressing the soft curve of her breast. Her eyes held his, and she controlled the inner revulsion she felt.

Jacques turned and left her, and she could hear his deep, throaty laughter as he walked away.

"I'd like to have a knife at his throat for a while," Mary hissed.

"Never mind him. Get Jessy and Alice. We're going to take a bath!" She hurried to the wickiup. "A real bath. Clean hair and skin. I don't think I've ever looked forward to anything quite so much." She paused inside the cool, dark, empty wickiup. "Except you, Seth," she whispered. "You were the only thing that really made me happy. Now I look forward to such silly things. Oh, Seth. *Why* did all this have to happen? Why do I have to go on living? Why can't I die and be with you again?" She fell to the dirt of the floor and cried.

"Morgan, is it true what . . ." Jessy paused as she saw Morgan. She knelt by her and took her in her arms. "Ah, Morgan, you're the strong one among us. Don't you give way. If you give up, we won't have anything to hold onto."

"Seth is on my mind constantly, every second. Everywhere I look I see things that remind me of Seth. Even trees, Jessy! Even trees remind me of Seth. He was huge, the biggest man I ever saw. Not awfully tall, but big. His arms were as big around as my waist. And he was so handsome." Morgan smiled and the tears began to clear. "I had to fight women off him constantly."

"What's wrong with you two?" Mary's querulous voice sounded through the wall.

Morgan wiped her eyes. "I'm all right now. Let's go

take a bath." She turned to smile at Jessy. "Thanks for listening to me."

"Morgan, I've decided this Seth of yours never existed." Her face was serious. "No man could be both kind and good-lookin'."

Morgan flashed her a brilliant smile. "Seth is special." Happily she raced toward the water, leaving Jessy to notice that she had said "is," as if her husband were still alive.

Jessy was the last one to the water and was surprised to see all of the Indian men, Jacques, and some of the Indian women standing there with the three white women.

Jacques's deep laughter came to her. "My Indians do not take baths, and they are very much interested in someone who does. They want only to watch."

"Well, I ain't takin' my clothes off in front of no Indians." Mary turned back toward the camp.

Jessy laughed. "What about you, Morgan? I think bugs have nested under my skin, it's been so long since I took a bath. I'm not gonna let a few staring Indians keep me from getting clean." She sat on the ground and began to pull off the tall moccasins. Seconds after she stood up, she was completely naked and ran happily into the cool water.

The other three women had watched speechlessly. The Indians and Jacques began to laugh as Jessy happily dived under the water, her smooth round buttocks coming to the surface.

"It feels great," she called.

"She's a fool besides being a slut," Mary muttered. "These animals need no more temptation. I wouldn't be surprised if one of them attacked her."

Alice clung to Mary, her face fearful.

"You sure you won't join me, Morgan? I can feel two months' worth of dirt and bugs floating away. Toss me my buckskins, will you? Might as well get them clean."

Morgan picked up Jessy's clothing and started to throw them to her.

"You know . . . if they wanted to, they could tear our clothes off at any time. What difference does this bath make?"

"You're right, Jessy." Quickly, Morgan undressed and walked into the water.

"Lord, Morgan! I think you've started a fight." Jessy gestured toward Jacques, who was smiling at one of the Indians. The Indian made an obscene gesture that even Morgan understood, and she turned away.

Jacques laughed and called to her. "Did you hear that, Golden One? Running Bear offers me six horses and four blankets to let you be his third wife. Would you like that? It is a good price, and he is a brave warrior."

Morgan looked at the Indian, his hair heavy with grease and his face stained with remnants of paint and food. Involuntarily, she shuddered. Recovering herself, she met Jacques's eye. "Do you think Madame Nicole will offer only six horses and four blankets, or do you think I am worth more?"

Jacques looked at her full breasts rounding above the surface of the water, her small chin and flashing eyes, and the great mass of golden hair cascading about her. He threw back his head and laughed. "You will bring a great deal more from Madame Nicole—I will make sure of that."

"Morgan, you have more guts than any three people put together."

"Not really, Jessy. It's just that I don't really care. If I can get to San Francisco, maybe I can escape and get back to Seth's ranch. At least there I'll be close to him."

"No matter what, Morgan, you're lucky—lucky to

have had a love like that, even for a while. Just once I'd like to fall in love with a man and have him love me in return. I mean real love, not like those men that paid my pa."

"Paid your father!"

"Don't tell Alice or Mary, but my father put me out to whore when I was thirteen. You can see why I felt no regret when the bastard died."

Too stunned to speak, Morgan stared.

"I shouldn't have told you," Jessy said quietly and began to swim away.

"No," Morgan caught her arm. "I was just thinking how I always hated my father, and I never even knew him. I guess we never know what we should be thankful for. If it hadn't been for my father, I'd never even have known Seth." She stopped and her eyes opened wider. "If I hadn't met Seth, he would still be alive."

Jessy's fingers dug into Morgan's flesh. "Morgan! You've got to stop blaming yourself! You can kick yourself for the next fifty years, and you still won't change the past. Remember Seth with all the love you have for him, but stop hating yourself."

Morgan frowned at Jessy. "Are you sure you're only sixteen? You sound more like ninety."

Jessy laughed. "Let's get out of here before they change their minds about leaving us alone."

They finished their baths and washed their hair and clothes. They put the wet buckskins on their bodies to dry. The sun was barely visible on the horizon, streaked with brilliant colors. As Morgan sat by the campfire in front of the wickiup, trying to smooth the tangles from her hair with only her fingers, Little Flower came to stand beside her. Absent-mindedly, Morgan smiled at the young Indian woman. Little Flower left and returned in seconds holding a beautiful tortoise-shell comb. She gestured to Morgan and Morgan nodded. Little Flower sat behind the blond woman and began combing her long tresses, while Morgan held the baby.

"What do you think you're doing, letting that animal touch you?"

Morgan hardly noticed Mary's anger, preferring to ignore it. Mary turned away in a huff.

When Little Flower had finished, Morgan asked to borrow Little Flower's knife. After a second's hesitation, she gave it to her. Morgan cut off a thick golden curl and tied it with a long piece of grass. She put the piece of hair into the fastenings at the top of the baby's cradle board.

Immediately, Little Flower grabbed the cradle board and ran to show the other Indian women and her husband.

"What's going on? What's all the noise about?" Jessy asked.

Morgan laughed, looking down at the baby pulling at the thong ties on her shirt. She told Jessy about the piece of hair.

"Well, it must mean somethin', 'cause here comes the bossman himself."

Jacques explained to Morgan that the piece of hair was considered a great gift and she was to choose a gift in return.

"I'd like my freedom."

"That is not Little Flower's to give. Choose something else."

"I don't want a gift, just her friendship."

"She will be insulted that you do not accept a gift from her." At the look of puzzlement on Morgan's face, he turned and spoke to the pretty Indian woman with a few soft words. Her face brightened and she ran to her wickiup.

Quickly, she returned and handed Morgan a silver and turquoise bracelet. The turquoise was a work of art, worked inside the metal in hundreds of little ovals, like daisies going round and round. The bracelet was surprisingly delicate.

"It was taken from a Zuñi warrior. They make beautiful things, no?"

"Tell Little Flower it is beautiful, and I thank her very much."

When Jacques had repeated her words, Morgan leaned over and kissed the Indian woman's cheek. Little Flower said something.

"She says you are now sisters."

"Sisters! Bah! Sisters to these filthy wretches! I'd rather be dead!"

Jacques turned to Mary's scowling face. "For you, that may be arranged very soon."

Later, Morgan always hated to remember the trip across the desert. Never had she imagined such a horrible place existed. They broke camp before full daylight and camped again before the hottest part of the day. There were no more campfires. The rich stews they had enjoyed were now memories. They ate dried meat and dried cornmeal. Water was strictly rationed, and the dry food stuck in their throats.

Morgan clamped her hands over her ears to block out the whimpering of Little Flower's baby. His mother did not have enough water to replenish her milk supply, so the baby was hungry. Morgan shared her water with Little Flower until Jacques found out.

"Do you think I go to all the trouble of bringing you across the mountains just to have you blow away? If you give more of your water away, I will kill the squaw and then the baby will have no milk at all."

One good thing came of the journey across the desert. Jessy and Mary stopped quarreling for a while, neither had the energy for it. During the hot afternoon, they lay in the scanty shade, barely able to breathe the scorching air. The horses were kept under crude shelters, rigged each day.

Eventually, gradually, they began to encounter

208

green plants and they knew that San Francisco was near. Morgan felt the ring she kept on a rawhide thong around her neck, and dreamed of Seth.

Early one morning, Jacques and two of the Indians saddled horses for the four women captives, and, leaving the other Indians in camp, they began the last leg of the trek into San Francisco.

~ *Chapter Fourteen* ~

AFTER three days of hard riding, they arrived in San Francisco in the dead of night. Jacques led them down alleys to the side of a three-story frame house. The women were too tired to notice much about their surroundings. A small, pretty mulatto girl opened the door.

"Get Madame Nicole right away. Tell her Jacques is come."

The girl scurried away, and quickly a large-breasted woman with masses of coal-black hair appeared in the doorway. Her skin was beautiful, flawless and unlined. She might have been beautiful, except that she weighed nearly two hundred pounds. Surprisingly, she carried her weight as if she were a young girl. Her walk was graceful and her movements were delicate.

"Jacques! How good to see you!" Her voice was pretty and young. There was a slight French accent that was very becoming.

Jacques threw his arms around Madame Nicole and lifted her enormous body off the ground. The woman blushed like a schoolgirl. "Jacques—you devil! How I have missed you!" She slid down across his body to plant a kiss on his mouth. After several seconds, they broke their embrace.

"There aren't many real women left," he said, giving the large woman a knowing look. "So I brought some

211

of those skinny little gals those half-men of yours like. I think you're really going to like one of 'em."

She looked at him quizzically. "I am not about to lose you, am I, Jacques?"

He smiled at her, looking her up and down. "It'd take all four of them to make half the woman you are."

She smiled at him, a smile of pure joy. "Later we will find out if you mean your words. But first, business." Immediately, she changed from lover to business-woman, and assessed each of the tired, dirty women.

"The blonde, *oui*?"

Jacques winked his reply. "Could hardly keep my Apaches from her. Real looker when she's clean."

"Good! They are just in time for Christmas. We are going to make four men very happy this Christmas."

Madame Nicole clapped her hands twice, many bracelets flashing. Instantly, four serving girls appeared. She gave orders, and Morgan found herself escorted up some narrow stairs to a bedroom. The sight of the bed, the first she had seen in months, held her entranced. She walked toward it as if hypnotized.

"No, no!" The girl took Morgan's arm. "Madame will not allow anyone so dirty to sleep in her clean bed. Carrie will bring water. You must bathe first." She led Morgan to a chair and moved a screen to reveal a large, red porcelain tub on gold claw feet. The girl, Carrie, arrived, and soon the tub was full of steaming hot water. Morgan allowed herself to be undressed and then she stepped into the tub.

The water seemed to soak through her body, even to her bones, and she enjoyed the rough scrubbing the girls gave her skin and scalp. She was stepping out of the tub into a heated towel when Madame Nicole entered.

The large woman appraised her as if she were a piece of furniture. "Ooh la la! You are by far the best of the four. In fact, you may be the best I have ever presented. You will bring a very high price."

Morgan stared at her in contempt. "What right have you to sell anyone? I am a person, not an article of merchandise."

The big woman threw back her head and laughed. "So, a crusader. I sometimes forget that such as you still exist. So often the women Jacques brings me have lived in poverty all their lives. They find all this"—her hand took in the room—"a dream. They like the luxury and the cleanliness."

Morgan clenched her teeth. "But your people kill their families! My husband was killed."

"Oh, yes, that is necessary." She dismissed the subject. "We cannot have angry relatives coming after our women. I would lose all my clients. Anyway, men are easily replaced."

"Not all men!"

"So you had not been with your lover long enough for the bloom to wear off. After your hands had cracked from the lye soap, and your body had worn out from bearing his children, you would be glad to trade for a life like this."

"No matter what, this is a whorehouse! I won't be used!"

"The women Jacques brings me, I do not use here in my house. They are sold to very wealthy men. They often marry well later, or if their lover tires of them, he settles sums on them that leave them comfortable for the rest of their lives." She paused and stared at Morgan. "Yes, you will do very well. You are even prettier when you are filled with rage."

Nicole took a few steps to the mirror and watched as the servant girls finished drying Morgan and dressing her in a pink gown. "You see, I like to know my girls, and I try to pick men who will fit their types. Your Jessica already loves it here. It will be easy to find a

213

man for her. And Alice . . . we will find her an older man, one who will protect her and pet her, and she will be very happy. Mary needs a man to hit her now and then.

"And you, Morgan? What type are you?"

Morgan glared at her. "I am not any 'type.' I am a person and I cannot be put into a category."

"Ah, but you have just described yourself. You need a man who will tell you his problems. One who will listen to you and to whom you can listen. And as a lover, you need one who will let you plan the moves sometimes, one who will let you control him sometimes, but not too often."

Morgan stared at her in astonishment. She was too close to the truth. Embarrassed, she turned away from the woman. She saw too much.

Nicole laughed. "You see, I am right. Every woman and every man fit into little niches. The world is too old for anything to be new. Come now, get into bed. We want you pretty and fresh tomorrow. There are a lot of things to do to prepare for our Christmas special."

In spite of her anger, Morgan fell asleep instantly.

For three days, Morgan lived amid a flurry of dressmakers. After a while she got used to standing nude in front of several women and even an occasional man, as they wrapped fabric around her and pinned things in place. She was not allowed out of her room or to see the other three captives. She missed Jessy and wished they could talk.

After the first three days she was left alone, but was still not allowed to leave the room. She found the door unlocked, but when she started out the portal, her way was barred by an enormous black man who held a whip coiled in his hand. Madame Nicole informed her later that Samson would always be there. He seemed never to sleep.

They gave her one of Mrs. Weston's latest romantic novels to read, but she angrily tossed the book aside after a few chapters. She could not read about flowers and romance when her own life was so harsh.

When the first of the dresses was finished, Madame Nicole informed Morgan of a tea to be given in their honor. There they were to meet some of the eligible young men of San Francisco.

Morgan marveled at the woman. She seemed to have no contact with reality as Morgan understood it. An outsider would have thought the four women were Nicole's beloved daughters instead of her slaves.

Morgan was led into a room of gold and white. The chairs and couches were covered in white velvet and there was a white rug on the floor. All the wood, including the mirror frames, was intricately carved and gilded.

"Morgan!"

She and Jessy ran to one another, their arms extended. "You're beautiful!"

"Ain't I though!" Jessy's red hair had been toned down with, Morgan guessed, a color rinse. Her lean body was beautifully enhanced by a soft violet dress. "It's her, though, that's done the most changin'," she whispered to Morgan.

Morgan was startled to see that meek little Alice was hardly recognizable. "She's been standin' in front of the mirror since she came in. Mary's havin' fits because the girl will hardly look at her. After all Mary did for her on the trip."

Alice held her chin high, barely nodding toward Morgan. She kept twisting one way and another to see herself from every angle. Mary was on the verge of tears, pleading with Alice to come sit by her.

Jessy and Morgan exchanged looks, Jessy rolling her eyes to the ceiling. They both covered their mouths to suppress their giggles.

215

"They been treatin' you good, Morgan? This is the finest place I ever even seen. Decked out like this, I look like a lady. Madame says all the men who come here are gentlemen. I'd sure like to get me a real gentleman."

"I don't really care, Jessy."

Jessy looked at her friend in sadness. "I never saw nobody pine over anybody as long as you have."

The door opened and Madame Nicole entered, followed by two very handsome young men. "Ladies, may I introduce Mr. Leon Thomas and Mr. Joel Westerbrooke?"

Morgan considered laughing. Was this an ordinary afternoon tea?

Mary's voice reached her. "We're held here as prisoners against our will. Would you help us? Get the sheriff!"

The two young men turned away, their faces crimson. Immediately, Samson appeared from nowhere. Mary was taken away.

Later, Morgan could remember little of the conversation. Alice and Jessy had talked to the young men eagerly. Morgan watched it all with little interest, and was glad when it was over.

Nicole came while Morgan was eating dinner in her room. "You were smart to be quiet this afternoon. Men dream of a quiet, beautiful woman. It is by far the better game."

Morgan worked hard at controlling her anger. "I was not playing any game."

Motherly, Nicole patted her shoulder. "Already San Francisco is hearing about Madame Nicole's little celebration, and it is rumored that a sensational beauty is to be offered. I thought I would reassure you. The sale is by invitation only. All these men have impeccable taste and a great deal of money." She smiled at Morgan.

"I doubt if you would be smiling if *you* were about to be sold like an animal."

Nicole laughed aloud, a deep laugh. "How ever do you think I got into this business? Actually, *chérie*, the sale is very exciting. I would give a great deal to be as young and as beautiful as you. To be auctioned off, to be fought over by many handsome young men—yes, that is very exciting. It happens only once. You should enjoy it."

She looked again at Morgan's furious face. "The young! They are so full of causes! This one would like to miss showing her beautiful body to men who will appreciate it. She would rather share it with only one man, one who will soon grow used to it and be bored by it. You are so lucky, Morgan, and you do not even realize it. Youth vanishes so quickly. Use it! Enjoy it!"

She realized that her sentiments meant nothing to Morgan. "Bah! Youth is wasted on the young. Goodnight."

The day before Christmas, Morgan was left alone. She napped and dreamed of Seth. All day her thoughts of him were especially strong. Late in the afternoon, she heard a music box playing and turned toward the sound, to the dresser. In the mirror she saw not her own reflection, but Seth's. He was staring at her with hatred, his features contorted. She stood frozen in horror. Then there was a muffled crash. The tinkling music was gone, and Seth's face vanished.

She was still locked in her place when Madame Nicole and two servant girls entered. Instantly, the large woman knew something was wrong.

"Morgan! What's wrong? You're shaking." She held Morgan's shoulders, but the young woman continued to stare at the mirror. Nicole turned to the mirror and saw nothing. She put herself between Morgan and the glass.

"Tell me."

"I saw . . . I saw . . ." Morgan's voice was a harsh whisper.

"What did you see in the mirror? Girls! Make the

217

water *very* hot." The three women undressed her and put her in the tub.

Gradually, Morgan began to lose her vacant stare and Nicole breathed a sigh of relief. "What did you see in the mirror?" she asked quietly.

Morgan's voice held no emotion. "My husband."

"But Jacques said he was dead. You only thought you saw him." Her eyes caught Morgan's and held. Something in them told her the truth: this vision been no wishful imagining. *"Mon Dieu!"* she exclaimed and crossed herself. Abruptly, she left the room.

Tonight, when Madame Nicole opened the sealed bids, she knew who would win Morgan. If only he *would* bid. This night she would say her rosary many times before sleeping.

The two young girls were quieter than usual as they dressed Morgan. Her clothes were especially fine, the lace on her chemise handmade. Her corset was satin and embroidered with tiny rosebuds. The dress was also satin, a rich emerald green. It was simply cut and unadorned, but very low in front, exposing her lovely shoulders.

The girls worked long on her hair, arranging it high on her head in loose, fat curls and waves. They kept checking the number of pins to hold it up, trying for as few as possible. Twice they removed all the pins and watched their artwork fall down her back in beautiful disarray. After the third try, they seemed satisfied. Their mood lightened as they became more deeply involved in their task, and they giggled often.

"Madame Nicole is very pleased with you. She says you may be the best girl ever offered. The men will be very happy."

"We'll show you off just right. Carrie and I have done this lots of times, but never with anyone as pretty as you. Sometimes we use makeup on the body, but you don't need it at all."

As Morgan's silence lengthened, they stopped talking.

"Now you just stay right here while we go get ready. Don't do anything to muss yourself."

It seemed only minutes before the two girls reappeared. Morgan gasped at their costumes. Their dresses were black with tight long sleeves and very low square-cut necks. The gowns were pulled in very tight at the waist, and the skirts flaring out dramatically. The dresses ended at mid-thigh. The girls' legs were covered only by sheer black silk stockings. Each had on black high-heeled pumps.

Morgan had never seen a woman expose her legs before. If the dresses had reached even to just the ankle, they would have been indecent. But this was beyond her imagination.

"These are our special dresses for the sales. Aren't they pretty?"

"But so much of you is exposed! How can you appear before men like that?"

"Like this? Honey, you're going to expose a lot more tonight."

Morgan stared at the girl. "What do you mean?"

"Carrie didn't mean a thing. Now you come along." Over Morgan's shoulder she gave Carrie a stern look.

Morgan met the other three women in the hall, each attended by two servant girls dressed exactly like the two beside Morgan. The four captives barely nodded to one another, each apprehensive about the events to follow.

They were led to a narrow backstage area. They could hear the muffled coughs and voices of men—many men—on the other side of the curtain.

Madame Nicole rushed to them. "Girls . . . be careful they do not muss their dresses. It will be Mary first, Jessy, Alice, and last"—she looked adoringly at

Morgan—"our Morgan." She was gone, and soon they heard polite applause.

As Nicole addressed her audience, her voice purred. "My dear gentlemen: The first lady is Mary. Mary will need some taming to overcome some of the unpleasant aspects of her personality. But as our Mr. Shakespeare has noted, there are ways to tame a shrew." Polite laughter. "I apologize for the need for Samson, but I hope you will agree with me that Mary is well worth the extra effort."

They heard the soft sounds of an orchestra.

"What do you think is going on?" Jessy leaned toward Morgan.

They heard Mary's voice from the stage. "No!" Then the crack of Samson's whip.

Alice looked anxiously at the other two women, quickly losing some of her recently acquired courage. They heard Mary sobbing. After a few moments the music stopped and they heard the tearing of paper.

"Mr. Thomas Millsant has just made a purchase," Nicole called out cheerfully.

There was a rustle of curtains at the other end of the stage, and the three women turned to see Mary, her face buried in her hands, her body gleaming in the dim light.

"Oh, my God! She's naked!" Alice seemed ready to faint.

Before Jessica could speak, her maids were hurrying her to the other side of the curtain. Morgan had a glimpse of Jessy's frightened face before she disappeared.

Again Morgan heard Nicole sketching the personality of one of "her" women. She exclaimed over Jessy's sweetness and complaisance. Again there was music, but there were no screams of protest from Jessy. There was polite, interested applause when the music stopped.

Morgan did not look at the opposite end of the stage

when Jessy left it. She tried to make her mind blank, to will it somewhere other than where it was. She knew now what was to happen to her. Alice walked past her. Only vaguely did she hear Madame Nicole expounding on Alice's virtues and virginity.

It seemed only seconds had gone by when she heard applause, much louder than before, and Madame Nicole's voice announcing the winner.

Her two servants helped her stand up. They smoothed her hair and dress. Morgan heard Madame Nicole.

"Now, gentlemen, the one you have waited for, the one all San Francisco has heard about. I must warn you now that if the bids are not high enough, I will reject them all. Now we will show you our jewel."

The music began and Morgan was led out onto the stage. She was glad there was so much light in her eyes, because she could not see the men in front of her. She tried to concentrate on something pleasant, but could find nothing.

The girls walked her back and forth across the stage and then, as she knew they would, they began to undress her. As they removed each layer of clothing, they turned her around to show off all the parts of her. Morgan was aware of low, quiet male voices.

Her body was bathed in the pink light the hundreds - of candles gave off. It took the assistants nearly half an hour to remove Morgan's clothes. Finally, she stood clad only in high-heeled pumps and black silk stockings, held in place by lace garters just above her knees. The girls turned her around and removed the pins from her hair, allowing it to cascade down her back.

It was then that the applause broke out. It seemed thunderous, as if hundreds of men were out there. She heard chairs moving back, scraping the floor. She wanted to run, to hide, but the girls held her arms and Samson blocked the exit.

They led her off after what seemed hours. They had walked her back and forth again, while her hair was down.

The girls put her arms into a robe and she collapsed into tears on the bed in her room. Madame Nicole came in close behind her. "You were sensational! My sale will make history! A standing ovation!"

"You got what you wanted. It's over for you, but for me it is only just beginning. I'm sold to God only knows who. To some man who will use me in any way he pleases."

Nicole loved her girls in her way, and it hurt her to hear the venom in Morgan's voice. She took her in her arms, Morgan sobbing on the woman's ample breast. "No, *chérie*, I am not without feeling. For years I held these sales in New Orleans. This is only my second sale in San Francisco, and because of you I am already a great success. You have made a new name for me, and I am grateful."

She held Morgan's shaking shoulders. Looking into her tear-filled eyes, she explained, "I was young once. I do know what it means to love someone, truly love someone. I have given you a new chance in life. I did not take the highest bid, and I pray no one will find this out. Your benefactor will suit you well while your broken heart mends. When you are well again, when your mind is as beautiful as your body, you will be able to begin again, to look for another love."

Morgan wiped her eyes. "I don't understand what you're saying, what you mean."

Nicole stood up. "You will, and I hope that someday you will not hate me. It is not easy to sacrifice a good profit. Girls! Get Morgan's traveling outfit. Mr. Shaw has a carriage waiting." She gave Morgan a nod of farewell and left.

"Mr. Shaw! Such a handsome man." Carrie rolled her eyes.

"Madame Nicole will tan you if she finds out what you're saying." Both girls giggled.

"Why are you acting like this, first Madame Nicole and now you two? What's wrong with this man, this monster she's sold me to?"

The girls looked at one another and dissolved in giggles. Their fingers were shaking so that they could hardly finish the closings on Morgan's chocolate-brown cape.

"Get out of here—do you hear me?" Morgan's voice was low, but getting louder as her panic rose. "Get out!"

Quickly, the girls left the room, clicking the door closed behind them. Immediately it opened again. Morgan didn't look up, but continued staring at her hands. "I told you to get out. I've had enough of . . ."

She looked up into the eyes of an extremely handsome man. He was probably in his forties, but his skin was clear and youthful. His hair was blond and waved back from his head. His eyes were blue. His shoulders were wide and his chest thick, tapering to slim legs.

Morgan stared, speechless. He seemed too perfect to be real. He motioned for her to look in the mirror. What she saw startled her. Their reflections were very similar. Their hair and eyes were surprisingly alike.

"It's as if we were brother and sister, don't you think? I was startled at the resemblance myself, when I saw you inside. Turn around and let me look at you." He took her chin in his hand. "Mmm, yes. I was afraid Nicole had used makeup to cover flaws, but I can see there are none."

Morgan jerked her head from his hand. "I assume you are Mr. Shaw."

"You do not have to say that as if I were an insect. Yes, I am Theron Shaw. You may call me Theron."

"Well, Mr. Shaw," she emphasized the words, "what do you have planned for your slave?"

223

"My slave? Well, I guess you would feel some hostility after that rather vulgar performance of Nicole's. But I do have plans for you. It's rather late now and I am tired. Tomorrow is Christmas Day, and we can spend the entire day discussing your future. Shall we go?"

"My wish is your command."

"I can hardly wait for you to stop this ugly sarcasm. You will stop it, won't you? I mean, it's not your normal personality to be so cynical, is it?"

She didn't answer, but he was beginning to puzzle her.

"Just let me say goodbye to my friend." Morgan heard Jessy's voice behind her and turned to hold out her arms. "I got me a pretty man. My girls say he's really rich and a real lover, too."

Her smile showed real happiness. "They told me the trick Madame Nicole played on you. I'm real sorry, Morgan, you deserve better."

"Are you coming, Jessica?"

"Be there soon, love."

"Hear that? He calls me Jessica. You cheer up and maybe we can visit each other soon. Goodbye." They kissed one another's cheek once more and parted.

Theron helped Morgan into an elegant carriage. They didn't speak until they had stopped in front of a simple, white, two-story house. It was new but unadorned, unlike many of the new houses.

The inside was unlike anything she had ever seen. Theron looked closely for her reaction, and her surprised gasp pleased him.

"So you like it?"

"It's beautiful. I've never seen anything to compare with it."

"Well, you see, this is my business. I am an importer and a collector. Most people decorate their houses in whatever is in fashion at the time, but I choose whatever I like from any period of history I like. That is why you see Chinese porcelains mixed with carpets from Morocco. That blue chair is Italian, late seventeenth century. I was told that it was made especially for a king, but the dealer wasn't sure which king." His eyes laughed.

Theron ushered her to a beautiful staircase, the curving handrail held up by carvings of flowers and vines.

"This staircase came from your own South. The house burned down, and this was one of the few things left undamaged. Are you familiar with Renaissance paintings? Brueghel, Rembrandt, and a new man—Ingres. I like the curve of this woman's back, don't you? Physically impossible, of course—but a lovely line."

Morgan was having difficulty absorbing everything.

"Morgan, you're tired. Please forgive me. Here is your room. I'm afraid you will have to take care of yourself tonight. I had no plans to bring a guest home tonight. Jeannette will take care of you in the morning. Is there anything I can get you? Something to eat?"

Mutely, she shook her head. He bade her goodnight, leaving her standing at the closed door, her little bag of night things on the floor.

The beauty and taste of the house had been a shock to her, but the bedroom was breathtaking. The walls were covered in a pale blue silk, lightly patterned. The ceiling was white. The floor was a highly polished parquet, with white rugs scattered about. The bed was enormous, hung in the same material as the walls. There was a low dressing table, a highboy, and a glass-fronted cabinet, all of the same honey-colored wood as the floor. The cabinet held several intricately carved jade statues. There wasn't one article in the room that didn't look as if it had been made especially for this room.

It took a few seconds for her to regain her senses, to know that Theron would soon be coming to the room to exercise his rights as her owner. Quickly, she took off the brown traveling dress and stepped into the pink gown Madame Nicole had given her. The gown looked sleazy in the lovely room.

She brushed her hair with the brush she found on the low table. There was a matched set for nails and hair, about twelve pieces made of a rich green marble. She climbed into bed and blew out the lamp. She waited expectantly for a few minutes, planning what she'd say to convince Theron to give her back her freedom. The day proved too much for her, though, and she fell asleep quickly.

When she awoke, it was morning and the sun was streaming in through two French doors. A young woman in a black-and-white maid's uniform was smiling at her, showing even, perfect teeth.

"Good morning. Mr. Shaw said I wasn't to wake you, but since you are awake, I'm sure he'd like you to join him for breakfast."

"I'm sure I have no choice in the matter," Morgan muttered.

The maid looked at her with a puzzled expression. "I am Jeannette. Mr. Shaw says you are to be his new assistant."

It was Morgan's turn to look puzzled. "Assistant?" She saw Jeannette frown slightly at her cheap whore-house gown.

"Excuse me, ma'am. I will find you a robe." Jeannette was back in seconds with a brilliant blue satin robe, trimmed with marabou at the neck and around the bottom. "Lovely, isn't it? Mr. Shaw has exquisite taste."

Theron was seated at the breakfast table reading a newspaper. When he saw Morgan, he rose and took her hand to escort her to the chair beside him. "I hope you slept well."

Morgan was now wary of this man. When the butler stepped from the room, Theron turned to her. "Really,

Morgan, there is no need to look like a scared rabbit and cringe from me. You will have every servant for blocks talking about how I beat you."

Before she could think of what to say, the butler returned with a plate covered by a matching porcelain dome. He set it in front of her, removing the lid.

"Oeufs demi-devil!" Morgan exclaimed. "It's been a year since I had eggs prepared like this." She took a forkful as she looked into Theron's astonished face. "Delicious! Your chef must be complimented."

"You know French cooking?" Theron obviously thought this was too much to hope for.

"Yes. I studied for some time with a French master chef."

He smiled, and his face resembled a Greek god's. "We are going to get along splendidly."

Their talk was about food and cooking for the rest of the meal. Morgan had time to notice the gleaming white tablecloth, the blue-and-white Limoges china, the silver accessories, and the blue-and-white carnations floating in a silver bowl.

"Jarvis, we will have coffee in the conservatory."

Morgan took Theron's arm as he led her through an archway at the end of the living room. The room was half of a dome with rounded panes of glass set in strips of dark wood. It was filled with lush greenery and orchids of every color. In the middle of the room stood a white marble statue of the classical Greek man, his body perfect. It could easily be a statue of Theron. Morgan turned toward him.

"I see you notice the resemblance. I found it in Greece." He turned away to stare at a cattelya orchid. Morgan realized he was embarrassed at the apparent vanity in having a statue so like himself.

"You were going to explain my future to me today?"

"Yes." He was relieved to have the subject changed. "I have already told you that I am an importer of fine art objects. I have lived and worked in New York most of my life, but when I heard gold had been discovered here, I knew there would be a need for my business. When men discover gold, their wives need ways to spend it. First, they have their husbands build them enormous houses, and then they fill them up. That is where I come in. I supply things for them to buy—lovely, beautiful, expensive things. I also make suggestions as to what to buy. Unfortunately, money is not often accompanied by good taste."

Morgan sipped her coffee. "Where do I fit into this?"

"In Europe or in New York, my job would pose no problem. There, people understand me. But here! This new gold takes a farmer or laborer and makes him a millionaire overnight. With all his new-found wealth, he is still ignorant. He dresses his fat, sweating wife in purple satin and thinks she is a lady—he thinks every man wants her." He paused. "I'm sorry, I am getting too emotional about this.

"I have learned that I need a companion, a woman to assist me when I talk to these ignorant people. Alone, I seem threatening. Also, the husbands are more likely to go along with their wives' extravagances when a beautiful young woman is in the room."

"Is this what you want me for? Your assistant?"

"Yes," he said simply.

"But I don't understand. Why did you have to buy someone from a brothel? You could hire someone."

"You make it sound very simple, but it is not. You have not caught the gold fever. You haven't seen what it does to people. The women who come here come with their husbands or fathers, and they don't want jobs—they want to spend their days in the sun shaking little pans of rocks. It's very difficult to hire anyone for a steady job these days. Besides, as you see, I cannot bear ugliness. Farmers' daughters rarely appeal to me.

"I had an assistant for a while, but she left me for one of those loud drunkards who had a few hundred dollars' worth of gold dust in his dirty pockets." His voice held contempt.

"I don't usually attend such things as Madame Nicole's human auction. But a friend of mine, Mr. Leon Thomas, remarked on the resemblance between the two of us, and I was intrigued. Madame Nicole offered me an invitation. I buy things for a living . . . beautiful things. And when I saw you, I made an offer."

"But you can't buy people!"

"Please!" He lifted his hand in protest. "Let's not go into that again. Madame Nicole said your husband was dead and that you are alone. I need an assistant and you need a home. Couldn't we just call this an intelligent business arrangement?"

"A business arrangement?" Morgan whispered. Tears came to her eyes as she recalled saying those same words to Seth, less than a year ago.

"Excuse me. I believe I've said something wrong again."

"No, it's not you. It's an old memory, but still very fresh in my mind. I have not gotten over my husband's death yet. Sometimes I am afraid I never will."

There was an embarrassed silence.

"As I was saying, you could work for me and learn my business and stay with me until your purchase price is paid. You will have every luxury."

She considered this for a moment. She could go back to New Mexico to her father's ranch. She knew that under the circumstances, she would qualify to inherit the estate. But what would she do alone on a ranch? Perhaps it would be better to work for a living.

"What is included in this business arrangement of yours besides decorating?"

He smiled at her, looking so much like the marble statue. "If you mean do I plan to become your lover, the answer is no. Though you are beautiful, you do not interest me in that way."

A sudden memory of her mother's chef, Jean-Paul, came to her. She understood, and returned his smile. Madame Nicole had indeed done her a favor. "Yes, I'll accept your job."

"Good! Now we can start to work. Jeannette says the clothes you brought with you are atrocious. I can imagine Madame Nicole's taste." He shuddered delicately. "Since we are so much alike in coloring, I know what colors suit you best—rich, bright, vibrant colors."

"That's just what my mother-in-law said. No pinks or beiges for Morgan—reds and blues and blacks."

Theron put her arm through his and patted her hand. "We're going to make a team, you and I. We'll be talked about everywhere. Look." He paused before a full-length mirror and she was startled again at the similarity between them. Streaked blond hair, gently curling . . . brilliant blue eyes . . . the same full lips. "Of course, I'm probably old enough to be your father, but I somehow doubt that I am." His eyes twinkled and she laughed.

"I think we're going to enjoy our partnership."

The following weeks were almost a fairy tale. Theron was a pleasant companion and a wonderful observer of people. Together, they laughed at the posturings of the *nouveaux riches*. Theron's impeccable taste enhanced Morgan's beauty. Soon she was a celebrity in San Francisco. Heads turned toward them wherever they went. There were constant invitations.

Men encouraged their wives to hire Theron to help them spend their wealth. Many times Theron had to rescue Morgan from the grasp of a too-ardent husband.

Jessy sent Morgan an invitation to lunch with her at a fashionable new tea shop. It was one of the few times Morgan had ever been anywhere in San Francisco without Theron.

Jessy and Morgan hugged one another, glad to be together again. Morgan noticed that Jessy's cheap taffeta dress was frayed and stained, but the happiness in her eyes overshadowed any money problems.

"He's been havin' some bad luck in the gold fields lately. Made too many bad investments."

"But you are happy, Jessy? That's what matters."

"Oh, sure. Me and Tom still get along swell. I got me a new lover on the side, too. Now don't look so shocked, Morgan. I'm not like you. I never could love one man at a time. Tell me about you. I was upset when those two girls told me what kind of man Madame Nicole sold you to. Maybe you got a lover by now too?"

Morgan laughed. "Jessy, I need you around all the time. Sometimes my mind gets lost for days in Louis XIV furniture and French enamels. You always seem to know just what you want."

"I do know that furniture, no matter how pretty it may be, is no replacement for a man. Now answer my question—you got a lover yet?"

Morgan was serious. "There's only been one man in my life and that's all I want. No one will ever replace Seth. Jessy, don't look at me like I'm crazy. I am happy, as happy as I can be without Seth. Theron and I are friends. He is good to me and I enjoy decorating."

"You're right, I do think you're crazy. But as long as you're happy, that's all that counts. I need to go, or Tommy'll decide I've left him and throw my things out. You know, I couldn't tell him I was meetin' you. If he ever found out I knew the famous gorgeous Morgan, he'd nag me to my grave to get to meet you." They parted laughing.

In May, when Morgan had been with Theron for nearly five months, the new wagon trains from the East began pouring in, each loaded with people aiming to try their luck in the gold fields. The Chandler wagon was among these.

~ *Chapter Fifteen* ~

THE Chandlers had already had a long, hard trip from Vermont. They were driving two wagons, one filled with farm implements and some basic mining equipment, the other carrying household goods. Ed Chandler was glad when he met the big man, Seth Colter. It had been all he could do to take care of a wife and two rather active young ladies all by himself. His daughters were pretty, and it seemed that every young man on the twenty-six wagons in the train was courting them.

Mr. Colter had said little about himself, just that he was heading west. Ed had offered him a job immediately. If he'd help with the stock and the wagons, he'd have his meals cooked by Ed's wife and daughters, and someone would care for his clothes.

Ed laughed to himself as they shook hands on the deal. Seth looked at him questioningly. "I'm not sure I've done you such a favor, Mr. Colter."

"Why's that, Mr. Chandler?"

"I have two daughters, both experts at breaking hearts. I'm afraid they may cause you some problems."

Seth's face was serious. "I don't think I have to worry about a broken heart."

Ed Chandler frowned. There was something far too serious about this young man.

Early the next morning, Seth rode out to the wagon train and met the Chandler women. Ivy Chandler's eyes were forever darting around, watching her daughters.

The girls, Gladys and Sudey, were both pretty. They were tall, big-boned girls with beautiful auburn hair. Gladys was seventeen and Sudey eighteen. When their father introduced Seth, they stared and nodded. Seth tipped his hat and left them.

It was a minute before the girls recovered, Gladys first. "Papa, why didn't you tell us about Mr. Colter?"

"I did, yesterday." He smiled. He knew exactly what they meant.

"Where does he come from?"

"Is he married?"

"Girls! Please. I know next to nothing about Mr. Colter. I met him just yesterday and offered him a job."

"Do you think that's wise, Ed? I mean, we really know nothing about him, and we will be spending three months very close to him."

"Three months!" Gladys sighed.

"A stranger. A tall, handsome stranger!" Sudey joined.

"Girls! I want no more of that. Mr. Colter is an employee of your father's. Even though we are in the wilderness, there is no excuse for unladylike behavior."

Both girls adopted looks of shame and contrition. The second their mother's back was turned, they turned to one another and grinned. Watching, their father could hardly contain his laughter.

"Don't encourage them, Ed," Ivy whispered to her husband.

During the day, Seth often rode ahead of the wagons to look for fresh game. At night the new settlers circled their wagons into a fortress against danger.

"Could I get you some stew, Mr. Colter? I made it myself."

Seth smiled up at the girl, giving her his full attention for the first time. "Yes, I'd like some, especially since you made it yourself."

Gladys glowed from the compliment and smiled as

she saw Sudey frowning at her. "Coffee, Mr. Colter?" Sudey asked.

Ivy Chandler watched her two daughters warily. At night when she and her husband were alone in the wagon bed, she talked to him. "Ed, you have to speak to your daughters. They're too forward. Since Mr. Colter came, they're not even speaking to the other boys on the train. They pester the poor man till he can hardly get his work done."

"Ivy, they're not causing any harm. I remember when we were courting. You seemed to turn up everywhere I went."

"Edward Chandler! Are you saying I chased you?"

Ed laughed. "No, dear. It was all just coincidence, I'm sure. But Mr. Colter seems sad. Even in the middle of several people, he seems alone."

"I've noticed that, too."

"I think two pretty girls fighting over him may be just what he needs."

Both Gladys and Sudey had made many efforts to get Seth's attention, but they both felt their failure.

Gladys was pleased when she saw Seth walking away from camp alone. She let him get a few yards ahead and then began running after him, calling his name. When he turned toward her, she bent her ankle under her and fell.

Quickly, Seth was kneeling by her, taking her foot in his large hands. As he kneaded the foot and ankle, he watched her face for signs of pain. There were no such signs, but Seth didn't mind. He had known only one woman who hadn't played games to get him. He did not expect to meet another.

"Does it hurt?"

"Oh, yes," she cried, trying to squeeze out a tear.

"Let me help you up." He put his arm around her shoulders and she leaned against him. She took one step and collapsed to the ground.

"I'm so sorry, Mr. Colter. I don't seem to be able to

walk at all. Maybe you could get my father for me and he could carry me back to the wagon." She looked coyly up at him through her lashes.

Easily, chuckling to himself, he bent down and picked up the large girl.

"Mr. Colter! You don't have to carry me. I'm much too large to be carried."

"You hardly weigh more than a bird, Miss Chandler," Seth lied.

Ed Chandler was upset at first to see his daughter injured, but when he noted the smile on Seth's face, he guessed Gladys's trick.

Sudey was furious with her sister. At night in the wagon, she viciously grabbed her sister's ankle. "You weren't really hurt. You had no right to act like that!"

"And who says I have no right?"

"He's mine. I've wanted him ever since I first saw him!"

"Well, so have I." She turned to her sister, smugly. "You can't imagine what it's like to be held in his arms. He's so *very* strong."

Sudey leaped at Gladys, catching some of her hair in her fingers.

Their screams brought their mother.

Ivy Chandler lectured the girls for some time on their behavior toward Mr. Colter. She reminded the girls that they knew very little about the man, that it was possible that he had a wife and several children somewhere.

The girls stayed away from Seth for a week. Sudey looked out from the wagon one night and saw Seth sitting alone by the dying fire. Quietly, she left the wagon and joined him.

"I couldn't sleep," she explained.

"Coffee?" He poured her a cup.

She rubbed her upper arms. "Nights in the mountains get awfully cold, don't they?"

Seth stepped to his horse and got a blanket from his

bedroll on the ground. Sudey stood up as he put it around her shoulders and lifted her face to be kissed.

Instinctively, he kissed her. She molded her body to his. Her lips were very receptive, but Seth felt nothing.

Angrily, he pushed her from him. "I think you'd better get back into your wagon."

Sudey smiled up at him, happy, oblivious.

Seth watched her go, his hands clenched by his side. Damn you! Damn you, Morgan! He went to his bedroll and stretched out. He tried to remember Sudey's kiss, but all he saw was Morgan. He compared every girl to Morgan. Sudey had yielded to him, but all he thought of was Morgan's body. It was a long time before he went to sleep.

After the kiss, Sudey became very possessive of her father's helper. She took care that his shirts were mended and his plate was always full. But the longer they spent on the trail, the more Seth stayed by himself.

When Ivy Chandler questioned her daughter about this new possessiveness, Sudey told her of Seth's kiss.

They were coming close to the edge of the desert when Ivy confronted Seth with Sudey's admission.

"I just want to know what your intentions are, Mr. Colter. My daughter is very young and very forward, I know . . . but I'd like to know where you two stand."

"I'm sorry, Mrs. Chandler. I did not mean to take advantage of your daughter. I'm sorry it happened. As for intentions toward your daughter—I have none."

"Are you married, Seth? Do you have a wife somewhere?" Her voice was gentle. She saw the pain her question caused.

"Yes, I have a wife somewhere. Though, at the moment I don't know where."

She put her hand on his shoulder. "You carry a heavy weight with you. I hope you will find peace someday."

JUDE DEVERAUX

Ivy told her daughters of Seth's wife. They were both upset, but they finally decided to turn their interests elsewhere.

Crossing the desert was more of a hardship than anyone had imagined. Everyone on the train turned his thoughts to dreams of water. It was a tired, ragged group that arrived in San Francisco in May of 1850.

238

~ *Chapter Sixteen* ~

"Remember, if you ever need anything, just look us up," Mr. Chandler called to Seth.

The girls watched him walk away, leading his horse. "Whoever his wife is, she's a very lucky woman."

"I want to marry a man just like him, big and quiet, who walks just like that." Both girls watched Seth, then giggled.

"If Mama heard you, you know what she'd say."

"I know, but it's hard for Mama to understand—she was never faced with a man like Seth Colter. Any woman who would leave him must be crazy."

Seth tied up his horse and walked into the saloon. An explosion of laughter came from three well-fed men in business suits at a near table.

"Ol' Charlie here paid three thousand dollars for some Chinese wallpaper just because the little gal said she would personally supervise its hanging. Three thousand dollars for three days' company! Pretty expensive, huh?"

The man with the red face laughed. "Of course, he *did* get to keep the wallpaper."

"That's *all* he got, though. He sure didn't get anything else."

Again, the explosive laughter.

"The smartest thing that pretty boy ever did was buy

the little lady from Madame Nicole. My wife loves that fella, but I never could abide him. He's so pretty. I thought he belonged on the mantelpiece instead of walking around. But with that sweet little Morgan, he can spend all the time he wants at my house. Course it sure costs me a lot for the opportunity of lookin' at her."

"Hey, mister, we say somethin' to interest you?" The man's tone was slightly belligerent.

Seth smiled, slow and easy. "I was just listening. Heard the name Morgan. Used to know a girl named Morgan."

"Come set down with us and tell us about your Morgan. I can't believe there could be another woman like San Francisco's Morgan Colter."

Seth tried to hide his emotions. It *was* Morgan! And the little bitch had the gall to use his name. You'd think she'd at least use another name. "Seth . . . Blake's my name." The three men introduced themselves—Charley Farrell, Joe Beal, and Arthur Johnston.

The red-faced man was Joe. "Our Morgan's a real beauty. A little blond thing, big blue eyes and a body—wooeee." He grinned and looked to the other two men for agreement.

"Couldn't be the Morgan I knew. The one I knew was probably not as pretty as your horse." He grinned and took a sip of his beer. "This Morgan of yours sure sounds like something. What's the chances of getting a, shall we say, private showing?"

The three men all started to talk at once and Charley quieted them. He leaned back in his chair. "Well, Mister Blake, this little gal comes real high. I mean real high." He gave furious looks to the other two men to quiet their protests. "You see, she used to work at Madame Nicole's place, a real classy cathouse. You practically have to show your teeth along with a carriage full of gold just to go look at one of Madame

Nicole's shows. Well, this little Morgan was the star at Madame Nicole's place—used to go on stage and have two girls undress her for everybody to see. Of course, that was a special-invitation show only." Again he gave warning looks to the two other men, both of whom were staring, open-mouthed, wondering at this fantastic story.

"Now she's left Nicole's and works for this blond feller. He's so pretty, and he looks like Morgan. They're a real pair, struttin' around town, goin' to the opera. Well, as I was sayin', this little lady is expensive. She and this feller sell you things for your house. If you've got enough money and buy enough stuff for your house, you get a little extra on the side. You know what I mean?"

Seth managed a smile, one that didn't quite reach his eyes. "I guess I do know what you mean."

Charley continued. "Art, here, just finished decorating a whole house, and it was a real pleasure, wasn't it?"

Arthur nodded, silently.

"See, me and Joe are still workin' on our houses. So far, I've only spent three thousand dollars, and that ain't near enough for me to enjoy it yet."

Art coughed nervously. "You come to try your luck in the gold fields, Mr. Blake?"

Seth drained his beer. "Yes, I think I will." He turned back to Charley. "Whereabouts does this Morgan live?"

Charley could hardly contain his laughter. "Boy, you won't have a chance dressed like that. Even at Madame Nicole's she wouldn't entertain no goldminer. You need fancy duds like these." He gave Seth directions to Theron's house and Seth left the saloon.

Charley waited until the big man was out of the building before he allowed his laughter to escape. "The man'll try everything to get her. He'll see her and think she's for sale and . . ." He realized the other two men weren't sharing in his laughter.

"Come on, men. Don't you see the joke? Can't you see ol' Theron's face when that big dumb cowboy makes an offer for his little jewel?"

"Charley, Miss Colter is a lady, and you know about Nicole's sales. Morgan Colter didn't entertain in no whorehouse and you know it. I don't care about the cowboy, but if Morgan or Theron heard, they could do us damage."

"And besides, I like the little gal. She's a nice lady, and she keeps to herself. And nobody's even seen the inside of her room, even though everybody's tried."

"Oh, hell! Can't a man have a little joke? I was only funnin' the man." He finished his beer. "Let's get out of here. Charlotte's got Morgan and her pretty boy comin' to tea and she wants me there." He looked at the other two reproachfully. "A man can dream, can't he?"

Seth's senses were reeling. She was here! She was in San Francisco. A real classy cathouse, the man had said. Did she leave Montoya, or did he get tired of her?

Without conscious thought, he followed the man's directions to Theron's house. He stood staring at it for a long time before he saw the door open.

"Theron, shouldn't we take some of the upholstery samples? Charlotte may want to change her mind about that awful brocade."

"Morgan, will you never learn? That woman would never change her mind, not unless you held a gun on her. We could try that, couldn't we? 'Lady, either you pick what we say, or you die,'" he mocked. "How's that?"

"Oh, Theron, sometimes I wish we could. What is it with these people and purple?" She was smiling and turned in Seth's direction an instant before he disappeared around a building.

Her knees gave way and she grabbed Theron's arm for support.

"Morgan, what is it? Jarvis, go to the Farrells' and tell them Morgan is ill, that we can't make it." Theron picked Morgan up and carried her upstairs to her room.

Seth watched from the street, his rage mounting by the second. He turned and left the area.

"*Seth*. It was Seth, Theron. I saw Seth."

"But Morgan, Seth is dead. It must have been someone who looked like him."

"Theron!" Her eyes blazed. "It *was* Seth. He's alive. I have to find him." She started up from the bed.

"Not now you don't. I don't like your color. Jeannette, get Morgan some tea." He looked at Jeannette knowingly and she nodded.

"Theron, you have to understand. There is a reason that I have to find him now, without delay. He may hate me. He may think I left him for another man. He was told I did."

"How could he believe that? Morgan, you don't realize how much you talk about that man. I'd really like to meet him, because I'm sure he has a golden halo and his feet are supported by little clouds. If something is good . . . anything—art, food, wallpaper paste—you compare it to Seth. If it's bad, then it's not like Seth."

"Theron, please!" She looked at him in desperation.

"Here's your tea." Again, he and Jeannette exchanged looks. "Drink this and then we'll talk about finding your Seth."

Morgan sipped at the tea and then, at Theron's urging, drained her cup.

"Now, let's go." She swung her legs off the bed, then put her hand to her forehead.

"Theron! You put something in the tea. How am I going to find Seth? How am I . . . He hates me . . ."

"She's asleep. Good."

"Mr. Shaw, what's wrong with her? I've never seen her so upset. Do you think she really saw her husband?"

"I don't know, but I plan to make a few inquiries while she sleeps. A man with sandals and a white robe should be easy enough to find, don't you think?"

"Sandals?" Jeannette looked puzzled and then smiled. "Mr. Shaw! You shouldn't say things like that."

"If she wakes up, try to keep her calm. I'll be back soon."

Theron spent the afternoon and part of the evening trying to find Seth. He knew very little about him except that he was large. The bartender at one saloon seemed to remember a man like that, but he wasn't sure. Two wagon trains had arrived in San Francisco that day and he'd been pretty busy. It was well into the night when Theron returned home.

Morgan met him at the door, but she knew from his face that he'd been unsuccessful. She sank to her knees, dissolving into tears. "Seth. Seth." Her cries were close to hysteria.

Theron held her, rocking her gently. In the five months they had lived together, they had become very close. Theron thought of Morgan as his little sister. He enjoyed teasing her and, at times, protecting her.

"Morgan, sweet, don't cry. We'll find him. If we have to turn the town upside down, we'll find him. I'll send men into the gold fields to look for him. Whatever it takes, we'll find him. Now, please calm yourself. I can't stand to see you cry."

When Morgan couldn't stop her tears, built from months of loneliness and longing, Theron carried her back to bed.

"Morgan, please, I'm getting too old to keep climbing those stairs," he teased. Morgan's unresponsiveness sobered him. "If you'll rest, I'll go out again and look for him. Now."

Theron left her, worried about the frantic look in her eyes.

It took Seth only a few seconds and the flash of some gold to get the little tailor's promise to have a suit altered in a few hours.

It was night when he left the shop. No longer did he fit in with the tired, dirty prospectors in from the East. The charcoal gray suit and white shirt set off his hair and tanned skin.

His long strides took him to the rather quiet, unassuming house on First Street. A carriage pulled up and two men went to the door. A tall butler opened it, smiled, and ushered the gentlemen in.

Seth knocked on the door. The butler looked him over carefully. "Yes?"

"I am new to San Francisco, just arrived today, and I heard that some enjoyment might be had at Madame Nicole's."

"Just a moment, sir, and I will see." He closed the door. Within moments it reopened and Seth saw an enormous woman with beautiful black hair.

"Madame Nicole, of course." Seth bowed slightly. His eyes raked over her, making her feel as beautiful as her vanity allowed. "Seth Blake at your service, ma'am."

"Well, Mr. Blake, Edwards tells me you'd like to visit my humble establishment."

He smiled at her, showing deep dimples.

"Mr. Blake, I declare you can certainly charm a girl." Her eyes swept down his massive chest. "I believe I just may keep you for myself." She possessively took his arm and led him into the large drawing room.

"Will you be in town long, Mr. Blake?"

"I'm not sure yet. I have a ranch in New Mexico. I thought I might try my hand in the gold fields."

She led him to a table covered with various hors

d'oeuvres and wines. When Seth refused refreshment, she asked him more questions.

"Tell me, Mr. Blake, what would interest you tonight? Nicole has a wide variety of beautiful young women."

"Well, I saw one today that interested me. I believe she once worked for you—a little blonde, blue eyes. I believe she now works with an importer?"

"Ah, Morgan," Nicole smiled. "She was here for a while, yes. But she was sold right away."

"Sold?"

"Yes, twice a year I have a sale of beautiful young women. The highest bidder wins the lady. Morgan was the most beautiful woman yet offered in San Francisco."

Nicole did not see the muscles clenching and unclenching in Seth's jaw. He had hoped it wasn't true, that the men had lied. "So she did work here then?"

Nicole did not want to tell the handsome and possibly rich young man that she had never had such a beautiful girl work for her. Her reputation might suffer.

"Yes, I have many beautiful young women working for me. Let me show you a few." She clapped her plump hands and three women in thin, nearly transparent gowns entered the room.

Nicole had been around men for many years and could sense their needs. Something was troubling this young man, something deeper than simple need for a woman. He hardly looked at these. Nicole raised her hand and dismissed them.

"Seth, I don't know you, but I think I know your problem. You're in love."

Seth raised one mocking eyebrow.

"Go to her. Tell her you love her. Take her by force if you need to, but let her know how you feel."

Let Morgan know how he felt! Yes, he'd tell her. He tell her how much he hated her. He smiled. "Yes, I think you are right. Goodnight, Madame Nicole."

Nicole laughed when he was gone. She wished she were that young woman. It would be wonderful to hold that man in her arms.

Jeannette blew out the light in Morgan's room, glad to have finally gotten her to sleep. She closed the door quietly and went downstairs to her own room.

Seth made no sound as he opened the French doors and stepped into the room. Even by moonlight the beauty of the room was obvious. He walked to the dresser and touched her brush and comb, taking his time making his way to the bed.

Her hair was spread all around her and tangled in one fist. She made a little hiccough as she slept, as if she had been crying.

He reached out a hand and touched a golden tress with one finger. It was so soft. He hadn't remembered how soft her hair was. She moved, kicking the covers below her waist. She had on a satin gown of deep, rich apricot. The ties were loose in front and the fabric gaped open to expose the soft curve of her breast.

Too many things flashed before him: Morgan sunning herself on a rock in the canyon, Morgan cooking his breakfast and then sitting in his lap to feed it to him.

And then the note. Those few words, telling him she loved Joaquín.

Seth's eyes lost their softness. He put out his hands to clasp her neck, but then stopped. He had loved her, loved her from the first. He had stood back while she made up her mind whether she wanted to be a woman or not. He had waited and watched, for a long time. He had killed three men for her. Cat Man and his two cohorts had been sitting peacefully by their campfire. He had not even given them a chance to go for their guns. He had killed them and ridden away. For her!

He began removing his jacket. When he had removed

all his clothes, he lifted the light blanket and climbed into bed with Morgan.

Gently, he began caressing her soft breast. He brought his lips to hers, barely touching their sweetness, then delicately nibbling at her lower lip. In her sleep, Morgan felt the longed-for touch of Seth. She moved against him, parting her lips. The tip of his tongue traced the outline of her lips.

His kisses traced a sensuous path across her cheek to her earlobe. His teeth nipped the tender piece of flesh. "Morgan," he whispered. She nuzzled closer to him. "*Mi querida.*" Her eyes opened slowly, languidly, her arms going up to encircle his broad shoulders.

She opened her eyes fully and then opened her mouth to scream. Seth silenced her lips with his own. Her eyes were wild and she began to struggle.

Quickly, he put his fingers over her lips. "Don't you know your husband?"

She looked at him with astonishment for one long moment and then tears rushed to her eyes. "*Seth.* I knew it was you. I *knew.* Oh, Seth! What happened?" She pulled him to her. "Seth, I love you. I love you so much." She couldn't see his jaw clench, his eyes freeze. "Seth . . . did Joaquín finally admit that he—"

His hand covered her mouth. His eyes were dark with passion. "Later, sweet. Later you can tell me all about it."

Doubt flickered a warning in her mind. But he was so urgent.

"Have you missed me? Did you think about me?" His hands moved across her body, making her ache with longing. Her arms pulled him closer and she arched against him.

"Yes, oh yes," she whispered into his ear as she kissed it, pulling the earlobe between her lips.

"You're eager for me, aren't you, Morgan?" Again,

she had the awful feeling, the doubt. What was strange about Seth?

He removed her gown. Her body screamed for him to take her. His caresses were tantalizing, making her lose her senses. It was as if she were only a body, only desire.

His lips traveled down her neck, the weight of his body pressing on her. Her fingers pulled him closer. He felt her urgency and this made his kisses even slower.

"Seth, Seth," she moaned over and over.

His lips traveled down her body, across her breasts, one hand holding hers to keep her clutching fingers still, the other softly kneading her inner thigh. His lips traveled down and down, touching all of her.

When he reached her feet, he kissed each of her toes, raking the soft fleshy part against his lower teeth. "Please, Seth, now, now."

Abruptly, he turned her over, his teeth and tongue and lips making a trail across her smooth, perfect skin.

When he reached her neck, he turned her over and began to make love to her. He kept his lips on hers to still her loud moans. They reached their peaks together.

They lay quietly for a moment, wrapped in ecstasy. Their bodies were one, and inseparable.

Seth moved to lie beside her. He kissed her neck, her eyelids.

Morgan's body was on fire. Her fingertips were extremely sensitive, the nerves wonderfully alive. They sought Seth's body, searching the length of his broad back, feeling each muscle and the texture of his skin. She kissed his neck, running her tongue along the muscles, the sinews.

Her fingers entangled in the hair on his chest, her lips following the sensitive path of her fingers. Her hands found his maleness and lingered, gently stroking until she heard low sounds from Seth's throat.

She climbed on top of him and this time, slowly, they

came to new heights of desire and finally collapsed in one another's arms, sated.

Content, Morgan slept, her cheek against Seth's chest, the hairs tickling her nose. Seth's low voice woke her from the first happy sleep she had had in many months.

"Did you do this with the men at Madame Nicole's?"

"Mmmm?" she snuggled closer to him. Seth was here, alive and in her arms. She kissed his chest.

"Was Joaquín a good lover? Did he make your hips move and your hands claw?"

Her eyes flew open. "Seth, must I tell you . . . ?"

He roughly pushed her from him. "No, I must tell you. I know about them all. I know about Madame Nicole."

Her hand flew to her mouth, her eyes were wide. "No."

He stepped out of the bed, reaching for his clothes. "Tell me, did you react for all of them as you did for me? No wonder you're such an expensive whore. Tell me, how much do you share with your 'partner'? Does he set you up or do you find your own men?"

"No," she whispered, the tears coming to her eyes. She was on her knees in the bed, her damp, tangled hair falling about her. "No, Seth. That's all wrong."

"Well, ma'am, you are certainly fetching like that. I don't imagine you'd pleaded with many men. Does it hurt your vanity to find that you can be walked away from? I know you are used to doing the walking."

Her sobs were choking her, her body shaking.

Seth almost reconsidered, but quickly he picked up his hat and walked to the French doors. "I remember some time ago, when you left a light in the window so I could climb to your bedroom. It's ironic, isn't it?" He paused and reached into his jacket pocket and withdrew several gold coins. He tossed them to the floor beside the bed. "You can share that with your decorator friend. Goodbye, *wife*." He made the word sound ugly. And almost instantly, he was over the balcony.

When Theron found Morgan an hour later, his patient was calm, sitting quietly against the back of the bed. Something was very wrong. He preferred her hysterics to the icy calm he saw in her eyes now. He sat by her, took her cold little hand.

"What's happened?"

She turned to him and smiled. It was a smile Theron had never seen before, and it made chills run down his spine. "I have just had a visit from my husband, the man I've loved so long, the man I've dreamed of day and night." Her voice was flat.

"After he had used my body and made me react, he taunted me, accused me of having many men."

"Morgan, I really don't understand any of this. Why would he want to hurt you so? Doesn't he understand our relationship?"

She laughed. "I don't believe my husband understands anything. He wouldn't allow me to explain. He saw only the wrong side of everything." Morgan began telling Theron of her marriage to Seth, how she had asked him to marry her, had fought her feelings for him. She told of Seth's jealousy and Joaquín's treachery.

"He never even asked you if the note was true? It never occurred to him that you had been taken against your will?"

"It is ironic, isn't it? He has tried, judged and hanged me—and I am innocent. I don't believe I want to talk anymore, Theron."

The look in Morgan's eyes frightened him. Always, she had a kind word. Always, she smiled. But now her lips curved into a snarl.

"Maybe we could find him. Find him and tell him the truth of what has happened to you—that none of it was your fault."

She turned on him, eyes flashing. "I should go to him and tell him that I am innocent? What should I do, plead with him, beg him to forgive me—for nothing? I loved him and he should have been able to see that. I told him so tonight, but he chose to ignore it. He believes I was one of Nicole's whores. What if I had been? What if his pure little Morgan *had* been tarnished by other men? Should I kill myself in that case? He didn't care enough for me to even listen to me, to find out what had happened to me all this time."

She took a breath and leaned back against the pillows. "He was not the man I thought he was. I never want to hear his name again."

"Morgan, please listen . . ."

"I would like to sleep now. I believe Mrs. Farrell will want us to spend the day discussing her dining room, and I need strength to face that woman's taste. Goodnight."

Theron kissed her forehead, blew out the lamp, and left the room.

Morgan fell asleep, remembering Seth's back as he disappeared over the balcony.

Morgan became more and more involved in her work with Theron. In the next months, she tried constantly to keep herself from thinking of Seth, from fully realizing that he was alive. Did he have a mistress? Was some other woman taking care of him?

All she had to do was find him, tell him that Joaquín had forced her to write the note, that she had not had any other men . . . No! How dare she even think of pleading with him! He was a vain, arrogant man and she wouldn't lower herself.

Gradually, Theron's customers noticed the difference in Morgan. Before, she had met the men's advances with smiles and jests. Now she tended to sneer at them. She no longer returned their flirting with friendly jibes.

The evenings she spent with Theron often turned into brooding silences. Before, they were hardly ever out of one another's sight; but now Theron spent some evenings alone.

"Take it away, Jeannette. The very sight of food nauseates me."

Jeannette took the tray and set it on the dresser. Then she held her hand to Morgan's forehead.

"Stop it! There's nothing wrong with me. I just don't feel like eating."

Jeannette was calm. Theron had told her about Seth's attack on his wife. "No, ma'am, there's nothing at all wrong with you. I'd say that, in a few months, you'll be perfectly all right."

"Months! Don't be absurd! I'm just not feeling well. A few days' rest and I'll be fine."

"I should say in about six months, you should be quite yourself again."

"Six months! Jeannette, will you stop raving like a lunatic and take that food away? Even the smell of it makes my stomach turn and . . ." Her face drained. She met Jeannette's stare.

Smiling, the maid picked up the tray and started to the door. "I'm sure Mr. Shaw would want the doctor to check you, to confirm the time. But I think he'll say six months."

When Morgan was alone, she leaned back in the bed. "No. It can't be," she whispered. Her hands went to her stomach. It was hard, but had a slight new roundness. "A baby . . . what will I do with a baby? A baby whose father hates his mother?" She remembered her own fatherless childhood. It had hurt her in many ways, being raised without a man around.

The doctor's visit confirmed what Jeannette had known for some time and Morgan hadn't even guessed at.

Theron was delighted with the news. "A baby in the house! Delightful! Wondrous! We'll make the guest room into a nursery. Chinese décor, don't you think? Of course, I'm very partial to Chinese. Or how about Italian, some clean lines, very fluid? Color. We can do oranges and siennas, or the cool colors."

"Theron, please. I've just found out about this. I don't know what I'm going to do yet."

"Going to do? Well, of course you're going to stay right here. Jeannette and I will take care of you. Come along, Jeannette, let's let Morgan rest for now. We'll see you in the morning. I'm rather tired, too. This has been a very exciting day."

Alone, Morgan's thoughts whirled. A baby, her own child. She smiled. Yes, she wanted this baby, very much. She needed someone to care for, to care about.

But how should she or he be raised?

Her life with Theron was pleasant, but a baby needed more than a mother who decorated people's homes, a mother whom the townsmen took great delight in trying to pinch. What if her child found out this mother had been sold in a public auction at a brothel? What about Morgan's inheritance? She had not thought about it in a long time, but if she had a child, she wanted him to be raised in security.

She would go to Albuquerque and meet with her father's lawyers. Then she'd take her child and go back to Kentucky, and Trahern House.

The thought of Trahern House brought tears to her eyes. Many times when she'd been so happy with Seth, she had laughed at Trahern House, thinking how lonely and barren it would seem to her after her life with Seth. Ah, but now she wouldn't be alone. She'd have her child.

It took Morgan a week to convince Theron of the wisdom of her plan. She would return to New Mexico and then to Kentucky.

"Morgan, how can you leave? You're like my little sister. What would life be like without you? Please stay."

It wasn't easy to think of leaving Theron or the luxury he provided for her. When she left him, she'd be enitrely on her own, taking care of herself and responsible for another life as well.

A stage line had recently been started, connecting the Santa Fe Trail with the gold fields of California. It was on this stage that Theron booked Morgan's passage.

The goodbyes were tearful. "If you ever need anything, you know where you have a friend," Theron told her as she mounted the high steps into the stagecoach.

The return trip to Santa Fe was awful. The coach swayed and bounced with every rock the wheels hit, and there were thousands of them.

They stopped only long enough to change horses, the passengers being forced to grab whatever they could and to eat in the coach. The windows had pieces of canvas that rolled down over them, but a closed coach, with the six unwashed and sweating people, was unbearable. They talked at first, one man in particular trying to get Morgan's attention, but after the first few days they were all too tired for conversation. In the beginning Morgan had tried to keep her face and hands clean, but when she rubbed her neck and dirt rolled off in her hand, she gave up.

When they arrived in Santa Fe, she was too tired, hungry, and dirty even to remember why she had come. Her legs were cramped and she could hardly stand.

"Here, let me help you with that." Someone took her hand baggage and she turned to meet a pair of familiar eyes.

"Frank!" she cried, the weariness of her body making her vision blurred.

"Morgan!" Frank picked her up and swung her around. "Last time I saw you, them outlaws had carried you off."

Her eyes clouded. "An awful lot's happened since then." She turned away, frowning. If he thought of her as Seth did, he'd hate her, too.

"Hey, little gal!" He squeezed her again and set her down. "Don't you go lookin' like that. I heard every word of the story from Jake. I don't know your side of it, but I sure don't believe you left Seth for Joaquín."

"You don't?"

"Hell, no. Anybody could see the way you two followed one another around. I never saw two people so stubborn as you two. Both of you head over heels in love and neither of you admitting it."

"Oh, Frank! Thank you."

"Let's get you out of here. I bet you want to clean up. I'll take you to the hotel, and then tomorrow, after you've rested, we can go to the ranch."

"No, I can't go to the Colter ranch."

"Just hush now and I'll take care of you. I won't put up with your bullheadedness. Tomorrow you go to the ranch. It's where you belong, especially with that young 'un you're carryin'."

Her eyes flew to his, open wide.

Frank laughed. "Always have had an eye for the ladies. Only thing that's changed about you is that curvy little belly. And with six kids of my own, I sure know what causes that."

Morgan was grateful to Frank for taking care of her. She was content to stand back and let him order her a bath and dinner in her room. Once alone, she scoured herself in the hot water and ate greedily. It was still only about six in the evening when she fell into the soft bed.

Late the next morning, Frank came for her with a buckboard. She had rested and she felt strong enough to protest about going to Seth's ranch, but Frank refused to listen.

"That's your home. Of course you're going there."

"But, Frank, I need to go to Albuquerque and see my father's lawyer."

"All right, you can visit there later, but first you go home. Lupita will be waiting with open arms and hot tortillas. You couldn't ask for more."

Morgan was grim. "What about Jake? And Paul? Will they greet me with open arms? The woman who ran off with another man? You don't even know for sure that the baby I carry is Seth's."

Frank grinned. "You're even more stubborn than I remember. I know that that little one you're carryin' is yours. That's good enough for me. If Seth Colter and you been in the same town for the last few months and he ain't the father, then there's something wrong with him, not with you. Now, if you've finished your lunch, we'd better be on our way."

As they made the long trip to the Colter ranch, Morgan tried not to think of what would greet her there. They talked of Frank's family, whom Morgan had never met, and of life in general in New Mexico. Morgan told Frank about the hundreds of people pouring into San Francisco each week. She talked about Theron and the work they'd done, making him laugh over her stories of the people and the wealth they didn't know how to handle.

Lupita heard the wagon long before she saw it. She walked slowly out to meet them. Since Seth and Morgan had both gone, a change had come over the place. There was no laughter anymore. Jake and she ate their meals in the big kitchen while Paul took his outside. Paul didn't like the gloom of the inside.

She recognized Frank instantly, and thought he'd brought his oldest daughter with him. But something about the smallness of the form next to Frank made her start. "It couldn't be," she whispered. And then she began running toward the wagon.

JUDE DEVERAUX

"Señora Colter! You've come home!" The large
woman practically lifted Morgan out of the wagon. She
clasped her tightly in her arms, Morgan returning the
hug.

"Lupita, you better be careful how you handle our
little mother-to-be."

Lupita gasped, held Morgan at arm's length, and
then hugged her again.

258

～ *Chapter Seventeen* ～

"FRANK, you must stay to help us celebrate Señora Colter's return."

"Please, Frank, I need your help. I need someone here who believes in me."

Both women looked up at Frank, their eyes imploring.

"No, Morgan, you don't need me. Not when you have Lupita fighting for you. I've got to get home. The wife'll want to know what kept me overnight in Santa Fe anyway. I may need *you* to come defend *me*. Jake's a hummingbird compared to my Louisa."

Lupita and Morgan watched as Frank rode off in the buckboard. When he was out of sight, they turned to one another.

"Lupita . . . I . . ."

"There's no need for you to explain anything. I never believed a word of it. Now, let's get out of this sun. If there's going to be a baby, then there are many things to be done."

"But, Lupita, I can't just come back here to live, not after all that's happened. Frank nearly forced me to come."

"And he was right. This is your home. This is where Seth's baby should be born."

Morgan stopped. "Seth's . . . How do you know? What makes you so sure it's his baby? I've been gone a long time."

"Señora Colter," Lupita laughed, "you do not have to explain anything to me. Jake and Paul will need explanations but I do not. Now come on inside or that baby will get a fever from the sun."

Morgan turned startled eyes to her rounding stomach. Her hand went to the mound. She had so recently learned that she was to have a baby that she hadn't had time to think of it much yet, to get used to its constant presence.

"Yes," she smiled up at Lupita. "We will have to take care of her."

"Her? Already you know what it will be?"

Laughing, their arms around one another, they walked to the house. It was cool within the thick adobe walls. The familiar rooms brought Morgan home at last. Everything had been good in this house. All the many happy memories came flooding back to her.

She turned to Lupita, her face reflecting joy at being home.

"You are right. This is my home. This is where Seth's daughter will be born." She watched as Lupita's grin widened. "Yes, it's Seth's child."

Lupita again ran to Morgan and hugged her tightly. "I knew you'd find one another. I knew it. When will the Señor join us? Why did he ever allow you to travel alone? I will have many words to say to him for this."

"No, Lupita. Seth doesn't know about the baby. He won't be coming here." She paused. "Now you will let me explain."

"No! It does not matter. What is between you two is your business. Come into the kitchen and let me feed you two girls."

"Two girls?" Morgan laughed when she realized Lupita's meaning. "Lupita, do you think we could make some *empañaditas* this afternoon?"

The rest of the day was blissful. It was good to remove the whalebone corset she had worn in San Francisco. Lupita's cool cotton blouse and skirt felt marvelous against her body. She brushed her hair, glad not to have a maid standing nearby waving a hot curling iron.

"Now you look like yourself. The chickens all ran and hid from you before."

"Yes," Morgan laughed. "I feel like me again. Like I've really come home. Lupita, no matter what happens, I have a right here, don't I? I want my baby born here." The tears came once again. "This is where I was happiest. Where Seth and I were happy."

"Yes, Morgan, no one will make you leave. Seth's child will grow up here."

"Look at me. Sometimes I think I've spent the last year crying. I think we ought to get started with the cooking. Does Paul still eat as much as he used to? Of course, it was always Seth who could eat more than the rest of us put together," she laughed. She wiped her eyes with the back of her hand. "It's not going to be easy, is it, Lupita? I know Jake believed Joaquín's story."

Lupita looked at her with sympathy. "No, it won't be easy. But soon it will all be worth it, Morgan."

As Morgan began putting flour and butter together, she said quietly, "I like being called Morgan by you."

That evening when Jake walked into the house and saw Morgan, he was torn. He wanted to kill her. And at the same time, he wanted to leave and never see her again. He stood rooted, staring at the young woman who had caused everyone so much misery.

Lupita spoke first. "Paul, you come in, too, and welcome Morgan back."

"Her! It's because of her that Seth left. It's not right when a man has to leave his own home. We should get the sheriff for what she's done. Get tired of your lovers, did you, honey?"

Defeated entirely, Morgan turned to leave. "It's no use, Lupita. I'll go." Then she saw the gun in Lupita's hand, aimed at the two men. "Lupita! No! It doesn't matter. I'd rather leave than cause all this trouble. Please."

"You're right. Get out! We don't want you." Jake took a step toward her, in spite of Lupita's revolver. "He almost died because of you. When he got over all the wounds, he was still sick. Sick over your treachery."

Lupita stepped between Jake and Morgan. "Jake, we have known one another a long time and I'd hate to use this, but one step closer to her and I'll shoot you in the leg." Lupita's eyes were hard. "She has a right to be heard, a right to tell her side of what happened."

"She has no rights! She almost killed him!"

"I mean it, Jake. Not one more step. Now you two sit there and listen." She gestured with the gun to the couch.

"Lupita, this isn't going to work. You can see they hate me. No matter what I say, they'll never believe me."

"The note! We saw the note you wrote Seth. How could you run off with that Montoya when you had Seth?"

Morgan had turned to the bedroom, to get her bags. She just wanted out of the house, away from these people—two men who hated her unfairly and a woman who was ready to shoot someone for her. Jake's accusation brought her back to reality. It was the same as the night Seth had come to her room. She had begged him to listen to her, but he had been too selfish to bother. That night began to come back to her . . . all of it. She whirled on the two men.

"I've had enough of the Colter men to last me the rest of my life! You accuse *me* of treachery? Did it occur to you that your precious Seth ever did anything wrong? Yes, I wrote a note to Seth, a note I thought was going to save his life. Yes, go ahead and look at me in disbelief.

"I don't know why I bother with you. Yes, I do! I am sick of being accused of things I didn't do.

"The night of the party, I waited and waited for Seth. I hardly talked to anyone; all I wanted was for him to come to me." Morgan laughed.

"When he did come, he threw himself into a rage because I had dared step outside with Joaquín. You were right, Jake, when you said it was foolish to want Joaquín rather than Seth. I never even considered Joaquín. Never. I loved Seth and no one else. After Seth stormed out, I followed him. Joaquín went with me—to help me find him, he said. After several hours of riding, Joaquín took me prisoner in a strange house, tied and gagged me."

The first flush of Morgan's anger was gone now, leaving her weak. She sat down, staring at the empty fireplace. When she continued, her voice was quieter. "Joaquín said he'd kill Seth unless I wrote the note. He said that if Seth believed I'd run away, he'd hate the Colter ranch and sell it to him."

"Why? Why would Montoya want this little place?"

Morgan didn't look up. "Something about water rights. He said Seth could cut off the water from the Montoya ranch at any time." She missed the looks of confirmation exchanged between Jake and Paul.

"But after I wrote the note, he came back to tell me that he had killed Seth. I knew then that Seth had died hating me." She was silent for a while.

"What happened?" Jake's voice was gentle.

Morgan looked up at him and smiled an ironic smile. "Oh, very little, actually. Joaquín paid a Frenchman to remove me. The Frenchman took me and three other women across the country and sold us to a brothel owner in San Francisco. She auctioned us off to the highest bidder, after what you might call an unveiling ceremony."

Morgan laughed. Her speech became higher and more rapid. "I was lucky. A man bought me and was good to me. He never touched me. I was happy, after all the horror.

"Then Seth appeared. He was alive. He came to my room. He made love to me. I was so happy, happier than I'd ever been in my life. I told him how much I loved him. Then the accusations started. He believed Joaquín, not me. He would not listen to me at all. He wanted to know why Joaquín had left me. He found out about the brothel, but he thought I had worked there as a whore. He . . . he . . . ."

Lupita was on her knees in front of Morgan, gathering her in her ample arms. "Get out and leave her alone. She's been through enough. And I hope you both feel what I think you feel."

Sheepishly, the two men rose and walked toward the front door. Then Jake turned and went back to Morgan. He gently pushed Lupita away and took Morgan in his thin arms. His voice was husky. "We've all done you a wrong, Morgan. I know Seth and I know his father. Under their calm faces, they're jealous men, often given to yelling first and then asking questions. I'm right sorry we made the same mistake." He pulled away from Morgan and looked at her, his hands on her shoulders. "Can you forgive us? Will you stay here with us?"

Morgan smiled at the old man. "I don't know, Jake. I hadn't planned to come back to the ranch. Frank insisted that I . . ."

"Of course she'll stay. We have a baby on the way. A little boy just like Seth." Lupita smiled broadly.

"It's a girl," Morgan answered her. "A nice, sweet, little girl."

"A baby!" Paul was astonished.

Jake recovered from his own astonishment. "Yes, a

young 'un, you numbskull. Morgan's going to have a baby. We'll teach him to ride a horse, brand cattle . . ."

Morgan laughed. "It's going to be a girl and I'd like to get her into the world before you start teaching her how to ride a horse."

"He'll learn to use a rope, too, just like his pa."

"*She* will learn to make pastry, just like her mother. Lupita, I'm starved."

Everyone laughed together. "Babies need lots of food for growing. Let's feed this one."

It was a happy group that sat down to dinner. Lupita quietly put the gun back in the cupboard where she always kept it for emergencies. It was good to have laughter in the house again. If only Seth would come back. She offered a silent prayer to her favorite saint for his safe return. "Maybe he will come before the baby is born," she whispered.

"But, Jake, I can't stay here. What if Seth comes back? I don't want to see him. I don't ever want to see him. Not after what he did. I begged him, Jake, begged him to listen to me."

"Now, girl, don't get so riled up. We'll cross that bridge when we come to it. First thing you need is for someone to help you with the baby. Who else you got?"

There was no one. She couldn't go back to her Uncle Horace and Aunt Lacey. Seth's parents would take her in, but that would be the same as staying on the Colter ranch.

"You see, you know there's nothing else to do. So stop worrying and eat somethin' for that boy."

"Girl," Morgan added absent-mindedly.

After the first few days on the ranch she began to relax. The house was familiar and the people cared for her. She began to think more about her baby. Her stomach seemed to stretch a little each day. She rubbed the mound often, glad of its presence.

"Cecilia. What do you think of that name, Lupita?

I'm going to name her something very feminine. I get so tired of people's comments about my name."

"Cecilia is a good name. Another tortilla? They're hot."

"I don't know why I'm so hungry. It seems that no matter how much I eat, I just get hungrier."

Lupita smiled as Morgan coated the tortilla with freshly made butter. She poured her glass full of milk. "You're eating for two now."

"Yes, I guess so." Morgan's mouth was full. "I guess I should worry about getting fat, but somehow, I don't care. I feel sort of like a . . . a big pillow, just content to do nothing. I don't even worry about Seth coming. It seems nothing matters to me. I just want to have Cecilia."

Morgan looked up as Jake came into the kitchen from outside. "Are you still eating, girl? Did you know it's time for the noon meal and you're still eating breakfast?" He turned to Lupita. "She's going to pop her skin. Why do you let her eat so much?"

Morgan held up her arm and looked at it. Jake was right. The skin was tight and almost shiny. Her ankles and legs were the same way. Somehow she didn't care. She smiled up at Jake. "I'm glad it's lunchtime, because I'm hungry."

Jake watched her with growing concern as she ate constantly throughout the meal. After lunch, Morgan announced that she planned to take a walk. Jake was relieved to see her get away from Lupita's stove.

Later, as Jake was in the barn, he saw Morgan make her way slowly past the open door. "Morgan," he heard Lupita call. He watched in disbelief as Lupita fastened a cloth bag to Morgan's back. "In case you get hungry," he heard Lupita tell her.

Jake started to give his opinion of Morgan's food needs, but thought better of it. Whenever he spoke out, Lupita ignored him and Morgan smiled sweetly at him and then went on eating. She already ate more than the other three of them put together.

As Morgan's size increased, so did her placidity. She had not been so calm since she'd left Trahern House. Nothing bothered her. The emotions that had once raged inside her no longer concerned her. She thought of nothing but food and the baby's name. All of them were names for girls.

She spent mornings with Lupita. Whenever she forgot what she was supposed to be doing, and stared into space, Lupita quietly finished her task for her. After lunch, she walked. She walked for hours, very slowly and awkwardly. She never had a definite path in mind or even seemed to remember later where she'd been. Lupita always made sure her knapsack was filled with food, and Morgan always returned the sack empty.

As the weather grew colder, Jake tried to stop her from her long walks, but she never seemed to hear him. He couldn't understand her dreaminess, and he was worried about the way she looked.

Morgan's entire body swelled and stretched. After the first few months, she could no longer get her feet into her own shoes. Lupita brought her an old pair of *huaraches* to wear. Morgan still wore Lupita's clothes. The Mexican cotton blouse that had once swallowed her tiny frame now nearly burst at the seams. Her plump shoulders and bosom strained against the embroidered fabric.

One day as Jake and Paul watched her heading toward the trees for her daily walk, Paul commented, "A duck. She looks just like a duck." They both laughed at the apt comparison. Morgan heard their laughter and waved.

"She's somethin'." Jake watched her go. "Even if you told her to her face she looked like a duck, she wouldn't care. Sometimes when you talk to her, she don't even hear you."

"Women! I never understood them, especially one that changes as much as Morgan. She's all sweet when Seth's here and then she comes back spittin' fire. Now she's like one of the hens, just settin' on her eggs."

Jake grinned, showing his near-toothless gums. "That she is, a hen on her nest."

January of 1851 was very cold, and there were some days when Lupita made Morgan stay in the house and forget her walk. Morgan was just as content to sit by the fire, nibbling on *bizcochitos* and *empañaditas*, as she was walking.

The baby became more and more active. Morgan rubbed her enormous stomach and was pleased with each kick. She never thought of the actual birth, only of the time when she'd hold her daughter in her arms.

In the ninth month, Morgan stopped her walks altogether. Her hands were swollen too badly to sew and her feet no longer fit the old *huaraches*.

Jake became more nervous with every passing day. "When's that baby going to be born?" he demanded.

Neither Morgan nor Lupita paid any attention to him.

"You women don't seem to understand that that child is very close to being my grandchild. I'm worried. I've seen lots of women going to have babies, but never one to gain as much weight as her."

Morgan smiled at him. "Lupita, you know what I'd really like to have? Strawberries. I can taste them, so red and juicy. In Kentucky, we used to have the sweetest strawberries. And peaches! The juice would run down your arm. I think I could eat a bushel basket of peaches. And—"

"See! That's what I mean. It just ain't healthy for a woman to eat that much, or even a man to eat that much. She's so fat now somebody has to help her in and out of the chair. That baby's going to smother to death. Lord! If that baby ain't born soon, I'm goin' to go crazy." He grabbed his coat and stormed out into the cold air.

As Paul watched him go, pipe in hand, he heard Morgan. "And blackberries. I'd risk a body covered in chiggers for a pint of blackberries right now." He laughed to himself.

Lupita had begun to sleep in the big house. When she heard Morgan stirring in the bedroom, she was quickly in the room with her. Morgan was trying to change the bedclothes.

At the sight of Lupita, she began her explanation. "I guess Jake is right—I do eat too much. My stomach hurts and when I finally did go to sleep, I woke up again to find I'd wet the bed. I hope you won't tell him; he'll worry even more."

Lupita went to Morgan and guided her to a chair. "Now sit down and I'll change the bed. Does your stomach still hurt?"

"Yes, it . . . oh . . . Lupita. The baby! Lupita, it's the baby, isn't it?"

"Yes. Very soon now you will have a new baby."

"I'm so glad. Victoria. How about Victoria?"

"What the hell's going on in here? I suppose she got up to get something to eat."

"Out! We are going to have a baby."

"Oh." Jake's face became somber. "I'll get the doctor." He turned toward the door.

"I need no doctor meddling in this. I have felt the baby and he is in the right position. I've delivered too many to let some man tell me what to do. Now get out, both of you," she said as Paul came in the front door. "I'll call you when we have a new little Colter."

The delivery was easy. It seemed only minutes before Lupita was saying, "There's the head. Push again. Good. Slowly . . . ah."

Morgan fell back on the pillows, her hair damp with sweat. "Victoria. Let me see my little girl."

"Morgan, little madonna, your little girl is a boy. A very large and healthy boy."

Quickly she finished washing the baby and wrapped him in a clean cotton blanket. Morgan put her arms out to the baby. Lupita finished cleaning the mother and checking to make sure there were no complications with the afterbirth.

She could hear Jake and Paul in the next room. "They'll want to see you, now. Is it all right?"

"Yes. He's beautiful, isn't he, Lupita? Lots of hair, too. Look at his little hands."

Quietly, Jake and Paul looked down on Morgan and her new son. "He's going to be as big as his pa."

"What's his name? Cecilia?" Paul laughed.

Morgan smiled up at him. "Adam. My own sweet little Adam." As she said the name, Adam screwed up his face, opened his mouth and let out a lusty yell.

"The baby is hungry. You will have to leave now and we will quiet him."

"Hungry!" Jake was indignant. "He's been eating like a pig for nine months and now he's not ten minutes old and he's hungry!"

They all laughed while Lupita shooed the men out. Morgan and Lupita were alone with the baby. It was some time before Morgan's milk was enough for Adam's huge appetite.

In the morning, Jake was relieved to see that Morgan ate only a normal breakfast. Lupita laughed at him. "You think your little girl is going to look like me? No. It was only the baby wanting so much to eat. She will soon be as slim as she was before. You will see. Already Adam gives her much exercise. He is a healthy baby."

From the day of Adam's birth, he never lacked for someone to give him attention. It seemed to Morgan that sometimes she had to fight to get to hold her own son. At first she had been almost afraid of him, but she soon realized his strength. He loved water and happily drenched his mother when she bathed him.

For the first three months, Morgan was content to stay in the house and see to the needs of her young son. But after a while, she began to grow restless. Gone was the placidity of her pregnancy. She began to ride for a short time each day and the weight she had gained melted off her, leaving her body smooth and slim once again.

As she studied her body at night, she found very little change. Her breasts were fuller because she was still nursing him, but her stomach was again flat and her legs were slim. She remembered her pregnancy as if it were a long dream, and she shuddered to remember the enormous amount of weight she had gained. "Oh well," she murmured aloud, "at least there won't be any more children." The thought brought Seth to mind, and for the first time in months, she again felt anger and resentment. He had treated her unforgivably.

Lupita's cottons once again swallowed Morgan. So, on one of his trips into Santa Fe for supplies, Paul returned with Mrs. Sanchez and several bolts of fabric. For three weeks Mrs. Sanchez stayed at the Colter ranch, and the three women sewed constantly on Morgan's new wardrobe. There were two riding habits, several day dresses, and more dresses for shopping or visiting. Morgan had brought evening gowns from San Francisco.

Morgan wrote to Theron often, and he was delighted with the news of the baby. Theron and Jeannette were well. He had not hired another assistant. His clients still asked about her. As always, Theron begged her to return.

His letters always made Morgan a little sad. Although she was surrounded by people she loved and who loved her, there were times when she was lonely.

By August, 1851, Adam was six months old. He was a happy child and liked everyone. Frank came to visit and Adam was immediately taken with him. Frank car-

271

ried him about on his horse and Adam laughed happily. Sometimes Morgan accused Jake and Paul of making fools of themselves over the little boy.

In September, Morgan turned twenty-one. Lupita planned a party. Morgan wore a deep blue satin gown that Theron had bought her. When she tried it on, she was surprised to find it loose.

"You have lost too much weight. You do not eat enough. I have watched you and you are pining for something—or someone."

Morgan shook her head as the larger woman pinned the waist of her dress. "That's silly, Lupita. I'm perfectly happy. I have everything I need right here."

"Except a man."

"I have Adam."

"Yes, *señora*."

"Lupita, don't use that trick. I am happy and I mean it, and stop playing the docile servant."

"Whatever the *señora* wants."

"Lupita!" But she was gone. Morgan smiled to herself. She's wrong, she thought, I've just lost weight because I try to keep Adam from crawling into the stove. Anyone would lose weight running after Adam. She kissed her sleeping son, his blond hair curling about his face. He moved and made a few sucking motions with his mouth. A deep dimple appeared briefly in his cheek. Just like Seth, she thought. Just like Seth. She tried to brush the idea from her mind and went outside to greet her guests.

Many of the people there that night were strangers, and Morgan was glad when the party was over. When she had removed her satin gown and slipped into her plain cotton nightgown, she gazed at the bed and began to cry.

"What's wrong with me?" she asked. "I have everything, but I want more." Her voice woke Adam, and

272

she was glad to go and comfort him. It was a long time before she went to sleep.

The snows began early that year and the winter dragged on and on. Adam seemed to grow some each day, and she and Lupita were busy sewing clothes for him. Jake and Paul whittled wooden horses and cows for him, gradually creating an entire wooden ranch, complete with house, barn, fences, wagons, and men. Lupita filled the little toy house with furniture and food. She even made a replica of Adam. Adam rewarded everyone with squeals of laughter and a sometimes rather sticky hug.

Morgan's memories of Seth increased day by day and she began to be very restless. She wanted to go away from the ranch for a while. She worried about Seth's return.

In February, Adam was one year old. Lupita and Morgan baked an enormous cake, and Frank and Louisa brought their six children to share in the celebration. Adam was shy around the other children for a few minutes, but quickly recovered. Frank tossed Adam into the air. "Goin' to be as big as your pa, ain't you?"

Jake grinned. "Looks more like him every day. Doesn't seem to have his pa's stubborn streak though, or at least not yet."

Lupita watched as Morgan's face whitened at the mention of Seth. Lupita knew the memories tormented her and she felt the pain her little mistress felt.

Soon after Adam's birthday, Morgan wrote to her father's lawyer in Albuquerque. She stated briefly that she had fulfilled the terms of the will and would like to know about her inheritance. She hoped she and Adam could go away together, possibly even to Europe.

She waited expectantly for weeks for an answer to her letter, but none came. She thought she might write again, but Lupita told her to wait a bit longer. The mails in New Mexico were very slow.

Now when Morgan went for her morning ride, Adam went with her. Often they took a basket of food to make a picnic.

Neither of them saw the pair of eyes that watched them every day. As the sun was going down and Jake, Paul, and Adam walked around the house, none of them sensed their quiet observer. Once the horse Adam played near was stung by a wasp, and the horse reared. Only Adam saw the strong brown arms that pulled the unsteady toddler from beneath the iron-clad hooves.

It had been nearly two months since Morgan wrote the letter. She sat under a tree some distance from the ranch house, a place where she often brought Adam to play and picnic. The stream that watered the ranch flowed here, and the grass was green and the shade cool. Their horse, grazing nearby, whinnied, but for the moment Morgan was lost in thought. She decided to send another letter to the lawyer. Why hadn't he replied?

"Eat." Adam smiled at his mother as she lifted him from the horse.

"No, not eat. I'm mama, remember, Adam?"

"Ma ma ma."

"Yes, that's right. Look Adam, a butterfly." She pointed, but Adam continued to stare at his mother. He tried to form words, but none would come. His eyes lifted from Morgan's to an area just behind her head. He laughed at what he saw there.

Morgan laughed with him. His dimpled smiles were infectious. Still smiling, she turned to look at what he saw. Her hand flew to her mouth in alarm. Quickly she stood up and held Adam behind her. He struggled to see around her skirts.

An Indian sat majestically on a black-and-white

pony. He was slim, his hair straight and black, falling just to his earlobes. It glistened in the morning sunlight. He was naked from the waist up. There was a rawhide strip around his neck which held a little leather pouch, decorated by black and red beads.

His legs were clad in buckskin with fringe down the sides. He looked exactly like the Apaches who had taken her to San Francisco. Her voice shook. "What do you want?"

The Indian dismounted fluidly. He stared at Morgan and at Adam and took a step closer. Morgan turned and picked up Adam, pulling him close to her. He pushed her away. He wanted to walk, not to be carried. Mortan pulled him even tighter.

"Go away. Leave us alone." Adam frowned at his mother. What was wrong?

"I'm really sorry to have frightened you so. Allow me to introduce myself. I am Gordon Matthews."

Morgan's eyes widened. The Indian's voice was deep, rather musical. It was refined. His words were carefully articulated and the endings sharply pronounced, unlike the Kentuckians Morgan had always known.

He watched her closely, as if waiting for something. When she pulled Adam closer, Gordon shrugged and sat down on the bank of the little stream.

"Yes," he said. "You do look like your pictures." He turned and smiled up at her, showing even, white teeth. "I really shouldn't do this, I know. Uncle Charley used to say I played at being an Indian. It *is* really rather ostentatious of me, isn't it?"

"Osten . . ." Morgan loosened her hold on Adam, who had decided to remove the trim from her riding habit. She was confused.

"I really enjoy the game, and I get to play it so seldom these days. On the ranch the men like to forget that I'm half-Indian. So I like to dress up whenever I

275

can. I have a great deal of trouble with my hair. You see, it tends to curl, so I have to use a little lard on it. I'm sure my ancestors would disown me for not using buffalo grease, but these are modern times, are they not?" He paused.

"Morgan, please sit by me. I may get a cramp in my neck if you keep standing."

Morgan took a step farther from him. "Who are you? How do you know my name?"

Gordon sighed and then stood up. "I think one needs to keep in better shape to play Indian." He rubbed his neck. "The name Gordon Matthews means nothing to you?"

"No."

"Your father never mentioned me in his letters?"

"My father? Letters?"

"Morgan, please. Stop being so frightened. I won't hurt you. Here, let me take Adam and then we can talk."

Morgan twisted her body so that Adam was farther from him.

"It's your decision, but he is ruining your habit. Adam—look." He held out the beaded pouch and Adam reached for it. Gordon held his arms to Adam and Adam lunged toward him. Gordon caught the sturdy boy. "Another year and he'll be bigger than you are, Morgan. Now, let's sit down."

Gordon sat down again, took off the pouch, and gave it to Adam, who happily toddled off with his prize.

"He's a very handsome young man. I believe he's going to look like his father. Seth is a large man, isn't he?" Gordon turned back to look at Morgan. "You know, you look very much like your father when you frown like that. All right, since you don't know, I'll explain. Uncle Charley always said I took hours to get to a point. My father always said my education had interfered with my thinking. They were probably both correct." He chuckled ruefully.

"I am serious, Morgan. Unless you sit down, I won't explain one thing. My neck is really beginning to hurt."

Morgan's mind was whirling. This was preposterous. He looked like an Indian, one of the dirty Indians that had traveled with Jacques. But he sounded like an educated Yankee. She sat down on the bank, several feet away from him.

"I run the Three Crowns."

"Three Crowns?"

"You really don't know, do you? Your father and my father were partners in the ranch south of Albuquerque, the ranch called the Three Crowns. My father was killed in an accident three years ago."

Morgan saw a look of pain cross his face. Adam came back to them and pulled at the silver bracelet on Gordon's upper arm. Gordon smiled at the boy, removed the bracelet, and handed it to him. Adam promptly put it in his mouth, tasted it, and then walked away again, holding Gordon's possessions, one in each hand.

"He certainly is an energetic boy. I'll wager he never gives you a moment's peace."

"Go on with your story, Mr. Matthews."

"Gordon. I don't understand how you know nothing of your father when he knew everything about you. There are pictures, drawings of you, everywhere in the house. They show you at every age. A lot of them are of you on horseback, and some are of you peeping out a carriage window."

"No one drew pictures of me. How could they be of me? I never saw my father again after we left New Mexico. My mother refused to answer my questions about him."

"Hmmm. This is a puzzle! I guess you don't remember much about New Mexico. After all, you were about the same age as Adam when you left."

"I remember riding in a wagon and being very thirsty."

"That would have been the trip to Kentucky. Your mother was such a stubborn woman. When she made up her mind to leave, she did. She refused to wait for the guide your father hired.

"Of course, the ranch was really nothing in those days, just a little adobe shack. And your mother had to cook and clean for two men and me. She was expecting you then, and she was so clumsy. She hated the dirt and the dryness. Pa and I used to hear her complaining to Uncle Charley—that's your father—for hours each night about how rough her skin was, how tired she was, how she hated everything."

Gordon reached across the distance between them and took Morgan's hand. "Smooth, yet I know you do a fair share of work on this ranch."

She pulled her hand back. "How do you know what I do around here?"

"I've been watching." Gordon laughed at the astonished expression on Morgan's face. "I told you it's too seldom that I get to play at being an Indian. So when the chance arises, I take it. These rather suit me, don't you think?" He motioned to the buckskins covering his slim, muscular legs.

Adam toddled back to Gordon and his mother. He had trouble holding onto both his treasures, so Gordon put the pouch around Adam's neck and hung the bracelet on the leather thong along with the pouch. Adam grasped at a flower, and came away with only part of the head. As he dropped it in his mother's lap, he fell heavily backwards. He quickly got up and ran away, stumbling every few feet.

"You were so much like Adam when you were his age, but of course on a smaller scale. You had that funny streaked blond hair even then, curling around your face. You smiled a lot then and, like Adam, you thought no one was a stranger. I think I adopted you from the moment I saw you, when you were about

278

twenty minutes old. The day I came home and you were gone, I cried until I was sick. It was a week before I could eat again."

"Gordon . . . I . . . this is so new to me. The impression I have of the time I was in New Mexico is so different. My mother hardly mentioned it except to tell of the miseries she suffered."

"I know a lot about your mother, too. No"—he held Morgan's arm—"Adam needs to fall hundreds of times before he learns to walk. Let him be . . . We always assumed those letters were from you. The ones after Uncle Charley's death were from some man, some agency. I guess they were always from him."

"What letters?"

"About a year after you left, the letters started coming, one a month, very regularly. I never read one, but Uncle Charley told us in detail what was in them. It's funny to realize you knew nothing about us and we knew so much about you. I grew up hearing about little Morgan every day. Remember the time you fell off your horse when you were eight and cut your leg? When the doctor sewed it, you screamed so loudly that the groom had trouble quieting the horses in the stables."

"Yes, I remember," Morgan said quietly. It was still impossible to believe that this man could know so much about her.

"Pa and Uncle Charley and I always looked forward to those letters, and the sketches. My favorite is of you taking your first jump, when you were about seven. Your little hat was mostly over your face."

"This is too much! My mother never told me about my father, nothing good, anyway. I grew up with little thought of him. Trahern House and my mother were my whole world. And then the will! I hated my father then!"

"Yes," Gordon looked away, embarrassed. "I tried to talk him out of that, but Uncle Charley said, 'That

279

damned woman's made her hate men. If I don't do something, she'll rot in that big old house and dry up just like her mother did.' I suggested he stipulate that you come out here, but leave out the part about your having to get married. But he said that as soon as word was out about the will, lots of young men would be swarming around you. That's what he wanted for his pretty little daughter. He knew your mother had made you afraid of people, especially men. He just wanted them to come to you so you could choose any one you wanted. It wasn't meant to be an ordeal."

Morgan stared ahead at the little stream, lost in her thoughts. She had thought her father wanted to punish her for some reason. He had only wanted to help her. She *had* been afraid of men, afraid of everything, and he had known all about it. He had prevented her from retreating. He had cared about her, cared very much.

Gordon jumped to catch Adam as he nearly tumbled into the icy water. "There now, why don't you stay up here?" Unperturbed, Adam sauntered after more flowers.

"I was really surprised when you asked Seth Colter to marry you."

Morgan's head jerked up. "How do you know that?"

"Possessing a superior intelligence, I deduced it. After Uncle Charley died, the letters kept coming for a while. I was furious when I read what your Uncle Horace had planned. I was very nearly on my way to Kentucky when the last letter came and said that you had married Colter. I wrote a letter to one of Uncle Charley's old friends in Kentucky and got all the gossip, about how Colter was such a prize catch and he had eloped after meeting you only once. I knew that anyone who had been reared as you had did not captivate 'prize catches' in one evening. Besides, the agent had already told me how Horace dressed you. So I put two and two together. And I was right!"

"Yes, you were right. For a while it worked out well

. . . Adam!" Morgan jumped to her feet, but Gordon lithely ran after Adam and again caught him before he fell into the stream. Gordon tossed him into the air and Adam laughed loudly. "I'm Gordon. Can you say Gordon?"

"Or."

"Good enough. 'Or' it is."

"Eat. Eat." Adam squealed.

"Good idea."

"Gordon, this is all too much for me to take in. You've upset all the beliefs I've had about my father, even my mother."

Gordon smiled. "Well, then, let's take Adam's advice and eat. I'd like to sample some of the cooking you learned from Jean-Paul. He cost Uncle Charley a *fortune*."

"My father paid for Jean-Paul?"

"Of course. You don't think your mother would have let a man into her house without a great deal of persuasion, do you?"

Morgan spread out the picnic lunch. "There's something I've never understood. Why did my mother's father leave Trahern House to his son-in-law rather than to his daughter?"

Gordon put a tiny quiche in his mouth, handed one to Adam, and laughed. "Old Morgan Trahern was a smart one. He knew how spoiled your mother was. He left everything to his son-in-law because he knew his daughter was too headstrong to control that much property. He also hoped to keep her from leaving your father. But Uncle Charley was too soft. He could have made her stay with him in New Mexico. He tried to get her to leave you with him, but—" Gordon filled his mouth again and shrugged. "—Uncle Charley never pushed anyone."

Morgan's eyes flashed at him. "Except me. He used his will to push me to do what he wanted."

Gordon smiled at her. His eyes sparkled. "Still

281

angry, huh? Well, it looks like it came out all right." He rubbed his cheek on Adam's head.

They finished their lunch quickly. "Excellent, Morgan. Jean-Paul was worth it."

"Merci beaucoup, monsieur."

"Now! Let's go back to the house."

"Gordon, wait."

"No, I know what you're going to say. 'I wouldn't give you a plugged nickel for a dozen gol-danged Injuns.' That sound like Jake?"

Morgan had to laugh because Gordon's imitation of Jake sounded so much like him.

"Watch this." Quickly, Gordon went to his saddlebags and got a bar of soap. Within minutes, he had soaped and rinsed his hair in the stream and then returned to his horse for clothing. He stepped behind some trees and a few minutes later emerged in a light blue cotton shirt and darker blue cotton pants. He looked nothing at all like an Indian.

He smiled at Morgan's astonishment. "Sky Eyes, the Comanche warrior, has changed into Gordon Matthews, ordinary but rather attractive white man."

" 'Sky Eyes'?"

Gordon looked at her fiercely, then rolled his eyes. "Sapphire-blue eyes that captivate women in four states, and you didn't even notice."

Morgan laughed, the first good laugh she'd had in a long time.

"That's better. Now you look more like the little girl who used to ride with me on my pony."

"Or. Or." Adam tugged at Gordon's pant leg, wanting to be picked up.

They all rode back to the house slowly, Adam riding in front of Gordon. Morgan had too many thoughts for further talk, so Adam and Gordon kept up a conversation between themselves.

Jake was waiting for them, close to the house, with a

rifle. Morgan felt that, as much as anything, he didn't like another man so near Adam.

"This is Gordon Matthews. He and I are partners in the ownership of the Three Crowns. It's . . ."

"The Three Crowns! Glad to meet you, Mr. Matthews. I've heard about the Three Crowns since I first come to New Mexico. You say Morgan's your partner?"

Jake warmly clasped Gordon's hand. As they walked together toward the house, Gordon turned and caught Morgan's eye. He put two fingers to the back of his head and wiggled them, like feathers. Then he winked at Morgan before returning to the conversation with Jake.

Morgan laughed at Gordon's play. She felt better than she had for a long time. She hurried after Adam, who was trying to catch up to the two men.

Supper that night was fun. Adam decided he wanted his chair moved next to Gordon's. "Gor," he learned to say.

Morgan sat quietly with her own thoughts through the others' conversation.

"How many head of cattle you run on a place like that?" Jake asked. "What about Injuns? Any trouble with them?"

Morgan felt Gordon's silent laughter at the question. After supper, the two of them walked outside together, Adam toddling behind.

"I can feel the difference between the altitudes of Santa Fe and of Albuquerque." As Adam's steps slowed, Gordon picked up the boy, who snuggled against his shoulder.

"Come live with me, Morgan."

She didn't move, but stared ahead.

"I know something's wrong here. No one mentions Seth's name, yet I feel he's still alive."

"Yes, he is," Morgan whispered.

283

"Whatever's happened is your business. I don't need to know, but I do know that your father would have wanted you to come to the ranch. I know I'd like for you to come. I'm a bachelor. My father's people are in the East. My mother's people are Comanches and, in spite of my games, I know little about them.

"There are too many memories for you here, Morgan. Come back with me. I'll make a home for you and Adam." He stroked the hair of the sleeping child.

"I don't know, Gordon. I really don't know you. But what you say about there being too many memories here is correct. Let me think about it and give you an answer soon. Right now, I need to put my son to bed."

She walked ahead as Gordon followed with the dozing Adam. "Do you know that I've loved your mother since she was twenty minutes old? I don't care where your father is, because I plan to move heaven and earth to become your new daddy. Would you like that, son?" He kissed the dimpled cheek of the boy. "We'll go to the ranch. And inside of a year, I'll be your pa."

It took Gordon two days to persuade Morgan to go with him to the Three Crowns. The major opposition came from Jake; he couldn't stand the idea of Adam's leaving.

"I have to, Jake. What if Seth returns? I can't be here then. I don't want to see him."

Gordon could hardly control his elation as he loaded the wagon with Morgan's and Adam's clothes. "I'll send a hand back to return the wagon, and he'll let you know that we got there safely."

The goodbyes were tearful. "Send us letters. Tell us about yourself and the boy. The house will be sad without you," Lupita cried. Paul gave Adam two more carved wooden horses for his ranch house. Jake took it the worst, almost refusing to see them off.

Adam waved to them for a long time, enjoying the

unusual pleasure of riding in a wagon. By the time they reached Santa Fe, he was fretful and Morgan was glad to stop. She wanted to purchase fabric for some new clothes for him. The days were getting longer and the afternoons hotter. Gordon had told her it was much warmer farther down the mountains toward Albuquerque.

Gordon had taken Adam with him and promised to meet Morgan by the wagon in an hour. Morgan's last stop took her to a new shop, one she'd never seen. It carried imported silks and velvets, handmade laces, as well as the sturdy cottons she needed for Adam. She didn't hear the footsteps behind her.

"Well, Mrs. Colter, it is such a surprise to see you here again."

"Miss Wilson." Marilyn Wilson was the last person Morgan wanted to see. "How have you been? Is this your shop?"

"I've been quite well, thank you, and yes, my father bought this shop for me about six months ago. I hear you came back alone from San Francisco."

Morgan clenched her hands into fists.

"Tell me, how is Joaquín Montoya? Wasn't it strange how he and his sister packed up and left for Spain that way, just a few days after their party?"

Before Morgan could answer, Marilyn continued, "All of Santa Fe thought it was strange how you and Joaquín rode off together right in the middle of the party. Of course, as I mentioned to Seth, you two had spent a great deal of time together already."

"You . . ."

Neither of the women heard the shop door open.

"Then, of course, all of Santa Fe knew Seth spent the winter alone on the Colter ranch."

"Ahem." Both women turned to see Gordon and Adam. Adam let go of Gordon's hand and ran to his mother to show her the little wooden trees Gordon had bought him.

Morgan picked her son up. "Pretty, aren't they? They'll go with the rest of your ranch. Oh—Miss Wilson"—Morgan acted as if she had just remembered the woman's presence—"let me introduce my son to you. Adam, this is Miss Wilson." Adam looked at the woman for only a second and then began jabbering to his mother about his trees. He smiled, showing dimples so like Seth's.

Gordon took Adam. "I guess it's time we left Santa Fe." He didn't like the lightning atmosphere between the two women.

As they got to the door, Morgan turned back. "I guess all of Santa Fe doesn't know about my son. I think you'll agree there's no doubt who his father is. Goodbye, Miss Wilson."

In the wagon, Morgan was quiet at first. Then, a few miles outside of Santa Fe, the tears began to flow. Gordon pulled the wagon over under some large cottonwoods. Without a word, he set Adam on the ground and then lifted Morgan from the wagon. He held her in his strong arms and let her cry. He sat under a tree and rocked her gently. Adam heard his mother and came to investigate. When he realized she was crying, he began to cry, too. Gordon tried to keep one arm around each of them, but the more one cried, the more the other cried.

It took him a few minutes to realize that Morgan was laughing. "What's so blasted funny?"

"You. The look on your face. Two people crying in your arms and you trying to comfort both of them. I never saw such frustration."

Gordon grinned at her. "I'll have to remember the look for the next time you cry, so I can make you laugh. Anyway, it was worth it for a chance to hold you."

Gordon's seriousness made Morgan realize her position. She quickly moved from his lap and gathered Adam to her. Adam was happy again when he saw his mother smile, and ran to explore a nearby sound.

"You want to tell me about it?"

Morgan shook her head.

"Who was that woman, anyway? You seemed to know one another pretty well."

"Know one another! I've only seen that . . . viper a few times in my life. And each time, she's caused me problems. Her vicious tongue helped break up my marriage!"

"No. It was Seth's temper and jealousy that caused the rift between you."

Morgan looked at Gordon in puzzlement.

"Jake told me the whole story."

"Jake told you! He had no right. Does he tell *everyone* he meets, or just overnight guests?"

"Calm down, Morgan. He thought I should know, and he's right. He said it was Seth's fault and that you had every right to be angry."

"Angry! I believe I feel an emotion a little stronger than anger! I never want to see him again, not after the way he treated me. When we get to the ranch, I'm going to have my father's lawyer arrange a divorce."

Gordon felt like doing his best Comanche war yell at this news. "Morgan." He lifted her chin and smiled at her, but her deep frown still remained. "Oh, no."

"What is it?"

"That's my best melt-the-girls smile, and it didn't even make you lose your frown. I must be losing my touch."

"Gordon," Morgan smiled, "what would I do without you?"

"I hope you never find out." His eyes betrayed his seriousness, and Morgan looked away, embarrassed.

They spent the night camping. It was the first time

Morgan had slept outdoors since she had been taken to San Francisco by Jacques.

"Warm enough, Morgan?"

"Yes, I am. Gordon, thank you for taking Adam and me back to the ranch. I needed a change, and you came at the right time."

Gordon settled into his own bedroll. "Purely selfish, Morgan," he whispered to himself.

~ *Chapter Eighteen* ~

"HEY, mister, watch where you're goin'!" The man, one
eye twitching, squinted up at Seth. "You sick or somethin', mister?"

Seth stared at the man, unseeing. "What?"

"You hear about the gold out at Cypress Pass? From
what I hear, it's the biggest strike yet. You goin'?" He
stared up at Seth. "You sure you're not sick?"

"No, I'm fine. Where is this Cypress Pass?"

"No need to ask that, just follow all these people."
He put out one grimy hand and gestured to the confusion around them.

Seth looked at the people in the streets for the first
time. Work. That's what he wanted—work.

"These people are going to look for gold?"

"Boy, mister, where you been? Sure, that's what's
goin' on. The whole country knows about the gold and
here you stand in the middle of it and . . . Listen, bud,
just go over there to the general store and get some
gear. The storekeep'll know what you need." He
watched Seth turn toward the store. "And get some
clothes. Those duds are too fancy for the gold fields . . .
You sure get all kinds out here." He muttered this last
remark to himself.

As Seth walked toward the store, he turned back.
Morgan, his brain screamed. I'll go back to her, I can't
stand this. His mind raged at him and he saw her face,
the tears running down her cheeks. He heard her say, "I

love you, Seth," over and over. But after what he'd done, she'd never take him back. What about Montoya? What about this Shaw that she lived with?

He stopped walking. No, it was over. He and Morgan were finished. She'd chosen her life and it didn't include him. He'd had his revenge on her and now he could go ahead with his life. He'd mourned enough last winter. He remembered Morgan's sweet little body, her golden hair tangling between them, the eagerness of her kisses. And "I love you, Seth," cried out in his mind again and again.

"No!" He clutched his hands over his ears. A man and woman turned to stare at him, then shrugged and continued walking.

It's finished. He turned again to the store. Yes, he thought, I've had my revenge. But why isn't it sweet?

The storekeeper barely looked up from his ledger. The sight of Seth, his impressive size, and the expensive suit he wore caused him to take a second look. "Help you, mister?"

"I need some things for panning gold."

The clerk sighed. They were all alike, young and old. The gold fever hit everyone. He reached under the counter, never leaving his stool. He caught the neck of a burlap bag and slung it onto the counter beside him. It rattled and clanged as it hit. "Fifty dollars, cash."

Seth counted out the money. "How do I find out how to use this stuff?"

The clerk returned his attention to his ledger. "Ask anybody at the site. Anybody over three years old can show you."

"Thanks."

The clerk watched the big man leave, shook his head, and looked back down at the ledger. He considered the panners fools. He'd made his own gold strike and had never had to break his back in the sun for months on end.

Seth went to the livery stable to get his horse. He

changed from the expensive suit to his sturdy cotton work clothes. Contemptuously, he tossed the suit into a corner of the stall. It had seen too many bad memories for him to want to keep it.

The moon was up and the way to the new gold strike was easy to find. By the time he reached Cypress Pass, the sun was just beginning to lighten the horizon. It took Seth very little time to find a place in the stream and to learn to use the gold pan.

After several hours of bending, his back hurt and his neck ached. His head throbbed and he felt the burned skin of his back through his shirt. The pain was good; he hoped it would block out his vivid memories of Morgan. He attacked the pan with new energy.

He didn't really see the sun set, only noticed that he couldn't see the pan any longer. He looked around and saw a man entering a tent, carrying a lantern. He walked toward the man.

"Twenty dollars for your lantern."

The man looked up at Seth in surprise, then grinned. A front tooth was chipped and discolored. "Sure."

Seth returned to the stream. The flecks of gold glinted in the lantern light. When the sun came up, he was still at it. The other gold panners paid little attention to the newcomer. They all knew how it was when the fever first hit.

By noon, Seth was beginning to collapse. His eyes blurred and his head was light and he had trouble holding the pan steady. Only vaguely did he feel the hand on his arm, see the hand that removed the pan from his grasp. In the back of his mind, something whispered, "Morgan," but he knew it couldn't be.

"Here, eat this."

He sat down heavily. As the smell of stew reached him, he realized he hadn't eaten for a long time. He took the plate and ate greedily. The pan was filled twice more before he felt he had eaten enough.

There were no more trees in the ugly little camp, so

he stretched out on his bedroll in the shade beside a tent. He was instantly asleep. The girl stared down at the big sleeping man and smiled. Although he was twice her size, something made her want to take care of him, like a little boy. She knelt down and caressed the hair at his temple. Then she started, and quickly looked to see if anyone had seen her. No one had. She went back to her parents' tent.

The sun was just going down when Seth awoke, the horizon pink. His first waking thoughts were of Morgan. It seemed he never remembered how things actually stood between them in those first drowsy minutes. He always reached out, expecting to find her near him. Then he remembered.

"I brought you some more food."

He looked up at the girl standing over him. Hair darker than Morgan's, not nearly as pretty, and . . . Damn it, Colter, don't compare every woman to Morgan.

Seth nodded his thanks to the girl and began to eat, slowly this time. "Did you bring me food earlier today?"

Shyly, she nodded, not looking up at him.

"I thank you. I'm afraid I lost track of time working out there. Another few hours and I might not have been worth saving."

Her eyes flew to his. They betrayed her opinion of his worth. She lowered her lashes when she saw him staring at her. "We're camped over there," she pointed. "There's Ma and Pa and Ben and me. Ben's my big brother." There was pride in her voice. "Ma and me cook for some of the men here, the ones who ain't got wives." She looked up at Seth questioningly.

"Well," he smiled at her, "I guess you can cook for me." The idea of a wife was too painful to Seth.

She smiled back at him. "I'm Lee Ann Coleman."

"Seth . . . Seth Blake."

She was beginning to lose her shyness. "Don't you have a tent, Mr. Blake?"

"Seth. No, I don't."

She was quiet and seemed to be considering something. "I saw you working out there. You must be awful hungry to strike it rich, or else you're trying to kill yourself."

Seth was serious. "Maybe a little of both."

"I got to be getting back now, Mr. . . . Seth. I'll bring you breakfast in the morning. You better sleep now."

Seth watched her go. The old dress was faded and patched, but clean. It fit her too tightly, showing her stocky little body. He remembered Morgan's lush curves and he saw her again as she had looked in the bedroom at his ranch. Damn! he thought, will she ever get out of my mind?

Lee Ann was up early the next morning, heaping Seth's plate with fried eggs and fried bread. As she went to get a steaming mug of coffee, her mother caught her. "Why can't he come to the tent like the rest of the men? What's so special about this one?"

"Oh, Ma, he's . . ."

Corinne looked into her daughter's eyes and then smiled. So that's how it was. She'd been about Lee Ann's age when she'd met Larry. "Go on then and take him his breakfast. But hurry back, 'cause I need your help."

Corinne watched her daughter go. She knew Lee Ann would never be a beauty—her little face was too plain for that, and her sturdy little body would never be elegant—but she had a good heart. Sometimes when she looked up at you with those liquid brown eyes, she could melt your heart. Corinne had no doubt that this new man was in some kind of trouble. Not law trouble, more likely a broken heart. Lee Ann always loved the helpless ones. Corinne sighed. Too often, once Lee Ann had them on their feet again, they'd go running off. Lord, she prayed, let this one be different.

Seth was already working when Lee Ann got there.

He stopped when he saw her. "I'm glad to see you. I could eat these flakes of gold, I'm so hungry."

Lee Ann sat beside the big man, her legs drawn up under her, and watched him eat. "I like to see a man eat. I just hate these puny little ones who eat three eggs for breakfast and call it a meal."

Seth remembered how Morgan and Lupita had always plied him with food and more food. He looked at the meal of Lee Ann's, the eggs and bread swimming in grease. It was a far cry from Morgan's brioches and cheese-filled omelets.

"You from around here?"

"New Mexico."

"We been through there once. Too dry for me. I like it better here."

Seth looked around at the dirty, barren camp. There were many tents and a few haphazard shacks. The trees had long ago been used for firewood. Even the stream was discolored with dishwater, cooking grease, soap-suds, and the leavings from hundreds of slop jars. He remembered the clean, clear hills and arroyos on his ranch.

Seth quickly finished his meal and went back to work. The more he worked, the more tired he was, the less he was able to think. Yet at night, under the stars, he often lay awake for hours remembering Morgan, every word they'd ever spoken, every caress they'd shared.

A month passed. The days began to run together. The other people in the camp had tried to be friendly, but Seth's sullenness made them withdraw. Only Lee Ann stayed by him, bringing his meals three times a day.

It was Lee Ann who got the tent for him. One of the diggers was giving up, selling out, going back east. She bought everything without even asking Seth. Seth told her to take what gold she needed from his ever-growing hoard. She marveled that he trusted her so much, but also wanted to scold him for not hiding his gold like her pa did.

When Seth fell onto the hard cot at night, he hardly noticed the difference between it and the ground he had grown accustomed to. He was used to Lee Ann's presence and took for granted that she kept his food hot until he was ready for it, kept his clothes washed, mended, and orderly.

One morning after Seth had been at Cypress Pass for two months, Lee Ann saw him packing his gear on his horse. His tent was already down and he was just rolling his blankets.

"Where you goin'?"

He missed the alarm in her voice. "This place is getting too crowded. Heard about a new place upriver and thought I'd try there for a while. The gold's played out here."

Lee Ann turned abruptly and started running back to her parents' tent.

Seth looked after her. He'd planned to stop and say goodbye to Lee Ann, but as he watched her go, he just shrugged. He didn't really care one way or another if he left the camp. He didn't really seem to care about anything anymore.

Lee Ann ran to her mother, breathless. "He's leavin', Ma, and I'm goin' with him."

There was no need to tell who "he" was. Corinne knew her daughter had thought of nothing but Seth Blake for two months. Corinne opened her mouth to protest, but one look at Lee Ann's eyes made her stop. She'd felt this way about Larry, too. There was no use trying to persuade Lee Ann to wait and get the man to marry her. Corinne and Larry hadn't been married until after Ben was born.

"I have to, Ma," she whispered.

The tears gathered in Corinne's eyes. "I know." She

hugged her daughter, a short fierce hug. "Well, let's hurry and get your things together. You'll have to take the mule."

"Oh, Ma, I can't. Pa needs him."

"That's all right. He needs his daughter, too. If he can spare one, he can spare the other. There, now, that's everything." They had hurriedly stuffed Lee Ann's two other dresses into an old carpet bag.

"You'll tell them for me, Ma?"

"I will. You be careful, now. And Lee Ann," she called after her daughter, who was already climbing onto the mule, "if anything happens, you come back, you hear?"

Lee Ann nodded and headed the mule away from the tent.

She's so young, Corinne thought, and so happy. Please, Lord, let it turn out as good for her as it did for me.

Lee Ann caught up with Seth about a mile out of the camp.

He smiled at her. "Goin' into town?"

"No, I'm going with you."

He stopped his horse. "You're what? You can't go with me."

She smiled up at him. "I certainly can. You need me—to take care of you."

"What about your parents? And I don't need anyone."

Lee Ann continued smiling. "Ma understands. She ran off with Pa, just like I'm goin' with you."

Seth's eyes narrowed, his voice was stern. "*You* don't understand. I said I don't need anyone, and we're not going to be like your ma and pa."

Lee Ann's smile of confidence didn't dim.

"You have to go back. Don't you understand? I have a wife!"

Only for a second did a shadow cross Lee Ann's brown eyes. "If you have a wife, then why ain't she here? You need someone here with you now, and that's me."

"My wife . . ." Seth began. He could see it was no use. There was a will of steel behind those soft eyes. "Don't expect anything from me, Lee Ann, because there's nothing left to give," he said quietly before he turned his horse toward town again.

As Lee Ann kicked her mule to follow, she thought, at least it'll be easier to fight a ghost than a flesh-and-blood wife. I'll make him forget. She was happy as she smiled at Seth's broad back, the bronzed muscles moving under the rough cotton shirt.

For months, Lee Ann and Seth traveled from one gold field to another. After the first few weeks, Lee Ann began to lose her natural happiness. Seth ignored all her attempts at any sort of a relationship. One night, when she had crawled onto his cot with him, he merely shrugged and turned away. In the morning, he had pulled her close to him and she was so happy she laughed aloud, the happiness spilling over her. The sound of her laughter made Seth look at her, shaking off the drowsiness of sleep. Abruptly, he pushed her from him.

She had thought he'd talk more when she lived with him, but if anything, he talked less. As the days wore on, she lost her smile, and went about her chores lifelessly.

Seth was aware of Lee Ann and it nagged at him that she was unhappy. He'd tried to get her to go back to her parents, but each time he mentioned it, she'd cry. He'd finally dropped the idea.

On one of their trips to town for supplies, they met Johnny.

"Are you staying long, Mr. Daniels?" The girl was a pale blonde. She seemed to have no eyebrows or lashes.

"That depends, Miss Emory, on whether you're going to be around." He flashed even white teeth at her.

Lee Ann watched the scene absently. The young man was hardly out of his teens, not like her Seth, she thought. She looked to where Seth was studying new harnesses. *Her Seth!* He didn't even know she was around, half the time. She looked back at the young man. He was very handsome, and the three girls around him thought so, too.

"My pa's camp is not far away. Maybe you'd like to come for supper some night."

"That I would, Miss Cookson, but I'm sure my appetite would disappear with something as pretty as you so near me."

Lee Ann looked at Miss Cookson. Her nose was positively hooked! She turned away in disgust.

"Girls!" An older woman summoned the three women. Reluctantly, they left, amidst flamboyant goodbyes. Lee Ann kept her attention on the groceries.

"Now, young man, what can I get for you?" The clerk addressed Mr. Daniels.

"I'm not sure. I've never cooked anything before. What do I need?"

Lee Ann felt her heart lurch at the need in the boy's voice.

"Beans, first of all." He handed the boy a bag of dried beans.

"Aren't they a little hard to eat?"

Lee Ann couldn't suppress a giggle. She was still laughing when she felt a hand on her arm.

"Allow me to introduce myself—Johnny Daniels, Miss . . ."

"Lee Ann." She couldn't give Seth's last name, and her parents seemed so far away.

"Well, Miss Lee Ann."

"No, just Lee Ann."

"All right, just Lee Ann, possibly you could explain how I make these"—he held out the dried beans—"fit to eat." Johnny's eyes sparkled and Lee Ann responded to the laughter in them.

Seth turned to see Lee Ann smiling into the boy's eyes. He had not seen her look like that in months. There had been times when Morgan had looked at him in adoration. He tried to wipe the image from his mind.

He walked toward Lee Ann and she introduced them. As Seth watched Lee Ann's face light up, he realized how much he owed this girl for taking care of him for so long. He was poor company even for himself, much less for this young girl.

"Why don't you invite Mr. Daniels to supper, Lee Ann?"

Both Lee Ann and Johnny were happy at the prospect. As they left the store, Seth heard Johnny whisper to Lee Ann, "Is he your father?"

Seth looked down at himself. He felt old. He didn't like what he had become. He remembered how happy he'd been in the few weeks when he and Morgan had been together.

All through dinner that night, as the three sat in the dingy tent, Seth watched Lee Ann and Johnny. The eyes were wide as they discovered mutual interests and explored backgrounds. Able to stand it no longer, Seth left the tent, needing the cool night air.

"Did we do something?" Johnny asked.

"No, he's like that. Moody. Tell me some more about your family."

Johnny frowned for a moment. He wanted to ask Lee Ann just exactly what her relationship to Seth was, but he didn't know her well enough. Seth was a strange man.

Seth walked for a long while. Damn you, Morgan!

299

Everywhere I look, I'm reminded of you. It's been nearly a year since I saw you, and still I haven't been able to get you out of my mind for even a few hours.

I want you! He stopped walking and stared at the moon. It was a revelation. No matter what you've done, I still want you, Morgan.

But how? He couldn't just walk into that fancy house in San Francisco and demand to see her. What could he offer her that she didn't already have? Why would she leave the wealth and luxury she had in California to return to a little dirt-poor ranch in New Mexico? He couldn't expect that of her. She had her choice of men. Already all of San Francisco worshipped her beauty.

Money! That was the answer. He would go to her when he could lay diamonds at her feet. His eyes narrowed. Or sapphires, like the ones she wore at Montoya's party. Whatever she wanted he would give to her. He loved her. It was time he admitted that to himself. He felt as if a great burden had been lifted from him.

Purposefully, he strode back towards the tent. He had to see to Lee Ann. He owed her a great deal.

"Lee Ann." He burst into the tent. She and Johnny drew apart from their first tentative kiss. Seth knew then that he could use Johnny to repay Lee Ann. "Johnny, how'd you like to move in with us? Lee Ann would love to have you, and maybe the two of us could make a little money."

"Yes, sir."

Lee Ann stared at Seth. She had never seen him so animated. It had crossed her mind that he might be jealous, and she was willing to give up Johnny for Seth. What ever had caused the smile on his face now?

Lee Ann thought Seth had worked hard before, but it was nothing to what she saw now. The three of them worked together in the fields. No longer were Lee Ann's days taken up with just cooking and caring for Seth.

Sometimes the three of them rode into San Francisco. Lee Ann and Johnny spent the days looking at the new shops and houses which seemed to spring up overnight in the rapidly growing city. But Seth never joined them.

Seth realized that San Francisco was going to grow. Hundreds of people poured into the town every day. The gold fever attacked them like a disease. Many of these people would eventually settle here. He began using the gold he found to buy land. He rented land to the gold diggers. He leased it to men to put up new buildings. But he never sold it. What he bought, he held onto.

Johnny and Lee Ann were content to let Seth use their money for them. But after eight months, they were tired of living in a tent. They wanted to get married and buy a little home of their own. Seth tried to persuade them to hold onto their land, but they wanted out. Seth bought their shares of land from them.

Their wedding was quiet and Seth envied them their joyful faces. How he wished he and Morgan could have met one another normally and had an ordinary courtship. They might still be together.

It won't be long, Morgan, he vowed.

Seth missed Lee Ann and Johnny. Without Lee Ann there to make sure he ate, he lost weight. And he worked even longer hours. He dedicated himself to panning more gold and to collecting his rents and buying more land. He noticed little else.

"Hello."

Seth looked up to see a woman with red hair and a too-generous mouth. Her clothes were dirty, but had once been good.

"Hello." He smiled back.

"Well. *Well!* Won't I be the envy of every woman in this here camp? Mr. Good-Lookin' hisself has spoken to me."

Seth looked puzzled.

The woman laughed loudly. "You ought to know, honey, that every woman in camp has been pantin' after you. Not only are you the best-lookin' man here, you make the other women's men all look lazy."

Seth liked her easy openness. "Well, I guess we ought to remedy that. How about if we get out of the sun and sit a spell?"

"Wowee. I sure would like that, Mr. . . . ."

"Blake. Seth Blake."

"Seth?"

"What's wrong?"

"Nothing really. Just the name Seth reminds me of someone. My name's Jessy."

"Well, Jessy, I'm very glad to make your acquaintance."

Seth brought Jessy a tin cup of water, laced generously with whiskey.

"Real good water," she smiled. "Your woman about?"

"I don't have one. Not here, anyway."

Jessy propped herself on one arm and studied Seth. He sat on a wooden box and leaned against the tent pole. His massive legs were spread in front of him. She imagined him without his clothes. She liked her imaginings very much.

"How'd you like to have a roommate?"

Seth looked at Jessy's unwashed hair, at the dirt on her neck. He grinned at her, showing dimples. "That's the best offer I've had all day, but I'm afraid I'm going to have to pass."

"Mmmm. Too bad. Maybe I could do a little cookin' for you?"

"Now that I'd like."

"Well, then . . . thanks for the drink and I'll be seein' you. Maybe we'll work out somethin', Seth. A man like you is too temptin' to give up after just one try."

Seth went back to his work. Jessy's visit cheered him. True to her word, she brought a heaping plate of indescribable stew. Lee Ann's cooking had been a royal feast compared to Jessy's.

"Could I get you anything else?" Jessy asked when he'd finished. "Maybe you could use a little company overnight?"

Seth laughed and thanked her for both the food and her offer, but declined.

Jessy hadn't been so attracted to a man since she'd been sold at Madame Nicole's. Jessy always remembered Madame Nicole's as the height of her career, for she'd made her body her career. She loved men, and they loved her open easiness, her willingness to laugh.

Jessy had been bringing Seth meals for nearly a month when she first mentioned Morgan.

"You know, I guess I'll always be partial to any man named Seth. I knew a girl once, a real beauty, who was married to man named Seth. You never saw anybody so in love—*real* love, you know what I mean? Well, her Seth was killed, and you would of thought it was the end of the world. A neighbor, can you beat that, a neighbor, killed her husband and because she wouldn't bed the guy, he sold her to a Frenchman and his Apaches. That's when I met her. She cried all the way across the country for her Seth. The first few weeks she kept hopin' she was gonna have his kid. When she found out she wasn't, I thought she was gonna go crazy . . .

"Oh well, I'm boring you. I gotta go."

"No!"

Jessy turned to look at Seth. His eyes were fierce and he almost frightened her. His hand on her arm hurt her.

"Tell the rest of your story." His voice was harsh.

Jessy was puzzled. Maybe he'd seen Madame Ni-

303

cole's show and knew enough of the story already to know who she was talking about. Jessy straightened up and ran a hand through her tangled hair. Maybe he remembered her being in the show.

"Oh, Lord. All kinds of things happened to us. The Frenchman sold us to a whorehouse, Madame Nicole's. It's a real classy place. Maybe you've been there?"

She watched Seth's nod.

"We didn't work there. They auctioned us off. Morgan brought the highest price."

Jessy failed to notice Seth's whitened face. "What happened to her, this Morgan?"

"Well, Madame Nicole sold her to a pretty-boy, you know what I mean? I thought it was a dirty trick, but Morgan didn't care. All she ever talked about was her Seth. Me, I'd rather have a live one than a dead one, no matter how great a man the dead one was.

"Hey, you all right? You don't look so good. My story do that to you, or my cookin'?"

"I guess it's the sun. I've had too much sun."

"Well, you don't look good at all, like you was taken sick. You better stay out of the sun the rest of the day. I really gotta go now. You need anything, just holler." She touched Seth's forehead. "You are a little warm. I'll come back later and check on you."

"Oh, God! Morgan, what have I done to you?" He sat on the little camp stool, his head in his hands. "What ever have I done?"

He started walking, as he always did when he was upset, toward the top of the mountain. Memories began to flash before his eyes, more vivid this time than ever before.

He saw the Montoya party. Marilyn had told him that Morgan and Joaquín huddled together in corners. But he saw that in a new light now. He knew Marilyn, knew her well enough to remember that she lied and schemed to get what she wanted. Marilyn would have been angry about his marriage, would have wanted him to think his wife had lovers.

The note! Why had she written the note? Jessy had said Joaquín had tried to force Morgan into his bed. He could have forced her to write the note. But why? She must have known he wouldn't release her after what she had learned about him. But Morgan wouldn't know that. She had such trust in people.

Oh God! What she went through! Montoya sold her to some Apaches, to be used in a white-slave auction! Seth had heard of Madame Nicole's auctions. They were becoming famous in San Francisco. He'd heard, too, that sometimes the women purchased there were reluctant about their new jobs. It was whispered that Madame Nicole came by them in a rather mysterious manner.

Then there were the men in the saloon, when he'd first come to San Francisco. It was obvious now that they'd lied to a stranger, just to see him make a fool of himself over something they knew he could never have. Morgan was not to be had. That was the point. That had been the crux of their little joke.

What she'd been through! He remembered the night he went to her room, how he'd ignored her declarations of love. He sat down on a rock, his head in his hands. What had he done?

Morgan, can you ever forgive me? Can I ever make it up to you?

He stood up, staring at the sun. "I'll make it up to you, Morgan. I vow here and now that I'll find you and make it up to you. I'll never doubt you again, no matter where you are or what has happened to you. If it takes the rest of my life, I'll convince you that I love you."

Seth began walking down the mountainside, slowly at first, and then with stronger strides. Well, Colter, you've had enough time to feel sorry for yourself. A year—no! it was over two years since the night he had sneaked into Morgan's bedroom. He smiled cruelly at himself. Two years of his life had been devoted to self-pity.

But he was through with that now. He was going to go to Morgan and fight for her. If she hated him, it would take longer. But he'd make her love him again.

"Seth! Where've you been? I was lookin' for you. I was afraid my cookin' might have killed you off." Jessy looked up at Seth. He seemed ten years younger. "What's happened to you? You look like somebody died and left you a gold mine."

Seth put his big hands on Jessy's shoulders and, to her astonishment, gave her a resounding kiss on the mouth. It wasn't the passionate embrace she'd hoped for, but it was a start. She smiled up at him. His eyes were sparkling. She'd never noticed the deep blueness of them before.

"I don't know what's come over you, but I sure like it. Hey! What're you doin'?"

Seth was putting the saddle on his horse. "Jessy, I'll owe you till the day I die. No matter what I do, I'll never be able to repay you. Here." He took a plump leather pouch from his saddle bag and handed it to her.

Jessy felt the bag and knew it contained gold dust and nuggets. "What's this for? I don't understand what I did—but I know what I'd like to do." Seth's good humor was infectious.

Seth swung onto his horse. "Jessy, it's been a real pleasure knowing you."

"Wait!" She ran after Seth and he stopped. "What did I do? You have to tell me."

"My name's not Blake, it's Colter—Seth Colter."

"Colter! You're—*you're* Morgan's Seth? But you were supposed to be dead."

"Morgan thought I was dead, but it takes a lot to kill me." He laughed. "Morgan's Seth. Lord, I hope you're right. Goodbye, Jessy, and if you ever need help, come to Santa Fe, to the Colter ranch." He reined his horse and started toward San Francisco.

"What about your gear? Your tent?" she called after him.

"It's yours."

Jessy stood and watched Seth until she could no longer see his broad back. "I'll be damned. Morgan's Seth. Who would'a thought he'd be alive." She remembered the way Seth had looked at her. "No wonder she pined after him for so long. Lord! What I wouldn't give to be her right now and have a man like that gallopin' after me."

She turned back to the barren camp and shrugged. Jessy was not a dreamer, and she did not spend time longing after something she could not have. The gold Seth had given her, the tent, and his panning gear were more than enough reward for her. "Imagine that— Morgan's Seth," she murmured as she entered Seth's tent. It was good to have a place of her own.

Seth's first impulse when he reached San Francisco was to break down Theron's door. He laughed as he realized he'd already used cave-man tactics on Morgan. This time, he was going to go slowly. He would not push her. He was going to woo her, court her.

The first place he went was back to the little tailor who had made the suit for him two years ago.

Seth grinned broadly at the man.

"You certainly look nicer this time," the tailor said. "Last time I was afraid to speak, afraid my head would be removed from my shoulders."

"It might have been, too. Tell me, could you fit me with another suit?"

"Let me guess. You want it in three hours?"

307

"I think you and I are going to get along fine. You think this could hurry you along?" Seth dropped several gold coins on the table.

The tailor smiled at him. "Mr. . . . ."

"Colter."

"Mr. Colter, it is a pleasure to do business with you. Let's get on with the measurements."

Later, when Seth was putting his rough cotton work clothes back on, the tailor said, "Mr. Colter, I am curious about something. When you were here before—what, a year and a half, two years ago?—you came in demanding a suit. Now it's the same thing. I know this is all caused by a woman, but I'd like to know if it is a different woman this time or the same woman."

Seth's laughter filled the room. "It's the same woman." He picked up his hat and was nearly out the door when he turned back. "And the woman is my wife."

The tailor laughed. It wasn't often a man was so particular when the woman was his wife.

Seth went to a hotel, ordered a hot bath, and impatiently scrubbed weeks of dirt from his body. He marveled at himself. For the first time in two years, he was alive. He had admitted long ago how much he loved Morgan, but nothing could have lightened his spirit like finding out that Morgan had really always loved him.

Seth spent another hour at the barber's and then got his suit from the tailor. "Good luck," the man called after Seth.

By the time Seth reached Theron's house, he was shaking. Damn! he thought. I'm like a bridegroom on his wedding night. Would Morgan slam the door in his face? A butler answered the door.

"I'd like to see Mr. Shaw, please."

The butler appraised him, and Seth seemed to stand up under his scrutiny. "If you will wait inside, sir, I'll see if Mr. Shaw is in."

308

Seth waited in the spacious hallway. So this is what Morgan had been living in for the past two and a half years! It was a far cry from the adobe house on his ranch. He was glad he had some money now, glad he could give her things like this.

"If you'll come this way, sir."

Seth followed the butler into a room of golds and rusts. He stared at the man coming toward him. He'd seen Theron once before, but had paid little attention to him. He was incredibly handsome, smooth and blond. His features and trim physique were almost too perfect.

"Mr. Colter, I believe."

Seth was surprised at Theron's use of his name.

"Oh, yes, Mr. Colter, I know who you are. In fact, I've followed your adventures all over the gold fields. I must commend you for your wisdom in buying land here. I believe you are on your way to becoming a very wealthy man."

"You have the upper hand, Mr. Shaw. I know nothing about you."

"Won't you have a seat, please? Anyone who has lived with Morgan has heard of the great and wonderful Seth Colter." Theron's voice had a slight sarcastic edge to it.

Theron walked to an oak cabinet against the wall. The front of it was carved in a high relief. It was very old. He pulled a knob, and the front lowered into a shelf, held in place by delicate chains. "Could I get you something to drink, Mr. Colter? A brandy, perhaps?"

Seth nodded and Theron handed him a large crystal snifter of brandy. They both paused and savored it.

"Now, what can I do for you on this beautiful afternoon?" Theron's eyes were cold. This was the man Morgan had cried for, had been ready to die for. Seth Colter had taken her devotion lightly, had flung it in her face, used it against her.

"I'd like to see my wife."

309

Theron put his glass down and walked to the window, hands clasped behind him. He must control his anger. This . . . Kentucky lout walked in here and demanded to see his wife. Where the hell had he been when she needed him? He hadn't even been with her when the baby was born. Little Adam! He probably didn't even know he had a son. He certainly didn't deserve Adam. Theron breathed deeply and turned back to Seth.

"Mr. Colter, it is my opinion that you have lost all right to your wife."

Seth toyed with the brandy glass. He smiled up at Theron, a cold smile. "As you say, that is your opinion. What is between my wife and me is our business alone."

He certainly was cool. "Morgan has been my close friend for some time now, and what concerns her concerns me. I believe you have lost your priority in her life."

Seth frowned into the glass. "You are right, Mr. Shaw. I've been so wrong. I've done some horrible things to Morgan. I'd like to start again. I'd like to say some things to her that I should have said a long time ago. A great deal of our trouble is the result of plain misunderstanding."

"Oh, so the long-lost lover has come to his senses at last and now rushes to his little bride's side. Well, Colter, you are too late. Nearly two years too late. Morgan's gone."

Seth was on his feet. "Gone? Where is she?"

"Did you think she'd stay here and wait patiently for two years while you made up your mind whether you wanted her or not?"

Seth sat down, heavily, clumsily, setting the brandy snifter on the table next to him. His voice was quiet. "Everything is my fault. I have always had such a temper. I am thirty-five years old, and still I've never learned to control it. I've never loved a woman before,

310

not the way I fell in love with Morgan. I couldn't stand it when I thought she didn't return my love. I didn't think—I just flew into a rage.

"You mentioned my investments. I made those for Morgan. I decided some time ago that I loved her no matter what she'd done, even if she *had* worked in a . . . brothel. Even if she was your mistress. I decided I didn't care, that if she could be bought, then I would buy her. I set about making money.

"Today I found out what a fool I had been, what I had done to Morgan. She should hate me. I know she must, and I deserve it. But I still love her."

He looked up at Theron, standing by the window. "I want to make it up to her. No matter how long it takes, I want to prove to her that I do love her." He looked down at the floor again. The room was silent.

Theron took a seat across from Seth. "Morgan left here not long after your, *ah* . . . visit."

Seth moved uncomfortably, not meeting Theron's eyes.

"She says she hates you, and she has reason to, but I believe she needs you. She is living now at her father's ranch, the Three Crowns."

Seth looked up. "Yes. I know the place."

"She is living there with a sort of foster cousin—the son of her father's partner, a very pleasant young man—of whom I believe Morgan is growing increasingly fond."

Seth watched Theron intently.

"If you want her, I'd suggest you go quickly."

Both men rose and stood facing one another.

"I know I haven't deserved your consideration, but I thank you, and I thank you for taking care of Morgan. Jessy seemed to think you two liked one another."

"Jessy? Ah yes, Morgan's friend. Jessy told you Morgan's story, then?"

"Yes."

311

"I looked for you for a long time after that night, even though Morgan refused to mention your name. When I did find out about you, she was already in New Mexico."

"I have a great deal to do before I can leave San Francisco. I need to take care of my property. As soon as I can, I'll be off to New Mexico—to Morgan." He took Theron's hand. "You won't regret trusting me. I know you care for her."

Seth left the room and Theron stared after him. He wondered if he'd done the right thing. Morgan was happy at the ranch with Gordon and Adam. He didn't know if he should have broken into her peace. But he knew how much she'd always loved Seth. And, of course, there was Adam now. No matter what, Adam was Seth's son and Seth deserved at least to see the boy.

He smiled to himself. He'd like to see Seth's face when he discovered he had a son. And Morgan's when she saw Seth! He laughed aloud. It was almost tempting to make the journey to New Mexico. He shuddered. New Mexico was too ghastly to even consider. How could anyone want to live in that wasteland?

Oh, well, he sighed. Back to work. Mrs. Osborne needed some new drapes. Morgan would have loved these. They were several shades of Morgan's abhorred purple, and the figures on them resembled gargoyles rather than the young ladies they were supposed to be. He still missed Morgan's cutting little remarks and, he had to admit, the stir they caused when they went places together.

It took Seth a week to take care of his business in San Francisco. He found a young lawyer, Tim Bradbury, who was disillusioned and disgusted with the gold fields. Seth was his first client. With Seth's holdings to administer, he was able to set up his own law practice.

He was grateful to Seth. To keep his gratitude, Seth gave him a share of the rents and a percentage of the profits from the sale of any land. Revenues were to be sent to a bank in Santa Fe.

His mind was clear when he set out for Santa Fe. He was free to give all his attention to his wife.

~ Chapter Nineteen ~

MORGAN was happily surprised by the ranch house of the Three Crowns. It was built in the Spanish tradition, like the Montoya ranch. It was enormous.

"What do you think?" Gordon asked her as they looked down on the spacious house from the ridge above.

The house was the same color as the surrounding countryside and seemed always to have been there. It nestled down amidst the piñon trees and the much taller cottonwoods.

"There's a river near the house." Gordon pointed to a strip of green not far from the house. "Are you surprised?"

"Very. It's practically a mansion. How many rooms does it have?"

"I've never counted them, but you'll have a lifetime to count them." Gordon looked back at Adam, who'd climbed into the back of the wagon and fallen asleep. "We'd better get Adam into a bed."

Morgan thought the inside of the house was even more beautiful than the outside. The rooms on the first floor were large and airy. They opened into a spacious courtyard, in the center of which was a tiled pool. Stone benches and statues were sprinkled among the trees and flowering shrubs.

"He's asleep." Gordon returned from putting Adam to bed. "Now, let's meet the servants and have dinner."

"Servants?" Morgan laughed. "I'm afraid I've be-

315

come accustomed to doing most of the housework myself."

"This is your home and here, if you want to, you can sit and eat chocolates all day."

"Chocolates! I needed you when I was carrying Adam."

Gordon looked puzzled and then smiled. "Oh, yes, Jake told me about your unusual eating habits."

The servants were lined up in the foyer, at the bottom of the stairs.

"Roselle, our cook. Martin is our butler and general factotum. This is Carol, who takes care of the upstairs rooms. Donaciano, who is our groom. Carol's sister, Magda, comes in during the days to help with the downstairs rooms."

Morgan shook hands with each of them. Roselle and Martin were married and had worked in the house since it was built. Carol was a young girl, in her teens, very plain and rather shy. Donaciano was just a boy, about twelve or thirteen. Morgan learned later that Gordon had adopted him when his parents drowned two years earlier.

Gordon escorted her into the room adjoining the foyer, the dining room. The pine table was enormous, with at least twelve large pine chairs. It was covered now with a snowy white linen cloth and set with the finest Limoges porcelain and crystal. The silver was heavy and ornate.

"Gordon! It's really beautiful."

Gordon smiled at her praise. He liked to live comfortably. "Roselle is an excellent cook, and I think you'll be pleased."

The meal was delicious, as Gordon had promised. Martin served the meal expertly. Gordon raised a glass of chilled champagne to Morgan. "To your new home. To the hope that you find peace and happiness here and that you stay . . . forever."

She smiled back at him. "I hope you're right."

By the time the meal was finished, Morgan felt her body drooping. Gordon put his arm around her and led her upstairs to her room. The room was feminine, a white lace bedspread on the bed. The covers were turned down to expose lace-edged pillows. Her nightgown was spread ready for her. Gordon left her and she quickly undressed and was asleep.

Gordon paused outside her door. "I love you, Morgan," he whispered.

Morgan awoke to the sounds of Adam's squeals of laughter outside her door. Hastily, she donned her dressing gown and went to investigate. Adam was perched on Martin's shoulders, gleefully banging him on the head with a wooden horse, screaming, "Eat. Eat."

Gordon followed closely behind Martin. "Morgan, we woke you. I'm sorry, but Adam was rather disturbed at waking and finding himself in a strange place."

Morgan smiled up at her energetic son. "Thank you for caring for Adam, Martin." She held up her arms and Adam tumbled into them, his weight nearly unbalancing her. Martin continued downstairs, rubbing his head.

"Now, where is this monster's room?" She smiled affectionately at her son as he grinned up at her, showing two large dimples. "You know, I have a feeling he is going to be even more spoiled here than he was on the Colter ranch."

Gordon smiled at her as he led her into Adam's room. As she began to dress Adam, she looked around the room. It was filled with toys and pictures of children. When he was dressed, Gordon helped the child onto a large rocking horse.

Morgan went to investigate the pictures—they were

317

all of one little girl. She looked questioningly at Gordon.

"Don't you recognize her?"

"They're . . . that's me, isn't it?"

"Every one of them. These were your toys. When my father and Uncle Charley built the house, he had the pictures put into the room. It's been more or less a shrine. Your father spent hours in here. Sometimes, after a letter arrived, he'd lock himself in here for an entire day. I'm glad there'll be a little more life in here now."

Morgan laughed. "With Adam, you don't have to worry about any place being dull—or quiet. Adam!" She tried to be heard over his shouts of happiness about the rocking horse. "Let's go eat breakfast." Adam stopped rocking immediately and quietly climbed off the horse. Seeing Gordon's puzzled stare, Morgan explained: "Eat. That's a magic word with Adam."

Gordon took Adam to breakfast. Morgan dressed in a sturdy cotton gown, one that fit perfectly and accented her curves. Then she joined them. Both Adam and Morgan ate heartily of the food Roselle prepared.

After breakfast, Roselle asked to keep Adam in the kitchen with her. Morgan consented, and while Gordon attended to the business of the ranch, she explored the house and gardens.

At lunch, Martin watched Adam constantly, and anticipated his every need. Morgan sighed, knowing that all the attention was not good for her impressionable son. When Adam began rubbing his eyes, Morgan took him to his room for his afternoon nap.

Gordon returned to the house and asked Morgan to go riding with him, to see some of the ranch. They rode along the little river and Morgan found an ideal place for picnics under a grove of cottonwoods. When she dismounted the mare Gordon had given her, she tripped and grabbed at her saddle to catch herself.

Gordon caught her in his arms, holding her close to

him. "I'm sure that this will be the highlight of my day."

"Oh, Gordon," she laughed, as she stepped away, "you're always teasing, just like . . ." She left her sentence unfinished.

Gordon's eyes were serious. "Believe me, Morgan, I am totally serious." She turned away to hide the consternation that flooded her face. She wasn't ready yet. Seth was too real to her. When his memory faded, then she'd be able to look at another man.

The candlelight dinner, alone with Gordon, was pleasant and Morgan relaxed with him. "To my beautiful little foster cousin, who changed into an even more beautiful woman," he lifted his glass to her.

Early the next morning, she heard Adam in the hallway. She opened her bedroom door and her small son found his mother's room. She crawled back into bed, watching him wander about the room, looking at rugs, touching jars on Morgan's dressing table, and knocking on the door that connected Morgan's bedroom to another room.

"There's no one there, Adam." Morgan rolled over and found herself looking into Gordon's amused eyes. He was standing in her open doorway. "It used to be your grandpa's room, but now it's empty."

Morgan moved down in the bed, bringing the sheets to her shoulders.

"Do you mind if I take Adam with me today? I'd like to show him the ranch and show him to the men."

Morgan sat up, the covers falling away. Gordon was like an older brother. It was difficult to think of him in any other way, in spite of his protestations to the contrary. "Gordon, you don't want to take Adam. You don't know what he's like. There are times when he's more than I can handle. You'll never get any work done."

"Leave him to me. If it's all right with you, I'll take him."

Gordon stepped out of the room and returned with a little sombrero. It had a beaded band on it. "I bought this in Santa Fe. I think it'll fit." Adam loved the hat, jumping up and down at the sight of himself in his mother's mirror, the long nightshirt flying and looking very incongruous with the hat.

"Are you sure you're ready to handle that all day?" Morgan laughed.

In answer, Gordon swept the laughing boy into his arms. "My pleasure. Now, cowpuncher, let's get you into some other duds."

Morgan heard Adam's laugh all the way to his room. She leaned back against the pillows. Yes, she thought, this is very pleasant. It was peaceful here. No memories assailed her. Gordon was wonderful, too. It would be very comfortable to fall in love with him, yes it would.

With Adam gone, Morgan found she had too little to do. As always, she wandered toward the kitchen. Roselle was surprised when Morgan rolled up her sleeves and plunged into kneading a large mound of bread dough. They both soon forgot the notion that they were mistress and servant, and became just two women, cooking and talking together.

"Gordon has always been such a lonely fellow, even as a little boy. My heart cried for him at times."

"Lonely? But Gordon doesn't ever seem to be sad at all."

"He covers it with his jokes and laughter, but it is not easy to grow up without a mother."

"Didn't his mother ever live with him?"

"No. She left soon after her son was born, returning to her own people. For all the jokes he makes, Gordon takes his Comanche relatives very seriously. He has never spent much time with them. Once when he was very young, an uncle came to see him and Gordon followed him around for two weeks. His Indian uncle showed him how to dress like a Comanche and told him to be proud of his Indian blood. Gordon was very upset to find the Indian gone one morning. Now he gets so upset over what the white man is doing to the Indians." Roselle cocked her head toward Morgan. "The men on the ranch try to forget he's half-Indian. They don't like the idea of an Indian boss."

Morgan nodded her understanding.

Lunch was lonely for Morgan, with both Gordon and Adam away from the house. She ate in the kitchen with Roselle and Martin, but realized that her newness in the household made them shy.

She went to her room to nap. For some reason, her thoughts of Seth were especially strong. As she removed her dress, she almost felt his hands on her body. The memory made her ache.

Gordon arrived later with a tired, sunburned Adam. Morgan, glad to be busy, washed the child and slipped him into a clean nightshirt. He was asleep as his mother finished buttoning the gown. As she kissed her son's cheek, she was reminded again of how much Adam resembled his father. She chastised herself for always thinking of Seth.

At dinner, Gordon was especially happy. "You should have seen them! I never saw grown men make such fools of themselves over anyone. All day they talked baby talk to him. Calhoun especially! 'Ooh wanta go for wide on horsey?' Adam just stared at them. Wouldn't go to a single one of them. Stayed with me." Gordon's eyes gleamed with pride.

Gordon put his hand over Morgan's. "I can't tell you how glad I am that you are here. I've been rattling around alone in this big house for years. Sometimes I slept in the bunkhouse rather than be alone in here. Roselle and Martin have been the true occupants."

Gordon kissed her check. He was handsome, easy to

laugh, and Adam adored him. What more could she want? she asked herself. Gordon's goodnight kiss had not sent shivers down her spine as Seth's kisses did. Don't compare them! she told herself. As she climbed into bed, she thought again how comfortable it would be to be in love with Gordon.

The days began to fall into a routine, and Morgan was content, if not deliriously happy. Gordon often took Adam with him in the days, and in the evening he entertained her with stories of how the men tried to entice Adam from him. It seemed they never succeeded.

When Adam was gone, Morgan spent her mornings in the kitchen and her afternoons riding, improving her skills on the mare. Adam and she often took a picnic lunch and spent the afternoons together by the river. It was a little greener, but otherwise a lot like the place where they had spent their afternoons at the Colter ranch.

They had been at the Three Crowns for three months when Gordon first mentioned the divorce. Seeing Morgan every day and not touching her was agony for him. He wanted to know how she felt about Seth. He wanted the way clear for himself, with no ghosts between them. He loved her enough to wait for her.

They were at dinner. "Morgan, have you made any decisions about Seth?"

Morgan looked up, startled. Even the mention of Seth's name made her stomach contract, the skin of her scalp tighten. "I don't want to discuss him." Roselle's *coq au vin* suddenly lost its appeal.

Gordon watched her closely. It seemed that what her eyes said and what her lips said did not match. "Would you consider a divorce?"

A divorce, a permanent separation from Seth, from Adam's father. She must be sensible. "Yes, I believe it would be appropriate. But I don't know where Seth is.

I'm sure he must be found before there can be a . . . divorce." She hated the word, hated the whole idea. "I don't want to see him again."

"Then I'll contact John Bradley and see what can be arranged."

They were quiet the rest of the meal. They had coffee outside in the courtyard. Morgan was occupied with her own thoughts. Why is the idea of a divorce so distasteful to me? Because it makes me feel like a failure? She argued with herself over the absurdity of the idea, but she knew her answer was correct. Of course, it wasn't her fault, only Seth's. Seth and his temper.

"More coffee, Morgan?" Gordon interrupted her thoughts.

Gordon knew now it was going to be a tough fight. Morgan said she hated her husband, but he could see the lie in her eyes. Something had to be done.

When Morgan and Adam had been at the Three Crowns for six months, Gordon decided to have a welcome party. Morgan had met very few of the neighbors who sparsely dotted the countryside. She was glad to arrange the party, glad to cook, and to decorate the house. Gordon was happy to come home every night to Morgan and Adam. For the first time in his life, he wasn't lonely. His happiness would have been complete if he hadn't sometimes caught a glimpse of longing in Morgan's eyes.

~ *Chapter Twenty* ~

IT was the day of the party when Gordon saw the big man riding toward him. The easy, straight way he sat his horse showed unusual confidence. Gordon watched with interest as the stranger approached. He wasn't an ordinary drifter, and he was older than he appeared from a distance.

"They tell me you're the boss." The stranger's voice was deep, soft, very pleasant.

"I guess I am. My name's Gordon Matthews." Gordon extended his hand and found it engulfed in the man's larger one. It was hard and calloused from work.

"Dave Blake." He smiled and Gordon had a sudden flash of recognition. What was familiar about the man?

"I'd like a job."

"What experience do you have?" Gordon knew he was going to hire the man even before he answered.

"I used to run my father's plantation in the East, and I've worked out here about six years."

Gordon smiled back at him. "I can always use a good hand. You're on. That's Boyd, my foreman, over there. He can put you to work." He watched the man turn his horse and ride off. The way he moved his hands was naggingly familiar. Yet he couldn't remember having seen this man before.

The rest of the day, he watched Dave work. He wasn't like most new hands. He didn't wait to be told what to do. It was as if he'd been working on the ranch for years. The other men took to him quickly, liking the quiet way he stepped in. Yet they held him off, too, and did not bombard him with questions.

Gordon noticed one of the younger members of the crew asking Dave what he should do when he'd finished the task Boyd had assigned him. Gordon watched his foreman for signs of hostility. But Boyd, never an ambitious man, was content to let Dave take over where he could. On the ride back to the bunkhouse, Gordon sought out the new man.

"Dave, I watched you work today, and I want to say welcome to the Three Crowns."

Dave smiled at his employer, and again Gordon tried to remember whom Dave reminded him of.

"We're having a little party at the house tonight. Everyone's invited. Plenty of beer and hard stuff and all the food you can eat."

Dave laughed, his laughter deep. "I'm afraid you might get more than you want. After a day like this, I could eat my horse—even the horseshoes. What's the occasion?"

"Morgan and Adam have been living with me for six months now, six very happy months."

"A party because two men have moved in with you."

Gordon was puzzled for a second, then grinned broadly. "Come tonight and meet my guests. I think you'll be pleasantly surprised." He left to return to the house. Dave was certainly going to be surprised all right, after thinking of Morgan as a man.

Adam was just running down the stairs when he saw Gordon. Morgan ran close behind Adam. The boy leaped, knowing Gordon would catch him. Gordon held Adam close and looked up at Morgan. She was beautiful. She had just washed her hair and it hung down her back, still slightly damp.

326

"One of these days, he's going to jump at someone and miss. How was your day, Gordon?"

"Now that I'm home, it's a beautiful day." He kissed Morgan's cheek, put Adam down, and the three walked to the courtyard to look at the party preparations. "I hired a new man today."

"Oh?"

"The strangest thing." Gordon had his mouth full, and Morgan looked up sharply.

"Gordon, stop eating those! I have them arranged in a design and you'll mess it up. Now, what was strange?"

"This new man I hired. I know I've never seen him before, but I feel like I know him. The way he walks, certain ways he moves. It's like I've seen them hundreds of times."

"Maybe you're just imagining it."

"I guess you're right. I'll go get ready now. You going to wear that?" He looked at her everyday cotton dress.

"Don't be silly. I have a dress you've never even seen before. The silk is from Italy and it is gorgeous."

"With you in it, it will be."

Morgan watched him go, smiling. Gordon was so pleasant. She constantly wondered at herself for not being in love with him.

Dave walked into the bunkhouse and then busied himself while listening to the men talk.

"A real looker, ain't she?"

"Nearly bust my britches every day when I see her ridin' by on that horse."

"Maybe a good fairy'd give me three wishes and I'd give 'em all to be that saddle."

"I'd rather be the horse. She can ride me bareback."

As the laughter exploded again, no one noticed the new man leave the room. And no one noticed that he wasn't with them when they left for the party.

Dave returned to the empty bunkhouse to take his time bathing and dressing. The suit fit his body closely, emphasizing his muscular frame. The silk of the shirt offset the dark, nubby weave of the vest. He took his time, and when he started toward the house, the party had been going on for hours.

When Morgan came down the stairs, Gordon gasped. He had never seen anything quite so lovely. The emerald-green dress reflected in her eyes until they were the same color. Her hair was piled on top of her head in large, fat curls, while more curls cascaded down her back, all the way to her waist. Her delicate little ears were exposed where the hair swept upward, and she wore tiny diamond-and-emerald earrings that sparkled when she moved. The dress hung just off her shoulders and low across her breasts.

"Morgan, you're more beautiful then I thought possible. I don't know what to say."

"Do you like my hair?" She turned around and he touched a soft curl.

"It's lovely. I've never seen so much hair in my life." He looked at her questioningly. "Is that all yours?"

Morgan giggled. "Sir, it is not at all polite to ask a lady what on her person is real and what is not."

Gordon eyed her voluptuous figure. "At least I know some things are genuine."

Morgan laughed at his compliment. "Shall we go?"

Gordon took her arm and leaned close to her. "You smell nice, too." His lips touched her cheek and moved slowly to her waiting lips. His kiss was gentle, soft, and very pleasant. Morgan smiled up at him. She enjoyed his kisses, and might even grow to love them.

All eyes turned toward them as they entered the courtyard. For the thousandth time, Gordon wished Morgan's father had written his will to specify that his daughter must marry Gordon. He had hinted broadly, but Uncle Charley had laughed and said that feudal times were past, that the will he was writing was bad enough. He wanted to insure that Morgan would have her choice of several men.

For Morgan, the party was too much like the party at Joaquín Montoya's. The couples, all strangers, mumbled polite wishes as Gordon introduced her. He was so proud of her, he fairly strutted. She liked being beside him and felt comfortable on his arm.

Morgan hardly knew any of the ranch hands, having seen them only from a distance. After "good evenings" were exchanged, neither she nor Gordon noticed their conspiratorial looks.

Morgan had been standing for hours. She must have said "thank you" a thousand times. The faces of the people ran together and she had long ago given up trying to remember their names. She was considering going upstairs to check on Adam, but she had already used that excuse to escape twice.

She smiled at a large woman in a purple satin dress. Lord, but I hate that color, she thought. She saw Gordon coming toward her. Maybe she could persuade him to take her upstairs for good. She frowned slightly as she saw him veer off to the right, to the shadows a little behind her.

"Dave! I thought you weren't coming. I want you to meet the 'man' I'm giving the party for. Remember, I told you you'd be surprised.

"Morgan, I'd like you to meet the new hand I hired today, Dave Blake."

Gordon watched Dave's face for his reaction. "Dave, this is Morgan Colter."

He turned sharply at the crash of the punch glass. Morgan's face was totally without color. She was staring at Dave. "Morgan, what's wrong?" He looked from her to Dave, who seemed to be the cause of Morgan's distress. "Do you know Dave?" There was dread in his voice.

"No, I don't believe we've had the pleasure. Maybe I remind Mrs. . . . . Colter of someone she's met before."

"Is that it, Morgan? Does Dave remind you of someone?"

Morgan stood staring, speechless.

"I think I'll take Morgan upstairs. Something about you has upset her."

"Please do. I'm very sorry to have upset you, Mrs. Colter. Maybe you'll forgive me when you find I'm not the same man you think I am. Goodnight." He watched as Gordon led Morgan away.

Morgan still hadn't spoken when they reached her bedroom. Gordon picked her up and put her on the bed, her hair spreading around her.

"Morgan, what's wrong? Do you know that man? Does he remind you of someone?"

"Yes." Her whisper was hoarse.

"Who?"

"Seth." He barely heard her. Seth! My God! He had been afraid she was still in love with her husband, but if she reacted this way to a man who only resembled Seth! He stroked the hair on her forehead. "I'll send Carol up to help you undress. There's no need for you to come downstairs again. When everyone is gone, I'll come back."

Carol had come and gone, and Morgan lay in the bed in her nightgown. It had taken a long time before she could begin to think. Now the first shock of numbness was beginning to wear off.

Seth was here! She hadn't seen him since the night he had come to Theron's house. That horrible night when he had accused her of—She stopped. She didn't want to remember. What did he want here?

The shock of seeing him again had caused her more pain than she had thought possible. She had hoped that living with Gordon would make her forget Seth. She hadn't had enough time! She needed time to get to know Gordon, to forget Seth.

He can't do this to me! The tears collected in her eyes and ran down her cheeks. Adam and I are happy. We have a home now. Why can't he let us be?

She wiped away the tears as something occurred to her—she didn't have to let him upset her! No, she didn't love him anymore. She knew him for what he was. This time he wouldn't be able to charm her, because she knew now what lay behind his dimpled smile. She knew how to handle this. She would totally ignore him!

She sat up straighter in the bed, and smiled. Mrs. Colter, he called her. Well, Mr. Blake, you will be another hired hand, just as Boyd and the others are. No special favors, and no recognition, either. If he had come in spite, to punish her for crimes he believed she'd committed, he was going to be surprised. She wouldn't allow him to upset her. He no longer had any control over her.

She answered Gordon's knock. His concern faded rapidly when he saw Morgan's smile.

"Feeling better now?"

"Yes, much better."

"Morgan, I just wanted to tell you that you'll have to remember that Dave Blake is an entirely different person from Seth. Just because a physical resemblance is there doesn't mean they're at all alike."

"You're perfectly right. Mr. Blake is another man. It was such a shock, that's all. I don't know how I'll ever make it up to him. The poor man. He must have thought I was insane."

Gordon patted her hand. He was still shaken by Morgan's feelings for Seth. "I doubt that. You're much too beautiful for any man to take offense at anything you do."

Morgan laughed. "Did you know that at one time I was considered very plain?"

Gordon ignored her question. The idea was too absurd to consider. He kissed her forehead, blew out the light, and left her.

Before Morgan fell asleep, she saw Seth's smiling face. He hadn't changed at all. He was still very handsome.

Seth sat under the stars for a long time after the party ended. The carriages were gone and the bunkhouse was silent.

He had almost left the party when he first saw her. He had watched her for over an hour, being careful that she didn't see him. He had known right away that she was bored. Morgan had never liked a lot of people around her. She was happiest when there were just the two of them. He had seen the way Gordon hovered over her, always watching her, protecting her. It was obvious that Gordon was in love. That's what had made Seth want to leave. But as he watched Morgan's face, he knew she didn't return Gordon's love. He didn't know if he'd been joyous or sad when he saw that she was not in love with Gordon. Part of him wanted her to be happy, at whatever cost to himself, but the other part was selfish and wanted her to be his alone.

Where was this Adam that Gordon had mentioned? He'd said the party was for Morgan and Adam. Maybe she loved Adam. Adam! What was he like?

Seth rubbed his hands on his thighs. He felt he'd won one round in the battle for Morgan, but it had taken a lot of his strength. He dreaded the outcome of the next round. This was a fight for his life.

It was still very early when Morgan heard her son banging on her bedroom door. "Mama, eat. Mama, eat. Horse."

332

Drowsily, Morgan left her bed and opened the door for him.

Still mostly asleep, Morgan stumbled back to the bed. Adam ran ahead of her, reaching it before she did, and began bouncing up and down on the mattress. "Horse. Horse," he shouted. "Gor, horse."

Morgan smiled at her sturdy son. "Well, my talkative little son, I take that to mean that you are ready for Gordon to take you on his horse?"

Adam smiled at her, pleased she had understood.

"You little imp! You may have everyone else on this ranch hanging on your every monosyllable, but not me." She lunged at him, catching the tail of his nightshirt. Adam collapsed on the bed, laughing helplessly.

Hearing the commotion, Gordon came to Morgan's open bedroom door to investigate. The sight of Morgan and Adam wrestling on the big bed made him laugh. Then he grew serious as he watched Morgan. She wore a thin muslin gown and it was wrapped tightly about her body to expose smooth, golden legs. As she pulled Adam to her, the outline of her breasts swelled, full and sensuous. He felt little beads of sweat on his upper lip.

Feeling another presence in the room, Morgan turned. She saw Gordon and followed his eyes to her exposed legs. Hastily, she pulled a sheet over her body.

"Gor! Horse! Eat!"

Even with the sheet pulled to her neck, Morgan was beautiful. Her hair tumbled about her shoulders in a disarray of fat golden curls, some honey-colored and some almost white. Her face was slightly flushed. Gordon recovered himself just in time to catch Adam as he jumped from the bed into Gordon's arms.

"Good morning," she murmured.

Gordon's face broke into a wide grin and he looked at Adam. "Good morning. You sure are a lucky man, Adam. I'd like to crawl in bed with your mama some morning."

Morgan gaped at Gordon. Never had he said anything like that to her before.

As Gordon turned to leave, Adam in his arms, he smiled back at her. "You really should close your mouth, Morgan, beautiful though it is."

By the time Morgan was dressed, Gordon had dressed Adam, packed some bread and cheese, and left the house. She ate breakfast alone, trying not to remember that Seth was somewhere on the ranch.

"Hey! Gordon's bringing Adam today!" Seth heard the men yelling in the bunkhouse. Well, she certainly has picked a popular man this time, he thought. As the men all left through one door, Seth quietly made his way to the other door. He wanted to postpone meeting Morgan's new lover as long as possible. His horse shied away from him when he angrily tossed the heavy saddle onto its back. Of course, she had every right to take on a new lover, after the way he'd treated her.

But she was his wife!

Whoever this Adam was, he was going to have to fight Seth for Morgan's love and Seth meant to fight any way he could.

"Dave, are you in here?"

Seth didn't want to talk to Gordon. Probably wants me to shake the bastard's hand. If he's a pretty little fop, I may put my fist through his face. Even if he's twice as big as I am, I may try to do it anyway.

"Dave! There you are. There's someone I want you to meet. This is the *real* boss of the Three Crowns. This man's word is law."

Now I know I'm going to hit him, Seth thought. Slowly he turned, jaw clenched. He saw only Gordon.

"Adam." Gordon looked down and then behind him. He laughed, turned, and picked the boy up. "This is Adam Colter. Like I say, he's the real boss of this ranch. Adam, this is Dave Blake."

Gordon looked from one to the other. Neither spoke. Man and child stared at one another with an incredible intensity.

Gordon had never seen Adam be still so long, or be so solemn. Then Gordon saw the resemblance. No wonder Morgan thought this man looked like the boy's father. They both had the same shade of blue eyes, the same wavy hair, though Adam's was honey blond while Dave's was darker. Adam would someday be as large a man as Dave Blake.

"Morgan's right."

Without moving his eyes from Adam's piercing stare, Seth asked, "About what?"

"Well, Morgan said you resembled the boy's father. You two could easily pass for father and son."

Seth looked at Gordon and grinned, showing dimples like Adam's. "Is that so? Well, I've taken a real liking to this boy. Do you mind?" He held out his arms to Adam.

"No, not at all, but he won't usually leave me. We're pretty good pals."

Adam fell into his father's arms with no hesitation. Seth held the boy, running his hands over his arms and legs, over the back of his head. He smiled at the boy and Adam returned a mirror-image smile.

"Yes, sir, I do like this boy."

Gordon straightened his shoulders. "Well, we need to get to work." His voice was cool. Don't be silly, he told himself. Maybe Adam just feels a kinship with the man because they look alike. It doesn't mean anything. He tried to calm himself. He turned to saddle his own horse, and another beast felt the brunt of someone's anger.

Seth carried Adam into the morning sunlight. "Well, son, you are certainly a surprise. And you're one more reason why I have to get your mother back. It's not going to be an easy task."

335

Adam smiled up at his father and put out a hand to touch his cheek. "Horse."

Seth returned the smile and kissed the small hand, so like his own. "No, son, I'm not a horse. Less sense than one sometimes, but I'm what is known as a daddy. Can you say 'Daddy'?"

"Da da." Adam laughed delightedly, always happy saying new words.

"That's close enough."

Gordon came to stand by them. "Adam, are you ready to get on the horse?"

Adam smiled at his friend, content with Seth. He made no move to go to Gordon. "Da da."

Gordon looked puzzled and then laughed. "His first attempt at 'Dave'. Morgan complains that no one except her tries to teach him new words. She'll be glad to hear this one."

"I hope so."

Gordon took Adam and put him on the front of his saddle and them climbed up behind him. They waited as Seth mounted. Adam took one look at Seth on the horse and lunged toward him. Seth caught him and put him in front of him. The saddle could barely hold the two of them.

Gordon had to laugh. "You know, it's not easy for me not to be jealous. For six months now, Adam has been like my own son. Sometimes he'd rather stay with me than go to his own mother."

Seth tried to make his voice sound light, and Gordon didn't notice the way the big man's hands tightened on the reins. "The mother! Now she's a beauty. It must have been like having her for a wife for the last six months."

Gordon laughed aloud. "I wish you were right. That's what a lot of men think, but Morgan has a mind of her own. She has . . . problems . . . concerning the boy's father. But some day—maybe. I'm going very slowly with her right now."

"I would have thought living in the same house with a beautiful young widow was the kind of situation men dream about."

"It's a dream all right, but that's all. Oh . . . and Morgan's not a widow. She's still legally married." He started to turn his horse away and then looked back. "I must be as silly as Adam. I don't usually discuss my private affairs with the hands."

"I thank you for the confidence."

"Well, here's where we part. You're to work with Boyd today and I'm leading another crew. Adam, are you ready to go with me?"

Adam pressed his back closer to Seth's chest. "Da da." Gordon shrugged.

"Well, it looks like you're stuck with him."

"My pleasure." His hand was on the boy's knee. "I can't imagine anyone I'd rather spend the day with." ·

"I'm not sure you know what you're asking for. When he's tired, he can really be a nuisance. Right now he's happy, but—"

Seth tousled the boy's hair. "There's no need to worry. I'll take care of him as though he were my own son." Seth reined his horse toward Boyd and the other men. His son's little body near his own felt comfortable and familiar, as if they'd known one another for years.

The other men looked up sharply as they saw the new hand with Adam in front of him. Gordon never allowed the boy out of his sight. But then they shrugged. There was something about Dave Blake that made a man trust him, something even the nineteen-month-old Adam must feel.

All day Seth stayed with his son. It was true that his work would have been easier without Adam to look after, but Seth had been by himself too long to begrudge a little extra work now. Whenever Adam stepped too near a skittish horse, a large hand was there to guide him to safety. Seth felt a peace that he hadn't experienced in a long time. He was content now to take his time with Morgan, to go slowly, to give her time to trust him. Now, he had Adam.

Morgan was nervous all day. As soon as she entered the kitchen, she cut herself. She stared at the cut unseeing. Roselle bandaged it for her. Later, when she was removing a hot tray of rolls from the oven, she forgot to use a potholder. Roselle smeared her palm with cool butter and told her to leave the kitchen. Morgan didn't understand.

"Mrs. Colter, something is wrong today. Go outside, ride your horse, read, but please stay out of the kitchen."

Morgan removed her apron and went to the drawing room. Roselle was right, something was wrong. Seth Colter had come back into her life. She knew he must have seen Adam by now. What did he think of his son? Maybe he didn't even realize Adam was his. That would be just like him—he'd probably think Adam was Joaquín's son, or Theron's.

She picked up *Jane Eyre*. She scanned pages, anxious for Jane and Mr. Rochester to get together again. As she read, she began to realize that she was seeing herself as Jane and Seth as Rochester. She remembered clearly every muscle of Seth's body. She put the book aside and wandered from room to room, checking to see if anything was out of order.

Lunch was a lonely meal, adding to her nervousness. She had Donaciano saddle her horse and rode to her favorite place by the river. She spread a blanket and wished Adam were there to keep her busy. The thought of Adam brought visions of Adam and Seth together to her mind. I wonder how Seth felt when his own son preferred Gordon? Adam would rather be with Gordon than with anyone else in the world.

It was hot, and the place was alive with dragonflies and numerous other flying insects. Morgan removed her riding boots and stockings, wiggling her toes, glad to be rid of them. It wasn't long before she fell asleep.

She awoke dazed, not knowing where she was, her body stiff from the hard ground. The sun was low. It was well past time for her return. Hastily, she tried to pin her hair back into its careful coiffure, but finally gave up. Pulling the pins and ribbon out, she thrust them into her pocket.

She rode quickly back to the house. Breathless, she tossed the reins to Donaciano. "I'm late. Would you give her a good rubdown, please? I need to go— Gordon and Adam will be here soon."

Donaciano was willing to do anything for his young mistress when she smiled at him like that.

She started running toward the house and then turned to call thank you to Donaciano. She caught her breath as she ran into something; a hand caught the back of her head and tangled in her hair.

She looked up into Seth's sparkling blue eyes. His hand was burning her skin, causing chills down her back. Their eyes locked, each seeing only the other, oblivious to the rest of the world. Seth's hand moved along the back of her neck, fingers caressing the tendons, touching each muscle. Along the scalp, her hair was warm, almost hot. Involuntarily, Morgan's eyes began to close. It had been a long time . . . Her eyes flew open. He was staring at her with a slow smile, a smug smile. She jerked away from him but he held her easily.

"There you are, Dave. I wondered where you'd gone." Gordon looked from Seth to Morgan and Seth dropped his hand from her hair. Immediately Gordon felt the tension between them.

"Mrs. Colter ran into us, running from the barn."

Only then did Morgan notice Adam in his father's arms. The boy slept peacefully, his head cradled against Seth's shoulder. She turned startled eyes to Gordon.

"I know. It's the strangest thing. I never saw Adam take to anyone as he took to Dave. He spent the whole day with Dave, and no matter how many times I tried to get him to come with me, he refused to leave. The way they stared at one another, you would have thought they'd known one another all their lives."

"I'm afraid the boy's worn out. If you'll show me his room, I'll carry him to bed."

Seth's smile infuriated her. He was so smug, just because Adam liked him. Well, Adam was just a little boy. He didn't have much knowledge about all the dishonesty in the world. She smiled back at him, icily. "Mr. Blake, isn't it? I am quite capable of putting my own son to bed. Adam." She put her hands under the sleeping child's arm, trying not to touch Seth. Adam opened his eyes only slightly and saw his mother. He went to her willingly and she carried him into the house.

Gordon watched her go, astonished by her rudeness. "Dave, I really must apologize for Morgan. I've never seen her rude to anyone before. She's really not like that. Actually, she's a very warm person."

"That's all right. She just seems to have taken a dislike to me. Maybe I ought to forgo your invitation to supper."

"No, please don't. I owe you something for taking care of Adam. I know it's not easy to do a full day's work and keep an eye on a toddler at the same time. By the way, my foreman says you do one hell of a day's work, and that you know exactly what you're doing, too."

"It seems I get along with animals and children a sight better than I do with women." They laughed together.

"Well, I trust Adam. Anyone he likes is all right with me. Now let's go wash."

Morgan began undressing her son. He was dirty and needed a bath, but she didn't want to wake him to give him one. She washed his face and hands and began to put his nightshirt on him. He frowned once and fluttered his eyelids when she jerked his arm too sharply.

"I'm sorry, sweetheart." She kissed his cheek and finished dressing him more gently. Damn him! Why did he have to come back? Now that he's seen Adam, he'll probably never give me a divorce. I'll never be able to lead my own life.

Maybe he wanted the money, the money she offered him to marry her. But, somehow, she didn't think that was it.

She tucked Adam into his bed, brushing the hair from his forehead, and kissed him. She sat a minute, looking at her sleeping son. He was always such a whirlwind of activity that it was pleasant to see him quiet.

She went to her own room to dress for dinner. She chose a filmy sea-green dress, a gift from Theron. She had chosen it to match the jade treasures in her bedroom. She began to pin up her hair and then, on second thought, left it down, adding a ribbon that matched the dress. Just the way Gordon likes it, she thought, as she studied her reflection. And Seth—No! She wouldn't think that way.

Tonight was Gordon's night. She would be especially nice to Gordon. She would forget Seth, forget his laughing eyes, forget his touch. Yes, tonight would be the beginning of a new relationship with Gordon, and Seth Colter would be out of her life for good.

She started down the stairs. At least tonight she wouldn't be troubled by Seth. She could relax, alone with Gordon.

"I'm sorry I'm late, Gordon. I had to get Adam to bed. He was so tired after being with that awful Mr. Blake."

"Morgan!" Gordon's tone was sharp. "We have a guest." His eyes sent warning.

Seth's large form was visible now, inside the dining room. His eyes were teasing. His smile was slight but his dimples were deep, betraying extreme amusement. Amusement at her embarrassment!

"I'm sorry, Mrs. Colter, if your son was so disturbed by my presence."

"I'm sure Morgan didn't mean that, Dave." He looked to Morgan for support. "It's just that . . ."

"Would you mind if we ate now? I am starved." Morgan's voice was honey-sweet and she looked at Gordon lovingly.

Gordon frowned. This wasn't Morgan at all. What was the matter with her?

She entered the dining room on Gordon's arm, turning her back slightly on Seth.

"I'm sorry we're still in our work clothes, but we got back too late to change."

"Mrs. Colter would put us to shame, no matter what we wore." Seth smiled at Morgan's look of fury.

"Yes, she would. I don't believe I've seen that dress before. Is it new?"

She looked a challenge at Seth. "No. My former employer, Theron Shaw, gave it to me."

Seth offered no response. He sipped his wine and smiled into Morgan's eyes.

So that's how it was: He didn't care at all. Well, she didn't care either.

They sat quietly as Martin served dinner.

"Tell us about yourself, Dave. You said you'd been in the West for some time."

"Yes, Mr. Blake, do tell us about your life. You

must have done a great many *very* interesting things."
Her voice was close to a sneer.

Gordon was embarrassed. She was really carrying
her dislike too far. He would talk to her after dinner.
He didn't like having a guest mistreated.

Morgan ignored the looks she was getting from
Gordon.

"There's not much to tell, really. For the last two
and a half years, I've been working in the gold fields in
California."

"The gold fields! I've lost several men to gold fever. I
considered going myself, at one time."

"It's not a pleasant way to live. Dirty, and the work's
almost unbearable at times."

"You seemed to have enjoyed it. You stayed for over
two years. That's a long time; a lot of things can happen in two years." She looked at Gordon affectionately.

"Yes, whole lives can be created in that amount of
time."

She knew he meant Adam. He had not taken her
meaning. "People can start new lives, if old ones are
finished."

Seth merely smiled.

"Well, this conversation is becoming too philosophi-
cal for my poor Indian brain."

"Indian?"

"There now, I've told the house secret. My mother is
a Comanche. But I know little about the Indian way of
life. My mother left me when I was a baby and returned
to her people."

Morgan looked up at Gordon, her eyes gentle. "But
there are times when you make a very convincing Indian, Sky Eyes." Her voice was low, caressing.

Gordon was puzzled. You would have thought they
were sharing a lover's joke. He laughed, but he was
confused.

Morgan turned to Seth. He was smiling placidly, as if he hadn't even noticed.

Seth was now listening to Gordon, and Morgan was able to look at Seth, unobserved. His broad shoulders and thick chest were clothed in rough cottons. He was not clumsy at all, sitting amidst the silver and porcelain. When one large hand carried a fragile crystal glass to his lips, she wondered at the ease with which he controlled his strength so the glass didn't break. His shirt was open at the throat and showed blond curling hair on his chest. She remembered the color of his skin, a great expanse of dark honey and then lighter below his waist. His thighs were so muscular. She even remembered his toes. She shuddered.

"Morgan, are you cold?"

"No, not at all." She tried to make her voice light. At all costs, she must avoid Seth's eyes.

"What is this dessert?" Seth asked.

Gordon turned to Morgan for the answer. *"Babas au rhum,"* she murmured.

"Ah, yes, now I remember."

"Are you familiar with French cuisine, Dave?"

"Yes, somewhat. I had a brief encounter with the food once. I grew quite attached to it."

"Morgan plans all the menus and often cooks a lot of the food. You should taste her breakfasts—they are really delicious."

"I should love to share Mrs. Colter's breakfast." He looked at her across the top of a delicate porcelain cup. His eyes dropped from her face to her breasts.

Morgan stopped her hand midway before it flew to cover herself. He had no right to look at her like that! It was as if she were completely naked. She looked to Gordon for defense from the animal across from her. But he was busy with his dessert and had seen none of their exchange.

The meal was finally at an end, and Morgan realized

her body ached from tension. She wanted to relax now, to be alone.

"Would you care for brandy and a cigar, Dave?"

"Yes, I would."

"Morgan, would you like to join us?"

"No. I think I'll have some tea in the courtyard. It's cooler outside. If you would bring it, Martin?"

"Morgan's right, it's a beautiful night."

"Then maybe Mrs. Colter would allow us to join her."

"Morgan, would you mind?"

There was no acceptable excuse. So, silently, the three of them entered the courtyard. There was no moon, and they could hardly see one another.

Gordon broke the silence. "The skies here are so clear, the stars so bright. If I liked nothing else about New Mexico, I'd love the night sky."

"You speak with some knowledge."

Morgan jumped. Seth's voice was near—too near. She could almost feel his breath on her.

"Have you spent much time in the East?"

"Quite a bit, unfortunately. My father sent me to Harvard."

"Really? You were probably the first Indian to graduate from Harvard!"

"I'm sure I'm the only one, but since they never knew about my mother, it's not something I can publicize."

Seth laughed, quiet and low, a laugh Morgan remembered well.

"I'm sure the people in the East feel the same about Indians as people do here."

"Yes. Every little man needs someone to hate. Dave, would you keep Morgan company for a few minutes? I'd like to go and check on Adam."

"I'll go, Gordon. There's no need—"

345

"I want to. After all, I didn't get to see him all day. Dave stole the boy completely away from me."

She watched Gordon go, seeing only his outline in the darkness. She grabbed frantically for words. "The first time we saw Gordon, he was dressed as an Indian. I was scared to death of him, but Adam wasn't. He liked him right away. Sometimes he'd rather go to Gordon than to me." Her voice was fast, high-pitched. She made herself stop talking and took a sip of tea. Why doesn't he *say* something? He came here to punish me. Now why doesn't he get it over with?

"He's a fine boy, Mrs. Colter."

Mrs. Colter! Why did he keep up the pretense when they were alone?

"I believe Gordon will return in a few minutes and I need to get up early in the morning. We're going after some mustangs tomorrow. So, if you'll excuse me . . . The dinner was delicious and the company delightful. Goodnight, Mrs. Colter."

Morgan stood alone, speechless, and watched Seth go. How very cool of him. Goodnight, Mrs. Colter, indeed!

What did he want here? Why had he come back? Why was he such a coward that he couldn't even come out and tell her what he wanted? She had never known another person so unfeeling.

She put aside her tea cup and left the courtyard for her bedroom. She began to undress. She'd fight Seth with all her strength, she vowed, slipping under the covers.

The knock started her and her heart began to pound. "Come in." Her voice had a slight quiver in it. When she saw Gordon, she quieted.

"Are you all right, Morgan? When I got to the courtyard, you were both gone."

"I'm fine, Gordon." She looked away. Why couldn't her heart pound at the sight of Gordon? Why?

"He upset you, didn't he?" Gordon's voice held a tinge of anger. "Did he say something to you while I was gone?"

"No. He was a perfect gentleman."

Gordon studied her eyes for a moment and then relaxed. "Good. I like Dave. He's experienced and the men like him.

"Today a fight broke out between a couple of the men. Tim came to tell Boyd and me, but before we got there, Dave not only had stopped the fight but had the men laughing as well. Boyd never got the hands' respect like that. And Adam adores him."

"Please, Gordon, I'm tired of hearing about this man's virtues." Gordon was staring at her. He'd guess more than she wanted him to know if she weren't careful. "I'm sorry. I'm glad you and Adam like him. I just need a little more time before I trust someone completely."

Gordon smiled at her. "You can have all the time you want." He kissed her on the forehead. "I guess I should be glad you dislike him. I've always been afraid that if Seth Colter walked through the door, you'd fall right into his arms. It's good to see you dislike a man just because he resembles Seth. Goodnight."

Seth found it difficult to sleep. The few moments alone with Morgan in the dark garden had been hell. He had had to leave. He couldn't have stayed there another minute without taking her in his arms.

She was the same insecure little Morgan he'd met years before, but there was also a different air about her now. She looked people in the eye. She wasn't afraid of her own body. She didn't hide under yards of fabric. She was a woman now and, if possible, even more exciting than before.

Even so, it was not Morgan's lovely face that floated

347

before Seth as, at last, he fell asleep. The face was much smaller, round, and distinctly dimpled.

Morgan was groggy when she heard the knock. She couldn't seem to open her eyes, and didn't really want to. She heard Adam's squeal in the hall, and then the door opened.

"Horse!" Her son's demands were unmistakable. She turned over and gradually focused on Gordon and Adam.

"I'll take you on a horse in a minute."

Morgan frowned. "He's never going to learn to talk if no one ever makes him ask for what he wants."

"You're certainly in a bad mood this morning."

"I am not. I just didn't sleep well." She started to get out of bed.

"You just stay there. I'll take care of Adam and send Carol up with a breakfast tray."

"Adam needs a bath and . . ."

"He'll just get dirty again around the horses. Morgan! Get back in bed or I'll put Adam in there with you."

Morgan smiled. "You win. No one needs to be tortured like that."

"Good. Now go back to sleep and Carol will be up in a couple of hours."

Morgan tried to sleep, but after a few minutes, she knew it was a useless effort. She got out of bed and hastily donned her riding habit. Gordon and Adam were just leaving as she entered the room.

"Going riding, Morgan?"

"Why else would I wear a riding habit?" She continued toward the dining room, then stopped. "I'm sorry. I didn't mean to snap. Yes, I thought I'd take lunch and a book, and go to the stream."

"That sounds like a good idea. Maybe you'd feel better if you were outside for a while."

"There's nothing wrong with the way I feel! I just—" She closed her mouth. Nothing came out of it right any more.

"I want to take Adam with me again today. That is, if he'll stay with me and not go to Dave."

She wanted to scream. Her life was filled with the doings of Seth Colter. He was already beginning to control Adam, and Gordon liked him so much. She kept her mouth closed. No matter what she said, it would be wrong. Someone would defend Seth.

She turned to Martin. "Would you please have Roselle prepare a lunch in a basket for me?"

She kissed Adam goodbye, promising him a good scrubbing when he returned, and saw them out the door. She hurriedly ate breakfast and got her book, quilt, and the picnic basket. As usual, Roselle had packed enough for several people.

The air cleared her head and made her feel better. At the stream, she spread the quilt under the cottonwoods and settled down to read the rest of *Jane Eyre*. It was quiet, with only the sounds of the birds, the locusts, and the stream. She wasn't aware of it when she slept.

Gordon turned to see Dave riding toward him. Adam was slumped against the big man, his head down. Gordon sighed and wondered if he'd ever get used to the boy's preference for Dave.

"Gordon, I think you'd better take Adam back to his mother. It looks like two days in the saddle in a row are too much for him."

"Pull that rope a little tighter or you'll lose him. I can't go right now; I need to stay here. I don't think Morgan's at the house, but I guess Carol can take care of him. Wait a minute! Morgan should be at the stream. Why don't you take Adam and leave him with her? It's closer."

349

Gordon gave him directions. He hoped that, if Morgan got to know Dave better, she'd like him.

Seth stopped on top of the ridge and looked down at his wife. Her head rested on one arm and the other was sprawled, palm up, across an open book. How could she possibly be anyone's mother? She looked only about six years old herself.

Carefully, Seth dismounted and picked Adam up. He secured his horse and walked quietly toward Morgan. He put Adam on the quilt on one side of his mother and then sat down on the other side. Adam turned onto his stomach. Just like his mother, Seth thought.

Seth wanted to stretch out beside her, take her in his arms. But he'd lost that privilege. He smiled at Adam. At least his son harbored no ill will toward him.

Seth tentatively touched a lock of golden hair, then stopped as he realized her eyes were open and staring at him. There was hostility in them, and wariness. His heart ached. How could he have caused such a look?

"I brought Adam." He nodded to the sleeping child on her other side. "He was too tired from yesterday to last today. Gordon told me where you were. I hope you don't mind my disturbing your peace."

Adam stirred. He rubbed his eyes and then went to his mother. She sat cross-legged, now, staring at Seth. Adam sat ungracefully in her lap. He looked up at Seth and smiled. "Da da."

Morgan was startled.

"He's probably trying to say 'Dave.' "

Morgan looked at Seth in total distrust, knowing he'd probably been teaching Adam to say "Daddy."

"Thank you for bringing him to me." She looked away, her heart pounding.

"Eat!" Adam saw the picnic basket. "Chi'en."

Morgan laughed. "I believe that's supposed to mean chicken. He learns new words every day, but sometimes it's not easy to understand them." She watched as Adam dug into the basket. He squealed when he found that he wanted. With great pride he displayed a chicken wing, a trophy.

Morgan avoided Seth's eyes. "Most children's first words are 'Mama' and 'no,' but Adam's first word was 'eat.' In fact, I don't believe he's ever learned to say 'no.' "

Finally she turned to him. His eyes were gentle. She felt her throat tighten. He turned toward Adam.

"I can't imagine a better word than 'eat.' "

Adam turned to Seth. He liked conversations with his favorite word. He handed Seth his prized chicken wing and beamed at him. "Eat."

"It seems you've passed the test, if Adam is willing to share his food with you."

Seth smiled, a delighted smile that Morgan often saw on Adam. "I'm glad to pass his test." There was a slight emphasis on "his."

She looked away. It was still too painful to be so near him. She would be glad of the time when he was just another man to her, when she could look at him and not remember how it was to kiss his neck, his eyes. "I guess you'll have to stay for lunch. Adam seems to want you, and he tends to be rather spoiled. He makes a fuss when he doesn't get what he wants."

Seth's eyes grew sad. Adam sometimes used the same trick on her to get what he wanted. She always melted when he looked like that.

"I'm glad Adam wants me."

She wanted to scream at him. Why did he play this politeness game? Why didn't he tell her what he wanted from her and then leave her in peace?

Seth opened the picnic basket and Adam made a grab for the tin flask held by his father.

"Say what you want, Adam."

Adam's eyes gleamed. "Milk."

351

Morgan had to laugh. "It's just as I thought. He probably knows the English language better than I do. He's just too lazy to say the words. I'm glad someone else forces him to talk."

Seth's eyes were proud. "I have a special interest in this boy."

Morgan remained quiet through the meal, listening to Seth as he taught his son new words.

Abruptly, Seth stood up. "I have to go back to work now. I thank you for lunch." He turned toward his horse, then looked back at Adam, who was watching him avidly. Seth dropped to his knees and put his arms out to the boy. "Give Dada a hug?" Adam ran to his arms and Seth kissed the boy's cheek. "You take care of your mama and I'll see you later."

Seth tipped his hat slightly to her, and his eyes raked her body. Again, she felt naked under his gaze. Her hands flew to cover herself, but she caught them midway. Seth seemed to read her thoughts and laughed quietly. She and Adam watched as he walked up the hill and mounted his horse. The way Seth walked only added to her frustration. It seemed everything reminded her of days past.

She looked down at Adam, still watching Seth on his horse. He waved again. Her anger rose. Seth was trying to win Adam's affections in order to get to her. He thought that when he had the boy in the palm of his hand, he'd get Morgan again. Well, he was wrong.

Adam was content to stay with his mother after lunch. He stretched out on the quilt beside her and she read to him from *Jane Eyre*. He fell asleep quickly.

When Adam awoke, Morgan returned with him to the house. Adam decided he wanted to go back outside on a horse, and Morgan had her hands full persuading him that he was going to be given a bath. Later, when her son stood before her, clean and shining, he grinned at her. He seemed to know when he had given her an especially difficult time and just when to charm her. She tickled him until his squeals of delight were heard all over the house.

Roselle had dinner waiting for him and asked to be allowed to put the child to bed. By that time, Morgan was glad to let someone else take over the care of her active son.

At dinner, Gordon was full of talk about Dave. It seemed she was bombarded all the time with praise about Seth. She longed to scream out the truth about Seth Colter.

She was glad Seth wasn't sharing their dinner, but she kept looking across the table to where he had sat the night before. As Morgan took a bit of Roselle's *boeuf bourguignon*, she wondered if Seth was eating properly. The cook for the hired hands was a little man who reminded her of Jake. He generally liked pinto beans and fried cornbread. What did she care? Seth could starve to death. It would only serve him right.

She went to bed early and fell asleep quickly. She remembered Seth as he was on his knees with his arms outstretched.

Morgan did not see Seth for three days. She told herself that she was not getting enough rest, that that was why she jumped at the sound of a door opening. Her face fell when she saw only Martin, or Roselle, or even Adam at the door, but she thought it was just because she hoped to see Gordon. Yes—that was it. She was falling in love with him. She ignored the fact that she felt just as disappointed whenever Gordon appeared.

She tried not to allow herself to think about Seth. But there were times when she caught herself staring into space, remembering the way he looked astride a horse. Then she would curse him and fervently wish he had never returned to interrupt her life.

At night she slept poorly, often reading far into the night. The strain was beginning to tell on her.

Early one morning, she was baking *madeleines* for Gordon and Adam. She had slept very little the night before, and there were bluish shadows under her eyes. It was hot in the kitchen with both ovens going, and Morgan's hair escaped from the soft arrangement into damp curls on her neck and forehead.

"Why don't you go outside for a while? Take your horse and go to the stream."

"I really can't, Roselle. There's too much to do, and I need to watch Adam."

"Adam is no problem. I've had five children of my own. I can certainly handle one little boy. Now you go outside. You don't look so good."

"A ride would feel good. I'll go and change."

Roselle laughed and put her hands on Morgan's shoulders, pushing her toward the door. "You don't need a fancy riding habit. Go get on your horse and ride. This is New Mexico, not Kentucky. Women here do not own even two dresses, much less riding habits."

Morgan smiled in gratitude. "You're right. Thank you."

Donaciano was asleep in a stall when she got to the barn. Quietly, so as not to disturb him, she led her mare outside, taking a bridle from the wall. She stood on top of a barrel to mount the horse. She looked around carefully to make sure no one saw her and then tucked her skirt up into the waistband. It was good to be free, unhindered by long skirts. On impulse, she removed the pins from her hair and let it fall free.

She guided her horse to the place by the river. She had not been there since Seth had brought Adam to her, four days before. She wanted to return. She wouldn't let Seth keep her from doing what she wanted.

She slid from her horse, and quickly removed her shoes and stockings. She splashed icy water on her legs and thighs, face and arms, and unfastened her blouse to the top of her breasts. She had a sudden impulse to remove all her clothes and stretch out in the water. Instead, she leaned back on the bank, her hands clasped behind her head.

Roselle had been right to make her get out of the house. This was her favorite spot. She smiled up at the sunlight filtering through the cottonwoods.

"You really should tie your horse."

Morgan jumped to her feet. A few feet away, Seth was tying her mare's reins to a branch.

"If something scared her and she ran, you'd have a long walk back to the house."

"What are you doing here?"

"I come here often in the mornings. I liked it when I was here before, so now I come whenever I have the chance." His eyes went to her unbuttoned blouse. "I find the scenery especially beautiful."

She felt the blood rush to her face. "What do you want here? What do you want from me?" The anger she had been holding back for so long threatened to erupt.

Seth's voice was quiet. "I want nothing from you that you are not prepared to give."

"Give? I gave you everything I had and you—"

Seth's eyes were sad. "I'm sorry. I'll leave. I didn't mean to disturb you." With a few quick strides, he was gone.

Morgan sat down heavily. Somehow, she felt defeated. Why couldn't he rage at her, or drag her into his arms? Anything but this constant politeness, this self-effacing manner of his. She angrily wiped away her tears. What was wrong with her? She had planned to ignore him, but she was the one who was being ignored. She mounted her horse and rode around, directionless, for an hour before she returned to the house.

She heard Gordon in his study. He sounded angry. Morgan had never known Gordon to be angry. "Damnation! What do you mean, it's 'something you always meant to do"? Why the hell didn't you tell me that when you signed on?"

Morgan's hand flew to her mouth. "Seth," she whispered aloud. Then she straightened, trying to compose herself. Good, she thought. He's leaving. I'm glad. Now Adam and I can continue our lives without interruptions. She started up the stairs, but turned quickly when the study door opened.

Gordon was frowning at Boyd. The tall foreman was putting a roll of bills into his shirt pocket. "And I don't want to see any of you again," Gordon shouted at Boyd's retreating back.

"Gordon, what's wrong?"

"Gold fever! My foreman and three of my best men are leaving in the morning. They wanted this month's wages." He threw up his hands. "I sometimes wonder if it's worth it. You can never get any help."

Morgan put her hand on his arm. "It's not the end of the world. You'll find someone else."

"Sure I will, but then this damned gold fever will hit them and *they* will leave. Wait!"

"What is it?"

"I have an idea. I'll be back in time for dinner."

He ran from the house.

Morgan was just getting Adam ready for bed when Gordon burst in. "I just hired Dave as my foreman."

"Dave?"

"You haven't forgotten Dave already, have you?"

"No, of course not. I just wonder if it's wise to hire someone you hardly know. After all, he's been here less than a week."

"Well, I've watched him and he works as hard as any two men. And Adam likes him, don't you, boy?" The child went to Gordon, and Gordon carried him to his bed and covered him lightly. He blew out the light and he and Morgan left the room.

"I've invited Dave to supper tonight. We have a lot of things to discuss. That is—if you don't mind?"

"Why should I mind what Mr. Blake does or does not do? He is of no concern to me."

Gordon paused at the top of the staircase and looked at Morgan. She was especially beautiful in the half-light in the hall. He kissed her cheek and then his arms went around her. Lightly, his lips touched hers.

Morgan wanted to feel the blood pounding in her head as it had when Seth kissed her, but there was no such feeling. Gordon broke from her abruptly.

"Dave, I didn't hear you come in."

Morgan turned to see Seth at the foot of the stairs, his brow creased. She patted her hair and adjusted her dress.

"Good evening, Mrs. Colter. I hope you are feeling well."

"Very well, Mr. Blake." She turned loving eyes up to Gordon. "Very well indeed."

Gordon led her down the stairs. He and Seth began to talk of the ranch. Martin held Morgan's chair for her. She tried to listen to the conversation, but she knew little about the work done on the ranch. She was acutely aware of Seth's presence, however, and kept her eyes averted.

She didn't see Seth's eyes on her, or note the way Gordon broke off talking to follow the larger man's glance. Morgan sat quietly, pushing her flan about in the bowl. She had eaten very little.

"Morgan?"

Gordon's voice caused her to start. She looked up into Seth's smiling eyes. "I'm afraid we're being rude. Why don't we have coffee in the courtyard?"

"What about your business?"

"It can wait. Dave and I will have plenty of time to discuss it later. Right now I'd rather spend my time with a beautiful woman. Don't you agree, Dave?"

"I'm afraid I agree more than I'd like to admit."

"Martin," Gordon turned to the butler, "we'd like coffee in the courtyard."

"May I, Mrs. Colter?"

Morgan looked warily at Seth's proffered arm. She chided herself for being so silly.

"Of course." His arm was larger, harder than she remembered. His body was so incredibly warm. Images of the times she had been cold and had snuggled against him for warmth danced in her mind. She took slow, even breaths, trying to calm her frantically beating heart.

"You two go ahead. I want to get a couple of cigars."

The courtyard was still and quiet, with only a cricket's sounds. She removed her hand from his arm.

"Are you happy here, Morgan?" His voice was gentle. It was the first time he'd called her that.

"Yes, I am." She hesitated. There was no anger now. "Why are you here, Seth? Why couldn't you leave me alone?"

The moonlight played on Seth's hair, turning it silver. They held one another's gaze. Neither of them heard Gordon's footsteps.

"I want you. It's that simple. I decided I couldn't live without you, no matter what I thought you had done."

"What I had done! I have done *nothing* wrong."

"I know that—now. I met your friend Jessy and she told me everything. I had the whole story wrong."

Morgan tried to control the anger she felt surging through her. "Let me see if I understand you correctly. As soon as you discovered that I wasn't the . . . what you thought I was, you decided you'd take me back?"

"No, Morgan. That's not what I said. I decided a long time *before* I met Jessy that I wanted you and needed you, even if I had to buy you."

"Buy me! Why, you insufferable . . ." She stopped as Gordon noisily entered the courtyard.

"It took me longer than I thought it would." He

quickly took in Morgan's stormy face and Seth's help-lessness and bewilderment.

"I'm rather tired tonight." Her voice was curt. "Goodnight, Gordon. Goodnight." She did not look at Seth, but merely inclined her head in his direction.

The two men watched her leave. "Well, Dave, shall we go to my study and get down to business?"

Morgan tore her dress from her body and collapsed on the bed, nude. "Of all the despicable, insufferable—" She was at a loss for words. "He'll take me back! After all I've been through. After all the pain he's caused me, he decides he'll come back and forget everything. How generous."

This has all happened because I tried to save his life! I should have laughed at Joaquín and told him to go ahead. How could I ever have loved such a man?

She grabbed a vase from the table by the bed and hurled it at the bedroom door. It made a loud crash, mollifying her just a bit. "Damn *all* men except my son! *My* son, and no one else's!"

Below, in the study, both Seth and Gordon looked toward the ceiling as they heard the crash. Neither made any comment.

It was after midnight when they concluded their business. As Gordon walked past Morgan's room, he saw there was no light coming under the door. Everything was quiet. He went to his own room and removed his coat, vest, and cravat. He loosened his shirt and lit a cigar.

Gordon needed to think. He knew that Seth Colter and Dave Blake were the same person. It should have been a bigger surprise than it was. He realized in retro-spect that everything had pointed to this: the way Mor-gan had reacted to "Dave" on the night of the party; her nervousness since then; and the way she had started flirting with him—but only when Seth was near.

Right now she fought Seth, but Gordon knew it

would be only a matter of time before she admitted her passion for him.

What about his own love for Morgan? There were still times when just the sight of her made the blood in his temples throb. But that was beginning to be less painful. In fact, the last time he'd been in Albuquerque, he had been interested in some of the young women he'd seen there. Could he learn to love elsewhere? Could he get over his love for Morgan? Gordon thought he could.

Right now, he needed to do something to help his little cousin. Seth had done a terrible thing to her, not believing in her. But it was not really unforgivable.

What they needed now was to be together more, to be around one another constantly. Then their bodies would overrule their stubborn minds.

He could be the instrument for their getting together again. Tomorrow, he would begin.

As he fell asleep, he sighed and wished he had been reared in the simpler society of his mother's people. If Seth wanted Morgan, he'd just present her father with more horses than anyone else did. There wouldn't be any discussion about dishonesty, or forgiving—just simple bartering. Tomorrow he would move Seth into the house. There was a connecting door between her bedroom and the one next to it. He imagined it would be easy to fix the lock.

Seth was also just falling asleep. He had spent an hour cursing himself for his clumsiness. Everything he'd said to her had come out wrong. From now on, he thought, I won't let her bait me. I won't try to explain my reasons for coming back. I'll talk only about the present.

He'd tell her that he loved her, that he wanted her, over and over again. But there would be no more explanations. His resolutions made, Seth slept.

~ *Chapter Twenty-One* ~

BREAKFAST had begun before Morgan entered the room.

"I'd like to take Adam with me today, if you don't mind," said Gordon. "Adam has taken such a liking to Dave. It's strange how alike they are. When Adam first saw Dave, he went right to him. You'd expect a boy to react that way only to his own father. And the way Dave protects the boy! I sometimes think he'd lay down his life for Adam."

"All right! I've heard enough about the great Dave Blake. Could we please talk about something else for a change?"

"Why, of course." Morgan didn't see Gordon's suppressed smile. "Remember your father's lawyer, the one you wrote to, in Albuquerque?"

"Yes."

"Well, Mr. Bradley and I have been corresponding lately, and I checked with him about a divorce."

Morgan's head came up abruptly. "Divorce?"

"Yes. You remember we discussed it. Mr. Bradley says you'll need to find your husband before the action can be carried out."

Morgan jumped up from the table. "But he left me alone! He didn't even know about Adam. I should think that would be sufficient reason for a divorce!"

"Ah, yes . . . Adam is another problem. Before he was born, a divorce would have been a lot simpler.

361

Now, of course, there is the possibility that the courts would award Adam to his father."

Her mind went blank. She sat down again. "What do you mean?" Her voice was harsh.

"Well, I briefly told Mr. Bradley about your troubles in San Francisco. I assured him that you were totally innocent, but he said that no matter what the truth of the matter was, your stay at Madame Nicole's would look very bad on paper. And later, you lived with an unmarried man—Theron. It all looks bad."

"But none of that was my fault!"

"That wouldn't really matter. Seth's lawyer could use those facts to tarnish your character."

Morgan sat quietly, her hands folded in her lap. She couldn't even imagine losing Adam.

"There is a way."

"How?"

"If we found Seth and persuaded him to waive all rights to his son."

Morgan felt helpless, defeated. "He'd never do that," she whispered.

"How do you know? We'd have to find him and ask him."

She stood up. "Please excuse me, Gordon, I'm not very hungry this morning." How do I know? I know because Seth loves his son very much and he would never give him up. Never.

Gordon smiled. He really shouldn't have lied that way. Not lied, really . . . but bent the truth. Mr. Bradley had said all those things, but had added that there were ways of getting around the situation. Gordon had simply neglected to mention them to Morgan. It was for her own good, though. Someone had to stop her from ruining her life.

"Well, Adam, shall we go ride a horse?"

Adam grinned, showing little white teeth. "Ride horse."

"Very good. A few more days and you'll be able to argue with your mother."

Morgan spent the morning helping Roselle in the kitchen. After lunch, she went to Gordon's study to work on the household accounts. She tried a hundred times to make the horizontal row of numbers match the vertical row.

"Mama."

She looked up to see Adam running to her, arms outstretched. She was glad for the excuse to leave the hated numbers. "What happened to the pink-and-white cherub who left here this morning? I think this boy must have lived all his life with coyotes. Do you have a kiss for your mama?"

Morgan looked up to see Seth's large form smiling down on them. "I brought him back. He needs a nap in the afternoon. It's too tiring for him to ride in the sun all day."

She began to inform him that she was perfectly capable of caring for her own son, but choked back the angry words. "That's very thoughtful of you." She looked down at Adam's head. He was sitting in her lap, his back to her. He was perfectly still, a sure sign that he was tired. She shifted him to one side in preparation for lifting him.

In one stride, Seth was across the few feet separating them. He took Adam in his arms. His hand brushed her breast. It was as if a torch had touched her. Seth looked into her eyes, but she turned away quickly, hiding her reaction.

"If you'll show me where his room is, I'll put him in bed for you."

"I'll . . ." She saw in his eyes that he'd have his way. "Follow me."

"With pleasure." His eyes were on the sway of her

skirts as they went upstairs. She felt the blood rush to her cheeks again.

"Just put him here on the cot. I need to undress him before I put him in bed."

Seth carefully deposited the sleepy Adam on the cot, and began unbuttoning his shirt.

Morgan started to intercede, but he brushed her aside. "I want to. I don't get to spend much time with him, and I want to, whenever I can."

Morgan stood back and watched as Seth awkwardly removed Adam's shirt. It was funny to see the rugged little body treated as if it were eggshells. Adam, for some reason of his own, decided not to bend his arm. Seth worked for several minutes with no result. Adam's eyes were half closed, but she knew he was very much awake and enjoying his father's increasing frustration.

A giggle finally escaped her.

Seth whirled on her. "What's so funny?" he demanded.

"You. You act like he's a piece of handblown crystal. I assure you he is very strong. I could show you bruises he's made on me—" She stopped because Seth's eyes were twinkling.

"I'd like that."

"Like what?"

"To see your bruises."

She looked away and stepped in front of Seth to tend her son. Adam's eyes opened wide. "Yes, you little imp, you know I won't put up with your nonsense. Now let's get out of these clothes."

She began to undress Adam quickly, all too aware that Seth had not moved from his place behind her. She could feel his breath on her neck as he leaned nearer to watch.

"Is that how it's done?" His voice was low and very close.

She turned to answer him. His face was only inches

from hers. His eyes were slightly hooded, the lips parted and sensual. Her breathing became more shallow as she saw the strong neck and the blond hair that curled above his open shirt. She knew the look well. She had often fallen into his arms when he had looked at her like that.

"I remember a time when you undressed a larger man."

With all her strength, she turned back to her son. She did not respond to the thigh that pressed against hers. She turned away from Seth and bent to pick up Adam. Seth moved in front of her and easily picked him up, put him into the bed, covered him, and kissed his forehead. He stared down at Adam for a minute.

"He's a good-looking boy, isn't he?"

She could swear Seth puffed his chest out. She looked at him in disgust. Her voice was cutting. "Yes. All the Traherns are handsome people."

Seth's eyes teased. "I know one little grandaughter who's a beauty."

She glanced away.

Seth looked around the room for the first time, walking to a group of drawings on the wall. He turned startled eyes back to Morgan. "This is you, isn't it?"

"Yes."

"But how did they get here? I thought you left New Mexico when you were a baby."

Morgan explained briefly about the agent her father had hired, and why he had written that preposterous will.

Seth threw his head back and laughed. Adam turned over in his bed but did not waken. Morgan opened the door and they both went into the hall.

"Would you mind telling me why my story is so amusing?" Her voice was hostile.

"Because I thought that will of your father's was one of the meanest things I'd ever encountered. But he was

365

a sly one. He knew all along about that crazy mother of yours and the way she'd raised you."

"My mother was not crazy!"

"I shouldn't have put it that way. I'm sorry."

"I've found that a lot of things my mother taught me were perfectly true."

"Such as?"

"Men! Men are not to be trusted. They use women. Women are better off without them."

She didn't see Seth move, but all at once, she was in his arms. Before she could think, his lips found hers, quietly at first and then searchingly. Her arms went around his strong, hard body, pulling him closer. Her long-withheld passions came to the surface, and she felt she was falling.

Her body acted by itself, pressing her softness against his muscular thighs and hips. Her mouth opened under his and she returned his thrust with an eagerness of her own. Her lips moved with his. His lips sought her neck, traveling down the tendons with little nibbling bites, causing chills along the curve of her spine and on her legs. "I love you, Morgan. I've always loved you."

The words pierced her brain, recalling a time when she had said those words to him. She remembered his sneer. She couldn't let it happen again. She wasn't going to fall in love with him again and be hurt like that. He was not trustworthy. It might happen again.

"No," she whimpered. "No."

Somewhere in the back of his mind, Seth heard her protest. He loved her. He could not hurt her, not again. She wasn't ready yet. He'd gone too fast. He must leave, get away from her, because he wouldn't be able to contain himself much longer.

He would wait. There'd be another time, a time when she'd welcome him. He held her at arm's length. Her eyes held passion and rage. He smiled down at her and tenderly kissed her forehead. Her breath was soft and warm, still coming in gasps.

He turned and ran lightly down the stairs. Holding his hat in his hand, he stopped in the doorway and looked back up at her. He grinned at her. "I'm glad you still remember me."

Morgan stood for a long time, staring at the closed door. Remember him! She wanted to follow him and tell him what a selfish oaf he was, and how conceited. To think his kiss meant anything to her!

She went shakily downstairs to the study to finish balancing the accounts. She sat at the thick pine desk and began adding figures. But after a few minutes she turned and gazed out the window, unseeing. She stayed that way for a long time.

Morgan looked at the clock and realized the entire afternoon had passed. It was nearly time for dinner. Hearing Adam's squeal from the kitchen, she went to investigate.

Adam sat on a stool at the big work table in the center of the kitchen, shaping pieces of gingerbread.

"Those are the ugliest people I have ever seen. Why do some of them have four eyes?"

"I believe, Mrs. Colter, that some of those eyes are supposed to be ears."

Morgan tweaked Adam's ear. "Ears don't grow beside your nose."

Adam laughed and pushed her hand away. "Ears." He put a piece of raw dough in his mouth.

Morgan left the kitchen and went upstairs to change for dinner. Since Adam's nap had been so late, she decided, he could eat with Gordon and her tonight.

When Morgan entered the dining room some time later, the first thing she saw was Seth's broad back. He was impeccably dressed in the suit he had worn the night of the party. Morgan felt her anger rise again. She would have to tell Gordon to stop inviting him to dinner so often.

"Oh, Morgan, I hope you don't mind my inviting Dave to dinner tonight. I'm finding I can learn a lot about ranching from him."

She had no time to construct an answer before Martin entered, holding Adam's hand. Adam immediately ran to Seth, his arms outstretched.

"How are you, Adam? I haven't seen you in hours. Did you have a good nap?"

Adam smiled at his father and pointed to the table. "Eat."

"This boy certainly knows what he wants." Seth put Adam on a stool, next to what was fast becoming his own chair. The two sat directly across from Morgan.

"Might I say, Mrs. Colter, that you look especially lovely tonight? Red becomes you."

"Thank you," she said tonelessly. She just wouldn't look at him. She had a brief vision of the beautiful red dress she wore—wore for Seth—at Joaquín's party. It had disappeared on that horrible night, along with all her dreams.

Morgan stared at her plate as Seth and Gordon talked about the ranch. It seemed even Adam had deserted her. Of course, a mere mother always took second place to food. It infuriated her that Seth cared for the boy so easily. Adam's plate was never empty, and Seth saw to his needs as if he'd been doing this for years. Adam's placid acceptance of his father also made her angry. She was being betrayed by the person she loved most in the world.

Morgan was startled when Seth pushed his chair back. "If you'll excuse me, I think I'll put my . . . partner to bed." His smile was innocent, but she knew what he had wanted to say.

When they were gone, Gordon turned to her. "I'm glad he's gone, because I want to talk to you about something."

She opened her mouth to say that she was glad he was gone for any reason, but she closed it again.

"I know there'll be no problem, but I did want to discuss it with you first. For the good of the ranch, I'd like Dave to move into the house."

"What?"

"You know that trip I've been planning to New York will be soon. I don't like to leave you and Adam here alone. I'd like to have a man here in the house to protect you."

"Protect me! Has it ever occurred to you that maybe I need protection *from* Mr. Blake?"

Gordon was instantly concerned. "Has he ever mistreated you?"

"No, he hasn't . . ."

"Good. I thought I knew Dave better than that. Adam, of course, adores him. I just can't get over the way the child has taken to him, as if . . ."

"I've heard this before. Why do you think it is necessary for Mr. Blake to move into the house?"

"Morgan, I don't like to bear the entire responsibility for running this ranch. I'm afraid to leave, even to go to Albuquerque. Just when I think I can relax, something happens, like Boyd and the other men quitting to go to the gold fields."

"What makes you think Mr. Blake won't run off somewhere, too?"

"For one thing, he's older, more settled than the other men. And if I pay him more and offer him a room in the house, those would be incentives to stay. Dave's different. He shouldn't be treated like just another hired hand."

"So you plan to allow him into the house."

"He deserves it. Look at the way he cares for Adam. I wouldn't trust Adam with any of the other men. They're likely to put him down somewhere and forget him. Not Dave."

"Must I be plagued day and night with sermons on

this man's virtues? I'm sure if we knew all there is to know about Mr. Blake, we'd know things of which he isn't proud."

"I'm sure there are. But no one's perfect. Then you really have no specific objection to Dave moving to the house? The good really does seem to outweigh the bad."

Seth returned. "Dave, I've just talked to Morgan about your moving into the house, and she would be happy to have you."

They had already discussed it! Her opinion meant nothing. Gordon ignored the look she shot him.

"I thank you very much for the invitation, Mrs. Colter. I hope I prove to be of assistance to you and your son."

Gordon forestalled her reply. "I've taken the liberty of having Carol prepare your room." Gordon again ignored the look Morgan flashed at him. "Come upstairs and I'll show it to you. It was Morgan's father's room."

Morgan didn't follow them. She was furious with Gordon for planning all this without her consent. It wouldn't be easy to stay away from Seth when she saw him every morning at breakfast.

Her *father*'s room? Hadn't Gordon said that? Morgan nearly toppled the dining chair in her hurry to get upstairs. Her father's room was next to hers, and there was a connecting door between them!

They were in the room and Morgan stared at the door that led to her room. She tried to catch Gordon's eye, but failed.

"If you'll excuse me, Mrs. Colter, I'll get my gear from the bunkhouse."

She held her tongue until she heard the downstairs door close. "He can't have this room! It's right next to mine!"

"Morgan, have you seen the other bedrooms in this house? The housekeeper your father and mine had when this house was built decorated every bedroom for women, except three—the one Adam has, my room, and this one. I can't see Dave with a pink coverlet and chintz curtains."

"We'll redecorate, we'll . . ."

"Don't be silly, Morgan. The door locks from both sides." He walked to the door and demonstrated that it was firmly locked. "It's as if there were no door."

"It's not the same at all," she murmured.

"Morgan, I know it was a shock, seeing Dave for the first time. But his resemblance to someone you dislike is not his fault. The way you treat him is not fair. He's a very warm person when you get to know him . . . Well, it's been a long day." Gordon yawned ostentatiously. "I think I'll go to bed. I'm sure Dave can find his own room."

"Yes, I'm sure he can."

Gordon did not fail to note the sarcastic tone in her voice.

Locked in her own room, she removed her gown and put it away carefully. She stepped into one of her favorite nightgowns and sat before the mirror to unpin and brush her hair. She stopped in midmotion when she heard Seth enter the room next door. She listened. Drawers opened and closed. The wardrobe door clicked. She heard his boots drop to the floor.

It's as if he's in this room, she thought. She looked toward the connecting door. There was silence, and then she saw the light under his door go out. She went to her own bed, blew out the lamp, and snuggled under the covers. She was feeling that peaceful relaxation just before sleep comes, when the words carried through the door to her. "Goodnight, *mi querida*." Seth's voice was a caress. The familiar endearment relaxed her even more and she fell asleep easily.

Seth stared at the room. He was glad to be out of the bunkhouse. Every time one of those men had made a crack about Morgan, he had had a difficult time controlling himself. Now there was only one thin door separating her from him. He was calm for the first time in weeks. He hadn't liked the idea of her being alone in this house, alone with Gordon. Even if there didn't seem to be a romantic love between them, she was his. He meant to keep her that way.

He laughed at himself. Now, Colter, that's what caused all your trouble before—your possessive jealousy. This time he wasn't going to ruin things. After the long kiss this afternoon, he knew she still felt something for him. It wouldn't be long before that little door would open. He drifted off to sleep, confident.

Adam was awake especially early the next morning. He tumbled out of his bed, opened his door, and sleepily made his way to his mother's room, just as he always did. Seth heard the stumbling steps and hastily donned his pants and intercepted Adam before he could pound on Morgan's door.

Adam opened his eyes in surprise when Seth swept him up in his arms. His father put his finger to his lips and Adam understood. The little boy snuggled against the strong chest and closed his eyes. When Seth deposited his son in the big bed, Adam immediately turned on his stomach and went back to sleep. Seth removed his pants and climbed back into bed, leaving the hall door open. Soon both father and son were asleep.

When Morgan woke, she had a feeling something was wrong. She opened her eyes, frowning. The sun was up and there was a long ray of sunlight seeping in under the curtains. It was later than usual. She was so used to her son's waking her up and then climbing into her bed and going back to sleep that she had learned to sleep through the disturbance. She turned to Adam. He wasn't there!

Disregarding her robe, she ran from her room. The

door to Adam's room was open, but he wasn't in the room. Gordon's door was closed. She was alarmed. He couldn't disappear, not her little Adam. Tears blurred her eyes. She looked down the stairs. He could have fallen down them in his long nightshirt. She must calm herself. Maybe Roselle or Martin had taken him to the kitchen. She listened, but there were no sounds downstairs. Her hand flew to her mouth. Then she saw the bedroom door next to her own standing slightly open.

She pushed the door open, brushing away the tears in relief as she saw the little curly head just above the covers. She offered a silent prayer of thanks. She'd been so silly. She should have known that Seth's presence would upset everyone's life. She shut her eyes in exhaustion.

Seth opened his eyes to see Morgan standing near him. He might move his hand and clasp her waist, but he lay still. Her eyes were closed and she was breathing deeply, her breasts thrusting forward under the thin gown. The gown fit her perfectly, hugging her body closely to the waist and then flaring out softly in a bell shape. It was a deep, rich blue with long, tight sleeves that curved out at the wrist. The neckline covered her collarbone and then plunged deeply, almost to the waist, edged by cream-colored lace. Her hair was rumpled and fell about her to the waist. Never had he seen her more desirable. He caught her hand in his and her eyes flew open.

"I—" she began.

"You don't need an excuse to be here." She tried to pull her hand away, but he held it easily, caressing the fingertips.

"I came to find my son. He usually comes to my room. When he didn't, I was worried."

Seth's eyes were gentle. He pulled her hand to his mouth. He kissed the fingertips, raking the sensitive tips across his teeth. Her scalp tightened.

"Stop it!" His grasp on her hand was firm.

"I am limiting myself to only your fingertips. I like that blue thing, especially the lace."

Her hand covered the lace which played hide-and-seek with the soft curve of her breasts. She looked straight at him, one eyebrow arched, challenging. "Theron bought me this gown. He bought me many beautiful things."

"Theron," Seth murmured. "Nice man. Not your type, though. Lovely house." He was concentrating on his pleasant task. His teeth made little bites in the palm of her hand.

"Seth, will you stop that!"

"I don't plan to. I may stay here all day and make love to your hand. You used to love it."

"When did you meet Theron?" She had to think of something else or her whole body might start shivering.

"When I asked him where you were. You have the sweetest little veins in your wrist." He nibbled at them.

"Seth! Theron told you where I was? Why would he do that?" She made one supreme effort and succeeded in jerking her hand from Seth's grasp. She took a few deep breaths to calm herself.

Seth gave a disappointed sigh and sat up in the bed. The quilts fell away to his waist, exposing his massive chest. The movement caused Adam to stir. He sat up and rubbed his eyes.

"Morgan, sit down, please, and I'll tell you about Theron." He nodded toward Adam, quietly staring from one parent to the other.

She sat carefully on the edge of the bed.

"I told Theron what a fool I'd been. He agreed. But I told him how much I loved you and that I wanted a chance to win you back."

"Oh, yes, you loved me—*after* you found out I was pure."

Adam watched his mother. He didn't like her tone of

voice and he began to frown, her agitation scaring him.

"That's not really true, love." Seth's voice was calm. "I admitted to myself a long time before I met Jessy that I loved you." He continued before she could protest, "I would have come to you then, begged you to let me live with you. But I didn't think you'd want me, poor as I was, not after the way you were accustomed to living, with Theron. Did I mention that I am a rich man now?"

Her look was steely. "Twenty-five thousand dollars should make you quite comfortable."

Seth was puzzled. "Twenty-five . . . ? Oh, the money you offered me to marry you. I told you that never meant anything to me."

"How am I to know what to believe? Now you tell me you always loved me, but I remember some other things you said to me, such as accusing me of selling my body. You didn't seem to love me then. Tell me this: When am I to believe you, and when am I not?"

Seth didn't lose his slow, even smile. "I deserve your abuse. I deserve everything you have to say about me. I was a fool. I was hurt and jealous and I struck out at you.

"I want to make it up to you, Morgan. I love you and I plan to stay near you until you love me again, even if it takes years."

"You seem confident that everything will work just as you plan. What if I told you that I loved someone else and that I couldn't love you?" She looked toward the bedroom door.

Seth's smile broadened. "I've seen Gordon kiss you, and I've kissed you. If you love him and hate me, then I prefer your hatred. It has more fire."

"You—!" She struck him on the chest with her fist, but it was the same as striking an adobe wall, for all the damage it did.

Seth enclosed her fist in one of his, then encircled the

375

other wrist with strong fingers. He pulled her to him, crushing her helpless arms between them. He entangled his hand in her hair, cradling the back of her head. He touched his lips to hers, sweetly, and then with a demanding eagerness. He forced her mouth open. Morgan responded fully, meeting his demands with more of her own.

Adam had never seen his mother kissed before, and he wasn't sure her moans didn't mean Seth was hurting her. He hit Seth's shoulder with his fists. "Mama. Mama."

Morgan heard her son and began to return to reality, forcing herself away from Seth.

Seth extended his now-empty arms to his son, to reassure him. "I don't know whether he's trying to protect you or me."

"You?"

"A little fire goddess like his mother could easily destroy a mere mortal like me."

She raised her hand to him again, but his teasing smile reminded her of what had just happened.

Angrily, she lifted Adam into her arms. "You're going to have a long wait if you think I'll ever fall in love with you. I've made all my mistakes already."

She heard Seth's laughter behind her.

At breakfast, Seth ignored Morgan. Although she had planned to ignore him also, she found it infuriating that he should act as if she weren't even in the same room.

After Seth and Gordon left, Adam played in the courtyard with his wooden ranch set. Morgan needed to finish her ledgers and promised herself that she would not even think of Seth. But she looked up sharply each time someone passed the open study door.

At lunch, Adam proudly showed his mother his gingerbread monsters, explaining them in a mixture of gibberish and words. He went back outside for a while before his nap.

Morgan went upstairs to make sure the rooms had been cleaned properly. She hesitated at Seth's room, but then entered. His things were always neat, more so than hers ever were. She opened a drawer. He had too few shirts, and some of them needed mending. Angrily, she slammed the drawer shut. What was she doing? He was not her responsibility any longer. Let him care for his own shirts!

She ran into Carol, an armload of clean linen nearly falling from her arms. "Is anything wrong, Mrs. Colter?"

"No!" She fairly shouted at the girl. Morgan regretted it immediately, but Carol had already scurried away.

"Now he's making me yell at the servants," she mumbled as she hurried to her own room. Hastily, she donned her riding habit.

In the kitchen, she asked Roselle if she'd put Adam to bed for his nap, and she went outside to ride her horse. She started for her favorite place by the river, but she knew Seth went there, and she didn't want to see him. She remembered a pond that Gordon had shown her on the first day they'd toured the ranch together. It was an especially hot day and the sun was merciless. She loosened the high neck of the habit. The mare felt the heat, too.

The pond was a wider place in the river, forming a little pool, surrounded by tall cottonwoods. Gordon had said there would be cattails later in the fall. She dismounted, leading the mare to the trees. It would be good to splash her face with water.

She was startled by the sound of several horses beyond her, near the pond. Always cautious in the untamed New Mexico wilderness, she tied her horse and went to investigate before blundering into trouble. As she rounded a tree, she saw Seth leading several mustangs to water. As the dusty horses drank, Seth dismounted and walked to the edge of the water, letting his own horse drink.

Could she go nowhere without seeing him? She stood very still, knowing that any movement would cause him to turn and see her.

Seth removed his hat and wiped the sweat from his brow. Then he looked around. Morgan held her breath. She was thankful she'd worn her dark green riding habit.

Seth did not really see the place where Morgan stood, half hidden in the dense underbrush. Quickly, he removed his clothes and stepped into the water. He splashed himself, enjoying the coolness. Morgan looked on in fascination at the magnificent body she had once known so well, the powerful arms and shoulders, the muscles that stood out in his thighs.

Seth was used to the dangers of New Mexico, where a second's heedlessness could cause one's death. Over the years he had developed a second sense concerning these hazards. He stood still. He knew someone was watching him. He pivoted on one foot and faced Morgan, who gasped. Their eyes locked and held.

"Care to join me?"

She didn't answer, but whirled on her heel and returned to her waiting horse. She returned to her favorite spot and allowed the horse to drink before returning to the house. She tried not to think of Seth.

At dinner, the sight of Seth caused the blood to rush to her face. She refused even to glance his way during dinner. As they walked to the courtyard, Seth whispered, "Did you enjoy your bath as much as you enjoyed mine?" Blushes covered her body, and she was glad for the darkness.

~~~ *Chapter Twenty-Two* ~~~

IT had been a little over two weeks since Seth had come to the Three Crowns. Since the time Morgan had seen him in the pool, she had avoided him. She saw him even less now than she had when he'd lived in the bunkhouse. He took his responsibilities as foreman very seriously and often missed dinner to straighten out some problem on the ranch. Even when Morgan came down to breakfast, she found he had already been at work for hours. What free time he did manage, he spent with Adam. Morgan sometimes felt Seth paid more attention to Roselle than he did to her. She was, of course, glad of that.

It was on one of the rare mornings when the three of them breakfasted together that Gordon made his announcement. "My letter finally came. I'll be leaving for New York."

"What?" She dropped her spoon.

"Morgan, I've told you about this trip for months, so don't look so surprised."

"Adam and I will go with you."

"Sit down. You are not going with me. It will be a hurried trip and Adam is too young to have to travel for days on a stagecoach and then on a train. I won't hear of it. It's too dangerous."

Seth turned to Gordon. "Is it ranch business that takes you to New York?"

"Morgan's father once heard about some cattle bred

379

in the Scottish Highlands. He thought they might adjust to New Mexico, so he started working on getting them here. After several years, they'll soon arrive in this country. I figure if I'm not there to meet the ship when it docks, they'll sell my cattle to someone else."

"When are you leaving?" Morgan's voice was soft.

"Right after breakfast."

"Today! You'll be leaving *today*?"

Gordon stared at her a moment. "Yes. The letter took a long time coming and now I'll barely make it there in time for the ship. Martin is packing for me now."

After breakfast, Morgan tried again to persuade him to let Adam and her go with him.

"Don't worry. I'll be back shortly, and Dave is here to take care of Adam and you."

"Adam, yes—but not me."

Gordon looked weary. "If I didn't trust Dave as much as I do, I wouldn't leave him here alone with you. When you get over your hostility, you'll trust him, too. I have to leave now or I'll never make the stage. Kiss me goodbye?"

"Gladly." She happily slid into Gordon's arms and lifted her lips for his kiss. Gordon was the man she wanted to love.

With great effort, he resisted her lips and placed a chaste kiss on her forehead. "Now, get Adam so I can say goodbye."

Morgan held her son and they both waved to Gordon. When she turned back to the house, it seemed empty already. Adam squirmed out of her arms. He ran to the kitchen and she followed him. Tonight she would be alone with Seth. Without Gordon's presence, he could talk to her about anything. She began planning the night's meal, remembering Seth's favorite dishes without realizing she was doing so.

She worked all day on the meal, glad to be too busy

to think. Roselle put Adam to bed for his nap. Morgan rested for a while when the house was quiet. She worked again in the kitchen until it was time to bathe and dress for dinner. Roselle took charge of Adam.

From the back of the wardrobe, she took a dress that she had rarely ever worn before. It was simply cut, a deep golden yellow, embroidered with tiny sienna rosebuds around the neckline. The neckline was the reason she seldom wore the dress. It fell across her shoulders and the top of her breasts, stopping just above the rosy peaks. When she stood in front of the mirror, she remembered the last time she'd worn the dress. Charley Farrell had gaped at the enticing sight and she had been embarrassed at the open-mouthed stare he'd worn all evening.

She briefly asked herself why she was wearing this now when she and Seth were to be alone. She'd never worn it for Gordon. She told herself that she was wearing this only because she hadn't worn it in such a long time. She dabbed perfume on her wrists, behind her ears, and in the deep shadow between her breasts.

Carol came to tidy the room. "You look especially lovely, Mrs. Colter," the girl remarked shyly. "Mr. Blake will be very pleased."

"Mr. Blake—!" She cut short her remark.

"Will there be anything else tonight, ma'am?"

"No, Carol. You may go home. Be sure and say hello to your parents for me, and take them some gingerbread."

"Thank you, ma'am." She turned to leave, but saw Seth in the open doorway. He put his finger to his lips, conspiratorily. Carol did like Mr. Blake so much. He was always teasing—like Adam, except grown up. She left and closed the door behind her.

Morgan, at the mirror, heard footsteps behind her. "I don't need anything else—" She stopped when she felt his lips on the back of her neck, sending little shivers throughout her body. She closed her eyes, but opened them quickly when he moved away.

She whirled toward him. "What are you doing here?"

Seth smiled lazily at her and stretched out on her bed, his big, handsome figure nearly dwarfing the lacy, crochet-covered bed. "I live here, too, remember?"

"I just hope *you* remember that this is not your room. And may I remind you that this is my ranch, not yours."

"*Mi querida*, stop fighting me. I am looking forward to dinner. Roselle says you spent all day cooking, that you prepared a very special meal." His eyes were teasing.

"I did not! I like to cook and today I wanted to, so I just made a few things." She turned her face away, took a deep breath, and turned back. "Kindly get off my bed and out of my room."

He moved his hips slightly, as if testing the bed. "Do you sleep well on it, or do you find it too large for one person?"

"Seth Colter! Get out of here!" She started toward him. Seth opened his arms to her and she backed away.

He sat up on the bed, feet over the side. "That another dress Theron bought for you?"

Morgan saw a slight frown crease his brow, and she felt momentarily triumphant. "Yes. Do you like it?" She bent over just slightly so her breasts swelled even more precariously over the top. "It's strange that you are just now noticing this dress. Most men notice it immediately."

The little imp is trying to make me jealous, Seth thought. He smiled at her. His eyes raked her body, devouring her. "When I look at you, my little wife, I see you as I always remember you—wearing nothing but your hair ribbon. So it takes me longer to notice your clothes."

"You—"

"If you try to throw something, I will have to restrain you." He held out his arm. "Let's go to dinner."

Seth sat across from Morgan. She refused to speak to him. They were into the second course, and Martin had left the room.

"Martin will know something is wrong if you keep your silence. He'll think we've had a lovers' quarrel." He raised his voice. "Tell, me, Mrs. Colter, about your travels in San Francisco."

She smiled up at him. "I met some very interesting people, some gentlemen." She emphasized the title.

Seth was serious. "Do you remember a Charley Farrell?"

"That's funny. I thought of Charley just tonight. Mr. Farrell is not a man one should think of too often. Theron and I did a lot of work for his wife. A pleasant woman, but the most atrocious taste imaginable."

"What about Farrell? Did you know him?"

"More than I wanted to, I'm afraid. Theron rescued me several times from his greedy little hands. Finally he told Mr. Farrell that if he didn't stop his attentions, we would not return. I think Theron also threatened to tell his wife. Charley was deathly afraid of her." She sipped her wine. "Where did you meet him?"

Seth looked down at his plate. "Just over a beer once. I didn't really know him."

Morgan didn't understand Seth's sudden seriousness. If anyone should not be taken seriously, it was Charley Farrell.

Martin removed the last of the dishes.

"That was a feast," said Seth. "It seemed I couldn't get enough of everything."

"Well, if anyone could, you did. I don't believe I've ever seen anyone eat as much as you did."

He grinned at her. "I'm a growing boy. I need my strength."

383

"Martin, we'll have coffee in the courtyard—if that's all right with you, Mr. Blake."

They went outside and stood silent, listening to the New Mexico night sounds. There were coyotes near, howling. Seth walked to the little tiled pool. "It's nice to be here with you, Morgan. If I didn't know better, I'd think Gordon planned going away."

Morgan hid her face. The thought had crossed her mind, too.

"Remember the days we spent in the canyon, below the Indian ruin?"

"No."

He turned startled eyes toward her and then laughed. "Why don't you come over here and let me kiss you?"

"Stop it, Seth, or I'll go inside. All of that is over. We're just . . . acquaintances now."

"Good! Now that we're acquaintances, we can become friends. And then we can become lovers."

"Seth, you are impossible!"

"I hope you mean it's impossible for us not to love one another. Did you ever ask yourself why you asked *me* to marry you, and not one of the other men at the Ferguson ball?"

"I heard you had a ranch in New Mexico." She could hardly tell him she had liked his muscular thighs! She laughed.

Seth cocked his head and looked at her strangely. "Well, little one"—he walked toward her—"I think I'll go to bed." He put his hands on her shoulders and she drew back. He pulled her to him, their bodies close but not touching. Then he kissed her, lightly, on the cheek. "Goodnight, my wife." He released her and was gone.

She stood staring at the place where he had been. He had no manners! He should have walked her to her own bedroom instead of leaving her standing alone in a darkened garden. Angrily, she mounted the stairs. His door was closed and all was quiet in the big house. She pulled the pins from her hair and hastily removed her dress, carelessly tossing it over the back of a chair. She pulled a nightgown from the drawer, a thin muslin gown, almost transparent. In bed she tossed and turned, not even understanding the reason for her restlessness.

Seth smiled as he heard her movements. Oh, yes, sweet . . . you do remember the time in the canyon.

It wasn't long after Morgan fell asleep that she began to dream. She was back with Jacques and he had one hand on her hair, a knife at her throat. The Indians were watching. Then she saw Seth, heard his voice, calm and patient. "I'm here, sweetheart. There's no need to worry, *mi querida.*"

She woke up slowly, fighting the horror of the dream. Seth held her in his lap. Her arms encircled his neck and held him tightly to her. He spoke softly, using sweet words while caressing the back of her head. She cried softly.

"Do you want to tell me, little one?"

The story came pouring out in a torrent. She told him about Jacques, about the dream. Then she told of Joaquín's treachery, of the search that night for Seth, and then about the note. She told about Madame Nicole and how, on the night of the sale, she had seen Seth in the mirror and heard a music box. She didn't see the color drain from his face as he remembered the night before Christmas when he had smashed the little box.

Morgan sobbed out the story of her humiliation on the night of the auction. She told about her fondness for Theron. She told of that night when she had been so glad to see Seth, of how she'd prayed that he hadn't died, even though she had thought it was a hopeless prayer. There were tears in Seth's eyes. "I'm sorry, sweet one. I'm here, now, and I won't leave you again."

She was like a child. He cradled and rocked her. She needed his tenderness. And she desperately needed the release the tears brought. Gradually, her breathing quieted and he knew she was asleep. Gently, he put her in bed and pulled the quilt about her. She made a small sucking sound, like Adam. He kissed her cheek and the tears that remained in her eyelashes.

Reluctantly, he went to the door between their rooms. It was locked. Puzzled, he left the room through the door to the hallway. Out of curiosity, he tried the door again from his side. It opened.

Gordon, he thought. Somehow Gordon had found out about them and had arranged that they be alone together in the house. Of course, it wouldn't have been difficult to discover the truth, what with Morgan constantly shouting, "Seth Colter! You—!" It was music to his ears. If he guessed correctly, Gordon planned to stay away until he received word that Morgan and Seth were together again.

Adam had just raised his fist to bang on his mother's door when a big hand turned the unreachable knob. He looked up to see his father, his finger to his lips. Adam quietly followed Seth into the room, stopping to look down on the sleeping woman.

Seth planted a soft kiss on the little pulse point below Morgan's ear. She smiled in her sleep. Adam grinned up at his father and decided to imitate him. The boy's mouth missed the mark, falling loudly and succulently on his mother's ear. Instantly, Morgan's eyes opened and her hand flew to her ear.

Adam and his father laughed together in conspiracy. "The two of you! I can't even sleep peacefully!" She had to laugh. They were so much alike. "At least you should behave better than your son. He has the excuse of extreme youth."

Seth's grin broadened and Morgan could swear his chest puffed out at least another two inches.

"Why are you strutting about this morning?"

"That's the first time you've ever admitted that he's mine."

She frowned. "Of course, he's yours. Just look at him. I don't guess two people could look more alike."

Seth looked at his son adoringly. "I know, but I like to hear you say it anyway."

"You're worse than Lupita's roosters. He *has* to be yours. You're the only man I ever—" She hadn't meant to say that. He had no right to know.

Seth sat down heavily beside her. "I'm the only man who's ever made love to you?"

She looked away, absently watching Adam, who was pulling the lace trim from a pillowcase. "Yes," she whispered.

He grabbed her shoulders, pulled her to him, and kissed her loudly and heartily on the mouth. "I know it shouldn't matter, and I love you no matter what, but that makes me very happy. Son, before you destroy your mother's bed linens, how about a piggyback ride downstairs?" Adam climbed on his father's back and they stopped in the doorway. "Why don't you stay there? I'll give Adam to Roselle and I'll come back and join you."

Morgan rubbed her mouth, then her ear. "I already have had two bruising kisses this morning. I certainly don't need any more."

"Maybe on second thought, I'll just push Adam out the door. He can yell all he wants—we'll never hear him." He closed the door quickly, as the pillow hit the door. Adam kicked his father in the ribs, laughing with gusto. He liked this man because exciting things always happened around him, like his mother throwing a pillow at them. She never did those things around other grown-ups. "Horse. Horse," he screamed.

At breakfast, Seth suggested that Morgan bring Adam to the river for a picnic lunch. He'd try to get away to join them.

387

"Well, it may be difficult. I have a lot to do." He was taking too much for granted.

"What is so urgent?"

He sounded as if she spent her days lounging in bed. Her voice was hostile. "This is September, so I have a lot of food to put up for the winter. And there's the household accounts, and . . ."

Seth looked down, contrite. "I just thought Adam might need a change of pace today."

Morgan turned away. "If I can get away, maybe we can go."

"Good!" She knew his pain had been an act. He kissed her cheek. "Have a good day, wife."

"Stop calling me that. Someone may hear."

He smiled at her. "I hope so, wife."

"Wife." Adam imitated his father.

"Oh, no. You're going to have the strangest vocabulary when Gordon returns."

"Gord?" Adam questioned.

They laughed together at their son.

Adam spent the morning playing with his ranch. The men of the ranch had spent some of their evenings carving new pieces. Now it was too big to carry inside at night. Seth had built a canopy over it, to protect it from the rain.

Morgan paid special attention to the cleaning of Seth's room and then spent two hours working with Roselle on a delicious picnic lunch.

When everything was ready, she and Adam went to their special place near the river. Seth was not there, so she spread the quilt and sat down with Adam. She recited nursery rhymes to him, illustrating them on the slate board she often packed.

"How're my wife and son?" He looked at Morgan innocently when she frowned at him. He was becoming far too possessive. Morgan immediately opened the picnic basket.

"*Brioches!* Morgan, you don't know how often I

388

used to think about these little rolls. In California, I ate some of the worst food imaginable. Jessy cooked for me for a while. I don't know how I survived it. Jessy would take a skillet and throw in some eggs with a generous helping of eggshells." He demonstrated with hand gestures. "When some of the eggs were still mostly raw and some were so hard you couldn't tell them from the skillet, she'd serve them to you. Now don't ask me by what magic Jessy was able to use one skillet and get the eggs to come out at opposite degrees of doneness. I was always too smart to ask."

Morgan was laughing helplessly.

"Wait, I haven't told you about the biscuits. They were so chewy that you put your fingers between your teeth, like this, and stretched them as long as your arm could reach. Now, explain that. No one dared ask about those biscuits. They were such a marvel that we rather looked forward to them."

Morgan held her stomach as she laughed. She could just imagine Jessy making biscuits like that. She'd had a taste or two of Jessy's cooking. She'd love to send a recipe for those biscuits to Jean-Paul.

As Morgan laughed, Adam held his slate to his father and said, "Horse."

Seth wrote on the slate: *Seth loves Morgan with all his heart.* He handed the slate to her. She looked into his eyes and saw that what he wrote was true. She wiped the laughter tears from her eyes, erased the slate, and drew Adam's horse.

"I have to get back to work now. Kiss me goodbye? On the cheek?"

She laughed at him for playing the same tricks as Adam did when he wanted something. "All right, I'll kiss your cheek." She stood up and leaned toward him, and as they both knew they would, they clung to one another. When their lips met, there was no resistance from Morgan.

"You won't forget me?" He smiled down into her half-closed eyes. He turned to Adam. "A hug for your daddy, son?" Adam ran to his father's arms and Seth tossed the boy into the air and then rubbed the stubble of his whiskers in Adam's neck. The child screamed with delight. Seth left them both, waving.

When they returned to the house, Adam took his nap and Morgan undressed and lay on her bed. When had she realized she still loved Seth? Maybe when she'd seen the slate and knew he could be trusted completely. Yes, this time he could be believed and trusted.

What about what he had done, that horrible night in San Francisco? Somehow, the memory wasn't so clear anymore. Now there were memories of Seth playing with Adam, Seth comforting her after a bad dream. She didn't know if he had changed, if maybe some little thing might still set him into a jealous rage. She didn't care.

She would let the future take care of itself. She had him near her, and that's where she wanted him to stay. If he wanted her, then she was his.

Dinner was pleasant and Morgan relaxed and enjoyed the freedom that admitting her love for Seth had bestowed on her.

Afterward, they drank *café au lait* in the courtyard. Seth sat on a stone bench and put his arm across the back. Morgan watched him closely, hoping he'd ask her to join him. It seemed that for weeks she had fought his aggression, and now he left her alone! He finally patted the seat beside him and looked at her questioningly. She tried to keep calm, to walk toward him sedately and not run into his arms.

They sat quietly together. Morgan realized she felt safe, at home here beside Seth. She had never felt that way in San Francisco or even on the Colter ranch. For some reason she thought of Jake, of the way he had been so angry with her for always eating. She laughed.

"Share it with me?"

"What?"

"What were you thinking about that made you laugh?"

"Jake and the way he used to get so mad at me."

"Why would Jake ever get mad at you? I wrote them all when I came here, so they'd know I was still alive. I'm afraid I didn't tell anyone where I was when I was in California. But tell me, what made Jake mad? Maybe that you'd even speak to me after the way I acted at Montoya's party? I guess he knew we'd . . . ah . . . spoken." His eyes twinkled.

"That was part of the problem. You see, when I was carrying Adam, I ate."

"I don't understand. How could Jake be upset about that?"

"When I say I ate, I mean I ate *constantly*, for six months. I ate anything Lupita cooked."

Seth laughed softly. "I've been doing that for years."

"That's what I mean. I ate as much as you and it made me the same size as you."

Seth smiled in disbelief.

"You remember how Lupita's cottons always swallowed me? By the time Adam was born, they barely stretched across my body."

"But Lupita's twice as big as you are! I would have liked to see that. I'll bet you looked like a little barrel." He smiled down at her. "You seem to have lost all that weight."

Morgan's heart beat faster as she looked up into his eyes. He'd kiss her now, and she wanted him to.

"I think it's time to go to bed."

She took his arm, feeling the muscles under the smooth fabric. Her heart was pounding and her ears rang. He stopped with her outside her bedroom door and leaned down, his lips very close to hers. She closed her eyes and then opened them instantly when she felt his kiss on her cheek. She frowned.

"Goodnight, *mi querida*." He was gone, into his own bedroom, the door closed.

She undressed angrily and flounced about the room before finally going to sleep.

Seth had misinterpreted her frown. He decided to go slower with her. She probably still needed time to learn to trust him.

∼ *Chapter Twenty-Three* ∼

WHEN Morgan woke, the house was quiet. As she stretched her arm across the bed, she looked up in alarm, then lay down again, quietly. Adam was with his father again. She turned over on her back and then yawned, stretching luxuriously. It was good to admit she loved Seth. For the first time in a long while, she was at peace. Who knew what could happen now?

She tossed the covers aside and bounded out of bed. She looked at herself critically in the mirror. She brushed her hair just slightly, pulling a few curls close to her face. She nodded at her reflection, then giggled. "Why, Morgan Colter, you are becoming positively vain."

In the hall, she saw that both Adam's and Seth's doors were closed. She took a deep breath to calm her shaking body. What if he didn't want her anymore? He could have decided that she wasn't worth all the effort. As she lifted her shaking hand to knock lightly on the door, she reminded herself of all the times Seth had chided her for her lack of self-confidence. She could ride a horse and she could cook, but it still always startled her when men stared at her.

There was no answer from within, so she silently opened the door and tiptoed to Seth's bedside. He had thrown the sheet back from his body, exposing his full, broad chest. Lightly, she touched the hair at his temples. His eyes flew open and she stared into them, losing herself in the depth of feeling she saw there. Without a word between them, he held out his arms and she went to him.

For a moment they just held one another. Morgan felt she'd come home: the arms were safe. Here at last was peace. Her restful state of mind left her as Seth began kissing her hair, her eyes, nibbling on her ears. She had had enough quiet.

"I love you so much." His soft breath made chills on her legs and down her spine. "I've tried to be patient, but it's not easy. I want you. I need you. Can't you tell me you have a little feeling for me? I know I did a terrible thing, but can't you find forgiveness in your heart?"

There were too many questions to answer. Her mind was leaving her, her body taking control. Seth's lips were on her, his body touching hers. She wanted to tear the gown from her body, wanted her flesh to touch his. "Yes," she murmured.

"Yes, what?" He was kissing her neck—not just kissing it, but making love to it as if it were the only part of her body.

"Yes, I forgive you."

He pulled her from him and held her at arm's length. "You forgive me?"

"Yes, I do. I may regret it, but it seems I do forgive you for all the horrible things you've done."

"Horrible! I'll show you who's horrible." He pulled her close beside him, and he began tickling her, and rubbing the morning stubble of his beard against her neck and cheek. She laughed hilariously, enjoying the familiar play of Seth's love. But something was wrong. A second sense told her there was reason for alarm. The warning grew louder and louder in her mind, screaming over her laughter, her joy at holding Seth in her arms once again. *Adam!* Where was Adam?

"Seth." She began to push him away. The alarm blocked out all passion. "Seth! Where's Adam?"

"He's probably still asleep," he whispered into her ear. His hand was on her body, stroking the soft curve of her hip.

"No. Adam never sleeps late, at least not in his own room. I have to go see. Something's wrong."

Seth drew back and stared down into her face. He saw the concern, the fear. He started to tell her how silly she was, but he stopped. He'd have the rest of his life to talk about Adam. Right now she needed reassurance. "Well, go then. And then you can come back here. Better yet, I'll go with you and then I'll make sure you come back with me." He held her close to him as they went to Adam's room. "I don't plan to let you out of my room for at least two weeks. Adam can pound on the door for hours, but I need you more than he does. See," they stood in the child's doorway, "he looks like a little cherub."

Morgan frowned. Adam was too peaceful. Something was wrong. Every morning Carol had to remake Adam's bed from the sheets up because he tore everything off during the night. This morning the light quilt was still tucked in, not in its usual place on the floor. Quickly, she crossed the room and smoothed his hair from his forehead. His face was hot, very hot.

Her face drained of color and she turned to Seth. Instantly, he was beside his son, his large hands holding the boy's head. His neck was swollen and his skin was almost burning. Adam whimpered at his father's touch. Seth's face held the same look as Morgan's. "I'll get the doctor." His voice was harsh, reflecting a depth of fear he'd never known before.

Minutes later, Morgan heard him running down the stairs, and then there were the sounds of a horse's hooves.

Morgan was numb. She dropped to her knees and took her son's little hand. It was so dry and so very, very hot. Adam had never been sick. He couldn't be sick. He was too little to bear pain. "Adam, sweetheart," she whispered as she held the listless little hand to her cheek.

Adam's eyelids fluttered. "Mama." His voice was rough, barely audible. He swallowed and his eyes screwed up tightly as he tried to stand the pain.

"I'm here, baby. Mama's right here and Daddy's gone for the doctor. When he gets here, he'll make you well. You'll feel better then. The doctor will make it all stop hurting."

"Mrs. Colter!" Roselle entered the room. "I heard Mr. Blake running down the stairs. Is everything all right?" She stopped when she saw Morgan's face. Never had she seen such bleakness, such despair. She looked at Adam, too quiet, his mother holding his hand. "Adam!" She touched his burning little forehead and her eyes drooped.

Once before, this had happened. She was reliving that time. Her little girl had been like Adam, and about his age, too. Sarah, her sweet, always-active little girl. One morning she'd found her in her bed, so quiet and so hot. In less than a week, she'd died. She'd never really gotten over Sarah, or the pain of washing and dressing that sweet little body for the final time. Please, dear God, don't let it all happen again.

"What can I do?" Morgan's eyes implored the older woman.

Roselle tried to control her rising hysteria. "Did Mr. Blake go for the doctor?"

"Seth. He's not Mr. Blake, he's Seth Colter, Adam's daddy." She stroked Adam's hand and arm.

"I thought so." Roselle had to calm herself and calm Morgan. She left the room and returned with a dress and underclothes. She lifted Morgan from her knees and began dressing her, as if she were a child. She kept up a steady stream of talk. "It's probably just one of those childhood things, the things children always get. I'm sure he'll be well in no time at all."

"Adam's never sick. He's never even had a bad cold."

"Well, then, it's time he had one." Roselle tried not to let the fear into her voice.

"He's so still. Why isn't he yelling, 'Eat, eat,' like he always does? Adam." She fell to her knees again. "Mommy will get you some chicken. Would you like some chicken? Or cookies? Would Mommy's baby like some cookies?"

Adam made a great effort to open his eyes. Morgan gasped at the pain she saw in them.

Roselle put her arm around the other woman's shoulders, forcefully lifting her. "Please, Mrs. Colter, sit here." She pulled a chair close to the bed. "Adam doesn't want to eat now. Just wait until the doctor comes. He'll know what to do." She started toward the door. "I'll send Carol up with some breakfast for you."

When Morgan was alone, she felt the full fear rising in her throat, threatening to choke her. For some reason, Roselle's statement that Adam didn't want to eat was more frightening than his extraordinary quiet or even his fever-ridden little body. Adam always ate. He was born hungry and his little life was controlled by food. His first word had been "Eat!" It had not been a quiet attempt at the word, but one day it had just exploded from his lips in a demand. She remembered how she and Jake, Lupita and Paul, had all laughed. Adam had ignored them. He had demanded food and he expected it to be served to him.

Adam didn't want to eat. The words repeated themselves over and over in her brain. His face was flushed, the fever making his cheeks a vivid red. That couldn't be Adam, she thought. Adam was always a blur of motion. He's playing a game, to make me bake him some cookies. Yes, that's what he wants. I'll bake him thousands of cookies, but I can't go to the kitchen now because I must be here when he opens his eyes.

She stroked his forehead. It was so dry. Adam was

usually wet. He sweat all the time, just like his father. He played hard, running and laughing so much that perspiration often soaked his hair.

"When you get over your bad cold, Adam, Mommy will bake you some cookies, and some little cakes with lots of icing. We'll write 'Adam' on them and 'horse' and 'eat' . . . and we'll draw pictures."

Adam opened his eyes and stared at his mother in bewilderment. He didn't understand what was happening to him. In his whole life, the only pain he'd experienced was scraped knees and skinned elbows. When those things had happened, he'd gone to his mother and her kisses had made the hurt stop. Now his mother was here and the pain didn't go away. He didn't understand, not at all.

Morgan didn't know how long she sat there. She was vaguely aware of Roselle and Carol entering and leaving the room. A few times she heard someone telling her to eat. The lump was still in her throat and she knew she could swallow nothing. Didn't they understand that if her baby couldn't eat, then neither could she?

She heard voices outside the door and recognized Seth's. He'd have the doctor. She felt relief flood her body. "The doctor's here, baby. He'll make you well. He'll make the pain go away."

She ran to meet Seth. "Where's the doctor?"

"He's coming. Is he any better?"

"No, Seth. He's so hot. So hot, and he's so little."

Seth held his wife's hand. It was cold. They went together to Adam's bed. Seth's fears mounted. In the few hours since he'd been gone, Adam looked as if he'd shrunk. His entire face was red, splattered with ghostly white splotches.

"This is Dr. Larson, Morgan, and this is Mrs. Colter."

"Our son, doctor! He's so little and he hurts. He's never been sick before."

Seth took her arm, quieting her. He noticed she'd said "our son." He was glad she was ready to admit their relationship because, in his haste, he had given the doctor his real name.

"I'll do what I can, Mrs. Colter."

The doctor, an older, corpulent man, pulled back the covers and began to examine Adam. As he pulled up Adam's nightshirt, Morgan gasped at the redness. Seth's grip on her arm tightened.

"I think this is the culprit." He turned Adam's leg to show a bump, large and inflamed, on the calf of his left leg. "It seems to be some kind of insect bite."

"Some kind? *What* kind? What kind of insect bite?!"

"That, Mrs. Colter, I don't know. I've seen a couple of these cases, but not many. A lot of people think it's some kind of tick bite, but no one knows for sure."

Morgan sighed. It didn't matter what the cause was, just the cure. "What do we do now? How do we make him well?"

"There's not much I know to do, really. If the boy's healthy, he'll fight it off. But if not, then you ought to prepare yourself."

She smiled at the doctor. Her hearing wasn't working at all. Through the mist, she heard Seth's voice.

"There's absolutely nothing we can do?"

"Try to get some liquids down him. And pray. That's all anyone can do. He'll probably have diarrhea soon, and he'll need to replenish the water he loses."

The fog was beginning to clear. What did he mean, "prepare yourself"? The doctor was leaving. She pulled away from Seth. "You can't leave! My baby is sick. He needs you! You have to help him."

The doctor's eyes were sad. He looked up at Seth as the big man took his wife's shoulders in his hands. At

Seth's silent nod, he left the room. God! he thought, there were times when he hated his job.

Her voice was high, rising higher. "He can't do anything? My baby is sick and he can't do anything? He says to prepare myself."

Seth's fingers bit into her shoulders. "Listen to me. Adam is sick, very sick. He needs you. You can't indulge yourself in hysterics now. Do you hear me? Adam needs you."

"Yes." Her chin came up. "Adam needs me."

"Now the doctor said to try to get some liquids into him, and that's what we're going to do. Adam knows you best of all and he trusts you. You'll feed him."

"Feed him, yes."

"I'm going to the kitchen to tell Roselle, and when I come back, I want you in that chair and quiet. Adam needs his mother now, not some crazy woman tearing her hair. Do you understand?"

"Yes. Adam needs his mother."

Morgan sat obediently by Adam's bedside. Carol entered. "I'm sure he'll be all right, Mrs. Colter. My little brother has fevers all the time, but he always gets well."

Morgan tried to smile at the girl.

Seth returned carrying a steaming bowl of beef broth. "I'll hold him up while you feed him."

Adam's eyes hardly fluttered when Seth lifted him. Seth was shocked by the incredible heat emanating from the child's body. He felt so fragile in Seth's arms. He opened his eyes when the warm spoon touched his lips. He swallowed and then his eyes screwed together in pain as the liquid went down his throat. He moaned in agony. He turned away from the spoon his mother held and looked at her in question. Why did she want to cause him pain?

"It hurts him, Seth. He can't eat it."

"Try again." Adam kept his lips sealed, refusing

more of the broth. Seth lowered him. "We'll try again later."

Carol came into the room carrying clean towels and a basin of warm water. She also held diapers. Seth stared at the diapers. Adam hadn't worn them in months.

His mother and father bathed the fevered child and changed his gown. Then they sat down to wait. There was nothing else to do.

The house was silent. No one made any loud noises. Morgan bathed her son's face continually. Roselle brought food, but neither parent touched it. They watched their son, locked together in one purpose.

"I feel so helpless, Seth, I just don't know what to do. Adam has always been such a sweet child. Everyone has always loved him. The only time he's ever selfish is when someone threatens his food. Now—" She wiped a tear from her eye. "—now he can't eat."

"Morgan!" Seth's voice held a warning. "I don't know what to do. If only there were something . . . someone . . ."

He dropped his head onto his hands, his elbows on his knees. "I never know what to do. I nearly died once, when Montoya shot me. Lupita said I had a fever for two weeks. She said . . ." He stopped and looked up at Morgan. "Lupita," he whispered. He stood up. "Lupita!" He shouted her name. "I'll go get her. Lupita will save my boy. I know she will. I'll get her."

Morgan ran to her husband. Here, at last, was hope. "Can you do it, Seth? Can you get her here soon? It took us two days to get from your ranch to here."

"I'll do it. Hell won't stop me. Lupita will save him, I know she can." He stared down at his wife. He kissed her mouth hard, quickly. "Take care of him. Get Roselle to hold him and you feed him. I'll be back as soon as possible—with Lupita." He pulled her to him and held her for a few seconds. "God knows Adam, and

401

He'll take care of him. He won't let anything happen to our little boy." He released her and was gone. Within seconds, she heard the horse's hooves.

"Mrs. Colter, you really should eat. You must keep up your strength."

"Could you get me some milk for Adam? Maybe that will coat his throat and hurt less."

Adam took very little of the milk, whimpering in pain when his mother tried to make him drink it. She gave in to his helpless pleas and set the glass aside. She moistened his lips with a few droplets of water. She bathed his body.

All night she sat by his bed, watching for any signs of change. There were none. In the morning, he began to moan and toss about on the bed. He began to sweat and the dreaded diarrhea started.

"Roselle, you'll have to help me. We need to get fluids into him, or he'll lose everything."

Together, they tried to force him to drink the liquids, but they did not succeed. Most of it spilled down his front.

Roselle watched her mistress as she changed Adam's gown. Her hair was a tangle of snarls, her dress was covered with stains from trying to feed Adam. There were bluish circles under her eyes.

They heard a horse outside the house and Morgan ran to see who it was. Her shoulders drooped when she saw Martin. Of course it couldn't be Seth. He hadn't had time to get back yet.

"Martin's been to the bunkhouse to tell the men about Adam, and that Seth will be gone for a few days."

Bunkhouse? Oh, yes, there was a ranch . . . but she cared nothing for it right now.

"Mama. Mama." Adam's head turned on the pillow. He was asleep, or seemed to be.

"I'm here, baby. Mama's here." His little palm was wet though she had just washed him.

Hours later, Roselle brought tea for Morgan. Adam's body was hot again and he made feeble attempts to kick off the light quilt, but he had no strength. She tried again and again to feed him.

Roselle handed Morgan the cup and saucer and, automatically, she took it. The porcelain dishes rattled against one another as she held them in her shaking hands. She sipped the tea, finding it an effort to do so. Her whole body seemed to be trembling.

"You have to get some rest, now. Stretch out here and I'll stay with him while you sleep."

"Yes." She was weary, but when she lay on the cot, her body remained tense.

"Mama." She was at his side instantly. He was cold now, and even his teeth were chattering. Roselle ran for more blankets, and Morgan held her little son tightly in her arms. His body seemed to become more frail with each passing moment. She tried to get him to drink some hot milk, but his little throat was too sore.

In the late afternoon, Roselle got Morgan to drink some hot broth, and again tried to persuade her to sleep on the cot. She had Martin carry a loveseat from downstairs into the room. Morgan sank onto it and leaned back into the corner. Adam was still, sleeping peacefully again.

Morgan didn't know when she fell asleep, but when she woke, there was a quilt over her and Roselle smiled at her from across Adam's bed. She was grateful to the woman and said so. The sleep gave her new energy. She renewed her vigilance, this time trying to coax apple juice into the little body.

Seth rode hard all the way to Albuquerque. At the livery stable, he gasped out his reason for hurry and soon there was a fresh horse saddled and ready to go. In the middle of the night, he galloped to a stop at a homestead between Albuquerque and Santa Fe. The owner of the adobe house understood about the hurry.

He loaned Seth a horse and refused his offer of money.

"Your horse will be here when you return with the woman who will help your little boy. I will have another ready for her also. No, keep your money. Juan Ramón may need a friend someday. Then you can repay him."

Seth rode the horse harder than he had ever driven an animal before. He reached his ranch in the late afternoon.

Lupita was standing in the middle of the chickens when she saw the lone rider coming toward them. Her first thought was for the horse. No one had a right to work a horse like that. She couldn't see his face, but she knew it was her Seth. Something had to be very wrong for him to treat an animal so cruelly.

She dropped the basket of chicken feed, picked up her skirts, and began running. Jake, in the barn, dropped a bale of hay at the sight of the overweight woman running. He shouted for Paul and ran after Lupita. He knew that only Seth could cause her to lose her usual calm.

Seth pulled the horse to a stop and dropped to his feet beside Lupita. He looked awful—sunken, dirty—and his eyes were crazy, burning. "Adam. A fever. Some kind of tick," he gasped out at her.

She needed no more explanation. "I'll get my medicines." She started running back to her little house, behind the main house. She passed Jake and started to give orders, but closed her mouth. The old man would be useless until he'd seen Seth.

Seth was running beside her, Jake following. "What's he like?"

"There's a high fever and a knot on his leg, swollen and red. The doctor said it was an insect bite, maybe a tick."

"Adam! This is Adam you're talkin' about? I knew the little girl shouldn'ta taken him away. Now he's sick." He watched Seth. He had known the big man

404

since he was a little boy and he knew Adam must be very sick to cause the terror he saw now in Seth's face.

"Seth! It's good to see you!"

Seth absently shook Paul's hand. He watched impatiently for Lupita to come out of her house.

"Adam's sick," Jake whispered. "Seth's come to get Lupita."

Paul understood what was needed. "Jake, you get some food." At Jake's look of bewilderment, he added, "Dump some beans on Lupita's tortillas and get them ready to go. I'll get two horses saddled."

"Come with me." Jake motioned to Seth. "You and the little gal make up?"

"Yes. I guess so. I don't know. My head's groggy. I can't think. What's keeping Lupita?" He seemed to remember Jake and put his hand on his shoulder. "I'm just worried now. I'll come back when . . . when Adam's well and I'll visit with you then. I have missed you."

"I understand. Here's your *burritos*. They're not like Lupita's, but they'll fill you up." He wrapped them in a cloth and Seth stuffed them in the pocket of his vest.

Lupita was just leaving her house. She carried a large cloth bag. "I am ready."

Paul handed over the reins of the horses, and Seth helped Lupita mount. It had been a long time since she'd ridden a horse and already the muscles and tendons on the inside of her thighs hurt from the unaccustomed stretching.

"You take care of our boys, you hear, Lupita? And then you bring *all* of 'em back with you," Jake called after them. He turned to Paul. "It's goin' be a long time waitin' here and not knowin' what's happenin'." They turned back to their work, silent.

Lupita used all her strength to stay on the horse, but even so, they had to travel much more slowly than Seth had alone. Once Seth apologized for making her ride so hard. She dismissed his statement. "For Adam it is worth

405

it." She tried to wipe some of the haggard, drawn look from his face. "I have seen this tick before—it is not so bad as you think. There are many medicines I can use." Seth's trust in her made her swallow hard. She prayed that her words were true.

They changed horses at the homestead. Seth promised to return the extra horse, and he swore to himself that the poor farmer would have some new livestock as soon as he returned to his own ranch.

The moon of the second night was high when they reached the Three Crowns. Seth lifted Lupita from her horse, throwing the reins to Donaciano. The tired woman followed, stumbling, as he led her into the big house.

"They're here!" Morgan's voice was incredulous. She ran to meet them, throwing herself into Lupita's arms with such exuberance that she nearly knocked the plump woman down. "I knew you'd come. Please save my baby, Lupita, please. He's so little . . ."

Lupita pushed her firmly away and walked to Adam's bed. The child was dry and hot and his little cheeks, once so healthy, were sunken, as were his eyes.

"How long has he been like this?"

"I don't know. Nearly four days, I think. The time is all mixed up in my mind. What do we do first?"

Lupita was studying Morgan intently. "Heat water. I am going to make some tea."

"Tea! We don't need tea when my son is so sick." She was screeching.

"Seth!" Lupita turned to the weary man, slumped by his son's bedside. "I can care for Adam, but I cannot care for both of them at once." She nodded her head toward Morgan, who watched Lupita with an unnatural light in her eyes. "Is there someone else who can help me?"

"Me. I'll help." Morgan stepped forward. "I'll do whatever you say, Lupita."

"You! Look at you. Another few minutes and I will have two patients."

"May I help?" Roselle stood at the door in her dressing gown.

Lupita appraised her. "Yes. I will need someone."

"I can't leave my baby. He needs me."

"He does not even know you are here. Seth, take your wife to the kitchen and feed her good. And you eat, too. Then wash her, put her in a clean nightgown, and then into bed. And you do the same for yourself."

"No, I can't . . ."

Lupita's eyes were as hard as diamonds. "You do everything I say or I will leave."

Morgan allowed Seth to lead her from the room.

Roselle watched them leave. "You wouldn't really leave?"

"Of course not." The answer was snapped back.

"I've tried to get her to eat, to sleep, but she wouldn't."

"I have been caring for sick people and bringing babies into the world since I was just a girl, and I have learned that you do not ask tired mothers anything, you give orders. If they do not obey, you give them a reason why they must. Now, let us go to work. I need water to brew a tea."

"He won't drink anything."

Lupita arched an eyebrow at her. She didn't tolerate disobedience from her helpers, either.

Roselle left the room to get water.

Seth led Morgan to the big work table in the middle of the kitchen. He put bread and cheese, cold chicken, and milk in front of her.

"I can't eat, Seth, really I can't."

"Lupita's right. Neither of us is any use to Adam. We'd be in the way."

Roselle entered to get the hot water. Morgan stood

up to follow her out. Seth unceremoniously pushed her back into her chair. "Eat!"

Morgan began to eat, at first lightly and then with gusto. She hadn't realized how hungry she was. "I guess I was hungry," she mumbled through a mouthful of bread and cheese. "He is going to be all right, isn't he?"

Seth held her hand, squeezing the fingers. "Now that Lupita's here, I think he will be. Finished?"

"Yes." Her body felt so heavy, worse than when she'd carried Adam. She must rouse herself, because she had to go back to Adam. She'd been away too long. She started wearily toward the door, her eyes blurring.

Seth grabbed her skirt to stop her.

"Adam might call for me." Her goal was the kitchen door—such an ordinary thing really, but now it seemed impossible.

Seth lifted her in his arms.

"I'm too heavy. You . . ."

"Heavy! You nit! You hardly weigh more than Adam. Now that I'm here, you are going to be taken care of. Right now I am going to put you to bed."

She leaned her head against Seth's shoulder. It felt good to depend on someone else for a change, and there was no one she'd rather trust than her Seth. She sighed. "Her Seth" once again.

He set her on her feet again in the bedroom. "Get out of that dress and tell me where you keep your nightgowns."

"Third drawer." Her hands were shaking as she fumbled with the buttons. Seth was in front of her and pushed her hands away as he unfastened the row of little buttons. She watched his face and knew that he, too, was very tired. She touched his hair. It seemed that the more tired he was, the more gray there was in his hair. Right now he looked like an old man.

She stepped out of her dress and Seth began to unlace her corset. She let out a sigh as it fell to the floor. She thought she'd probably never get used to that tight, stiff thing binding her waist and rib cage. Seth removed her chemise and she stood nude under his gaze.

"Why do you wear that thing? You have red marks all down your body where it cut into you." His big hands rubbed at her sides, briskly.

She felt slightly uneasy under his touch. "My gown."

"First, a wash." He pulled her to the basin on the table and began washing her face and hands. She stood still, enjoying the way he scrubbed at her skin. He dried her and then slipped the clean, soft nightgown over her head. "I should be hanged for covering all this up." His hand lightly caressed her breast. "If I tried to take advantage of you now, it'd be like making love to a wet dishcloth." He smiled into Morgan's drooping eyes. "I think I'll wait. Let's go, little one."

Again he picked her up and carried her to the bed. She was practically asleep before he had tucked the covers about her. Seth started toward the door.

"Where are you going?" she murmured.

"To my room. Lupita seemed to think I need some sleep, too."

"Stay with me. I need you."

An incredible joy surged through him. "Yes, *mi querida*, I'll stay with you . . . for as long as you want."

Morgan immediately turned back onto her stomach and went to sleep. Seth took his time washing himself, and then he removed his clothes and climbed into the bed beside his wife. "Damn nightgown!" he murmured as he pulled her close. Their bodies fitted together with an old familiarity. Seth's breath became slow and even and he, too, slept.

Adam didn't know who held him or who forced the bad-tasting tea down his throat, but he knew the voice of command. It hurt terribly, but no matter how much he complained, the cup was always there again. His body hurt and ached so much, yet someone kept lifting him, turning him, and putting hot cloths on him. He didn't like this at all. He wanted to be outside. "Horse," he whispered, but the word didn't come to the surface.

Lupita forced several herb teas down Adam's throat, each laced with powdered rose hips. She and Roselle wrapped his little feverish body again and again in hot, steamy towels. Toward dawn, the fever began to lessen, and Lupita collapsed on the little sofa. She hadn't slept in nearly two days, and now that she knew there was nothing else she could do except wait, she fell asleep instantly. Roselle tiptoed from the room. No matter what happened now, there would be a need for food.

"Eat." The word didn't come out as loudly as he had planned. He tried again, but his mouth still didn't work. He looked at the big woman asleep beside his bed. Who was she? He was wet all over his body and he was hungry and thirsty. Where was his mother? He'd go to her room. She'd get him something to eat.

He started to move but his body didn't obey. It hurt, and his head hurt, too. "Mama," he whispered, and the tears began to flow. He felt so awful and there was no one with him except this woman that he didn't know.

Lupita opened her eyes to see Adam's face screwed up and tears rolling down his cheeks. Her tears followed, because she knew the danger was over.

"Ah, little one. You will be safe now." She immediately set about making the little boy comfortable. She changed his clothes and bed linens, talking to him soothingly all the while.

Adam decided he liked the woman. And he seemed to remember her voice from somewhere. But he was still hungry and he still wanted his mother. "Mama," he whispered again.

"Yes, I'll get your mama for you."

Lupita tried two doors before she found Morgan's

room. She paused a moment to stare at the sight of Morgan and Seth curled together in the big bed. She was glad they were together again. There was no need to wake both of them. "Morgan." Seth stirred and rolled away from his sleeping wife. Lupita touched her shoulder. "Morgan, Adam is calling you."

"Adam?" she murmured sleepily, eyes still closed. Then suddenly they were wide open.

"The fever is broken. He will be well. I will go back now. You come when you can."

Morgan jumped from the bed and ran to her wardrobe. She snatched a dressing gown and rapidly thrust her arms through the sleeves and tied it.

Adam whimpered slightly when he saw his mother. She held him close and he was comforted by her presence. He looked tired and he'd lost weight, but for the first time in a long while, his eyes were clear and focusing.

Seth came into the room, his eyes riveted on his son. He held the boy's hand and ruffled his hair. "I'm glad you're going to get well, son." Morgan saw the tears in his eyes. No matter how much she ever doubted Seth's love for her, his love for his little son was never in question.

Seth came to Morgan's side and took her in his arms. "I have to see to the ranch now. After four days without supervision, it's probably near bankruptcy. I'll try to get back for dinner, but if I can't, I'll send word." He kissed the tip of her nose. "I love you." He released her and left the room.

She stared after him for a second, but she couldn't worry about Seth now. Adam was still very sick and he needed her.

Morgan spent the entire day with Adam. She spoon-fed him, read to him, and drew pictures on his little slate. Lupita slept most of the day and Roselle stayed downstairs except to bring food.

"Mrs. Colter, why don't you go for a ride?" said Roselle next afternoon. "Adam is asleep, and I'll be here if he wakens. You need some fresh air."

"I know, Roselle, I guess I should. But I'm afraid he'll wake up and need me. I'll get over the feeling, but I came so close to losing him that right now I'm almost afraid to close my eyes."

Roselle agreed. Had her little girl lived, she would have felt the same way about leaving her.

When Lupita entered the room, Morgan ran to her and hugged her. "It seems I'm always saying thank you for all the things you do for me."

"I did not save the boy for you . . . only maybe a little for you. If anything had happened to him, my Seth would not think so highly of me. I cannot have that." She grinned at Morgan. "Also, remember, Adam is one of my children."

Adam gave Lupita a tentative smile when he heard his name. The woman was becoming familiar to him very quickly.

Lupita caressed the hair by his temple. "Now you will grow as strong and as big as your daddy. I think I will go to the kitchen and see how this Roselle is feeding my children."

"Her cooking is a lot different from yours."

"Hmph! That is why the child was so sick. He needs more chili. I'll see what I can make for supper."

"Chili! That sounds marvelous. How about a green chili stew with potatoes and meat? The three of us could eat here, together."

Lupita smiled at her. "Yes. The three of us together. That is nice."

In a short time, the two of them were happily eating quantities of green chili stew and freshly made tortillas. Morgan fed Adam a beef broth flavored with green chili. He ate all of it, and drank some milk. Once he smiled at them, the first time Morgan had seen his dimples in a long time. There was a milk mustache on his upper lip, and he said, "Eat."

The women had laughed together. "Now I know for sure that he's going to be all right," Morgan declared.

"Food has to be interesting, or it is not good to eat. He would not eat before because the food had no taste."

Adam put out a hand toward his mother's tortilla and she broke off a piece for him.

Martin came into the room. "Mr. Colter said to tell his wife"—his eyes twinkled—"that the ranch is falling apart. He'll be very late tonight, since he needs to put it together again."

Morgan laughed. "Thank you, Martin. Who brought the message?"

"A young hand called Tim."

"Well, take him to the kitchen and give him some green chili stew and tortillas. There's enough, Lupita?"

"What you think—I cook only a little bit for the three of us?"

"And Martin, you and Roselle help yourselves."

"We already have. The smells from Lupita's cooking were irresistible."

"Oh, Lupita," she laughed when Martin was gone, "I spent an entire year training with a French cooking master, and none of my food ever gets the raves your food does."

Morgan turned back to Adam. She felt slightly guilty because she hadn't really thought about Seth all day. She was too concerned with Adam, always aware of how close she'd come to losing him. She put her hands on the small of her back and stretched.

"It is time for you to go to bed."

"I'll sleep in here, in case he wakes in the middle of the night and needs anything."

"No. You will go to your own room and sleep. I will stay in here. If he needs you, I will call you."

Morgan knew when she was attempting a losing bat-

413

tle. She was asleep as soon as she snuggled under the covers.

It was late when Seth got back to the house and he stopped outside Morgan's door, his hand on the knob. He smiled in anticipation because he knew they could not possibly sleep together in the same bed for the second night in a row without making love.

He looked down at himself. He was dirty and tired. And in the morning, Morgan would be running into Adam's room. No, it would have to wait. When he made love to his wife for the first time in years, he wanted time to caress her and touch every part of the body he'd once known so well. With a sigh, he turned to his own room.

Morgan awoke early. She still wasn't used to Adam not banging on her bedroom door. She threw on a dressing gown and went to her son's room. Immediately she knew something was wrong. The room was a mess. There were towels on the floor, a tea kettle beside the bed. Both Adam and Lupita were asleep. She sat down heavily in a chair. It came back to her with renewed force that she had come very close to losing her son. Last night, while she slept, she had almost lost him again. If Lupita hadn't been with him . . .

Morgan turned and saw Lupita's eyes open. "What happened?" Her voice reflected her despair.

"Nothing happened. He was restless so I made him tea."

"What about the towels?"

"I had them ready in case the fever returned, but it did not."

"He had a relapse, didn't he?"

"Morgan, no! I was just being cautious, but he needed no more treatments."

"Why didn't you call me?"

"You weren't needed. Nothing happened. I—"

Seth entered the room and looked in puzzlement

from one woman to the other. "Is something wrong?"

"Adam was ill again last night," said Morgan. "He isn't over it at all. He's still very sick."

Lupita threw her hands into the air, mumbled something under her breath in Spanish, and then turned to Seth. "Adam is all right. Last night he was restless and I was afraid it was the sickness again, but it was not. Your son is getting well quickly and there is no more danger."

Morgan looked skeptical. "I'm just worried, that's all."

"Well, I believe Lupita." He kissed the woman's forehead. "Let's all go downstairs and eat breakfast. Carol is here and she can stay with Adam."

"I'd rather stay with him myself."

"Of course, you stay with Adam if you want. That way I'll have Lupita all to myself." He winked at the large woman. As he kissed his wife's cheek, Seth was vaguely aware that Morgan wasn't even looking at him. He frowned slightly when she turned away quickly.

Seth and Lupita sat at the breakfast table. "There really is nothing wrong, is there?"

"No, nothing. I am just an old mother hen and I wanted to be safe. I am sorry I did not clean up the mess before Morgan saw it. It is good to eat with you again, to see you again."

"Lupita, I can't thank you enough for what you've done for Morgan, and Adam, and for me. I knew you'd come when we needed you."

"Of course, I come. Is everything all right now, between you and the *señora*?"

"It's coming along. It isn't easy to forgive what I did to her."

"She must see how much you love her."

"No, I don't think she does. Sometimes I think she does. Maybe she doesn't trust me. I just try to wait and be patient."

"Wait! You do not need to wait. You should not wait. She is your wife. Take her."

Seth smiled indulgently. "It's not like that. I've lost rights . . ."

"Rights! She is a woman and you are a man. And besides, you love each other."

"I want Morgan to make up her own mind when she wants to come to me."

"She can't make up her own mind. I know Morgan very well. All her life she has had people tell her what to do. She has never had a chance to be her own self. At first, she spoke the words of her mother, and then she had an uncle to control her, and then she had you. Even in California, she was pushed and pulled by others."

For some reason, Seth felt a need to defend his wife. "She made up her own mind when she asked me to marry her. That took courage."

"Yes, I know all about that. Even then she bought someone to control her. I am sure she sensed that you were a strong man. Another woman might have told her problem to everyone. Then she would have had her choice of many men. But Morgan has always been too sheltered to make choices."

Seth sipped his coffee. Lupita was right.

"Now she needs someone to help her." She nodded her head toward the stairs. "She loves that little boy. But if someone does not help her, she will let him rule her life. She is a little girl herself."

Seth sat silently for a moment. He had always been too involved with Morgan to look at her clearly, like Lupita did. Seth had always blamed Morgan's mother, but he'd never realized that he filled the same place Mrs. Wakefield once had.

"I thought I might go home tomorrow."

"So soon?"

"Yes. The boy is fine. He does not need me, but Jake and Paul do."

416

"Lupita, I wish you'd stay. It's been a long time since I've seen you, and you know what you've always meant to me."

"I must go home. Soon, I hope the three of you will come home, too."

"Yes," Seth grinned. "I'd like that. It would be nice to be on my own place again. I hope we will go. Maybe when Gordon gets back, I can leave. I'll bring my wife and son with me. Morgan hasn't really . . . accepted me as a husband, yet."

"Accepted! These modern men! In my day, women did not choose their husbands; their parents told them who their husbands would be. That is what should have happened here."

"What if Morgan had gotten Jake instead of me? Then where would I be?"

She turned to snap at him and then saw his teasing eyes. "We are too long at this meal. We both have work to do. Let's get started."

Seth kissed her on the cheek as he left for a long day on the ranch.

Lupita again spent her day with Adam and Morgan, talking and quietly laughing together. Lupita didn't like the worried look Morgan's eyes always held when she looked at her little son. The older woman could not convince her that he was out of danger.

At dinner, Morgan again refused to leave Adam. Seth saw the alarm and fear in her eyes and he agreed. He, too, was not completely satisfied that Adam was really well.

Seth and Lupita ate dinner alone and enjoyed talking about the Colter ranch. Seth was entertained by the stories of Morgan's pregnancy.

As Seth led Lupita to her room, they stopped to look in on Adam. Morgan lay curled up on the cot.

"No, don't wake her." Seth put a restraining hand on Lupita's arm. "Let her sleep."

"She should sleep in her own bed. There is no need for her to stay in here all night. Her son is fine."

"Let her stay. She needs the reassurance that he's well. When she wakes, she'll see him. Then she won't worry."

"Someday you will remember my words."

"Lupita, did I ever tell you how pretty you are when your eyes flash like that?"

"You!" She couldn't stop her giggle. How easy it was for this big handsome man to reduce her to an eighteen-year-old *señorita*!

Lupita fell asleep quickly, but Seth tossed about in his big empty bed for a long time.

The sun was barely up when Seth awoke. He pulled on some pants and padded towards Adam's room. Morgan was asleep, one arm hanging off the side of the cot. He kissed her mouth. Her eyes fluttered open. Seeing Seth so close to her, she put her arms up to him, pulling him closer. As his lips fastened onto hers, she heard Adam's plaintive voice: "Mama. Mama."

Instantly, she was wide awake. She rolled quickly away from Seth to the other side of the cot and went to comfort her son.

Seth laughed. "I never thought my own son would become my enemy."

Morgan's face was serious. "He's still a very sick child. He needs me."

Seth turned away. "I need you, too," he whispered. He looked back, chiding himself for his selfishness. "I'm going to take Lupita home. It'll be a slower trip than before, so I'll probably be gone for at least a week."

Morgan was hardly listening. "You want something to eat, Adam? Lupita made some apple juice for you."

"Morgan, did you hear what I said?"

"Something about a week?"

"I'm going to be gone a week, to take Lupita back to the ranch."

"Yes. Well, don't leave before I say goodbye to Lupita. I owe her a great deal." She turned back to Adam.

Seth left the room angrily. Just when I thought things were going well, she doesn't even seem to know I'm alive. I liked it better when my presence made her throw things.

Morgan ate breakfast with Adam while Lupita and Seth ate downstairs. Seth avoided all discussions about Morgan. One of the hands hitched a wagon while Lupita said her goodbyes. Morgan wanted the older woman to stay in case Adam's fever returned, but this time Lupita didn't even argue with her. She shrugged. Let the young ones solve their own problems, she thought.

"I am glad I do not have to ride a horse again." She frowned, as though in pain.

"After two days on this thing, you'll wish you had a soft saddle to sit on."

They traveled for two days in the springless wagon, over hole-riddled roads. When they reached the ranch, at sunset on the second day, they were hot and dirty and tired.

Jake and Paul ran to meet them. Seth picked up the little man and whirled him around. His grip nearly crushed Jake's frail body. "Just as skinny as he always was. When's he gonna get some muscles? He looks like a girl."

Paul shook the big man's hand. "I reckon the boy's all right."

Seth beamed. "Thanks to Lupita here." He put his arm around her ample shoulders.

Embarrassed, Lupita pushed his hand away. "You be careful or you might hurt yourself, trying to get your arms around me."

"Hurt myself! Why, Lupita, you're no bigger than a tadpole."

She looked at him as if he were crazy.

Seth winked at Jake and then swooped Lupita into his arms and ran with her to the house.

Jake's chest puffed with pride. "That's my boy," he declared.

They had a lot to talk about at dinner. Lupita didn't tell the entire story, but she said that Morgan and Seth were together again. Jake entertained them with more stories of Morgan's pregnancy. "We was scared to death she'd fall down an arroyo. The way she was built, she'd still be rollin'."

Seth shook his head. "I just can't imagine Morgan like that. Are you sure you aren't exaggerating, maybe just a little?"

"Well, let's just say that after the seventh month, she quit usin' the back door."

Seth frowned, not understanding.

"It was too small. She had to go in and out the big front door."

They all shared in the laughter.

Seth spent two days on the Colter ranch. Jake and Paul ran the place competently, and he could find no fault with any aspect of their management. Seth told them of the more complex problems of running the Three Crowns. "You could put the Colter ranch in the house, maybe just in the dining room."

"The little girl's sure gonna hate givin' all that up, ain't she? All them servants and all?"

Seth didn't want to discuss with anyone—even himself—the possibility that Morgan might not want to return with him. She and Adam had been happy at the Three Crowns without him, and she might want to stay there. If that's where she wanted to stay, then he'd stay with her. He needed to be near her, and his son.

On the morning of the third day, he hitched the

wagon and prepared to leave. Lupita packed an old Indian basket with food for him to eat along the way, and several boxes more to take to Juan Ramón. Seth tied a milk cow to the back of the wagon, a gift to the farmer who had helped when Adam was ill.

After goodbyes, the three watched him go. "I don't understand all this to-in' and fro-in'. Why don't the three of them come back here and live, where they belong?" There was no answer for Jake.

Seth stopped in Santa Fe and bought Adam a little metal toy train from one of the passengers on a wagon train. People were still streaming out to California.

He decided to buy some fabric for Morgan, and as soon as he walked into the store, he saw Marilyn Wilson.

"Seth! How are you?" she purred. "It's been so long since I've seen you." She possessively took his arm and rubbed her overly ripe breast against it.

"Hello, Marilyn."

She missed the coldness in his voice. "You're just as handsome as always. I heard you were in California. I imagine that's real excitin'."

He looked her up and down. Her dress was a gaudy taffeta of red and green stripes. Her hair wasn't too clean. "You would probably like the gold fields."

Again, she missed his tone. She was encouraged by his looking at her body. "I guess you knew about my shop. My daddy bought it for me."

"No, I didn't know." He could hardly look at her without remembering the lies she'd told the night of Montoya's party. If I had known, he thought, I would not have come in here.

"But your . . . Mrs. Colter"—she spat out the words —"was here."

"Was she? She never mentioned it to me."

"Oh? Well maybe she also forgot to tell you about the man she was with. Very good-looking. And the little boy—he seemed to resemble the man. She was probably just taking care of him, although she did say he was her son."

Seth laughed at himself. How could he ever have believed this woman's lies? "Gordon is a friend of ours and Adam is my son."

"Well, Seth, love," she had her hands on his arm, "if that's what you think. Of course, Joaquín left town about the same time as your wife, and I've always wondered—"

"Good day, Marilyn." He left the store. He felt dirty for ever having touched the woman.

After Seth left, Morgan began to spend all her time with Adam. She fed every meal to him, allowing no one else to feed him. At night, she awoke frightened and was frantic until she was sure Adam was all right. During the day she'd sit for hours, just staring at him while he slept, holding his hand.

Roselle constantly tried to get her to go outside. She was pale and had lost weight. After the first few days, she wouldn't allow Carol to clean Adam's room; she wanted to do it herself. She didn't go to the kitchen to cook any longer, but gave Roselle instructions about what to prepare. Adam had lost his appetite, and Morgan needed to coax and plead with him at every meal.

Seth was surprised to find the front door locked during the day. When Martin opened it, Seth thought the man looked older, and sad.

"It's good to have you back, Mr. Colter."

"It's good to be back. Could you have Donaciano carry a bath to my room? Is Morgan out riding?"

"No, sir, she's with Master Adam."

Seth raised his eyebrows. 'Master' Adam? He bounded up the stairs, three at a time.

He stopped at the door and stared at the sight that

greeted him. The room was airless, dark, and smelled bad. Morgan, her hair pulled once again into a tight little knot, was coaxing Adam to eat. "Please, sweetheart, eat something. For Mommy."

"No!" Adam yelled the word at her and pushed the cup away, nearly upsetting it.

"Morgan?" Seth's voice was a whisper. She turned. He gasped at the sight of her. She had on the same dress she'd been wearing when he left, and there were food stains all over it. But her face was what frightened him: her eyelids were drooping, and the bluish circles under her eyes were now almost purple. Her skin was pale. She had an expression of great weariness.

"When did you get back?" Her voice was hoarse.

"Just now. What's going on here?"

"I'm trying to help Adam get well."

"Trying to—!" He tried to control his rising anger as he went to the window and threw back the curtains. The sunlight revealed the room to be even dirtier than it had first appeared.

Morgan followed him to the window and closed the curtain. "No. You mustn't. It hurts Adam's eyes."

Seth grabbed her shoulders. "Morgan, how much sleep have you been getting?"

She looked away. "Enough."

He pulled her chin up so she met his eyes. "Answer me."

"Adam needs me sometimes in the middle of the night. Aren't you going to greet your son?" She turned away and smiled at Adam.

For the first time, Seth looked at his son. Except for having lost a little of his tan, he looked healthy. Seth smiled at his son. Adam turned away and picked up a spoon by his bed and began to bang on a little metal tray. "Mama!" he demanded.

Morgan looked at Seth in explanation. "That's for when he wants me."

423

"What happened to his learning to talk?"

"He'll learn to talk. Right now, he just needs time to recover."

"Morgan, he should be outside. In the sunshine."

"No! I told you sunshine hurts his eyes."

"Well, it never did before." He stepped nearer Adam. "You want to go with me on a horse?"

Adam looked up at his father with a bored expression and then turned to his mother and began to whine, "Mommy."

Morgan lifted the covers and put her hand underneath.

"What are you doing?"

"Checking his diaper."

"But he hasn't worn a diaper in a long time—just the few days he was sick."

"But he's still weak, Seth, very weak."

Adam threw Seth a look of hostility and continued his whining.

"I think you ought to leave now. Adam needs his rest."

He had been dismissed! He turned and left the room before rage began to control his thinking. He stormed into the kitchen where Roselle and Martin were drinking coffee together. "What the hell's going on here? I leave for one week and what do I come back to? A shell of a wife in a filthy dress who hasn't slept in a week, and a son who whines and demands! What happened to the little boy I left here, the one who smiled and laughed? Do you know what she was doing when I walked in? *Begging* him to eat! My little son, whose whole life is controlled by food! She's up there pleading with him to eat.

"He's finally learned to say no, and from what I heard, he says it quite often. And that goodamn spoon on a tray—"

"Mr. Colter, we know. We've been watching it all happen."

"Well, something has to be done about it. Maybe I'll be able to reason with her at dinner."

"Then you'll be dining downstairs?"

"Of course, we will. Where else would we eat?"

"Mrs. Colter no longer uses the dining room. She takes all her meals in the nursery with Master Adam."

"When did you start all this *Master* Adam?"

"Mrs. Colter thought it was more fitting to the young sir."

"Young . . . !" He spun around and left the room. He doubted he'd ever been angrier in his life. He had to calm himself. After a bath and a shave, maybe he would feel like reasoning with her.

When he'd finished, he was still angry, but he realized that some of this was his fault. Lupita was right. Morgan needed someone to control her life.

She was sitting beside the bed, reading to the little boy. Adam was frowning, so unlike his old dimpled self.

"Morgan, are you ready to go down to dinner?"

"I'll stay here. Adam may need me."

He lifted her under her arms. The dress was wet. "How long has it been since you've had a bath?"

"I don't know. I guess I've been too busy lately."

He pulled her to him, his arms around her. "I don't care. I still love you. Come eat dinner with me and then I shall personally give you a bath."

Behind them, Adam made a whining, petulant noise.

Morgan tried to pull from Seth's grasp. He held her, but she looked at him with fierce eyes. "Let me go!" she snarled at him. Surprised, he dropped his hands. She went to her son's side, feeling his forehead. She sighed in relief.

"Morgan, he's not sick any longer. He's perfectly healthy. All he needs is to get up and run, maybe ride a horse."

Morgan faced him, hands on hips, her face shrewish. "Ride a horse! The doctor said his illness was caused by some insect bite. He probably got it *while* riding a horse. Now, if you want to stay here, be quiet. I have a sick child to care for, and he needs my attention."

Seth could swear he saw a look of triumph in Adam's eyes. He left the room, closing the door behind him.

Dinner was a lonely meal. Seth stared at his plate. He'd sworn to wait for her even if it took years, but he couldn't stand by and let her ruin her life and their son's as well. What was he going to do?

He especially didn't like what she was doing to his son. The little boy he'd grown to love and the whining tyrant upstairs were two entirely different people.

Colter, he thought, you've stood back too long. There's only so much a man can take before he has to assert himself.

Upstairs, he decided not to go to the nursery again. He wanted to see no more of what he'd seen today. He lay awake a long time, thinking. It wasn't an easy plan he came up with, but it was a necessary one.

In the morning, he went back to the nursery. Morgan was asleep. She looked worse than he remembered. He kissed her cheek and she jumped, awake instantly.

"Did you sleep well?"

"Adam had a restless night."

"Poor boy. How is he feeling this morning?"

"I think he's better, but I'm never sure. It's such a chore to get him to eat now. Roselle is making crullers today, and I hope I can coax him to eat at least one."

Seth smiled at her. "Would you like to join me for breakfast?"

"No, I ought to stay with Adam. He might need something."

"You're right, dear, he may need something."

Morgan returned his smile. She was grateful for his understanding.

He kissed her cheek again. "I may be late tonight.

426

I'm sure there are a lot of things to do on the ranch."
He watched as Morgan wiped Adam's brow. The older
man squinted his eyes in threat to his son and he could
have sworn he saw the hint of a dimple. In the hallway,
he chuckled to himself. At least his son wasn't ignorant.
Adam was playing a good thing for all it was worth.
The problem was Morgan.

Seth spent the day organizing men, assigning work
crews, and arranging plans. When he got to the house,
everything was dark and everyone was in bed. Roselle
got up when she heard Seth in the kitchen.

"Mr. Colter, I've kept food warm for you."

"Roselle, I hate to do this to you. I know it's late,
but could you wake Martin? I have something rather
important to discuss with you."

It was very late when the three of them finally got to
bed. As Seth sank into the soft mattress, he smiled. He
felt better than he had in a long time. Everything was
ready. He did not look forward to this. He hated himself, but it had to be done.

~~ *Chapter Twenty-Four* ~~

WHEN Morgan awoke on the cot, Adam was still sleeping. She was tired, but the minor aches she felt were worth it if Adam was well again. She couldn't forget those horrible days when he'd been so ill, so near death. She'd gladly give up part of her life to keep him well, to protect him from further illness. It was her fault that Adam had been so sick. If she had not given him so much freedom, he would never have been so ill.

Something was wrong in the house—it was too quiet. People were usually stirring by now. Roselle could be heard in the kitchen, and Carol always brought breakfast upstairs for the two of them. Adam opened his eyes and moaned. She flew to his side. Always, in those first few seconds, she fought a rising panic.

"Are you hungry, baby? Eat?" She pantomimed the last word.

Adam nodded curtly, his lower lip extended in a pout.

"Carol is late this morning." She went to the door and looked out. The hall was empty. "I can't imagine where everyone is." She called for Roselle and Carol but there was no answer. "Adam, sweet, mommy must leave you for just a few seconds. You rest and I'll be right back."

She opened the bedroom doors next to Adam's room. The rooms were all empty. She stopped at the top of the stairs and called again. There was still no answer. She ran back to Adam's room. "Mommy has to go downstairs. She'll be back very soon." She kissed his forehead. Where was everyone? How could they desert her and a very sick little boy? There was also fear. It started at the nape of her neck and moved down her spine.

The dining room was empty. She knew Seth always ate breakfast downstairs. The kitchen was empty, with the stove cold and nothing on the big work table. The fear inside her began to spread. Something must have caused their disappearance.

She tried to calm herself. There had to be a simple explanation for all this. At the same time, she wanted to run back upstairs and protect Adam.

The kitchen door was open and she walked outside. The sunshine hurt her eyes. She had not left Adam's room for nearly two weeks, and she squinted against the glare. The barn door stood open and she hurried toward it. Her legs were weak from disuse. It was dark and cool in the barn. She saw no one. She heard a movement from an empty stall and breathed a sigh of relief. She had a vision of the time she'd caught Donaciano asleep in an empty stall. She'd certainly be glad to see the boy now!

She took two steps toward the stall, and then— blackness! She was suffocating! Something very heavy was on her body, covering her. She couldn't breathe. There were hands, many hands, pulling and twisting her. She began to fight, but there was no fighting the enormous weight of the thing that was cutting off her breath. She screamed, but even to her the sound was slight. Where was everyone? Was she truly alone with her attacker?

As she was moved a few feet, she tried to remain standing, but the long skirt tripped her and she fell to her knees. There were rough, cruel hands handling her. She felt them on her wrists and there was something else, too. It was a rope! If only she could breathe! She fought her unseen foe, struggling while gasping for air. But she couldn't even ascertain the direction in which her enemy stood.

The thing on her head, covering her entire body, weighed her down. Her neck was going to break under the weight of it. She began to breathe deeply. It was no use struggling. She tried again to scream.

She struggled to stand on her feet but fell forward onto her face. More hands tied a gag around her mouth. Another cloth was tied across her eyes. The enormous weight was lifted from her body. She breathed deeply of the cool air, glad to fill her lungs once again.

She could see nothing. Hands pulled her to her feet. Then she was thrown, roughly, and something hit her in the stomach. She was being carried upside down. She tried to push away with her tied hands, but met only with a wall. Something clasped her legs together in an iron grip.

Abruptly, she was stood upright, on her feet. She could see light through the blindfold, feel the sun on her body. She turned at the sound of a voice. Someone was near! Please help me, her mind cried. Please! My little boy needs me!

It was very much like the time she'd been taken by Cat Man, but that time she had been sure Seth would rescue her. This time she was not so sure he would, not after the way she'd been treating him. She was tossed astride a saddle and instinctively grabbed the pommel. Her attacker mounted behind her, and she kicked back sharply with her right heel. She heard his indrawn breath. She started to kick again, but an arm was fastened around her waist and, as she lifted her foot, it tightened, cutting off her breath. It relaxed when she lowered her foot.

They rode for a long time. She couldn't see. She

concentrated on breathing slowly and deeply, and on balancing herself on the horse. She heard the horse's hooves occasionally splashing in water, as if they crossed several streams. Sometimes she felt her attacker's thigh muscles, pressed against hers, as he urged the horse uphill. She was weak from two weeks of little food and even less sleep.

She began to gather her senses. Maybe this madman who held her was just one of many. Maybe they'd already killed Roselle and Martin—and Seth! Would Seth be safe? She hadn't thought much of Seth lately, but now she was very concerned about him. How could she have ignored him so much lately?

Abruptly, she was taken off the horse. She stood quietly, holding her balance. She heard footsteps behind her and then a door opened. Hands guided her through the door, up the one step over the threshold.

She listened. She sniffed the air and soon discovered burning logs. He began circling her. She heard his slow, easy footsteps.

His hands were on her shoulders, then on her head. She felt the tie that bound her hair being pulled away. The hands were spreading her hair, combing it with gentle fingers. She stepped away from him, but the grip on her shoulders tightened.

The hands were on her waist, encircling it, the thumbs in front as they moved upward to touch the undercurve of her breasts. She stood still, rigid. He touched her face, his palms on her cheeks.

He began unfastening the little buttons down the front of the soiled cotton dress. No! She shook her head. She made a noise in her throat. His hands worked slowly. She felt the bodice part and knew the corset and underlying chemise were exposed.

She felt a tugging, and something cold touched her shoulder. She jerked away, falling to her knees. She sat back, ready to kick her assailant. Her shoulder hurt and it was warm and damp. Blood! He'd cut her.

She stood very still. A cool cloth was placed on her cut shoulder and the pain stopped. She felt a tug again on the shoulder of the dress, and it fell away on one side. She felt another tug and then a tearing sound. The dress had been removed from her body. She heard footsteps and then felt extra heat from the fire. He had burned the dress!

She felt sharp little jerks as the laces on her corset were cut. Then it, too, fell away. She breathed deeply when the constricting garment was gone. He tore off her chemise and threw both it and the corset on the fire.

Hands went to the back of her head and unfastened the blindfold. Everything was a blur and then her eyes began to focus ...

"Hello, little wife. Oh, no, I plan to leave the gag on for a while. I have a great deal to say to you, and I don't want any interruptions."

She leaned forward to cover herself, her eyes pleading with him to allow her to shield herself.

"As you can see, I burned your clothes. I plan to keep you just like that for some time." He sat in a chair by the fireplace. "Come here, a little closer. I want to really enjoy you." He took her arm and she tried to jerk away, but he held fast.

"You're really angry, aren't you?"

She nodded vigorously, staring intently.

"I will explain. I am a very patient man, but I am not a martyr. I was willing to wait for you for years, as I've told you, but the way things were going at the Three Crowns would have tried the patience of a saint. How many women can say their husbands have made only one mistake? It was a big mistake, and I was rather ah ... unpleasant ... about it. And it did cause a great deal of misfortune for us both.

"Morgan, if you keep frowning at me with such ferocity, your entire forehead will be wrinkled in two days. I know I'm simplifying things, but I've stood by now for nearly a month and watched you 'leading your

433

own life,' and I believe you are only making a mess of it."

She started to pull away from him, but he pulled her onto his lap, her head on his shoulder, legs across him "I like this very much.

"I don't know if I can go on talking to you." His voice was husky as he stroked her thighs. "It was such a surprise when I first saw your body. And every time I've seen it since—too few times—I have marveled again at the perfection of it.

"Morgan, I love you so much." He ignored the loud noise of protest she made in her throat. "I thought everything was solved when Gordon left, but then Adam got sick and I had to leave to take Lupita home. When I returned, I knew something had to be done, and done quickly. You need someone to guide you, to care for you. I leave you alone for a week, and look what happens! You quit eating, bathing—you smell awful, you know—and you turn my nice, laughing little boy into a whining monster.

"Every time I have been away from you, terrible things have happened. I left the wagons on the way to New Mexico, and Cat Man took you. I was late to a party and, well . . . you know what happened then."

She turned her head away.

"I just couldn't do it anymore," he switched subjects abruptly.

She looked at him in question.

"I couldn't stand by and let you make a fool of yourself. You need me."

She jerked her head up, chin out.

"You're very good at pantomiming. You do need me, and these last few days prove it."

His voice was lower. "Would you like to know what I have planned for you? I plan to keep you here until you get over your anger. That may be a year or so. And then we'll wait until you admit that you love me. Oh, you think that's impossible, but I assure you it's not

434

Meanwhile, while you're making up your mind about your feelings for me, I plan to drive you wild with passion."

Her eyes widened and her body stiffened.

"Not right now, though. First, I'm going to bathe you, feed you, and let you rest for a time. Maybe." He looked at her golden skin. "I should like to see you just as you are for a while, a long while. I hope you like it here because Roselle—yes, Roselle, and don't look as if she were a traitor, she nearly gave me away at the barn—Roselle packed enough food to last us a month. If that isn't enough time, I'll lock you in here and go get more. You, dearest"—he kissed her nose—"are my prisoner of love."

He rubbed the stubble of his whiskers on her stomach, and she laughed against her will.

"Do I perceive a softening? I'll remove the gag if you won't scream—not that anyone would hear you, but because it grates on my ears." He removed the cloth binding her mouth.

"Seth Colter! You are the most horrible—"

He closed her lips with a kiss, a sweet kiss.

"You can't escape, so just relax." He kissed her again, this time with more passion. His lips touched hers as he talked. "Morgan, sweet, did anyone . . . ever tell you . . . that . . . you . . . stink?"

"You!" She bit his shoulder hard.

He stared in puzzlement at the bright drop of blood gathering there and then laughed. "I guess that repays me for your shoulder. I wouldn't have cut you except you jumped like a jackrabbit."

"Seth, Adam needs me."

"That, love, is where you're wrong. Adam does not need you. At least for a while he doesn't. The way you were acting, I could imagine Adam thirty-two years old and still being diapered by his little old mother, who hadn't had a bath since he was two years old."

Morgan started to protest, but then a giggle escaped her. It was such a silly picture. "Was I that bad?"

"Another week and he'd have forgotten how to walk. He'd already forgotten how to talk."

"But why all this?" Her glance included the cabin and her still-tied hands.

"What would you have said if I'd said, 'Morgan, let's go spend a couple of weeks alone in a mountain cabin'?"

"Well, I would have—"

"You'd have found two hundred excuses why we couldn't go."

"But why the gag and tying my hands, and the tearing off of my clothes?"

"You had to be gagged or you would have screamed all the way here, and I didn't feel like fighting you all the way." He grinned at her, showing deep dimples. "Removing your clothes was my lustful idea. I guess I'm a pirate at heart, a kidnapper and ravisher of young girls." He tickled her with his beard.

"Seth"—she was laughing—"will you untie my hands now?"

"No."

"No?"

"Not until you've had a bath. You smell worse than the men in the bunkhouse."

"Seth!"

"I mean it. If a bear came in here right now, he'd think you were his mate."

"You!" She tried to raise a tied hand to strike him "Why can't I have a romantic lover, like the ones in novels?"

"Which one of those characters do you want? The one who throws you to the ground and has his will of you, or the on-his-knees, hand-kissing type?"

"I don't . . ."

"Just tell me, my Guinevere. I am your Lancelot "

She giggled.

"Well, sir, the rules of chivalry definitely state that knights do not tell their ladies that they—stink."

"My sweet—ah, maybe sweet isn't the right word . . . My love—believe it or not, I do still love you—royal ladies do not stink. They take baths."

"Fair knight, will you lead this lady to her bathing chamber?"

Seth unceremoniously dumped Morgan from his lap. He strode to the door and opened it. "Your bathing chamber awaits."

"It's cold out there. Let's heat some water in here."

"I have a large bar of scented soap, and I plan to use the entire thing on your lovely body."

"That's all right. I have grown up now, and I can bathe all by himself."

His eyes raked her. "I can see that you have grown up, and that is precisely why I plan to bathe you. Now if you don't want to get raped, you better go outside where I can cool off."

She hesitated.

"Oh, no, you don't. If you don't bathe, I promise I won't rape you."

She scurried out into the cold mountain air, throwing him a look that made him catch his breath.

At the water's edge, she turned to him. "What about these?" She held up her tied hands.

He reached for his knife. "On second thought . . ." He sheathed the knife.

"Seth, they hurt."

His eyes relented for a second. "I don't believe you. Remember, you're my prisoner. Most husbands would have left the gag on."

"Seth."

"If you don't hurry and get your bath over, you'll freeze. Now I'm not sure how to do this. I'd hate to ruin a good pair of boots. Aha! I have the perfect solution." Quickly, he removed his clothes and boots, and Morgan had only a brief glimpse of his magnificent body before he pulled on her bound wrists. "Come, slave."

She gasped as the water touched her. "It's too cold."

"That's all right, you'll be warm soon." He began rubbing soap on her, mixing it with some fine sand he carried in a little bag. He scoured her vigorously, all over, until she thought her skin was going to come off. He didn't listen to her pleading. He rinsed her body, then soaped her again, gently this time. He stopped abruptly and began soaping himself.

"You aren't going to leave me soapy, are you?"

Without a word, he pulled her to him and held her close. The soap on their bodies felt good. They rubbed together, their lips drawn to one another. Morgan's tied hands touched his manhood, and when she felt him shudder and heard his sharp intake of breath, she tightened her grasp. Their kisses became serious.

Seth stepped away from her to his clothes, and quickly cut the rope that bound her hands. He gently laid her down on the sweet grass near the stream.

He entered her with an urgency that Morgan more than met. The long-denied passions carried them to a violent wave.

After their first frantic passions were spent, they clung to one another, their hearts pounding in unison, their panting breaths drowning out all other sounds. Morgan felt a great release from tensions she hadn't even realized she carried.

Seth rolled from her. They lay side by side, not touching or speaking. Twilight gathered around them, and the stars were beginning to show.

"You know, when they find us here together, our bodies frozen, they're going to wonder what the hell that white slimy stuff is all over our bodies. Let's wash this off. And I'm starving. After I eat, I want to start all over again."

"You mean with the blindfold and the gag?" she teased. "What was that heavy thing you threw over me? I thought it was going to break my neck."

"Heavy thing?" He looked puzzled and then laughed. "That was a quilt!"

"It couldn't have been just a quilt. I thought I was dying of suffocation."

"You're going to die of the cold if we don't go inside." He pulled her into the stream and they rinsed quickly. Together, they washed Morgan's abundant hair.

Seth grabbed her hand and pulled her to the cabin. "One minute I can't get you to take a bath, and the next I can't get you out of the water." When they were inside, he pulled her close. "Did I ever tell you I love you?"

"Never."

"Not once?"

"Not a single time."

"Good, because I don't love you. I worship you. You're my . . . wife. Yes, my wife. Morgan," he said seriously, "do you feel anything for me?"

"Only a passing fancy." She saw the hurt look in his eyes. "Seth, I've loved you from the moment I saw you at Cynthia Ferguson's ball, and I guess I'll always love you, no matter what."

She watched as he walked toward the door. His naked body was bronze in the firelight. His broad back tapered to a slim waist and trim hips, all on those muscular legs that Morgan had first noticed.

"Where are you going?" she asked.

"To get my clothes, and chop some firewood. There's food in that cabinet."

"Food?"

"Of course. You do remember how to cook, don't you?"

She put her chin up. "I'm a valued prisoner. I do not do menial labor."

His eyes narrowed. "If that food isn't started by the time I get back, there'll be big trouble." His eyes caressed her body lingeringly. "I have a lot of work to do tonight, and if I know my 'business partner,' I'll need a lot of strength."

He left, shutting the door behind him.

Morgan leaned against the back of the chair and inhaled deeply of the evening air.

How very far she had come in just a little time. Her old dream, a solitary life in Trahern House, no longer meant anything at all. She needed no more dreams. She had all she could ever want . . . a home, her son, and her Seth.

She turned toward the cabinet. It was time to prepare the first of many meals.